DemonWars

TOR BOOKS BY R. A. SALVATORE

DemonWars

FIRST HEROES

R. A. SALVATORE

TOR®

A TOM DOHERTY ASSOCIATES BOOK
NEW YORK

This is a work of fiction. All of the characters, organizations, and events portrayed in these novels are either products of the author's imagination or are used fictitiously.

DEMONWARS: THE FIRST HEROES

Copyright © 2014 by R. A. Salvatore

The Highwayman copyright © 2004 by R. A. Salvatore

The Ancient copyright © 2008 by R. A. Salvatore

All rights reserved.

Maps by Joseph Mirabello

Chapter opening illustrations by Shelly Wan

A Tor Book
Published by Tom Doherty Associates, LLC
175 Fifth Avenue
New York, NY 10010

www.tor-forge.com

Tor® is a registered trademark of Tom Doherty Associates, LLC.

ISBN 978-0-7653-7616-9 (trade paperback)

Tor books may be purchased for educational, business, or promotional use. For information on bulk purchases, please contact Macmillan Corporate and Premium Sales Department at 1-800-221-7945, extension 5442, or write specialmarkets@macmillan.com.

First Edition: February 2014

Printed in the United States of America

0 9 8 7 6 5 4 3 2 1

Acknowledgments

As with everything I do, this is for Diane and our children. Their support through this long journey has made it wonderful, indeed.

For this book, I also have to give my heartfelt thanks and appreciation to Mary Kirchoff. She found me in a slush pile twenty years ago and gave a (kind of) young writer a chance, and then two decades later found me again and brought me to Tor Books to continue my DemonWars work. So to Mary, a dear friend, a fabulous editor (again!) . . . but most of all, a dear friend.

Doing this book gave me something I've wanted for a long, long time—the chance to work with Tom Doherty. Tom is old-school publishing, maybe the last remnant of the days when every decision didn't have to go up one chain of command and down the other. He doesn't talk a good game, he does a good game. All I can say about my expectation compared to my actual experience is: As advertised. I'm proud to be a part of the Tor family now. Top to bottom, I've dealt with nothing but competence, enthusiasm, and a constant reminder that, at the end of the day, this is supposed to be fun.

Contents

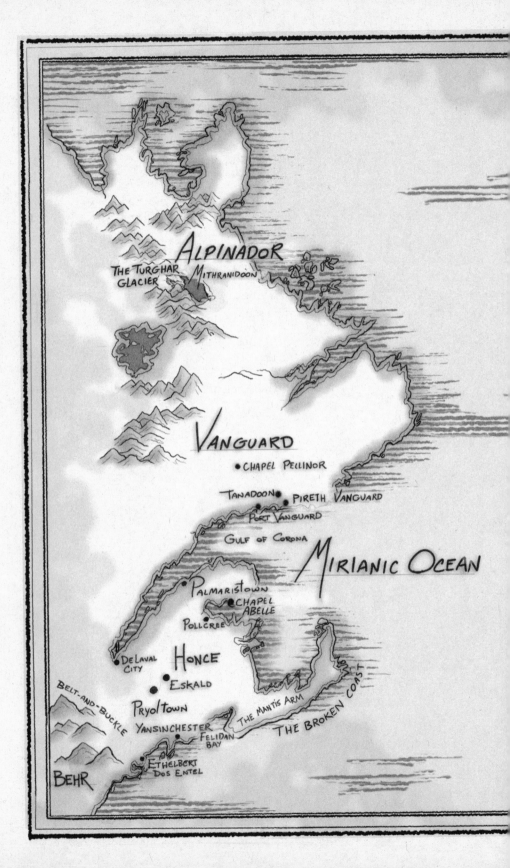

The Highwayman

God's Year 74

Seventy-four Years after the Death of Blessed Abelle

Harkin cracked his whip with an urgency wrought of terror. Orrin slumped next to him, a spear buried deep in his side, bright blood flowing freely, staining his brown woolen tunic a dark and ugly red black.

"Come on, run!" Harkin urged his team, and he cracked the whip hard again. He couldn't help but consider the terrible irony of it all. He had been transferred from the front lines of battle—in a war that had been raging since he was a young man—to the seemingly safe job of driving Prince Yeslnik about the growing lands of Greater Delaval. And now this—to be caught and killed on the road!

The horses dug in and pulled hard, but an undeniable drag slowed the coach. "Orrin, you hold on!" Harkin cried to his injured friend, and he shifted his hands just enough so that he could pull back the slumping man, who seemed as if he would tumble from his seat.

Harkin glanced all around frantically. He heard Prince Yeslnik shout, though the words were lost in the tumult. He heard Prince Yeslnik's wife, Olym, scream in fear. When the coach hit one straight, flat stretch of the tree-lined road in the southeastern reaches of Pryd Holding, Harkin dared to stand quickly and look back. The coach was dragging a tangle of logs. "Ah, you cunning beasts," he lamented, for the bloody-capped powries had hit the coach with some sort of grapnel, affixed by rope to the logs.

Harkin's mind tumbled through the possibilities. He knew that he had to do something; it was only a matter of time before those bouncing logs caught on a tree or some other obstacle at the side of the road and either stopped the coach or, more likely, tore it apart. He couldn't go back to free the grapnel while they were charging along, and he couldn't stop. He knew the truth. He had seen the bright red berets. He had heard the grating voices and the guttural shouts. These were powrie dwarves, and powries showed no mercy.

"Come on," he called again to his straining team, and he cracked the whip once more.

Good fortune got them through the straight section of road without any serious entanglements, but Harkin knew that the flagstone path twisted and wound around many stones and trees, down into dells and into sharp-cornered turns over ridges. "Bah!" He snorted in dismay, and he pulled back hard on the reins, bringing the coach to an abrupt halt. Before the wheels had even fully stopped turning, Harkin looped the reins about the bench seat and leaped to the ground. "Stay inside, my prince!" he cried to Yeslnik as he ran past the door's open window and around the back of the coach.

He followed the rope to the grapnel, and found it secured underneath the carriage. Cunning powries, indeed! They hadn't hit the coach with a spear or anything like that, but rather had set a trap in the road to hook it from beneath.

Harkin started to bend and even dropped to one knee, starting under the coach frame to free it, but the thought of crawling on the ground, so vulnerably, with powries closing, had him gasping for breath. Instead, he drew out his short bronze sword and began hacking at the rope with all his might.

"You fool! What are you doing?" cried the prince, leaning out and hanging on the now-opened door. "Why have you stopped? I am the nephew of the Laird of Delaval!"

"We cannot go, my liege," poor Harkin tried to explain. He hacked with all his strength, and finally the rope snapped. Yeslnik saw it and cried out in dismay, and then he saw a spear come arcing in and hit the coach near Harkin.

"Get back in, I beg you, my liege!" Harkin cried, and this time Yeslnik didn't argue.

Harkin scrambled around the coach and back up into his seat. If he could just get them moving . . .

The reins were not there.

Harkin's gaze went forward to the nervous team, and there, between them, he saw his doom. For there stood a powrie, a smile on its leathery and wrinkled face, white teeth showing behind the long hairs of an overgrown red mustache.

"Ye lookin' for these, me lord?" the dwarf asked, and he held up and jiggled the reins. "Aye, but ain't yer horses tired from yer stupid run?"

Harkin could hardly draw breath as he heard other dwarves moving around the sides of the coach, for the powries' reputation preceded them. They were not here for treasure, other than human blood.

The dwarf in front dropped the reins and drew forth a long, curving knife with a wicked, serrated edge. "If ye don't fight, it won't hurt as much."

Harkin's mind whirled—he didn't want to die, certainly not like this! "Wait!" he cried as he heard the coach creak behind him and knew that a dwarf was beginning to climb on it. "I got something for you. Something that'll get you all the blood and money you want!"

The dwarf in front held up his hand, and the one creeping near Harkin stopped.

Poor Harkin heard the coach door open, and a moment later, he heard Prince Yeslnik's wife scream, followed by a protest from the prince himself.

"Aye, that one," Harkin improvised. "He's noble blood, and his laird'll pay whatever you want to get him back. Money and people—it won't matter to Laird Delaval, as long as he gets the safe return of his precious nephew."

"Hmmm," the dwarf in front mused.

Harkin could hear more movement and shouting from behind, but no sounds of battle yet joined. The dwarves were waiting, he believed and prayed.

"What're ye thinking, Turgol?" asked the one in front. "Ransom? That be our game?"

"Nah," said the dwarf to the side and behind Harkin, and he nearly fainted when he realized how close this second one actually was. "Lots o' work in that, and we're to rile up a laird? Nah, kill 'em now, I say. Three humans to brighten me cap."

The dwarf in front began to nod and smile all the wider, and he opened his mouth to speak.

"Oh, wrong answer," came a voice from above—a human voice and not the grumbling chant of a powrie. Harkin and the dwarves turned, their gazes flying up, up to the high boughs of a wide oak tree.

And there he sat on a limb, a smallish man dressed head to toe in a black outfit of some exotic fabric. He wore a mask black as night that covered more than half his face, with holes cut out for the eyes.

"If it was just a business deal—a good one—then perhaps I could have wandered along on my way without interfering," the mysterious man said. "But since you insist . . ."

As he finished he shoved off the branch and came flying down at the coach.

"By the gods!" Harkin cried, and he fell back, throwing his arm up in front of him, expecting the man to go crashing through the coach.

The powrie behind Harkin shrieked but instead of retreating, lifted up a heavy battle-axe.

The dwarf roared and swung trying to bat the man in black out of the air. But amazingly, the axe whipped below the descending man, as if he had some-how slowed his fall. And he didn't crash through the coach roof—as he should have after falling from so high—but rather touched down firmly on it right behind the swinging blade. He fell as he hit, absorbing the impact with a for-ward roll following the swing of the axe, and he came up tangled with the dwarf—at least as far as the dwarf was concerned. For the man's balance as he rolled fast to his feet remained perfect, and as he leaped down from the coach his hands caught the dwarf so that the dwarf had no choice but to go flying away with him.

Again the man landed in perfect and easy balance, as the powrie crashed down hard beside him, sprawling on the ground, its axe flying away.

"Not a graceful sort, now is he?" the man asked a pair of powries standing before him, their mouths agape. He jabbed his elbow back as he spoke, for he had cleverly landed right beside the open coach door, and a simple shove from that elbow had it swinging closed. "I beg your pardon, Prince Yeslnik, but would you please remain inside while I finish my business out here?"

The two dwarves recovered, roared, and charged; and the man sprang into a forward somersault right over them. He touched down, running, turning as he went, and drawing from over his shoulder the most magnificent sword that any of them—man or dwarf—had ever seen. Its blade gleamed silver, shining in the morning light, and tracings of delicate vines ran the length of it. Most wondrous of all was the hilt, all silver and ivory, the pommel shaped as the head of a hooded serpent.

The powries swung and rushed right in, one thrusting a spear, the other stabbing with its own sword, a weapon of bronze.

Two quick, sharp raps turned both those weapons aside. The man retracted his blade to his right, spun it end over end suddenly, and it disappeared behind him.

The foolish dwarves kept coming.

Out from the left now stabbed the silvery sword, forward, a quick tap to the side to push the dwarf's sword wide, and then ferociously ahead to stab the powrie in the chest. The man came forward at the same time, turning at the last second so that the thrusting spear flashed past him. He caught that spear shaft in his right hand as he stepped closer to the dwarf, tearing free his sword from its falling comrade. Too close to use the weapon effectively, the man tossed the sword up into the air, and predictably, the powrie's eyes followed its ascent.

The man hit the powrie with three short left jabs—short but amazingly hard. The dwarf staggered back a step, dazed.

The man caught the sword as it fell, and his hand flashed out, smashing the snake pommel into the dwarf's face. He had to turn as another dwarf came at him; and as he did, he flipped the sword and stabbed straight behind him, plunging the magnificent blade through the stunned dwarf's chest so forcefully that its tip exploded right out through the creature's back.

The man let go of the hilt again, his hands moving in a side-to-side blur before him to confuse the next attacker. Somehow those flashing hands evaded the stabbing powrie sword. The man's right palm slapped the blade out to the dwarf's right, while the lightning-fast fighter brought his left hand under the dwarf's arm, backhanding it out even further. Suddenly he grabbed the dwarf's wrist and pulled it between them. His right hand bent the dwarf's wrist, overextending the ligaments and bringing a howl of pain. A sudden brutal jerk took the strength from the dwarf's fingers, and the man slid his hand down, pulling free the powrie's sword.

"You only get one chance," he said, throwing the dwarf's arm out wide, slapping him across the face with his left hand, then grabbing the powrie by the hair, and forcefully tugged it back.

The dwarf growled and started to punch, but his forward movement only served to present the man with a clear line to an exposed throat.

The sword slid in, turning the growl to a gurgle, and the man pushed on.

The dwarf wasn't punching anymore but was frozen in place, staring up at the morning sky, its arms out to the sides and twitching.

The man was gone, leaving the powrie's sword in place.

Another dwarf pursued, with several more circling as if to cut the man off, for it seemed as if their enemy were unarmed now.

The man remedied that as he came upon the dwarf he'd skewered with his sword. The man dove into a sidelong roll right over the dwarf, catching his sword's hilt. When he landed on his feet on the other side, with two powries rushing up in front of him, he had his sword in hand. He put it to sudden and devastating work, launching a series of short back-and-forth slashes, striking their weapons in succession. Somewhere in the side-to-side blur, he thrust out, once and then again, and one of the powries staggered back, bright blood erupting from its shoulder and chest.

Now the man's sword went into a tight circular motion around the remaining dwarf's sword. He had the dwarf watching the dazzling display: he knew from its spinning eyes.

A fatal mistake.

The sword then changed its angle, and, with a sudden shove and a cry that came from somewhere deep inside, the man threw the dwarf's weapon out wide and stiffened the fingers of his free hand as he stepped forward, thrusting that hand straight out, his fingers driving into the powrie's windpipe.

The dwarf shuddered and staggered back, all its body jerking in death spasms.

"Who shall be next?" the man asked, spinning and bringing his sword into a series of left and right diagonal cuts.

But none of the remaining dwarves wanted anything to do with him! They were off and running, scattering to every direction.

The man laughed and looked at the coach, where the Prince of Delaval was peeking out and slowly opening the door and where the unnerved driver was staring at him from above. "They always run when half are down," the man calmly explained. "If only they would play it out to the end, they might find me growing tired."

As he finished, he launched into a series of leaps, twisting and striking out with his sword, a barrage that would have likely taken down any ten enemies standing too near.

"Or perhaps not," the man said with a salute.

"Who are you?" Prince Yeslnik asked.

"My reputation has not preceded me? I am wounded."

"The Highwayman," Harkin said.

"Thank you for that," the man in black replied. "I would hate to think that all my hard work these past months has been for naught."

Prince Yeslnik slid out of the coach. "Your reputation does not do you justice, my friend."

"Why, thank you."

"You will be rewarded." Behind the prince, the Highwayman could see his female companion staring out at him from the coach, leaning toward him eagerly.

So predictable a reaction from these fair ladies of court.

"And pardoned," the excited prince went on, "for any crime of which you have been accused. You will live the life of a wealthy and free man, from one end of Honce to the other."

"As if that was yours to give," said the man. "'Tis a big place."

"Then in Delaval Holding at least," Yeslnik said. "You may walk freely in Delaval."

"I have no desire to travel to Delaval."

"Well . . ."

"But a reward does sound fine, and so I will take it . . . now."

Yeslnik seemed unsettled, but he composed himself quickly and turned to the packs tied on the back of the coach.

"A hundred silver coins, then," Yeslnik offered.

"I prefer gold."

The prince glanced back at him, a momentary flash of anger betraying his true feelings. "Gold, then, a hundred pieces."

"Surely you have more than that. You did come to collect your uncle's taxes from Pryd Holding. You know—we both do—the burden Delaval places on the people of Pryd in exchange for keeping them free from the advances of Laird Ethelbert."

Prince Yeslnik stood up very straight. "Name your price then."

"Why, all of it, of course," the Highwayman said.

The prince looked shocked.

"You see, I lied when I told the powrie that it gave the wrong answer. I agree with it! Taking you hostage for ransom would be a terrible choice."

There was no missing the threat in those words, and Yeslnik's bluster seemed to melt away.

"All of it," the Highwayman repeated, "and be glad, stupid prince, that I have no need for human blood. My mask is black, you see."

He walked over past the prince and right up to the woman who was hanging half out of the coach. How her green eyes sparkled as he neared, and her breasts heaved with excitement.

He reached up as if to stroke her face.

And tore the bejeweled necklace from her neck. She gave a little shriek and lifted her hand over her tiny mouth, and her eyelids fluttered as if she would swoon.

"Surely a beauty as radiant as your own needs no baubles," he said sweetly.

She stammered and tittered, and the Highwayman glanced back at Prince Yeslnik, offering a look of pity.

"Such substance," he said as he turned back to Olym, masking his sarcasm beneath a voice that seemed husky with awe.

She sucked in her breath and brought her hand up before her mouth again; and this time, the Highwayman took a closer look at the shining emerald ring she wore. He took that hand in his own and kissed it.

Then he took the ring.

She didn't know whether to protest or to swoon, and behind him, the Highwayman heard the growls of Prince Yeslnik. He offered a salute to one and then the other, then stepped behind the coach where he freed two packs bulging with coins. Slinging them over his shoulder as if they were weightless, he seemed to fly away, with a great leap that brought him to the top of the coach. He glanced at the driver and his slumping companion, then moved closer to inspect the wounded man.

The Highwayman closed his eyes and placed a hand on the wound. His focus brought warmth to his hand, and that warmth brought some healing to poor Orrin.

"You turn and get him to Chapel Pryd," the Highwayman instructed Harkin. "The brothers will help him—his wounds are not as grave as they seem."

Harkin nodded stupidly.

The Highwayman bowed to him, turned and bowed to Prince Yeslnik, then leaped again, even higher, back to the low branches of the tree from which he had come.

In a matter of only a few minutes, he had arrived, rescued, robbed, healed, and vanished.

PART ONE

God's Year 54

CHAPTER 1

Walking in the Clouds

Brother Bran Dynard stepped out of his room into the brilliant morning light. The sun reached down through the few patches of cloud, which were really no more than jagged lines of white torn by the fast winds. Bright flashes dotted the terrace and the bridges, as puddles from the night's rainfall caught the rays of morning and threw them back into the air with exuberance.

Brother Dynard walked across the landing to the waist-high railing and leaned over, looking down at the clouds that drifted across the mountainsides below him, then looking past them to the valley floor, hundreds and hundreds of feet below. Though he had grown up just north of the mighty Belt-and-Buckle mountains, though he had sailed around the eastern fringes of that great range, right under their shadow, Dynard could never have imagined looking down on the clouds.

Looking down on them!

He noted the sparkle of the river snaking through the valley, weaving around the sharp stones and red-streaked rock that seemed to grow right out of the mountains. In the six years he had been here, this view of the strange land that the nomads of Behr called Crezen ilaf Flar, the Mountains of Fire, had never ceased to amaze Dynard and had never ceased to send his heart soaring with the possibilities of . . .

Of anything. Of everything.

When he had left Chapel Pryd of the Honce holding of the same name on his *Journey Proselyt* (as the monks called their evangelical missions) seven years before, weary Brother Dynard had never expected any of this. He had served the Church of Blessed Abelle well, so he had thought, through his twenties and past his thirtieth birthday; and it had come as a surprise to him when Father Jerak had pointed him south for his mission. "Go to the desert of Behr," the elderly Jerak had told him one cold and wet winter's day in God's Year 47. "If we can turn the good people of Honce from the dark pagan ways of the Samhaists, then surely even the beasts of Behr will not be beyond the call of Blessed Abelle."

"The beasts of Behr," Dynard quietly mouthed, and how many thousand times had he sarcastically repeated that denigrating phrase used by the fair-skinned people of Honce when referring to the darker-skinned people of the great desert to the south of the Belt-and-Buckle. The Behr were nomadic tribesmen, wandering the windblown sands of the desert from oasis to oasis, from the sea in the east to the steppes far in the west. They rode misshapen beasts—humped horses—and spoke in gibberish, so said the men of Honce who knew them. An excitable lot, they were, by all reports, quick to laugh and quicker to anger, and fierce in battle—as would be expected of any animal, so the general reasoning in Honce went.

Thus it was with great trepidation that Brother Dynard had sailed on one of the small, shore-hugging fishing boats from Laird Ethelbert's domain. He hadn't known what to expect of the southerners; could these people even properly communicate? Were they merely savages or animals?

His string of surprises had begun before he had stepped off that fishing boat, for the structures of Jacintha, the largest settlement in Behr, exceeded anything Brother Dynard had ever before seen, even in the great Honce city of Delaval. White towers topped with brightly colored pennants captured his imagination that morning on the boat. And to this day, what he most remembered about Jacintha was the colors of the place, the brilliant hues and dazzling patterns of the clothing and the rugs. So many rugs! The city seemed to be one sprawling marketplace, anchored by the great houses of the tribal sheiks, more elaborate and beautiful than any of the castles of Honce, and shining pink and white with polished stone. The city bristled with energy, with life itself; and it was there that Brother Dynard believed he truly began his journey and found his heart once more. Before Jacintha, he had walked with weariness, dour and depressed, but a few weeks in that place had him alive again and ready to spread the good word of Blessed Abelle.

He spent many weeks in Jacintha, learning the ways and the language of Behr and coming to recognize the ridiculousness of the labels his people placed upon these civilized and cultured people. Then came the months when Brother Dynard had traveled with the nomads through the stinging, windblown sands and in the shadows of the great dunes. He spoke with the tribesmen about his faith, of the great Blessed Abelle who had found the sacred isle and the gemstone gifts of God. He showed them the gemstone powers, using the gray hematite, the soul stone, to heal minor wounds and afflictions. And they had listened, and they had been amused and tolerant, though not amazed at all, to Dynard's surprise. A few even seemed genuinely interested in learning more about this wondrous prophet who had died nearly a half century before. From those potential converts, Dynard had heard of this place, Crezen ilaf Flar, and of the mystics who lived here, the Jhesta Tu.

According to his guides, these mystics could perform feats of magic simi-

lar to those Dynard had displayed, only without the use of any props, gemstone or otherwise.

And so, on a blistering summer day nearly six years before, Bran Dynard
had arrived in the valley below his present perch, in the dry bed where the
spring waters now ran as a river, at the base of the magnificent staircase, built
into the mountain wall, that wound up to the lower terraces of this mountain
monastery, the Walk of Clouds.

Thinking back to that day now, it seemed to Dynard to be a lifetime ago.
And indeed, in the six years since, he had learned more about himself, about
the world, and—he truly believed—about God, than in the three decades he
had lived before that.

And he had learned about love, he silently added as his gaze drifted to the
solitary figure who had come out on the open walk to perform her morning
exercise ritual. Warmth flooded through Dynard as he gazed upon SenWi.
Ten years his junior, with delicate, birdlike features and shining black hair
that hung to her shoulders, the brown-skinned woman had won his heart almost upon first glimpse. She smiled often—continually, it seemed!—and filled
her steps with a bounce and twirl that made her movements more of a dance
than a walk.

Dynard watched her precise turns and twists now, as she wove her limbs
gracefully and slowly through the ritual of practice, stretching her muscles
and playing one against the other in moves to strengthen. The wind gently
ruffled her loose-fitting clothing—the off-white ankle-length pants and her
rose-colored shining shirt, decorated with intricate embroidery of flowery
vines. The light material rippled and whipped, but beneath the clothing stood
the anchor of a solid form.

For there was a strength about SenWi, though she wasn't much more than
half Dynard's weight.

How could she ever love me? Dynard wondered as he looked down upon the
beautiful creature, with her round face, dark brown eyes, and her delicate lips,
perfectly shaped and balanced and brought to a pouting peak so that a hint of
her white teeth showed when she assumed her typical expression, as if she
were always smiling.

How different she was than he, how much more beautiful! Brother Dynard could not help but make these comparisons whenever he looked at her.
Her nose was a button, his a hawkish beak. Her body was smooth and flowing,
her every movement like the bend of a willow in the wind, while he had ever
been a stiff-legged and somewhat hulking figure, with one shoulder forward.
His black hair was thinning greatly now, more and more each day it seemed,
and his once sharp jawline now possessed ample jowls.

SenWi had not fallen in love with him at first sight, as he had with her.

How could she have, after all? But she had listened to his every lecture and participated in every discussion with him in those first months after his arrival, often staying late after all the others had retired, to press Dynard for more stories of the wide world north of the mountains. Dynard could still remember the moment when he had realized that her interest went beyond curiosity in what he knew and had seen, when he had realized that she wanted the stories, not for what they revealed about the world but for what they revealed about him, about this strange white-skinned man from another world. Through Dynard's tales, SenWi had discovered his heart and soul, and somehow—miraculously as far as he was concerned—had fallen in love with him and had agreed not only to formally wed him but also to travel with him back to his home in Pryd.

But first they had their respective tasks to complete.

The thought brought Brother Dynard's gaze to the row of clay pots lining the back of another terrace. The mere sight of the pots, wherein pieces of iron had been placed with wood chips, brought to mind all the condescending and dehumanizing slurs of these southern peoples that Bran Dynard had heard throughout his lifetime. "Beasts of Behr" indeed!

These southern people had found a new way to prepare iron, to strengthen it considerably by transforming it into a metal they called silverel steel. The process was difficult, the items made of it very rare. For a Jhesta Tu mystic, one of the very highest trials was to take this steel and to craft with it a light and mighty sword.

SenWi had been working on hers for years—every day, one fold a session. Brother Dynard remembered the day her work had begun, marked by a grand ceremony that had all the four hundred mystics of the Jhesta Tu assembled on the terraces, praying for her success. Amid the hum of their intoning, the blessed roll of silverel steel had been borne up the mountain stairway by the younger members of the sect. Thin enough to ripple in a gentle wind, the piece was just under four feet wide and, if unrolled, nearly twenty feet long.

Great heated stone wheels had pressed the metal to this thin state, so thin that the entire roll weighed but a few pounds. It had to be light, for this roll—all but the tiny pieces that would be trimmed at the end of the process—would become SenWi's sword, one inch at a time. That was her task: to take this piece of marvelous metal to a specially designed table that had been constructed within her private rooms for the single purpose of crafting her weapon. Many times had Brother Dynard asked about that secret process—asked SenWi and all the masters of the Walk of Clouds who had so warmly welcomed him into their home.

But, alas, this was one secret they would not tell.

Dynard couldn't complain, for the generosity of these mystics had been more than he could ever have imagined. They listened to his stories of Blessed Abelle, of his Church and its precepts, of his hopes of spreading the word. They didn't deny him the opportunity to preach his beliefs to any in the Walk of Clouds, for these mystics saw Bran Dynard as a source of increasing their knowledge, and to them that was all important. In return for his gifts of the gospel of Abelle and his instruction in the use of the magical gemstones, the Jhesta Tu had taught him their disciplines spiritual, mental, and martial— though he hadn't become very accomplished in the latter! They had welcomed his questions and welcomed, too, the blossoming love between this strange man from the northern lands and one of their own.

And they had given Dynard perhaps the greatest gift of all: they had taught him to read their language, which was quite different from that of Honce. And they had loaned him a copy of the Book of Jhest, their defining tome.

So many of their secrets were revealed within the pages of that massive tome: the lessons of concentration, of movement memory, the dance of the fighter, the dance of the lover. It was all there, and the Jhesta Tu masters offered it freely to this visitor from afar. They had provided Dynard with a similar-size and length book, but one whose pages were as yet unlettered, and had bade him to copy the work so that he could take the duplicate back with him when he returned home, and share it with the people of the northern kingdom.

"But would that not compromise your tactics and understanding of battle?" a shocked Dynard had asked when he had been presented with the intriguing prospect.

Gentle old Master Jiao had answered without hesitation, "Any person capable of understanding our martial dance will have first taken the time to learn the language of Jhest. Even then, the words are meaningless unless one first absorbs the wisdom of the Book of Jhest. Without that wisdom, without that totality of understanding, there is no power; and in one who finds that totality of understanding, there is no threat."

Every day, as SenWi went to her work in which she would accomplish but a single one of the thousand folds that would form her sword, Brother Dynard retired to his own room and sought to precisely copy a few lines of the weighty tome. He had done quite a bit of similar scribing in his first years as a follower of Abelle and always before had approached the task with trepidation, though with devotion. For bending over the table, quill in hand, had brought him aching shoulders and neck, and had left his eyes bleary. His new friends, though, even had an answer for those maladies, in the form of the morning exercises they had taught him, the gentle stretches and the connection to the earth beneath his bare feet.

He stared down at SenWi, glad that she was not aware of him at that moment of her own sweet dance. She rose to the ball of one foot, lifting her arms gracefully as she did, extended her other leg, and used it to send her in a slow turn. As she came around, her left arm swept across, with her right following, fingertips to the sky, moving straight out from her chest. Her balance shifted and she smoothly landed on her other foot. A series of shoulder twists followed, each arm coming forward in turn, hands sweeping in a rotating motion as they retracted to the opposite shoulder, then slicing back across her chest and rolling forward once again.

She went down in a sudden waist bend, her feet turning, and then she rotated back to her right, where she repeated the motions.

It looked like a dance, a graceful celebration of the wind and the earth and life itself, but Brother Dynard understood it to be much more than that. This was the basic martial training of the Jhesta Tu, and each pivot was designed to put the warrior face-to-face with another opponent. The form on which SenWi was now working, *sing bay wuth,* was designed to defeat three opponents; Dynard had watched it in fierce practice sessions and had come to appreciate its worth.

Even if it had been but a dance, the monk from the north could not deny its simple and graceful beauty.

Nor could he deny the beauty of the dancer, whom he loved beyond anyone he had ever known.

SenWi ended her exercise, standing perfectly erect and still. She closed her eyes and steadied her breathing.

Dynard understood the posture. She was aligning her *ki-chi-kree,* the line of spiritual energy the Jhesta Tu believed ran from the top of one's head, the *ki,* to the groin, the *kree.* To the Jhesta Tu, this *chi* was the line of power, of balance, of strength, and of spirit—the very energy of life itself. Finding perfection of that line, complete alignment, as SenWi was now, was the key to true balance.

She finished by lifting her arms up, thumb tips touching, index fingers touching, in a salute to the morning sun. And then she bowed low as she brought her arms back to her sides, her whole body perfectly still except for the bending at her waist.

Brother Dynard gave a great sigh as the woman walked back into her private quarters to resume work on her sword. Then he, too, faced the rising sun and went through his practice. Not nearly as proficient as SenWi, of course, he nevertheless managed to get through *sing bay du,* a routine designed to battle two opponents, front and back, with some measure of grace. Then he came to the part he most enjoyed: the stance of the mountain. He found his line of *chi,* head to groin, and consciously extended that life energy down his legs and through his feet, rooting himself to the stone of the wide terrace. A strong gust of wind blew by, but Dynard didn't budge. He felt the strength of the earth grasping him, becoming part of him, and felt as if he wouldn't flinch if a large man charged into him at full speed. Once he had achieved the posture, he allowed himself to absorb the sensations of the morning: the smell of the flowers, the warmth of the sun, the soft feel of his light clothing brushing his skin.

He saluted the sun, he bowed, and he went inside to his work.

He couldn't help but notice his old clothing hanging on a rack just inside the door. Like all the common folk of Honce, each of the brothers of Abelle wore a simple woolen tunic that reached to the knees and was typically belted at the waist with a leather cord. The brothers also added a coarse woolen traveling cloak, dark brown in color. Dynard considered that tunic and cloak, then looked at the silk clothing the Jhesta Tu had given him.

"Beasts of Behr," he said with a chuckle and a shake of his large head.

The monk rubbed his face and moved to the desk, where two books sat open and quills and inks of various colors waited.

A s she had advanced through the ranks of the Jhesta Tu, SenWi had found her private quarters moved forward and forward, and now, as a budding master, the young woman's rooms were at the very front of the house and cave complex built so high on the mountainside. Several windows lined the front wall of her two-room abode, facing south and east. They were open holes in the stone wall, but SenWi usually kept the heavy drapes pulled aside, except on the coldest of winter nights and when she was at her private work.

Fresh from her morning exercise, she moved to close those drapes, but paused, catching a glimmer of slanting morning sunlight streaming in to illuminate the ivory and silver hilt and crosspiece of her sword. SenWi walked over and gently stroked the carved piece, fashioned to resemble the flared, curving neck of one of the great hooded vipers known in the steppes of To-gai. Shiny silver and smooth white ivory intertwined through the length of the hilt, an artwork in and of itself. SenWi let her fingers trace the crafted lines, taking satisfaction in the solid grip she had created beneath the illusion of beauty. The neck tapered just a bit down to the crosspiece, which was comprised of two thinner rods of shining steel. Even these had been worked intricately by SenWi so that they bent at their respective ends to form snake heads. Above the crosspiece was a steel rod, just under three feet in length.

SenWi looked across the room, to the roll of thin metal, much of it already folded to form the sword's blade. Those first few folds had been critical, for SenWi had to leave an exact opening into which this center pole could be inserted, joining blade to hilt.

SenWi released the hilt and stared at it, hardly believing that years had passed since she had begun this process, since she had crafted the hilt. She remembered the day when the masters had returned it to her, smiling all, with the news that she could begin to craft her sword.

How many thousands of hours had she toiled in this one pursuit, this singular goal? Only now, with the end clearly in sight, did SenWi appreciate how well spent those hours had been. For she had learned so much about herself in these last few years. She had found the limits of her discipline, had learned the patience of a true craftsman. She couldn't help but smile as she recalled days, weeks even, when she had managed to craft only a single line of scales on the serpent-headed hilt. And now she worked on the blade no less meticulously, bending one by one the hundreds of folds that would comprise it. Each one of those folds consumed the working hours of a single day.

Even on those days when SenWi was able to complete the single fold easily, she could not then go on. There was no "getting ahead" in the crafting of a Jhesta Tu sword. There was only the process, methodical and disciplined.

The woman drew the heavy curtains closed and moved across the small room to the special metal table and the rolled steel. She felt the heat more profoundly with each step forward, for under the table was set a small oven, which she had fired up before going out to her morning exercise. She picked up another block of coke, slipped a heavy glove onto her left hand, and used an iron poker to pull open the small round hatch. She tossed in the fuel, then paused and watched as the orange glow increased, as lines of smoldering fires ran like living caterpillars across the face of the new block. Above it, waves of heat climbed, funneling into the seams of the furnace and table so that it would be properly distributed.

SenWi closed the furnace hatch and moved to the side of the table. To her right lay the beginnings of the shaped blade, with the unfolded metal sheet running to her left like an unwound bolt of silk. Just past the blade, farther to the right, was a raised edge, the apex of the heat zone, slightly glowing in the dimly lit room.

A small diamond-edged rule and cutter, fashioned with a concave edge designed to fit tightly against the edge of the blade facilitated the next part of the process. When SenWi slowly and precisely ran it across the thin sheet, it drew the line of the next fold and also drew a lighter line indicating the breadth of the overlap area. With her bare hand, she lifted the blade and brought it up and over, using all of her focus and discipline to set it precisely in place, so that the scratched line rested perfectly along the raised and heated edge.

Then she removed her glove and let the metal sit, while she went across the room and prayed, finding her center of focus, aligning her *ki-chi-kree*. When the appropriate time of heating had passed, she took up a pair of tiny hammers and moved back to the table.

SenWi began to sing softly, finding a rhythm and cadence. She began to dance around the table, her hands working slow circles, tap-tapping the metal atop the raised edge, but gently, so as not to tear the already thin sheet. It went on for nearly an hour: the soft singing—chanting really—the graceful steps, each bringing her arms in reach of a different point of the crease; and the continual tapping. Never once in all the days of her work had the woman touched the formed blade with those hammers, despite their proximity. That was the discipline of the dance and the movements, to strike precisely along that single, definitive line.

When she was done, she dropped the hammers and quickly put on the heavy gloves. Moving fast now, she folded the blade back over the raised bar with even pressure, so that the fold line was perfectly in place with the edge of her previous work. She pulled it as tightly as her honed muscles would allow and held it there, squeezing, for a long moment. Satisfied, breathing heavily, SenWi then poured water over the length of the blade, smiling at its hissing protest.

She was equally quick to dry the blade, thus hardening the fold.

Then she prayed some more, and added more coke to the oven.

Then she prayed some more, and when she judged that the table surface was again hot enough, she hoisted a long, thin block of heavy stone and set it in place atop the blade. And another, and another, until the whole blade was covered, the weight of the stones forcing the folded metal tight against the blazing metal surface.

SenWi went to take her morning meal. She hoped that she would see her lover there, though she knew that he was nearing the end of his scribing and was working furiously so that his finish would coincide with her own. Bran Dynard wanted them to be on the road in late spring or early summer at the very latest.

Her work this day wasn't nearly done, of course. When she returned, she had to remove the stones and cool the blade, and then she would use a diamond-encrusted file to finish the tip of the last fold, scraping it down, hour by hour, so that it fell into exact place of the triangular sword tip.

Tomorrow, she'd do it again, exactly the same way.

Enough tomorrows would produce the sword. And they would give her the sense of accomplishment and ownership: that she had taken a simple sheet of metal and so crafted it into a beautiful weapon, a true work of art, an extension of her martial training.

He wasn't shivering with cold—winter was surely loosening its grip on the land—but his fingers trembled so badly that he had to stop.

Brother Dynard sat back, gave a frustrated snort, then stood up, abandoning the moment that he thought would bring him triumph. He paced away from the desk, determined not to look back.

But he did glance over his shoulder, to see the large volume, the Book of Jhest, opened wide, with all but one of its many pages turned over to the left now.

Only one to go. Half, actually, for in the second book similarly opened on the slightly inclining desktop, that last page was half written. Half a page to copy of all the great tome—except for the still-blank two opening pages, which were customarily left so that the scribe could preface the work after completion with a letter to its intended recipient. Up to this point, Dynard had been moving on a roll, momentum gained for the final push and with the hope and expectation that this morning would mark the last day of his copying.

Then had come Dynard's moment of doubt. For the first time since he had embarked upon this task of expanding his boundaries of understanding and spirituality itself, the monk from Honce had come to realize that this particular part of the journey would be a finite thing: that his work here would end.

For months, Dynard had been lost in the swirls of the Jhesta writing, the gracefully curving lines and symbols drawing him into contemplation as surely as any chanting ever could. The concentration of exact copying brought him into that same trancelike and prayerful state of meditation. For months, his work had been his purpose and his life; he knew that he could not underestimate the importance of this. This tome that he would bring back to the north could change the very scope of the Church of Blessed Abelle.

Those thoughts weren't the source of his trembling now, though. With the end of this part of his spiritual journey so clearly in sight, Brother Dynard had finally begun to look toward the next road—the physical road—across the deserts to the coast and north to the mountains and, finally, the sea.

He knew well the perils of that road: the robbers and knaves, the warfare between the rival tribes of the Behr, the snakes and great cats and other monstrous animals, the dreadful and often vengeful power of the sea itself. Even if he arrived back in Honce, around the mountains and into Ethelbert Holding, the road inland to Pryd was a graveyard for foolhardy travelers.

Dynard looked back at the book. Had he done all of this, had he buried himself within the curving lines of understanding and enlightenment, had he created this copy, this artwork, only to have its illuminated and illuminating pages rot in a gully in the rain? Or to have those soft pages used by some ignorant knave to wipe the shite from his arse?

His chest heaved in short gasps. He closed his eyes and told himself to calm down. In a sudden fit of nervous energy, the monk raced out of the room, down the hallway, then out onto the terrace.

The wind blew fiercely this day, dark clouds rushing overhead. Few of the Jhesta Tu were outside, no clothes were drying on the lines, and most of the flowers had been brought inside. His fears churning his stomach, his arms and legs trembling, Brother Dynard walked to the far edge of the terrace, to the rail and the thousand-foot drop to the valley below. His knuckles whitened as he grasped that railing, partly to secure himself and partly out of anger—anger at himself for being so weak in the face not of failure but of triumph.

"I am surely a fool," he said, his words whipped to nothingness by the gusting wind. A self-deprecating chuckle was similarly diminished, as the monk considered the simple humanness of his failure. He recalled a day from his youth in Chud, a small village across the forest from Pryd. With his father, mother, and two sisters, young Bran Dynard had been walking the forest path, a pilgrimage of sorts, to see the new stone chapel being built by this new Church that was sweeping the land, and sweeping the Samhaist religion before it.

Bran's father had never followed the Samhaists and held some anger against them that young Bran did not understand. Not until years later, after his father's death—indeed at the occasion of his father's funeral in Chud—would he learn that his father's twin brother had been sacrificed by the Samhaists; they always killed one of any twins, considering the second born to be an appropriate offering to their gods.

On that road that long-ago day, the family had come to know that they weren't alone. Sounds to the side of the path, in the shadows of the forest, had warned them of robbers, or worse. They moved more swiftly—the smoke of Pryd's fireplaces was in sight up ahead. Bran had seen the sign of danger first, a flash of red in the dark shadows, and on his call of "Powries!" his father had gathered up his younger sister, his mother had grabbed the hand of the other girl, and all had sprinted for the village. For powries, the bloody-cap dwarves, were not ordinary thieves seeking gold or silver—of which the family had none. They sought only human blood in which they could dip their enchanted blood-red berets.

To this day, Dynard didn't know whether or not there really were powries on that forest road. Perhaps it had been a redheaded bird or the bright behind of a wild tusker pig. But he remembered that flight and the sensations that had accompanied it. Barely into his teens, he had dutifully taken up the rear, his father's spear in hand, and had even lagged behind the others so that his engagement with the powries would not force any of them, particularly his father, into the battle. What Dynard remembered most keenly was that he had not been afraid. At that first sighting of the red, he had been terrified, of course; but during the run, his helpless family before him, he had felt only a sort of elation, the pumping of his blood, the determination that these monsters would not wash in the blood of his loved ones, whatever he had to do.

It wasn't until the very end, his family already reaching the wooden gates of Pryd and with only fifty yards left before him, that young Bran Dynard had felt the return of fear, of a terror more profound than anything he had ever known. He was not carrying the spear, but he didn't even know at the terrifying moment that he had dropped it.

By the time he reached the gates, his cheeks were wet with tears, and he stood there before his family and the townsfolk who had come out to see what the commotion was all about, trembling and sobbing and feeling a failure.

A couple of the townsfolk had laughed—probably not at him, though it seemed that way to the teenager. His father, though, had clapped him hard on the shoulder and tousled his hair, thanking him for his courage over and over again.

Bran hadn't believed him and felt himself a coward, but then one man dressed in cumbersome brown robes had come forward and had wrapped him in a hug. He pushed Bran back to arm's length and saluted him. That was when Bran Dynard had first met Father Jerak of Chapel Pryd.

"Is it not strange that only at the end of our run, when the goal seems attainable, that we allow our fears to surface?" Jerak had said to him, and those words echoed now in his mind as he stood on that balcony of the Walk of Clouds.

The monk stepped back from the railing and turned into the fierce wind. He spread his feet shoulders' width apart and brought his arms up before him, entwining his fingers and lifting them high over his head. He found his center of energy, his *chi*, as the Jhesta Tu had taught him, and he extended that line of power down through his legs and feet and into the stone of the terrace.

He stood against the breeze, rooted as firmly as any tree, as solidly as any stone. With his internal strength, he denied the wind, and while his light clothing flapped wildly, Brother Bran Dynard did not move the slightest bit.

In that place and in that time, he found again his heart. Some time later, he went back inside, back to his work; and before the last rays of the sun disappeared from the light of his western window, he closed both books, his task complete.

Only reluctantly did SenWi relinquish her hold on the diamond-faced file, laying the wondrous tool, one of only three such items in all the world, down at her side.

There was no need to continue; the sides of the triangular tip were smooth and even, and no amount of working them would make them more perfect.

The tip was done. The wrapping was done. The final heating and beating of the metal was done, including the attachment of the blade to the hilt and crosspiece. Earlier that same morning, SenWi had finished her own scribing, marking the lines, both delicate and bold, of the flowering vines enwrapping the length of the blade. These symbols, so precise, tied the sword back to the Hou-lei traditions, the warrior cult from which had long ago sprung the Jhesta Tu. There could be no mistaking one of these blades, for there was nothing like them in all the world. The wrapped metal ensured that the blade would only sharpen with use, as layers wore away to even finer edges.

Looking at her sword now, this weapon of few equals, crafted with her own hands, SenWi felt a sense of her past, of her kinship to those who had come before, perfecting their methods, defining the very nature of her existence in their accrued centuries of wisdom. She appreciated them now, more fully perhaps than ever before.

With hands moist and trembling, SenWi lifted the sword and felt its balance. Assuming a two-handed grip on the hilt, she stepped into a fighting stance and brought the weapon slowly through a series of thrusts and parries, as she had done so many thousands of times with wooden practice blades on the terraces of the Walk of Clouds.

She knew that a wondrous journey was before her, with the man she loved, on a road that would lead her farther from her home than she had ever imagined.

Holding this sword, this tie to her past, this tangible reminder of all that she had learned, SenWi was not afraid.

In a display of dazzling colors and sound, of snapping pennants and richly colored clothing, the entire body of Jhesta Tu mystics stood on the terraces, flying bridges, and walkways of their mountain monastery. They sang and played exotic instruments: carved flutes, harps small and large, and tinny, sharp, and strangely melodious four-stringed instruments the like of which Bran Dynard had never before seen.

Sounds, smells, and colors everywhere greeted the couple as they made their way along the terraces. Propelled by the dance-inspiring music, Brother Dynard picked up the pace as they neared the end of that last terrace, the entrance to the long stone stairway that had been carved into the mountain wall eons ago. As they approached, SenWi paused, holding his hand and holding him back.

The monk looked at his new wife and recognized the myriad emotions flowing through her. This was the home she had known for most of her adult life; how terrifying it must now be for her to walk down these steps, knowing that perhaps she would never again make that long and arduous climb.

Dynard waited patiently as the moments slipped past, as the celebration continued around them. He noticed the great masters of the Jhesta Tu, standing in a line beside the stairway entrance, and he saw SenWi's stare focusing that way.

One by one, those masters nodded and smiled, offering both permission and encouragement; finally SenWi glanced over at Bran, smile widening, then pulled him along.

Down the couple went, away from the Walk of Clouds.

Neither of them would ever return.

CHAPTER 2

My Dear Brothers

My dear Brothers of Blessed Abelle,

    I had no idea how wide the world really was. I thought that in my studies I had learned the truth of our lands, of God and of Man. I believed that within the tomes of the philosophers and the fathers, and within the writings of Blessed Abelle himself, I could find the entirety of human existence and purpose, and the hope of ascension beyond this physical experience.

This is what we all hope, of course. This is our prayer and our faith and our reason. These truths shown us by Blessed Abelle have loosened the fear-inspired hold of the Samhaists, and rightly so!

Knowing all of this prepared me for my *Journey Proselyt*, so I believed. With wisdom in hand, I could travel the world secure in my beliefs and in the notion that I could extend those truths to those I encountered. My confidence in the teachings of our faith lent me confidence in the validity of my mission. And, of course, such conviction of the ultimate truths of our faith also bolstered my own courage, for my understanding of what will ultimately befall me, of the existence my spirit will find when my physical being is no more, grants me freedom from fear of the specter of death. Faith led me out of Chapel Pryd. Faith allowed me to place one foot before the other, to travel through lands unknown and dangers unforeseen, though surely anticipated. Faith allowed me to meet peoples of other cultures and lands, and to tell them with confidence of the revelations of Blessed Abelle and the sacred gemstone gifts of God.

With all that knowledge and all that confidence, I hardly expected to find, out there in the world so wide, cultures and ways beyond my expectations. With all the surety afforded by the supreme calm of blessed insight, I hardly expected that I would find my horizons widened even more!

I pray to Blessed Abelle, as do we all, and to the God he showed us; and there is no tremor in my voice—not of doubt, at least!—unless it is the usual shakiness I feel when I attempt to communicate to those so far greater than I.

And yet, my brothers, for all the beauty of Blessed Abelle and for all the completeness of serenity in his teachings, I found myself with eyes wide and heart opened once more. For I have discovered that we who follow the words of Blessed Abelle are not as alone in our faith as we assume. For I have traveled among the Jhesta Tu, generous in spirit and wise in nature. The Jhesta Tu, who understand the same sacred powers offered by our godly gemstone gifts. These mystics, ancient in their ways, are as akin to Blessed Abelle as any man might be. They, too, have found the strength of God, not from gemstones falling from heaven to the shores of holy Pimaninicuit Isle, but within themselves! With energy internal, they replicate the beauty of godly magic.

Are these Jhesta Tu who we shall become?

I do not know, and I do not elevate them above Blessed Abelle, surely. And yet I must insist that from these Jhesta Tu we will find a continuation of our own road to understanding. We must learn from them as they will learn from us—and they have already shown the willingness and the hope that such will occur.

Thus I have copied the Book of Jhest, the foundation of understanding of the Jhesta Tu. In the final measure of my mission, this will prove the most fundamental and important accomplishment of all. Study the Book of Jhest, I beg each of you, with eyes wide and heart open. Infuse yourself with its wisdom and blend the revelations within with the truth we know from Blessed Abelle.

I walked a road with sure strides, but I had no idea that the road would take my spirit to places it had not yet tread. I walked a road to enhance the lives of those pagans I encountered, but I had no idea that the road would brighten my own understanding. I am not afraid of these revelations and the greater scope of miracle, and neither should you be.

Turn these pages with reverent hands. Bask in the words of wisdom of the Jhesta Tu, and find in them enough similarities to show us that the only falsities in our understanding of the truths of Blessed Abelle are the limitations that we naturally place upon those teachings. This was my wont, for never did I imagine the true width of faith's horizon.

Penned this day of Bafway, God's Year 54
Brother Bran Dynard, humble servant of Chapel Pryd

CHAPTER 3

Prydae

With backs stooped from hours and hours of heavy labor, the peasant workers building the road south of the holding of Pryd were most commonly seen with their hands placed firmly on their aching lower backs. They didn't look behind them often as they dug and smoothed the ground between two forested hills, for if they did, they would see the stone tower of Castle Pryd, red pennant emblazoned with the black wolf waving in the brisk breeze above it: a poignant reminder of how short a distance they had actually gone in these weeks of brutal labor and how inconceivable—to the peasants, at least—a distance they had yet to go.

Work had begun on the project in the summer of the previous year. The road itself was not an elaborate affair, merely a widening and smoothing of the existing southern cart paths, with the ground pounded flat and strategically reinforced with wide flagstones. Laird Pryd had been quite pleased with the progress made in the late summer weeks and those of autumn, but all those involved—particularly the peasants pressed into this hard labor—had been quite dismayed to find, when the snow had at last relinquished its grip on the land, that much of their work had been damaged by the frost heaves of the unusually harsh winter.

"At least I won't be needing to clean under me fingernails," one man griped to another as they stood beside the road in a moment of respite, their heavy flagstones set on the ground before them, upright and leaning against their bare, badly bruised, and always scuffed shins.

"That's because ye got no fingernails," the other replied, and he held up his own hand, filthy and battered. "By the time we make the mountain shadow, all of us'll be missing more than that, I'm thinking."

"Bah, but you're the fool, for we're not to live long enough to ever cool in the shadows of them great mountains."

"Come on, then, the two of you," came a call from up the road. The pair turned to see a soldier of Pryd, splendid astride his tall horse and in his shining breastplate of bronze. With each pace of the mount, the hard sheath of the short sword on the soldier's hip made a clapping sound against the iron studs of his leather skirt. "They're needing stones up front. Now get about it."

Both peasants sucked in their breaths, bent their knobbly knees, and hooked their arms under the bottoms of the large stones, then hoisted them and began waddling away.

"Weren't that Doughbeard's boy?" one gasped to the other when they had moved beyond the soldier's range of hearing.

"Aye, and ain't he looking all pretty up there on his fine horse?"

"So many o' them young and strong ones do, while our old bones creak and crack."

"Creak and crack! And swim in the mud and horses' shite."

"And work all the day and all o' the night," said the other, taking up the cadence and the nonsensical rhyme.

"Until them soldiers be out o' our sight!" the other went on, and he cackled with laughter between the grunts.

His friend started to cackle as well, but broke off, feeling an impact and the sound of a sharp rap against the front of the stone he was carrying. He staggered back a step, managed a "what?" and then lost his words and his breath as he recognized what had struck his stone was a stone-headed throwing axe now lying on the ground before him.

Had he not been carrying a flagstone against his chest like some unintended breastplate, that axe wouldn't now be on the ground, he knew.

"What are ye about?" his friend asked, staggering to a stop and turning. He followed the ashen-faced gaze of the stunned man to the weapon.

"Bloody caps!" the man shouted, and he dropped his stone and ran back toward his friend, who still stood there, holding the stone that had saved his life, and staring slack-jawed at the axe.

"Go, old fool! Go!" the fleeing man shouted, grabbing his friend's shoulder as he raced past, turning him; but as he did, his friend lost his grip on the stone and it crashed to the ground, clipping his foot and bringing a great howl from him.

The fleeing man didn't wait, didn't slow at all. He ran back up the road, toward that fluttering pennant, screaming "Bloody caps!" at the top of his lungs.

Y our scouts were correct," young Prince Prydae said to the guard captain standing beside him. They had moved secretly into place, under the cover of the brush and trees to the side of the road. A hundred yards or so farther down the road, all the workers were running and waving their arms frantically, the calls of "Powries!" and "Bloody caps!" filling the air.

The nobleman slid his leather gauntlets onto his hands and stepped into his chariot—the most magnificent war cart in all the holding. It was bordered on three sides by waist-high walls of hard oak and leather, a running black wolf painted on either side, silver trim running the length of it. The wheels were heavy and sturdy, with spokes as thick as a strong man's forearms, and hubs set with scythe blades that stuck out for more than a foot. The pulling team, a pair of Laird Pryd's strongest horses, pawed the ground, eager to run.

To any onlookers, young Prince Prydae did not appear out of place there. He stood strong and tall, his blue eyes set with determination in a face not unaccustomed to scowling. When he did so scowl, Prydae's thick brow furrowed such that it formed a triangular chasm atop his long, thin nose; and people in all the region for many years had known to beware the "sharp shadows of anger" from the men of the line of Pryd!

Prydae's other features were no less powerful: a strong chin and high-boned cheeks that bespoke his noble heritage. His black hair was neatly trimmed about his ears; and thick sideburns ran down to touch the thin jawline beard, which blended in with a thin goatee and mustache, as was the fashion of the day. He wore a bronze breastplate, fitted perfectly to his muscular frame, leaving his arms bare. Many nobleman warriors had taken to wearing iron instead of the softer bronze, but Prydae preferred this piece precisely because the soft metal had allowed his craftsman to decorate it with grand designs. Right at the ridge below the breasts was a line of running wolves, three across and nose to tail. The back of the piece boasted clever swirls and geometric shapes, and even contained the "fisted P," a letter formed from an upraised forearm and cocked and balled fist, the emblem of the line of Pryd.

Prydae did use iron for his open-faced helmet and for the metal greaves overlaid onto thick leather breeches. His belt was leather, too, wrapped in a bright red sash of fine fabric; and complementing that, a red ribbon was tied about Prydae's right upper arm, a black one tight about his left biceps, a sign of his station in the Holdings of Pryd. Only Prydae or his father, Pryd, could by law wear such distinctive armbands within the holding.

"Well, my friend, shall we go and remind the peasants of the importance of the House of Pryd?" the young nobleman remarked, turning a sly smile at the garrison captain.

"Indeed, my liege."

"Take care the powries, for they are no easy foe."

"Yes, my liege."

Prydae gave a nod to his trusted soldier, a man handpicked by his father to watch over him, then cracked his whip. The horses burst from the brush, charging up the short incline to the road and thundering down onto it, the chariot bouncing wildly. Prydae held his stance securely, urging the galloping horses on even harder.

He cracked the whip above his head and waved the peasants out of the way—and how they scrambled, diving from the road!

Prydae soon came in sight of the one mounted soldier who had been at the forefront of the work area and was now bringing up the rear of the fleeing peasants, shouting at them to run for their lives. The man was lurching, one shoulder forward, and Prydae noted the flash of red behind him, the telltale shimmer of the blood-soaked berets.

More peasants dove to the side; one was not quite fast enough and got clipped by Prydae's team and sent flying from the road. Before the young nobleman, the wounded soldier seemed hardly in control of his mount anymore, but the well-trained horse veered out of the way just in time, leaving the racing chariot a straight line to the charging bloody-cap dwarves.

Those powries were odd little creatures, each standing under five feet, with a broad, thick torso and shoulders at least as wide as those of a large man, but with spindly little limbs, whose size was exaggerated by the bulky, padded, and metal-stripped armor the dwarves wore around their barrel-like torsos and by the fact that the powries were almost always bearded, with bushy, wild-flying hair sticking out from under their caps. Prydae was seasoned enough not to underestimate the strength in those spindly limbs, though—as he was reminded now by a dwarf, near the front of their charging line, who carried an iron-headed axe so huge and bulky that few humans could have wielded it.

With typical ferocity, the ten bloodthirsty dwarves didn't turn from the sudden appearance and charge of the prince and his entourage.

Prydae grasped one of the small iron-tipped spears set at the front of his chariot, and hoisted it high. Before him, the powries parted ranks, some scrambling wide, others barely sidestepping the charging horses, no doubt to try to strike at him as the chariot raced past. Prydae let the scythe blades of his wheels handle the immediate threat, the spinning weapons slicing deep into the surprised dwarves, taking a leg from one, disemboweling another, and hooking the leather tunic of a third, who was trying to scramble aside, pulling it along in a bone-crunching tumble. Then the prince threw his spear deep into the chest of a powrie at the side of the road.

He had no time to grab another spear, for a dwarf at the left side of the road before him was already launching an axe his way. Prydae shifted his reins to his right hand and cracked his whip at the dwarf with his left. He felt the thump as the axe smacked against his breastplate and bounced aside, clipping his chin and drawing a line of blood.

Prydae growled through the pain and pulled hard on the reins, wanting to slow his team, wanting to get back around in time to repay that particular dwarf before his soldiers killed them all.

As the chariot slowed, Prydae let go of the reins altogether and grabbed his shield and leaped from the chariot back, drawing his sword as he went.

The powries were scattering now as the full force rolled over them; in those initial moments of combat, more than half were down. Prydae did not lose sight of the axe thrower in that turmoil, noting the dwarf scrambling toward the trees. Running full out, Prydae's longer legs chewing up the ground, he caught up to the wretch in the shadows of the nearest boughs.

The powrie spun to meet the charge, an axe in either hand. It wasted no time, but came forward wildly, slashing left and right.

Prydae dodged back, avoiding one cut, and got his shield out in front to block the second. His arm went numb under the force of the heavy blow, and good luck alone prevented him from having his arm cloven, for the axe crunched right through his wood and leather shield, hooking in place.

Prydae retracted the shield arm hard, tugging the axe along with it. The powrie started to tug back, but it saw the danger as Prydae stabbed ahead powerfully with his iron-bladed sword.

Metal rang against metal as the powrie cunningly parried with its free axe. But the dwarf lost its grip on that second, trapped axe, with the prince spinning and tugging it free. Prydae threw his arm out behind him, dropping his shield and hardly interrupting his momentum as he charged forward, stabbing again and again.

The powrie frantically slashed with its axe, clipping Prydae's sword, though the prince was already retracting it anyway. The powrie managed to retreat enough so that the prince's next strike fell short of the mark.

More important to Prydae was that he saw his attacks were keeping the dwarf moving and dancing, preventing it from reaching for its third axe that Prydae saw strapped behind its left shoulder. Fortunately, since its left hand was the empty one, the dwarf could not both fight and retrieve the remaining weapon.

And Prydae was determined not to give the creature a chance. He stepped boldly ahead, and the powrie's axe rang out against his thrusting sword. He stepped and slashed; the powrie darted back to his left, just under the blow, then riposted hard with a slash and back slash of the axe, forcing Prydae to throw back his hips. When the powrie tried to use this apparent opening to toss its axe to its left hand, freeing the right so it could easily reach its other weapon, Prydae came forward again.

The powrie had barely caught the axe in its left hand. Recognizing its own vulnerability, it simply threw the weapon forward.

But Prydae didn't flinch, ignoring the dull metallic ring as the axe bounced off his breastplate. The powrie had its right arm back, reaching for the axe, presenting Prydae with a fine opening through the armhole of its jerkin.

The nobleman warrior took that opening. He slammed in hard against the dwarf, wrapping his free arm around the beast to keep its arm trapped between them, while his sword sank deep through the armpit.

The pair went down hard, the impact of the ground only furthering the sword's bite. His face barely inches from the powrie's grimace, Prydae heard its growl and groan. He felt the wretched little creature tense beneath him, tightening every one of its muscles as if it meant to simply crush the sword within it!

And still the powrie growled long and low, a rumbling breath of denial.

It went on and on and on, and Prydae did not let go, did not lessen the pressure on the stabbing blade. He tried to turn his sword, which brought a different pitch to the powrie's groaning protest, and the vicious dwarf even tried to bite Prydae's face.

But there was little energy in its lunge, and gradually Prydae felt the powrie's muscles relax. The growling stopped and the dwarf lay very still, eyes wide and staring at Prydae with hatred.

They were dull eyes, though, with no life behind them.

Prydae pulled himself off the dwarf and yanked his sword free. He stood and surveyed the area. One fight was still raging, but his soldiers seemed to have it under complete control, with several of the mounted warriors surrounding a single dwarf who already had at least five spears sticking from him.

"Seven of ten dead, my prince," a soldier reported, trotting his mount up beside the blood-spattered nobleman. A shriek rent the air, and the pair glanced over to see the surrounded powrie finally go down. When it tried to rise, one of the soldiers guided his horse over and had the beast stomp the dwarf flat.

"Eight," the soldier corrected. "Two have fled to the forest, but we will hunt them down."

Prydae nodded, then moved toward his abandoned chariot. "And what of my people?"

The soldier quickly dismounted so that he would be walking beside his prince and not towering above him. "A few minor injuries," he explained. "One man dropped a heavy stone on his foot as he tried to flee. That might be the worst of it. With all the talk of powries of late, the peasants were well prepared to run away."

"Double the guard along the road," Prydae ordered as he reached the back of the chariot. He paused and reconsidered. "Nay, triple it. We have no need for another display of force anytime soon. The peasants understand that we protect them; their complaints will be fewer. So let us dissuade the fierce dwarves or any other monsters that might be about from even beginning such a battle."

"Aye, my liege."

Prydae waved the man away and pulled himself up into the chariot. The well-schooled team had not continued after he had leaped from it, nor had they veered off the road. Prydae turned them around until he had them trotting back down the road toward the castle of his father.

He kept his eyes straight ahead, a look of "royal calm"—as Laird Pryd liked to call it—upon his face as he guided the magnificent chariot past his soldiers and the gathering of appreciative peasants. The soldiers fell into ranks behind him, adding to his splendor; the peasants called his name, cheering.

Prydae held his royal calm and slowly paced his team past them all. The battle had gone exactly as he had hoped it would. When reliable reports of powries gathering in the area had come to him, along with many reports of grumbling among the workers, he had seen the potential of quelling both problems. And so he had lain in wait with his choice warriors, and with one decisive charge they had defeated the powrie threat as well as the chorus of complaints. And not a soldier was badly injured, and the few injured peasants would likely heal.

It had been a good day's work.

Chapel Pryd, a stone structure that could hold nearly four hundred people in its wide and long nave, was only a short walk from the much more dominating stone structure of the holding, the castle of Laird Pryd itself. But to old Father Jerak, the number of required paces to go from one building to the other seemed greater and greater each day.

He could count those paces, too, and easily for the increasing stoop of his back had his eyes looking at his feet, and it was only with increasing effort that he was able to look up. He didn't complain, though, as he and Brother Bathelais made their way up the narrow stair to Castle Pryd's portcullis and then past the guard towers and up a longer flight of stairs to the audience halls of the laird, which were set more than halfway up the tall tower that served as the principal keep.

They were welcomed without question and admitted without formal introduction, for visits to Laird Pryd of the two presiding holy men of his holding were not uncommon and of late had become a more-than-weekly matter.

As usual, Laird Pryd was sitting on his huge oaken throne, its arm rests gilded, its high back bejeweled. He was the same age as Father Jerak, and, indeed, the two had known each other for more than forty years, since the then-young Jerak had been assigned to Pryd Holding after his training in the mother chapel of Abelle, along the coast to the north. Unlike Father Jerak, though, the laird didn't so obviously show his age. He sat straight and tall; and while his hair was now more salt than pepper, and perhaps his blue eyes did not hold their previous luster, he kept his shoulders squared, his jaw high, and his beard and hair meticulously trimmed.

Behind him and to the side stood another aged man, with hawkish features and a scowl that only intensified whenever the monks of Abelle entered the room. Jerak paid Rennarq, Laird Pryd's close adviser, no heed, but Bathelais always took note of that scowl. Rennarq was rumored to be a staunch Samhaist, though not openly, of course.

The two monks moved up before the throne and bowed to their laird. Jerak was glad that Bathelais held his arm, for without that support, he feared that he would have tumbled at Laird Pryd's feet.

"You seem rather tired today, old priest," Laird Pryd remarked, and at his side, his sentry snickered.

"Our work has been long, Laird," Brother Bathelais answered.

"That is the way of things."

Jerak forced his eyes up to meet those of the laird. Whenever Pryd made that particular remark—"That is the way of things"—his tone became dismissive. "That is the way of things," Jerak understood, meant that there was nothing Laird Pryd meant to do to remedy it.

"We have come to discuss the matter of your son," Father Jerak said.

"The matter? Whatever matter my son might have is hardly a concern of yours."

Father Jerak bowed in deference at the not so subtle reminder that he and all the brothers of Abelle were allowed and recognized in Pryd Holding at the sufferance of the laird. Again, the old monk was glad of the physical support of Brother Bathelais.

"He drives the peasants hard, Laird," Jerak said.

"Their work is important."

"We spend all the night with the soul stones, Laird, alleviating their aches and trying to mend fingers cracked from digging and hammering and carrying those huge flagstones."

"I am grateful for your efforts, I assure you. But that is your duty, is it not?"

"Their maladies outpace our abilities to heal them," Father Jerak began to explain, trying to keep his voice steady in the face of Pryd's continuing dismissive tone.

"Winter will come soon enough, we all know, and they will have the quiet months in which to recover."

"My laird—"

"This business only aids your Church, as well, can you not agree?" Pryd interrupted. "My son, serving as my voice, shows the peasants the way to a better life through their toil. That toil begets suffering, of course, and so you serve a heroic and healing role, one that no doubt enamors the peasants of your Blessed Abelle. I believe that my son's tactics serve you well in your continuing duel with the Samhaists for the souls of the people." He offered a smile that sent a shiver coursing along Jerak's spine, and Jerak glanced past him to note the scowl of Rennarq.

"Ah, those marvelous and sacred gemstones," Pryd went on. "So much more convincing must they be when you put them to use in such a practical and helpful manner as healing the injuries and maladies of dim-witted peasants!"

It was a joke, of course, and one that had Laird Pryd and all his guards laughing, but only with great effort was Father Jerak tactfully able to join in.

"Perhaps there is a compromise to be found," the old monk suggested.

The smile disappeared in a blink from Pryd's face. "All the lairds have agreed on the construction of these roads, and for good reason."

Before he could go on, a side door of the audience chamber banged open and Prydae strode into the room, still wearing his battle gear and still with the stains of powrie blood and of his own, where dried blood had crusted on his beard.

"Powries," he explained. "A band on the road."

Father Jerak gasped.

"Our healing skills will be needed at the chapel," Brother Bathelais said.

Father Jerak noted the dismissive look young Prydae turned on the holy men at that moment, a typical response from the prince, whom Jerak believed viewed the Church of Abelle as a rival to the power and wealth of his forthcoming inheritance. No doubt, Jerak supposed, that crafty old Rennarq often whispered disparaging remarks into Prydae's ear.

"Yes, some of the peasants were injured," Prydae said, looking back at his father. "Unfortunate."

"As they often have been injured since you began your work on the roads," Father Jerak dared to say, and Brother Bathelais gave his arm an insistent squeeze.

"Truly, I should think that you would wish the roads completed," Prydae was quick to reply, "that you can spread the word of your God and bring more and more folk under your control."

"They are not under our control, young prince," Father Jerak corrected. "They serve beside us because they, too, see the truth of the word of Blessed Abelle and the hopes of eternal life and redemption."

Behind the throne, Rennarq snorted.

"As you will," Prydae said with a bow.

Father Jerak stared at the prince a moment longer, then turned back to Laird Pryd and gave a stiff bow. He and Brother Bathelais took their leave immediately, knowing that they had much work to do.

"Step lightly with the brothers of Abelle," Laird Pryd warned his son as soon as the holy men had gone. "Their Church is displacing the Samhaists in the hearts of the commoners and is fast becoming a dominant force in all Honce. It would not do your aspirations well to turn them against you."

"You overstate their hand, my laird," Rennarq dared to put in.

"And you have stubbornly denied the obvious for more than a quarter of a century, my old friend," Pryd replied.

"The lairds rule Honce, not the Church," Prydae remarked, and then pointedly added, "Not either Church."

"And the wise lairds will see the Church of Abelle for what it is and use it to their best designs," Pryd went on, directing his words to his son. "There is talk of unity in the land, the likes of which I have not heard in my lifetime, the likes of which have not been known in Honce since the Samhaists ruled both body and soul." He looked back at Rennarq again, and teased, "The golden age of Honce?"

Rennarq couldn't help but smile at that, and he didn't voice his belief that such an estimate might not be far from the truth.

"That talk is fostered by the agreement to build the roads," Prydae observed. "What laird has refused his resources in this endeavor?"

"None of the thirty," Pryd answered. "Because the driving force is that Delaval City, on the Masur Delaval, has proceeded with their road building, with or without our agreement."

"I have heard the marvels of the Delaval roads," said Prydae. "Lined in iron, so say the traveling skalds."

"Indeed, and in this endeavor, if we are behind, we risk irrelevance. The world is changing before our eyes and it is up to us to determine where we will fit into those changes. Think of the trade when the roads connect! And we will be better able to move our armies."

"To drive the powries from the land."

"And to exterminate the goblins," Laird Pryd said, his old eyes gleaming, for he still felt the pangs from a wound in his hip, an injury received in his youth from a goblin spear. "We may tame the land, at long last, but only if we are able to work in coordination with the other lairds of Honce and only if we can keep the peasants content through the years of trial they will no doubt face.

"And that is where the brothers of Abelle will prove their usefulness. Their gemstones heal the wounds even as their promises of eternal life strengthen the spirit. The Samhaists ever ruled by fear, but the brothers of Abelle have found a greater means. They guide with promises that no man or woman could resist. See the light of Abelle and you will find eternal rest. Hear the words of Abelle and you will one day be reunited with your loved ones who have died. What mother could deny her desire to one day see again her lost child?"

"These promises have been made before, many times," Rennarq reminded.

"But the brothers of Abelle strengthen such promises with the gemstones," Laird Pryd explained. "They have the gifts of God to prove their words."

Prydae looked at his father, studying the man from head to foot. "You believe them," he said at length. "You believe the way of Blessed Abelle."

Pryd shrugged, but he wasn't quick to offer a denial.

The prince looked back at Rennarq, whose expression clearly showed that Prydae's words had hit the mark.

"Would it be so bad a thing if Abelle were proven right?" Laird Pryd replied. "If his promises were true? You are a young man yet, my son, and do not concern yourself with questions of what might follow this life. Even in your battles, you do not believe that death will find you. But I am old—every day I awaken to feel the creeping of age in my bones and in my heart. Many are the nights that I close my eyes and wonder if I ever shall open them again."

Prydae walked to the edge of the dais and sat down. He had never heard such words as this from the unshakable Laird of Pryd before. A frown creased his face as he considered the words of his father and mentor.

"The peasants cheered you in your splendid armor?" Pryd asked.

Prydae glanced back at him, and did manage a smile. "Four powries fell to my hand—my soldiers will claim that I killed six single-handedly. Of course the peasants were appreciative."

"As they should be. We offer them protection. We give them their very lives, every day. And we ask little in return."

Laird Pryd gave a chuckle as he considered his own words. "Nay," he corrected, "we ask nothing of them. We demand what we must, and they have no choice but to comply. That is the way of it."

"They would be wandering sheep, fodder for the powries, without us," Prydae reminded, and his father nodded.

"As it has always been and as it will always be," the laird remarked.

T he young one is brash and headstrong," Bathelais observed, not for the first time, when he and old Jerak finally walked out of Castle Pryd's main gates.

While Bathelais's words were spoken in a jesting and almost dismissive manner, Father Jerak didn't share his amusement. "And we both know that the wretch Rennarq whispers in his ear," he said. "Prince Prydae cares nothing for the suffering of the peasants. I wonder if he even hears their groans."

"Like so many noblemen, he views the world beyond the concerns of the individual," reasoned Bathelais. "He sees the gains the roads might bring to all of us, beyond the pain some might suffer in creating them."

"That is the place of the laird, it would seem," said Jerak. "What, then, might be the place of the Church of Blessed Abelle?"

The seemingly simple question set Bathelais back on his heels, so much so that the old monk walked right past him and continued alone for many moments. For in that seemingly simple inquiry, Bathelais saw many deeper questions. Was Father Jerak insinuating that it was the place of the Church to work against the lairds, as the Samhaists had done, often and futilely, in their string of miserable failures? Though it had made great gains in its seventy years of existence—particularly in the fifty-four years since the death of Father Abelle and the creation of the new Honce calendar—the Church of Abelle was still in its infancy. Missionaries armed with gemstones had traveled far and wide, and every holding in Honce had a chapel of Abelle of one sort or another. And yet it was clear to Bathelais, as it had been earlier to Jerak, that their very existence was under the sufferance of the individual lairds.

With a wave of his hand, Laird Pryd could order the Chapel Pryd dismantled, stone by stone, and all of the brothers expelled from his holding. Or worse.

Bathelais hurried to catch up, and found Father Jerak talking away, as if he hadn't even been aware of his companion's absence.

"The people will love us because we salve their wounds," Jerak remarked, and he picked up his pace, for he could hear the crying and groaning within the chapel now and knew that the wounded were waiting. "We must remain worthy of their trust, that they can trust, too, in the message we bring. But we cannot feed them, can we? We cannot protect them from the monsters of the world, can we?"

"Then what are we to do?"

Jerak stopped and slowly turned to face the younger brother, straining his stiff neck so that he could look Bathelais in the eye. "In serving the lairds, we serve the people of Honce," he said. "Never forget that."

CHAPTER 4

Sailing to Civilization

It was comforting to smell the salty air and to see the dark swells of the Mirianic again, and with good fortune on the road, Bran Dynard and SenWi made the city of Jacintha at just the right time of year, barely a week before the summer solstice, when the fearsome ocean could be well navigated. The spring storms were behind them and the dark waters had calmed somewhat.

Even in the summer, it was not easy to find transport around the eastern spurs of the Belt-and-Buckle mountains and to the land of Honce. All of the boats sailing around Jacintha were coastal vessels, and the coastline to the north was rocky and treacherous. Still, for those daring enough to try the journey, there were fine profits to be had in Honce.

Dynard and SenWi wound up on a merchant vessel, a square, flat-bottomed, and high-sided craft set with a single square sail and rows of five oars on either side. Though he could use the extra hands at the oars, the merchant sailor, a man so leathery and wrinkled and hunched over that some questioned whether he was human or powrie, had been reluctant to take them on. Only after Dynard had used his soul stone on the sailor's blistered feet, alleviating the man's pain, had the deal been struck; and even with that, Dynard and SenWi found themselves laboring at the oars almost continually throughout the journey.

"And if we see some sharks, you're sure to be the ones getting fed to them!" the sailor said every time he passed the couple, always offering a wide and ridiculous two-toothed smile.

Given the sword SenWi had beside her, Brother Dynard rather doubted that.

The small craft had to swing so wide of the coast to avoid the treacherous rocks that the journey from Jacintha to Ethelbert Town, a mere fifty miles as a bird might fly, took them nearly a week. But they got onto the sandy beach that lined the harbor without serious incident, and with just the cracked lips and sunburned skin that any extended stay on an uncovered boat guaranteed.

"Lucky ones, aren't you, that we saw no sharks?" the wrinkled sailor cackled as he walked between the couple, and he gave SenWi an exaggerated wink. Then he stopped and turned, assuming a pensive posture.

"Once more with that stone of yours?" he asked, lifting his bare foot up.

Brother Dynard was in too fine a mood to resist, so he produced the hematite, the sacred soul stone, and brought it before his eyes, quietly reciting the prayers that would allow him entrance to the gray stone's depths. He continued to pray for some time, then pressed the stone against the sailor's battered, sea-soaked, and rotting appendage. Dynard felt the stone's magical energies reaching out even before the old sailor gave a moan of relief.

The boat slid against the sand beneath the shallow waters then, and the sailor pitched backward, though with the extraordinary balance that only a seaman could ever achieve, he caught himself before he tumbled to the deck. He gave another cackle and stomped his healed foot hard on the deck, then even did a little dance of appreciation.

Dynard and SenWi dropped off the side of the boat, into water that came halfway between Dynard's knee and waist. They hardly noticed and hardly cared, for they were on dry land in seconds, navigating through the crowd that was coming down to see the southern boat and its exotic wares.

"It is one of the greatest cities of Honce," Dynard was explaining to SenWi as they moved up the slope of the beach and more and more of Ethelbert came into view. Many cottages were spread about the lower reach of the community, which was built on several layers climbing into the foothills of the great mountains.

Brother Dynard paused and spent a long while more fully surveying the scene, then closed his eyes and tried to compare it to the vision of Ethelbert he had known as he had sailed out of the place nearly ten years before.

"The city has grown," he remarked, as much to himself as to SenWi. "When I last journeyed through here, most of the folk of Ethelbert lived in those caves up there." He pointed to the south, where the ground climbed sharply and where many cave openings could be seen at many different levels, connected by ladders, most with balconies carved in the stone before them.

"It is not as primitive as it might seem," Dynard quickly added as he considered the view, and how the structures of Ethelbert paled beside the marvels of Walk of Clouds or the great man-made stone structures of Jacintha.

SenWi offered him a comforting and nonjudgmental smile.

To the southwest of their current position, Dynard pointed out Castle Ethelbert dos Entel, though he hardly needed his guiding finger to show SenWi the structure, which so dominated the landscape. It was built against the cliff wall; indeed, the bulk of the place was within the cliffs themselves, tying into the natural limestone caverns common at the lowest levels. But this castle, worked and expanded generation after generation, was much more external than internal, with huge round towers, sweeping walkways, and a magnificent gatehouse that seemed as if it alone could hold all the people of the town.

"Come," Brother Dynard bade her, taking her delicate hand in his own. "Let us see if Laird Ethelbert will grant us audience."

Focused on that thought, his mind spinning as he came to fully comprehend that he was back in his homeland, Brother Dynard hardly noticed that the farther he and SenWi got from the beach, the more curious grew the stares of the Honce folk.

Similarly, when Dynard approached the sentry at Castle Ethelbert and introduced himself and stated his wishes for an audience, and the man responded, "You come bearing gifts, brother monk?" it almost escaped Dynard that the sentry was looking directly at SenWi.

Several flights of stairs later, Dynard paused by a tower window to take in a wider view of the land. Only then could he comprehend how dramatically Ethelbert Holding had grown in the last decade. Out to the west of the city, the great forests had been felled to make room for many more houses—and even more striking—for tracts of land for farming.

The sentry led the pair through a short corridor that took them into the smoky inner chambers of the complex, where stone walls were mostly covered by ancient tapestries of sailors and great battles, and sculptures of the line of Ethelbert lairds decorated every hallway. The couple soon found themselves before the present laird of the holding, a burly, sun-hardened man with curly black hair and eyes the color of the sea under a blanket of gray clouds. He was older than Dynard by a dozen years, but seemed fit enough to travel the world, battling goblins and powries every step of the way.

"Greetings, Laird Ethelbert," Dynard began with a bow. "I doubt you remember me, but once have I come before you."

"Yes, yes," the older man said. "From . . . Pryd, was it?"

Brother Dynard looked up, smiling widely. "Indeed it was, my laird. I am Brother Bran Dynard of Chapel Pryd, returned from the desert of Behr."

"With a fine trophy, I see," said Ethelbert, tilting his head to regard SenWi.

"My wife, SenWi," Dynard said. He looked at SenWi as he spoke, so he didn't see Ethelbert widen his eyes at the declaration that the two were married.

"Greetings, L—Lair . . . ?" She looked at her husband for support.

"Forgive her, Laird Ethelbert, for her command of our language is not yet complete." He draped his arm over SenWi's shoulders and pulled her close. "I am teaching her, but it was much more important for me to learn the southern languages during my years there."

"I see," said Ethelbert, his tone a bit flatter. "Well, what might I do for you, good brother? I am sure that Father Destros would wish to speak with you. Do you know Destros?"

"Was he Brother Destros when last I came through?"

"Yes, that would be right. Only recently has he assumed leadership of our chapel. Poor Father Senizer was forced aside by issues of his health, I am sorry to say. You might speak with him, as well, but I fear that he will not comprehend your presence and will have no memory of your previous visit."

"Your holding has grown greatly since my last journey through, Laird," Dynard remarked. "I congratulate you."

"No less than has grown your Church, good brother. The teachings of the brothers of Abelle, and those marvelous stones you command, have put the Samhaists in retreat throughout the lands of Honce. Every holding has a chapel now, of course."

Dynard couldn't contain his smile at that. He squeezed SenWi close again and grinned at her.

"And now we are all hard at work on the roads," Laird Ethelbert went on. "You will find your traveling far easier on the trails just west and north of my holding, and though you will have to pass through lands still wild, you will again find solid roads awaiting you as you near Pryd, if that is where you plan to go."

"It is indeed. My mission is ended, more successfully than I could ever have imagined. Have you word of Father Jerak and Pryd Holding?"

"None of Jerak," said Ethelbert, "but Laird Pryd is well, and his son is making quite a name for himself in driving back the powrie threat."

Dynard nodded and smiled, though the news did catch him a bit off his guard. Prydae had been a mere boy when Dynard had left the holding, after all, and the sudden realization that the boy was now a man came as a stark reminder to him that he had been gone a long, long time.

"I will see to it that you are escorted to the borders of my holding when you are ready to go," Laird Ethelbert said. He came forward in his seat and motioned to the nearest sentry, indicating that the audience was at its end. "Is there anything more you would ask of me?"

"No, Laird, you are most generous," Bran Dynard said with a bow. He started to walk away with SenWi and the guard, but Ethelbert waved him back suddenly.

"Approach closer," the laird said, waving him right up to the throne.

Brother Dynard glanced back at SenWi, who kept looking at him over her shoulder and at the guard, who kept pulling her along to the doors.

Ethelbert put his hand on Dynard's wide shoulder and pulled him close.

"Have I offended you, Laird?" the confused monk asked.

"Me? No, no. But I offer you now a word of advice. Call it my respect for the Church of Abelle, or perhaps it is merely that I am fond of a man such as yourself who dares travel the world. I traveled extensively in my own youth, you know."

"Indeed, I had heard as much, Laird."

"To the desert of Behr on several occasions," Ethelbert explained. "I would tell you then, with worldly knowledge and a better understanding than you possess, perhaps, of man's failings, that you would not be wise to so openly announce this dark-skinned creature as your wife."

Brother Dynard reflexively pulled away, staring hard at the laird. "Am I to be embarrassed?"

"Of course not. Her beauty cannot be denied. But you must understand that Ethelbert Holding is unique among the lands of Honce in our understanding and acceptance of the southern race of Behr. You'll not find . . ."

The laird paused and smiled warmly, if a bit resignedly. "Well, take my advice as you will, good brother. I congratulate you on your safe return and on the knowledge and happiness you have seemingly discovered."

"For so long, I feared my journey to Behr," Dynard admitted. "I had been taught that the people south of the mountains were animal-like, and so you can imagine my surprise when I witnessed the beauties of Jacintha, and when I . . ." He paused, seeing that Laird Ethelbert was holding up his hand.

"Again I congratulate you, good brother, and take pleasure in welcoming you home. I pray that you will find your forthcoming journey through the lands of Honce as enlightening as your travels south seem to have been." He waved to the now-closest guard as he finished, and Brother Bran was escorted out of the room to rejoin SenWi.

"What did he want?" SenWi asked, using the language of Behr.

"Nothing important at all," Dynard assured her, and he leaned in and kissed her on the forehead. "A private welcome for a returning countryman."

Dynard was not so blind as to expect that SenWi believed that explanation, but she did accept it.

As she accepted the curious stares of those they had passed on the way up to the castle, he supposed.

CHAPTER 5

Long Roots

With great effort, his limbs wearier this night than usual, old Father Jerak pulled on the brown robes set with the red trim that marked his station in the Church of Abelle. The news had just come in to him that an adulteress had been caught, and now, predictably, old Bernivvigar was demanding his rite of justice. Father Jerak could well imagine the scene of eager onlookers, and he had personally witnessed the look upon the Samhaist Bernivvigar's face several times in the past: the satisfaction, a calm so profound that it reeked of savagery, as if this act of brutal retribution and the willingness of the laird and the people to go along with it somehow denied the changes sweeping through the land with the ascendant Church of Abelle.

There came a soft knock on Jerak's door, and it creaked open. He turned to see brothers Bathelais and Reandu.

"Are you ready to go, Father?" Bathelais asked, his tone appropriately somber.

"If anyone can ever be ready for such a journey as this," Jerak replied, and he started toward the door.

"The legacy of Samhaist justice," Bathelais said with a shrug that made it clear to Jerak that the younger man was not so upset by the rite.

"The woman is guilty," young Reandu declared rather bluntly, and both of the other monks turned their surprised gazes upon him. Reandu—a short man with close-cropped black hair and a solid, if diminutive, frame—shrank back beneath those looks.

"There is always the question of proportion, brother," Father Jerak quietly offered. "In this case, the proportion of sin to punishment was determined long ago, and it has not been within our province to modify its balance. Someday, perhaps, we will see a different measure of things and convince the lairds of our enlightened position. For now, though, our duty is to acquiesce to the law humbly and to bear witness to its legitimacy."

Jerak paused, as if considering his own words. "But it is a long journey."

The three monks swept up four other brothers before they had exited

Chapel Pryd. By the time they had gotten outside, they could see the bonfire marking the ancient Stone of Judgment already burning brightly.

"Try not to reveal your enjoyment of the spectacle, if indeed you do find it amusing," Laird Pryd said to his son. Lying on his goose-down bed and wearing only a cotton nightshirt that reached to his ankles, the Laird of Pryd Holding didn't seem quite so formidable this particular evening. Laird Pryd had taken ill that very day, and now his eyes were sunken and darkly ringed, contrasting starkly to the chalky color of his face.

"You are the eyes of Pryd this night," the laird went on. "Your presence sanctions the event under the laws of the holding."

Prydae, dressed in his full military regalia, bronze breastplate and all, bowed.

"You need do nothing but bid Bernivvigar to commence," Laird Pryd explained. "Take your seat and bear witness; the old Samhaist will preside over the course of events. He takes great pleasure in these things, you see."

Prydae felt a bit of hesitance, leading to an expression that his perceptive father did not miss. "This will not be a crime paid for with coin," Pryd said.

Prydae looked at his father directly and nodded.

"Bernivvigar is not to allow that in these times," Pryd went on. "The Samhaists feel the press of the Church of Abelle, you see, and what have they to offer the peasants but the surety of order contained within their codes of strict justice?" Pryd raised a hand and dropped it on Prydae's forearm. "You are prepared for this?"

Prydae shook his head at the whole question. "I will not disappoint you, Father," he said, and he gave a low bow.

Laird Pryd waved him away.

As he exited the room, castle guardsmen sweeping up in his wake, Prydae considered the events. There could be little doubt of how the evening would proceed, given the claim of the wronged husband that he had actually caught his wife in the arms of another man. And, as his father had said, Prydae's role was minimal; he was just there to give the weight of law to the proceedings.

Prydae hardly even realized that he was rubbing his hands with anticipation as he moved out into the warm summer night.

Whatever he might feel while witnessing this particular form of punishment, it would surely be exciting.

He noted that the brothers of Abelle were already at the clearing. Old Father Jerak and the others stood and sat off to one side, many with their heads bowed and hands folded in prayer. Not far from them stood Rennarq. Prydae knew that the man had come out here, though Rennarq was not acting as an official of the laird this night. Prydae's father wouldn't allow that, for where the Samhaists were concerned, he didn't consider Rennarq to be possessed of objectivity.

Most of the townsfolk were in attendance as well, even many of the children. That surprised Prydae for a moment, but then he realized the point of it all. Harsh justice demonstrated civilization, of course, and reinforced societal expectations of behavior. Let the children learn these lessons young, and learn them well, and perhaps fewer of them would find themselves in the same situation as the guilty woman.

The guardsmen set the chairs they had brought from the castle in the proper place at the left side of the large, flat stone that old Bernivvigar would use as his dais, the customary spot for the Laird of Pryd to bear witness. When Prydae took the chair center and forward of the others, the customary seat of his father, the gathering predictably began to murmur and whisper among themselves.

Prydae stood up and stepped forward. "Laird Pryd is taken ill this night," he said loudly, silencing them all, then he offered a reassuring smile and patted his hands in the air to calm the gasps and fearful exclamations. "A minor case of the gripe, and nothing more. Laird Pryd has bidden me to serve as the voice, the eyes, and the ears of Castle Pryd this evening."

Nods of assent and even some scant cheering came back at Prydae, and he took his seat once more. He recognized the importance of this night then, all of a sudden. He was the obvious heir to Pryd Holding, as his two older siblings were female. There were rumors of half brothers, but they were all by women Laird Pryd had never formally recognized as wives, and so had no claim to the throne. No, it was Prydae's to hold, and soon, too, he believed. Often of late he had seen the weariness in his father's face when the formalities of the day had ended. Prydae's exploits in battle were helping to smooth the way to his ascent but presiding over so important an event as this, he realized, was no less vital. The people of the holding had to believe in him as their protector and as their adjudicator.

Only then did Prydae understand the significance of his father's advice to not reveal his amusement at the spectacle.

The crowd stirred and went quiet as the minutes turned to an hour. The bonfire marking the clearing before the stone—the signal from Bernivvigar of the significance of this night—burned low, casting them all in dim shadows.

Finally, a tall, lean figure made its way down the forest path and out onto the flat stone. The Samhaist did not bend with age, as did Father Jerak and even Laird Pryd. And Bernivvigar was taller than almost any other man in Pryd, standing above six and a half feet. He had wild, almost shaggy, gray hair and a long, thin beard that reached halfway down his chest. He wore his simple light green robe, the Samhaist habit, and sandals that revealed his dirty feet and his red-painted toenails. He carried an oaken staff that was nearly as tall as he, with a knobbed end that made it look more akin to a weapon than a walking stick. A necklace of canine teeth framed his beard and clacked when he walked or when he turned quickly to settle his sharp gaze on one or another of the onlookers.

He looked at Prydae only once, gave a slight nod, then squared up to face the general gathering and lifted his arms high.

"Who claims grievance?" he called. The crowd went completely silent, all eyes turning to the left of the stone, near where the monks were sitting.

A young man, his face covered in snot, his cheeks streaked with tears, stepped forth from that area and staggered up before the stone and the Samhaist, which put his head about level with Bernivvigar's feet. "I do," he said. "I seen them." He brought his arm up and wiped it across his dirty face.

"Bring forth the accused woman," Bernivvigar commanded.

The crowd parted and a group of men—soldiers of the Laird all—forced a young man and woman forward, prodding them with spears and slapping them with the flat sides of bronze swords. Another man, a commoner, bearing a sack in one hand and a pole ending in a small noose in the other, came out after them and moved toward the low-burning fire.

Prydae gave a profound sigh at the sight of the accused. He knew them, the woman at least, and understood that they were young—younger than he at eighteen by two or three years. Callen Duwornay was her name; he knew her family. Startled, Prydae realized that Callen was the daughter of one of Castle Pryd's stablemen.

She was quite a pretty young thing, and Prydae had many times thought of taking her for a night of his pleasure, as the laird and his offspring were wont and legally entitled to do. Her soft hair was the color of straw, and it hung below her shoulders, cascading from her face in silken layers. Her eyes were not the customary blue of the folk but a rich brown hue—not dark, but true brown. Her smile was bright and even, and often flashed—there was a life and lustiness about her, a scent of womanhood and enthusiasm that all fit together, in light of these charges, to Prydae.

Such a waste, he thought, and he worked earnestly to keep his expression impassive. He was bearing witness and not passing judgment. Some traditions overruled even the desires of the son of the laird.

As soon as her hands were untied, Callen brought them up to brush back the hair from her face, but since she was looking down, it fell right back.

"And the other?" Bernivvigar instructed.

A young man, barely Prydae's age, his blue eyes darting about like those of a terrified animal, stumbled through, jabbed hard by a spear and off balance because his hands were tightly tied behind his back. He seemed as if he could hardly draw breath or as if he were about to burst into tears at any moment.

"Are these the two?" Bernivvigar asked the cuckold.

"Aye, that's the one," said the wronged husband. "Oh, I seen him. Right on top o' her! And I paid good money for her. Silver coin and three sheep."

"Which will be repaid in full—nay, thrice—of course," Bernivvigar said, aiming his words and his glare at the cheating young man. "Thrice!" he repeated strongly.

"Y-yes, yes, me lord," the man stammered and he tried to bow, but tumbled against the hard facing of the stone that served as the Samhaist's platform, then fell. The crowd began to laugh and taunt, but the monks kept praying, and Prydae did well to keep his composure.

"You will be working for years to pay off the debt, you understand," Bernivvigar said.

"All me life, if need be!"

"Then you admit your crime?"

The man, up on his knees now, chewed his bottom lip, then looked from the old Samhaist back to Callen.

Prydae watched him with great interest, noting the emotions tearing at him. The man obviously loved that young woman, and he knew of course what his admission would do to her. He would be branded and indebted, but that paled beside Callen's fate.

A long minute passed.

"We will need two sacks this evening," Bernivvigar said loudly, and the crowd cheered.

"Yes, I did it!" the accused man suddenly blurted, and he started to cry. "We did. Oh, but she bewitched me with her charms." He fell forward, facedown on the ground. "Pity, me lord. Pity."

On a nod from Bernivvigar, a pair of guards moved over and roughly pulled the groveling man aside.

"Have you anything to say, woman?" the Samhaist asked.

Callen didn't look up.

She knew she was doomed, Prydae observed. She had gone past hope now, had settled into that resigned state of empty despair.

"Now comes the fun," Prydae heard one of the guards standing behind him remark.

They took the guilty man first, throwing him roughly to the ground. Two men sat on him to hold him still, while another pulled off his trousers. The cuckolded husband, meanwhile, went to the bonfire, where a flat-headed iron brand had been set in place, its end now glowing. By the time he lifted it in his gloved hand and turned, the guilty man was staked to the ground. He lay on his back, naked from the waist down and with his legs spread wide and held firmly in place by leather ties.

Gasps of excitement and even appreciation, accompanied by a few sympathetic groans, marked the husband's stride as he moved between those widespread legs. The guilty man began to whimper, and all the louder when the cuckolded husband waved the glowing iron before his wide, horror-filled eyes.

"P-please," he stammered. "Mercy! Mercy! I'll pay you four times, I will! Five times!"

The glowing brand went in hard against the side of his testicles.

Prydae had seen several battles in his eighteen years. He had watched men chopped down, squirming and screaming to their deaths. He had seen a woman get cut in half at the waist by a great axe, her top half falling so that she could see her own severed legs, standing there for a long moment before toppling over. But never in all the battles had the young nobleman heard a shriek as bloodcurdling and earsplitting as that from the man sprawled before him.

The man jerked so violently that he yanked one of the stakes from the ground. That hardly did him any good, for as he tried to kick his leg over in an attempt to cover up, he merely brought the tender flesh of his inner thigh against the side of the hot iron.

His face locked in a fierce grimace, the wronged husband pressed harder and slapped the flailing leg away. Finally he stepped back, and the wounded man, sobbing and wailing in agony, flipped his leg over again, trying to curl up.

The guards pulled him up from the ground, and when he tried to duck, one kicked him hard in the groin. He doubled over and fell back to the ground, and so they grabbed him by the ankles and unceremoniously dragged him away, through the jeering and laughing crowd, many of whom spat upon him.

When finally it settled again, Bernivvigar turned his hawkish gaze upon Callen once more. "Have you anything to say?"

The woman sniffled but did not look up.

A nod from him had the guards eagerly stripping off her clothing.

Despite the gruesome surroundings, Prydae couldn't help but take note of the pretty young thing's naked body. Her breasts were round and full and teasingly upturned, and her belly still had a bit of her girlish fat, just enough to give it an enticing curl. Yes, he should have taken her for a night's pleasure, Prydae realized, and he sighed, for now it was too late.

Again the aggrieved husband went over to the fire, where the handler was preparing the adder, exciting it and angering it by moving it near the hot embers. With a wicked grin, the dirty man handed over the catch stick, its noose now securely holding the two-foot-long copper-colored snake right behind its triangular head.

The husband glanced back when he heard Bernivvigar say, "This is your last chance to speak, woman. If you have any words of apology or remorse, this is the moment."

Callen started to lift her head, as if she wanted to say something. But then she slumped back, as if she hadn't the strength.

Prydae watched the husband, noting his wince as the guards drew the large canvas bag over his wife's head, pulled it down, then pushed her roughly to the ground and forcing her legs inside. Now she flailed wildly and struggled, until one of the guards kicked her hard in the back.

They drew the drawstring of the sack, and kicked her again for good measure, and she lay there, sobbing quietly.

The crowd began to murmur, urging the husband on; and, indeed, there was a hesitation to his every step toward her.

Prydae watched him intently, seeing him pause and imagining the tumult of feelings that must be swirling within him. That hesitation seem to break apart all of a sudden, as the cuckold painted a scowl on his face and moved to the sack with three quick strides. One of the guards pulled up the tied end, and the other pulled open the mouth of the bag.

"Don't ye miss," the guard holding the open end said, and he gave the cuckold an exaggerated wink.

The cheering grew louder; the husband looked around. Then he thrust the catch-stick forward, shoving the adder's head far into the bag. With quick hands, the guards helped him force the rest of the squirming snake in, and the husband released one of the drawstrings and pulled back the empty catch-stick.

The guard drew tight the string and tied it off, then jumped back, letting the sack fall over.

The crowd hushed; Prydae found himself leaning forward in his chair.

For a long while, nothing.

There came a slight movement as the snake began to stir. The woman screamed, and the sack began to thrash.

They heard her cry out, and a sudden and violent jerk of the sack brought every onlooker to hold his breath and seemed to freeze the scene in place. The sack held still for a moment, then came another jerk, the woman within no doubt reacting to a second bite.

And again and again.

It went on for many minutes, when finally the bag went still.

The snake handler cautiously moved over and slightly opened the tied end, then jumped well back.

Sometime later, the adder slithered out.

Prydae sat back in his chair, chilled to the bone.

"Stake her up at the end of the road," he heard Bernivvigar say, "that all the workmen might be reminded of her crime."

With that, the old Samhaist turned and walked away, and the crowd began to disperse.

"It'll take her two days to die, unless an animal gets her," Prydae heard his guard say behind him.

"Aye, and with the poison burning her, head to toe, all the while."

The prince sat very still watching the sack. One delicate bare foot had come out of the end and was twisting slowly in the dirt and twitching.

Prydae finally managed to turn his eyes and consider the monks. Father Jerak was staring at the departing Samhaist, his expression obviously uncomplimentary. The prince noted the young and stern one, Bathelais, had his arms crossed over his chest, eyes set determinedly. Bathelais seemed the most accepting of the group, standing in particular contrast to the monk beside him, a young man Prydae did not know, whose look of horror and distress was so pronounced that the prince had to wonder if the man's eyes would freeze open. Obviously, most of the monks had no liking for this severe Samhaist justice, but they hadn't the power to do anything about it. In times past, the adulteress would often have been spared the sack, with a confession and if she were properly broken of spirit before going in. But now, Prydae understood—as did his father, as did Bernivvigar and the monks of Abelle—this scene was about much more than the life of one pitiful little peasant girl.

It was about an old Samhaist's declaration of his continuing importance.

This was justice in Honce, in God's Year 54.

CHAPTER 6

Along the Rim of Time's Circle

They traveled the wide and smooth way out of Ethelbert Holding for many miles to the west, then turned to the north, where the road fast dwindled to a simple cart path, a pair of wet, muddy ruts in the grass.

"Laird Ethelbert is more interested in pressing forward to Delaval City than to my home of Pryd, apparently," Dynard said with a laugh, for the work on the road extended beyond their vision to the west.

"I prefer the untamed lands," SenWi said, and when she glanced at Dynard, she had a little sparkle of excitement in her dark eyes that the monk could not miss.

He tightened his grip on her hand and strode more boldly forward. Soon after, the couple had left all signs of the road behind them and moved along an even less defined trail, where underbrush obscured the cart ruts and great trees crowded overhead.

"I know the land, even after all these years," Dynard assured her. "In two weeks' time, we will find Chapel Pryd. We'll not get lost."

"Little is the care if we do," SenWi replied. "The unknown road oft brings unexpected joys."

Her reference to Dynard's own journey brought a blush to his cheeks. "And oft brings unexpected dangers," he replied. "The land is rife with powries and goblins, so said Laird Ethelbert. Even when I left, the beasts were all about."

"I am Jhesta Tu," SenWi reminded him, the words drawing Dynard's eyes back to the ivory and silver hilt of the sword that pointed diagonally above her left shoulder.

He squeezed her hand again, and they strode off along the forested trail.

Later that same night, on a hill open to the stars above, SenWi ran her hand over the sleeping Bran's shoulder. The air was warm, but the evening breeze carried a slight chill that amplified and tingled as it moved across the perspiration that still clung to SenWi's naked body.

Bran slept soundly, his chest rising and falling in a smooth, contented rhythm. Their lovemaking had been particularly energetic that night, with

Bran almost ferocious in his advances, and as urgent in the act itself as he had been in their first encounter, years before in the Walk of Clouds.

Was he trying to reaffirm his love for her to himself? SenWi had to wonder. Was his insistence of action a way for him to defy the obvious disdainful glances that he knew the two of them would face among his unworldly, even intolerant, people?

SenWi smiled the thought away, not over concerned. Had her beloved Bran Dynard felt any more at ease during his first days in Jacintha or among the xenophobic tribes in the desert of Behr? Had he not been a curiosity of sorts when first he had come to the Walk of Clouds, with his chalky skin and strange ways, his words of Blessed Abelle and magical gemstones?

SenWi understood. In making love to her that night, under the stars in the summer breeze, Bran had tried to prove to her that he loved her beyond anything else and that there could be no severing of that tie. And he had tried to prove to himself, she presumed, that the curious and doubting expressions of other people mattered not at all.

His sleep was not restless.

"My love," SenWi whispered, her words floating on the evening breeze. She bent low over Bran and kissed him, and he gave a little grumble and rolled onto his side, drawing yet another amused smile from SenWi.

She held faith in his love for her, and never doubted her own for him, and she was doubly glad of that now.

For she knew.

With her Jhesta Tu training, her senses attuned so well to the rhythms of her own body, the mystic knew.

She brought a hand down to her belly.

T hat is it?" SenWi asked in a halting voice. She was gaining a better command of the Honce language, for she and Dynard had been speaking that alone for the last week of traveling. She moved around the side of the rocky jut on the hillside to stand beside her husband, and followed his gaze to the distant dark shape of a formidable castle, anchored in the back by a wide, round tower.

Dynard's grin gave her the answer before he verbally confirmed, "Castle Pryd, home of Laird Pryd, who hosts my chapel." He glanced to the west, and noted the sun, now more than halfway to the horizon.

"This night only if we travel long after . . . *bokri*," SenWi answered his unasked question.

"Sunset," Dynard translated. "*Bokri* is sunset, as *bonewl* is sunrise." He extended his hand to her. "Tomorrow morning, then. I am anxious to return to my home, 'tis true, but I will miss our time alone."

SenWi took his hand and followed him and didn't disagree at all with his observation. The weather had been fine and the company better over the days since they had left the bustle of Ethelbert Holding. It had rained just once, a light sprinkle one dark night, but even in that, SenWi and Bran had huddled and laughed under the sheltering lower boughs of a thick pine, and barely a drop had touched them.

The Jhesta Tu mystic had enjoyed the journey as much as her companion. They had laughed—mostly Dynard laughing at her as she struggled to master the language—and basked in the scents and sights of the unspoiled Honce wilderness in the late summer. They had been fortunate thus far, for the only monster or dangerous animal they had encountered was a single adder that slithered into their campsite one night. Dynard had reached for a stick, but SenWi had intervened, moving low to face the serpent and swaying her hands rhythmically to calm it and entrance it. With a lightning quick strike, the Jhesta Tu had caught the adder in her grasp right behind its head, and had gently carried it far from the camp, where she then had released it.

She remembered now the image of Bran Dynard when she had returned to the camp, as he sat there, shaking his head and grinning widely and chuckling with obvious admiration. "You have learned *ki-chi-kree*," she had said to him. "You, too, could have calmed and caught the serpent."

To that, Dynard had laughed all the louder and had equated his own command of the Jhesta Tu understanding to that of SenWi's grasp of the language of Honce.

Since they had agreed that they need not make Castle Pryd that night, they walked leisurely and on a meandering road, with SenWi often rushing to the side to further explore some interesting sight or sound. For their camp, they chose a bare-topped hillock, and from its apex as the sunlight began to fade they could just make out the southernmost reaches of the new and expanding road, less than a mile away.

"Your world is changing," SenWi remarked as they stared down at that significant development.

"Greatly, I would guess, when these roads are connected. But for the better," Dynard added, turning a grin SenWi's way. "Better to spread the word of Abelle. Better to take the healing powers of the soul stones to the ends of the land."

"Better to move about your armies?"

"If in the pursuit of the monsters that plague the land, then yes."

SenWi nodded and let the conversation go at that. She was Jhesta Tu, and so she had studied the history of the southern lands of Behr extensively. Many times over the centuries had empires arisen, building roads and marching their armies all about. Most of those roads were lost again now, as were the empires, reclaimed by the desert sands. History moved in circles, the Jhesta Tu believed, a hundred steps forward and ninety-nine backward, so the saying went; and that understanding was based on solid evidence and a collective, often bitter, experience. How many people through the ages had thought themselves moving toward a better existence, toward paradise itself, only to be thrown back into misery at the whims of a foolish ruler or by the stomping of a conquering invader?

SenWi wondered then if the roads of other empires had crossed this land of Honce, ravaged by time and swallowed by regrown forests. She expected as much.

She fell asleep comfortably in Bran's tender embrace that evening, her vision of the stars above and thoughts of eternity taking her to a quiet and peaceful slumber. Like all Jhesta Tu, she had trained her body to remain alert to external stimuli even in the deepest sleep, and she awakened sometime near midnight to the distant sound of coarse laughter, drifting on the summer breeze.

SenWi extricated herself from her husband's arms and slowly rose to her feet, staring off to the north, toward Pryd. She saw the flicker of a torch through the trees, perhaps halfway to the firelight glow showing in the windows of Castle Pryd. The commotion and new lights were somewhere down by the end of the road, she figured.

She heard Dynard stir and crawl over beside her, where he wearily rose to his knees. "What is it?"

Some more laughter filtered through.

"A party?"

"No," SenWi quickly answered, for she recognized that there was little joyful mirth in that grating sound. It was more taunting and wicked in timbre. "Not a party."

She began to dress, and not in the flowery white clothing she typically wore through the days, but in a black suit of silk—the dress of a nighttime hunter.

"You mean to go down there through the darkness?"

"In this instance, the darkness might prove our best ally," she replied in a grave voice. She started off down the northern side of the hillock, pulling her silken shirt about her as she went.

Dynard grabbed his clothes and rushed after, not wanting to lose sight of SenWi in the night. The woods could be confusing and disorienting, he knew, but he knew, too, that his wife could find her way unerringly.

A few minutes later, the monk found himself crouching behind a bush beside SenWi. She motioned for him to hold his place, and she crept forward toward the flickering torchlight and harsh-toned conversation. The hairs on the back of Dynard's neck were standing on end now, for he could recognize the language of the speakers, if not the words, and knew them to be powries.

He felt SenWi tense before him, then he moved past so that the scene came into view. A group of five powries stood at the end of the road, prodding, poking, and taunting a young woman, naked and battered, who had been strung up by her wrists, her feet a foot off the ground.

One powrie said something Dynard could not understand, and the others began to laugh.

"Ack, but ye're a pretty one, ain't ye?" the spindly-limbed little dwarf then said to the woman, speaking in the language of Honce. She didn't even groan in response, just hung there, twisting slowly and seeming very near to death, if not already there. The powrie poked her naked belly, sending her into a little swing, and the others laughed again.

"Pretty and with bright blood, eh?" the powrie said, and with a sudden movement, the dwarf brought a knife up and across the inside of the woman's thigh, opening a large wound. Now she did cry out, softly and pitifully, and she tried to wriggle away, but the powrie caught hold of her and slapped his beret against the flowing blood.

The other dwarves hooted.

SenWi leaped out of the brush, bringing forth her magnificent sword.

"Be gone from here!" she commanded.

The powries stared at her for just a moment, then howled and lifted their own weapons.

SenWi's sword spun over in her right hand, went behind her back, and reappeared on the other side, and she thrust her left hand forward, taking the powrie with the fresh blood on its beret in the side and sending it away with a shriek. She retracted her sword immediately, then flashed it left to right, parrying a swinging powrie axe. SenWi let go and left the sword out there, engaged with the axe, as she spun a tight circle, catching the blade back in her right hand as she came around. Using her momentum, she slid the blade hard across the axe and thrust ahead, forcing the powrie to suck in its belly and scramble back.

SenWi couldn't finish the move, for another powrie came in hard at her side. Across went her sword, slashing the tip from the iron-headed spear and forcing the newest attacker into an overbalanced posture.

The other powries came in hard. She spun and she leaped, kicking out and punching as often as thrusting her sword. Blades came at her from every angle, but she bent and swerved, dodged and parried, with precision.

———

Brother Dynard had hardly registered that his wife had even moved! Still crouched in the brush, he tried to make sense of this whirling and furious combat before him, tried to call out to SenWi. But he couldn't hope to find his voice, and didn't know whether to cheer or to scream in terror at the wild melee, the slashing swords, the ring of metal.

Up SenWi went above a pair of thrusting spears, and she kicked out, scoring solid hits on the faces of each attacker. But the dwarves didn't fall, and one of the tough creatures even began to laugh at her.

Dynard knew that he had to help. As wondrous a warrior as SenWi was, she couldn't hope to win against five powries!

He started to come forth, but stopped cold, wondering what in the world he might do. He had no weapon, and even if he had, Dynard understood all too well that he was no match for the average powrie. He scrambled about, his eyes glued to SenWi's continuing flurry, and finally settled one hand into his belt pouch.

Dynard brought forth the smooth gray stone and held it up before his eyes.

The soul stone.

Her fighting was completely defensive now. SenWi ducked and turned from weapons that came in at her from every side. The dwarves coordinated their attacks well, leaving her little opening, but one of the five was lagging, she noted. In her initial attack, she had hit him hard, her sword digging a deep wound. He was trying to keep up with his four friends, but his thrusts shortened every time, as he winced and curled over that torn side.

SenWi wanted to focus on him and finish him off, but the other dwarves had her turning continually. She leaped over one swiping axe and threw her leg out wide to avoid the stab of a spear. As she landed, she brought her forearm up to accept the smack of the spear she had beheaded, for the dwarf was now using it as a club. As her arm connected, she shoved it out wide, then stepped in and stabbed at the dwarf with her sword.

But again, she had to pull up short and spin to deflect the charge of another, the dwarf lowering his shoulder and trying to bowl her right over. She hit him with three short jabbing punches to turn him, then crossed hard with the snake hilt of her sword, cracking his jaw.

The tough little creature staggered backward but did not fall.

Brother Dynard chanted and clutched his soul stone, trying to find his concentration and his center, seeking his *chi* so that he could send it fully into the swirling gray depths of the magical stone. He heard SenWi's breathing, heard the growls of the ferocious dwarves.

He heard his love grunt as a powrie connected with the wooden shaft of its spear, and he opened his eyes.

He snapped them shut immediately and concentrated again on the issue at hand. He couldn't go out there physically, he knew, for his appearance and incompetence would likely hinder SenWi more than aid her. Thus, he had to go out there spiritually. He had to find his center and free his spirit through the use of the soul stone.

The sounds of battle grew distant suddenly, and Dynard felt as if he were falling through cool water. And he was standing there, looking back at himself, on his kneeling physical body.

His spirit turned and willed himself forward into the fray. He denied his trained revulsion as he approached one powrie and accepted the invitation of its corporeal form.

In he went, against his understanding that this usage of the soul stone—insinuating himself into the body of another free-willed creature—was among the most trying and repugnant possibilities offered by the gemstone. To possess another was the temptation of the stone and the danger of the stone, and was an act frowned upon by the brothers of Blessed Abelle, an act specifically damned by Abelle himself in his writings.

But this time, with SenWi in so difficult a position, Dynard accepted the danger and the moral ambiguity and fought past his revulsion. His spirit dove into the powrie.

He sensed the creature's surprise and horror, and he knew that it would instinctively react to possession with a fierce battle of willpower. But for just a moment, the powrie was off guard, confused, and in that split second, Dynard took control. He saw through its eyes; he felt its limbs as if they were his own.

He made the dwarf throw its axe to the ground, turn, and leap upon the dwarf nearest him, bearing both to the ground.

Then Dynard felt the sudden attack upon his spirit, the rebound of the dwarf's free will. He envisioned a dwarvish shadow tearing at the fabric of his own spiritual silhouette.

But he held on stubbornly, with willpower and with the dwarf arms he controlled.

SenWi had no idea what had just happened, why one of these vicious dwarves would tackle another, but she didn't pause to ask questions. Her sword went out to the right to block a spear, then she rolled her blade about the weapon repeatedly in rapid succession.

Instead of retracting, the dwarf came forward, but SenWi had anticipated the move. She retracted her arm, then struck straight out, like a serpent, once, then again and again.

The dwarf staggered backward.

SenWi sprang into the air, tucked her legs, and went right over backward as the dwarf opposite her, the wounded one with the knife, charged in with a roar. She landed lightly right behind the creature as it stumbled past, a perfect opportunity to strike hard.

But she didn't, diving sidelong instead at the remaining battling powrie, who was obviously thinking to follow her in pursuit of the knife wielder.

SenWi's sword whipped over, coming in diagonal down strikes at the too-slow dwarf, slashing shoulder to hip one way, then the other.

The dwarf tried to get its axe up to block, but SenWi seemed one movement ahead of it each time, her sword coming across and down repeatedly.

The dwarf's tunic hung ragged, with lines of blood beginning to show, and the dwarf continued its futile efforts to block. Not once did it hit SenWi's sword, and it began to retreat—to inevitably stagger backward.

SenWi's sword blazed in diagonal circles, each one scoring a hit.

And she stopped suddenly, reversed her grip on the sword, and thrust it out behind her, just in time to meet the roaring charge of the knife wielder. He came forward anyway, for he couldn't break his momentum, and ran right up against SenWi. For a moment, he seemed frozen in time, impaled to the hilt on her blade, and then his eyes slowly turned up to meet hers.

He roared and tried to strike, but SenWi whirled and ducked under the blow, moving out to the side of the dwarf, where she gave a great tug on her sword.

Powries were made of tough stuff indeed, but so was the steel of SenWi's sword, and strong was its impeccable design. The blade tore through the powrie's innards and ripped out the side, and the dwarf staggered. It tried to cry out, but only a thick flow of blood rushed out of its mouth.

SenWi spun her sword, using its momentum to center her own balance once more as she turned.

That dwarf was down and dying; as was the one she had slashed so many times; as was, she was glad to see, the one she had poked thrice. That one was still alive, kneeling and groaning. The other two were up again, off to the side, staring at her incredulously.

They turned and ran off.

SenWi took one step to follow, but stopped at once, turning to regard the hanging woman, then glancing over at the bushes where a shaken Dynard came stumbling forth, soul stone in hand.

"I—I possessed him," the stumbling monk explained.

SenWi responded with an absent nod, but was already focusing on and moving toward the woman. She looked up at the rope and then at her sword, but then snapped the sword back into the scabbard across her back, recognizing that the woman was too near death to handle the trauma of a fall.

The Jhesta Tu brought her palms together before her and again fell into that line of energy, that center of power, that ran from the top of her head to her groin. With a deep exhalation, SenWi breathed that power forth into her arms, coursing down to her hands and her trembling fingertips.

She felt the heat building in her hands even as she reached out to the dying woman.

She placed a hand on the tear in the woman's thigh and sent forth her healing energy, and accepted the woman's pain as her own.

She felt something then, in the blood, some uncleanliness.

But she didn't relent, forcing her energy into the woman, lending her strength.

A soft groan escaped the battered woman's lips.

"SenWi, do not," came a sharp cry behind her, drawing her from her concentration. She glanced over her shoulder to see an ashen-faced Dynard staring at her wide-eyed. "Leave her alone."

SenWi's jaw drooped open in disbelief.

"She is an adulteress," Dynard explained, "or some other such sin."

"This is how your order deals with sinners?"

"No, no, not the brothers of Abelle. But this is not our province. This justice is the tradition of the land, since long before Blessed Abelle walked the ways of Honce. In the half century of our Church, we have made some gains and offered some concessions. This is the doing of the Samhaists, who once presided over all the folk as the clerics of Honce. The lairds have not seen fit to change."

"This is justice?"

The accusatory tone had Dynard back on his heels. "It is the way of Honce. The woman was convicted, no doubt, and given to the snake."

The snake. SenWi's head snapped around, and only then did she fully realize the other wounds; fang marks. She understood then the sensation of uncleanliness in the blood, for it was rife with poison.

She swallowed hard and stared at the woman, who seemed more alive, just a bit, as if the healing hands had made some progress. The poor, battered girl gave another little groan.

"I will not watch her die," SenWi declared.

"It is not our place."

"Choose your own place as you will," she granted. "I will not watch her die." She folded her palms and fell into her *chi*, then went back to her healing work with renewed energy.

A moment later, to her great relief, Brother Dynard was beside her, soul stone in hand. With a look and helpless smile at SenWi, he pressed his free hand against the woman and began his own healing, using the magical stone.

A few moments later, the two looked at each other again, and SenWi nodded and motioned for Dynard to grasp the woman. SenWi then pulled forth her sword and leaped into the air; and with a sudden and swift strike, she cut the woman free.

She helped Dynard guide the poor girl to the ground.

"Your cloak," SenWi instructed, and Dynard shed his woolen robe, and he and his wife managed to wrap it about the shivering woman. Then Dynard picked her up gently in his arms. "Come along," he instructed SenWi. "The powries might return with their friends."

He started off into the forest, to the side of the road. "We cannot take her to Pryd, for they will merely throw her in the sack with the snake again and hang her once more," he explained. "But there may be a place."

"Chapel Pryd?"

Dynard nearly laughed aloud at the notion, for he knew well that Father Jerak, kindly as he could be, would not go against Laird Pryd in this matter. Nor would Dynard, in all good conscience, even involve the others of his order in this crime.

No, this burden was his own.

CHAPTER 7

To the Side of Things

The middle-aged man stared out the partly open door for a long and silent moment, then finally seemed to breathe again and stepped back, pulling the door wide. "Can it be?" he whispered, and he held up a candle before him. He was of medium build, a bit shorter than most men, with a shaggy head of black and gray hair, and with several days of beard evident on his face. One of his eyes was quite dead, showing only milky white, but the other held a lustrous blue-gray sparkle.

Brother Dynard put on a wide smile. "Garibond, my heart fills with joy at seeing you alive and well." He stepped inside the dimly lit stone house, and in doing so, stepped out the lake, for this stone structure was constructed on a rock out in the water, a dozen feet from the shore along a sometimes submerged, sometimes revealed, shoal. The house was built in two parts, with this, the lower level, right at the lakeside, and a higher, drier structure a dozen feet above and farther from the shore, on the higher rocks. Even with the two structures, connected by a cave and stone extension, there was little elaborate workmanship showing about Garibond's home, just two stone-walled rectangles with thatched roofs.

"Bran in the flesh! Back from his travels around the world!" Garibond Womak replied. He stepped forward and clapped Dynard hard on the shoulder, then wrapped him in a great hug, which Dynard comfortably returned.

Garibond leaped back. "Come in," he bade. "Come in! You must tell me every detail." His enthusiasm melted almost at once, as he noted the grim expression on the face of his long-lost friend.

"I need your help," Dynard said seriously.

"Have I e'er shown you anything but?"

With an appreciative nod, Dynard stepped back outside and splashed across the shallows to the shore, returning a moment later with the unconscious young woman in his arms.

Garibond's good eye went wide.

"We found her at the end of the new road," Dynard explained.

"Where Bernivvigar left her to die, with the blessing of Laird Pryd."

Dynard nodded.

"Are you mad?" Garibond asked. "The woman was convicted and executed. She met the adder in the sack—to the joy of the folk who went to watch, I am certain," he added, his voice taking a sour note. "You cannot—"

"I could not leave her out there. I—we—met powries dancing about her, ready to take her blood."

"Dead is dead. Probably better that way than from the slow poison of the snake."

Dynard just shook his head and moved to the side, gently laying the woman down on a thick bearskin rug elevated on a wooden frame near the still-warm hearth.

"You had to know the truth of her predicament," Garibond protested. "You've seen old Bernivvigar's work before."

"I could not leave her."

"They'll put you in her place, you fool," protested Garibond. "You cannot go against the word of Laird Pryd. Your own brothers of Abelle were there in attendance, bearing witness."

Dynard held out his arms helplessly, and Garibond gave a great sigh.

"You said 'we,'" Garibond remarked. "Who was with you, and more important to your own skin, where is he now?"

The smile returned to Brother Dynard's face and he stepped back outside and motioned off into the night. A moment later, SenWi appeared at his side in the doorway. "Not he. My wife."

Garibond's good eye went wide again, and widened even more as he came to understand the truth of SenWi's exotic heritage. "But she's a pretty one," he managed to say at length.

"Will you help us?"

"What would you have me do?" Garibond answered skeptically. "I'm no healer."

"Just let us stay here for a bit, that we can tend the girl and keep her safe and warm."

"You're to be the death of me."

"I know you can hide her—can hide us," Dynard said with a grin, and Garibond gave a sigh. "He has tunnels beneath this house," Dynard explained to SenWi. "Keeps him safe from powries and goblins." He turned back to Garibond and, with a wide grin, added, "Though I thought you'd have slowed enough by now for them to catch you before you got your old arse into the hole."

"Bah, them stupid ones don't even come around here. If they did, I'd be more likely to stand and kill them all before I'd run like a child into the tunnels!"

Dynard knew the truth of the bluster, but he didn't press the point.

Garibond's smile proved short-lived. "Tunnels or no, she won't be safe if Lord Pryd—or worse, his son, Prydae—discovers that she is missing," Garibond said.

"Prydae?"

"Aye, Prydae. A boy when you left. A man now. A young warrior with as much fight and mettle as the father ever knew, who makes his reputation daily against the goblins and the powries."

Again Dynard was reminded of how long he'd been gone. He looked at SenWi and gave a helpless laugh and shake of his head. "The world moves on without me, it would seem."

"Young Prince Prydae would not take well to your disruption of old Bernivvigar's holy ritual."

"Murder is holy ritual?" SenWi asked, her eyes going wide, and she looked up at Dynard for support.

"Not murder," the monk tried to explain, but he found little heart for the distinction he offered. "The Samhaists carry out the executions and other punishments of convicted criminals."

"This young girl was a murderess?"

"An adulteress," said Garibond.

SenWi looked to Dynard, who explained the crime in the woman's native tongue. That explanation did little to alleviate either her confusion or her disdain, however.

"Appeasing the Samhaists has always been important to the lairds," Garibond reminded Dynard. "You know that."

Brother Dynard paused to study his friend before answering. "But you will allow us the use of your home?"

"Shut the damned door, old fool," Garibond said. "And come along to the upper house where it's more dry—and bring along a log or two to throw upon the fire. I've some stew I can heat." He gave another sigh and looked at SenWi. "And for you, pretty one . . ." He turned to Dynard with his pause.

"SenWi," the monk explained.

"Yes, SenWi, pray you go behind that curtain and find more blankets for the poor girl."

"Prince Prydae will see the powrie tracks and think no more of it," Dynard assured his friend.

"Or he will follow your own to my house, and Bernivvigar's next ceremony will feature four sacks."

That brought a laugh from Dynard, though he knew well that Garibond was hardly joking.

A short while later, with SenWi tending Callen by the hearth in the upper house, Dynard and Garibond sat opposite each other in comfortable chairs of wood and skins a few feet back, telling the woman of Behr the tales of their long friendship. The two had been fast friends since childhood, and Garibond had even tried to enter the Church of Abelle at the same time as Dynard. But the court of monks had seen that Garibond's motivation was strictly one of loyalty to his friend and not wrought of any sincere belief in the Church and its precepts, and so he had been refused even before Dynard had set out from Pryd Holding to the mother chapel in the north.

Their friendship had not been as tight when Dynard had returned a few years later, the two explained to SenWi, and they both blamed circumstance and no lessening of their almost-brotherly love. Dynard had been busy in the town and chapel, right up to the time when he had departed for the southland, after all; and Garibond only very rarely went to the town, preferring the solitude of his small farm east of the community.

"Sometimes it is easy to forget those things that are truly most important to us," Dynard reflected.

"And this one has always been getting me in trouble," Garibond said suddenly, and he jabbed his accusing finger in the air Dynard's way.

"Or the other way around!" Dynard argued.

"'Twas your own idea to take the ripened tomatoes from farmer Filtin."

"'Twas my idea to take only the ripened ones after you dragged me to his fields," came Dynard's not-so-subtle correction.

The two laughed, and SenWi did as well, until Garibond began to pat his hands in the air and whisper for quiet, reminding them that his house wasn't that far out of town, after all.

"What are you doing to her?" Garibond asked SenWi then, for she had bent over the gravely injured younger woman and slid her hands under the blanket around the poor girl's midsection.

"She is offering her healing powers to the poor girl," Dynard answered.

"Callen," said Garibond. "Callen Duwornay. She was indeed guilty of the accusation of adultery, from what little I heard, but she's not deserving this fate. Poor girl indeed."

He studied SenWi as she slid her hand back out and shifted to put it back from a different angle. "She uses no soul stone," he remarked.

"SenWi is Jhesta Tu," Dynard replied.

Garibond shrugged. The name likely meant nothing to anyone north of the mountains, Dynard knew.

"Just one of the many marvels I have to share with you," the monk said, and he began recounting his journeys then, from the road to Ethelbert to the sea voyage around the Belt-and-Buckle and all through the wild deserts of Behr to his culminating exploration at the Jhesta Tu monastery. He spoke with passion and true admiration as he detailed those years spent at the Walk of Clouds with the devoted mystics, and his story lasted until the eastern sky had begun to lighten with the coming dawn. Garibond didn't point out the lateness of the hour and neither did SenWi, whose work with Callen was hardly finished.

"What are you going to do?" Garibond asked somberly when at last Dynard settled back in his chair.

"In the morning, I return to Chapel Pryd with SenWi."

"Take care," Garibond warned. "Things have changed in the ten years since you left, my friend."

"How so?" Dynard asked, responding to the alarm in his friend's voice.

"The work on the road is hard on the people; and Laird Pryd, like all the lairds of Honce, is determined that his holding will not be outdone in this endeavor. But the land is not tamed—less so than even when you left, I would say."

"Laird Ethelbert spoke of goblins and powries."

"The powries are as thick as trees, as you saw for yourself," said Garibond. He paused and looked curiously at his friend. "How did you get rid of the beasts? You've never been a warrior."

Dynard led Garibond's gaze to SenWi.

"Interesting," Garibond remarked.

"So you are not surprised to hear that we encountered powries?"

"The bloody caps are all about," Garibond explained. "They've left me alone, for the most part. I don't know why. Mayhap they think my dirty old blood will soil their berets."

"Or it could be those tunnels beneath your house," Dynard said with a wink.

"Perhaps you should move closer to the town," SenWi offered in her halting command of the language.

"Ah, that would kill me sooner than any powries ever could!"

"Fie the day that we granted them the safety of our coast," Dynard added, and Garibond nodded.

"A group of powries came to the shores of Honce many years ago," Dynard explained to SenWi. "Perhaps a score of years ago now. The lairds chose not to confront them, but parlayed instead, granting the dwarves a region of the coast as their own. We have come to regret that generosity."

"Your own Church did not oppose the decision," Garibond reminded, to which Dynard could only hold up his hands.

A long pause ensued, and Garibond's last statement led Brother Dynard back to the meetings he would face in the morning. "How fares Father Jerak?"

"He is getting very old, and looking even older. Rumors say that Brother Bathelais has assumed most of his duties now."

That news saddened Dynard but did not surprise him; Jerak had already been an old man when Dynard had set out on his mission, after all. Nor did it alarm him in any way. He and Bathelais had been friends before he had left, and, from what he knew, Bathelais was possessed of a good heart and a clear mind.

"More important is the passage of the title of laird," Garibond explained. "Laird Pryd is robust yet, so many say, but he was not at Bernivvigar's court last night. Day by day sees the rise of Prydae."

"A good man?"

Garibond shrugged. "That would hardly be my place to judge, though I have heard nothing contrary to that. His courage against the powries cannot be dismissed, and the soldiers of Castle Pryd follow him with great loyalty. He is as proud as he is fierce, some say, but whether that will prove a strength or a weakness in these days of change, who can know?"

It occurred to Dynard to ask about how this young and rising prince might view the Church of Abelle, but he held the question private. Garibond wouldn't likely know the inner workings of Pryd's Church of Abelle, since he wasn't one to visit Chapel Pryd. Had he ever gone to the place after the monks had turned him away, except on that one occasion to see Dynard off on his mission?

The conversation drifted away then, and so did the three companions, falling into light sleep right where they sat. Sunlight awakened them soon after, though, streaming in through every crack and opening in Garibond's old house.

"And what am I to do with her?" Garibond asked when Dynard and SenWi moved immediately to collect their packs.

Dynard looked to SenWi.

"She will not likely awaken today," SenWi said with confidence.

"And we will return to you this very night," Dynard promised. He looked all about, then reached into his pack and pulled forth his most-prized possession, the transcribed Book of Jhest. He stared at it for a few moments, wondering whether he should reveal it to Father Jerak immediately upon his return to Chapel Pryd. A nagging thought in the back of his head, undefined but forceful, made him reconsider, and he glanced all around. He moved to the back of the two-roomed upper house and pulled open the partially hidden trapdoor, revealing a narrow shaft. He tenderly wrapped the tome and went down the hole with it. He returned a moment later without the book, to see his two companions, particularly Garibond, watching him intently.

"More trouble you're bringing to my house?"

Dynard looked at his friend. "It will not remain here for long," he promised, and Garibond merely smiled and shook his head—a familiar look that sent Dynard's thoughts careening back to the garden raids of their youth.

"First sign of the laird's men, and Callen's going down the hole, as well," Garibond warned.

"Gently, I trust."

"Quickly."

Dynard smiled, knowing the truth of his compassionate friend.

Another fine, warm summer day surrounded Dynard and SenWi as they moved back to the end of Pryd's lengthening road. Workers and soldiers were all around, some studying the myriad tracks, others looking to the empty pole where Callen had been strung.

"To think that they meant to work all day under the shadow of the hanging woman," Dynard quietly remarked as he surveyed the scene, while he and SenWi were hidden from the sight of the crew. He noted that the powries had apparently returned after the fight and retrieved the bodies of their fallen. Still, the signs of the struggle clearly remained, a puzzle that the folk milling about the area were trying hard to decipher.

"Are you ready to meet them?" Dynard whispered. He couldn't suppress a helpless chuckle when he regarded his wife, who seemed so uncomfortable dressed in a typical Honce woolen tunic. The dress was normal for the land, true, but wearing it, SenWi hardly seemed like any normal Honce citizen.

SenWi looked up at him, her typically calm expression telling him all he needed to know. He took her hand and rose, then crossed out onto the open ground before the work area.

Calls for them to "stand and be counted!" assailed the couple almost immediately, and soldiers drew out their short swords.

Dynard couldn't help but grin as he noted those weapons, of bronze and iron, and compared them to the sword that SenWi had strapped across her back.

The soldiers approached cautiously, fanning out to flank the couple.

"Be at ease, soldiers of Laird Pryd, for I am of your town, returned now to my chapel," Dynard said to them.

"That's Bran Dynard!" one of the workers yelled out, and a host of murmurs erupted.

"Indeed," said the monk. "The time of my mission is ended, and so I return to Pryd."

"I do not know you," said the nearest soldier, a large man with knotted muscles and a broad and strong chest. Although hardened like a seasoned veteran, he was less than twenty years of age, by Dynard's estimation, perhaps no more than sixteen.

"I am of Chapel Pryd," he explained. "You would have been no more than a boy when I departed."

"It is that monk," said another of the soldiers, and he slid away his sword and moved closer. Nods of agreement came from all around and the warriors relaxed.

Dynard's relief was short-lived, though, for he noted their expressions as they scrutinized SenWi, showing a range of emotions from lewd to curious to dismissive, as one might view a goat or a cow. It was that last expression, offered by the powerful younger warrior, that most unnerved the monk, showing the warrior's complete disregard for the dark-skinned southerner.

"'Twas powries who ran off with the girl," Dynard said, drawing them all back to him.

"What do you know of it?" asked one, apparently the leader of the group, a slender, tall warrior of about Dynard's age whom the monk thought he recognized, though he could not recall the man's name.

"Captain Deepen," the man introduced himself, and Dynard nodded his recollection.

"We came upon them last night, and did battle," the monk explained. "They were too numerous for us to retrieve the girl, but we drove them away."

"And yet you escaped?" Deepen asked, obvious doubt in his tone.

"Because of your gemstones, no doubt," another remarked.

"More the work of my wife," Dynard explained, looking to SenWi, and he didn't miss the horrified expressions all around him as he proclaimed this diminutive woman, the stranger to Honce, this "beast of Behr," as his wife. Dynard steeled himself against that response and recounted the battle in full, dramatizing SenWi's prowess and sword work, and leaving out only the not-so-small detail that he and SenWi, and not the powries, had run off with poor Callen.

"Laird Pryd will hear of this," Deepen decided and he reached out as if to take Dynard by the arm.

The monk recoiled. "I am for Chapel Pryd straightaway. Too long have I been out on the road. I will speak with Father Jerak, and will come to the summons of Laird Pryd, of course, if I am so called."

The captain eyed him suspiciously, then SenWi as well, but he did back away a step, clearing the way to the road.

"Where'd you find that . . . one?" the young and powerful warrior asked Dynard, and the man strode up to study SenWi more closely.

"She is my wife, from Behr," he replied, and the man gave a burst of laughter.

"And your name is?" Dynard asked.

"Bannagran," said the warrior, and he looked at Dynard, chuckled again, then walked away.

Dynard took SenWi by the arm and led her along quickly before the soldiers could reconsider, before they perhaps grew more interested in, and concerned about, the weapon strapped across her back.

In short order, the couple were long out of sight of the workmen and the soldiers, walking quickly down the road. Dynard slowed their pace when they came to the outskirts of Pryd Town and in clear sight of Castle Pryd, considering again the expressions on the faces of those folk at the battle scene, looks from soldier and peasant alike, as they regarded his foreign wife.

How might his brothers of Abelle respond to her?

He wondered if perhaps he should have left SenWi with Garibond.

B y the Ancient Ones, it is impossible!" Garibond said to Callen when he came back from his chores to find the woman sitting up in bed, the blankets wrapped about her shoulders. "The poison had you, girl."

Callen kept her head bowed, but Garibond saw her brown eyes glance up at him from behind the screen of her wheat-colored hair.

"The woman—of Behr no less!—saved your life, girl. She gave you healing." He shook his head in disbelief.

Callen rose, unsteady for a moment. "Have you clothing for me?" she asked, and the tremor in her voice reflected the ordeal she had suffered.

Garibond nodded at the foot of the bed, where a tunic and traveling cloak were set out.

"I will be gone this morn," Callen said, and she moved to the clothing and began to dress, discarding modesty in the face of necessity.

"Now, take your time," Garibond said. "Where will you go?" He started for Callen, but held back until she had slipped the tunic over her head.

"Where will you go?" he asked again when she turned back to him.

"I've family in the west," she answered. "They will see to me."

"You've friends here," Garibond replied.

Callen stared at him for a few moments, then tightened her lips and shook her head. She was afraid, he could plainly see. She knew that she was a danger to any who showed her kindness.

"You need food and rest," Garibond remarked, and he rushed across the way and pulled open a cabinet and began searching for some food he might offer. "You cannot go out there now, not so soon. They'll see you and guess the truth of it, don't you see? You should let all the whispers of Callen Duwornay die away before you venture out anywhere where you might be seen. Memories are short, don't you worry, and soon enough, strong and with all health returned, you'll find your way." He finished hopefully, and turned with a loaf of bread in one hand and a cooked chicken in the other.

But the door was open and Callen was gone.

CHAPTER 8

Forward Looking

With a great and steadying sigh and a glance back to SenWi, Brother Dynard pulled open the large oaken door of Chapel Pryd and walked inside. Like all of the Abelle chapels in Honce, the place was dimly lit and smoky, with few windows and many candles set about.

"May I help you, Brother?" said a younger monk Dynard did not know. The man moved up to him, his posture open and inviting, for obviously he had recognized Dynard, in his brown tunic and robe, as a fellow brother of Abelle.

Before Dynard could answer, he heard his name called out from across the way, through the inner doors of the chapel and in the main area.

"Dynard!" cried Brother Bathelais. "Is it really you?" The monk came rushing out from those doors to stand right before the returned brother, and he took Dynard's hands.

"Greetings, Brother Bathelais," Dynard replied, and he was glad that Garibond had mentioned this man the night previous, for he would not have recalled the name otherwise. "Long has been my road, across ocean waters and through desert sandstorms! It is good to be home."

"Father Jerak will wish for a full recounting as soon as is possible."

"Of course."

"You are Brother Bran Dynard, who went to Behr?" the younger monk asked. "I hope to serve my own mission soon in that same land!"

"And better will you be if you are so blessed," Dynard said to him.

"You have brought back trinkets and insights, perhaps?" asked Bathelais. "And tales of conversion?"

The unintended irony of that last statement was not wasted on the transformed monk.

"I have tales more wondrous than anything I expected," Dynard answered, smiling with sincerity. How he longed to show his brethren the beauty he had seen and insights he had gained. How he hoped that his journey to Behr, and more particularly to the Walk of Clouds, would help transform the Church of Abelle into something more wonderful and insightful.

With that thought in mind, Dynard turned from Brother Bathelais and called out for SenWi.

He turned back in time to see the astounded expressions of both the monks when his beautiful Behrenese wife walked into the chapel. Bathelais even made the sign of the evergreen before his chest, a triangular movement that was fast becoming a staple signal of devotion among the followers of Blessed Abelle, for Blessed Abelle had reportedly lived for three years sheltered under the boughs of the sacred evergreen tree.

"This is SenWi," Dynard introduced as the woman moved up beside him, and he casually draped his arm across her shoulders and pulled her close to his side. "My wife."

He saw Brother Bathelais fighting hard, but with only limited success, to keep the incredulity off his face.

Brother Dynard didn't think much of it at that time—how could the man not be surprised, after all?

Little did Brother Dynard understand.

Three dead powries, so he said," Captain Deepen told Prince Prydae. "Who can know what powers the beast of Behr brought with her?"

"Bah, but Prince Prydae killed five in the last fight!" one of the other soldiers in the room blurted.

Prince Prydae accepted that accolade with a nod, though all in the room, including the speaker, knew it to be an exaggeration. Prydae could claim only four kills in that particular fight, and three of those would more correctly be credited to his chariot than to his battle prowess. While he would accept the compliment, the prince recognized that if the returning Brother Dynard had spoken truthfully about the foreign woman's exploits, they were well worth noting.

He saw one young, promising, and amazingly strong warrior, Bannagran by name, looking at him almost apologetically.

"You did not see her sword?" the prince asked Deepen.

The captain shrugged. "Just the hilt of it, and that alone was impressive."

"The peoples south of the Belt-and-Buckle are well known for their crafts," Prydae admitted. "On my last journey to Ethelbert Holding, I saw this clearly. Keep a close watch on this visitor. I would know her movements."

Captain Deepen bowed. "She is with Brother Dynard now in Chapel Pryd."

"Any news of Callen?"

"The powries took her, so said Brother Dynard. If that is the case, then we'll never find enough of her corpse to bother about."

"Make sure that you take down the hanging pole early in the morning,"

Prydae instructed. "It may serve to remind our workers of a powrie presence, and I'll have no such distraction at this time. We have far yet to travel and much more road to construct before the season's turn, and many are already grumbling that they must be back to their fields before harvest."

Captain Deepen bowed again, and Prydae motioned that it was time for him and the others to go. As soon as he was alone, the prince took up his favorite mug and filled it with mead, which he drank quickly. Then, not satisfied, he moved to a small cabinet across the castle room. He pulled open the door and sorted through the metal flasks within, at last settling on one nearly full of a light brown liquid, a fine Vanguard whiskey.

Again he filled the mug, and he wasn't slow to drain it.

All the while, Prydae kept glancing at the door on the right-hand side of the audience room, the portal to his father's wing of the castle. Pryd was still in bed and still feeling ill, and Prydae was beginning to worry that perhaps his father was more sick than he was admitting.

That notion elicited a myriad of thoughts in the ambitious young man. He was ready to assume the mantle of Laird of Pryd Holding, so he believed—indeed, that was a day he had anticipated for most of his life. But Prydae had hoped for a more gradual transition. There were so many nuances to every duty, it seemed, such as his attendance at the trial and sentencing of the adulteress and her illicit lover. Laird Pryd understood these subtleties quite well; he knew how to make the peasants love him even as he broke their backs with difficult labors or took the bulk of their crops and coins.

Prydae cocked his arm back and only at the very last moment stopped himself from throwing his mug across the room.

He would never rule with that type of tact and wisdom, he feared. He was not possessed of his father's diplomacy.

He finished the whiskey in one large gulp, then tossed the mug aside and stormed through the door to Pryd's private chambers. He found his father in bed, lying on his back, his eyes sunken and circled by dark rings. Prydae was struck by how frail the laird appeared. Only a few days before, Laird Pryd had ridden in the courtyard, inspecting his soldiers, and at that time it seemed as if the laird could have led them all into battle and would have claimed the most kills of all with his fabulous sword. He had started to cough a bit that same day—just a tickle in his throat, he insisted—and it had sounded as if it was nothing serious.

And now he lay in bed, coughing and pale, his bowels running as water and his breath smelling of vomit.

"How fare you today, father?" Prydae asked, kneeling beside the bed.

"I curse my age," the old man said with a laugh that sounded more like a wheeze.

"One of the monks who had gone off on his mission has returned," Prydae explained. "A Brother Bran Dynard, back from Behr—I do not remember him."

"A man of little consequence, no doubt."

"He brought with him a brown-skinned woman with strange eyes."

With great effort, Pryd managed to lift one hand and offer a slight, dismissive shake.

"Yes, it does not matter," Prince Prydae mumbled. "Powries took the executed adulteress," he started to say, for he cut himself short, realizing that this event would mean little to his father.

He took his father's hand and kissed it, then clasped it. He felt no strength there, and little warmth, little sense of life at all. He knew that he had to get the healers back in here with their soul stones, and had already arranged a meeting with Brother Bathelais for that very night.

Prydae also understood the limitations of those healers.

Again the prince had to follow two diverging lines of emotions, for beside his fear and pain at watching his father's diminishing health, there was another type of fear, one rooted in ambition and eagerness. He gave his father's hand a slight squeeze, then placed it back atop the old man's chest. He was held there for just an instant, staring at his father and feeling the hints of coming grief, and then he was propelled away by the hints of coming responsibility.

By the time he reached the room where Brother Bathelais waited, his step was brisk and alive.

"There is word that Laird Pryd does not fare well," the monk said as soon as Prydae, after glancing both ways in the corridor to ensure that no one was watching, entered the private room.

"Age wins," the prince dryly returned. He took a seat across the hearthstone from the monk.

"I will send Brother Bran Dynard, who is only just returned, to his side posthaste."

"Not that one," Prydae quickly replied. "Nor his exotic concubine."

"You have heard, then."

The prince nodded.

"And you do not approve?"

"The Church of Abelle approves? You would open your texts and hearts to a beast of Behr?"

Bathelais let the sarcasm go with a resigned shrug. "Perhaps I should tend to your father myself."

"To what end?" the prince asked. "Will Laird Pryd again feel the vitality of youth?"

Bathelais looked curiously at the young man.

"For that is what we will now need in this changing world," Prydae went on. "The roads will connect us all—perhaps as early as the summer after next. What challenges might Pryd Holding find in that new reality, when cities coalesce in a myriad of alliances?"

"Your father's experience—" Bathelais started to say.

"Is founded upon the old reality of individual holdings," Prydae interrupted. "It is time for all of us to look forward."

Bathelais settled back in his chair, his eyes widening as Prydae continued to stare hard at him, driving the implications of his point home with the intensity of his gaze.

"Yes, perhaps Brother Bathelais should be the one to tend ailing Laird Pryd," Prydae remarked.

The monk wiped a hand across his mouth but did not, could not, blink.

"How fares old Father Jerak?" Prydae asked.

Bathelais jerked in surprise at the abrupt change of subject. "H-he is well," he stammered.

"For such an aged man."

"Yes."

"His successor will be determined as much by the laird as by the Church of Abelle, of course."

Bathelais sucked in his breath, and Prydae smiled, marveling at how easily he had taken control of this meeting. The prince settled back comfortably in his seat. "Tell me more of this Brother Dynard fellow and of the exotic goods that he brought back from his journeys through the wild lands of Behr," he bade, his wide smile showing interest, amusement, and most of all an understanding that Bathelais was in no position to refuse.

CHAPTER 9

The Dangerous Concubine

There may perhaps be a place for your concubine here at the chapel, though I warn you that your behavior is unseemly," Father Jerak said.

"She is my wife," replied Brother Dynard, biting his emotional response back. He knew that Jerak's error was neither benign nor a simple misconstruing of his relationship with the woman of Behr.

"Your concubine," the old monk bluntly stated, confirming Dynard's understanding.

"She is as much a part of my heart as any wife could be," Dynard protested. He looked across the small room at Brother Bathelais for support, but found none forthcoming on the icy visage of the monk. "Any ceremony—and of course I agree to such!—would be a formality, following the vows of marriage SenWi and I already exchanged in southern Behr."

"Vows unrecognized by the Church of Abelle."

"True enough, Father, and so I say again that I willingly submit—"

"Your concubine will agree to forsake the ways of the Jhesta Tu?"

The question nearly knocked Brother Dynard from his seat.

"For, of course, no brother of Blessed Abelle can enter a sanctified union with a woman who is not devout in her faith to Blessed Abelle. Would you not agree, Brother Bathelais?"

"Of course, Father Jerak. The logic is self-evident."

Brother Dynard rubbed his hands over his face and tried to sort out his thoughts in response to this unexpected barrage. He had always recognized that there would be some resistance to the exotic SenWi, resistance from within and without the Church, but he had never imagined gentle Father Jerak to be so stubborn, determined, and apparently prejudiced against the Jhesta Tu.

"Well?" Father Jerak asked.

"Well?" Brother Dynard helplessly echoed.

"Will this woman, SenWi, willingly renounce the ways of her current religion and devote herself to understanding and following Blessed Abelle? Do you suppose that to be the case?"

Brother Dynard couldn't find the words to answer, but he was already shaking his head anyway.

"Nor do you believe that she should move away from this cult, do you, brother?" Jerak accused.

"Father, there is a joining here of beauty and possibility," Dynard started to explain.

"In you and SenWi?"

"In Abelle and Jhest," Dynard continued.

"Brother, you went to Behr to enlighten, not to be enlightened."

"But if such was an unintended consequence—" Dynard started to argue, but Father Jerak held up his hand to cut him short.

"Brother," the old monk said gravely, "do you ask me to detail the possibilities before you if you have moved away from the teachings of Blessed Abelle?"

Brother Bran found it hard to breathe. How could he explain to Father Jerak and to doubting Brother Bathelais that he had not moved away from Blessed Abelle through learning the ways of Jhest, but rather that he had enhanced his understanding of magic—gemstone and other—and thus of godliness? How might he best illustrate to these suddenly hostile brothers that, far from being a threat to the glory of Blessed Abelle, the ways of the Jhesta Tu would only enhance the beauty of the Blessed One's teachings?

After a long pause wherein Brother Dynard could merely shake his head and mumble under his breath helplessly, Father Jerak cleared his throat.

"There may be a place for your concubine here at the chapel," he said. And he sat back and smiled, as if he seemed to think that he was acting quite generously. "I would ask for a measure of discretion, though. You, we all, must serve as examples to those around us, after all, and while your physical needs are understandable and perhaps undeniable, you would do well . . ."

Brother Dynard wasn't listening, for his mind had wandered down a sand-swept Behrenese road and to a place that he realized he badly missed at this terrible moment. Had he erred by returning to Honce? To his Church and his home?

Father Jerak's voice trailed off, and Dynard, thinking that his inattentiveness might have caught the man's attention, hurriedly glanced back up.

There sat Jerak, seeming perfectly content, having had his say.

Brother Dynard simply had no answer and no argument.

I trust her not at all," Prydae told his father. "The idea that a dangerous and armed beast of Behr is living right beside Castle Pryd bodes nothing good."

"Rest easy, my son," Laird Pryd replied. He seemed his old self again after his weeklong bout with sickness—through no fault of Brother Bathelais, who had done little in the way of real healing, Prydae knew. "This Brother Dyn—what was his name?" the old man asked Rennarq, who stood in his customary spot behind the throne.

"Brother Bran Dynard, my laird," Rennarq dutifully replied. "A man of little consequence, so I was told. By you, I believe."

"But this woman—" Prydae started to say.

"Yes, she would indeed seem more formidable, my laird," Rennarq agreed. "By all reports, she slew several powries in fair combat in a single fight."

Prydae did not miss the man's emphasis on the notion of "fair combat," the subtle reference Rennarq was making to his own exploits in an armored chariot.

"She is in the care of the monks?" Pryd asked.

"Yes," Prydae answered before Rennarq could, drawing Pryd's gaze back his way. "Brother Bathelais has informed me that this beast of Behr will likely remain in the chapel as a worker."

"What would you have me do in that case?" asked Pryd. "Am I to deny her my trust when the brothers of Abelle have seen fit to take her in?"

"It is not within their province to deny your claim," Rennarq put in; the harshness of his tone served as another reminder of his general feelings toward the brothers of Blessed Abelle.

"She should be surrendered to the laird until her disposition can be properly determined," added Prydae.

"You fear her," Laird Pryd remarked as if suddenly realizing it. "Or is it, perhaps, that you fear that her reputation will outshine your own?"

Prydae narrowed his eyes and crossed his arms over his chest, one foot tapping on the stone floor. A moment later, Laird Pryd laughed at him.

"Forgive me, my son." The old man was quick to explain, "I have seen this creature from Behr from afar, and she is but a wisp of a thing."

"Who slew several powries in combat," said Rennarq, for no better reason, apparently, than to thicken the tension in the air.

Laird Pryd stopped laughing and turned to offer a stern glance to his long-time friend, then turned back to his son.

"Would you have a stranger, a foreigner, a beast of Behr capture the hearts of the peasants as a hero?" Prydae asked. "A foreign creature who is allied with the brothers of Abelle and not with the Laird of Pryd Holding?"

Put like that, Prydae's words seemed to have a greater effect on his father. Laird Pryd settled back in his chair and assumed a pensive pose.

"She should be surrendered to Castle Pryd at once," Prydae pressed now that he had his father's sudden interest. "Father Jerak is not over fond of her anyway, from what Brother Bathelais has told me. I doubt he will argue against your request."

"You would have me take her into Castle Pryd, and what—imprison her?"

"Until we can understand her true nature and her intent in being here, yes."

Laird Pryd paused and took a couple of deep breaths, then looked back over his shoulder at Rennarq, who merely shrugged.

"I will go and speak with Father Jerak," the laird agreed, and with some effort—a lingering weakness from his illness, perhaps—he pulled himself off his throne.

A wave of dizziness had SenWi leaning back in the cool shadows of an alcove, broom in hand, when the main door banged open and Laird Pryd and his entourage entered the chapel. The woman watched him with interest, measuring his strides and recognizing that something might be amiss here.

SenWi had been uncomplaining, accepting the position offered her by Brother Bathelais as a cleaning servant in the chapel. Dynard had not been pleased of course, but SenWi had counseled him to patience. At least the two of them could spend some time together by this arrangement, which was much better than an alternative that had him serving in this dark place, with her somewhere away. As a disciplined Jhesta Tu, SenWi didn't fear work, after all.

Without apparently noticing the woman hidden by the shadows, the laird and his escorts swept through the room and down the side corridor toward Father Jerak's private quarters.

SenWi stepped out of the alcove and glanced all around. She knew that this was an unusual visit, and she sensed something deeper, some notion that the secular leader's presence here had something to do with Bran Dynard's return. Seeing no one watching her, SenWi leaned the broom against the wall and moved off, silent as a shadow. She headed down the corridor, turning the corner to see the laird enter Jerak's private room. SenWi paused at the wall and gathered her concentration, then lifted her *chi*, lightening her body weight as she scaled the decorated wall.

She crawled sidelong atop a ledge, moving right above the now-closed door to a transom, so she could look down upon the private meeting. They were exchanging formal greetings, and SenWi reconsidered her course. What was she doing here? What business was this of hers? Shaking her head at her foolishness, she began to ease away, but stopped short, when she heard Laird Pryd say to Jerak, "It would not be wise for the brothers of Abelle to harbor a dangerous animal."

"We are assessing her," the old monk replied.

It hit SenWi then that they were speaking of her. As she quickly moved away, she heard Laird Pryd say something about the need for proper security during such assessments.

She hit the ground running, slipping back into the main area of the chapel and then out the door. She thought that she should go to Dynard but wasn't sure where he might be. In the tiny prayer rooms, likely, but he would not be alone.

SenWi went out and around the corner of the building, moving into the alleys between the chapel and the castle. She found a quiet, secluded spot and leaned back against the brown stone wall, overcome by lightheadedness.

Her hand went instinctively to her belly, to the child growing there.

They are going to tell you that I must be turned over to Laird Pryd," SenWi told Dynard, in the language of Behr.

"They will not—" Brother Dynard started to argue, but he stopped short and leaped forward, grabbing his suddenly swaying wife. "Are you all right? SenWi!"

She put her hand comfortingly on his shoulder and managed a weak smile. "I am with child," she explained. "I am pregnant with your child."

Suddenly it was Dynard who needed the support to stand.

He gasped out a few unintelligible sounds, then, his eyes moist, he hugged his wife close, burying his face in her black hair and wondering if anything in the world could be more wonderful.

Finally, after a long while, Bran managed to move back to arm's length. "My Church will sanction our marriage only if you disavow the teachings of the Jhesta Tu."

SenWi's expression went cold immediately.

"Which of course you cannot do," Dynard quickly added. "Nor should you. I embrace Jhest as wholly now as I did in the Walk of Clouds."

"But your brethren will not approve."

"Not yet," he admitted. "These things take time. I will show them the truth, SenWi. It is my place in the world now—well, that and serving you as husband and our child as father." He couldn't suppress a grin, but his smile did not soften SenWi's concerned expression.

"I will teach them and persuade them," he promised her, taking her by the shoulders so that she had to look at him directly, had to see his determination.

"They will insist that I am handed to the charge of Laird Pryd," SenWi countered. "I heard them myself. He fears me, for some reason."

"Or he wishes to learn from you. Might it be that Laird Pryd has heard of your exploits against the powries?"

"He likely would have, since you boasted of it to his soldiers."

"Then perhaps he wishes to have you teach his soldiers or his son."

SenWi's lips went very tight and she shook her head.

Brother Dynard hadn't expected any different reaction, of course, for he understood that the Jhesta Tu weren't about to divulge their secrets of combat. To the southern mystics, the learning of martial arts was part of the process of learning the Book of Jhest, and to remove the specifics of combat from that overall process went against everything they believed. Dynard had made the suggestion of intent only to place a less menacing twist on the laird's apparent interest in SenWi, to try to lighten their shared fears.

"I just mean—" he started to explain.

"I am vulnerable now," SenWi interrupted, and she took Bran's hand and placed it on her belly.

He could hardly draw breath. He turned his hand over and clasped SenWi's tightly, pulling her close. He looked up at the sky as late afternoon turned to twilight. "Come," he bade her. "We will get you out to Garibond's house, where you will be safe. I will tell my brethren that you have departed for Behr, that you could not accept the terms of their demands." He was thinking as he went, improvising. "And I will remain steadfast in my support of your choice. I will teach them—I *must* teach them. I see my duty now to my brethren as clearly as Blessed Abelle must have seen his own when he discovered the glories of Pimaninicuit and the sacred gemstones. This is my place in life." He looked back down at SenWi's delicately curving belly and added, "My place in the wider world."

The couple went out soon after, as darkness fell across the land.

Before the dawn, Brother Bran was on his way back to Chapel Pryd, clutching the Book of Jhest, his expression one of complete determination.

He would teach them.

CHAPTER 10

The Loss of Control

SenWi awakened with a start and immediately tried to rise. A wave of nausea sent her tumbling back to the cot, and she gave a little cry.

As soon as she saw Garibond coming through the door toward her, she realized where she was—in the tunnels beneath his house—and she remembered her last conversation with her husband. Dynard had wanted to return at once to Chapel Pryd with the Book of Jhest. He was convinced that he would sway the brothers of Abelle, that he would enlighten them as he had been enlightened.

SenWi didn't believe it for a moment. She had counseled Bran against returning—or at least against returning with the book.

But he was angry, livid over the dismissal of their marriage by his brethren and outraged at the notion that SenWi would be "turned over" to anyone.

The discussion had gotten heated, SenWi remembered, with Dynard shaking his head so violently that it seemed as if he were using the movement to physically deflect her nay-saying.

Then, in the excitement of the moment, the dizziness had returned, had knocked SenWi off her feet. She remembered being carried to a cot and gently laid on it by Dynard. She remembered his bending low and kissing her, and leaving her with the promise that he would make them understand.

She settled back down and closed her eyes, finding her center and inner balance.

"Trust Bran," Garibond was saying as he came and straightened the blanket over SenWi. "He's a good one. He'll let them know the truth of it all."

SenWi kept her eyes closed and remained focused internally, though the man's words did register with her. She didn't doubt Garibond, nor did she lack faith in the abilities of her husband—hadn't he won over the entire enclave of the Walk of Clouds? But SenWi understood, where these other two apparently did not, that the monks at the chapel—Father Jerak and Brother Bathelais—already understood the truth, at least from a practical point of view. They understood perfectly well that Dynard honestly believed that he had found an extension of their religion, a supplement that strengthened and did not diminish the words of Blessed Abelle.

SenWi believed the same thing.

But she also recognized that the folk of Honce would not likely open their ears to that call. Nor would the monks, nor could they at this time when their religion was vying for the approval of the lairds.

She was desperately afraid for her husband, but SenWi couldn't hold her focus upon that. She was Jhesta Tu, attuned to the rhythms of her body, and she was beginning to understand that something was very wrong inside her. The lightheadedness, the overwhelming weakness, the nausea—all of that could be explained simply because she was with child. But there was something more, she understood. It wasn't just the symptoms but the intensity of them. She had seen other Jhesta Tu women through their pregnancies, women who were not nearly as accomplished in the way of Jhest as she, and they had almost always been able to use their *chi* to overcome any and all symptoms.

That was the problem here. When SenWi tried to find her center, to align her thread of life energy, she could not. It was as if that line of energy were somehow creased and unbalanced, and the problem went far beyond the normal bounds of what a pregnancy might cause. SenWi knew that, but she had no answer.

She did have a guess, though. She thought back to the poor battered girl hanging by her wrists from a pole at the end of the road.

SenWi put a hand over her face and fought hard against her welling tears.

"He'll be all right," Garibond said softly, and he stroked her black hair. "You must trust Bran."

She started to shake her head to explain her deeper concern, but it didn't matter.

Brother Bathelais wasn't opening up. Brother Dynard could see that clearly as he sat across from him. Dynard clutched his precious Book of Jhest to his chest, huddling over it like an eagle protecting its kill.

"You presume much, Brother, to think that we are in need of further enlightenment," Bathelais said slowly and deliberately. "The teachings of Blessed Abelle are not open-ended and inviting of addition."

"But even Blessed Abelle was ignorant of the truths of the Jhesta Tu," Brother Dynard said before he considered his words. As soon as they left his mouth, Bathelais widened his eyes and recoiled, and Dynard knew that he had erred.

"Th-those truths are extensions," Dynard stammered, trying to bring back a level of calm that seemed fast eroding. As he spoke, he uncurled from around the book and slowly presented it to Bathelais. "Contained herein are beauteous revelations that enhance all that Blessed Abelle has taught us."

"Then you are saying that Brother Abelle was not God inspired? You are saying that the words God spoke to Brother Abelle were not revelations of divine truth but merely revelations to him of a truth that already was known to man?" Bathelais shook his head, a sour look on his face. "A truth already known to the beasts of Behr?"

Brother Dynard forced himself to continue to present the book. He even leaned closer so that Brother Bathelais couldn't ignore the large tome.

Finally, his face a mask of suspicion, Bathelais took the great book and set it upon his lap. Still looking at Dynard, his eyes narrow, he flipped the cover open and read Dynard's letter—a two-page introduction that was virtually the same argument that Dynard had been making to him for more than an hour now. When he finished Bathelais paused and looked back at the hopeful Dynard—and to the enlightened monk, Bathelais seemed more bemused than intrigued.

Could his mind be so closed? Brother Dynard wondered. Was his heart so encased in absolutes that he would not allow for an expansion of the beauty he had learned?

Brother Bathelais turned the next page and glanced down, perplexed. "What is this?" he asked.

"It is written in the language of Jhest, one similar to that of Behr," Brother Dynard tried to explain.

"I did not know the beasts could write."

The continuing racism struck hard at the heart of Brother Dynard. He wanted nothing more than to reach across and grab Bathelais and give him a good shake! He wanted to tell Bathelais about the culture of the southern people, about the intricacies of their language—which in many ways was superior to that of Honce—about their clothing of silk, and the fabulous colors of their rugs. He wanted to describe artifacts he had seen, hundreds of years old, predating any known art in all Honce. He wanted to tell Bathelais about the architecture of Jacintha, an ancient and wondrous city. He wanted to do all of that; he thought it imperative that his brethren came to see and appreciate this reality.

All he could do was point at the book, although emphatically.

"What would you have me do?" Bathelais asked. "Admire the curvature of your lines?"

"I will instruct you in the language."

"Could you not have simply translated the work?"

"It would not be exact," Brother Dynard explained. "And it was a condition of the Jhesta Tu that any who would peruse their secrets do so in their language—learning the language is part of the discipline required to truly appreciate the knowledge contained within, you see."

"A condition of the Jhesta Tu? They do not willingly share their insights?"

"They do not proselytize, no," Brother Dynard replied. "Theirs is a light that must be attained by the willing, not forced upon the reluctant."

"Are you not proselytizing right now?"

The question had Brother Dynard nonplused. He finally managed to string a few words together in a coherent fashion. "I am not Jhesta Tu."

If Brother Bathelais was convinced of that, his expression did not show it. "What are you, then?"

"I am your brother," Dynard insisted. Though he believed that with all his heart, he could not infuse his voice with any strength under the increasingly hostile stare of Bathelais.

Brother Bathelais looked back at the cursive and stylized writing on the page, then gently closed the book as his eyes rose to regard Dynard once more. "And you will teach us how to read this language of the Jhest?"

"I will."

"And when we read this book, we will learn that Blessed Abelle was not wholly correct?"

The form of that question left it unanswerable by poor Dynard.

Brother Bathelais stood up, the tome wrapped in his arms. He looked hard at Dynard for a moment longer, then gave a curt nod, turned, and left the room.

Brother Dynard sighed and slumped in his chair, glad of the reprieve. He held no illusions that this initial discussion of the delicate subject had gone well.

She stood before the rising sun, her breathing perfectly even, her stance completely grounded, not a muscle twitching.

She focused on the sun, climbing slowly above the eastern horizon. She imagined its rays permeating her, linking with her *chi*, and she used the vertical climb of that burning orb to focus her inner strength on the vertical line of her *ki-chi-kree*. In the sun, SenWi found balance. In the sun, she found inner warmth.

As slowly as the great ball rose, she lifted her arms before her. As so many minutes passed and her arms lifted before her face, she brought her hands together, linked six fingers, and pressed both thumbs together and index fingers together in salute.

The sun continued its climb and her arms moved as if lifting it. She meant to stand here until noon, until her arms above her head were in complete concert with the heavenly cycle. But she didn't make it. As her hands began to lift above her forehead, SenWi felt a stretch in her belly, constricting at first and then suddenly so painful that it had her doubling over and clutching her midsection.

The line of her *ki-chi-kree* could not hold the straightened posture; her life energy had been wounded, and badly—and not just her own, she feared.

"The snake venom," she whispered, her teeth clenched. She understood it all then. When she had healed the poor girl, her own inner-heated hands had taken the venom of the adder into herself. But how had that so wounded her? A Jhesta Tu mystic could do this, with little danger, for the Jhesta Tu mystic could overcome poison with ease.

And then SenWi understood; and her breath came in short gasps and she wanted nothing more than to scream in outrage.

A Jhesta Tu mystic was possessed of the inner discipline to defeat poisons. But the unborn child of a Jhesta Tu mystic . . .

He knew as soon as Father Jerak entered the room with Brother Bathelais that things had not gone well between the two of them, for the old man's face was locked in such a scowl as Brother Dynard had never before seen.

"You have come to question Blessed Abelle?" Jerak asked, and it seemed to Dynard as if he were trying, quite unsuccessfully, to keep the bitter edge out of his voice.

"No, Father, of course not," Brother Bran answered.

"And yet, there is this," Father Jerak said, and he turned, extending his open hand toward the Book of Jhest that Brother Bathelais still held close to his chest.

"Father," said an exasperated Dynard, "as I tried to explain to Brother Bathelais, this book, these truths of Jhest, are no threat to our order or the teachings of Blessed Abelle. If we are to believe in divine inspiration, then are we to claim sole province over it?"

"And thus you believe that this ancient order"—again he indicated the book—"received this divine inspiration many years before Blessed Abelle?"

Brother Dynard felt as if he were sinking. He could clearly see on their faces that they had made up their minds. They weren't questioning him now in hopes of understanding. No, they were allowing him to damn himself and nothing more. "It is not . . . There is no threat here," he tried to explain. His frustration turned to hopelessness when a pair of armed soldiers of the laird appeared in the doorway.

"Where is the woman?" Father Jerak asked.

When Dynard continued to stare incredulously at the soldiers, Jerak repeated his question in even sharper and more insistent tones. Then Dynard did look at him, and old Jerak's scowl seemed even more pronounced.

"Where is she?" he asked again.

"She left." Dynard's thoughts were swirling. He tried to concentrate, reminding himself that he had to cover for SenWi at all costs, that he had to be convincing! "She could not tolerate the prejudice and the unwillingness."

"The unwillingness?" came Father Jerak's sharp reply. "To convert to her heathen ways? Did you expect to come here with some false prophet from the land of beasts and undo the blessings of Abelle's teachings? Did you believe that your revelations of a few tricks from these . . . Jhesta Tu creatures would turn us aside from our path to spiritual redemption? Brother Dynard, did you truly believe that one misguided brother—"

"No!" Dynard shouted, and he sat back and went silent as the soldiers at the door bristled, one even drawing his bronze short sword halfway from its sheath. "No, Father, it was never my intent."

"Your intent? Wherever did you come to the conclusion that your intent meant anything, Brother Dynard? You were given a specific mission, entrusted with a duty to spread the word of Abelle to people deserving, though ignorant. You were sponsored by and of the Church of Blessed Abelle. You were sent by our arrangements and with our money. You seem to have forgotten all these things, Brother Dynard."

Dynard couldn't give voice to any objections. For he could not argue with Jerak's reasoning. He thought the man's perceptions skewed, to be sure, but in looking at all of this from that viewpoint, it struck Dynard for the first time that these brothers of Abelle were afraid of the Book of Jhest.

Truly afraid.

"You misunderstand," he finally found the courage to reply. "The Jhesta Tu—"

"Are heathens in need of enlightenment," Father Jerak finished.

The silence hung in the air like the crouch of a hunting cat.

"Do you not agree, Brother Dynard?" Jerak said.

Dynard swallowed hard.

"Where is your concubine?"

"She is my *wife*," Dynard insisted.

"Where is your concubine?" Jerak asked again.

Dynard's lips went very tight. "She left. This place, this chapel, this town. This land of Honce itself. She could not tolerate."

"She would go south and east then, back toward Ethelbert Holding," Father Jerak reasoned, and he turned toward the soldiers as he spoke. Both men nodded. He turned back to Dynard. "She'll not get far."

Panic coursed through Dynard and he licked his lips and glanced all around. "Leave her alone," he said. "What reason . . . She has done nothing."

"Be easy, Brother Dynard," Father Jerak said. "Your concubine is in no danger as long as she has truly departed this holding. Laird Pryd has promised me this."

"What are you saying?" Brother Dynard demanded, and he leaped out of his seat and moved to tower over the stooping Jerak. But Bathelais was there, staring him down. The soldiers came forward suddenly, interposing themselves between the furious Dynard and Jerak.

"Brother Bran Dynard, it becomes apparent to me that you have lost your way," Father Jerak said, stepping back to give the soldiers access to him. "Perhaps you are in need of some time alone to consider your true path."

On a nod from Jerak, the soldiers reached for Dynard, who roughly shrugged them away.

"She is my wife," Dynard stubbornly insisted, and he started to take a bold step forward. But before he could shift his weight, the pommel of a sword slammed him hard on the back of the neck. One moment, he was moving for Father Jerak, the next, he was staring at Father Jerak's sandals. And he felt as if the stone floor beneath him was somehow less than solid, as if it was rising up, its cool darkness swallowing him.

He knew not how much time had passed when he at last awoke, cramped, in the dark. The dirt was muddy beneath him, the ceiling too low for him to even straighten up as he sat there. He heard the chatter of rats and felt some many-legged creature scramble across his foot.

But all he could think of was SenWi.

What had he done to her by bringing her to this place?

What had he done to their child?

CHAPTER 11

The Power of the Written Word

Father Jerak sat quietly in his private chamber, staring at the troublesome book. It pained him to see his former student so seduced. He had been overjoyed when he had first heard that Brother Dynard had returned to Pryd Holding from his mission in the wild southland, for many monks were not returning. The world was a dangerous place, after all, and Behr was considered one of the wildest regions. In his last visit to the mother chapel in the north on the rocky coast of the Gulf of Corona, Jerak had learned that of those brothers who had gone to spread word of Blessed Abelle outside Honce—to Vanguard or Alpinador across the gulf to the north or to Behr in the south, less than one in three had returned. Even if every traveling brother not already confirmed dead came back to his respective chapel, that number would not exceed one half of those who had gone forth.

Thus, Jerak had been pleased to learn that Bran Dynard, ever a favorite of his, had come home alive and well.

No, not well, Jerak reconsidered, and he looked again at the book on the small table. To Jerak's thinking, it would take a monumental effort to ever get the wayward brother well again.

There came a soft knock on his door, and Brother Bathelais entered.

"He is contrite?" Father Jerak asked hopefully.

"He has not spoken since we put him in the dungeon," said Bathelais. "He hardly registers our presence when we go to him with food and drink. The only reaction I have seen from him at all was one of surprise and perhaps satisfaction when I asked him yet again the course of the missing Behr woman."

"He was pleased that she has eluded us these three days," Father Jerak said. "And likely now we will never find her."

"Perhaps that is for the best."

Father Jerak didn't disagree, though he doubted that Laird Pryd or Prince Prydae would agree. Those two had urged him forcefully on this decision regarding the disposition of Brother Dynard. Never would Jerak have imprisoned Dynard—certainly not in the wretched and muddy substructure of Chapel Pryd! As angry as he had been, and remained, over Dynard's transgression concerning these southern mystics, Father Jerak had hoped to gently persuade the man back to the fold. He had even for one moment considered having Brother Dynard teach a younger brother, Bathelais likely, to read the flowing script in that cursed book, that he might then expose to Dynard the fallacies of the text.

But Father Jerak understood well that he and his brethren were secure and welcomed only under the sufferance of Laird Pryd. Though Jerak had seen a threat in Dynard's failings, Laird Pryd had seen more. Or perhaps this anger at Dynard was more the working of the laird's proud son, Jerak mused. There were rumors that the heroic prince hadn't taken well to the tales of the Behrenese woman's battle prowess.

Either way, it didn't matter—not now. The die was cast, and appropriately so, Father Jerak believed, though perhaps it had been thrown a bit harshly.

"I fear that if we await contrition before releasing Brother Dynard from his cell, then he will die in there," Brother Bathelais said, drawing the older monk from his contemplations. "Though perhaps that would be the best course for all."

Father Jerak answered that with a scowl.

"Better even for Brother Dynard," Brother Bathelais quickly added. "His path is a road to eternal damnation. Perhaps he has not yet transgressed too far for divine salvation."

"Unrepentant sinners are not welcomed by Blessed Abelle, who sits at the feet of God," Father Jerak tersely reminded.

Father Jerak paused, then, and studied Bathelais, but the man did not respond.

"Keep him incarcerated another week," the old monk ordered. "By then we should know the more about the missing woman."

"And if she has not been found?"

"I have no desire to see Brother Dynard dead in our filthy dungeon. If the woman is not found and our wayward brother has not repented, we will accommodate him more comfortably in a room within the chapel proper."

"A cleaner cell?"

"But a cell nonetheless," said Father Jerak. "I am willing to spend as much time and energy as we can afford to bring Brother Bran Dynard back into the ways of the order, but he will not proselytize this bastardized version of the message of Blessed Abelle. That is not a point of debate."

"Laird Pryd will agree to this?"

Father Jerak shrugged, unsure, and especially if the missing woman was not found. "Laird Pryd will see no threat in Brother Dynard as long as we keep our reins on him tight. And I assure you, Brother Bathelais, that Brother Dynard will know no freedom until he sincerely repents." That last statement chilled Father Jerak's bones even as he spoke the words. He hadn't thought of this matter in those drastic terms before—not to their obvious conclusion. That conclusion loomed before him now, powerfully so. Brother Dynard was more than merely a wayward brother in need of repentance or, absent that, of excommunication from the order.

Brother Dynard, by bringing the Book of Jhest, by his insistence on blurring the lines between the Church of Blessed Abelle and this mystical southern cult, was a threat to the Church—one the fledgling religion could ill afford, particularly with the continuing pressure of the Samhaists.

Threats to the Church could not be tolerated.

A week later, SenWi had not been found, to the increasing frustration and anger of Prince Prydae. But, true to his word, Father Jerak had ordered a haggard and ill Brother Dynard brought from the dungeon and placed in a secure room in the chapel. Dynard had lost a great deal of weight, and his body was covered in sores from the standing water and mud. His muscles had already begun to atrophy, and it took two brothers to help him up the stairs and into his new prison: a windowless room on the chapel's second floor.

That night, Father Jerak went to him, the Book of Jhest in hand and Brother Bathelais in tow. He dropped the book on a table near the bed where the ragged-looking Brother Dynard was half sitting—and it seemed as if only the wall was holding the battered heretic up.

"Have you something to say to me?" Father Jerak asked.

Brother Dynard looked up at him, then at the book. "You wish me to translate the tome for you?"

Father Jerak's expression grew very tight and he scowled at Brother Bathelais. "He is to have no visitors. His chamber pot will be replaced every morning and he will be served meals in accordance with the other brothers." He spun back to face Dynard. "But you will not leave this room. Understand that edict, foolish brother, if a brother you remain. Upon pain of death, you are not to leave this room."

Brother Dynard's expression didn't change, the fallen monk didn't flinch as he sat there staring at Father Jerak, though whether that was through stubbornness or a simple lack of strength the old monk couldn't tell. Father Jerak snatched up the book, motioned to Bathelais to follow, and stormed out of the room.

"You did not even ask him about the woman," Brother Bathelais remarked when they were out in the hallway and Bathelais had locked Dynard's door.

"You heard his response."

"A misconception regarding your request? He may have thought that his release had been incumbent upon our lessening our opposition to this supposed knowledge he has brought back."

"The mere fact that he still harbors any uncertainty concerning that tome, or that he still holds, as his tone evinced, any desire to share the words confined within its pages, is all the proof I need that our wayward brother has not come to the truth. Let him fester through this season and the next. When winter's first winds blow against the walls of Chapel Pryd, we will return to him."

Brother Bathelais did wince at the harsh sentence, but only momentarily, and he said nothing, deterred by the power of Father Jerak's scowl.

She was having a good day, relatively speaking. SenWi had found some measure of energy and strength that morning, and after nearly three weeks of seclusion inside Garibond's house, she had dared to go out into the sunshine. She stayed close to the cottage by the lake, though, well aware that the authorities of Pryd Holding were seeking her.

She managed her Jhesta Tu training ritual that day, as well, and though a light-headed weakness did return, SenWi pressed through the ritual to completion. She was still outside, sitting in the shadow under the eaves of the house, when she saw Garibond approaching, returning from one of his rare visits to the town. She rose unsteadily, but quickly found her balance and her center, and moved to greet the man with a hesitant hopefulness.

She saw from his expression that things in town were not well.

"Where is Dynard?"

"You should not be outside," Garibond remarked, and he glanced around. "They are still looking for you."

"Where is Dynard?" He started to go by her, but she caught him roughly by the shoulder and held him back. "Tell me."

"He is alive but under guard in the chapel, so I heard. You and Brother Dynard are the talk of all the town, of course."

"They are not mistreating him?"

"Who can know what the brothers do," Garibond replied, and he gave a frustrated sigh. "I doubt you'll be well treated if Prince Prydae and his soldiers find you, and that is our main concern."

"No."

"Yes! There is nothing we can do for Dynard, and do not forget that it was his choice to return to Chapel Pryd. I promised him that I would look after you, and I'm not about to go back on my word."

SenWi's expression clearly revealed that she wasn't buying the argument.

"This is likely part of the process," Garibond went on more forcefully. "Dynard knew that it would be no easy task to persuade the monks."

"Where is the book?"

Garibond shrugged.

SenWi looked out toward the distant keep tower, her thoughts spinning as she suddenly came to recognize the potential depth of this problem. "You must return to town, to the chapel itself," she improvised. "I will know more of Bran and of the Book of Jhest. You must do this for me, at once."

"And mark my house for suspicion?" Garibond argued. "Shall I pause and visit Castle Pryd before my return and simply tell Prince Prydae that the woman he and his soldiers seek is safely hidden in the tunnels, or will you remain outside to greet them?"

With her limited command of the language, it took SenWi some time to understand the sarcasm in the remark.

"I cannot do it, girl," Garibond said bluntly.

SenWi didn't argue any further, for her thoughts were already moving in another direction. With her returning strength came the return, she understood, of her responsibilities to her husband and to the prize he had carried from the Walk of Clouds. So deep in contemplation was she that she hardly noticed that Garibond had moved to the door and had pulled it open.

"Come along inside, then," he said. "I've brought some fine spices. I'll make us a stew."

SenWi didn't argue.

Long after supper, with darkness spreading across the land, SenWi sat across from Garibond as he half sat and half reclined before a roaring fire. She said nothing, and brushed off his feeble attempts to begin a conversation. She watched and she waited, and when at last he nodded his head in slumber, she went to her travel sack and rummaged through it, producing the suit of black silk.

She changed and went out into the night, dark and silent, trotting swiftly toward the town and Chapel Pryd. She spent a moment trying to recall its layout, then moved to the base of the northern wall. There was only one window here, set high up.

SenWi fell into herself, grasping the energy of her *chi* and twisting it so that it battled against the natural pull of the ground. Then she picked out handholds in the wall and began to climb, moving steadily and easily—almost as if she were weightless. She arrived at the window in short order and squeezed through, entering the bedroom of Father Jerak himself.

SenWi resisted the urge to awaken him with a choke hold that she might force the information from him. No, such a bold course could prove catastrophic for her husband, she knew. She slipped across the room and through the door to the antechamber, and before she took another step, she saw one of her missing prizes.

The Book of Jhest lay there right before her, opened upon a wooden pedestal beside the low-burning hearth fire. Many other books were set haphazardly on shelves flanking that hearth; and even from this distance, SenWi could see the dust that had gathered on them. Was that the fate that awaited the product of Bran's long toil?

Her fingers trembled as she felt the smooth pages of the opened book, and she promised herself that she would come back through here on her way out after locating and securing the release of her dear husband.

She moved away, but before she even reached the door, a renewed wave of nausea washed over her and nearly buckled her legs beneath her. Black spots flitted before her eyes, and it was all that she could do just to stand there and not fall over. Instinctively, SenWi clutched at her belly and it took all of her considerable willpower to bring her breathing quickly back under control.

"Bran," she whispered helplessly, and another wave brought her to one knee. She knew that she was in trouble. Her physical exertion in running all the way out here and, even more so, her mystical exertion in scaling and levitating up the wall, had been too much, she only now realized. She thought of the days she had spent in Garibond's house, incapacitated beyond anything she had ever known, barely conscious and without the strength to even stand. What might it mean for Bran if she fell ill here?

With that troubling thought in mind, SenWi glanced back at the Book of Jhest. Then she looked past it, to the shelves and the piled, disheveled tomes. Glancing all around, improvising as she went, SenWi searched the deepest recesses of the shelves and found a book of roughly similar size to the one sitting on the pedestal. She meant to tip the pedestal to the floor toward the open hearth, and nearly did so as she swooned, but fortunately, she caught herself at the last moment.

She didn't want to make a ruckus that would awaken Father Jerak and half the chapel, after all!

Regaining her balance and a measure of her strength, SenWi placed the Book of Jhest off to the side, then gently lowered the pedestal to the floor, lining it up with the hearth. She then opened the other book, taken from the shelf, and placed it on the embers, and after blowing on those orange coals for a bit, managed to set the book aflame.

SenWi glanced back at the crowded bookshelf and wondered how effective the ruse might prove. For good measure and taking care not to obviously disturb the dust, she jostled the remaining books on the shelf to better hide the theft. With no other options before her, she gathered up the Book of Jhest, and with a rueful glance at the room's other door—the one that would lead her deeper into the chapel and hopefully to her imprisoned husband—she staggered back the other way, back into sleeping Father Jerak's bedchamber.

She squeezed out onto the windowsill and glanced down the twenty feet or more to the ground. SenWi told herself how important this was, reminded herself of the grim consequences of failure—for her, for Bran, and for the precious book. She felt inside herself again, found the line of *chi*, and tried again to free herself from the bonds of gravity.

Father Jerak stirred behind her, and she knew she could wait no longer. She turned and slipped down from the windowsill.

And then she was falling.

She arrived at Garibond's house many hours later, after the dawn, dragging one broken leg, barely conscious, and trembling violently in the grip of a high fever.

She was still clutching the book.

CHAPTER 12

The Inspiration of the Season

She heard the birds singing every day but never did she open her eyes at their inviting call. She felt the movement around her and knew it to be Garibond, and occasionally heard his whispers.

But it too was distant, and nothing that could bring her forth from the damaged shell of her physical body.

She tasted the cool water and warm broth when he managed to get some into her mouth, but they were sensations of another time and place, of another world altogether, it seemed.

For most of SenWi's thoughts remained inward, sharing herself with her unborn child, offering her love and her warmth, watching the awakening of consciousness. It seemed to her such a beautiful and comforting thing that a piece of Bran and a piece of herself should create an entirely different and independent little being. She felt its presence keenly within her own corporeal coil, and knew after a time that it sensed her as well.

One morning, SenWi heard the birds more distinctly, though it seemed to her as if they were fewer in number. Hardly aware of the movement, she blinked open her eyes. Curtains covered the room's small window, but the brightness stung her nonetheless, and it took her a long time to resist blinking her eyes tightly closed.

She lay there as time passed. She knew not how long—hours perhaps—before the door was finally pushed open and Garibond, looking weary and downtrodden, walked in.

He moved by the bed, a small cup in hand, and it wasn't until he was even with SenWi's head that he noticed her looking back at him.

He jumped back, his eye opened wide, and he nearly dropped his cup, his hand suddenly shaking so violently that its contents splashed over its sides. Finally he managed to set the cup down on the small table by the bed, and he nearly fell atop SenWi, scrambling to get close.

"Are you there?" Garibond asked.

"Garibond," she replied, and with great effort, she managed to bring one hand up to stroke the man's strong, hairy arm.

"By God, I thought you'd never awaken," Garibond whispered. "All these days and weeks . . ."

His admission of time's passage struck SenWi hard, and she, too, opened her eyes more widely. "How long?"

"You've been away from me for almost five weeks."

SenWi found her breath hard to come by. "Bran?" she gasped.

Garibond's smile comforted her.

"I saw him just two days ago," he explained. "Every passing week, the brothers at the chapel afford him more liberties, though he is not yet able to move about unrestricted, and certainly not out of the chapel. He longs for you—I heard that in his every word! But he cannot come to you, for fear that you would be discovered. Laird Pryd and that son of his are a stubborn lot."

SenWi had no idea what he was talking about at that blurry moment, but she was thrilled that her dear Bran was apparently alive and well. "Some day," she replied, and left it at that.

Garibond nodded and started propping up her pillows. "Let us sit you up a bit," he explained. "You have to get some food in you."

SenWi's face scrunched up, for the thought did not appeal to her, but that only prodded Garibond on more forcefully.

"For the sake of the child in your swollen belly," he said, and SenWi felt his hand touch her there. When she looked down to regard that gentle hand, she saw that she was beginning to show her condition. "A woman with child has to eat," Garibond insisted. "You're feeding two!"

SenWi nodded and didn't resist as Garibond helped her to sit up, and then he put the cup to her lips and let her sip its broth contents. Before long, she had drained the vessel, and Garibond smiled and went out to get her some more.

That, too, she drank, and she was feeling better with each sip of the warm liquid that washed down her parched throat.

"We will get you a solid and hearty meal as soon as you're able," Garibond assured her. "I promised Dynard that I would take care of you, and I'm not about to let your stubbornness get in the way of that."

SenWi even managed a smile, albeit a weak one.

Brother Dynard's eyes and thoughts were fixed on the wider world beyond Chapel Pryd's open gate as he swept the falling leaves from the courtyard's paths. It was late morning, and already he had been out longer this blustery autumn day than he had in many weeks.

SenWi was somewhere out there, pregnant and ill. Every fiber in Brother Dynard urged him to run off to her bedside, to hold her and kiss her, to tell her that he loved her, and to help her back to him. Nothing else in all the world, not even his beloved Church, seemed to matter beside that image of stricken SenWi, for though Garibond had assured him in their brief meeting that she was strong and would pull through, Dynard had heard the undercurrent of fear in his seemingly confident tone. SenWi was in trouble, and for her own sake and despite his every desperate desire, Dynard could not go to her.

He was gaining some measure of freedom here, at least. He had only recently learned of the accident in Father Jerak's chamber and the destruction of the Book of Jhest, and while his spirit sank at the great loss to his brethren, and while his heart ached at the thought of his most precious work undone, all that paled in comparison to his fears for SenWi and his unborn child.

Until very recently, Brother Dynard had believed that his greatest contribution would be that book he had so painstakingly transcribed. But now he knew the truth: his greatest achievement would not be measured in copied words but in living flesh, in his child.

He prayed that SenWi would fight through this illness that had befallen her and that one day he would be able to see their child and hold their child.

Ironically, Dynard recognized that the destruction of the book had probably facilitated his best chance in seeing SenWi or his child again. From what he had learned over the last weeks of his increasing freedom, Father Jerak had visibly relaxed since the book had burned. Perhaps Jerak saw in its destruction the threat of wayward Brother Dynard lessened, or perhaps he was just growing tired of his vigilance. Either way, it didn't matter to Dynard, as long as the result put him back where he belonged, in SenWi's loving arms.

Brother Bathelais called to him, and that reminded him to keep the broom moving. He glanced back to his superior, who was standing on the chapel's stone stoop. When Dynard returned his focus fully to his sweeping, Bathelais called to him again, bidding him to come inside.

Dynard moved into the shadows within the chapel door tentatively, for he had caught a hint of anger in his superior's tone. Bathelais, waiting for him just inside, stood impatiently, tapping his foot on the stone, his arms crossed over his chest.

"Yes, Brother?" Dynard asked, keeping his head bowed and his gaze to the floor.

"We have received word concerning you from Chapel Abelle," Bathelais explained.

Dynard's gaze came up, eyes wide. Was it possible that his return had attracted the notice of the leaders of the great mother chapel itself?

"Of course we dispatched a courier to Chapel Abelle with word of your return and your surprising cargo, book and human," Bathelais explained. "Your fall from the teaching of Blessed Abelle is no small thing—not as inconsequential as your death might have proven."

Dynard accepted those stinging words without argument.

"The brothers at the mother chapel will speak with you," Bathelais went on. "As soon as winter lessens its grip upon the land, you will travel north to deliver a full accounting of your journeys in the land of Behr. A pity that the book does not survive, for I am certain that it would have proven of great interest to our brethren."

Brother Dynard felt his knees grow weak beneath him, and it took all his control to stop from falling over. "W-when?" he stammered, for all of Bathelais's words beyond that first simple statement had flowed right past him.

"At the first onset of spring," Bathelais repeated, "as soon as the roads are clear."

"How long? I mean . . . where will I . . . will I return to Chapel Pryd?"

He saw from the expression of Brother Bathelais that his panicky questions were inciting more than a bit of curiosity, and it was only with great effort that Brother Dynard managed to find some measure of control. Behind the placid façade he managed to paint upon his face, his thoughts were swirling and tumbling. He had to get word to SenWi, had to find some way for her to meet him on the road. How could he not? How could he walk away from this place, from her, from his child?

His child!

If he were to depart in the early spring, the baby would have just been born. How could he leave?

How could he not? he realized a moment later. Even if he turned away from the Church of Blessed Abelle now, he would hardly be a free man, and certainly not free from their suspicion and watchfulness. If he went to SenWi, then SenWi would be found.

"Is there something wrong, Brother Dynard?" he heard Bathelais say, and when he looked at the man, he recognized that the question had likely been asked several times already.

"No, no," he blurted, and he took a deep breath and forced himself to calm down. "No, Brother Bathelais, of course not. It is just that I am weary of the road."

"The knowledge you brought back with you from Behr is important to us, of course. If we are to send any more brothers into that vast southern land, as we surely will, then the information you provide may help keep them safe."

"There are fewer threats to us in the southern lands than you believe," Brother Dynard dared to reply, but he did so absently, his mind still caught on the horrible notion of this impending separation from his dear SenWi. In the silence that ensued, Dynard felt the gaze of Bathelais upon him and looked back at him.

"I offer this as your friend," Bathelais sternly said. "When you are before the brothers of Chapel Abelle, you would do well to adjust your thinking more clearly in compliance with the edicts of the Church concerning the people of Behr. You would do well to remember, Brother Dynard, that you went there to teach them, not to be taught by them."

Brother Bathelais stared at him hard a few moments longer, then spun on his heel and stormed away.

Dynard leaned heavily on his broom, needing its support.

It wasn't until nearly a week after awakening that SenWi realized just how badly her leg had been injured. The limb would not hold her weight. Even using her Jhesta Tu powers of healing and concentration, SenWi knew that it would be a long time before she walked again, if ever.

That wasn't her primary concern, however. Her body was in such a weakened state that she could hardly find her line of *chi*, and even less so, that of the child within her. The battering she had taken, from that day she had used her powers to draw the poison from the poor condemned girl on the road, went too far, SenWi feared. Now every day was a struggle—to get enough nourishment in her to keep her child alive, to keep herself active so that her muscles would not atrophy any further, to regain her focus and enough strength so that she could get herself and the child through the trials of labor and birth.

She spent many hours sitting by the window, admiring the beauty of the vibrant coloring appearing on the leaves of the deciduous trees. SenWi had never seen anything like the autumn foliage or the dance of the leaves as they tumbled from the trees, catching the wind and spinning through every unpredictable fall. Bran Dynard had told her of the seasons in his homeland, something unknown in southern Behr, and Garibond had expanded upon that information now that he had the visual elements showing clearly before them. The leaves would fall and the trees and the land would go dormant through the winter season, with its blowing snow and bitter cold. And then in the spring, the buds would bloom anew, renewing the cycle of life.

SenWi found that notion comforting through the long days, and she used it to bolster her resolve at those dark times when she felt as if she must fail.

All would be better in the spring.

"They believe the book destroyed," Garibond said to her, surprising her as she sat deep in thought by the window one blustery day, the air alive with spinning leaves. "Even Dynard."

SenWi looked at him, tilting her head, not sure of how she should take that.

"He is devastated by the thought that his work of all those years is no more," Garibond went on, and SenWi nodded.

"But you did not tell him."

Garibond shrugged. "I would do anything to lessen his pain at this time—and most of that pain comes from his separation from you and not from the loss of the book. But, no, I did not tell him. I feared that someone might be listening."

SenWi turned her head, scrutinizing him all the more. "You feared that he would be foolish enough to again try to foist that book upon them."

Garibond didn't answer.

"He is a stubborn one," SenWi admitted with a laugh. She leaned over to the side then, bracing herself through every inch of the difficult motion. She slipped her hand under the bed and with great effort brought forth the Book of Jhest. "Do you read?"

"I am one of the few outside the Church of Abelle who does, yes," Garibond replied. "I learned very young, alongside Bran."

SenWi set the book on her lap and drew it open. "Come, then," she said. "I will teach you the language of Jhest. You will see what your friend has spent the last years of his life creating."

Garibond hesitated.

SenWi didn't allow herself to blink. Her duty was coming clear to her now. She didn't know when or if her beloved husband would return to her, and she could hardly be confident of her own health throughout the ordeal of this pregnancy.

She needed someone to trust.

Her child needed someone to trust.

"Come," she insisted. "We've not much time." When Garibond reacted to that comment with obvious discomfort, she added, "The sun is already nearing its apex."

Garibond stepped back out of the room, but only to retrieve a second chair.

CHAPTER 13

Orphan Born

Searing lines of fire ran through her ravaged body, but SenWi did not cry out. They were down in a smoky tunnel where Garibond thought that they would be safer during this trying and noisy process. Up above, the air crackled with energy as bolts of lightning split the sky; and the sulfuric residue, that peculiar smell and tingle of a thunderstorm, permeated even down here.

Garibond continued talking about the weather, about how unusual it was for a thunderstorm at this time of year. Winter had barely let go, with little snow remaining and three weeks left until the equinox. "These storms are usually for the middle of spring," Garibond explained, trying to sound excited and engaging. His voice trailed away, for he saw clearly that SenWi wasn't paying him any heed, that she was locked in a life-and-death struggle against the waves of agony.

Never had he felt so helpless. He hadn't ever watched a woman give birth before, and now here he was, serving as midwife, as the only support, and her pregnancy had not been going well for many months.

He bent low and whispered, "What can I do for you?"

SenWi didn't answer, other than to take his offered hand and squeeze hard.

Inside her, SenWi felt as if someone were grabbing her line of *ki-chi-kree*, pulling and jerking it back and forth. She tried to find some sense of center, some focus of energy, but there simply was none. Spasms shot through her as if they were drops of acid being splashed within her.

She reached with all her powers to try to touch her child, to try to find its life energy. And there was something strong in her womb, a powerful force. But it was not aligned, she understood; it felt as if the thread of this one's *chi* had been frayed.

SenWi couldn't pause and consider that. The pain and sense of urgency were too great. They tore at her and pressed the air from her lungs. She transferred all her pain to her breathing and used that as her focus, puffing in short gasps, gradually developing a rhythm that she transferred to her thumping heart.

And she felt Garibond's hand, a tangible connection to the physical world.

She squeezed that hand with all her strength and let the pain flow through her clutching fingers to dissipate beyond her corporeal being.

But more pain built within, faster than she could let it flow from her; and deeper within, the pressure built against the inside of her birth passage. She felt her skin ripping, felt a sudden surge of agony and a contraction of her muscles so powerful that she was certain they must be tearing themselves apart. It went on and on, and she had no sense of time's passage.

Garibond wasn't holding her hand anymore, and she had to fight off a wave of panic, thinking that she must have fallen away from all the world.

She felt him between her legs, then and heard his shout.

"Push!"

He called to her again and again, and each repetition gave the failing woman a little bit more to hold on to. SenWi gathered all her strength, all her energy, and all her disciplined focus. She lifted the thread of her *chi*, balling it into a formidable force just above her struggling child. Then, as surely as if she were pushing with her hands or legs, she forced that energy down, down.

Her skin ripped a bit more, and then she felt a rush of sudden coolness, a great release of pressure, and all her lower body went comfortably numb.

She lay there for some time in the cool darkness of semi-consciousness, her body falling into a deep state of relaxation, muscles sinking into the bed as if she were being swallowed by it—and that was a sensation that the battered and exhausted woman welcomed. Moments slipped past in blissful emptiness, with not a spot of light marring the blackness or a whisper of sound defeating the silence.

Not a whisper of sound.

Not the beating of her heart.

Not the cry of a newborn baby.

She was dying. She knew that, and she didn't fight it. Not then. Perhaps it was time for her to surrender.

Her child was not alive. SenWi realized that her child was not crying, was making no sounds at all. She concentrated her life energy and grabbed at her heart, forcing it to beat. She sent her thoughts back through that blackness, as if she were climbing out of a deep hole, and she finally saw a glow of light. She raced for it, desperately now, as she realized that her child was not yet alive.

Her eyes opened and the room came into focus. She saw Garibond standing off to the side, the child on a table in front of him, blue and still. He glanced back at her, and SenWi could see his tears.

Garibond shook his head.

SenWi rolled off the bed and to her feet. She swayed and staggered and nearly fell. She felt the warmth of her own blood running down her legs, and knew that she was bleeding too heavily. But she forced herself into a stumbling walk to the table, where she placed both her hands on her child.

It was a boy, a beautiful boy, a perfect boy.

His life force was so weak, barely a sliver of energy in his little body. Nor was that thread of energy straight, the typical and expected line of *ki-chi-kree* from forehead to groin. No, she sensed that her child's life line was interrupted at many points, was wavering where it should have been straight and solid. He was not perfect, SenWi realized with horror. He was damaged, badly so; and SenWi knew that it was from the snake venom she had willingly taken into herself when she had healed the condemned girl. As the venom had attacked her, so it had assailed her defenseless infant.

That realization didn't slow her in the least. Garibond grabbed one of her arms and cajoled her to relent and go lie down. He might as well have been grabbing at iron.

Was it guilt driving her? Was it anger?

SenWi didn't care. All that mattered to her was that her baby wasn't breathing, that her baby was damaged, perhaps fatally. She found the connection to his life energy and threw her own into him, offering herself fully to him. She let her *chi* energy flow out of her and into the child.

The blood splashed down her legs. Garibond's cries became more insistent. "Lie down, woman!" he shouted in her ear. "Your blood's running!"

He tugged and tugged futilely at her. "Too late for the little one!" he insisted.

SenWi felt him let go, and then he came back with a thick cloth and placed it hard against her, trying to stem the blood flow. It didn't matter, she knew by then, and she accepted the sacrifice as she came to feel the life force of her child strengthening.

The baby opened his eyes and gasped his first breath, and then he began to cry.

To SenWi, that sounded like the sweetest music ever sung.

She felt her own life energy spasm, a wild dispersal of strength and reflex that jolted her away from her child. She staggered back a step and would have fallen.

But Garibond was there, gently catching her and laying her back down on the bed. She tried to ask for her baby, but was too weak to give voice to her words. Garibond understood, though, and he took up the child and gently placed it on her chest.

SenWi heard the baby crying. She wanted to tell him that it was all right. She managed to hold the baby in her arms and feel his softness and the warmth of his breath against her neck. And suddenly, he wasn't crying anymore, but had settled in comfortably.

The torch-lit room began to darken once more, the black tunnel's sides rising around SenWi. Regret filled her for just a moment as she considered all that she would miss. She threw that emotion aside at once and considered that her baby was alive, that she had given him existence and then had breathed life into him.

To SenWi, there was no price too great for that.

She let the blackness rise, because she knew that she could not resist it. She felt the baby's breath and softness to the last.

H e hated leaving the child alone, but Garibond didn't know what else to do. Dynard had to know of the babe and of the fate of SenWi, whom Garibond had buried on the small island on the lake, the island where a younger Garibond and Bran Dynard had spent many of their finest childhood days.

Two weeks had passed since the child's birth, and Garibond still had not named him. He couldn't bring himself to do it. The baby seemed healthy enough, if very frail and thin.

Garibond hurried all the way into town that cold and wet late winter day. He concocted a story of illness, a general soreness in his legs, that would get him into Chapel Pryd, begging healing from the brothers. So when he got in sight of the town, he slowed and began walking awkwardly, favoring one leg.

He found no resistance at the chapel doors. The common area was nearly deserted this day. Garibond limped in and took a seat.

"May I be of service to you, friend?" asked one of the brothers, a younger man Garibond knew as Brother Reandu.

"The cool rain's got into my bones," Garibond explained. "I've come to beg a bit of healing, if that is possible. I'll be putting my crops in soon enough, but I doubt I could bend over to work the ground."

The monk nodded. "I have not seen you regularly in church—it is Master Garibond, is it not?"

"Aye, that is my name. Garibond of Pryd. I live a long way out, brother, and with my weakened knees, the journey is painful. Perhaps if you gave some healing to me, I would be a more frequent visitor in the chapel, bringing donations, what little I have, every time."

The monk smiled at him—a look of sarcasm and not warmth.

"Brother Bran Dynard, he promised me some healing if I could return to Chapel Pryd after the snows," Garibond insisted. "He did, your—our God as my witness."

The doubting smile only widened.

"Go and get him, then!" Garibond insisted. "Go and tell Brother Dynard that his old friend Garibond is here. He'll take that cleverness from your face, I do not doubt."

"That would be a rather long walk for me, friend Garibond," Brother Reandu replied, "for your friend Brother Dynard is not here. At the bidding of Father Jerak, he has gone north to Chapel Abelle. I doubt that he will return before the next winter."

Garibond fought hard to keep his eyes from widening with shock and fear. What was he to do now?

"Shall I ask Father Jerak to come and speak with you? Or tend your sore knees, perhaps?" Reandu asked.

Garibond scowled. "Have you any healing to offer my old bones?" he asked.

"The gifts of God are not without recompense," Brother Reandu recited. "You would find Chapel Pryd more accommodating to your pains if you more regularly attended the sermons of Father Jerak and Brother Bathelais."

With silver coins ready for the passed basket, Garibond thought. He turned his gaze from the useless Brother Reandu and slowly rose. He continued to limp slightly as he made his way out of the chapel, then hardly at all through the rest of the town. Once past the gates, Garibond picked up his pace steadily until he had broken into a run, propelled by fear more than anything else.

SenWi was gone. Dynard was gone.

Leaving him with a child to raise, at least until the following winter.

Brother Bran Dynard huddled under his heavy cloak, bringing his hands to his chest. He had wrapped his fingers in fur, but that was hardly sufficient against the biting cold wind. Head bowed, leading a donkey, the monk plodded along. Only a week out from Pryd, with perhaps a hundred miles behind him, Dynard had found that winter had not yet let go. All the shady areas near the road were still covered in snow, and the road itself was icy in many places. More than once, Dynard had slipped and fallen hard to the ground.

All that he had thought about when leaving the chapel was SenWi and Garibond. She would be close to delivering the baby now, he knew, if she had not already.

How he wanted to go to her!

But he could not, for he had left Chapel Pryd escorted by soldiers—Prince Prydae had arranged an escort to the northern edge of the holding. Even after that, Dynard had been aware of eyes watching his every move, scouts for the prince and for Father Jerak, no doubt. If he turned in the direction of Garibond's house, he would give it all away.

Thus he had continued along the northern road, hoping only that he would reach Chapel Abelle and be done with his business quickly.

"Ack, ye let me have yer cloak then," he heard a harsh voice cutting asunder the smooth notes of the wind. Dynard straightened and looked up, left and right; and as one patch of blowing snow thinned before him, he saw a diminutive but undoubtedly solid figure standing in the road.

"Ye give me yer cloak now," the powrie—for of course it was a powrie—said again.

Brother Bran swallowed hard. He kept as still as possible, but his eyes darted all around. Where there was one powrie, there were usually more.

"Come on then. I'm freezing me arse off out here," the dwarf insisted, taking a step forward. "Ye let me use the cloak a bit, and then I'll let yerself wear it in turn, and both of us'll get through this wretched storm. Come on then."

Poor Dynard didn't know what to do. He thought of attacking the dwarf, but his hands were so cold he doubted he could grasp a weapon.

He knew that he shouldn't trust a powrie, but still . . .

This was not a normal circumstance.

Dynard reached up and undid the tie about his neck, then pulled the cloak back from one shoulder.

"There ye go, giving me a good target," said the dwarf.

Dynard didn't see the sudden movement, but he saw the spear flying his way. He tried to dodge or duck, but he was too late.

The spear drove into his chest.

He was only half aware that he was sitting. He was only half aware as the dwarf pulled his cloak from him, laughing.

He was only half aware when the dwarf wiped its beret across the bloody wound in his chest.

Then the powrie kicked him in the face, but he didn't feel it.

All he felt was the cold wind, slowly replaced by the colder chill of death.

PART TWO

God's Year 64

CHAPTER 14

Taming Honce

Heavy rain poured down, ringing against the metal armor and running in sheets across the steep slopes of the rocky coastline. Bright flashes of lightning rent the air, their accompanying thunder reverberating through the stones.

Prydae looked down across the jagged, blood-soaked rocks and shook his head, his long brown hair flying. The warriors had dislodged the powries again but had gained only a few score yards of ground. The dwarves had merely retreated to the next defensible high ground in this up-and-down terrain of one fortresslike stone ridge after another. And there they were digging in, no doubt, and preparing the next ridge after that one for their next retreat, forcing the humans to battle for every inch of ground.

Bannagran walked up beside his prince and dropped a trio of berets at Prydae's feet. "You claim them as your own, my liege," he said.

Prydae looked at his dear and loyal friend. Bannagran was a giant of a man, not so much in height, though he was several inches taller than the norm, but in girth. His shoulders were nearly twice as wide as Prydae's—and Prydae was no small man—and his bare arms were as thick as a man's thigh, with the corded muscles one would expect on the hammer arm of a blacksmith. His black hair was long and dripping in the rain like Prydae's, and though he tried to keep his beard short and his cheeks clean shaven, as was the style of the day, the long days and difficult conditions were allowing that beard to get away from him. Even with that scraggly look, however, Bannagran kept a youthfulness about him, with a broad and often-flashed toothy smile and cheeks that dimpled. His face often turned red, either in mirth or battle lust, and that set off his dark eyes and eyebrows, which seemed, really, like a single thick line of hair.

Prydae glanced down at the berets. So Bannagran had killed three more in the latest fight; he was making a reputation for himself that would resound from one end of Honce to the other before this campaign was done. Who could have known the prowess this warrior would come to show or the strength? In the early days of their adventuring, a few years before in Pryd Holding, Prydae had always outshone his friend. No more, the prince knew. Prydae was more than holding his own, despite the loss of his prized chariot and fine horse team in the first week of fighting, but Bannagran had caught the notice of every laird in attendance, and no champion wanted to challenge this one.

"Take them," the warrior said again. "More than a few here're complaining openly about the mud and the rain and the shit and the blood. They're needing a hero to keep them steady on the line when them dwarves come back at us—and you know the vicious little beasties will do just that."

It was hard to argue with that. Prydae looked around, following the moans and sharp shrieks of the wounded. So many wounded and so many dead. The folk of Pryd Holding who had accompanied the prince on this journey to the eastern coast had been away from home for more than two years now—and nearly half, at least, would never be returning.

"Bloody caps coming!" came a cry from far to the right, and Prydae and Bannagran looked down the line to see a wave of dwarves swarming over the crest of a stony ridge and charging toward the human line. Archers let fly, but their barrage hardly seemed to slow the fierce dwarf advance. Prydae scooped the three berets and tucked them into his belt in plain sight.

"Right beside you, my liege," said Bannagran, and he moved in step next to Prydae.

The prince was glad of that.

"They're going against Ethelbert's line," Prydae remarked as the dwarves bunched together at the base of one ravine and began scrambling up. Above them, the men of Ethelbert Holding threw rocks and launched arrows, but the dwarves growled as one and pressed through the volley.

"Take the men down," Prydae said suddenly.

"My liege?" came the surprised response.

"Bring the men of Pryd into the gully. We'll cross below the fighting and when Ethelbert drives the powries back, they will find the metal of Pryd Holding blocking their retreat." Prydae turned, a tight grin on his face. "Yes, they'll have the high ground coming against us, but they'll have no coordination across their line."

"Yes, my liege," Bannagran replied, and Prydae recognized and understood the hesitation in his voice, but also the loyalty. Bannagran immediately began calling the men of Pryd to order.

"Onward!" Prince Prydae cried, and he lifted his sword high into the air and led the charge straight ahead and down the rocky slope. They swept into the gully, then turned south.

"Find defensible ground!" Bannagran ordered. He sent a couple of men up the slope in the east, farther from the battle, to ensure that no more powries could rush to join the fray. Wouldn't the Holding of Pryd bury more than a

few of her menfolk if powries on ridge lines east and west caught them holding the low ground in between!

Before Prydae's forces could position themselves, the dwarves above to
the west, apparently seeing the vise closing about them, began to break ranks
and came charging back down the slope.

"Tight groups!" Prince Prydae cried. "See to your kin!"

Half the dwarves tumbled in their flight down the steep ground, but if
that bothered the hardy, barrel-chested folk, they didn't show it. Like stones
rolling, they hit the lines of the men of Pryd.

One dwarf came up before Prydae and launched an overhead swing, but
Bannagran, standing beside his friend, brought his own axe across to intercept, catching the dwarf's axe just under its head and holding it fast.

Prince Prydae wasted no time but stabbed straight out through the opening, driving his sword deeply into the powrie's chest. The dwarf staggered back
but did not fall.

Prydae jerked hard on the sword, then pulled it free and struck again, a
fountain of powrie blood washing over his arm.

But still the dwarf didn't fall, and the vicious creature even tried to swing
its axe now that Bannagran had retracted his blocking blade.

Bannagran was the quicker, though, his axe thumping hard into the dwarf
beside the embedded sword. The powrie staggered backward, sliding off Prydae's blade and stumbling to the ground.

Prydae turned to congratulate his friend, but the words caught in his throat
as he realized that Bannagran was in trouble: a pair of dwarves were stabbing
and slashing at him, forcing him to stumble sideways. Without even considering the danger, Prydae swept past his friend, his short sword stabbing hard at
one powrie and driving it back. Across he swung, his iron blade ringing
against the bronze sword of the other dwarf, which snapped at the hilt.

The powrie threw the pommel against Prydae's face, but the prince only
shouted all the louder and charged in, stabbing with abandon.

He felt Bannagran rush behind him to finish the other dwarf.

When both powries finally fell, Bannagran clapped Prydae on the shoulder, and the two spun, looking to see where they could fit into the continuing
brawl. One group of Pryd men nearby was sorely pressed by a trio of dwarves—
until the prince and his champion leaped into the fray.

Prydae paused and glanced up the slope, to see the men of Ethelbert Holding cutting the remaining dwarves into smaller and smaller groups. More and
more of those powries broke and ran. "Come along then, Laird Ethelbert," Prydae muttered under his breath, for if the army of the southeastern holding didn't
immediately pursue, he and his men would be even more sorely pressed.

And at first it did seem as if the men of Ethelbert would hold their defensive position on the high ground.

"Come along!" Prydae shouted in frustration, for he knew that every second of hesitation would cost a Pryd man his life. "Come along!"

Laird Ethelbert himself appeared among the ranks on the ridge line, scanning the unexpected fighting down below. He locked eyes with Prydae then. Smiling and nodding, he ordered his men down to the aid of their Pryd comrades.

Their charge shook the ground, a continual thunderous rumble amid the flashing storm. Powries broke left and right; some tried to cross the ranks of Prydae's men, all in a desperate effort now to get away.

And many did escape, but many did not, their blood running with the rainwater along the stones of the gully.

Through it all, Bannagran and Prydae kept on the move, joining wherever the human line seemed in danger of breaking, standing strong over fallen friends to keep the deadly dwarves at bay.

When it was done, Bannagran held a handful of berets out to Prydae, but the prince smiled and shook his head. "I have enough of my own this time."

Bannagran returned that smile and nodded. Between his work and that of his liege, nine powries had been sent to the otherworldly halls of their ferocious gods.

"Take the ridge to the east!" Bannagran ordered the men of Pryd. "No retreat to the west! One less gully to cross on our march to the sea!"

Those men who were able trudged up the slick eastern slope and began settling in among the many large rocks. Prydae remained in the gully, moving among the injured, offering comfort and calling for brothers of Abelle to come with their healing gemstones. He stayed with one gutted man—a boy, really, of about fifteen winters. Prydae took the boy's hand in his own and locked stares. He could see the terror there.

"I'm dying, my prince," the boy gasped, blood accompanying every word out of his mouth.

"Priests!" Prydae cried.

"Won't do no good," said the boy. "Prince Prydae, are you there? Prince Prydae?"

"I am here," Prydae yelled at the boy, who no longer seemed to be seeing in the land of the living. Prydae clutched the hand tighter and called again, desperate to let this young warrior know that he would not die alone.

"Oh, but it's cold, my prince," the boy cried. "Oh, where'd you go, then?" His hand fumbled, clasping and pulling Prydae's. Prydae tried to call back to him, to offer some words of comfort, but his voice caught behind the lump in his throat.

"My prince, it's so dark and so cold. I cannot feel my feet or my arms. It's all cold."

A shiver coursed Prydae's spine.

The boy rambled on for a short while, grabbing frantically at Prydae's arms, while the prince tried to soothe him and tried hard not to let his voice break. Then suddenly the lad quieted, and he opened his eyes wide, his face a mask of surprise, it seemed. He gripped Prydae so tightly that the prince feared he would crush his forearm, but then that grip relented, and the boy's hand fell away.

A monk of Abelle arrived then, soul stone in hand. "Too late," Prince Prydae said to him, and he placed the boy's hand on his chest.

The monk stared at the Prince of Pryd. "I'm sorry," he said. "I was tending another. . . ." He started to point back along the gully, but Prydae stopped him—and when he grabbed the monk's arm, the prince saw that his own hand was dripping with blood.

"You could have done nothing for him anyway," he said as if it did not matter, and in his heart, Prince Prydae knew that he could not allow it to matter. "The wound was too great."

"I am sorry," said the monk, and Prydae nodded and rose. He started to walk away, but hesitated there for some time, looking at the dead boy, remembering his own past adventures a decade before, when he was more slender, when his eyes held a youthful luster, and when he thought he could conquer the whole world.

"We lost seven more, though it could go as high as a dozen," reported Bannagran, coming to his side. "And I am thinking that we should surrender that eastern ridge and pull back to the west, for we're out in front of the rest of the line."

"The southern men did not advance?"

"Laird Ethelbert retreated as soon as the last of the dwarves went out over the eastern ridge," Bannagran explained.

Prydae scanned to the west, his lips going very tight.

"And probably wise that he did," said Bannagran. "None of the other lairds saw fit to advance, and we'd all be sticking out like a spur begging to be clipped."

Prydae looked at him.

"Those powries are not fools, my liege. They could use the same twist on us that we just used against them. Sweep in behind us and cut us from our kin."

Prydae looked all around and heaved a frustrated sigh. "Make sure that all the wounded and the dead are brought back behind Laird Ethelbert's lines," he ordered. "Then bring our charges all back to the crest north of Ethelbert. A fine fight, but no ground gained."

"No ground lost, either," Bannagran reminded him, eliciting a strained smile from his friend.

And a short-lived smile, as Prince Prydae continued to scan the rocky area. Wet, cold, and aching from head to toe, he was weary of this campaign. The combined armies of Honce had chased the powries to the coast in short order, but it had been day after day and week after week of fighting since.

"One ridge at a time," he muttered.

"That was among the most daring maneuvers I have ever witnessed, Prince Prydae," came a voice that drew both Prydae and Bannagran from their private thoughts. The two turned as one to see Laird Ethelbert walking his warhorse down toward them. He cut an impressive figure on the armored stallion, but it didn't escape Prydae's notice that the old man was not covered in the blood of his enemies nor in mud. Prydae had to wonder if Ethelbert had even drawn his sword. Was there a single nick along its iron edge?

"I grow weary of advancing one ridge and then retreating to the previous," Prydae replied.

"Three forward and two back," Laird Ethelbert agreed, for that was a fairly accurate assessment of their progress over the last three weeks of fighting. "But still, more than a few bloody caps met their end this day, thanks to the daring maneuver of the men from Pryd Holding."

"If Laird Grunyon and his men had closed from the south, more would lie dead."

Ethelbert shrugged. "Night is falling, and it will be a dark one. After this rout, the dwarves will not return before dawn. Take supper with me in my tent this night, my friend Prydae, and pray bring your champion with you."

Prydae watched the Laird of Ethelbert dos Entel as he turned and casually paced his mount away. Ironically, it was exactly that steadiness and solidity that for a moment unnerved Prydae. He couldn't dismiss the stark contrast of Ethelbert, in his shining and clean armor, so calmly walking his warhorse past the torn bodies of fallen men, some dead, others grievously wounded, some even reaching up toward him desperately. That's what it was to be a leader among men in Honce, young Prydae decided, the godly separation between laird and peasant, between noble and common. A rare gift it was for a man to be able to shine above the mess, beyond the touch of blood and mud and rain. Laird Ethelbert then stepped his horse right over one wounded peasant and paid the man no notice at all as he went on his way.

Ethelbert was above them, Prydae could clearly see.

The prince thought of the boy who had just died.

A peasant, a commoner.

Prydae shrugged and put the boy's dying words out of his mind.

Prince Prydae marveled at how adept this army had become in cleaning up after bloody battles. The Samhaist clerics accompanying the force went about their work with the dead, consecrating the ground in their ancient traditions before burying men of Honce, damning the ground below the bodies of powries, which would be left unburied. All of this was done under the judgmental eyes of the brothers of Abelle, who busied themselves with the wounded, not the dead, using their magical gemstones to bring some measure of relief.

The struggle between the two sects, a battle for the hearts of men, was not lost on Prydae. Nor were the various effects the two sects were having on the common soldiers. Those hopeful of returning home some day seemed to be favoring the brothers of Abelle, but as more and more died on the field, the Samhaists' promises and warnings of the afterlife seemed to be resonating more profoundly among those remaining.

Prydae looked to the west below the defended forward ridge, where screams and moans and sobs came forth continually, and he shook his head in amazement. For not far above the tents of the wounded sat a pair of Samhaists, staring down like vultures. The brothers of Abelle wouldn't give up the corpses easily to the clerics of the ancient religion, but they were too busy with those still living to prevent the taking.

The tug for hearts became a tug for bodies, a battle from birth that tore at every Honce citizen throughout his life, and even after, it seemed.

Neither Prydae nor Bannagran spoke as they crossed from the forward lines to the rear. They entered Laird Ethelbert's tent with little fanfare and, to their surprise, found none of the other lairds within.

Ethelbert smiled widely and warmly, bidding them to enter and to sit opposite him at the opulent—relatively speaking—dinner table that had been set out. To either side of the laird sat his four military commanders, accomplished warriors all, men whose reputations had preceded them to this war.

"I am so pleased that you could join me, Prince of Pryd," Ethelbert said when Prydae and Bannagran had taken their places. Attendants moved immediately to put their food—a veritable feast—before them.

Prydae was too busy staring at the cutlery of shining silver and cut glass goblets filled with rich wine to even answer.

"A proper laird must always take his accoutrements with him," Ethelbert explained. "We owe that to our peasants, you see?"

Neither of the men from Pryd questioned that aloud, though both their faces, especially Bannagran's, asked the obvious question clearly enough.

"What the peasants need from us is the hope that their own lives might not always be so miserable," the Laird of Ethelbert dos Entel explained. "Or that their children will know a better existence. That is always the way, do you not understand? A miserable peasant with hope is a miserable peasant pla-cated. We walk a fine line between breaking them altogether, which would lead to open revolt, and teasing them just enough to keep them happily working."

"Happily?" As soon as the word left Bannagran's mouth, Prydae jabbed him in the ribs with an elbow.

But Laird Ethelbert seemed to take no offense. He grinned and held up his hands.

"There is so much to learn about ruling the common folk," Ethelbert said at length. "I have spent forty years as leader of Ethelbert Holding and still I feel as if my initiation has only just begun. But the people of Ethelbert are happy enough, I would guess, and healthier than those in many other hold-ings, Delaval in particular."

Prydae perked up at the disparaging reference to the largest and most pop-ulous holding in all Honce. Set at the base of the great river that cut the main region of Honce off from the vast northern forests, Laird Delaval's city was more than twice the size of Ethelbert's. The river teemed with fish, the fields to the east of Delaval City were rich and fertile, and the wood brought in from the west allowed the Laird Delaval to build wondrous sailing ships that even Laird Ethelbert had been known to grudgingly purchase.

Laird Delaval's army, and his warships, were battling powries up the coast in the north, and with great success, by all reports. That success of his rival seemed to grate on Laird Ethelbert, from what Prydae could tell.

It all began to make sense to the warrior prince from Pryd Holding. The roads had brought the holdings of Honce closer together, had greatly in-creased trade and communication between them. Several lairds were ru-mored to be in secret alliance already. During this campaign, with so many armies marching side by side, Prince Prydae had come to envision a time, in his lifetime perhaps, when Honce would become a united kingdom under a single ruling laird. Of course, that presented the question of who that leader might be.

"We are scoring the greatest victories of all against the powries," Laird Ethelbert went on. "More of the vicious dwarves have died here than in the north, and I attribute that to the finer coordination between our forces." He lifted his goblet in a toast, and all the others followed suit.

"In the north, of course, there is little cooperation and a more-hierarchical command," Ethelbert went on, predictably now to Prydae, who hid his know-ing smile. "Laird Delaval is not interested in the plans and movements of his peers, unless those movements follow his precise instructions."

Prydae thought to point out that Delaval's force was many times greater than the combined armies of the other lairds up in the north beside him, but he kept silent.

"This battle will be done soon," Ethelbert remarked.

"We can hope for that," said Prydae.

"Indeed." Ethelbert held up his goblet again. "And when it is done, we must all be aware that Honce will emerge a different land than the one of scattered holdings which began this campaign. The roads are nearly clear of powries and goblins, from the gulf to the mountains, and our people will be able to trade even more vigorously outside their communities.

"Thus, we must anticipate the changes, my friends. We must prepare ourselves for the new reality that will be Honce. Smaller holdings, such as your own, will need allies, or perhaps even an overseeing laird of a greater holding to secure your defense."

So there it was.

Prydae felt Bannagran's stare upon him, and he turned to offer a comforting nod to his excitable and uneasy companion.

"An overseeing laird?" the prince calmly echoed.

"Various cities joined together in a greater and more powerful holding," Ethelbert explained.

"Are you asking permission to annex Pryd, Laird Ethelbert?"

The blunt question had Laird Ethelbert's commanders bristling and brought a slight gasp from Bannagran. But if Ethelbert was at all discomfited by it, he hid the fact. Again he seemed the calm man on a great horse, unbothered as he walked past the broken bodies of his inferiors.

"I am suggesting that you and your father begin to give consideration to your future," Ethelbert replied.

"We ever do. That is the duty of an independent laird above all, is it not?"

"Be reasonable, Prince Prydae. When this messy business with the powries is done, the world around you will be changed. You cannot deny that. Roads carry trade and they also carry armies."

"And Honce will no longer be a collection of separate holdings?"

"A few perhaps, or perhaps a single kingdom. We all see that. And you must understand that in the end, it will be Ethelbert or it will be Delaval. I offer you a peaceful alliance."

"You mean a subjugation."

"Not so. For all purposes, your land will remain your own and under your control, though, yes, I will speak for you in the greater affairs of Honce. I will require some taxes, to be sure, and your share of the men to serve in the forces who will defeat all challenges. But for the family of Pryd, life will hardly change, and certainly not for the worse."

"And if we refuse your generous offer?"

Ethelbert shrugged. "Who can say what will happen? Will an army from Delaval march upon you?"

"Will an army from Ethelbert?"

The commanders bristled again, one even rising, but Laird Ethelbert merely laughed. "Of course not," he said. "We are comrades in arms, joined in common struggle. I admire your independence, young Prince of Pryd. It is one of the reasons that I come to you so early with my offer and the reason I do not wait until you have more wine inside of you to openly make this offer." He shrugged and laughed again. "The plague and the sea took my offspring, you have no doubt heard. I am childless. The line of Ethelbert will end with my passing. If I had a son as worthy as Prydae, I would die content."

Prince Prydae tried hard to keep his emotions from his face. Was Ethelbert hinting at a greater alliance here? Did he imply the lairdship of his holding would pass to Prydae?

"But enough of speculation," Ethelbert said jovially. "We have fine food to share and a fresh victory to better consume our conversation. Drink heartily and eat until your belly rumbles with content, I pray you!" He held up his goblet again.

"To Prince Prydae the Bold!" he declared.

Prydae noted that two of the four Ethelbert commanders seemed less than thrilled at that though they did lift their goblets to him.

CHAPTER 15

The Stork

Bransen Garibond consciously thrust one hip forward and then the other, rocking his frail body so that his legs alternately dropped in front of him. He was small for his age and desperately thin. His unkempt hair was black as a raven's wing, and his eyes, too, favored his mother's southern heritage, showing so brown as to appear black. His skin was more brown than most in the region, but not enough to show that he had the blood of Behr running through him, particularly in a land where the peasants were almost always dirty. Besides, no one ever looked closely enough to notice, for the more obvious distinctions of Bransen—like his awkward walk or the purple birthmark that circled his right arm—separated him from the folk of Pryd more than the nuances of his heritage ever could.

Over the years, the young boy had learned to give a hasty glance at each footfall, to determine if the foot was firmly planted so that he could continue. He couldn't feel the ground beneath his feet, and if he stepped on an uneven surface or put his foot down on an edge, he would stumble and fall. Bransen hated when he fell in a public place, for pulling himself up from a prone position was no easy task, and showed little in the way of grace to the gawking—always gawking—onlookers.

Fortunately for the boy, he knew every step of every road in the eastern reaches of Pryd Town, and all the way out to his father's house by the lake. He rarely fell these days, unless of course one of the other boys ran over and knocked him to the ground, just so they all could laugh at him while he flopped around.

I don't like to drool. I can't feel the drool. I don't know when I'm doing it. But they laugh, and even the men and women stare or turn away in disgust. The drool and the snot. Always it is on my face, and crusting my sleeves. I don't like it!

He heard someone cry out, "Stork!" and he knew he was doomed.

That's what they called him.

Bransen locked his eyes forward and forced his hips to rotate faster, propelling him along at a great pace for him, one jerking, stiff-legged stride at a time, his head lolling and his arms flailing all the while. But still, within a minute or two, he heard the footsteps behind him, a pair of boys running up close behind, and when that rhythmic trotting changed suddenly, Bransen knew that they had taken up a mocking "stork" gait behind him, falling into line.

He didn't stop his forward-leaning walk. He had come into town to buy some grain for Garibond, and he was determined to push through this inconvenience. He brought his arm up in a jerky motion and wiped it across his face, and though he unintentionally smacked himself quite hard, he didn't blink or show it at all.

After another minute, the two boys apparently tired of imitating and ran around him, blocking his way.

"Hello, Stork," said Tarkus Breen.

Bransen kept moving, but Tarkus bashed him in the chest with his open palm.

Bransen stumbled and had to work his hips frantically to keep from falling. "Leeeave . . . m-m-me . . . alone," he cried, his mouth contorting painfully as he tried to form the syllables.

Both boys laughed. Most people did when Bransen spoke.

"I . . . have to . . . b-b-b-buuy . . ."

The laughter drowned him out, and Tarkus slapped him across the face, silencing him.

Bransen narrowed his eyes and stared intently at his nemesis. In that moment, standing perfectly still, face locked in a determined and hateful grimace, Bransen did manage some measure of intimidation, did seem, for just an instant, as formidable and normal, as anyone else.

Tarkus sucked in his breath and even backed off a step. But the other boy came forward and shoved Bransen hard.

He wobbled and he scrambled, his hips swaying wildly, and then he fell, facedown to the dirt. He hadn't even been able to close his mouth as he hit, and now tasted dirt and blood.

Bransen fought hard against the tears welling up. He didn't want to cry; he tried not to cry in front of anyone anymore, other than Garibond. He could cry in front of his father; his father often cried with him.

I won't cry, he told himself over and over, but some sobs did bubble out. He heard someone shouting, but he was too upset to register the speaker or the words. He did take note of Tarkus mocking, "B-b-b-b-bye." Then he heard the boys run off.

His father, Garibond, had told him that his life would get better as he got older, but in fact, the last year had been the worst. Most of the menfolk, including the older boys, were away at the powrie war. Those older boys had never been kind to Bransen, but their abuse was usually more verbal than physical. Since they had left, though, the boys of around Bransen's age had taken free run of the town without restraint.

Bransen settled back down in the dirt, allowing himself to relax for a moment to get past his crying. He had to get up now that they were gone, and that was going to take all his attention and determination.

There was no time for tears and no use for them anyway.

But still . . .

As he started to rotate his shoulders so that he could roll to one side, his feeble arm finding a supporting angle in the dirt, Bransen felt a hand grab his shoulder. He stiffened immediately and closed his eyes, expecting a barrage of blows to rain down upon him, as so often happened.

The touch was gentle and supportive. "Are you all right?" came a soft whisper in his ear, a voice he knew and welcomed. He allowed his helper, a girl his age, to turn him over, and he looked into a beautiful face.

"C-c-c-ca . . . dayle," he stammered, and he looked up at her, soaking in her every aspect. She was not tall for her age and was thin, like all the peasants. But she had a softness to her, a rich and smooth texture to her skin, that many of the other poor commoners lacked. Her blue eyes seemed to glow when she smiled. Her whole face seemed to glow, for Cadayle blushed often, and almost always when she smiled. Her hair was long and mostly straight, the color of wheat, and it flowed like tall stalks in a windblown field.

"Oh, Bransen," Cadayle replied, and her smile brightened the day for him and helped him push his tears away. "Every time I see you, you are dirty!"

It was not an insult. Bransen knew that from the tone of her voice, and simply because it was Cadayle who had said it. She never insulted him, never hurt him. She never judged him, and even wiped the snot and spittle from his face without complaint. And most important of all to him, she always waited patiently for him to stutter through his broken sentences.

With Cadayle's help, he got back to his feet, and managed to offer his thanks.

Cadayle gently brushed the dirt off him. "Pay them no heed," she said as she worked. "They're stupid, is all. And they know they're stupid and they know you're not."

Bransen smiled, but he didn't believe her.

Still, it was comforting to hear the words.

Y ou've blood on your shirt."

Cadayle looked down to see that her mother was right, for a dirty red-brown smudge marred the left shoulder of her tan shirt. She looked back at her mother and shrugged.

"Were you fighting?" the woman demanded.

"No, Ma."

"Did someone hit you? Or did you trip and fall?" The older woman's voice went from suspicious to concerned as she approached her young daughter.

"It's not me blood, Ma," Cadayle explained.

Her mother began brushing at the smudge.

"It's Bransen's. The boys were beating him again. He cut his lip."

Cadayle's mother sighed and shook her head. "As if they've nothing better to do than beat the poor creature. The folk're nasty, Cadayle, meaner than you'd ever believe. How did you get yourself involved in it?"

"I yelled at them and they ran off. I just helped Bransen up, is all."

Cadayle's mother took her daughter's chin in her hand and forced the girl to look at her directly. "You listen to me," she said. "You did right in helping him. You always help him, or anyone else needing your help. I'm proud of you."

Cadayle was surprised by the sudden intensity in her mother's voice and the huskiness, as if her ma was holding back a flood of tears. Her mother pulled her in close, then, crushing her in a great hug.

"I'm proud of you," she said again.

Cadayle didn't understand why it was such a big deal to her ma, for she did not know that her mother had once been treated more horribly than she could ever imagine. She didn't know that her mother had once been thrown into a sack with a poisonous viper, then hung up by her wrists in the wilderness and left to die.

Only the generosity of strangers had saved her.

Come inside and be quick about it," Garibond said to Bransen when the boy at last returned to the homestead. Garibond put his hand on the boy's back and ushered him along more quickly, the older man's gaze darting about the tree line surrounding his small fields.

Bernivvigar was out there, Garibond knew, watching Bransen with sudden interest. Garibond wasn't surprised by that, other than the fact that it had taken the old and vicious Samhaist this long to take note of the crippled youngster. The Samhaists were not typically kind to such "inferior" people, for theirs was a brutal religion, ever searching for sacrifices to give their scowling gods, the dreaded Ancient Ones that haunted Honce. Like the second-born twin, cripples were considered appropriate gifts.

And now, Garibond suspected, Bernivvigar was watching Bransen.

Garibond watched the boy stagger across the room, pivot on one foot, and fall into a seat. His lip was blue and swollen on one side, and it looked as if he had chipped a tooth.

Garibond winced and silently berated himself for allowing Bransen to go into town that day. He had been against it, but Bransen, with his typical pig-headedness, had argued and argued. The boy was determined to live a normal life, but it would never be, Garibond knew. The folk of Pryd, the folk of any holding in all Honce, would never allow it.

The weary man thought back to the day of Bransen's birth, when SenWi had given her life to save him. She had thought it a generous deed, no doubt, but Garibond had to wonder. Many times during those early years when the extent of Bransen's infirmities had become clear, Garibond had entertained the thought of putting a pillow over Bransen's face and peacefully ushering him into the quiet realm of death.

It broke his heart to watch Bransen staggering around, to hear the insults hurled his way, to see the other boys mocking him with their "stork walks" behind him. It broke his heart to see the boy covered in blood day after day, whether from the bullying blows or from his own clumsiness. Would Bransen be better off dead?

The question remained inescapable for Garibond, but, in truth, it was already answered, and definitively. SenWi had answered it, with finality, when she had thrown her life force into the dying infant; and it was not in Garibond's province to go against that choice she had made.

He wanted only to protect the boy.

Bransen managed a crooked smile and said, "C-c-c-ca-ca-ca-Cadayle."

"Aye, boy," Garibond replied. "You lie down and rest and think of your little friend." He watched as Bransen settled down on his cot and on his pillow, which was formed of a folded and rolled silk suit of black clothing. In looking at that pillow, Garibond was reminded of how special, how magical, SenWi had been, and how magnificent were the works of the Jhesta Tu, for the pants and shirt and the soft, flexible shoes hadn't worn out in the least over the last decade, and Bransen's spittle and snot seemed to gain no hold on the soft and smooth material.

Garibond thought of the Book of Jhest and the sword of SenWi, both of which, like Bransen, had been entrusted to his care. He would protect them, as he protected the boy.

He looked at the frail figure lying across from him and wondered how in the world he could do that. He closed his eyes and tried not to think of the terrible fate that awaited Bransen if he should die before the boy. Or if wretched old Bernivvigar got his filthy nails on him.

The thought of the Samhaist had Garibond glancing back over his shoulder and out the door, which he quickly closed.

And barred.

CHAPTER 16

Hierarchy

W hat can you do for me?" Every word came out on a gasp of air, as old Laird Pryd lay on his bed, propped on a mound of pillows. Lying flat, the laird could not even draw breath; and even with the pillows, every inhalation was forced.

"We will pray," said Father Jerak. His head bobbed excitedly, as if he had just hit on a revelation.

Beside him, Brother Bathelais paled.

"Pray?" said Rennarq from across the room. "You will *pray*?"

"Yes, of course," offered Jerak. "We are priests, are we not? Praying is our wont." He chuckled as he finished, though no one else in the room was sharing his levity.

"Perhaps we might try again with the soul stone to make Laird Pryd more comfortable," said Bathelais.

"Perhaps you would be wise to do so," Rennarq replied.

Brother Bathelais nodded, but old Jerak—older than Laird Pryd even—scoffed.

"To what end?" he asked and turned to Pryd. "You are old, good laird. When we grow old, we die. The gemstones are no relief from the inevitable. They cheat not death, unless it comes for one wounded or prematurely ill." Again he laughed, apparently unaware of how out of place his words seemed. "Are you afraid of dying, Pryd? My old friend, I will join you in the next life soon enough, I am sure. As will you, Rennarq—and are you equally afraid?"

Brother Bathelais cleared his throat. "What Father Jerak means—"

"Has already been spoken," a scowling Rennarq interrupted.

"There is nothing?" Laird Pryd managed to gasp.

"My old friend," said Jerak. He moved very close to the bed and put his wrinkled hand on Laird Pryd's arm. He stared lovingly at this man who had been his liege for four decades. "Now comes the mystery. We are creatures of faith, for without it, we are nothing more than the goats and sheep that graze in our fields. I follow Abelle, and I believe his promise of redemption. You will find its truth before I do. Take heart."

Laird Pryd's face seemed as if it were frozen. "What can you do for me?"

Father Jerak fell back from the bed, and Brother Bathelais quickly replaced him. In one hand, he clutched his hematite, the soul stone, and he put his other hand flat on Pryd's chest. Bathelais concentrated and sent his healing powers through the stone, and it did seem as if Pryd did breathe a bit easier then, though only for a short time.

Behind Bathelais, Father Jerak began to pray, and behind him, Rennarq snorted and turned away.

Y ou raise their expectations," Jerak scolded his companion on their walk back from the castle to Chapel Pryd.

"I offer them hope."

"Where there is none, or at least, none for an outcome that cannot be. The laird will die within a week, likely this very night, and would so fail even if all the brothers of our order crowded about his bed, soul stones in hand." He glanced over at Bathelais, who was holding his arm in support but looking straight ahead.

"You disagree?" Father Jerak prompted.

"This is about more than the death of Laird Pryd, I fear. Prydae is off at war and you saw how Rennarq viewed us."

"Rennarq is a scowling idiot."

"One who will soon enough gain full power in the holding."

Jerak shrugged as if it did not matter.

"We fancy ourselves to be healers."

"We alleviate as much suffering as we can," Jerak corrected. "If I could cure age, would I need your arm to get through a fifty-foot stroll?"

"Your bluntness . . ." Brother Bathelais sighed and quieted.

"Speak your mind."

"You offered no hope to them, even if that hope was a false one."

"You suggest that I should lie to my old friend?"

Bathelais's hesitation was telling. "Bernivvigar was at Laird Pryd's bedside earlier this day and last night," he reminded.

"Preparing him for death. That is all the Samhaists do, of course. Their entire religion is based on the inevitability of death. They mete out harsh justice so that the common fools can see death firsthand, offering them an illusion of conquering it. And the Samhaists dismiss the dead as inconsequential even as they pretend to consecrate the ground that holds the corpse."

"And are we not an alternative to the Samhaists? Is that not the message of Blessed Abelle, that we are the light to defeat their darkness?"

"We are. We are a hope for life after death, but we cannot prevent the passage of the body from this world."

"Rennarq wanted more from us."

"Rennarq is an old fool."

"Laird Pryd hoped for more from our gemstones."

"I hope for more from our gemstones!" Father Jerak laughed again and shook his head, though the movement, with his stiff neck, barely registered. "Laird Pryd is afraid, and who would not be? He goes to that place from which none has ever returned. He goes on promises and prayers and nothing more. That is faith, my friend. And it is a terrifying thing when at last we are forced to take the great leap from life."

Brother Bathelais at last let it go, for he did not want to speak his thoughts bluntly. He believed that Chapel Pryd should put on a grand show to try to save Laird Pryd, that every brother should be constantly at the old man's bedside, praying and healing. He had made that suggestion to Father Jerak when they had first learned of Laird Pryd's sudden ill turn, but the old monk would hear none of it. Perhaps, Bathelais mused, Jerak was looking not so far down the road, when he would find his own deathbed. Perhaps he was forcing the laird to face it without pretense, as if to bolster his own understanding that no pretense would alleviate his own fears when the time came.

In any case, Bathelais feared that Father Jerak wasn't looking at the implications beyond the immediate political situation. This was about more than the impending death of Laird Pryd: it was about the future standing of Chapel Pryd itself.

That very night, the monks of Chapel Pryd were summoned to the castle.

"He will not last the night," one of the guards, another old man in this town of very old men and very young boys, quietly explained.

The two monks hustled by, as fast as Father Jerak could manage. They crossed from the gatehouse and climbed the four flights of stairs to the largest tower and Laird Pryd's private chambers. They came into the anteroom of the laird's bedchamber to find Rennarq inside, pacing nervously, along with several of Pryd's attendants and a pair of guards blocking the door.

"We will offer the sacred rite of passage," Brother Bathelais explained, and he and Father Jerak started for the door.

Rennarq nodded, not to them but to the guards, who promptly blocked the way.

Bathelais and Jerak turned curious expressions upon the old adviser.

"Bernivvigar is with him," Rennarq explained.

Bathelais furrowed his brow, and Jerak argued, "Laird Pryd is of the Church of Blessed Abelle, is he not? As he accepted the sacred rite of birth and the sacred rite of second affirmation, the sacred rite of passage is expected, and expressly granted."

"The Samhaists have rituals of their own to ease the way into death."

"Ours is to prepare the dying for their meeting with Blessed Abelle. On his word alone shall a man know the joy of paradise."

Rennarq shrugged. The guards did not move aside.

The two monks looked at each other with concern.

"Perhaps in the end, Laird Pryd was persuaded by the honesty of your rival," Rennarq said. "You could not cure him and neither could Bernivvigar, but at least the Samhaist never pretended that he could."

"Nor did we, against your protests," said Father Jerak, and Rennarq shrugged again and seemed not to care.

"This is madness, Rennarq," Father Jerak declared, and he straightened more formidably than he had in many years. "Laird Pryd long ago embraced the Church of Blessed Abelle and commissioned our chapel to be built right beside his own castle. There can be no doubt as to the road of his faith."

"A dying man chooses his own path, Father."

Father Jerak had to wonder about that. He was no fool, and was not unversed in matters politic. Jerak understood the reality of this moment. When Laird Pryd passed on, Rennarq would likely step in as ruler of Pryd until Prince Prydae returned from the powrie war—if that ever happened. This ending, right down to the call for the monks to quickly come to the castle, had been orchestrated by the shrewd old adviser for a very definite effect. Rennarq was sending a clear message to the brothers of Blessed Abelle—not one of outright rejection, perhaps, but one designed to remind them that they remained no higher than second in the hierarchy of Pryd—a very distant second.

"Let us go to him, at the end," Father Jerak said quietly, wanting to seem appropriately cowed for the sake of peace in the holding and the sake of the dying Laird Pryd. "Allow Laird Pryd the benefit of both blessings, Abelle and Samhaist. In the end—"

He stopped as the door to Pryd's bedroom opened. Old Bernivvigar stepped out, announcing at once, "The Laird of Pryd Holding has passed from this world to the ghostly realm. We are diminished as the ghosts about us grow stronger. Let us prepare an appeasement ritual to them."

Always it was about fear with the Samhaists, Father Jerak mused.

Bathelais, meanwhile, hardly registered Bernivvigar's words, so busy was he in scrutinizing and measuring the old Samhaist himself. The brothers of Abelle had a formidable opponent in him, Bathelais understood. Though no one really knew the man's exact age, Bernivvigar was at least as old as Jerak, and yet he was full of energy and the strength of life. By his own example of longevity and health, might Bernivvigar be silently enticing the folk of Pryd to lean the Samhaist way?

"The laird is dead, long live laird-guest Rennarq!" one of the guards proclaimed, and Bathelais's eyes went from the Samhaist to the new ruler of Pryd Holding. Never had Rennarq shown any love for the Church of Blessed Abelle.

Without another word, without a look at anyone—and pointedly none at all toward the brothers of Abelle—Bernivvigar walked past the monks and the others and left the castle.

"We will formally declare the transfer of power tomorrow morning," Rennarq said. He looked at the monks. "We are done here. You may return to your beds or your prayers or whatever it is you brothers of Abelle do at this hour."

"You and I must talk at length, laird-guest," Father Jerak replied, and Bathelais didn't miss the respect in his superior's voice, nor Jerak's insertion of the soon-to-be-formalized title.

"In time."

"Soon," Father Jerak pressed. "Most of your subjects are among the flock of—"

"In my good time, good father," Rennarq cut him off.

Father Jerak started to reply, but then just half nodded and half shook his head. He accepted Bathelais's arm and hobbled away.

CHAPTER 17

Offspring of Two Religions

Bransen watched Garibond at work on the small rock jetty one damp morning. The sky was low that day and soft with a misty rain. That heavy curtain kept the air still and only the slightest of waves lapped against the rocks.

Garibond sat hunched over, working with his nets and line. Every couple of minutes, he would straighten with a groan. He was getting older now—he had just passed his fiftieth birthday—and the toll of the hard work showed, particularly on wet mornings such as this.

Bransen knew that he should be out there helping with the lines and stitching the nets. Other boys his age were actually doing the fishing and the farming now, with so many of the older men off at war. That was why men had sons, after all, to take up the chores, that they could ease the toil on their old bones.

But not with me, Bransen thought. *I'm more trouble than I'm worth to him, and still he loves me so and never complains.*

At that moment, in that soft light and quiet air, Bransen wished that he could draw. He wished that his hands would stay steady enough for him to trace lines on a piece of parchment, that he could create a lasting image of his wonderful father out there, quietly toiling, uncomplaining, as constant and solid as the lake and the rocks. When he looked at Garibond, Bransen understood all that was good in the world. He felt nothing but unconditional love from the man and for the man; he would do anything to help Garibond!

But that was the rub, he knew, the source of his greatest frustration. For there was rarely anything at all that he could do to make the man's life easier—quite the contrary. Even when he went into town on errands, he knew that it was more for his own sake, for his expressed need to be independent, than for any true gain to Garibond. For more often than not, Bransen returned from town with goods spilled and lost in the dirt. He wasn't even ten years old, and he knew the truth of it.

How he wanted to go out to that jetty and help with the fishing nets! *I'd fall in, and Father would get wet pulling me out.*

The boy took a deep breath to throw aside the thoughts before more tears began to drip from his eyes. He swiveled his hips and did his stork walk back into the house, where he collapsed on his bed. Another day in the life of Bransen Garibond. Another day of unfulfilled wishes and of guilt.

He fell asleep and dreamed of fishing beside his father. He dreamed of walking, of running, even. He dreamed of telling his father that he loved him, without the spit flying and without turning a simple word like "love" into a rattling cacophony of half-bitten syllables.

"The clouds are lifting." Garibond's voice awakened him sometime later. "Do you mean to waste the whole of the day on your bed? Come along. I need to collect some vines."

Bransen managed to roll to one side and prop himself on his elbow. "I—I wou—wou—would just slo-ow you."

"Nonsense!" Garibond bellowed, and he walked over and helped lift the frail youngster from the cot to a standing position, and held on until he was sure that Bransen had found his footing. "And even if you do, I'd rather take three hours with your company than spend an hour alone."

The sincerity in that remark was all too clear to Bransen, defeating all his protests and arguments before he could begin to stutter them. He managed a smile and didn't even worry that parting his lips allowed a bit of drool to escape—because he knew that Father didn't care in the least. That mitigation wasn't complete within Bransen, though.

"Come on, then. I get lonely out there." Garibond ruffled Bransen's dark hair and turned to leave, but the boy made no move to follow

"You ch-ch-cho-ose this . . . l-li-l-l-life," he said.

Garibond, at the door, turned and watched him through the last half of the sentence, showing his typical patience with the painful speech but also wearing an expression of deep curiosity and concern.

"I did," he replied.

"You l . . . y-y-y-you . . . like alone."

Garibond sighed and dropped his gaze. "I thought I did," he clarified. "And now I prefer you."

"No."

Again Garibond put on that curious and concerned look.

"What is the matter, Bransen?"

The boy gasped and sniffled, his thin chest heaving. "I should be dead!" he blurted; the words carried emotions so powerful that for once he didn't stutter at all.

Garibond's eyes widened in alarm and he rushed to tower over the frail boy. "Don't you ever say that!" he cried, and he lifted his hand as if he meant to strike out at Bransen, who didn't flinch in the least.

"Y—yes!"

"No, and don't you ever think that! You are alive, and that's wonderful, for all the trouble. You're alive because your mother . . . because . . ."

Bransen stared at the man, not quite knowing what to make of the twisted and confused expression. It wasn't often that he had seen sensible and stable Garibond ruffled, and never to this extent.

The older man took a few deep breaths and calmed, then sat down on the cot and pulled Bransen down beside him, gently draping his arm across the boy's shoulders. "Don't you ever say that or even think that," he said.

"B-b-but—"

Garibond put a finger over Bransen's lips to quiet him. "I once thought the same thing," he admitted, "when you were born. And the trials you face pain me every day—probably more than they pain you, you're such a strong one inside. The Samhaists say that any child born less than perfect is meant as a sacrifice, and that is still the way in many towns.

"But not for you, because of your mother. I haven't told you enough of SenWi, Bransen, and what a special woman she was. You know that you got part of your name from her, and that she died when you were born. The rest of your name came from your father."

"G—Gar—"

"No," Garibond interrupted. "I gave you that surname, as was my right. Your father's name was Bran. Bran Dynard, a monk of the brothers of Abelle."

The boy's jaw drooped open wide, drool escaping unheeded.

Garibond turned, and turned Bransen, so that he was looking the boy in the eye. "I am not your father, Bransen, though no man could love any child more than I love you."

The boy began to slowly shake his head. Tears welled in his eyes and rolled down his cheeks, and he began to tremble so fiercely that Garibond had to hold him tight to keep him steady.

"Please forgive me," Garibond said. "You are old enough now. You need to hear this, all of it. You need to know about Bran, my dearest friend in all the world. You need to know about SenWi." He couldn't help but smile as he said the name, and a wistful look came into his good eye. "She didn't just die when you were born, Bransen. She gave her life to you so that you could live."

Bransen, stunned already, was even more surprised when Garibond, who rarely showed any emotion, leaned over and kissed him on the forehead. The older man rose, then, and slowly moved across the room to the trapdoor leading to the tunnels below.

"You were dying even as you were born," he explained. "You were too weak to draw breath, and SenWi wasn't much better off after the birth. But she was no ordinary person, your mother." He reached down and lifted the door, and then removed one of the side boards of the solid wooden casing. He reached into the hidden compartment and pulled forth a thick book, held it up, and blew the dust from it. "She was a Jhesta Tu mystic," he said, and Bransen had no idea what that meant, and he let his expression show it, as much as he could manage to let his expression show anything purposefully.

"A magical person," Garibond explained, "more so even than those brothers with their gemstones. Your father went to her land to convert her people to his religion and wound up seeing the truth in SenWi's beliefs." He presented the book to Bransen. "It's all in here. All the secrets."

"M-m-my . . . fath-fath-fa-ther?" The boy trembled, tears flowing more freely. *What are you saying to me?* his thoughts screamed at Garibond, though he knew that he would never find strength to voice the words. *You are my father! You! Not anyone else! How can you say these lies? Why do you wish to hurt me?*

"SenWi knew that you both were dying," Garibond went on very slowly, making sure that Bransen was hearing him past the obvious turmoil his revelations had brought. "So she used her magic to give you what was left of her own life, so that you could survive."

Bransen seemed to simply melt then upon the bed, his tiny body bouncing with sobs, and assorted shrieks issuing forth from his tortured mouth. Garibond rushed to him and held him and let him cry it all out. For more than an hour, he sat with the boy, gently patting him and telling him that he loved him and that it would all be all right. For more than an hour, he told Bransen that he was old enough to learn of these unsettling things, and promised the boy over and over that he would understand just how special he was when he heard the full story of his mother and father.

Finally, Bransen composed himself enough so that Garibond could pull him back up to a sitting position, and then the older man truly began the story. He told Bransen of his younger days with Bran Dynard, of how Bran had entered the Church of Abelle but Garibond had not. He spoke of Bran's travels to the strange lands south of the southern mountains, relating all the stories Bran had told to him of the Behr and the Jhesta Tu. His good eye sparkled when he talked of Bran's return to Pryd Holding, SenWi at his side, determined to enlighten his brethren about the beauties he had learned among the Jhesta Tu.

"That first day back was trouble, though," Garibond said in more somber tones. "Your father and mother came across a woman who had been tried and convicted before Bernivvigar."

Bransen shuddered at the name.

"He condemned her to death, and so she was bitten by a deadly snake and hung up to die slowly and painfully out along the southern road. Powries were there with her, dipping their caps in her blood!"

Bransen sucked in his breath, eyes going wide, fully caught in the tale now.

"But your mother and father fought them away," Garibond said, his voice showing his eagerness in injecting some real drama into the story and to paint Bransen's parents in the heroic light they deserved. "And then your mother—what a special lass she truly was!—used her mystical powers to cure the poor girl. Aye, but in that, she brought the poison into her own body, and it was that same poison that so hurt you, and her, in the end. Your affliction is because of generosity, my son. That might make it seem harder, I suppose, but to my thinking, it makes you no less a hero than your mother."

"Is—is—is she st-st-still . . . a—live?"

"The poor girl? Well, I've no idea, to tell the truth. If she's not, then it has nothing to do with that day, ten years ago. She left here of her own accord, walking with strength. And all because of your mother."

Bransen sat quietly and let that sink in, then turned a curious look up at Garibond. "B-b-b-but . . . my . . . fa-fa . . ."

"Your father?"

Bransen nodded.

"He was sent away by Father Jerak. Jerak did not much like your mother, for her powerful religion threatened him, I think. He didn't want to hear what your father had to tell him. So he sent your father away, to the north, to Chapel Abelle on the Gulf of Corona."

Bransen's curious look didn't abate.

"I don't know," Garibond admitted. "We never heard from him again. He may be up there at Chapel Abelle to this day, but Father Jerak's been telling me that he never got there at all. I do not know what to believe, Bransen.

"And I cannot believe that I told you all this in one sitting!" Garibond went on a moment later. "But you had to know—and you have to know that this changes nothing between us. You and me, we're family. Father and son, as far as I'm concerned. And don't you ever say to me again that you should die." He poked a finger threateningly at Bransen's face. "Don't you ever!"

Garibond couldn't hold the scowling pose, and he fell forward, wrapping Bransen in a tight and loving hug, and he held him there for a long, long time.

Garibond watched Bransen closely in the hours following their talk. He had placed so much on the shoulders of the frail boy—too much, perhaps.

Bransen, whose face was far too numb to show any but the most extreme emotions, seemed to move about with his typical posture and demeanor, giving Garibond few clues. He kept going back to the thick book, however. He'd stand beside it and run his fingers over the cloth cover, staring down, as if he were trying to somehow connect with his mother through those mystical pages.

"Do you know what a book is?" Garibond asked him on one such occasion.

Bransen jumped back from the tome, startled by the unexpected remark, and shifted to look curiously at Garibond.

Garibond smiled to reassure him, then walked over. "A book," he explained, gently pulling open the cover of the tome. He watched Bransen as he did, and was surprised at how the boy's eyes lit up, and at the sudden look of curiosity that crossed Bransen's face as he leaned in closer to see the gracefully curving letters.

"Your father penned it, one line at a time. It took him years." As he spoke, Garibond ran the tip of his index finger under the first line of the text, right to left as SenWi had taught him. When Bransen tentatively moved his hand toward the enticing letters, Garibond took him by the wrist and placed his fingers on the soft page. "Each of these lines is a letter," he tried to explain, and he scrunched up his face, wondering how in the world he might even begin to explain what a letter might be. He took Bransen's hand more firmly and moved it across one complete word, then spoke the translated word, "foot," out loud.

Bransen stared at him, then nodded and looked back at the page.

Garibond was tired from his long work that morning and even more from revealing so much painful information to Bransen. He wanted nothing more than to eat his supper and go to a well-deserved night's rest. But he could not deny the look on Bransen's face and, given his fears that he had overwhelmed the boy with sorrowful news, he understood his duty here.

Besides, after a few more minutes, after settling on the bed with Bransen sitting beside him, the book across their laps, Garibond found himself invigorated by teaching. He went through each of the letters, as SenWi had done with him. He pointed out and spoke aloud all the familiar words he could readily find on a page, then read complete sentences.

Garibond remembered SenWi's plea to him, that he teach the Book of Jhest to her child. He considered the high hopes, the promise held by the coming baby, and he had to fight back tears over and over again.

For now he considered the futility of this exercise. What might he really teach this idiot boy who could barely manage to walk and talk?

But Garibond quickly pushed those negative thoughts away, even managing a wide and sincere smile when Bransen stuttered out the word for arm. This exercise wasn't about the boy, the lonely older man soon realized, but for him. This was a way to reconnect with those lost to him, to hear again the voice of Brother Bran Dynard and that wonderful wife of his.

Finally, the daylight faded too much to continue and Garibond rose to leave, closing the book.

Bransen clutched it close and would not let go.

Smiling, nodding, Garibond let him keep it. A short while later, candle in hand, Garibond checked on the boy, to find him sleeping restfully—more so than Garibond had expected given the revelations of the day—his arms wrapped about the book, holding it close to his chest, his head on the clothing of SenWi.

CHAPTER 18

For the Line of Pryd

The smell of brine hung thick in the air; they could hear the waves crashing against the rocks beyond the few remaining eastern ridges, and with great hopes and great hunger to be done with this awful campaign, the men of the many holdings pressed forward. The intensity of their charge drove the bloody-cap dwarves before them, spurred by the common cry to "push them into the sea!"

Led by their eager young prince and by the mighty Bannagran, the men of Pryd Holding drove hard from the southern end of the line. Bannagran charged out in front, his heavy axe clearing the way of powries with powerful sweeps.

One dwarf got past that flashing blade and rushed hard at the large man's side, short sword leading. It clipped Bannagran's hip, and the man grimaced and turned. Out snapped Bannagran's hand, catching the dwarf by the front of its leather tunic.

Up into the air went the powrie, soaring over the ridge line to bounce down the rocky eastern side.

Two other dwarves pressed Bannagran furiously from the front, whacking at his blocking axe with their spiked clubs. He was forced back and slipped down to one knee, and the dwarves charged in for the kill. But Bannagran scooped up a large rock and hurled it forward, smacking one powrie squarely in the face. Up came the huge warrior, prodding the spiked tip of his axe straight ahead to halt the charge of the second dwarf.

The powrie had the better angle and tried to shove that axe aside, but so strong was Bannagran that even off balance, even with only one hand holding the axe shaft, he managed to keep the powrie at bay.

Bannagran got his feet under him, and he stood up and lunged forward, his other hand now slapping against his axe handle. He forged ahead, and the powrie gave ground and slipped a step to the side. Instead of following the movement, Bannagran snapped his axe the other way. Suddenly free of the entanglement, the powrie stumbled on the uneven ground, putting distance between himself and the axe—and that gave Bannagran enough room to maneuver and strike, his axe plowing into the dwarf.

He had to reverse his swing immediately, though; and he took the head from a second dwarf that was clambering over the rocky ridge.

Propelled by the warrior's gains, Prince Prydae led the rest of his forces in a sudden charge up the ridge. The powries broke before them, affording them the high ground and offering a moment of respite from the nearly constant fighting of that morning. As soon as he was clear, the prince rushed up beside his friend and clapped Bannagran on the shoulder. "We have met our objective and the sun has not yet reached its apex," Prydae congratulated.

"Our comrades have not shared in our good fortune this day," Bannagran replied as both of them looked northward, where the men of several other holdings lagged, mired in heavy battle with the fierce and stubborn dwarves.

"If I could offer them sons of Bannagran to spearhead their charge . . ." Prydae said, and when Bannagran turned to regard him, he found his prince smiling.

"I hear the waves!" one man cried from behind them, and that brought a cheer from all the men of Pryd.

Prydae's smile became a wry grin. "Is our work done this day?"

Bannagran saw the answer clearly in the man's expression. "It came to us too easily," he replied with a shake of his head.

"Let us press on."

"We risk leaving our support behind," Bannagran warned.

"To the east a bit, but then north," Prydae explained. "Let us turn the end of the line so that the powries cannot flee around us."

Bannagran looked back to the battlefield in the north, across the broken and rocky terrain. All seemed quiet in the east, after all, and the day's fighting was not half done.

Prydae clapped him on the shoulder once more. "You take half our charges and move straight north in support of the men of Laird Ethelbert. I will hold your eastern flank with the other half."

Bannagran fixed him with a knowing stare.

"I will spread my forces out in a secure line north to south," Prydae promised, "to ensure that I am not flanked." He clapped Bannagran once again and moved off, calling his men to order.

The daring young Prince of Pryd," Laird Ethelbert remarked when one of his commanders brought news of the unexpected northward curl of the army of Pryd Holding. "Ever out in front is that one."

"The powries break before his ranks," said the commander. "The men of Pryd have marked themselves well."

"Yes, particularly Prydae's large friend. One victory after another for the men of Pryd." Ethelbert smiled as he considered his own words. He wasn't jealous of Prydae's gains; quite the contrary: Ethelbert figured that Prydae's reputation would serve him well when he annexed Pryd Holding into the greater kingdom of Ethelbert, opposing Delaval. Though they remained far in the north, the men of Delaval had no doubt heard of Prydae's exploits here. What might their reaction be if Laird Delaval, attempting to take all of Honce for himself, ordered them into battle against the daring and cunning young prince and his soon-to-be-legendary champion?

"Tell your men to take the valor of Pryd Holding as their example," Ethelbert instructed his commanders. "Let us press forward as Prydae and his forces seal the trap. The more powries we kill now, the fewer we will have to kill later. Perhaps this day will mark the end of our troubles.

"So valiantly, one and all of Ethelbert!" the laird cried loudly. "The completion of our task lies before us this day, and the road home is at hand!"

With cheers reverberating along the line, the men of Ethelbert Holding charged forward against the fierce dwarves. Their advance inspired those armies of the lesser holdings flanking them to fight on more courageously.

Laird Ethelbert shifted his gaze from his own men to the army of Pryd, who were forming a line east to west, up one side of a ridge and down the other. Still the powries broke before them as they made their way north.

Ethelbert wondered if he might be watching the champion he would name as heir to Ethelbert Holding.

The powries continued to break ranks and flee, and the men of Pryd, led by their new champion, Bannagran, eagerly gave chase. Even those at the end of the line looked ahead more than behind as they swept along the ridge line.

Which was exactly what the powries had anticipated.

Standing in the center of the two lines, Prydae clearly saw the first signs of the counterattack. Powries leaped up from concealment in the rocks and pressed against the trailing edges of the Pryd line.

"Turn, lads! Close up the line!" he cried. "Hold, Bannagran! Tighten the ranks!" As he shouted, Prydae moved south along his trailing forces, and each step more clearly revealed to him the urgency of the situation. For this was no disorganized and desperate maneuver by the dwarves. The prince had to wonder if all his army's gains that morning had been but illusion. Had the powries allowed him, even enticed him along on his sudden push?

There was no time for Prydae to stop and think about it, for the fight was on at the southernmost end of the line, his soldiers already sorely pressed by a score of dirty dwarves. Into their midst charged the valiant prince, his sword ringing hard against a powrie weapon.

He turned the powrie blade and, with a burst of rage, leaped forward and struck hard, driving his sword deep into powrie flesh. He cried out to bolster his men; but it was hardly necessary, for his presence alone had already stabilized their defense and solidified their determination. Not a man broke ranks and ran.

For a moment, the powrie attack seemed to waver, as several dwarves fell, and others shied from the sudden presence of the mighty prince. But then came further proof to Prydae that this was not an improvisation by the bloody caps; for the second wave came on the length of the Pryd line, locking his men into place as they tried to reinforce the weakness along their ranks. And from the south and west, behind Prydae and his men, came a second group of dwarves, howling and hungry; and some already seemed to reach for their berets, as if the spilling of human blood was inevitable.

Prydae batted aside one thrusting sword, then backhanded to clip off the head of a spear. Then he ducked to avoid a second spear, thrown from somewhere in the rear ranks of dwarves. Acting purely on instinct now, Prydae roared encouragement to his men and forced himself to press on. For he knew that to run was to die, that the dwarves had them caught, whatever the outcome might be. And he knew that without his example many men would turn and run and that would spell doom for them all.

"Hold strong!" he yelled, parrying another sword blow, then thrusting forward to send a powrie spinning down in pain. "Fight them, I tell you! Hold strong! Bannagran!"

Above all the turmoil, Bannagran heard his prince's call. He brought his axe high to intercept an overhand chop by one dwarf, then stepped in, his sheer strength forcing the powrie's axe over its head. He gave a sudden jerk, throwing the powrie off balance, then caught the dwarf by the front of its shirt and lifted it into the air.

"Bannagran!" Prydae called again in desperate tones, and the mighty warrior threw the dwarf back into its fellows, forcing that entire section of the powrie line backward just a bit—enough for him to turn and locate his prince amid the confusion of the melee.

The huge man winced as Prydae swiveled away from one thrust and barely pushed a second spear aside. Bannagran's hopes soared for an instant, when Prydae not only intercepted a third blade but also suddenly turned and sprang forward, his sword taking down one of a trio of powries. The prince landed in perfect balance and began to fend against the remaining two.

Bannagran's hopeful nod froze when he noted, and Prydae obviously did not, that the dwarf on the ground was not quite out of the action.

"My liege!" he screamed, and he broke ranks and charged toward him.

Prydae never heard him. Prydae never noticed the dwarf on the ground, reaching for its spear.

Suddenly the prince felt a fiery explosion erupting through his groin. All strength deserted him and his arms dropped and his sword fell.

He was already falling before the nearest powrie slugged him.

Prydae hit the ground hard, his loins torn and bloody, fires of pain coursing through his body. He knew that the powries were closing to finish him. He knew that all was lost, but there was nothing he could do.

He had no strength even to cry out for help, his voice stolen by the crashing waves of agony.

He saw only a blur as a large foot planted itself on the ground in front of his eyes. A hollow sound echoed through his fading senses, and only distantly did he hear Bannagran, though he was straddling his prone form, as he cried out for the men of Pryd to rally round their prince.

Finally, Prince Prydae slipped into blackness.

Bannagran set himself solidly, a foot on either side of the prone and unmoving prince. All around him, the men of Pryd tried to rally, but the dwarves came on in force from all sides. They smelled blood, Bannagran knew, and nothing lured a powrie more fiercely than the notion that it might get to dip its shining red beret in the blood of a victim.

One dwarf came at Bannagran hard from the side, and he brought his weapon up to meet the charge, holding his large axe out horizontally and catching the dwarf's axe as it chopped for him. Hands set wide on his axe handle, Bannagran jerked his weapon, hooking the dwarf's axe under its bulky head and lifting it. The stubborn powrie didn't let go even when the tall human brought his hands up over his head, forcing the dwarf to its tiptoes.

Bannagran turned his weapon and shoved it out to the side, sending the dwarf into a half turn. He saw that the powrie was already winding up for a second swing as it finally managed to plant its feet, but he was the quicker, kicking the dwarf hard in the ribs and knocking it several steps away. It swung anyway, its flying weapon falling far short of the mark, and Bannagran took a step forward and stabbed straight out with his own axe's pointed tip. Stuck, the powrie staggered away.

But Bannagran couldn't afford to follow and finish the task, for all around him, his men were falling.

And there remained Prydae, lying so still.

A roar of defiance escaped Bannagran as he set himself determinedly over his prince and began battling a pair of dwarves. He worked his axe furiously, stabbing and slashing, spinning to meet a charge from behind, and even hopping so that he dropped his feet on the opposite sides of the prone man.

He got hit hard in the ribs but shrugged the pain away. As he spun again, his axe flying, his weapon came together with a dwarf's axe at an awkward angle, and it rode right up the shaft. With a growl and his tremendous strength,

Bannagran managed to wrest the axe from the dwarf's hands, but he clipped his own hand on the sharp underside of the dwarf's weapon, the blade cutting through his leather gauntlet and gashing deep into his skin.

Bannagran ignored the angle of his pinky finger, obviously severed and hanging in the torn glove. He couldn't afford to feel that pain at that time.

Not now. Not with dwarves flowing about him and his men, like water breaking over rocks.

Despite his roars of defiance and the brilliance and strength of his movements, Bannagran saw the truth. The men of Pryd could not hold back this force. Prydae was doomed, he was doomed, and all of Pryd's army was doomed.

He felt a twinge of regret and the guilt of failure, and he kept swinging and kept urging on his desperate companions.

Beside him, the powries took down another of Pryd's brave warriors and swarmed over him, chopping and stabbing, many already eagerly pulling off their berets.

The blare of horns rent the air suddenly, freezing man and powrie alike, and as he came to understand their source, Bannagran managed a sigh of tremendous relief.

"Ethelbert!" one Pryd man cried. "The Laird of Ethelbert is come!"

A great thrust, turn, and sudden swing had one dwarf flying away, giving Bannagran a moment to look back over his shoulder and regard the scene. Rolling through the rocky dale to the north came the forces of Ethelbert Holding, chasing the powries before them.

Hope suddenly renewed, Bannagran shouted to his beloved prince, "Hold strong, my liege! Our salvation is at hand! Laird Ethelbert is come!

"Fight on, men of Pryd!" the great warrior shouted, and he followed by cleaving a dwarf's head nearly in half. "The day is yet to be won!"

Powries swarmed Bannagran then, and he went into a fit of battle rage, his axe swinging and stabbing. They hit him with clubs and chopped him with their fine blades and stabbed him with their fine swords, but he paid them back many times over.

And he held his ground, his legs as solid as if rooted deep into the earth. He was only half conscious when another mass of powries came by him, but enough aware to hold his strike.

The men of Ethelbert Holding flowed past their Pryd brethren, driving the vicious dwarves away.

CHAPTER 19

The Way of Samhaine

Thousands lined the streets of Pryd Town on the day the men came home from war. Bright banners waved and horns blew from every rooftop. Women put on their finest clothes and danced and twirled with abandon, children cried out in joy, and all the air was full of music and vibrant sound and bright colors flashing.

Prince Prydae led the solemn procession of returning warriors. He sat astride a large roan stallion, riding somewhat gingerly but holding his shoulders proudly squared. Bannagran, with a multitude of new scars, rode beside him, but other than those two, the procession consisted of footmen alone. Dirty and ragged footmen. Men weary of war and dirt, ill nourished and battered. Men with hollow eyes that had seen too much. Men with heavy hearts that had known too much pain and too much sorrow. They and their comrades of the other holdings had driven the powries to the sea and had all but eradicated the threat of the vicious bloody-capped dwarves, but the victory had been long and costly. When Prince Prydae had ridden out of Pryd Holding three years before, he had led a column of more than three thousand men.

Barely twelve hundred had returned, and nearly half of those carrying wounds that would follow them for the rest of their miserable lives.

Still, as the procession entered the southernmost stretch of the town and became almost immediately engulfed in the sounds and sights of the cheering throng, to a man they found their spirits lifted, and Prince Prydae rode a bit straighter in the saddle, and Bannagran managed a smile.

They continued their march through the town and toward the castle, where Prydae would be formally crowned as Laird of Pryd Holding within the week. Couriers had told the prince of the death of his father; at the rear of the battlefield, Laird Ethelbert had even held a memorial for the lost Laird Pryd and a celebration for Prydae.

But Prydae hadn't yet been able to properly mourn his loss, and so his heart remained heavy as he moved along the road, despite the cheering and the dancing. These were his people now; this was his holding now.

He felt a twinge down low, an uncomfortable reminder that he would quite possibly be the last of his bloodline to hold the title of laird.

Prydae winced, and not from the pain.

"Are you all right, my liege?" asked Bannagran at his side, and Prydae realized that he had let his discomfort show on his face.

"It is all the same, yet all so different," he replied.

Bannagran nodded. "After the sights of war, it is indeed."

Even as he started to answer, Prydae's attention was caught by the spectacle of a young boy off to the side of the road up ahead. He was dancing, or moving at least, in an awkward manner, his head lolling from side to side, spittle glistening on his face. A man long in years, but still looking quite solid, sat on the ground beside him, obviously trying to calm him.

But the boy was clearly taken with the excitement and seemed on the very edge of losing control as he flailed about, cheering, or trying to, for the Prince of Pryd. Prydae made eye contact with the curious creature, and it seemed as if that link almost drew the boy forward as the prince walked his stallion by.

The boy staggered out; the man overseeing him tried to grab him, but the stiff-legged creature staggered forward suddenly out of the man's reach. The youngster lurched out into the road, arms flailing, legs striding this way and that without apparent control.

Prydae's expression turned to one of horror as the creature stumbled against the flank of his horse, against his own leg. He instinctively pulled his foot from the stirrup and kicked out hard, sending the boy staggering back.

"Control that beast!" the horrified prince said to the man who scrambled out to grab at the poor boy.

"Pardon, my laird," the man stammered. "We beg your pardon. He did not mean . . ."

Prydae wasn't even listening, and just marched his horse along.

A soldier from the ranks behind him rushed out and roughly pushed the man and the boy back from the road, both of them going facedown in the mud. Most of the nearby onlookers laughed, though one woman and a young girl hurried to the side of the fallen pair.

"My people, oh, joy," Prydae said to Bannagran. "The pleasure of lairds to suffer the likes of the peasant rabble." Had the prince been watching the continuing drama along the roadside with any real interest, where the woman and girl were helping the strange creature, he might have felt a flicker of recognition. That particular woman, after all, was the first woman he had seen executed.

Bannagran laughed at Prydae's sarcasm, taking it as a sign that his prince was feeling a bit better.

Prince Prydae wasn't surprised to see Father Jerak and Brother Bathelais waiting for him inside the castle—though he had hoped that the old wretch Jerak would already have gone to his grave. Rennarq, lean and sharp as ever, sat at the front of the throne room in a seat set just to the side of the throne, as was the custom; and Bernivvigar, yet another remnant of a past age, stood nearby, tall and straight as always.

"My prince," Rennarq said as Prydae and Bannagran swept into the room. The old man pulled himself from the chair swiftly and bowed low. "Heavy are our hearts with grief at the loss of your father."

Prydae's eyes darted from man to man, finally settling on Bathelais. "Old men die," he said. "It is the way of things." In light of that comment, the fact that the other three awaiting Prydae were all well past their seventieth birthday was obviously not lost on Bathelais.

"We are glad that you have returned to us, warrior prince," Bathelais remarked. "Greater is Pryd Holding now that the line of Pryd is restored."

Prydae managed to hide the smirk that wanted to leap onto his face as he regarded Rennarq's slight scowl.

"The line of Pryd?" Prydae asked of Bathelais. "And how eternal shall that line be, pray tell?"

An uncomfortable moment passed between them all, with the two monks of Abelle looking nervously at each other and Rennarq looking at Prydae, his gaze inevitably lowering, then going to the floor and his own feet.

Yes, they knew, Prydae reasoned. Of course they did, for the monks at the front lines would have spread word far and wide of the battlefield casualty, that the gelded prince of Pryd would likely sire no children.

Off to the far side, Bernivvigar dared to chuckle, and all eyes turned to him.

Prydae felt Bannagran tense suddenly, and he half expected the man to leap over and throttle the impudent Samhaist.

"To put your faith in the trickery of the upstarts is to invite disaster," old Bernivvigar cackled, and Prydae shot a look at the two monks of Abelle.

"Our brethren have saved many lives at the front," Father Jerak protested. "Prince Prydae's among them."

"Limited miracles, then?" Bernivvigar replied. "An interesting concept."

"And what shall the Samhaists offer Prince Prydae beyond your clever insults?" Brother Bathelais charged.

Prydae could hardly believe that these men were vying so, right in front of him, and daring to speak of him as if he weren't even there. Rather than interrupt, the prince let them go on a bit more. It seemed obvious to him that the tension between the competing religions had heightened of late, as was logical, given the monumental changes in the land and the desperate and competing work of both Samhaist cleric and monk of Abelle at the battlefield.

"We shall see," Bernivvigar replied to Bathelais, and he offered a look to Prydae then, designed obviously to give the prince some ray of hope.

"My pardon, my prince, who is soon to be rightful Laird of Pryd," Father Jerak interjected; and he stepped in front of Bathelais and fixed him with a scowl that silenced him. "The brothers of Blessed Abelle have prayed for you every day. We are pleased that your life was saved but sorrowful for your loss, which is a loss to all the lands of Honce. We have done all that we could, and will continue our efforts on your behalf. A collective of our most powerful brothers, with the soul stones of the greatest godly energy, can be called together at any time. Many would make the pilgrimage to the aid of Prince Prydae, no doubt, perhaps even some of our masters from Chapel Abelle."

"Though you know that you can do nothing," Bernivvigar immediately interjected. "Would you stretch out hope indefinitely to avoid the inevitable realization by Prince Prydae that there really is nothing your church has to offer him?"

"Perhaps you would do well to hold your tongue, old Samhaist," Father Jerak snapped back with uncharacteristic sharpness.

"I have held several tongues," Bernivvigar replied, and he brought forth his hand, palm up. "Cut from the mouths of undeserving fools, muting them so that others could be given back lost voices."

It took a moment for that remark, that notion of Samhaist doctrine, which often used sacrifice for supposed medical purposes, to truly sink into Prince Prydae; and when he fixed Bernivvigar with a serious look, the old Samhaist merely offered him a meaningful stare.

"Father Jerak," Prydae began, still staring hard at Bernivvigar, "I am not without gratitude for the work of your brethren out on the battlefield. Surely I would have expired had it not been for them. Rest easy here, I pray you, and know that the brothers of Abelle showed themselves well in the east. Let us end this useless bickering."

"Yes, my liege," said Jerak.

"We have other matters to attend," Rennarq cut in. "Prince—Laird Prydae should be crowned within the week. The event will heighten the celebration of our glorious victory over the bloody caps! Their scourge is lifted from the land, and never again will the men of Honce have to fear powrie raiders along our roads."

That last remark had Prydae and Bannagran exchanging looks, for it wasn't quite true. Victory in the east had been substantial, and the blood of thousands of powries stained the coastal rocks and had turned the tides red for many days. But Laird Ethelbert and Laird Delaval, the two men truly in charge of Honce's arrayed forces, had stopped short of eliminating the powries altogether. And both Bannagran and Prydae knew well that it was not because of battle weariness and not because the two lairds simply could not have pressed farther. No, the decision to allow the powries some escape had been a calculated one, as almost all the lairds at the front had learned. The powrie threat had to be kept at a minimum to allow for trade and for the coming consolidations the two great lairds planned. But at the same time, the powrie threat had to remain, at the edges of awareness, so that all the lairds of the land could keep their people properly afraid of the world beyond their borders. With tales of powries and goblins lurking in the forests, the peasants would not question the demands of their protector lairds.

"You may leave us," Prydae said to the monks, and he pointedly turned to Bernivvigar and added, "but you stay a bit longer."

The old Samhaist bowed and flashed a superior look Father Jerak's way. Brother Bathelais muttered as if intending to protest the slight, but Father Jerak silenced him with an upraised hand.

"It is good that the brothers of Blessed Abelle were able to save your life, good prince," Father Jerak offered to Prydae as he shuffled past. "An empty place would be Pryd Holding without the proud son of Laird Pryd."

Prydae didn't respond, other than to offer a quick nod.

"We have much to attend to, my laird-in-waiting," Rennarq remarked, and Prydae stared at him as if listening, but the door had barely closed behind the departing monks when Prydae turned away from the old laird-guest to focus on Bernivvigar.

"You speak of the sacrifice of a tongue to restore the voice of another."

"Indeed, it has been done," Bernivvigar answered. "Other sacrifices have not been so successful, of course."

"To what does this apply?"

"To anything, if the sacrifice is appealing to the Ancient Ones. I have seen men slaughtered so that others could rise up from their graves. I have seen eyes plucked out to make more worthy blind men see."

Prydae lowered his head and sighed.

"As for your . . . infirmity," Bernivvigar said tactfully. "You fear that you are the end of the line of Pryd."

"There is little left to dissuade me from the conclusion," Prydae admitted.

"Castrating another might bring relief, depending on the extent of your injuries and depending upon the whims of the Ancient Ones."

"The whims?"

"That is the way of the gods, my laird," Bernivvigar answered. "Among men you stand tall. Among the folk of Pryd Holding, you are practically a god yourself. But among the Ancient Ones, we are all rather small."

Prydae paused and considered the words for a moment. He licked his lips and glanced over at Bannagran, who nodded. "What would we have to do?" the soon-to-be-laird asked.

"Find a sacrifice, of course."

"What requirements?"

Bernivvigar laughed. "That he has testicles, my laird. Any man will do, though I would not recommend an old and shriveled specimen." A smile widened on the old Samhaist's face that set Prydae back on his heels, so obvious was its wickedness.

"There is a rather odd boy about the town," Bernivvigar remarked.

"Not that stork creature?" put in Rennarq, and Bernivvigar blinked slowly, holding fast to his smile.

"Why that one was ever allowed to continue to draw breath, I do not know. The Ancient Ones surely show no favor to a creature so inferior and damaged as he," the imposing Samhaist said.

"The boy on the road?" Bannagran asked Prydae. "The one who staggers with every step and has a face full of snot and drool?"

"A wonderful specimen, is he not?" said Bernivvigar. "Perhaps when I am finished with him—with your permission of course, my laird—I can mercifully put an end to his thoroughly wretched existence."

Prydae's conscience tugged at him. Could he do such a thing? Any of it? Surely, if his virility could be restored, the line of Pryd secured, it would be for the greater good. But still . . .

He glanced around at his secular advisers, focusing mostly upon Bannagran, who had become such a trusted companion under such difficult circumstances. The large man returned the look and nodded.

Prydae licked his lips nervously, then turned to Rennarq. "Do we know where this creature lives?"

CHAPTER 20

When All the World Turned Upside Down

Garibond watched as the woman he believed to be Callen Duwornay, who had stubbornly called herself Ada Wehelin, and her young daughter walked away from his house on the lake. "A good deed repaid," the man repeated, for that is what the woman had said when he had once more, upon their parting, thanked her and her daughter for their help in the town.

Garibond hadn't recognized the woman at first—Callen Duwornay was someone long out of his thoughts—and the truth of her identity hadn't even registered to him during their walk out to his house or during the short visit of the woman and her daughter. It wasn't until she was leaving, actually walking away, when she had uttered those words, "A good deed repaid." Even then, for a few moments, Garibond hadn't made the connection.

But watching her now, though her back was to him, the man understood the truth, beyond any doubt. That was her, Callen. Garibond was glad to learn that she was still alive, that she had gotten through her ordeal and had even managed, apparently, to remain in Pryd Holding—in Gorham's Hill, on the far western edge of the town proper, she had told him. Somehow seeing her alive bolstered Garibond's spirits, even beyond his simple sympathy and empathy toward her. Somehow, the fact that she had gone on, had even given birth to a beautiful daughter, made the sacrifices of SenWi and now poor Bransen, somewhat more tolerable.

All along, Garibond had known that SenWi had done right that day in healing the young woman, and never had she wavered on that matter, never had she expressed the slightest bit of regret. Seeing Callen and Cadalye reinforced the concept.

"Sh-sh-sh-she'sss—my frien . . . my frien . . . my friend," Bransen said to him, making his way over to join him at the window.

"What a beautiful little friend you've got there, Bransen," Garibond replied, and he draped his arm about the boy and pulled him close, in part to steady him but more because he just felt that he needed a hug.

"I-I-I'm going to m-m-marry . . . marry her."

Garibond's smile nearly took in his ears, and he squeezed Bransen up close to his side and continued to watch the departing pair. He knew that such a thing could never be, of course, but he simply said, "She'll be a fine wife to you." Why would he deprive Bransen of his dreams, after all? What else could the poor boy possibly have?

When he looked at Bransen then, his thought was only reinforced, for rarely had Garibond seen Bransen smile so widely. And Bransen didn't look back at him, didn't even seem to feel the weight of Garibond's gaze. No, he kept staring out the window at Cadalye, and he kept smiling.

Sometime later, when the mother and daughter were long out of sight, Garibond remarked, "Well, I must get myself cleaned up and get some dinner to cooking." He gave Bransen another hug, then moved off and went about starting a fire and heating some water for stew. As he stood there stirring the pot, Garibond wondered about the boy's smile. Glad he was to see it, after their humiliation in the town. How horrible that had been!

But more horrible for him than for Bransen, Garibond understood, if for no other reason than the fact that the poor boy was quite used to such humiliation. He second-guessed himself for all those occasions he had allowed Bransen to journey into the town on an errand. True, Bransen was always eager to go, and often begging to go, but had there been a single occasion in the last two or three years when the boy had gone to Pryd Town and had returned without mud on his clothing or blood somewhere? Given the experience today, Garibond realized more fully that many of those falls were far from accidental.

He thought of Dynard and SenWi as he stood there cooking, remembering his old friends. He watched the swirl of the stew, the thick liquid rolling back over to flatten the wake caused by the passing spoon, and that motion invited him to look more deeply into himself and his life. Garibond the hermit, he supposed, and he thought back to all the disappointments that had led him to this place. It hadn't been a sudden decision for him to move out here and settle in the abandoned shell of a cottage on the small rocky island. It had been a gradual drifting away from the disappointments he always seemed to find when around other people. He remembered when his sister had been killed by powries and how the soldiers of Laird Pryd, coming in just moments too late, had been more concerned with celebrating their victory than in worrying about Garibond's grief. While he had knelt there over his sister's body, the soldiers had cheered and danced, arguing over who could claim credit for which powrie killed.

"Aye, and what a wonderful life it's been," Garibond muttered over the stew.

The moment of self-pity passed quickly, as it always did with Garibond, and he turned his thoughts to the good things he had known, to Dynard again and SenWi, who had touched him deeply in so short a time. And of course, to

Bransen, that awkward and fragile little boy. Garibond chuckled as he considered how frustrated other people always seemed to get when Bransen tried to speak, turning a simple statement into a long ordeal. Garibond didn't think of things that way with Bransen; to him, the boy's stuttering only lengthened the moment of revelation, like having a hooked fish put up a good and long fight or watching a refreshing spring storm roll in from far away.

He looked up from the stew to Bransen, then, and found that the boy had again taken out the Book of Jhest, and was now gently moving his hands across the pages. Bransen was always at that book, it seemed, ever since Garibond had shown it to him and had spent many days with him trying to explain the lettering. For some reason Garibond didn't understand, Bransen seemed to take a kind of solace in just looking at the flowery text. At first, the man had worried that the clumsy child would damage the book, but it had quickly become apparent to Garibond that Bransen was taking more care with the tome than anyone else ever could.

So he let the boy play with the book as often as he wished, and he never concerned himself with the well-being of one of the most important artifacts he had to tie him to SenWi and particularly Dynard.

The two sat down to dinner a little later, the room full of the rich aroma of the fish stew and wood smoke. Several candles provided the light, for clouds had thickened outside, hastening the onset of dusk.

"Good lettering in that book," Garibond remarked between bites. "You like looking at it."

Bransen's face twisted into a crooked smile.

"Does it take you away from all of this?" the man asked. "Can you forget what happened in the town when you focus on the letters in the book? Bah, what fools are those soldiers."

Bransen's smile twisted even more, finally settling into a perplexed expression, or the closest thing the boy could approximate. He started to respond several times, and Garibond caught on that more than his inability to quickly verbalize his thoughts was holding him back. Finally, Bransen brought one hand over the table, fingers outstretched and palm down.

"This iiiiis . . . take," he said. His arm shook from the effort as he forced the palm to turn upward without any wild flailing.

Garibond tilted his head curiously.

"Nnnnnnnth. Nnnnnnnth . . . th-this iiiis . . . re-re-re-receeeeive."

"Of course," Garibond said quietly, and he took Bransen's hand and slowly guided it off the table. He could see that Bransen was growing quite excited, and knew that type of emotion usually foreshadowed some wild movement from the damaged boy. Garibond had little trouble in imagining bowls of his fresh stew flying about the room.

But then, even as he brought the arm over the table side, it hit him, and he froze in place, staring wide-eyed at the boy. "What did you say?"

Bransen's face twisted as he tried to form the words, and he started to turn his hand over again, though Garibond still held it.

Garibond did it for him and brought the arm back up over the table. "This is take?" he asked, not willing to wait through the stuttered explanation.

Bransen nodded.

Garibond turned the hand over. "Receive?"

The boy's smile answered it all.

Garibond leaped up from the table so quickly that his chair skidded out behind him. He scooped up a candle as he went to the book, and bent low to study its open pages.

And there it was, on the very page Bransen had left open, one of the Jhesta Tu explanations of the differences of posture, the connotations of movement and position. Those acting in anger or superiority, the text explained, often reached for something from another with their palms down—the inference being that they took what they wanted without regard. Like the soldiers on the road, pushing Bransen and Garibond away, like the prince himself, kicking the boy without regard.

Those who lived a receptive life, an open existence in which they hoped to, and expected to, learn from others, must reach out with their palms up, inviting compliance and sharing.

But how had Bransen figured that out? Garibond had never read him this specific page!

The man turned to regard the boy. "Are you reading this?"

The twisted smile, the awkward nod.

"Reading?" Garibond asked with a gasp.

Bransen gulped for air, as if he was setting his jaw muscles so that he could try to answer. He did start to stutter something out, but it was irrelevant to Garibond, who had been thrown into complete confusion. How could an idiot read? How could Bransen, a boy who could hardly master the simple movement of putting one foot in front of the other, begin to decipher the intricacies of Dynard's flowing script?

He shook his head in denial, then gathered up the book and moved over to the table. He surprised and frightened Bransen as he swept the bowls from in front of him, caring not at all that they crashed about the floor. He placed the book down and flipped the pages, coming to one of the early lessons the Jhesta Tu placed upon their beginning students. A student would be bound by the ankles to a heavy weight, then dropped into a pool that was just deep enough to keep the student, fully extended, under water. As with most of the lessons and pages in the book, Garibond possessed only a rudimentary understanding.

From what he gathered, the Jhesta Tu wanted to see if their students could free themselves without help.

The ending note of wisdom on this page—every page had one—went, "In the peace and solitude of the water, do we see ourselves."

"Re-re-reflec . . . reflecti . . . ti . . . tion."

"Yes," said Garibond. "Reflection. Like when you look into the lake with me. You see what you look like."

Bransen began shaking his head. "Nnnnnnno. No," he said, and he poked a finger at the text. "Innnn wa-wa-water . . ." The boy gave a great sigh and closed his eyes. He seemed deep in thought for a moment, looking inside himself, and then, in the clearest statement Garibond had ever heard him utter, he said, "In water we see ourselves."

So shocked was Garibond by the clarity of the words, that it took him a long moment to realize that Bransen was poking at the book, bidding him to look.

He read the indicated passage, and in light of what Bransen had just said, something dawned on him. The purpose of the Jhesta Tu test of water was to measure the inner calm of a student. All the students had been shown how to extricate themselves from the binding weights; at issue was whether or not they could do it under the extreme pressure of being underwater. This test was of a person's inner strength, his calm under duress. Garibond had always seen that, somewhat, of course, but the revelation here was not what was on the page in the Book of Jhest, but rather, the reasoning power of Bransen!

That, and the fact that the boy could read! How could that be possible?

Garibond looked at him, and wanted to say something, wanted to pour out all of his amazement and joy. Never before had he looked at Bransen in quite this way, and he wanted nothing more than to shout with happiness.

But he couldn't. He felt the lump welling in his throat and he could force no words past it. He reached out and tousled Bransen's hair, and managed to motion toward the boy's bed.

Then he gently closed the book and blew out the candle and waited for Bransen to settle onto his bed, which was really just a cot piled with dry hay, before blowing out the other candles in the room.

Garibond didn't go straight to his own bed. He went to the window and stared up at the sky, which was caught in the last moments of twilight. In a patch where some of the clouds had cleared, he could see the first twinkling stars, framed by the rolling dark edges of the overcast.

It was a long, long time before Garibond managed to get to bed, and the room was beginning to brighten in predawn glow before he finally managed to fall asleep.

Garibond heard the knocking, but it didn't register in his mind, as if it were coming from far away, perhaps, or as if it were part of another world.

Even the loud crash that followed merely made him blink once and roll over.

But when he heard Bransen cry out, "Nnnnnnnno!" his eye popped open and he rolled quickly out of bed to his feet.

He took in the scene immediately: there was Prince Prydae and his companion, the warrior of note named Bannagran. Bannagran held Bransen by the shoulders, his great strength keeping the poor boy almost completely still.

"When your laird comes knocking, you would do well to open the door for him," Bannagran said to Garibond.

"I—I was asleep," the man stammered. "My liege, is there a problem?"

"No problem," Bannagran answered. "We came for the boy and now we have him." The large man wheeled about, jerking poor Bransen so forcefully that his legs swung out wide.

Garibond, dressed only in his flimsy nightshirt, rushed to the door before them. "What are you doing?" he cried. "You cannot take my boy!"

"Cannot?" Prydae said, holding a hand up to silence Bannagran.

"But, my liege—"

"Exactly," Prydae interrupted. "Your liege. Your laird."

"But why would you wish to take him? He is just a child. He has never harmed anyone. Please, my liege, I beg of you to leave him alone. Mercy, my liege. Sweet mercy."

"Oh, shut up, you babbling fool," said Bannagran. "And get out of the way before I throw you through the door. The Prince of Pryd is in need of your son, and so your son will come to his service."

"What can he do? He is just a child, and infirm—"

"Not infirm for our needs, I pray," said Bannagran. He wrapped one arm around Bransen's chest and leaned back, holding the boy easily from the floor, then reached his other arm around and down the front to the boy's crotch and gave a squeeze that brought a squeal from poor Bransen.

"Yes, he is secure."

Garibond's eyes widened with horror, and he charged forward—or started to, for before he got a single step, Prydae had his sword out, its tip against Garibond's chest.

"I will forgive you that," Prydae said, "just once."

"Ah, I see that you have secured our sacrifice," came a voice behind Garibond, from the open doorway, and he turned around to see Bernivvigar standing there.

"S-sacrifice?" Garibond stammered, and then he steeled himself and straightened his shoulder. "You old beast! Begone from my home!"

"The boy will not be killed," Prydae assured Garibond, and there was something in the prince's voice, some bit of remorse perhaps, that made Garibond look back over his shoulder.

"He is needed," Prydae went on. "Take pride that this crippled creature will restore the line of Pryd."

Garibond's expression was one of pure incredulity. "What will you do to him? He's just a boy."

"The Ancient Ones oft accept such sacrifices," Bernivvigar said.

"You just said . . ." Garibond protested to Prydae.

"That he will not be killed," Prydae repeated.

"His life is not the sacrifice," Bernivvigar said, and there was obvious amusement in his tone. "This wretched little creature will restore to the new Laird of Pryd that which the powries took away."

Garibond's eyes widened, and he inadvertently dropped his gaze to Prydae's groin.

"If you utter a word of this, I promise that I will cut your face off," Prydae warned. "That for all of your life you will suffer the screams of revulsion, of children and women, and even men, who cannot withstand the horror of your ugliness. And if you utter a word of this, you will watch your wretched little boy die slowly and painfully."

Garibond hardly heard the words, his thoughts careening as he came to understand exactly what the old Samhaist had in mind. "You c-cannot," he stammered. "He is just a boy."

"The line of Pryd must continue," Prydae said.

Garibond's eyes darted all around, like a cornered animal. All the revelations of the previous day, all the wonderful realizations that there was actually some measure of intelligence within the stuttering Bransen, played in his mind, demanding an end to this sudden and unexpected tragedy. "Take me instead."

"Do not be a fool," Bannagran answered. "The boy is damaged and infirm."

"You should beg us to kill him when we are done removing his genitals," Bernivvigar said smugly. "He will have no need for his own virility, obviously. He should have been killed at birth—you know this to be true! So be satisfied that perhaps the little wretch will do some good with his miserable existence."

Bransen made a little mewling sound.

It was more than Garibond could take, and he wheeled around, fist flying, and connected squarely on the old Samhaist's jaw, sending him back hard against the doorjamb. As he started forward, Garibond heard Bransen cry out, and he turned about just in time to see Bannagran wading in.

The big man hit Garibond with a thunderous jab that straightened him and dazed him so that he could not even react to the wide-arcing left hook that caught him on the side of the face and sent him flying away to the floor.

Again he heard a voice, Bernivvigar's voice, as if it were far, far away, much like what he had heard before he had fully awakened that morning.

"Perhaps the older man would be better," Bernivvigar was saying. "How old is this boy?"

"Nine? Ten?" Bannagran answered.

"Not yet a man."

"Does that matter?" asked Prydae.

"It would be better if he had already reached manhood and was able to sire a child on his own," said Bernivvigar.

Garibond managed to turn to regard the Samhaist, standing in the doorway, leaning on the jamb, rubbing his jaw, and shooting Garibond the most hateful look Prydae had ever seen in all his life.

"Accept his offer and spare the boy," Bernivvigar advised.

A moment later, Bannagran's strong hand hoisted Garibond up to his feet, and the warrior began dragging him out. He managed to look back to the side, where poor Bransen was still trying to stand up after being shoved aside by Bannagran.

"Do not think your crippled son has fully escaped me," Bernivvigar muttered to Garibond as Bannagran hauled him past.

Poor Bransen spent all the day at the eastern window of the small house. He was still there when the sun disappeared behind the western horizon.

What will I do? How will I eat?

He wanted to rush out and run to the town to rescue Garibond—all the day, that had been his most pressing thought. But he couldn't rush and he couldn't run. He couldn't do anything. He couldn't even light a candle so that he didn't have to sit there helplessly in the darkness.

He wanted to stay awake, to stay alert, to be ready to do . . . whatever he could possibly do to help his beloved father. But eventually, Bransen's head dipped down to the windowsill.

His sleep was fitful, and he heard the approach of horses. He looked up, but they were already to the side of the window's view, splashing up the submerged walk to the front door of the cottage.

Bransen turned and tried to rise, but fell back repeatedly and was still sitting when the horses thundered away and the cottage door was pushed open.

In came Garibond, and he held up his hand to keep Bransen back. "Go to bed, boy," he said, and Bransen could tell that his every word was filled with agony.

Bransen started for his bed, while Garibond moved to the table and struck flint to metal to light a candle. Only then did Bransen see how bent over and haggard Garibond seemed; and when the man turned, candle in hand, Bransen nearly swooned, for the front of Garibond's nightshirt was drenched with blood, waist to knees.

"It is all right," the older man said. "You just go to bed."

Bransen fell onto his bed and immediately buried his face. He wanted all the world to just go away.

CHAPTER 21

For the Boy?

The rain splashed down all about him, spraying on the rocks and making the lake hiss in frothy protest. The drenching didn't bother Garibond but only because he couldn't remember a time over the last few weeks when he had felt anything but miserable. His wound had healed, or at least had scabbed over, but that was just on the outside. Bernivvigar's brutal work had left him sick inside as well, and he felt as if the festering sore were worming its way deeper into his body every day. Every morning, Garibond found pulling himself out of bed a trial.

The near-constant rain of the last days had added to his misery and had made his daily chores more difficult. The lake was up several inches, so that Garibond and Bransen had to abandon the lower house for the time being; that or watch their feet rot away from wading through ankle-deep cold water.

Garibond sat there and coughed through the morning's fishing. He didn't catch a thing, and knew that he wouldn't. The area of the lake near the island was not deep, a few feet at the most, and was not reedy; and the silver trout that normally could be hooked from the rocks of the small island wouldn't be milling about the shallows in this heavy downpour. Garibond stayed out there anyway, coughing and miserable, mostly because he couldn't find the strength in him to climb back to the house.

He knew that his situation was growing more dire. He knew that his health was fast deteriorating and, even with his stubbornness, he was beginning to recognize that he would not get through this ordeal on his own. He thought of going to Chapel Pryd to ask the monks for some magical healing. It wouldn't be easy to persuade them, and he knew it. His injury and illness were due to the order of Laird Prydae himself. Garibond wasn't a religious man in any sense of the word, and the distance he kept from the competing factions in Pryd Holding in many ways gave him a better understanding of each. Even from afar, Garibond understood the quiet war being waged between Bernivvigar and the brothers of Abelle. And the prize of victory, even more than the support of the peasants, was the sanction of Laird Prydae.

How could the brothers of Abelle help Garibond heal his current malady, given that?

Perhaps he should go instead to Castle Pryd, and beg the laird to ask the brothers for assistance.

The mere thought of it brought bile into the proud man's throat. Laird Prydae, as much as—or even more than—Bernivvigar had done this to him. Now was he to go and beg the man for mercy?

He slapped the wet rock next to him in frustration, and his hand was so cold and numb that he didn't even feel the sting. Was this numbness akin to Bransen's? he wondered.

That notion had him glancing back to the house, where Bransen was no doubt sitting on his bed with his nose deep in the Book of Jhest. That book had become Bransen's life of late, his tie to the past and . . .

"And what?" Garibond wondered aloud. Was Bransen finding solace within the pages of the Book of Jhest beyond anything he had ever expected of the boy? Certainly Bransen's apparent understanding of the text had been a surprise to Garibond, but what did the book—which Bransen claimed he had read cover to cover several times—now hold over him? Was he finding an escape within its pages from the misery of his tortured reality?

Garibond hoped that was the case. That was all he really wanted, after all. For himself, life had become a simple matter of survival, of getting through the days. His few joys were all tied up in Bransen's too-infrequent smiles. Garibond wanted nothing more, except for some relief from his pain. He didn't covet jewels or coins, and preferred to catch his own food over any banquet that Laird Prydae himself might set. He didn't want any companionship other than Bransen's.

As he considered these things, Garibond snorted and looked at the hissing water. Was there anything life could now offer him, to make him desire life? Responsibility for Bransen alone was keeping him going, he knew. And now, given his declining health, that, too, was beginning to worry him. What in the world would Bransen do once Garibond was gone? He couldn't fend for himself, and he had no real friends other than Garibond himself. At that moment, a crow flew past Garibond. He gritted his few remaining teeth, blinked his one good eye, and watched the black bird disappear into the film of heavy rain. A crow—a spy for Bernivvigar perhaps?

"Bah, you're just being an old fool," Garibond told himself, but he knew that he had reason to be suspicious. Bernivvigar's threat concerning Bransen had not been an idle one, Garibond understood, for Bernivvigar was not a man to make an idle threat. In the weeks since his ordeal under the Samhaist's knife, Garibond had seen Bernivvigar around the lake, often watching his house from afar, and he knew that the old wretch had never given up his desire to sacrifice Bransen.

He thought again of Callen Duwornay, or rather Ada, and her daughter who had befriended Bransen. Many times over the last few days had Garibond considered seeking her out and asking her to take in Bransen. But on every occasion, and now again, Garibond quickly dismissed the idea. How could he force this burden upon another, even one who owed her life to Bransen's parents? And how could Callen defend the boy if Bernivvigar came for him? Indeed, how could she defend herself, if the callous old Samhaist wretch discovered her true identity and that she had somehow escaped his punishment?

"Ah, what am I to do with you, then?" Garibond asked into the rain.

Some hours later, Garibond dragged himself back into the house, where he found Bransen sitting and reading, so engrossed that he didn't seem to hear Garibond enter.

"You like the book, don't you?" Garibond greeted, his typical refrain.

Shaking with every movement, Bransen turned his head and managed a half smile.

Garibond started to laugh, but caught himself short, feeling the crackling in his lungs. A wave of dizziness washed over him, but he caught himself on a nearby chair and managed to hide his weakness.

What was he to do?

"I know a place that has many more books you might enjoy," he said suddenly, hardly thinking of the implications.

Again Bransen turned, this time looking more confused than pleased or excited.

"Them monks in the chapel have shelves and shelves of books," Garibond explained. It had to be the monks, he knew, and it had to be soon—certainly before the next winter. "You would like that, yes?"

"J . . . Jh . . . J-J-J-Jhes . . . sst," Bransen stammered.

"Jhest? Yes, the Book of Jhest, penned by your father. But there are other books. So many more. Books of wisdom and history. You would like that, yes?"

Bransen nodded, but didn't seem overexcited about the prospect and turned right back to the Book of Jhest.

His reaction didn't matter. Garibond thought through all the options before him, and the only course possible seemed clear enough. He had to convince Father Jerak to take in Bransen and to care for him. That wasn't going to be easy. Certainly not. To Garibond's understanding, the monks of Abelle were not nearly as generous as they pretended.

Perhaps he could offer the monks something so they would take in Bransen. Perhaps that very book now open on the bed. Garibond quickly dismissed that notion, remembering the reaction of the Church to the book ten years before! Besides, how could he explain its existence, given that SenWi had made it appear as if the book had been burned?

Another thought came to him, an image of a marvelous sword wrapped in cloth in a dry place in his tunnels. Perhaps he could offer them the sword—a weapon unrivaled in all Honce. Yes, the monks could trade the sword to Prydae. Surely they would greatly appreciate its workmanship and the power it might offer to them in their battle for the affections of the young laird.

That was it, then, Garibond decided. The monks were his only option.

And it had to be soon, the crackling in his chest reminded him. For Bransen's sake. What would the young man even begin to do if Garibond dropped dead on the floor one morning?

He did hope that the monks would treat Bransen well, and that they would teach the boy to read the language of Honce and give him access to their books. Yes, he would have to make that a part of the bargain. Little in life other than reading offered pleasure to poor Bransen.

O n the first break in the weather, a couple of days later, Garibond set out from his house, leaving Bransen, as usual, with his face buried in the Book of Jhest. The boy's single-mindedness toward that book continued to amaze the man.

Garibond walked a wide and careful circuit of his house before heading to the road to Pryd Town, for he wanted to make certain that Bernivvigar was not lurking about. What defense might Bransen offer if the old wretch came calling?

Once on the road, with no sign of the Samhaist anywhere, Garibond remained uneasy and reminded himself with every fast stride to be quick about his business. To his relief, he found that he did not have far to walk, for a monk from Chapel Pryd was out and about, standing before one of the town's outermost houses.

Garibond recognized the man, though he didn't remember his name.

"My greetings, Brother," he said, moving up the short path toward the monk, who seemed to be just leaving the farmhouse.

"And to you," the monk replied. "I have no time to hear your woes, I fear, but must be straightaway back to Chapel Pryd."

"I know you," Garibond said in leading tones.

The monk paused long enough to look over the man carefully.

"I am afraid that your recognition is one-sided, friend."

Garibond tried hard to place the man, and finally, as the monk started away once more, just blurted out, "I was a friend of Brother Bran Dynard's."

Again the monk stopped and studied Garibond, his gaze soon dropping to the man's waist area, which told Garibond that he had been recognized. "You are the one the Samhaist took for Laird Pryd," he said.

"Aye, and that's a reputation to put forth, is it not?" Garibond said with a helpless laugh.

"I am sorry, friend, that you fell victim to the brutish old man," the monk said. "But there is nothing I can do to alleviate—"

"I'm not here about that, Brother . . ."

"Reandu. Brother Reandu."

"Ah, yes, I remember our meeting after my friend Brother Dynard left for the north. Has there been any word at all?"

"Brother Dynard is believed to have been murdered on the road," said Reandu. "That, or he rejoined the Behrenese woman and fled the land of Honce, as many brothers believe."

"He did not, for she did not survive." Garibond saw that he suddenly had Reandu's complete attention.

"What do you know of it?"

"I know that she is dead. Long dead, to the loss of the world."

"And yet you ask me of Brother Dynard?"

"Of him, I know nothing, beyond that he departed from your chapel ten years ago."

"Nor do any of us, Master . . ."

"Garibond."

"Master Garibond. I feel for your loss, for your friend and for . . . well, your ill treatment by Bernivvigar."

Garibond nodded.

"I need the help of the Church," Garibond stated. "Not for me and my ailments—those I accept well enough. But for my son."

Reandu looked at him curiously.

"You know of him, no doubt," said Garibond. "He is . . . unique and difficult to miss."

"The damaged one? The one they call Stork?"

Garibond winced at the disparaging name, but let go his anger for the sake of Bransen. "Yes, for him."

"If we believed that there was ever anything our soul stones might do for one so damaged, we would have undertaken the task years ago, Brother."

"You cannot heal his maladies, of course."

"Then what?"

Garibond gave a profound sigh, and was surprised at how painful this was. He had not considered how lonely his life might be, how much less fulfilled and fulfilling, without Bransen in it. "He is a lot of work, of course, and I am growing old—and more frail because of the Samhaist beast. I fear that I will soon not be able to care for Bransen."

Reandu's wide eyes betrayed his shock. "You would ask us to take him in?"

"I would. He needs protecting."

"We have not the means, brother. We are not a house for wayward—"

"Not wayward," Garibond corrected. "I do not ask you lightly to take this burden."

"You should ask a friend."

"I cannot, for I fear for the boy. Bernivvigar got me, aye, but that did little to satisfy his blood thirst. He wants the boy."

"Speak to Laird Prydae."

Garibond knew that he didn't even need to respond to that ridiculous suggestion. They both understood that Prydae wouldn't do much to go against Bernivvigar, not at present, at least. "I do not ask lightly you to take this burden," he repeated and then added, "nor without offering you gain for your Church."

Brother Reandu started to respond, but stopped short and looked curiously at him. "Gain for the church of Blessed Abelle? You are not a man of wealth or influence, good master Garibond."

"Rightly noted," he said dryly. "But I am in possession of an item that would prove quite valuable to you in your dealings with Laird Prydae."

He paused for effect. Reandu licked his lips and bade him, "Go on."

"Do you remember Brother Dynard's wife, the Behr woman named SenWi?"

"Yes."

"A mighty warrior, so it was said?"

"Her exploits against the powries were spoken of, yes."

"With an amazing sword, a sword more grand than anything in all the land of Honce?"

Reandu stared at him hard but did not respond.

"I assure you that if you heard any tales of that magnificent weapon, they were not exaggerated. Indeed, if anything, the people who saw the blade could not begin to understand its beauty and craftsmanship. It is a sword fit for a laird—indeed, it is beyond any weapon that any laird in all Honce now carries, or has ever carried."

"That is quite a claim."

"One I can back up, on your agreement to take Bransen into your chapel and care for him."

Reandu considered the words for a moment, then said, "I am not authorized to make such an arrangement."

"Of course, but you are capable of relaying my proposition to Father Jerak in the strongest possible terms."

"You would wish us to care for the boy until his death? For decades, likely?"

"Yes, but he is not without use. He can work for his meals, as long as the tasks are within his physical limitations. Oh, yes, and there is one more thing.

I want you to teach him to read our language and to allow him access to books."

"The idiot?"

"He is no idiot," Garibond snapped back. "Do not confuse physical deformity with mental weakness—it was a mistake that I long made. He can read, I am certain. It is a skill that will allow him to transcend the limitations of his flesh."

Reandu kept shaking his head, his expression sour, but he did reply, "I will take this matter to Father Jerak and Brother Bathelais."

Garibond could ask for nothing more. He nodded and rushed away, hoping that Bernivvigar had not learned in the meantime that Bransen was all alone.

He has her sword," Brother Bathelais mused aloud. He stared out the window of Father Jerak's audience chamber, overlooking the windy courtyard inside the chapel's outer front wall. Bathelais remembered Dynard out there sweeping the leaves. He remembered SenWi, a wisp of a thing, really, and quite beautiful in her exotic southern way. He had never seen this supposed sword, but he had met a few who had, and their description of it was nothing short of incredible.

"We are to take in this creature and care for him?" Father Jerak asked doubtfully. "Are we to throw wide our doors to all with maladies, then?"

"This is an exceptional matter, and an exceptional malady, perhaps," said Reandu. "And Garibond has assured me that the boy can do menial tasks and needs little care."

Father Jerak snorted.

"Perhaps this is an opportunity to display compassion," Reandu said.

"Have you not heard the chanting of the Samhaists at night?" Brother Bathelais interjected. "Do you not see Rennarq ever at Laird Prydae's side? What venom might he be whispering into Prydae's ear? This is the time for strength, Brother, not compassion."

"Less than a century ago, a wise man proclaimed compassion to be strength, I believe," Reandu replied. He knew from Bathelais's immediate scowl that perhaps he had crossed a line in invoking the words of Blessed Abelle.

"It might well be compassion that costs us nothing," Father Jerak remarked. "This sword—you have seen it?"

"No, Father."

"Then go to this peasant Garibond—both of you. Bid him to show it to you, and if you judge this sword as valuable as we believe, agree to his terms. I know this young Prydae, and if we are in possession of a weapon that will elevate his warrior status, it will prove a marvelous incentive to help us move the Sam-haists from his side."

"This boy, this creature, slobbers," Bathelais reminded.

"And we have duties appropriate for one of his idiocy," said Jerak.

At that point, Brother Bathelais sighed, looked at Reandu, and said, "Let us go, then. I pray the sword will be naught but a line of rust, but we shall see."

Garibond held the package up before him and slowly unwrapped the cloth holding the fabulous sword of SenWi. And as he pulled the layers of cloth from the weapon, he saw the layers of doubt melt away from Brother Bathe-lais's face. The silverel steel gleamed in the sunlight and the snake-head hilt sparkled. Not a speck of rust marred the blade, not a sign of wear or age. It was as SenWi had crafted it, and as she had left it.

"It has no equal north of the mountains," Garibond said with great confidence. "Not in all of Honce."

"It seems thin," Bathelais said.

"Because the metal is stronger than bronze and stronger than iron," Gari-bond explained. He drew forth the sword completely from the wrapping and waved it, then nodded to the two monks and snapped it suddenly to the side, where it cut deep into the trunk of a tree. He extracted the sword, pulled it back, then stabbed the tree, and the fine tip dove in to an impressive depth.

Again Garibond pulled the sword out, and he rolled it over in his hands and presented it hilt first to Bathelais.

The monk took the extraordinary weapon and moved it around slowly, marveling at its light weight and balance.

When both Bathelais and Garibond looked at Reandu, they saw that he was smiling, and that drew a nod from the ever-doubting Bathelais.

"Do we have an agreement?" Garibond asked, taking back the weapon. "You take Bransen in and you keep him safe from Bernivvigar. He'll work for you, and without complaint. You give him a chance."

"There is nothing we can do for the . . . boy with our gemstones," Bathe-lais said. "We will not waste the time and energy in trying."

Garibond suppressed his anger and managed a nod. He handed the sword to Bathelais and went to the house, emerging a few moments later with Bran-sen, who was carrying a large sack, beside him.

"The Stork," Bathelais whispered to Reandu.

Brother Reandu didn't respond and didn't let Bathelais see his disdain at the remark. In truth, Reandu was hardly certain from whence that disdain had come or why the name, which he himself had often used, struck him as so unseemly coming from Bathelais. He watched Bransen's awkward but determined approach. The boy was afraid, he could plainly see, but he also appeared eager to please. Perhaps behind the ungainly hip-swerving, stiff-legged strides and behind the smears of drool on his crooked face there was something else.

A boy, perhaps?

Just a boy?

CHAPTER 22

I Will Not Fail Garibond

Garibond said this is important. He needs me to work here, so the brothers will heal him and feed him. I will not fail Garibond. Bransen let this litany repeat over and over in his head, leading him through his dreary days at Chapel Pryd. He had come there full of hope and excited at the prospect of having so many people around him who, Garibond had assured him, would not push him to the ground or laugh at him.

They hadn't done anything like that, and that was good. Unfortunately, they also weren't really *around* him at all. He had been given a room in the substructure of the chapel, a windowless, empty little square of stone and dirt. There was only one way in or out, a ladder and trapdoor that Bransen couldn't hope to operate on his own. Thus, every morning, one of the younger brothers came and opened the door, then reached in and lifted him out so that he could go about his chores, which amounted to carrying the chamber pots down to the river for emptying and cleaning, two at a time. It took him most of the day, and at the end of his journeys, another brother set him back in his hole, along with a single candle, a flagon of water, and a plate of food.

That was Bransen's day, his life, his solitude. *I will not fail Garibond*, got him through it.

He knew that his work here was making life better for his father, for the man who had given so much to help him.

I will not fail Garibond.

Bransen brought his mother's black outfit with him and used it as a pillow. The soft silk smelled of her, he decided, and that gave him comfort. And it was comfort he needed, despite his resolve that he wouldn't fail Garibond, because as much as he missed the company of his father, he missed the company of his real father's work and of his mother's philosophy. He didn't have the Book of Jhest; he didn't have any books. He often tried to broach the subject with one of the brothers or another, but these men had no patience for his stuttering and never let him get the request out. In fact, they never really listened to anything he tried to say.

Every night as he lay there, every day as he made his uneven and awkward forays to the river, Bransen thought of that wonderful book and pictured its many pages. In his mind, he saw again the flowing script so meticulously copied by his father. In his mind, he recited the text, beginning to end, over and over again. He feared that he didn't have it perfect, but in the end, this was all he had.

As the days became weeks and the recital more rote, Bransen began to do something that had never before occurred to him. He began to roll the words in his thoughts and apply them to himself. He considered the source of Jhesta Tu power in the context of his own broken body, and searched for his *chi*. And he thought that he found that line of power, or what was supposed to be a line of power, for in him there were just inner flashes of energy, dispersing to his sides and his limbs, and no discernable and focusing line at all.

He thought that he must be doing something wrong in his inner search. Perhaps he was recalling the words of the book incorrectly. If only he could see it again, to compare his memory to its pages.

Several times, Bransen considered walking, along the riverbank to the little bridge that would lead him east to Garibond's house.

But suppose he angered the monks and they refused to help Garibond? Did he dare do such a thing?

If only they would listen to him long enough so that he could explain!

From a narrow window along the back wall of Chapel Pryd, Brother Reandu watched the boy stumble out through the mud, a pot sloshing and splashing at the end of each skinny arm. Strangely, those balancing chamber pots seemed to steady the Stork somewhat, though there remained nothing smooth about his movements and more than a bit of the contents of the pots wound up on his bare legs and woolen knee-length tunic.

Reandu sighed and wished that it could be different for this poor creature. He wished that he could gather up a soul stone and give the boy a more normal existence. That task was far beyond him, he knew. Far beyond any of them.

"But I will see to it that you are cleaned at least," the monk whispered, his words lost in the groan of the wind rushing through the narrow rectangular opening in the stone. He made a silent vow that he would begin assigning various brothers to take the last trip of the day to the river with Bransen, that they could scrub him clean before putting him back in his miserable little room.

He would have to get permission from Brother Bathelais, of course.

Brother Reandu gave a helpless laugh at that thought. Bathelais wasn't open to much of anything concerning the Stork. Keep him as far from the others as possible, give him enough to eat and drink, and make sure he doesn't freeze in his stone room at night. That was enough, by Brother Bathelais's interpretation, despite the fact that he, at the behest of Father Jerak, was preparing a grand celebration during which he would present the magnificent sword to Laird Prydae. Bathelais expected a large return for that gift—the brothers at Chapel Pryd who were knowledgeable about metals and weapons had told him that the sword was everything Garibond had claimed it to be and more.

But that optimistic outlook had done little to take the edge off Brother Bathelais concerning this poor, tortured creature.

With that in mind, and determined to at least help the boy wash the excrement from his legs, Brother Reandu went out from the chapel and quickly caught up with Bransen. The boy turned bright eyes upon him—and stumbled and nearly fell. In steadying him, Reandu got splashed by one of the chamber pots. He forced himself to hold back his automatic, angry response, reminding himself that it wasn't the poor boy's fault.

"Is this your last journey to the river this day?" he asked.

Bransen looked at him, as if in surprise. Of course he was surprised, Reandu realized. Had anyone asked him a question in all the days he had been at the chapel? Had anyone even spoken to him?

"Nnnnn-nyeah . . . nyeah, n . . . yes," the boy stammered.

Reandu had to take a deep breath to compose himself, the aggravating speech only reminding him all too clearly of why others like Bathelais simply could not tolerate being anywhere around this smelly one.

"Yes?"

The boy started to stammer.

"Just nod," Reandu prompted, and the boy did, and he managed a crooked smile.

Brother Reandu smiled as well.

"Uh . . . uh . . . I w-w-wa . . ." the boy stuttered.

Reandu shook his head and patted the air to try to calm the blabbering creature. Bransen responded and seemed to be trying to compose himself.

"B-book," he blurted suddenly.

"Book? What book?"

"Re-re-read b-b-boo-k."

"Read a book? You?"

The boy managed another smile and nod—or at least, something that approximated both.

"You want me to give you a book to read?"

Still the smile.

Then Reandu understood, as he remembered what Garibond had demanded of him as part of the deal. "You want me to teach you to read?"

"I r-r-re . . . re . . . read."

Reandu grinned and nodded and glanced back at the chapel. "Well, that was part of the bargain, I suppose. I should speak with Brother . . ." He turned back on the boy and winked. "I will see what I can do."

Bransen actually laughed at that, and the sudden jerk of his mirth overbalanced him and he fell to the mud. Reandu rushed over and picked him up.

"I cannot," Reandu started. "Do not expect . . . I must speak with Brother Bathelais. It is not my decision and I do not want to cause your hopes to soar."

Bransen was giggling with glee.

"You understand that?" Reandu asked, holding him steady and looking him right in the eye. "It is not my decision to make."

The boy stared at him—so stupidly, it seemed—and Brother Reandu thought himself a fool for even beginning to entertain such a thought as trying to teach this poor creature to read!

"Come along," he said. "The hour grows late and the river is still some distance." He hoisted one of the pots and helped Bransen gather up the other one, then took the boy under his arm and helped him to the river to complete his chores and so that both of them could get a much-needed washing.

B ransen was surprised, even frightened, when his overhead door opened unexpectedly late that night. A smile widened on the startled boy's face when he saw the face of Brother Reandu behind the glare of the candle.

"B-b-boo—" he started to say.

"No books, Bransen," Reandu replied.

The tone in the man's voice spoke volumes beyond the actual words to Bransen, a boy not unused to disappointment.

"Brother Bathelais will not be persuaded on this," Reandu admitted, and as Bransen's expression became crestfallen, he added, "You must understand, my boy, that our books are our greatest treasures. If you were to drool on them or dirty them—"

"No!" Bransen blurted.

"Even handling them causes damage," Reandu went on. "Please understand that it is not possible. Perhaps I can find some parchments on which a brother has spilled ink or otherwise damaged them. They might have words upon them. But you cannot read, of course."

Bransen started to stutter and pointed at the monk.

"Yes, Garibond wanted me to teach you to read," Reandu admitted. "But it would not be possible. I am sorry, boy. I wish that things could be different for you."

Bransen saw the true regret in Reandu's eyes, but that did little to fill the empty hole that had been dug in his heart. No books? Nothing at all but the dozens of walks to the river each day?

I will not fail Garibond, he repeated over and over and over as the trapdoor closed, leaving him with only the dim light of a single candle. Sobs and tears accompanied the litany.

He cried for many minutes, and only gradually managed to translate his heartbreak into anger. He picked up one of the many loose stones at the base of the wall and tried to throw it, but it slipped out of his hand and fell to the ground at his feet. He picked it up again, and again failed to propel it any distance. A third time he cocked his arm back to throw.

Symbols and curving script appeared in his thoughts, as if floating in the air before him. He held his pose and read the words, the words his father had meticulously copied, the words of *chi* and alignment, of the movement of muscles.

For one brief moment, it all came together for Bransen. For one beautiful and miraculous instant, one flicker of clarity in a decade of fuzziness, his core energy aligned and with a movement that could only be described as graceful, he threw the rock across the room to smack hard against the opposite wall.

Bransen stood in shock, staring into the darkness of the far end of the chamber. His legs quickly became shaky again as his line of life energy dissipated. But his mind held that moment of clarity.

Bransen shifted back to the wall and fell to his knees, then into an awkward half-sitting half-kneeling position. He lifted another stone and brought it against the wall and scratched out a shaky line.

No, that would not do, he realized as he studied the scratch.

Bransen concentrated more deeply. He remembered the writing in the book, the opening sequences. He could see them clearly in his mind, and his hand followed that guidance as he scratched out another line. He sat back and inspected his work. It was better than the first but still far from perfect.

The third line was a bit better.

The fourth line was better yet.

The hundredth line was almost perfect.

But the candle was gone soon after that, and Bransen allowed exhaustion to overtake him, there at the base of the wall on the cold, hard floor.

When he finished his chores the next day and was put back in his hole with another candle, he went right back to his real work.

And so it went, day after day, week after week.

Brother Reandu tried to convince himself that his inattention to Stork was merely a matter of his being too busy with his many duties. With several of the older brothers called away on missions or to Chapel Abelle, he was now the third highest ranking monk in Pryd, behind Father Jerak and Brother Bathelais.

His justifications held his conscience in check until one blustery, cold autumn night, the coldest by far since Stork had come to stay with them. Late
that night, Reandu checked on the window hangings along the lower chambers of the chapel, making sure they were secured against the wind, while
other brothers brought in wood to keep the hearth fires burning.

As he passed along the northeast corner of the building Reandu unconsciously glanced at the trapdoor leading to the substructure and to Stork's room.

How cold was it down there on a night such as this?

Brother Reandu took a torch from one of the nearby wall brackets and
moved to the trapdoor, pulling it open gently and as quietly as he could so that
he did not disturb the boy's sleep. He lay flat on the floor and poked his head
through the opening, and was relieved to find that the room, though a little
chilly, wasn't really uncomfortable and certainly wasn't dangerously cold. Hearing the boy's sleeping wheeze, Reandu brought the torch closer to the opening.

There lay Stork on his small cot, sleeping contentedly. The image warmed
Brother Reandu's heart. Perhaps in sleep, at least, the tortured boy knew some
peace.

He brought the torch back and began pulling himself up, but as he did the
torch moved. Brother Reandu froze in place, his attention grabbed by the
scratches, a hundred scratches, a thousand scratches, ten thousand scratches
on the wall!

The monk blinked many times as the writing—it had to be writing!—
became more clear, as the staggering scope of it began to be apparent. Now too
curious to consider the boy's slumber, Brother Reandu climbed down into the
underground chamber. He moved to the end of the wall nearest the boy's cot
and found what had to be the beginning of this work: a large scratch, a squiggle,
and nothing that made any sense to Reandu. Brother Reandu was no expert
on linguistics; in fact, he had been among the worst of the scribes during his
work at Chapel Abelle, but he instantly recognized patterns here, with words
repeated.

"Amazing," Reandu said, and he was quite amused. Had Bransen, in his
frustration, written his own book? Had he concocted a series of squiggles, a
gibberish all his own?

Reandu's smile disappeared and he turned to consider the sleeping boy.
Then he looked back at the wall, then back at the boy.

Then back at the wall again.

Even the first letter of the work was larger than all the others, a definitive
beginning point. How had Stork possibly known to do that?

Shaking his head, Reandu slipped out of the room and went right to the
door of Brother Bathelais.

He knew at once, as soon as Bathelais had squeezed into the cramped chamber beside him, that the older brother wasn't nearly as delighted. Bathelais stood there, staring at the markings, squinting and chewing his lip. He motioned for Reandu to follow, and they went back out of the hole.

"We will return in the morning, when we can study this without fear of disturbing the boy," Bathelais said.

"We should ask him about it."

"In time. I have little patience for listening to Stork stutter through some incomprehensible and ridiculous response."

Even though sympathetic Reandu always thought of Bransen as "Stork," hearing the name spoken by Brother Bathelais made him wince.

After more than an hour in the hole the next day, Bathelais's mood seemed to sour even more. He had brought with him some paper and charcoal and had done a rubbing of the work.

Reandu kept remarking that perhaps this was a miracle, but Bathelais just brushed him off over and over, muttering, "The boy has obviously seen a book."

"But to do such intricate work reveals an intelligence—"

"There are birds in Behr that can mimic human speech, brother. Should we kneel before them?"

Brother Reandu quickly realized that he would be better off remaining quiet as Brother Bathelais took over the investigation. He had little choice, in any event. He wasn't even invited to go along with Bathelais when he took the paper to Father Jerak later that day, and he only began to comprehend the level of Bathelais's disdain when the brother walked out of Father Jerak's room muttering, "Damnable Dynard, there were two."

Garibond was feeling particularly uncomfortable this day. He sat on the rocks beside the lower cottage, absently casting his line. He thought about Bransen; he was always thinking about Bransen, and he could hardly believe how lonely and empty his days had become since the boy had gone off with the monks.

But it was for Bransen's own good, he had to continually remind himself. That, or he would simply sit and cry.

He heard the horses, but was so entangled in his thoughts of his lost boy that the sound didn't register for several moments. When he finally glanced to the side, the riders—three monks and a pair of soldiers—were almost to the stones leading to his front door.

Garibond hurried to set his pole down and meet them. He recognized two of the monks and one large soldier that he knew to be Bannagran, the close friend of Laird Prydae. His presence more than anything warned Garibond that something was amiss, and he immediately thought of the Samhaists. Had they gotten to Bransen?

"Greetings to you, Brother Bathelais," he said, trying to keep the fear out of his voice.

"Where is it?"

"It?"

"Apparently, Brother Dynard kept another secret, did he not?" Brother Bathelais said.

Garibond rocked back on his heels, his mind spinning.

"You would be wise to speak openly and truthfully," Bathelais added. "For your sake and the sake of the boy."

"He is Bran Dynard's son," Garibond blurted, and he was surprised at the shock that came over Bathelais, as if he had caught the man completely off guard with the admission he believed the man to be anticipating.

"Bran Dynard," Brother Reandu said. "And SenWi." With both names, he emphasized the first syllables. "Bran and Sen," he clarified to those astride the horses about him.

"Bransen," said the third monk, whom Garibond did not know.

"When was the boy born?" Bathelais demanded. "Soon after Dynard departed?"

"Or soon before," Garibond admitted.

"And so the mother was here, all the while," reasoned the monk. "When all the holding was searching for the outlaw SenWi, she was kept safe through her pregnancy in the home of Garibond Womak." As he spoke, Bathelais looked at the soldiers, particularly at Bannagran, whose lips went very tight and whose dark eyes bored holes in old Garibond.

"She was no outlaw," Garibond managed to whisper, and his voice grew even weaker as all the riders began to dismount.

"Save yourself more trouble, and more for the boy, do not doubt," Brother Bathelais said to him. "Tell us where it is."

"SenWi is dead."

"Not the creature of Behr. The heretical book that Brother Dynard scribed. We know that there were two."

Garibond shook his head. "Two? No, there was only the one."

"Destroyed in the hearth in Father Jerak's room?" asked Bathelais.

"So I have heard."

Bathelais's smile became that of a predator that had finally cornered its meal. "And pray tell me how you heard of such a thing?" he asked. "Certainly few even in Chapel Pryd knew of the destruction, for few even knew of the work. How could Garibond Womak, who lives out here on the edge of the wilderness, know of such a thing as that?"

Garibond swallowed hard. "Word spreads quickly."

"Not that word!" Bathelais snapped. To the others, he said, "Tear out every stone of the walls if you must. I will have that book."

He looked back at Garibond, his scowl increasing. "Make it easy, master Womak. Your trouble has only just begun, and it will soon end, I assure you, but if you make it easy, then I will make your passing easy."

There it was. Bathelais had just branded him a heretic, and from that, there could be no appeal. He felt his knees go weak beneath him, but he stubbornly held himself up.

"For the sake of the boy, then?" Bathelais added.

The weakness was gone, replaced by a wall of anger. Garibond tried to respond with a barrage of insult and accusation, tried to scream out that this Church of Blessed Abelle was a sham under the leadership of Father Jerak, that Bran Dynard was the finest man he had ever known, and SenWi the finest woman, that all of the monks' pretense could not hide the awful truth.

He wanted to say all that, but all that came out was a wad of spit, aimed at Brother Bathelais's face.

The monk didn't flinch, and he slowly brought his arm up to wipe his face. He stared at Garibond hatefully all the while, and that was the last image he knew before a sudden burst of pain erupted on the side of his head and he fell away into blackness.

He awoke much later—he knew not how much time had passed—to the sound of voices and the crackle of wood. Immediately he was assaulted by a wave of smoke, stinging his eyes and throat.

And he felt the pain suddenly in his feet and shins. He squirmed and realized that he was lashed tightly, his hands behind his back and around a stake.

"I had hoped you would not awaken," came a sympathetic voice. Garibond managed to open his eyes enough to see Brother Reandu, with Brother Bathelais lurking right behind.

The waves of heat and smoke engulfed him. He heard himself screaming as the fires of Church justice curled the skin of his legs, as his woolen tunic ignited, and a million points of pain screamed out in protest.

He thrashed and he cried. And he choked and gagged, and couldn't find any air at all to draw into his burning lungs.

Just beyond the pyre, the soldiers, the monks, and a few curious neighbors watched the man pass from life.

"You could have made a grand spectacle and example of him," Bannagran said to Brother Bathelais.

"That is what Bernivvigar would do," Bathelais replied, and his voice was subdued and full of regret.

"It teaches proper respect."

"Respect?" Bathelais said, turning to regard the soldier. "This is an unpleasant necessity. This"—he held up the book the soldiers had found in a secret cubby in Garibond's tunnel complex—"is not an issue for public discourse." He looked down at the book for a long moment, then tossed it into the fire.

"This all ends here," Bathelais instructed. "All of it. Garibond is gone and the pagan tome is finally destroyed. We will speak of it no more."

And he went to his horse, and the others followed.

And the neighbors were left to watch the flames roar against the late afternoon sky and to bury the husk of Garibond's body the next day.

PART THREE

God's Year 74

CHAPTER 23

Walking—Awkwardly—in Place

Bransen stood in the growing darkness outside Chapel Pryd. At just under five and a half feet he was smaller than most men, and since he could not stand straight, he seemed even shorter. His battered, bony frame barely topped a hundred and twenty pounds, making him closer in weight to the average woman than man. His hair hung long and black and his beard was scraggly, unkempt whiskers dotting his chin and cheeks, along with splotches of angry-looking hives. The unique and purplish birthmark on his right arm had not diminished, yet another mar on a body so full of imperfection.

His teeth were straight and white, his best feature, but they were rarely seen, for Bransen didn't smile often. Every day of every week led him on the same journey through Chapel Pryd to the river. Every night found him in his underground chamber, whose walls were smooth and unmarked—as the monks had moved him to another room and regularly inspected his walls.

Only three things sustained Bransen: his memories of the Book of Jhest, whose words he recited in his mind every day as he went about his chores; the conversations and lessons of the brothers in the room above him, particularly when they used the formal speech of ancient times as they read stories of legendary heroism and valiant deeds; and finally, the few scraps of mostly illegible parchments that Brother Reandu had generously obtained for him, pages ripped from old and decrepit tomes and errant works produced by tired brothers. Reandu hadn't been able to teach Bransen any more than the basics of this form of writing, but playing with those pages and trying to make sense of the words had greatly benefitted the curious young man, at least in relieving the boredom of his life.

It was the Book of Jhest, transcribed in his mind, that truly sustained him.

Especially at moments like this. These few minutes each day, after his last trip to the river, afforded Bransen the privacy and opportunity to further explore those words of wisdom implanted in his mind.

Very slowly, Bransen visualized his *chi*, starting at his forehead. He moved his internal eye down the line, collecting all the scattered flashes of life energy as he went. His lips stopped quivering, the drool held back. His head stopped lolling and settled in balance. His shoulders straightened and his arms stopped twitching and flailing. He couldn't see it, but the red splotches that so marred his face disappeared, although the birthmark on his right upper arm did not.

He took a deep and calming breath as his inner eye moved down the line between his lungs and to his belly.

Bransen stood perfectly straight.

Bransen stood perfectly steady.

Slowly, he lifted his arms before him, then above his head. He brought them down to his sides as he rooted his feet into the ground. In that moment, Bransen, the boy they called Stork, was so strong, and he believed that he could hold his ground and footing even if Laird Prydae charged into him!

The young man took a few strides forward—not awkward and stiff-legged strides but real steps, powerful steps, balanced steps. "I am the son of SenWi and Bran Dynard," he said, and he did not stutter. "I am the child of Garibond, the boy he loves, the boy who loves him."

A wobble of Bransen's hip belied his calm posture. The moment of clarity was quickly passing, and a wave of exhaustion was following.

In another few moments, he was just Stork again, stuttering and gangly, drooling all over himself. But beneath that slimy and shiny covering and those crooked and twitching jaw muscles, Bransen was smiling.

Every day, he escaped the bonds of his infirmities. Only for a moment, perhaps, but that moment was more than he had ever dared to hope.

One day, he mused, he might tell Brother Reandu of his secret, and tell him in a voice strong and stable.

Perhaps that fantasy would take place, but Bransen remembered all too well the monks' reaction to his writing the Book of Jhest on his walls. He remembered the panic and the anger; and though he had not been punished, he saw the flash of hate and outrage in Bathelais's eyes, the implication and threat all too clear.

But he wanted to tell someone, and Reandu was probably his best friend. Or maybe he would get stronger, and maybe he would learn to sustain the power offered by his forcefully composed *chi* for longer periods—forever perhaps—and then he could go to Garibond and show him.

That was Bransen's deepest wish and hope: to return to his beloved Garibond, not as Stork but as a whole man. Wouldn't Garibond be proud of him! And if he could become whole, even if he were to continue working for the monks, he should be able to find enough time each week to go back and visit his beloved Garibond!

The young man picked up the empty chamber pots and staggered toward the chapel's back door, his simple dreams sustaining him through each labored step.

H as he spoken at all today?" There was no missing the contempt in Master Bathelais's tone, a simmering revulsion that seemed to be growing almost daily.

"No, master," replied Brother Reandu. "Father Jerak sits, staring into emptiness. It is almost as if he is looking at the past."

"He is, and seeing events as if they are only now unfolding. Last week, he demanded that I go to Laird Pryd to insist that he ease the burdens of those working on the road."

"The road?" Brother Reandu echoed, and then he grew even more startled as he added, "Laird Pryd?"

"It is an argument twenty years old," Master Bathelais explained.

"It is good that the masters at Chapel Abelle saw fit to convey the powers and title of master upon you, dear brother," said Reandu. "If we were at the discretion of Father Jerak now—"

"Father Jerak has no discretion," said Bathelais, and when Reandu started to balk at the bold statement, he held up his hand. "I say that with great sadness, brother. Long have I considered Father Jerak my friend—more than my friend. He has been as a father to me in more than Church ways."

Brother Reandu nodded. Father Jerak had ruled Chapel Pryd wisely and compassionately for many decades.

"You will need to formally announce your position as presiding father of Chapel Pryd very soon," Brother Reandu advised. "Our superiors offered you this at your discretion."

Bathelais rocked back on his heels. "You ask me to unseat my beloved friend."

"Will Chapel Pryd survive the weeks, months, even years we may have to wait for him to go and sit with Blessed Abelle? Master, Rennarq whispers in Laird Prydae's ear in favor of Bernivvigar even as the people shout the same, all the more loudly every day."

Bathelais's look turned icy.

"The Samhaists had more than a thousand people gathered at their bonfire last night." Bathelais winced at that.

"The people are angry," Reandu went on. "How many men are dying in the south? How little have they to eat, and less now that Laird Prydae has been forced to pay taxes to Laird Delaval."

"We are not responsible for the policies of Laird Prydae."

"But neither are we fulfilling our promises to the people of Pryd. We cannot heal their illnesses when so many of our resources are caught up in the greater issues of the holding. We cannot continue to tell them that our God is a benevolent God when their sons, husbands, and fathers die in the south. We cannot continue to tell them that our God is a bountiful God when their stomachs pinch with hunger."

"What would you have me do to alter the realities of our life in these dark days?"

"We are in need of a stronger voice in Chapel Pryd, with no confusion. Retire Father Jerak with all honor and respect, and speak out with a voice bold and full of conviction."

"And what will this voice say?" There was no missing the skepticism in Master Bathelais's tone.

"Speak out against the policies of Laird Prydae," Reandu pressed. "Against the conscription and the taxes. Against the suffering of the common folk. Bernivvigar embraces that suffering and says it will make the people more prepared for their ultimate fate. Are we any different from the Samhaists if we remain silently by the side of an oppressive laird?"

Bathelais's eyes flashed with anger for just a moment. "We are here at the sufferance of Laird Prydae," he reminded. "Prydae understands that if Laird Delaval is not successful in his campaign against Laird Ethelbert, then Ethelbert will annex Pryd Holding."

"And Laird Delaval will do the same if he wins," Reandu argued. "He already has, in everything but name."

"Name is an important factor to a man like Laird Prydae."

"Is that what all this is about, Master? The pride of one man? It is well known that Laird Prydae was ready to throw his sword to the side of Laird Ethelbert when he believed Ethelbert meant to place him in the line of succession of Ethelbert Holding. It is only because of Ethelbert's rejection, since the line will now end with the gelded Prydae, that our laird saw Delaval's offer as more tempting. And even that offer calls for the annexation of Pryd by Delaval upon the end of the line of Pryd!"

"You involve yourself too much in politics, Brother."

Reandu was a bit taken aback by the tone of warning clear and present in that statement. "The matters of politics are the only reality the people of our congregation know," he said.

"I do not recall Laird Prydae asking our opinion, Brother."

"Then what is our purpose?" Reandu blurted, but his bluster dissipated quickly under the threatening scowl of Master Bathelais. Reandu suddenly found his breath hard to come by, as so many implications of his continuing resistance flashed across Bathelais's eyes. Fear, frustration, and anger all rolled together within Reandu, gathering into a single, tangled ball that left him speechless.

"Go to your duties," Master Bathelais instructed. "If you truly wish to help me now, then help me find a way to positively distinguish us from the Sam-haists. I will take your words concerning Father Jerak under serious advise-ment, as I believe that you might be correct in your observation. Father Jerak cannot openly oppose Bernivvigar at this time. Father Jerak cannot properly clean himself at this time! But I warn you, and only this once, beware your words against Laird Prydae. I prefer a tentative hold on the people of Pryd to no hold at all, Brother, and your indignation is a sure way to the expulsion of the Church of Blessed Abelle from Pryd Holding."

Reandu continued to reel in unfocused anger and frustration, and could barely mouth out, "Yes, Master," as Bathelais walked away.

CHAPTER 24

The Laird's Manly Sword

Bannagran banged on the wooden door, his huge fist nearly dislodging it from its frame.

"You would be wise to open the door," he called. "You may need it when the battle comes north!" He hit the splintering wood again with a resounding thump that made the door lean into the hovel.

Finally, the door opened a crack, and the dirty face of an old woman appeared.

"If ye're coming for coins for yer laird, we got none left, master," she said.

"Not for coins," Bannagran replied. "And I trust that if you happened upon a few, you would know to deliver the proper amount to Castle Pryd."

"Then what? More food's what ye're wanting? Oh, but ain't we to keep enough to feed our own skinny bodies?"

"Not food," Bannagran replied. "A regiment of Laird Ethelbert has been sighted in the east. Men are needed."

The woman gave a cry and fell back, trying to close the door tight, but Bannagran's heavy fist knocked it open. He and the two soldiers accompanying him strode into the one-room hovel.

"Bah, ye took me husband and now who's knowing if he's dead? Ye took me brothers and not a one's to be found! What more are ye asking?"

"You have a son of fifteen winters," Bannagran replied.

"He's dead!" the woman shrieked. "I killed him meself. Better that than he get all chopped in some bloody field!"

As she spoke, Bannagran motioned to one of the soldiers, who moved to the hanging curtain that divided the room. A tug pulled it down, revealing a small cot, really no more than a wooden frame covered in hay.

The soldier looked back at Bannagran, who nodded for him to proceed.

"Dead, I tell ye!" the woman continued, her voice rising with obvious terror. "I put a pillow over his face while he slept. A peaceful way."

"If I believed your tale, then I would have you executed," Bannagran said matter-of-factly.

"For murder? He's me son, and I can kill him if I'm choosing."

"For stealing from Laird Prydae," the large man replied. "All the folk are the property of the laird, and you've no right to deny him his possessions. Whether he is your child is not important." He nodded and the soldier up-ended the cot, revealing a teenage boy and a younger girl, huddled together on the floor against the wall.

"Come on," the soldier said, and he reached down and hooked the boy under the arm and roughly pulled him to his feet.

The girl started crying; the woman rushed past to intercept.

But Bannagran caught her by the back of her tunic and easily held her in place. She tried to turn and swing at him, but he had her quickly wrapped in one powerful arm, and she couldn't begin to wriggle away.

"Ye can't have him!" she cried. "Ye can't be taking him! Oh, ye dogs!"

Bannagran squeezed her more tightly and hoisted her up so that his scowl-ing face was barely an inch from hers. "Foolish woman. If we do not go out and meet the threat of Ethelbert, his soldiers will knock down your door and knock down your house. They'll kill your boy when he hasn't even a weapon in hand to defend himself, and they'll take you . . ." He paused and offered a wicked smile. "Might be that you're too ugly to interest them, but that wouldn't be your gain. They'd take your daughter instead, every one of them would, and leave her torn and bleeding and broken. Perhaps she's old enough to bear a child—is that what you're wanting, old fool? Do you wish upon your daugh-ter a bastard child whose father you'll never know?"

The woman was crying so violently now that she couldn't answer. Nor did she offer any more resistance. Bannagran released her and shoved her back, then followed the two soldiers, who were flanking the subdued boy, out of the house.

"That makes twelve," one of the soldiers said when they were outside.

"Enough for this group, then," Bannagran explained. "Get him to the castle and fit him with leather armor and a weapon." He looked more closely at the boy, even reached over and felt the skinny biceps. "A spear for him. He couldn't hit anything hard enough with a sword to make a difference."

Bannagran quickly climbed onto his horse and turned the mount away, not wanting the others to see his continuing scowl. He found this duty dis-tasteful, and he was quite weary of pulling men—and now boys—from their families. He heard the woman's frantic shrieks and prodded his horse on more swiftly, wanting to put the noises far behind.

He rode away from the others and moved closer to Pryd Town, trying to ignore the haunted stares of the many people in the streets. Not a family had escaped the last six months of the war unscathed. Bannagran wondered if Pryd Holding would survive this wave of battle; an entire generation of menfolk could be wiped out if Laird Ethelbert persisted in his designs for conquest.

Already, more than three hundred of Pryd's menfolk were known dead—a hundred and fifty alone in the battle of Bariglen's Coe.

As he rode toward Castle Pryd, Bannagran thought back to those days of battle against the powries in the east, when Laird Ethelbert and his legions had held the flanking ground north of the men of Pryd. The laird of the great holding in southeastern Honce had rescued him, Prydae, and all the others when they had been caught in a powrie web. Even then, though, Bannagran had seen the first signs of coming trouble. The roads were complete, crossing Honce from Delaval City to Ethelbert dos Entel, through Pryd and Cannis and all the way to Palmaristown on the mouth of the great river, the Masur Delaval. With that network came the march of armies to push the powries back, and with that network came the march of armies to expand the influence of their respective lairds. Already, Palmaristown was under the rule of Laird Delaval, and all the Mantis Arm heeded the commands of Laird Ethelbert.

It was Pryd Holding's bad fortune to rest halfway between the two dominating lairds.

Castle Pryd's drawbridge was down over the newly constructed moat, and the great champion of Pryd, the most recognizable warrior in all the land, didn't slow as he thundered across the wooden bridge and between the gate towers—also newly built—and into the lower bailey of the rapidly expanding castle. He pulled up short and leaped down as attendants moved quickly to tend to his strong mount.

To his right sat the Laird Prydae's private chapel, with an open garden behind it for those occasions when Bernivvigar came into the castle proper to offer his prayers and blessings. This was the oldest building in the castle, dating back many generations, and was of a stone more gray than the main castle structure. The architecture of the chapel, too, was more primitive, with thicker walls and smaller windows. Past the chapel lay the only predominantly wooden building in the complex, the barracks, nearly empty now, as most of the men were off patrolling.

Directly ahead of Bannagran, opposite the main gate, sat the great keep, the tower of Laird Prydae, connected at its base to the castle's dining hall and audience chamber.

The two men standing guard at the keep's heavy wooden door moved quickly when they saw Bannagran's approach, pulling wide the double doors, then standing at attention, eyes ahead and unblinking, as their commander walked through.

The bottom floor of the keep, the only square room in the tower, was sparsely appointed, with only a pair of chairs set before the large hearth, a thick rug beneath them. Bannagran's eyes were drawn to that hearth and to the empty hooks above it. Not too long ago, Laird Prydae's magnificent sword, a gift of the brothers of Abelle, had hung there. But the laird had recently moved it to his private quarters, safely out of sight whenever any of the noblemen of Laird Delaval's court came calling. For when they came, they did so with their hands out, seeking money or goods, and Laird Prydae knew well that his sword, a creation far beyond anything any blacksmith in Honce could hope to forge, would be greatly desired.

That was the one treasure in all his holding that Laird Prydae would not surrender.

Bannagran was surprised that his friend wasn't down here taking his breakfast, as was Prydae's custom at this hour. The warrior moved for the stairs on the left side of the room but paused at the base when he heard a woman crying up above.

Somewhere behind her, Prydae cursed, "Harlot!" and then, "Rotfish!"

Bannagran put his head down and drew a deep breath. He knew the insults well enough, had heard Prydae launch them at women for a decade now. As ruler of Pryd, it was Prydae's privilege to take any woman in the holding, married or not, a tender child or an old hag, as his lover. "Lover" wasn't quite the right word with regard to Prydae, Bannagran supposed, for the scars of the laird's powrie wound would not permit it, despite the work of the monks with their soul stones, despite the many sacrifices of other men's genitals old Bernivvigar had offered over the years.

Inevitably, when he failed to perform, Prydae would blame the woman, calling her harlot and other similar insults, and "rotfish," a term usually reserved for a woman of no sexual imagination, who would lie still as a receptive, yet unmoving, vessel.

The woman, a pretty enough thing—as long as she hid her three-toothed smile—in her mid-twenties, came out on the top balcony and rushed to the highest of the four visible staircases, her clothing bundled about her, hardly hiding her ample charms. Her bare feet slapped on the wide wooden stairs as she scurried down to the next balcony, her face wet with tears.

Bannagran recognized her—he remembered the day he had taken her husband away to join a group marching south to battle.

She hardly glanced at him as she rushed past, sobbing at every step.

Bannagran watched her go, then looked back to the top stairs, where Prydae stood naked and half erect, his face red with frustration, his fists clenched in rage. "Rotfish!" he cried again, and he banged his hand hard against the wall, then moved back.

Bannagran shook his head and sighed, then moved to one of the chairs before the hearth and poured himself a drink of Prydae's wine. He took a seat and stared into the embers, some still showing lines of orange, wisps of smoke slipping out from the ash and drifting lazily up the chimney.

It was some time before Prydae came down to sit beside him.

"Useless bitch," the laird said, and he filled, drained, and refilled his wine goblet before offering more to Bannagran. "A sound other than a whimper, a movement beyond her drawing of breath—is that too much to ask?"

"You were close this time?" Bannagran asked.

Prydae set his goblet down on the arm of his large, upholstered wooden chair and rubbed both his hands over his still-red face. "Better if the powrie had taken it all," he said, "and taken, too, the desires that burn within me."

"You seek the treasure of a dragon," Bannagran remarked, "and have found its footsteps on several occasions. Is not the hunt worth your time, my liege?"

"I seek the honey of a woman," Prydae corrected. "And have seen the sweets before my eyes and within my reach, and yet I cannot grasp them! Is not the frustration more than any man should bear?"

Bannagran chuckled as he brought his goblet up to his lips and tasted the smooth red wine from the grapes of Laird Delaval's western fields. "The honey will be sweeter for your wait," he replied.

Prydae joined him with a chuckle of his own, but they both knew that this was much more serious than the frivolous pleasures of an overamorous laird. If Prydae could perform—and he had come so close on several occasions— and produce an heir to the line of Pryd, then the politics of all the regions would dramatically change, and for the betterment of Pryd Holding. The only reason Laird Ethelbert had not named Prydae as his successor and heir of all his holdings was because it had become apparent that the line would end with Prydae.

Conversely, that fact had brought Laird Delaval to Prydae's side; and the pact between Pryd Holding and the most powerful laird in all Honce was quite specific: when the line of Pryd ended, Delaval or his heirs would annex Pryd Holding, by contract and treaty.

A son to Laird Prydae could change the dynamics all across southern Honce, and positively on every account for Pryd Holding.

"How much less would be the frustration if the coals below weren't showing signs of fiery life," Bannagran said. He knew that he was, perhaps, the only man who could speak in such a manner to proud Prydae, for he alone knew the intimate details of Prydae's attempted liaisons.

"So close," the laird muttered, and he drained his wine, then moved to refill his goblet.

"Prince Yeslnik is fighting in the south," Bannagran remarked. "His banners have shone on the field—word has it that he is leading charge after charge."

"Your voice says that you do not think this likely."

"Prince Yeslnik is no warrior. Likely, his champions are riding forth in his stead, while he sits in the comfort of his carriage far behind. It would seem that outside of the small holdings, places like Pryd, the nobleman warrior is fast becoming a lost notion."

"Delaval was a great warrior, as was Ethelbert, who put his sword to the task only a decade ago, beside us in the east."

"Was, my laird," Bannagran replied, and he looked at Prydae doubtfully, for both of them knew the laird's last remark to be an exaggeration. In truth, Ethelbert's armor was rarely dirtied and never bloodied in all the months of their campaign. "Was," Bannagran repeated. "Among the lairds of Honce, I doubt that any could stand in battle more than a few moments before you."

"Ah, but in the bedroom . . ." Prydae replied with a mocking laugh, and he lifted his goblet in toast.

Bannagran didn't drink to that.

"Yeslnik will make a name for himself," Prydae said.

"Yeslnik's *champions* will make a name for him," Bannagran corrected.

"Can any less be said of Bannagran and Prydae?"

"Yes," the champion answered immediately and with complete sincerity. "The name of Bannagran is known—not once did Prydae claim the credit for the successes of Bannagran. Not once did Prydae need the achievements of champions to heighten his own claims to glory."

"You are kind, my friend." Prydae lifted his goblet to Bannagran for another toast, and this time, the warrior did lift his own. "There were occasions when I wore your powrie trophies as if they were my own."

"And more occasions when you wore trophies of your own victories."

"Perhaps it is nearing time for me to put the Behrenese sword to use," Prydae said. "Will we ride south, my friend? Two warriors, side by side, to help drive back the hordes of Laird Ethelbert?"

Bannagran paused and considered the words carefully, then slowly shook his head. "We will have all that we can handle should Ethelbert turn a portion of his force north and strike at us from the east. The work on Castle Pryd is not yet completed, and five thousand men would press us hard, even behind our walls. Laird Ethelbert has twice that to spare."

"True enough," Prydae admitted.

"You will find the opportunity to bloody the silver blade of your sword, I suspect and fear. Battles rage across the width and breadth of Honce." Bannagran needed yet another drink as he considered the truth of his words. All the land was in chaos. The roads had been built with the promise of greater trade and a greater ability to rid the land of the powries and the goblins. And at first, that promise had been realized, with the powries thinned to irrelevance and pushed to the sea, and the goblins all but eradicated throughout the land east of the Masur Delaval and south of the great Gulf of Corona.

But now the holdings were warring. Now Delaval and Ethelbert fought for dominance on a wide scale, while minor holdings battled over small pieces of valuable land. Even the powries had returned, or were beginning to, as reports of bloody cap murders seemed to increase daily throughout the land.

Bannagran drained his goblet. He didn't mind battle, didn't mind killing powries or slaughtering goblins.

But killing other men was something quite different, something that left him sour and empty.

CHAPTER 25

Straining the Quality of Mercy

It was a day like any other day. The same routines and chores, the same time for waking and eating and collecting the refuse from the previous night. A light rain fell through the humid early summer air, making the dirt clump about Bransen's sandaled feet as he staggered out from Chapel Pryd toward the river, a chamber pot in each hand.

He hardly felt the weight of the two buckets, though they were nearly full, for his grip had grown strong and sure. That much of his muscles, Bransen could control. As for the rest, he stumbled and had to realign himself continually after each awkward step, certainly living up to his nickname. It had been a rainy spring, and so Bransen was used to the muddy ground, and he was managing well enough, though with great concentration, his eyes set straight ahead, his every thought locked on his forward movement.

He didn't notice a figure move silently up beside him, or the foot that went out in front of him.

Bransen tripped and stumbled; the chamber pots at his side sloshed and splashed him. He caught himself and would not have gone down, but the foot kicked hard against the back of his locked knee, buckling it.

He heard the laughter as he crashed to the ground, the contents of the pots splashing over him, mixing with the mud on his face and sliding up his nostrils.

Bransen fumbled and finally managed to come up to one elbow and lift his head, spitting with each movement. Then he froze, seeing four legs—strong legs, the legs of young men—planted before him.

"Aye, Stork, you fell down hard that time," came a voice that Bransen knew, a taunting voice he had heard on many occasions for more than ten years: that of Tarkus Breen, who had been away at the war, so Bransen had thought. Now he was back, apparently. As Tarkus finished, he stamped his foot down hard, spraying Bransen's face with muddy water.

"Take care, Tarkus," said his companion—Hegemon Noylan, Bransen knew. "You'll bury Stork where he lies and only make it all stink worse."

"Bah, all right, then," Tarkus conceded. "I'll pick him up." The strong young warrior reached down, grabbed Bransen by the front of his tunic, and hoisted him to his feet. But then he shoved Bransen hard as he offered a phoney "oops!" and the poor helpless young man stumbled back and fell in a painfully twisted manner.

He had barely hit the ground when a boot came in hard against his back, jolting him.

"Hey, you nearly tripped me with the dolt," said the third of the group, a younger boy of about fifteen, Hegemon's little brother Rulhio. He gave another kick, this one more vicious, that set off an explosion of pain in Bransen's shoulder. Bransen grabbed at the wound and tried to cover up, but his inability to curl onto his belly made him roll back before Rulhio in a vulnerable position.

Bransen tried to scream as a muddy foot lifted over his face, ready to stamp him flat. The poor young man couldn't even manage to cry out properly, his face twisting and his voice gurgling. He couldn't even manage to bring his arm back across to block the blow. A moment later, he tasted blood with the mud—his blood, running from his nose.

Then he was up again, suddenly, hoisted by Tarkus.

"Aw, you hurt him," Tarkus said, and he threw Bransen forward.

Rulhio caught him roughly, turned him, and shoved him to the waiting grasp of Hegemon.

"Well, I don't want the wretched thing!" Hegemon proclaimed, and he sent Bransen hard at Tarkus.

And so it went, around the triangle of bullies, the three of them taunting, pinching and punching, and throwing him in turn. Bransen couldn't begin to put his feet beneath him, couldn't even twist his mouth to shout a protest. On one throw, he tripped as he started ahead toward Tarkus, and he toppled forward, crashing hard against Tarkus's waist and knocking Tarkus off balance so that he followed Bransen to the muddy ground.

Of course, though that made the other two howl with laughter, it infuriated Tarkus, and he punched Bransen even harder in the face, then hauled him back up. Before Bransen realized that he was standing again, Tarkus slapped one hand between his legs and grabbed him by the front of his tunic with the other. A twist and heave had Bransen horizontal and in the air, Tarkus lifting the thin little man right over his head. With Bransen up high, the powerful Tarkus began to turn.

Only then did Bransen realize that the commotion had brought a crowd of onlookers—men, women, and children.

Tarkus stopped short, then threw Bransen down. He landed on his back, dazed and out of breath. He heard the crowd, and it brought an ache to his heart that far exceeded any of the pain the three bullies had caused him. For most were laughing, while one or two expressed their sympathy for "the ugly little creature," mostly in the form of whispers along the lines of, "It's a pity that such a beast should have survived birth."

Tarkus's foot stamped on Bransen's stomach, and Bransen jolted into a curled-up position.

"Hey, we're not done with you!" Tarkus said, and he grabbed Bransen again and pulled him to his feet, violently shaking him.

Crying, bleeding from his nose and gums, Bransen offered no resistance as Tarkus wound up to pound him some more.

"Stop it!" came a cry. "You leave him be!"

Before Bransen could register the identity of the speaker, the distant familiarity of the female voice, a woman crashed hard into him and Tarkus. Bransen slipped and would have fallen, but Tarkus held his ground and held Bransen upright; and the free hand that was about to launch a heavy punch at Bransen instead shoved the woman back.

Bransen tried to cry out, "Cadayle!" but only managed something that sounded more like "Cc . . . c . . . ca-daaaa!"

Cadayle pulled herself up from the mud and came right back in—or tried to before Hegemon and Rulhio intercepted her and held her off.

"You leave him be!" she continued to shout. "He's done nothing to you! He's just a—" She stopped short, and Bransen saw that something had caught her attention and had caught the notice of both men holding her. He followed her gaze back to Tarkus and saw him looking back over his shoulder. And Bransen realized that the crowd had gone silent.

When Bransen finally managed to turn his head to see what the others were looking at, he understood, for there stood Bernivvigar.

The Samhaist towered over Tarkus and all the others, making them all seem insignificant. He stared hard at Bransen mostly, and there was no mercy in his awful glower.

Bernivvigar curled up his withered old lips and chuckled menacingly. Out of the corner of his eye, Bransen noticed the transfixed expressions on the faces of the three bullies and noted that Cadayle had apparently shaken off the trance. She twisted suddenly, pulling free of Hegemon. Her arm came forward suddenly, slapping Tarkus across the face.

That brought the three to action. Rulhio moved quickly to grab the young woman. Tarkus Breen reacted even more directly, stepping forward and punching Cadayle square in the chest. She tumbled backward and would have fallen had not the other two regained solid grips upon her.

"Oh, but you're to pay dearly for that, witch," Tarkus remarked.

A moment of clarity, in the form of outrage, surged through Bransen, and he cried, "No!" and lashed out with both arms, flailing away. He heard the laughter erupt all around, even from Bernivvigar, but that didn't slow him. He felt Tarkus's grip tighten on the front of his tunic and knew the man was regaining his composure and balance, but that didn't stop him.

But then his face exploded in pain, spraying blood, again and again as Tarkus pumped his free arm. Cadayle screamed; many in the crowd gasped, while others laughed; and Tarkus growled like some rabid animal.

Bransen's senses were fast deserting him under that barrage, but he did hear a distant shout of protest and then a sharp and thunderous report, as if from a thunder bolt.

People stumbled and people screamed, and Tarkus stopped punching.

"Let him go!" cried Master Bathelais, and he extended his hand and opened it, showing the gray graphite stones, crackling with power.

When Tarkus didn't immediately respond, Bathelais dropped his arm and fired another lightning blast into the ground, jolting them all.

"I said let him go, and I warn you that I will not offer any more warning blasts." Other monks scrambled behind Master Bathelais, several of them, including Brother Reandu, showing gemstones of their own.

Tarkus Breen eyed Bathelais defiantly, but he did release Bransen, giving him a shove that had him tumbling to the ground.

"You protect this wretched creature," Tarkus shouted loudly enough for all to hear, and he gave a derisive snort.

"We are measured by the welfare of the least among us, not the strongest," Master Bathelais said.

From the side, old Bernivvigar laughed.

So did many others.

Bransen saw that Master Bathelais was not amused, and when the master's gaze locked with his own for just a moment, he saw little true compassion there. In fact—and it hit Bransen hard—even Tarkus Breen had not looked at him with as much hate as Bathelais did now.

Bransen didn't dwell on it, though, as he tried to pull himself back up, especially when he heard Tarkus say to Cadayle as he walked by her, "This is not over, whore. I know where you live."

Cadayle spat at him, and she rushed to Bransen, helping him to his feet. She began brushing him off, to the catcalls of the crowd and in the face of the obvious disdain of Bernivvigar.

"Get back from him," came an unexpected assault from an unlikely source. Both Cadayle and Bransen looked at the approaching Master Bathelais. "Shoo, girl," Bathelais fumed. "You have no place here."

"B-b-but," Bransen started.

"Shut your mouth," the master commanded, and he grabbed Bransen by the shoulder and pulled him away from Cadayle, shoving him into the arms of the waiting Brother Reandu.

"Easy, Bransen," Reandu reassured him. "It's over now."

Bransen managed to turn to face Cadayle, and she smiled at him. Then she motioned to indicate that Bransen should go along with the monks.

"B-b-b . . ." Bransen stammered, trying to point out Tarkus and the threat to Cadayle. "B-b . . ." he stuttered, spittle flying everywhere.

"Oh, be silent," Master Bathelais scolded as he walked past, and then he added to Reandu, "Get him inside before I lose my compassionate humor and give him to the anger of the crowd."

Reandu kept reassuring Bransen and led him off toward the chapel.

Clearly, Master Bathelais was not pleased. Bransen heard him shouting long before he neared the room to which he had been summoned by Brother Reandu; and as he approached, the master's words became clearer.

"So now we are using gemstones to threaten the populace away from this . . . this . . . this abomination?"

"Master, we are brothers of Blessed Abelle. Blessed because of our capacity for compassion," Brother Reandu countered. "When we took him in, we discussed this very matter."

"We took him in to secure the sword, that we might strengthen our position with Laird Prydae," Bathelais corrected. "Never forget that."

Bransen froze in place and found his breathing hard to come by. The sword? His mother's sword?

"He is our charge," said Reandu.

"Then keep him inside from this day forth. Have him collect the pots and put them out by the wall, where a younger brother can take them to the river."

"Do you justify the actions of the three ruffians?"

"Can you blame them?" Bathelais argued. "In these times? They go off and fight and die, while he stays here and—and what, Brother Reandu? While he stays here and eats the food for which others toil in the fields or hunt in the forest?"

"Master!"

The room went quiet for a moment, and Bransen dared to peek in. Bathelais stood there, before one of two chairs set in front of a desk. His eyes were closed, and he finally seemed to settle down with a series of deep breaths, his large chest heaving.

"Once, I vowed never to use the magic of a gemstone in anger, unless it was against a powrie or goblin," Bathelais said.

"You hurt no one."

"But I scared them. I scared them all." He gave a little snort. "That has always been the difference between us of the Church of Blessed Abelle and Bernivvigar and the Samhaists. They held power through fear, but we . . ." He gave another disdainful snort and shook his head. "I believe now that when it comes down to the moment of crisis, our two religions are not so different."

Brother Reandu stiffened defiantly in his chair. "I refuse to believe that."

Bathelais snorted yet again. "Keep the pitiful creature inside," he said again, and he turned and walked away, heading for the room's other door.

Bransen waited for some time before staggering into the room.

Brother Reandu smiled widely as soon as he saw the young man.

"Come along," the monk said cheerfully and he moved to a small desk and brought forth a pouch. He dumped its contents, a cache of various gemstones, onto the desktop and produced a gray hematite. "Let me tend the wound that young man gave you."

Bransen moved over and managed, with Reandu's help, to get into the chair opposite. Reandu cupped Bransen's chin in his hand and tilted his head back.

"He hit you hard, didn't he?"

Bransen wanted to say that he didn't care, but he grunted. Too many thoughts swirled in his head for him to even begin to sort them out at that time. He was angry at the bullies and deathly afraid for Cadayle. He was terrified of Bernivvigar and very confused about the words of Master Bathelais and his simmering anger, apparently directed at him.

It was all too much, and it was all that Bransen could do to hold back his tears.

Then he jumped in pain as Brother Reandu touched his nose.

"Ah yes, he hit you hard," Reandu said, and he gave a comforting laugh. "This will not hurt you," he promised as he brought the soul stone up to Bransen's face.

Bransen instinctively pulled back as Reandu began to chant, putting himself in a state of focus and meditation as he gently brought the stone against the other's broken nose. Bransen's slight discomfort from the pressure of the stone lasted only a moment and was replaced by a warm feeling spreading through his nose and face. He felt the healing powers of gemstone magic for the first time, and he closed his eyes and basked in it.

And something wholly unexpected happened. Bransen saw his line of *chi* react to the soul stone, just in the upper areas of his body. He pictured it clearly, a lightning line of crackling energy suddenly coalescing and aligning to the call of the gemstone!

Bransen's eyes opened wide.

"Yes, it does feel good, doesn't it?" Reandu asked.

The moment passed quickly—too quickly—and Bransen slumped back.

"There, done already," said Reandu. "That feels better now, does it not?"

Bransen gave a head-lolling nod.

He was too surprised to begin to elaborate.

CHAPTER 26

Paralysis of Another Sort

When the trapdoor slammed shut, its reverberations felt to Bransen as if someone had driven a stake right through his chest. He sat in the near darkness of his barren and cold room, the light of a single candle the only barrier between him and a blackness so profound that he could not see his own hand if he waved it an inch in front of his face.

He was in emotional tumult, his thoughts flying from Tarkus Breen to Cadayle. Cadayle! Bransen could hardly believe that she had arrived in his moment of need. He hadn't seen her in years, and there she was, right when he most needed her, just as she had so often been before Bransen had come to Chapel Pryd. And as if all that turmoil and confusion, elation and fear weren't enough, Bransen saw the scowl of Bernivvigar and the trembling rage of Master Bathelais.

And one more thing swirled through his roiling emotions: the feel of the touch of hematite.

In his deepest dreams, in his moments of the purest concentration over the Book of Jhest, Bransen had not imagined anything as crystalline as the sensation that gemstone had provided.

Now he had to consider the hematite in a different light, and for a different purpose. He had tried to warn Brother Reandu that Cadayle was in danger. He had heard Tarkus Breen's whispered threat. But he hadn't succeeded and Reandu had merely reassured him that everything was all right, that bluster was just that and that the boys were "feisty"—yes, that was the word Reandu had used several times to describe the bullies—but were not criminals.

Bransen knew better. He had seen the look in Tarkus Breen's eyes. He had heard the hateful tone of Breen's voice. All that led him to the inescapable conclusion that Cadayle was in danger.

And no one would help her. And he was here, in a hole in the dark, hardly able to help himself.

Bransen forced himself to stand on his wobbly legs. He recalled the head to groin, conscious alignment of the energy line, of *ki-chi-kree*. Even though

Bransen could hardly hope to achieve or sustain such a state, the effort to do so allowed him to throw aside his jumble of thoughts, one by one.

He dismissed the humiliation he had suffered outside. He dismissed Bernivvigar's threatening glare. He dismissed the unsettling comments of Master Bathelais. He dismissed the implications of the reference to his mother's sword. He even put aside his thoughts of Cadayle.

Temporarily.

Now he was in control of his tormented body. Now he stood straight and strong, and he stretched his arms out, then brought them in slowly and in perfect coordination, working through some of the Jhesta Tu exercises.

With a deep breath, Bransen fell into stillness and let thoughts of Cadayle come back to mind, hearing again the threat from Tarkus Breen. He focused the inevitable rising anger into his meditation, into his determination.

He knew he had to do something, but how could he even begin?

He thought again of the gemstone, of the moment of not just physical wholeness, but of *easy* physical wholeness.

Bransen stepped forward, walking swiftly before this effort of smooth movement weakened him. He went below the trapdoor and pushed it open, hoping that no brothers were around in the lower levels of the chapel at this late hour.

Bransen lifted his arms and planted his hands firmly on the lip of the opening. Only as he pulled himself up did he come to understand that his years of torment, of twisting and struggling for every movement, had actually done something wonderful: his muscles were strong. Now moving with coordination, his often-flailing arms easily hoisted him out of his hole.

He was beginning to tire, though, as he walked across to the desk and he nearly fell with exhaustion, his mind beginning to lose focus, his *chi* beginning to scatter once more. With great effort, Bransen pulled open the small side drawer, where Brother Reandu had dropped the gemstone-filled pouch.

He pulled it forth and carefully emptied its contents onto the desk, then sifted through the stones to find the one he needed. As soon as he had the smooth gray hematite in hand, Bransen felt the cool pull of its depths. He had never been trained in gemstone use, and he had only rarely seen the brothers of Abelle employ them. He wasn't sure how to begin to access and employ the magic.

But he found himself in the swirl of the stone almost immediately, and he understood its properties clearly. Amazed, Bransen quickly realized that the mental state that permitted gemstone use was almost identical to Jhesta Tu concentration.

His arm was shaking again, so much so that he actually punched himself in his still-sore nose—which sent a wave of nausea rolling through him—as he lifted the soul stone to his forehead. Finally he got it in place, and he let his thoughts flow through its inviting depths and then back into his *chi,* starting right there at his forehead.

Bransen's breathing steadied, and his arms and legs stopped shaking almost immediately. He saw his line of energy coalesce and straighten, and he felt a harmony within.

A perfect harmony, even more complete than he had achieved in those few moments when Brother Reandu used the stone on him. The combination of Jhesta Tu and gemstone magic held his life energy, his *chi,* strong and tight.

Bransen stood straight. He wanted to move through some of the Jhesta Tu exercises, for all weariness had suddenly flown, but he couldn't bring his arm down. He wanted to revel in this feeling of freedom, this feeling that all healthy people took for granted. He wanted to stand there and bask in the moment or to jump for in joy in an impromptu dance.

Could Cadayle wait for him to calm down?

He began replacing the other stones in the pouch; with each one he handled, he felt its magical energy, and its knowledge of its various properties flitted through his mind. He felt the tingling of the lightning-inspiring graphite and the weightlessness afforded by malachite. He felt the inner heat of ruby, the protective shield of the serpentine, and the warmth and light of diamond. The stones seemed strangely familiar to him. He couldn't dwell on it now, though. He put the pouch away and returned to his chamber. He fumbled with his bedding and pulled forth the black silk suit. It was still in amazing condition, but a seam at the right shoulder had begun to open. Bransen knelt on the main part of the black shirt and with his free hand pulled the right sleeve off. Then he wrapped it around his head, using it to secure the hematite in place.

Gingerly Bransen tied the ends together and brought his hands down to his sides, then breathed a huge sigh of relief: the gemstone effect was continuing even without his hand holding the stone. The connection remained, and it was strong.

Bransen smiled as he considered the expressions he might elicit if he walked out of his hole and to Master Bathelais's private quarters! What would Bernivvigar think of him now? Would he apologize? And what of Tarkus Breen and his cohorts? Bransen was free of his limitations; Bransen was also schooled in the martial ways of Jhest. He felt confident that Tarkus Breen couldn't even hit him, let alone hurt him!

Indeed, what might the world think of the Stork now?

Bransen's smile disappeared and a wave of fear nearly buckled his legs, every hopeful possibility fast replaced by dread.

With that in mind, he removed his bandana. Working carefully, one hand holding the gemstone, the other manipulating the material, he brought the fabric over the candle and held it there, once and then a second time. When he put the bandana back on his head to hold the gemstone, he spread it over his face so that it covered his nose and all the way to his upper lip. An adjustment showed him that he had burned the eyeholes correctly.

Cadayle.

That one thought stayed with him. He quickly pulled off his tunic and began donning the black silk suit. He recognized one error almost immediately, though, for he had removed the right sleeve, showing his bare arm and the unique birthmark. Thinking quickly, Bransen removed his bandana and tore a narrow strip off it. He put his mask back in place, then tied the strip around his right arm, hiding the mark.

When he put on the soft shoes, he felt as if he could leap to the stars or run faster than any deer. He was complete, dressed in his mother's outfit of station and blessed by the powers of both Jhest and the Abelle gemstone. He blew out the candle and scrambled out of his hole, closing the trapdoor behind him; and he quietly crossed out of the chapel, across the courtyard, and out into the night. As he tried to get his bearings, he moved from shadow to shadow, though there were few people milling about anyway. Cadayle lived at the western end of town, he remembered from long ago, or at least she *had* lived out there.

Bransen ran off.

He *ran* off!

His legs moved swiftly and he didn't have to throw them by jerking his hips forward. His legs strode in balance, his feet planting firmly with each long running stride. Bransen couldn't believe the feeling of freedom, of elation, and pure joy. He had never imagined this release from the bonds of his infirmity. He had never imagined the feel of the wind in his hair quite like this. He almost felt as if he were flying; and to him, this ability to run was almost as much of a leap as true flight would have been to a normal man.

So rapt was he that he nearly forgot his purpose, and he had gone quite a long way before remembering Cadayle and the possible danger. He slowed—how he hated doing that!—oriented himself, and realized that he had no idea where he was, for never in his life had he been west of Castle Pryd.

The farther he got from the castle, the more sparse lay the houses, scattered about small fields, clusters of simple houses separated by walls of piled rocks. All the structures looked the same, one- or two-room hovels of plain stone with thatched roofs. A few had small gardens under their windows, flowers and vegetables with colors dull in the pale moonlight. Some cows lowed and a few goats skittered past Bransen as he made his way along the winding roads. Some of the houses had candles burning inside; and whenever he noted the lights, Bransen slipped to the window and peeked in, hoping every time that he had at last found Cadayle's house.

He walked for hours, all the lights going down, even the moon setting in the west, so that he was alone in the quiet dark. He went farther out than he had intended, out to where the houses were even more widely spaced, out where fields and forests dominated, and cows and chickens and goats far outnumbered people. Bransen had no idea that Pryd Town was this big, for there were certainly more houses here in the west than in the east where he had grown up, where Garibond lived quietly with few and widespread neighbors around the small lake. Given the scope of the town, the young man only then realized the magnitude of the task before him in even finding Cadayle, let alone protecting her.

Frustrated, but with the eastern sky beginning to brighten with the first light of dawn, Bransen sprinted back along the roads toward Castle Pryd, whose massive dark outline could be clearly seen even from this distance. The light was growing by the minute, and Bransen realized that he might have erred. He understood clearly that he did not want to reveal his new secret, he did not want the monks or anyone else to know that there was another side to the Stork.

Each stride became more desperate as Bransen realized that he wouldn't make it back to the chapel before the brothers had begun to stir. How would he explain himself? He thought of running right by, of going all the way out to Garibond's house, but his place was Chapel Pryd, especially since he had one of their prized possessions, a magical gemstone, with him.

Bransen sprinted. He thought of the Book of Jhest, about its lessons concerning breathing and stamina. He loosened his fists and let all his muscles relax, save those pumping his legs.

He passed Castle Pryd and moved to the side of the chapel, sidling up to one window in the room above his chamber. He peeked in and saw a couple of brothers sweeping and dusting. "Come along, Stork," one of them called.

Bransen fell back against the wall and held his breath, trying to figure out some escape. He thought that perhaps he should just slip in and tell them the truth.

And then he thought of the Book of Jhest, the book that seemed to have the answers to everything buried in its graceful lines of script.

Barely making a sound, Bransen turned back and studied the two working brothers, soon discerning their patterns, soon predicting their turns and movements. He found his timing and slipped over the stone sill and in the window, sliding down to the floor and crawling along it like a snake. He reached the trapdoor and paused, silent and still, watching the two brothers moving in the dim light. As one brother lifted a candelabra from the desk, Bransen lifted the trapdoor, just enough so that he could slither through the opening. He touched on the floor below hands first, and held himself there, his feet slowly descending and quietly lowering the trapdoor closed as they did.

Bransen dropped to all fours and breathed a sigh of relief.

"Stork!" he heard one of the brothers call more insistently.

Now he moved fast, to his bed, where he stripped and pulled his woolen tunic on. Last, and with great remorse, he removed his mask and the gemstone it held. He worried about keeping the stone for just a moment, until he realized that there had been several of the soul stones in the pouch, after all, and the brothers didn't seem to keep close watch on them.

Bransen tucked everything out of sight, and not a moment too soon, for his trapdoor banged open. "Come along, Stork," said the monk. "Daylight is wasting."

Bransen rose from his bed, or tried to, and only then did he understand the toll his previous night's exploits had exacted upon his tortured body. A wave of such weariness came over him that he staggered forward and dropped hard to the floor, blackness engulfing him. Only distantly did he realize that he was being hoisted from the hole. Only distantly did he hear the calls of the monks.

He awoke much, much later, with darkness again settled on the land. He was on a blanket on the floor of the room above his own, a monk sitting in a chair above him, his head to one side, his breathing rhythmical in slumber.

Cadayle.

The thought stabbed at him. Had he failed her? Was it too late to go back and find her house?

Bransen tried to roll over and rise, but before he even really began to pull himself up, the monk grabbed him by the shoulder.

"Easy, Stork. It's almost dawn. Come on, now, go back to sleep. You had us all worried. We thought you had just decided to die!" The monk gave a chuckle, and Bransen hardly paid him any heed, but he did clearly hear the man's next words.

"I suppose that might be a good thing for you, though, eh, Stork? Poor wretched thing. Might be that we'd all be better off, yourself most of all, in just giving you to Bernivvigar. Ah, you poor thing."

Bransen wanted to scramble into his hole and gather up the soul stone, then come back in a rampage and teach this fool better!

But he didn't and he couldn't. He slumped back and hoped desperately that Cadayle was all right.

He went through his duties absently the next day, and was glad that the monks had reduced his workload since the incident with Tarkus Breen. When he finally managed to get back down into his hole, he was relieved to find that the monks had not found his hastily hidden black suit and the stolen soul stone. A crooked smile crossed Bransen's face as he considered that. Why would they find any of it, after all, since none of them ever came down to see him? On the one occasion when he had found visitors in his subterranean lair, they had been too consumed by the writing he had done on the wall even to notice the roll of black material that had so long served him as a pillow.

Realizing his limitations, Bransen dared to slip out earlier that night. He had to move more carefully, as there were people around, but the sky was heavily overcast, and the darkness gave him ample opportunity to hide.

And he used the lessons of the book, the deeper understanding it offered of how individuals perceived their surroundings. As he fell into those words, it almost seemed to Bransen as if he could see the world through the eyes of those from whom he wished to hide; and moving past them without being noticed presented very little challenge.

Bransen felt as if he were truly Jhesta Tu, as if the secrets of the mystics were more than simply known to him but actually were a part of him. How could he move so gracefully with his newfound freedom so fresh? How could he run, and fast, when he had never done anything like that before? And yet, he knew how, as if he saw every movement of his muscles, as if he understood every twist and its result, as if his thoughts, his *chi*, had so perfectly aligned that his body had become a perfect extension of that life energy, perfectly guided.

As he walked to the west end of Pryd, Bransen moved through the various routines of Jhesta Tu fighting, working his arms in a series of movements both defensive and offensive. He thrust his hand forward or sideways, precisely snapping at the end of each strike as if to crush a windpipe or stiffening his fingers as if jabbing them through flesh.

Many more lights were on as he moved through the western reaches of Pryd Town, affording him a better chance to locate Cadayle. The shadow that was Bransen drifted through the lanes and small yards, one by one, peering into house after house. And finally, he found her.

She lived with her mother at the end of a lane in a small stone house with flowers all around the yard. She was inside going about her nightly routines. Bransen's heart leaped at the sight. He watched the two eat their dinner, laughing and talking. He listened as they sat before the small hearth later, sometimes talking and sometimes sitting silent, taking in the meager heat on this unseasonably chilly night.

When at last Cadayle rose and moved to a small cot and began to undress, Bransen froze and nearly panicked.

She pulled her tunic up, and Bransen turned away, putting his back to the wall and fighting for every breath. How he wanted to watch her, to bask in the beauty of her soft curves and delicate limbs! His curiosity and something deeper, something he didn't really understand, something deep in the base of his line of life energy, in his loins, tugged at him to watch.

But he knew that it would be wrong.

He stayed by the house until late in the night, protecting his dear Cadayle. And while he was there, he practiced the Jhesta Tu exercises, the precise movements designed to instill memory and precision into the muscles of a warrior.

Any Jhesta Tu mystic watching him would have thought he had spent years at the Walk of Clouds.

No trouble came to Cadayle that night, nor the next, nor the next after that. And through each night, Bransen was there, outside her house, keeping watch and examining, too, his newfound physical prowess and the implications that it might hold.

"How will Master Bathelais and Brother Reandu accept this change?" he asked himself quietly. The young man found himself speaking aloud quite often these nights. The sound of his voice, without the stuttering, without the wetness of unwilled saliva, without the tortured twists and tugs of uncontrolled jaw muscles, amazed him and pleased him in ways he had never imagined. "Or Bernivvigar? Yes, the old one will be surprised and not pleased. What will he say when I look him in the eye and declare him a criminal? What will he say when I knock him down and kick him hard for the pain he brought Garibond?"

Bransen's eyes gleamed as he considered that, as he pictured Bernivvigar helplessly squirming on the ground before him. He shook the dangerous fantasy away, when he reminded himself that Bernivvigar had acted on behalf of Laird Prydae. Would he challenge the whole of Pryd?

"Garibond," he whispered to the night. "My father of deed, not blood. You will see your efforts rewarded. You will see your prayers answered. You will see your son stand straight. I will tend to you as you did for me all those years. Never again will you have to sit huddled in the cold rain, trying to catch a fish or two to silence your growling belly. Never again will you stagger toward the house, an armload of firewood in your weary arms.

"Never again, my father."

As he finished, Bransen leaped high into the air and spun one leg flying out in a circular kick, muscles working in perfect harmony, joints moving smoothly and without pain. He heard the crack of wind at the end of that kick, so sharp and swift was its motion. He landed easily in a crouch, arms flowing side to side before him as if fending off enemies.

He stopped abruptly and looked back at the house. "Cadayle," he whispered. He tried to imagine the look upon her face when he revealed himself to her, when he showed her that he was the Stork no more—or at least, not all of the time. "My love, my all."

A sudden stab of fear stole his voice. He thought he would rush forward and profess his love to her, tell her that there was nothing in all the world more precious to him than her smile and her gentle touch, that there was nothing warmer to him than the feel of her breath.

He realized that she wouldn't reciprocate. He knew in his heart, then and there, that she would never be able to see past the shit-covered Stork, wallowing in the mud. How could someone as beautiful and perfect as Cadayle ever hold any feelings other than compassion and pity for the wretched creature he had been all his life?

"How could I begin to think myself worthy of you?" he asked the empty night.

No, not empty, he only then realized, as his senses reached outward and caught the movements of several forms, distant, laughter, and the crash of a bottle thrown to the road.

Bransen ducked into the shadows of a tree a dozen yards to the side of Cadayle's house. He stared back to the east, back down the lane, and noted the approach of five dark forms. He couldn't make out any details from this distance, but he knew at once that it was Tarkus Breen and his friends, come at last to make good on their threat. Bransen's hands trembled so hard that his fingers tapped against the rough oak bark. His legs turned weak beneath him and his mouth went suddenly dry.

"This is why you came out here," he reminded himself, but the words sounded hollow against the fear, the terror that was welling within him. He thought himself a fool, a pretend hero who kicked at the air and imagined he could do anything.

Anything at all.

For he was just the Stork, just a boy, who had never been to war, who had never fought back against anything other than pounding his dirty hand into the dirt after being thrown down.

A movement before him brought him from his thoughts, and he caught a flash, a reflection of glass in the starlight, as the bottle soared and smashed against Cadayle's door.

The three walked right past, taking no notice of him.

"Cadayle," Tarkus Breen called. "Come out and play, girl. I've a weapon too long sheathed!"

The others laughed.

The group strode right up to the house, one going left, another right, to ensure that no one got out.

Bransen wanted to shout. He wanted to charge at the group and demand they leave. He wanted to run back to town and call out the guard.

He couldn't bring himself to move. Not an inch. He couldn't bring himself to swallow, let alone cry out!

Everything seemed to move before him so slowly and yet very quickly as if his mind couldn't properly take in the unfolding scene. He saw candlelight inside the house. He watched a large man walk up to the door and kick it hard, and then again, knocking it wide open.

He heard a protest—Cadayle's mother.

And Tarkus Breen and two others went in.

He heard a scuffle, saw the two other men coming back around the house; and the sound of a slap jolted him straight.

Cadayle appeared in the door, wearing only a white nightshirt. She started to run out, but Tarkus himself caught her by her thick hair and tugged her back. She fell to her knees right there in the doorway.

Bransen shook violently. He silently cursed his cowardice. How could he watch this and not go to her? How could he stand here, ready to pee in his pants?

"Shut up, you old hag, and be glad that you're too ugly to feel the sting of our weapons!" one of the brutes shouted from inside. And Bransen jumped at the sound of another slap.

Cadayle crawled out and started to rise, but Tarkus's foot planted on her back and sent her sprawling to the ground.

In a moment, four of the five were around her, taunting her, while the fifth remained inside with her mother.

"You should know your place, girl," Tarkus Breen said. "You interfere where you're not wanted."

Cadayle looked up at him. Even at this distance, Bransen could see her eyes full of hate and fear.

"You defend that creature," Tarkus Breen said, and he spat upon her. "Do you not understand who we are and what we have done for you? We fight in the south and we die! We defend you, whore, and you side with that creature over us?"

Cadayle shook her head.

"You should welcome us with your legs wide," Tarkus Breen said, and he kicked her and started to roll her over. "You should be honored that we think you worthy of our seed!"

"Take her!" one of the others eagerly prompted, and the other three laughed.

Bransen told himself to move, ordered his legs to take him out there and intervene. And yet, he stood huddled against the tree, hardly breathing.

He looked at Cadayle, offering a silent apology for his weakness.

She didn't see him, but as if in response, she seemed to go, suddenly weak, all defiance falling into hopelessness, and she began to cry.

Those tears, lines of wetness glistening in the starlight, crystallized Bransen's thoughts. All his personal emotions fell aside in the face of that sight, of dear and wonderful Cadayle crying and broken, the surrender of the woman who had been one of the pillars of strength in his life.

Bransen was moving without even thinking. Bransen's subconscious and muscles were falling into the martial lessons of the Book of Jhest. He hardly realized that he was approaching the group; he hardly even saw the closest man, the big one who had kicked in the door, turn and stare.

Bransen slid to one knee as he came up on that man, who was just beginning to cry out in surprise. Without breaking his momentum, Bransen drove the heel of his right hand hard into the big man's groin, lifting him up to his toes.

Bransen sprang up, snapping his foot up to kick the man in the face. As the victim straightened, Bransen hit him a left, right-left-right combination, finishing with a left hook that had the man flying sideways. Bransen leaped forward going right past the reacting attacks of the two men at the sides of Cadayle and going right over her to land before Tarkus Breen.

Breen's arm flashed out, a knife in his hand, but to Bransen he almost seemed to be moving under water. Bransen turned his fingers upward and pushed the striking arm harmlessly wide.

Reacting on instinct, he leaped straight in the air, tucked his legs beneath him, then kicked out on both sides, stopping the charges of both men beside him. He landed with his arms crossed over his chest, then flung his arms out, the backs of his hands smashing against the faces of his attackers. Bransen slipped to the right, bending his right arm, then lashing out once and again with his elbow. He felt the crunch of the man's nose with the first blow.

He dropped as that man fell and snapped out his leg into the kneecap of the other attacker, stopping him short. The man stiffened and stumbled backward, and Bransen used the distance to begin a charge of his own, easily deflecting another stab from Tarkus Breen. Two short steps and he leaped and spun, turning nearly horizontal in the air, adding even more weight behind his kick to the man's midsection.

As one leg flew out hard, Bransen lowered his other leg. He landed, absorbing the impact by letting his knee bend deeply and using the movement to regain his center of balance as he dropped nearly to the ground.

Then, with all his strength, he came up hard and threw all his strength and weight into the move to gain enough momentum to again lift him from the ground. Around he went as he rose, sending his free leg into a circle kick. It was too high, and cut the air above Tarkus Breen's head as he ducked and charged ahead, arm extended.

But Bransen's kick had been too high on purpose, in accordance with the movements taught in the Book of Jhest. As Breen ducked, Bransen launched his intended attack, his other foot snapping straight up into Breen's face.

Bransen landed easily on both feet, Tarkus Breen staggering backward. To Bransen's left, an attacker was rising but scrambling away, one leg broken. To his right, a man squirmed on the ground and clutched his broken face. Behind him, Cadayle cried; and beyond her, the big man lay very still.

"Who are you? What do you want?" Tarkus Breen said, the confidence long gone from his voice.

"I am . . ." Bransen paused, as if awakening from a dream, as if for the first time actually realizing what he had done. While his body had come in here, fighting perfectly, his thoughts were stalled back at the tree. Now he was waking up.

But what was he to say? He recalled some of the brothers at the chapel complaining that the roads were becoming unsafe again, with powries and highwaymen. He recalled pieces of their stories of older times and great deeds. He seized on that without even thinking.

"I am the Highwayman," he said, hardly considering the implications.

Tarkus Breen wasn't listening, Bransen then realized, but had used the pause only so that he could gather himself for another attack. He came forward hard, slashing his knife back and forth.

But Bransen, though he had regained his awareness of himself, was no longer afraid. There was no paralysis in him, and the lessons of the Book of Jhest flowed through him as easily and fully as if he were reading the book. His line of *chi,* formed so solidly by his discipline and by that soul stone set under his black mask, held tight and straight, relaying his thoughts to his muscles perfectly, and calling them to action.

Breen's knife slashed, left to right, then back again, but Bransen retreated and veered, so as not to trip over Cadayle. Tarkus Breen followed, stabbing straight ahead. Bransen's hand pushed the strike out wide, but then his attacker surprised him by breaking off and turning back to Cadayle.

Tarkus Breen stabbed the knife out toward her.

He never got close to connecting.

For Bransen rushed back to Cadayle, catching Breen's wrist with his left hand. He lifted Breen's arm and went under it, turning it and forcing the bully to come up straight. Bransen kept twisting as he stood up straight. He lifted his right arm and drove his elbow against Breen's.

The snap of bone sounded like the breaking of a thick tree branch.

Bransen hardly heard it and hardly slowed, ducking under the shattered arm and turning to come face-to-face against the agonized man, the twisted and broken arm between them.

The look in Breen's eye—somewhere beyond pain, somewhere in the realm of shock and horror—was the first indication of something serious to Bransen. He leaped back, letting go, and Tarkus Breen stood still, his right arm hanging at his side, his left hand coming in slowly, trembling every inch, approaching the hilt of his knife, which he had driven hard into his own diaphragm.

Shaking fingers moved around the hilt and started to close, but Tarkus Breen seemed to lose all strength then. He looked at Bransen. His arm fell to his side.

He fell over dead.

Cadayle screamed, but Bransen hardly heard it. He knew his enemy was dead. He knew that he had killed a man.

He searched through the Book of Jhest for an answer to this sudden realization. He tried to remember to breathe.

Another woman's cry behind him took it all away, and Bransen spun and charged into the house.

A moment later, Callen staggered out, crying, one eye swollen. She caught the door with one hand as she passed and managed to pull it partially closed behind her. She stumbled to Cadayle, who rose to embrace her, and the two turned back to the house, to the sounds of fists connected repeatedly, to the sound of grunts.

The door slammed closed then exploded outward, the assailant flying through it backward. He hit the ground hard, groaned, and rolled over, giving the two women a view of his bloody face.

The Highwayman appeared at the door.

"Be gone, all of you!" he demanded of the beaten attackers. "Be gone and return to this place only on pain of death."

They staggered and scrambled, hoisted their friend with the shattered knee-cap, dragged Tarkus Breen's body, and managed to move away.

"They'll not return," Bransen said to the two women.

"How can we ever thank you?" Cadayle said to him breathlessly as she continued to hug her crying mother.

Bransen went to her and helped both women to rise. "No need, of course," he said, trying to show some measure of calm so that the two would follow that lead. "I consider it an honor to be able to help."

Despite his cool demeanor, Bransen was churning inside. How he wanted to pull off his mask and proclaim his love for Cadayle! How he wanted to kiss her and hold her and tell her and her mother that everything was all right. How could he blend this moment of heroism into a moment of personal revelation?

The sound of a neighbor's call defeated any hopes he might have. No doubt, the defeated gang were beginning to draw attention.

Bransen smiled and tapped his hand to his forehead in salute.

"Good evening to you, beautiful ladies," he said. "Blessed am I to be granted the good fortune to aid you this night."

"But—" Cadayle started.

"The look on your face is all the gratitude any man would ever need, and more than any man would ever deserve, milady," he said, and he thought himself clever in sounding like the monks when they told their great tales of old heroes. Stealing a line directly from one of those overheard stories, Bransen added, "In all a man's life, might he hope to see a single instance of such pure beauty as your face. I am the fortunate one this night." He saluted again as both Cadayle and her mother looked to the road and the neighbors' approach. When they looked back, he was already gone, melting into the night.

The road back to the chapel was a long one for Bransen. So many truths assailed him from every side, so many conflicting emotions. He had performed brilliantly. He had saved Cadayle and her mother, had beaten the bullies.

He had killed a man.

Out behind the castle, in the darker predawn shadows within a copse of trees, Bransen Garibond, the self-proclaimed Highwayman, fell to his knees and threw up.

CHAPTER 27

Catching His Mother's Spirit

The thrill of being out in the daytime had Bransen smiling widely, almost giddily, below his black mask all the way out to the small lake in the west. When he had heard—so soon after his return just before dawn—that all the monks had been summoned to the castle for the day, Bransen couldn't resist the chance to finally go out to his dear father's house. Now he could hardly contain his joy when Garibond's house came into view. Gray lines of smoke rose from each chimney, which struck Bransen as unusual, since Garibond typically only kept one hearth burning.

He skipped from tree to tree, moving through the shadows and even up in the lower branches as he went. He had been spotted a couple of times on the way out, as indicated by the shouts of distant people, but he thought nothing of it. Now, though, as he neared, he saw several forms moving around the small island: a pair of children and a pair of women, one of about his age and the other older, possibly her mother.

Had Garibond taken a wife?

Bransen swallowed hard, not sure what to make of it all. Were these Garibond's children running about his island? And who was the girl of his own age, for surely she couldn't belong to his father? He moved even closer and rushed past the house to a pile of rocks on the shore, affording him a view of the southern side of the small island. Both women were heading that way, and now he saw why. A pair of men sat on the rocks down by the water, fishing.

Bransen had to consciously steady himself, for neither was Garibond. Where was Garibond? Who were these strangers that had come to his house?

He started forward, thinking to go and ask them exactly that, but he paused, remembering his distinctive garments. It was one thing to be spotted running along the distant fields but quite another to go right up to someone. And if he asked about Garibond, wouldn't he be implicating his father as an ally? He knew not what retribution might be in store for him for his actions at Cadayle's house. Was he to be branded a hero or an outlaw?

He couldn't risk it, for Garibond's sake.

He stayed in place for some time longer, taking a look at each of the six people on the island, committing their faces to memory. If they came into town, he would find a way to ask, he decided, or he would come back out here dressed in his woolen tunic and walking in the awkward guise of the Stork. Yes, that might work. With the gemstone hidden, he could pretend to be the creature that everyone believed him to be.

It was all too surprising and all too confusing, and the sun was low in the western sky. The monks would be returning soon after dinner, so he had heard.

He sprinted back to the west.

D o these problems never lessen?" Prydae said, and he threw down his gauntlets upon the desk, stamped his hands upon the wood to steady himself, then turned his angry look back at Bannagran. "One man?"

Bannagran shrugged.

"One man, unarmed, defeated five?" Prydae pressed. "Five who served with our warriors in the south and are not new to the ways of battle?"

Again, the big man shrugged.

"There were spearmen in the trees, perhaps?"

"There were no spear wounds, my liege," said Bannagran. "Nor were any cut, except Tarkus Breen, who died on his own dagger."

Laird Prydae rubbed his face. Powries were all around once more. Bandits had been seen on the roads to the south and to the west, and now this—a daring attack by a single man against five! Here Prydae was, trying to focus on the titanic events in the south, on the war between lairds Delaval and Ethelbert and the implications to his sovereignty, if not his very survival—and trying to discern how best to collect the heavy taxes Delaval was demanding—and these minor distractions would not lessen at all.

"What of the other four?"

Bannagran shrugged again. "Keerson will not walk again without a limp, but beyond that, they will all recover with time. Except for their wits, perhaps, for they claim the martial prowess of this one to be beyond belief. He was possessed of the strength of ten men, they said, and he fought so quickly that it seemed as if there were three of him."

"They would say that to save their drunken pride, though, wouldn't they?"

Bannagran shrugged.

"Who was it?"

"He called himself the Highwayman."

"Wonderful." Prydae slammed his fists down on the desk.

"He is one man," Bannagran reminded.

"Who defeated five—unarmed when they were not."

"Five staggering drunks."

Prydae nodded, having to accept that.

"Our guests are waiting," said Bannagran. "We should not linger; I doubt that Father Jerak will be able to remain much longer."

"Does he even know where he is?"

"Doubtful. And if we don't get him out of here, it is likely he will shit himself soon enough."

Prydae laughed, then moved to the hearth at the side of the room and pulled the fabulous sword from its perch and slid it into his belt at his left hip. "Lead on," he bade his friend, and he fell into step behind the man who would announce him. Before they even began to descend the stairs of the tall keep, Prydae reached out and grabbed Bannagran's shoulder, stopping him. "We should go out in full splendor in the morning," he said. "It has been too long since I worked my chariot team."

"A show of strength to assure the people?"

"And to warn this Highwayman. Let him realize the terrible end of the road he has chosen to walk."

Chapel Pryd was strangely quiet the next day as Bransen went about his chores, collecting the chamber pots and setting them by the back wall. Not a monk seemed to be anywhere, except the one who served as attendant to Father Jerak, and the old man himself, apparently worn out from the excursion of the previous day.

Bransen wasn't using the soul stone, though he missed it dreadfully, as he missed walking straight and missed the sensation of running. Secretly, he never wanted to assume the posture of the Stork ever again. But playing his alter ego, this Highwayman, was physically exhausting to him, and, beyond that, he had no idea of how the brothers might react to his newfound health, nor to his pilfering their sacred gemstone. He had noticed, however, that even without the soul stone firmly secured against his forehead, he was finding a bit more control of his movements with every day. In Jhesta Tu terms, and using Jhesta Tu technique, Bransen was finding more and more solidity to his line of *chi*. With his meditation and focus, he could form that line and hold it, albeit for only short periods; but even when he was not consciously engaged in such Jhesta Tu disciplines, he found that his line of life energy wasn't dispersing quite as widely and wildly as before.

Given that, Bransen found himself in the strange position of consciously exaggerating his storklike movements. He wasn't quite sure why he should not reveal the changes he was experiencing, but he had a feeling that his cover as a helpless creature would serve him well for the time being.

On his fourth trip to the back wall, a chamber pot sloshing at the end of each arm, Bransen found the six previous pots still sitting there untended and unemptied. He put the two new additions down and looked about curiously. Where was his helper?

Bransen moved back into the main areas of the chapel's first floor and was struck again by how empty the place seemed. Not a brother was to be seen or heard. He staggered through all the main rooms, finding them unoccupied. He went to the front door of the chapel, which was opened wide, and glanced out into the courtyard, with its twin trees, left and right of the cobblestone path.

He was about to go back in and head right up to Father Jerak's attendant to inquire about it all, but then he heard the bells ringing and the trumpets blowing out in the town. Curious beyond any fear of breaking the rules, or of simple good judgment, Bransen moved down the chapel steps and across the courtyard to the open outer gate.

He saw many of the monks lining the main road of Pryd Town. He picked out Bathelais and Reandu among the throng, and it was indeed a throng, with all of the folk out there, waving and cheering. The Stork made his awkward way to Reandu and reached the brother just as the trumpets began to blow with even more urgency.

"Stork," Reandu greeted. "What are you doing out here?"

Bransen couldn't tell if the man was angry or merely surprised. "I-I-I . . . I didn-didn-didn't kno-kno—"

"Never mind," said Brother Reandu and he put his hand on Bransen's shoulder to quiet him. "Perhaps it is better that you came out. You should see the glory of Laird Prydae revealed!" As he finished, he pulled Bransen forward and helped him settle in place right at the road's edge. He even helped Bransen to steady his head and look toward the castle, where the procession had begun.

First came the soldiers of Pryd in their full regalia, bronze armor dully shining in the sunlight. They carried long spears, holding them vertical, gleaming tips up high and in perfect alignment with one another, showing the splendor of the discipline of these best-trained soldiers of Laird Prydae. The laird's various commanders walked along the side of the tight formation, calling orders and warning back any peasants who stepped too far out from the roadside.

Bransen watched in amazement as the procession paraded by, boots thumping the ground in unison.

Behind the common soldiers came three horsemen, including one Bransen knew well enough in the center. Bannagran seemed even more huge and more imposing on his armored mount! And clearly the legendary warrior commanded the attention of all the onlookers.

That is, until the man behind him appeared. In a chariot more grand than the one he had lost in the war all those years earlier, and with a team of two large and strong horses, Laird Prydae seemed the most splendid of all. He wore a new breastplate, replacing the many-nicked one that had gone off to the powrie war. This one, again of bronze, and again emblazoned with the running wolves, was studded with jewels that caught the sunlight in bursts of radiance. He wore an open-faced helm with a horsetail-like plume, dyed red. But armor, helm, and chariot seemed not to matter much when he drew forth his shining steel sword. He held it aloft and the crowd gasped and cheered and as one pointed at the marvelous weapon.

That sword could cut through a plate of bronze armor, so it was rumored, and it could fell a small tree with a single powerful stroke. That sword, it was whispered all around Bransen, would keep the powries at bay and make any imperialistic-minded laird tremble at the mere thought of warring with Pryd Holding.

That sword . . . was the sword of Bransen's mother.

The emotions sweeping through Bransen as he watched the procession and the proud laird were very different from those of the people around him. They saw inspiration; they showed awe. But for Bransen, there was only the sudden realization that this sword did not belong with the Laird of Pryd. This sword, his mother's sword, was his own to claim.

And so he would, he determined, and that very night.

When the chapel monks had all settled into their beds, the Highwayman, dressed in black, a soul stone pressed against his forehead by his tight mask, slipped silently out of Chapel Pryd and moved through the shadows to the wall of the great castle itself.

Bransen watched the wall top for signs of sentries, trying to spot their dark silhouettes against the moonlit sky. All seemed quiet.

He fell into his meditation, recalling the lesson in the Book of Jhest, recalling the day he had spent at the desk when first he had taken the soul stone. He considered the many revelations of the various gemstones, recalling the properties of malachite. Bransen gathered his *chi* and lifted it, replicating the levitational energy of malachite. He felt almost as if he were floating, though of course he was not. But he was lighter, his life energy battling against the pull of gravity.

Bransen lifted a hand to the stone wall, found a slight fingerhold, and propelled himself upward. Hand over hand he went, easily and spiderlike, needing no more than the ridge between two stones to provide him enough of a grip to move past.

He reached the top of the wall in short order and glanced all around. With no guards in sight, he moved silently along the wall to the point where it joined with the large keep. This tower was Prydae's own, Bransen had learned from various discussions among the monks over the years, and so this was likely where he would find his mother's precious sword. Again, he fell inside of himself and lifted his energy skyward, walking up the wall.

He passed one window and peered in, but saw nothing of interest in the candlelight. *Up higher,* he decided, and he moved along. As he neared the next window, this one along the back of the tower, he heard voices from within.

"A fine show, my liege," said a deep voice. Bannagran's, perhaps, Bransen thought.

"Every now and then, they need to be reminded," came the reply, a voice that Bransen did not know, dour and serious and gravelly with age.

"Perhaps it is a reminder that I need, as well," said a third, whom Bransen recognized as Laird Prydae. It also struck the young man that the laird's voice was quite somber. "I do not miss the sound and smell of battle," Prydae went on. "Yet I cannot dismiss the thrill that courses my body when I drive my chariot and draw my sword."

"It gives hope to the people," said the voice Bransen believed to be that of Bannagran. "You are their protector."

"And their laird, with all the privileges that entails," said the old voice. "The woman you chose along the parade route awaits you in your chambers, my liege. Use her well."

"My blood is hot with the sound of trumpets and cheers," Prydae said. "Perhaps this, at long last, will be the night for consummation."

Bransen heard the tink of goblets tapped in toast, and a moment later, the sound of footsteps receding, followed by the bang of a heavy door closing. He waited a bit longer before edging toward the window and peering in.

The room was dark, with only the glowing embers of the fire remaining to add to the slanted rays of moonlight that were sliding in through the narrow window.

Bransen held his position and glanced all around and down. Still he saw no guards walking sentry. After a few more moments of silence, he slipped into the room.

He moved away from the window, crouching in the darkness and allowing his eyes to adjust. Gradually, the distinctive shapes within the room came into clearer focus: the closed door across the way, the chairs before the hearth off to his left, the hearth itself.

And something set on the wall above the hearth.

Bransen sucked in his breath. Had good fortune shone upon him? Had he wandered into the very room that contained his mother's sword?

Silent as a shadow, he slipped to the hearth and saw the outline on the wall. It was a sword, a long sword, too long for bronze or iron.

Behind him to the right, the door banged open, and he saw the steel of the fine blade flash with the sudden intrusion of torchlight.

Bransen swung around to see a surprised Bannagran standing just inside the door, torch in hand and wearing only a tunic and loose breeches. The man's eyes were so wide that they seemed as if they might roll out of their sockets, and his jaw drooped open. But that dumfounded expression fast twisted into a wicked grin.

"Was it the Ancient Ones of the Samhaists or Blessed Abelle that put you here in my grasp?" the large man asked as he quickly set the torch into a bracket beside the door. "For truly such good fortune as this falls within the realm of divine miracle!"

He balled his huge fists and rushed forward.

Bransen sprang over the chair behind him, putting more ground and now two chairs between himself and the charging warrior. He landed in a defensive crouch and easily ducked away as Bannagran lifted one of the chairs and threw it at him. Then he hopped aside as the second chair flew through the air, swept away by the wrath of the powerful Bannagran.

The mighty warrior waded in with a wide-arcing left hook that the nimble Highwayman easily ducked, then came with a straight cross. Bransen's hand knifed up to deflect the blow, but Bannagran would not be so easily deterred. He launched a straight left and followed with a right, then back and forth in a sudden and vicious flurry, barreling forward like an angry bull.

Up came the Highwayman's hands one after the other, slapping left and slapping right, and ducking and swerving. A couple of glancing blows clipped him, but only at first, only while he was acting with his conscious mind instead of letting himself fall into the teachings of the Book of Jhest.

As the rhythm of the book flowed through his body, as his concentration became a pure interaction between mind and body, a fusing of the mental and the physical, and again it almost seemed to him as if his opponent were moving under water. Even the expressions of Bannagran's face as he roared in increasing frustration seemed an exaggerated, slow-moving thing, as the roar itself seemed to stretch out in the Highwayman's ears.

Now Bransen dared to counter, getting his hand up inside Bannagran's punch, deflecting it and launching one of his own. He hit the big man once, twice, thrice about the head with short, snapping jabs.

But Bannagran pressed on, ignoring the blows. And as he stepped forward, he dropped his right shoulder and launched a roundhouse punch that seemed to come from his ankle, his heavy right hand swooping in for the side of the Highwayman's head.

A right jab smacked into Bannagran's nose, but the big man didn't flinch. The Highwayman, in trying to drive his opponent back, didn't duck but bent his arm, his wrist against his ear to cover.

It was a perfectly executed block, a detailed maneuver in the Book of Jhest.

But neither that book nor the Highwayman had taken into account the strength difference between the diminutive Bransen and the giant and powerful Bannagran. Bransen's arm blocked the punch, but the weight of the blow sent him flying sideways. He staggered and nearly fell, but instead threw himself into a sidelong roll that brought him back to his feet near the wall.

In charged Bannagran, fists flying, but suddenly Bransen wasn't in front of him. Bannagran only began to understand how completely Bransen had out-maneuvered him when he felt the weight of the man in black crashing against his legs, tripping him headlong into the wall. He managed to get his arms up to absorb some of the jolt.

He spun immediately, launching a wide-flying right hook.

Bransen ducked it, dropping so low that his butt nearly touched the ground. Up he sprang into the air, lashing out with his feet, one and then the other.

But as he landed, he found that he had done little damage to Bannagran, for the big man went right back to the attack. And now he was altering the angles of his strikes, high and low, and seemed perfectly willing to accept Bransen's stinging counters.

Bransen's ear ached from the last blow, and he understood that it wouldn't take many hits from Bannagran to drop him!

The flurry intensified; Bannagran snapped off a series of crosses, then dropped and repeated with three left jabs in a row, though Bransen brought his knee up to block. Up went Bannagran, and Bransen jumped back a step, then came back in, his hands rotating in overlapping circles before him, offering no openings.

A left jab snapped in, and Bransen turned it, retracted his hand, and started to counter. Then he saw the blood pouring from his fingers, and then he noticed that Bannagran's hand was no longer empty. Bransen leaped back, glancing from the cut to Bannagran, to the long knife that the man now held.

A sweeping crosscut had Bransen sucking in his gut and leaping backward. Bannagran charged ahead, stabbing hard, but Bransen went around the outstretched arm in a quick roll, then sprinted past the man for the wall.

Bannagran cried out in victory and turned to pursue, then watched in amazement as the Highwayman seemed to run right up the wall, springing directly over him in a twisting somersault. The Highwayman landed lightly, and a second leap brought him to the top of an overturned chair. He sprang away again, gathering momentum, in a great leap that sent him flying across the room.

He landed right before the hearth, grabbed the magnificent sword by the pommel, and turned to face Bannagran. With a grin, Bransen yanked the sword in an upward and sliding motion, its fine edge easily severing the two leather ties securing it to the upturned hooks.

Bannagran skidded to a stop.

"You drew first," the Highwayman chided. "I was content to embarrass you with open hand. Now it seems I must kill you." As he finished, the Highwayman leveled the deadly blade Bannagran's way. "Which will you pray to, mighty Bannagran? The Ancient Ones or Blessed Abelle?"

The Highwayman took a fast step forward, thrusting the blade; but Bannagran leaped back, caught a chair by the arm, and whipped it across to block. Then, with strength beyond anything Bransen had ever seen, the big man stopped his swinging arm suddenly and threw the chair.

The Highwayman dodged it, barely, and spun in a pirouette, then fell into another defensive crouch.

But Bannagran hadn't pursued; he had run back to the open door, shouting for the guards. Bransen heard a commotion out there.

He ran to the window, turned to salute the big man, and promised, "We two will fight again, sword to sword or fist to fist!" Then he went out.

But not down.

Like a spider, the Highwayman moved to the side of the window and then up. He reached the top and pulled himself over even as the head of a guardsman poked out the window and began looking all around at the ground. "Did he fall?" the man cried.

Bransen put his back against the crenelated tower top and lifted the gleaming sword before his eyes. He felt the smooth steel and the keen edge and marveled at the beauty of the etchings running the length of the blade. This was the work of his mother as surely as the copy of the Book of Jhest had been created by his father. Bransen didn't know the technique that had gone into making this sword, of course, the folded steel and precise and disciplined toil. He didn't know that it had taken his mother years to craft it.

But he understood completely that this was no ordinary weapon, and from more than the exotic feel of the materials. The balance, the delicate work along the pommel, the light yet solid feel of the blade all hinted to him of the marvels within and of the discipline required to create this. He knew that his mother had made it, for he could feel her residual energy within the blade. The Book of Jhest had referred to weapons such as this and spoke about the bonding between the craftsman and the weapon, but only now could Bransen truly come to appreciate that truth. For in holding this magnificent sword, Bransen felt as if he were touching the mother he had never known.

Could she have foreseen this day? Could she have guessed that her sword would outlive her and would be handed down to her son?

A weight of responsibility fell upon Bransen then. His mother was a Jhesta Tu mystic, an accomplished warrior and philosopher. He had a lot to live up to.

He heard the commotion below him as Castle Pryd came fully awake, but he paid it no heed. Not now. Now, he was with the spirit of his mother as he had been with his father in those moments when he had possessed the Book of Jhest. This was so much more than a weapon, Bransen knew at once. This was a work of art, an extension of Sen Wi herself, imbued with her skill and her love.

As he continued to hold and contemplate the sword, he felt a warm, clear sensation that his mother was pleased, that she was looking down at him now and was glad that her sword was in the hands of her son, the child for whom she had willingly offered her own life force.

A long time later, the commotion around the castle died down, but Bransen could still see groups of soldiers with torches scouring the area. He poked a loop for the sword in the tied waistline of his trousers, gathered his inner strength, and climbed down the wall. Moving from shadow to shadow, the Highwayman was soon back in the chapel, and soon back in his little room.

And now he had one more thing he knew he must keep hidden.

CHAPTER 28

Alone, and so Be It!

The lines were not as intricate and flowing, but the patterns of the words were much the same. Bransen focused hard to keep his head from lolling about so that he could study those patterns and try to make some sense of them. It wasn't often that Bransen got any opportunity to view the writing of the monks. On those occasions when he was the Highwayman, he spent very little time in the chapel, only enough to get in and out along a direct route from his trapdoor to the window and back again.

So this morning, going about his rounds, when he saw the parchment unrolled and weighted down on the desk, Bransen quickly moved to inspect it.

How he wished that the monks had taught him to read their language. How he wished that so many of his empty hours could be spent engrossed in a tome filled with words of wisdom. Did the words of Blessed Abelle mirror those of the Jhesta Tu? He had already clearly seen and felt the similarities of Jhesta Tu meditation and the powers afforded by the sacred stones, and he had to believe that those commonalities extended into the relative philosophies of the holy men. Bransen suspected that the books of the monks would enhance his understanding and control of his life force, but, alas, Brother Reandu had made it quite clear to him that the brothers would not teach him to read.

He stood there for a long time, staring down at the script and wondering if he might somehow teach himself. So immersed was he in the lines and words that he didn't hear the door open across the way and the soft footfalls of an approaching monk.

"Take care with that," Brother Reandu said, and Bransen staggered and nearly fell.

Reandu steadied him.

"Taking respite from your work?" the monk asked.

Bransen stammered, trying to formulate an answer, but Reandu calmed him and quieted him quickly.

"Still intrigued by words?"

Bransen nodded.

"Well, please do not drool on this, my little friend. Do you know what this is?"

Bransen tried to shake his head, but it went in a circular motion instead, and sent his eyes spinning.

"It details instructions from the masters of my order," Reandu explained. "From Chapel Abelle itself, where the prophet taught and where he died. Perhaps one day I will find the means to take you there. Yes, you would like Chapel Abelle." Reandu's eyes sparkled and he began to wave his arms out to show the vastness of the place and to dramatize his nearly breathless words as he continued. "It is set on a high cliff overlooking the dark, rolling waters of the ocean. Waves smash against the rocks continually, like the thunder of God himself! You cannot stand atop that cliff without seeing the beauty of God, Stork. You feel small and great at the same time, as if you are part of something larger and more wonderful than yourself, than your life itself. The thunder of the waves pounds like the heartbeat of God, I tell you!"

He paused and looked back at Bransen. "You would like to see that place, wouldn't you?"

Bransen nodded eagerly and grinned from ear to ear, but the smile went away almost immediately as he came to consider what any journey away from Chapel Pryd might do. How could he take his clothing, the sword, and the stolen gemstone with him? How could he keep his secret, or find the hours of freedom in the guise of the Highwayman?

He caught himself in those thoughts and glanced anxiously at Reandu, who, thankfully, had not noticed his changing mood. Quickly, Bransen shifted the focus and the conversation by pointing emphatically at the parchment.

"An order from Chapel Abelle," Reandu explained, and he gave a sigh. "The world is a difficult place right now, Stork. Men are warring across the land of Honce as the lairds vie for supremacy and allegiance. And we of Blessed Abelle are caught in the middle. We are healers, not warriors, but some of the lairds wish us to use our gemstone powers to help them in their battles—and, indeed, many of the brothers are doing just that. And, of course, after the battles, we toil endlessly over the wounded."

Bransen understood that the man was not really talking to him, but rather was simply thinking out loud, as if he were trying to clear up things in his own mind.

"Thus come the troubling decisions concerning the disposition of the wounded," Reandu went on. "Are we to heal only those men who fight for our own lairds? Are we to ignore the cries of the enemy wounded? I do not know if I could do that, Stork. I do not know if I could allow a man to die, knowing that I might have healed his wounds.

"But it is not my decision, so declare the masters of Chapel Abelle. The decree before you states that we are to heed the desires of our laird regarding the wounded. If Laird Prydae insists that we let the enemy wounded suffer and die, then we must abide by his decision."

Reandu gave a shrug. "Do the colors a man wear so determine the value of the man? Does allegiance to a laird mean anything more to a peasant than the happenstance that he was born in the holding of that laird? Would a man of Pryd serve Laird Ethelbert with equal fervor if he had happened to be born in Ethelbert Holding? I think so, Stork, and so I am saddened by the choice of my masters."

Bransen looked back at the parchment, seeing it, suddenly, in a very different light. If the monks of Blessed Abelle were truly God inspired, as they claimed, then how could they abrogate their moral imperatives to the decisions of a secular man? It seemed a cowardly thing.

"Practicality has its place, I suppose," Reandu said, as if reading Bransen's thoughts or, at least, as if sharing Bransen's concerns. "Fortunately, the battle has not yet reached us here in Pryd Town, and with good fortune and the aid of Laird Delaval's thousands, it never will."

Bransen glanced over to see Reandu standing calm, his tirade ended.

"Come along, Stork," the man said. "You cannot avoid your duties."

Bransen lifted the room's chamber pot with one hand and offered his free arm to accept Reandu's guiding hand, and he shuffled along beside the monk toward the room's open door. Not willing to let go of this rare encounter with Reandu—at least, rare when they actually had time for a few words—Bransen stuttered out the name of his father and protector.

He made sure that he watched Reandu closely as he spoke Garibond's name, knowing, as was detailed in the Book of Jhest, that a man's initial reaction was often more telling than his subsequent words.

And, indeed, Brother Reandu's eyes did flash and widen for just an instant before he got himself steadied.

"Garibond?" Reandu echoed. "Ah, yes, old Garibond! A good man. A good man."

He was stalling, Bransen could tell, given his initial reaction.

"He went to the south, I believe. Yes, yes, to Ethelbert, from what I have heard. The sea air would be gentler on his aching bones, so he said."

Bransen wasn't entirely convinced, and he only half listened, focusing instead on the man's expressions and inflections as Reandu continued to tout the healing aspects of salty air and went on about the better, warmer, and sunnier climate of Ethelbert compared to Pryd.

Of course, Bransen knew, the monks could simply have offered Garibond healing sessions with their gemstones.

He didn't press the point, and he showed no outward sign of his doubt as he and Reandu exited the room and moved along toward the next door in the hallway. But then monks were rushing all around, responding to a commotion down the hall the other way, near the main chamber of the chapel's first floor. Immediately Reandu reversed direction, pulling Bransen along with him. They came to the end of the corridor to see many of the brothers assembled in line before Master Bathelais in the main chamber, with Laird Prydae himself and several soldiers facing them.

"Stay here," Reandu told him, and he rushed out to join Master Bathelais.

Bransen watched as Bannagran moved along the line of monks, lifting and inspecting their hands. The young man's eyes widened as he realized what was transpiring here, and he lurched over, placing the chamber pot down hard, then dipping his hand into its brown contents. He came back up as fast as he could, holding the pot once more in his filthy, shit-covered fingers—fingers that had been cut by Bannagran's knife the night before. How glad was Bransen that Brother Reandu had not apparently noticed the scar, the cut healed by the stolen soul stone and the meditation of Jhest, but still visible.

Bannagran finished with the monks then, and noticed Bransen as he turned back to his liege. He paused and studied the damaged young man.

He thinks I am the right size, Bransen thought, and he immediately staggered and lurched, accentuating his infirmity.

Bannagran started to approach and Bransen fought hard to remain calm. He wished that he had his soul stone with him, that he could become the Highwayman, if need be, and flee this place. He thought he was surely trapped.

But Bannagran stopped suddenly and looked down at Bransen's hand and the chamber pot. The large man crinkled his nose in disgust and gave the Stork a dismissive wave, then went back to join Prydae, Bathelais, and Reandu.

Bathelais dismissed the monks then, and they began to disperse, talking among themselves.

Bransen used the distraction to shamble along the general direction of the leaders, and he perked up his ears as he neared.

"Surely you do not believe any of the brothers hold any complicity in this theft," he heard Master Bathelais say.

"There was no rope," Bannagran answered, his voice low and grave. "No sign of a rope."

"It is hard to believe that anyone could steal the sword and so easily flee the forty feet down the side of the tower," Laird Prydae added, "unless of course the thief had the aid of a magical gemstone."

"Malachite," said Brother Reandu. "We have but two, I believe, in all of Chapel Pryd."

"And where are they?" asked the laird.

Reandu looked at Bathelais.

"I will order a complete inventory of all of our gemstones," the master said. "All of them, and I assure you that if any are missing, our aid will prove invaluable to you. There are ways to detect the usage of gemstone powers, my laird."

Laird Prydae nodded slowly, but he didn't seem very happy at that moment. "Are you so careless with your sacred gemstones that you know not even where all of them are now placed?"

Bransen took note of the embarrassed scowl on Master Bathelais's face. Of course, Father Jerak's unorganized ways were legendary among the brothers of the chapel, and the implication now was that perhaps Bathelais was not only inheriting but furthering the carelessness. That possibility seemed not to sit very well with him at that moment.

"We are no less vested in our gemstones than you are in your magnificent sword, my laird," Bathelais declared suddenly, with renewed vigor in his voice. "We will account for all of them, I assure you. If an outside contraband stone has been brought into the region by this man, this . . ."

"Highwayman," Bannagran spat.

"This Highwayman creature," Bathelais agreed. "There is no tolerance for this within our order. Any man found with a contraband gemstone will suffer the full wrath of the Church of Blessed Abelle."

"A man not of the Church in possession of a stolen gemstone is declared a heretic and burned at the stake," Brother Reandu added.

Bransen heard the contents of the chamber pot sloshing below his trembling fingers.

"Perhaps I will allow you that pleasure, if indeed this thief holds such a stone," Prydae said. "But not until I am finished with him. And know that he will welcome the consuming flames when I have shown him my wrath!"

Bransen nearly tumbled to the ground and felt as if he would throw up. Somehow he managed to get out of the room without attracting any more attention to himself.

What was he to do? Had he gone too far? Could he possibly explain to the brothers why he had borrowed the soul stone?

Unsure of himself, not knowing what to do next, the terrified man continued with his duties. The guise of the Stork would protect him, he tried to convince himself. How could they suspect him of anything when he could hardly walk?

He knew then that he had to be very careful. He could bring no attention to himself, and could not give any of them, not even Reandu, any reason to believe that there was any kind of intelligence inside his damaged physical form. And he had to take care in using the soul stone, apparently, if Master Bathelais's claims of being able to detect such magic were to be believed.

He had to be the Stork—just the Stork. His frailty would protect him, he hoped.

He desperately hoped.

Several days passed before Bransen dared to go out as the Highwayman again, days made longer by his burning desire to test his mother's magnificent sword. Now that he had it firmly in hand, moving through the training movements he had learned in the Book of Jhest, Bransen began to understand just how wonderful the weapon truly was. It felt as if it were an extension of his arm as he swung it; its balance remained perfect at nearly every angle, making it seem even lighter than it was—and although it was much longer than the average Honce bronze or iron sword, the thin steel blade of SenWi's creation *was* far lighter.

Bransen spent an hour and more playing with the blade, weaving cuts against imaginary opponents, defeating attacks and quickly countering with killing strikes.

Even when he finished the most taxing of practice routines, he was full of energy and brimming with eagerness. He had no destination in mind this night, so he glided through the shadows, taking in the sights, the sounds, and the smells of Pryd Town. It was generally quiet: a bird calling, some cattle lowing, a mother shooing her children into the house, an owl hooting. But Bransen stopped when he heard a sharp cry among the soothing sounds of the town winding down.

"But what am I to feed my children this night?" came a woman's voice.

"You have more," a man replied. "You know you do. I told you three days ago to be ready for this."

"But me husband's not returned from the south!"

"Then get on without him! Do you believe that any are having an easy time of it with the war, selfish woman?"

Bransen came up over a small grassy mound to take in the sights of the argument. A peasant woman, dirty and dressed in rags, was practically on her knees before one of Laird Prydae's soldiers, who had a bulging sack slung over one shoulder while he kept her at bay with his other arm.

"Just give me food for the night, then, so I won't be going to bed hungry," the woman begged, and she came forward suddenly, lunging for the sack.

The man slapped her aside.

Bransen, the Highwayman, started over the knoll, but stopped short and held his ground. Anger welled up inside him, but he suppressed it, reminding himself that anger was a warrior's worst enemy. Anger denied calculation. Anger led to errors.

He watched the soldier kick the peasant woman as she scrambled back toward her hovel, whining pitifully all the way.

Laughing, the soldier turned away. He pulled the sack from his shoulder and fished his free hand about inside, bringing forth a shiny tomato, which he promptly bit into as he started back toward Castle Pryd.

The Highwayman circled him, moving to a tree and up it and onto a branch overhanging the road.

"A fine night of thievery, I see," the Highwayman said as the soldier approached. Bransen hardly took note that he had slipped back into that peculiar way of speaking, emulating the monks when they told their stories.

The man stopped and threw aside the remaining piece of tomato, quickly drawing his short sword. "Who said that?" He glanced all around, even hopped in a circle, waving his weapon.

"An admirer," the Highwayman replied.

The soldier stopped and followed the voice to the tree that held the Highwayman.

"Truly," the Highwayman went on. "I do admire one who has found a way to so easily steal that which he desires. It shows cunning and efficiency, I think."

"Steal? Bah, I'm no thief! This is the laird's business and none of my own."

"Laird Prydae bids you to eat your booty?"

The man laughed. "Get yourself gone, and be quick. I've no time to suffer a fool. You interfere with the laird's tax collectors on penalty of death."

"Oh, but I am already so marked," the Highwayman said, and he dropped from the tree, landing a few paces in front of the soldier. The man fell back a step, surprised.

"Do you not know who I am?" the Highwayman asked. He drew out the sword that had recently been hanging in the private quarters of Laird Prydae, the sword that had incited a search of the whole town.

"You!" the soldier cried.

"Curiously said," replied the Highwayman. "Could I not claim the same of you?"

"You're . . . you're him!"

"Again, my point holds."

"You come with me!" the soldier demanded. "In the name of Laird Prydae, I arrest you!" He dropped the sack and presented his sword in a menacing manner.

The Highwayman suppressed a chuckle and instead backed off a cautious step.

"Come on, then," said the soldier. "I've been fighting in the south for a year now and think nothing of cutting you up."

The Highwayman glanced around as if he meant to run away. The soldier, predictably, rushed ahead, the tip of his sword barely inches from the High-wayman's chest.

"Now!" he said with a growl. "Last chance to surrender before I run you through."

The Highwayman sighed, feigning fright, and presented his sword hori-zontally before him. When the soldier reached for the offered blade, the High-wayman tossed it up into the air.

The soldier's eyes followed the ascent.

A right cross from the Highwayman staggered him backward, tumbling to his knees.

The Highwayman caught his blade as it fell and leaped forward in a spin, whacking the soldier's feebly presented sword across, then rolling behind the blade and up the man's arm, timing his turn perfectly so that he could drive his left elbow into the side of the man's face. He felt the soldier's sudden halt and reversal, and he dropped as the man cut a fast backhand, the short sword whipping above his head.

And the Highwayman came up fast, inside the soldier's reach, bringing the tip of his sword under the soldier's chin and forcing the man up on his tiptoes.

"I will hear your sword hit the ground, or I will hear the last breath of your life," the Highwayman calmly stated, and he inched his sword up just a bit to accentuate his point.

The short sword fell to the dirt beside them.

Up came the Highwayman's knee into the soldier's groin, as the Highway-man retracted his blade and stepped back. Again he spun, a foot flying to smash the lurching, bending man's jaw, sending him falling to the side and to the ground.

"The first rule of battle is to know your enemy," he explained, though the man was far from hearing him, or anything, at that moment. "The second is to prepare the battlefield. And the third, one you apparently have not read, my sleeping friend, is to make certain that your enemy thinks that you are less formidable than you are."

The man stirred and groaned and pulled himself up to his elbows and shook his head.

"Although I admit, such a tactic would be difficult to present, for one of your lack of skill."

The man growled.

"But you have learned, perhaps. I suppose that if we meet again, you will not be so easily deceived," the Highwayman said to him. "On that occasion, regretfully, I will likely have to kill you." He ended by putting his foot on the soldier's shoulder blades and stamping the man flat to the ground, adding the warning, "Of course, if you stubbornly persist now, we will never meet again in this lifetime."

Sometime later, the naked soldier, his arms twisted and bound behind his back with his own torn clothing, a tight gag tied in place, stumbled to the front gates of Castle Pryd.

Sometime later, the peasant woman found a cache of food inside the one small window of her house, as did several of her equally hungry neighbors.

Sometime after that, a voice awakened Cadayle. When she went to the window to investigate, she saw a bright smile below a black silk mask.

"Here, eat well with your mother this evening," the Highwayman said to her, and he handed in a worn sack of food.

"What are you doing?"

"I met with one of Laird Prydae's thugs," the Highwayman explained. "The laird has enough to eat, I think."

"You stole?"

"Well, it sounds harsh when you speak it in like that. I prefer to think of it as seeing to the laird's flock in the name of Prydae himself, and representing his better and more generous side."

Cadayle rubbed a bit of the sleepiness out of her eyes and took the offered food, then glanced back into the darkness of her small house. "If we are caught with this . . ." she started to warn.

"Then eat it!" came the easy answer. "Laird Prydae's men cannot see into your belly, now can they?"

"You play a dangerous game."

"That makes it more fun."

He finished with another wide and bright smile, and added only, "Eat well, beautiful Cadayle!" before he spun away from the window and disappeared into the night.

She pressed the food close to her breast, and she could feel the excited flutter of her heart.

The Highwayman danced away through the shadows, spinning his sword and leaping into battle against imaginary foes. He knew not why he had acted as a thief this night, knew not why he had suddenly taken this more dangerous fork in the road. But he couldn't deny the lightness of his step, the rush of blood throughout his body, or the thrill of his mischief.

Yes, he knew, he was the Highwayman, who defended the woman he loved, who took back his mother's stolen sword, and who, it now seemed, would not suffer the unfairness of Prydae's rules.

The image of gratitude on the faces of those he had fed this night was better than wine as he danced his way across Pryd Town and back to the quiet chapel.

CHAPTER 29

Almost Honest

All the town speaks of him," Prydae said, grinding his teeth with every word. He moved to the hearth and roughly threw a log onto the fire, for autumn was in the air, the wind chill and from the north.

More than a month had passed since the theft of his precious sword, which was now being used weekly—at least weekly—by the outlaw Highwayman, usually in stealing from Prydae's tax collectors and even some of his soldiers. The lone bandit was striking haphazardly, without any discernable pattern. Every time, he seemed to simply appear out of the darkness, quickly dispatch of any offered defenses—and thus far in a nonlethal, though usually painful, manner—take what booty he could, and melt away back into the night.

"They exult in the glory and cunning of the Highwayman!" Prydae growled.

"Not openly," said Bannagran, standing across the room and stripping off his cloak and wet boots.

"No, and that is all the more troubling. He is feeding them, you know. He is taking the requisitioned food from lawful collectors and distributing it among the peasants."

"We do not know that, my liege. And if we find any such evidence, rest assured that the offending peasant will be punished."

"You know that he is doing that!" Laird Prydae retorted, turning sharply on his friend.

Bannagran shrugged, not arguing.

"This . . . this miscreant, this common thief, becomes a hero among the people by throwing them a few scraps of food. And these disloyal dogs fall for the ploy. How fickle is their allegiance!"

"Times are difficult for the common folk, my liege," Bannagran reminded as he took a seat and began to rub his sore feet. "So many are off to the south, never to return, and our demands sorely press those remaining. Many families are headed now by the mother alone, without even an older son to help her in the fields."

"Laird Delaval presses me hard," Prydae argued.

"They have little to eat."

"They have as much as our warriors battling Ethelbert in the south!" shouted the Laird of Pryd. "Should I deny food and clothing to men spilling their blood so that these peasants, hungry though they are, might live more comfortably?"

"I am not arguing, my liege, but merely trying to explain why this Highwayman creature has so easily found the hearts of many."

"I want him caught." The words were accompanied by another crash as Prydae threw a second log into the fireplace. "I want him dragged to the castle and burned alive."

"The people will frown upon you," Bannagran warned, and it occurred to both men that Bannagran was the only man in the world who could have so bluntly said that to Laird Prydae.

"Upon me?" the laird asked. "Nay, the execution of this one will fall to our Abelle brothers, or to Bernivvigar, if not them. Either way, he will die."

"Deservedly so."

"Prince Yeslnik, favored nephew of Laird Delaval, is on his way," Prydae said. "Double the scouts upon the road and send patrols of the castle guard out to the ends of Pryd Town each night. Offer a reward for any whispers that lead us to this knave. We must put an end to this before the legend of the man grows and before Laird Delaval comes to know that we harbor such a secret."

Bannagran kept his expression impassive as Laird Prydae fell into the chair across from him, drawing a curious stare from his liege.

"What?" Prydae asked.

A slight smile turned up the corners of Bannagran's mouth.

"What?" Prydae asked again, before he took the cue from his friend and managed a smile of his own, which kept widening and became a burst of laughter that Bannagran shared.

"You are right, my friend," said the laird. "He is one man, one prickly thorn, that we shall pluck and discard soon enough."

"He strikes in the dark, from behind and by surprise, and against men ill prepared to defeat him. We learn from his every attack, and we will become better prepared."

Prydae took a deep breath and settled more comfortably in his chair.

"What will Yeslnik Delaval ask of us?" Bannagran inquired.

"More food, more gold, more iron, and more men, likely," Prydae answered. "The fighting in the south has not let up at all, and there is word that Laird Delaval has sent warriors to support the people of Palmaristown and their battle against the wild tribes of the north and west."

"He should focus his strength against Ethelbert first, and drive the man back before offering any truce," Bannagran reasoned. "This has gone on far too long already."

"Would that he would," Prydae agreed, and he went silent and turned back to the hearth, which had flared to life, hungrily eating the two new logs.

Bannagran folded his large and calloused hands behind his head, stretched his legs before him, wriggling his cold toes near the flames, and said no more.

Cadayle walked along the road to her house one dark night, her stride easy and her posture showing that she was unafraid. That calm demeanor was not unnoticed by the people in the neighboring houses, most of whom dared not venture outside after dark.

For the young woman, her own realization that she was unafraid struck her suddenly. Bandits were all around the roads of Pryd, and powries had been seen in several areas—one group had attacked some men not far from this very area. But Cadayle knew that she was not alone.

A small sack plopped to the ground before her, hitting with the jingle of coins. It fell open and an apple, shiny even in the starlight, rolled out.

Cadayle looked up to the tree, to see a now-familiar and not unexpected figure sitting astride a low branch, leaning back against the trunk.

"You should not be out after dark," said the Highwayman. "You never know what knaves might find you and ravish you."

Cadayle blushed, and was glad of the darkness.

The Highwayman, though he was at least fifteen feet up, swung his leg over the branch and dropped down, landing easily, knees bending to absorb the impact. He stood up straight before Cadayle, his smile wide—as it always seemed to be when he was with her.

"Well, are you not going to accept my gifts?" he asked, and he bent down and retrieved the bag and the apple. His grin became mischievous when he stood back up, and he held the apple out toward her, then pulled it back and took a large bite of it when she reached for it.

Then he offered it once more.

Cadayle put her hands on her hips and stared at him defiantly.

"You'll not share your ill-gotten goods with the man who ill got them for you?" the wounded Highwayman asked.

Cadayle couldn't resist, her expression brightening, and she took the apple and the sack. She looked inside the bag, confirming her suspicions when she noted the glisten of shiny coins among the remaining food.

"Money?" she asked.

"I have no need of it."

"If I go to market and spend it, I will draw suspicion. No one has extra coins, with Laird Prydae's tax collectors all about. Not unless they are hiding it from the laird, and that is not wise."

"People spend money in the market every day," the Highwayman replied with a shrug.

"But not so much."

"Then spend it a bit at a time. Buy something for your mother."

Cadayle paused and smiled, then lowered her arm to her side and lowered her gaze. A moment later, she looked back at the Highwayman. "Why do you do this?"

"Do what?" he replied. "You need the food, so I give it to you."

"No, I mean, why do you do all of this?" Cadayle clarified. "You live in the shadows of the night. What of the day?"

"I am alive every day."

Cadayle blew a frustrated sigh. "Do you serve with Laird Prydae's garrison? Are you a farmer? Did you fight in the war?"

"Are you an agent for the laird?"

Again she sighed and declared, "You're impossible."

"Not so, my lady. I am here." He dipped a polite bow.

"The laird is not happy with you."

"I would not expect him to be. In fact, I would be disappointed if I learned that he was."

Cadayle was about to remark that the soldiers were everywhere, it seemed, but the point was made for her with the sound of horses coming down the road behind them. Before she could react, the Highwayman grabbed her by the shoulder and pulled her from the road, the two of them rolling into the depression off to the side.

And not a moment too soon, Cadayle realized as a trio of soldiers came galloping past. Alarmed, she looked at the Highwayman—to see him smiling and to hear his laugh.

"The laird is not happy with me," he said with a grin. "I thought it best that you not be seen speaking with me."

Cadayle started to respond, but suddenly realized how close she was to this man, their bodies intertwined, his breath warm on her face. He, too, seemed suddenly caught up in the moment, and Cadayle wondered if he would kiss her.

And she realized that she hoped he would.

But he didn't. He rose and helped her up, then brushed himself off as she did likewise.

"Why do you do this?" she asked him again.

He stared at her for a long while, his face sober, his eyes, so dark and sparkling, locked onto her. "Because it is right."

Cadayle had no idea of how to take the conversation from there. *Because it is right.* She rolled those words over and over in her mind. She had heard many of her neighbors say such things, had even seen a few of them do such things on occasion. But never, in all her life, had Cadayle heard or seen that particular concept expressed by a man in power.

Because it is right. So simple, and so elusive.

"Sleep well this night, my lady," the Highwayman said. "Dare I hope that you might dream of me?"

The bold question had Cadayle back on her heels, but as it was accompanied by one of the man's typical sassy smiles, she let it go with a grin of her own.

He took her hand and kissed it, then bowed to her and danced away, leaping into the night and disappearing.

This was how it usually had gone between them over these last few weeks and their few encounters. Was that the real reason she had offered to take some eggs to a neighbor for her mother, and then tarried with the neighbors before heading home after darkness had fallen? Had she been hoping to see the Highwayman again? She knew the truth of it, of course—and was finding it harder and harder to deny that truth to herself—for Cadayle found herself thinking of the man more and more.

And as he had boldly asked, she was indeed dreaming of him.

*B*ecause it is right.

The words followed Bransen, too, as he made his way across the town and back to Chapel Pryd. It had been a good answer, he knew, and one that had certainly seemed to impress Cadayle.

But was it true?

Bransen chewed his lip as he considered that. The teachings of the Jhesta Tu demanded introspection and honest self-evaluation, and the Book of Jhest had shown him many techniques to strip away the inevitable defenses that any person would construct against such painful personal intrusion.

Bransen studied his feelings honestly. He recalled how he felt during all his actions these last weeks as the Highwayman. He knew, and came to understand even more with every step, that his efforts weren't quite as magnanimous as he had made them seem with that answer.

There was the matter of his pride.

There was the matter of his love for Cadayle.

Yes, he felt proud when he rescued someone from bandit, powrie, or tax collector alike, or when he saw the smile of gratitude on the face of a peasant after the heroic Highwayman had offered some food to quell the grumbling of his belly. He knew that pride was a failing—the Book of Jhest often referred to it as the downfall of great men—but there it was.

When he had answered Cadayle, Bransen had to fight hard to resist blurting out the truth. How he wanted to tell her that he loved her, and had loved her since he was just a boy, when he was the Stork and she would help him off the ground, when she chased the bullies away. He had almost said it, but he was too afraid. What would Cadayle think of the dashing Highwayman if she knew that he was really the dirty Stork?

So perhaps there were some personal reasons for his choices of late.

Because it is right.

"Well, it is right, is it not?" the young man asked when the chapel was in sight. "I am helping people desperately in need, as some have helped me. Would Garibond do any less?"

Satisfied with that, Bransen crept back through the window, across the room, and into his hole. He had defeated the demon of introspection and self-evaluation, and fell to his cot with the warm memory of Cadayle beside him.

He hadn't reached for the deeper self-evaluation, however, hadn't gone to the dark place in his heart where festered his frustration and anger, memories of his years of torment, thoughts of the missing Garibond and the horrible Bernivvigar who had once mutilated the man, and resentment at his continuing ill-treatment by the brothers who had taken him in and would not teach him to read.

It all sat there, buried within, quietly waiting.

CHAPTER 30

In the Hearts of Everyman

"An impressive turnout," Prince Yeslnik of Delaval said to Laird Prydae as the two ate on the balcony of Castle Pryd's grand dining and audience hall, along with his wife, Olym, Bannagran, and Rennarq. The prince from the huge city at the mouth of the great river, the Masur Delaval, was, in Prydae's estimation, a fine example of Honce nobility. Tall and lean, physically fit and deceptively strong, young Yeslnik sat with perfect posture, and was perfectly groomed, head to toe. His blond hair was trimmed in the fashionable bowl cut, halfway over his ears, and he kept his light beard and goatee trimmed close. His clothing, of course, was of the finest cut and the rich hues of expensive dyes, and he wore rings, bracelets, and a necklace of glittering precious metal and gems. It did not escape Prydae's notice that among the four rings Yeslnik wore, three were sparkling gemstones of obvious value, but the fourth was a set with dull gray soul stone.

Likely, it was an enchanted item, one of the sacred stones that had escaped the Church of Blessed Abelle, and probably as a gift from the brothers. Had they used this item to gain the favor of Laird Delaval? Certainly a soul stone ring, with its healing powers, would be a valuable asset to a nobleman.

Prydae made a mental note to speak with Master Bathelais about that.

Below the foursome, the dining hall brimmed with activity. All the brothers were in attendance, as well as the many substantial landowners within Pryd Holding. Notably absent was Bernivvigar, who had, not surprisingly, refused the invitation. The old Samhaist would not bend to secular leaders, and he had not been invited to sit on the balcony with the laird and prince. Prydae wasn't sure of how he viewed that. Was it principle or mere pride that guided the old wretch? In any case, it wasn't practical. The Samhaists had dominated the ways of Honce for centuries, and still held great power over the ever-fearful peasants. The only reason the Church of Blessed Abelle had leaped so greatly in stature among the lairds was their monks' accommodating attitude toward the nobility, the true power among the folk.

That, and the gifts they could bestow, like the ring Yeslnik wore and the sword—

The mere thought of his missing sword made Prydae wince, and he quickly covered it up by raising a goblet of wine to his lips.

"And I was pleased by the roadside reception, Laird Prydae," Yeslnik went on; and if he had noticed Prydae's soured expression, he did nothing to show it. "I see that your people understand the role Laird Delaval has played in securing their freedom from the grasp of greedy Laird Ethelbert."

Prydae thought it wise to not point out that his holding was pouring money, men, food, and other supplies into those efforts against Ethelbert. "They, we, are grateful that Laird Delaval has seen fit to side with us against the intrusions."

"Laird Delaval respects the sovereignty of the smaller holdings."

Laird Prydae didn't respond, but Bannagran nearly choked hearing that and covered up by coughing, and Rennarq merely rolled his eyes.

"Of course, Laird Delaval cannot settle all of the problems of Honce alone," Yeslnik continued.

Prydae wasn't surprised at the leading statement, of course. He knew that Yeslnik had come here to exact more resources. "More than half the men of Pryd Holding over the age of twelve are dead or off fighting in the south," he answered.

"There is more to fighting a war than soldiers."

"And we are, in every respect, thin, Prince of Delaval," replied Prydae. "Every belly in Pryd growls with hunger, and many of the peasants growl with mounting anger."

"How you control your peasants is no concern of Laird Delaval," said the prince.

"Kill a few and the others will quiet," his wife added, surprising the other four at the table. Rennarq gave a chuckle—one appreciative of Olym's understanding, it seemed to Prydae—and Bannagran cleared his throat.

So did Yeslnik, and he seemed a bit disconcerted by the bluntly callous statement. "Forgive my wife, I pray you," he said.

"For speaking that which we all know to be true?" Rennarq asked. "That which the Samhaists have understood for centuries?"

"Yes, well . . ." Prydae cut in, trying to change the subject, especially since peasant servants were coming to the table often. "My good prince, you must understand that our demands on the people of Pryd Holding have pushed them to the very edge of despair."

"Then push them over," Yeslnik was quick to answer. "Ethelbert is a stubborn foe and for every Pryd man killed, Delaval has lost two."

The fact that Delaval Holding had a population more than twenty times that of Pryd—plus a fishing fleet that easily kept its people fed—was yet another of those troubling details that Prydae thought it best to not mention.

"Bernivvigar will keep the peasants in line, my liege," Rennarq offered, and it was obvious to Prydae that he wasn't the least bit concerned with the common folk or their troubles.

"Our warriors die in the south for the sake of your holding, Laird Prydae," Yeslnik added. "Need I remind you of that? Men of Laird Delaval do battle with those of Laird Ethelbert for your good! Laird Delaval has sent me here because more is needed. More coin and more supplies. And we will expect you to keep your ranks well stocked with soldiers to replace those who fall. This is the critical moment in our struggles with Laird Ethelbert. His lines are near to breaking, and he has found more resistance to his plans of conquest and domination than he expected from the various lairds along the Mantis Arm."

Prydae kept his face emotionless. He knew that the resistance Ethelbert was facing was simply due to the deep pockets of Laird Delaval, who had made many of the other lairds a better offer, as he had done with Prydae. He also understood that Yeslnik's estimation of Ethelbert's weakness was more than a bit exaggerated. Many of Honce's lairds understood the truth of Delaval's offers: that autonomy was such only under the continued willingness and the fluctuating interpretations of Laird Delaval himself. If Delaval proved victorious in the struggles with Ethelbert, then, yes, Prydae would retain his power in Pryd Holding.

But that wouldn't stop the occasional visits from Prince Yeslnik or some other Delaval nobleman. And there were always demands to be met, after all.

"Bannagran here will lead the tax collectors out at the break of morn," Prydae assured his guest. "Your wagon will leave laden with supplies."

"With coin and other valuables," Lady Olym corrected before her husband could speak.

Yeslnik only confirmed that anyway, adding, "Your own wagons may deliver the mundane supplies to the south. I expect to remain another three days. Will that suffice for your collection?"

Prydae looked to Bannagran, who nodded.

"Three days, it is," Prydae confirmed. Noticing that Yeslnik wasn't even looking at him as he replied, he followed the prince's gaze to the man's wife, who sat there seeming perfectly giddy and glowing.

A moment later, not unexpectedly, Yeslnik said, "You will pardon me and my wife for a few moments, good Laird Prydae. We have something we must discuss at once." He rose up swiftly and took his wife's hand. He bowed, she curtsied, both abruptly, and they hurried off toward their private quarters.

"I expect there will be little conversation between them," Rennarq said dryly.

Prydae chuckled at the lewd innuendo, but Bannagran did not. "Laird Delaval's forces do battle for the good of Laird Delaval, not for Pryd Holding," he said.

Prydae disarmed that ire with a smile and a wave of his hand. "It matters not at all. For whatever reason, the army of Laird Delaval serves our purposes in their struggle with Laird Ethelbert; and so we do well to support our friend."

"In the end, we all see to our own needs," Rennarq added.

Prydae looked at the old man and thought that had been a perfectly Samhaist thing to say.

Bransen loved days like this, when all the brothers, with the exception of Father Jerak and one—usually sleeping—attendant, were away. He tied the soul stone onto his forehead and finished his duties in a matter of minutes, then took up a sack with his highwayman garb, removed the soul stone, and went out of the abbey in the guise of the Stork.

He made his way to the river, and there, when he was sure that he was alone, became his true self.

The Highwayman looked all around, feeling strange in this guise when the sun was still bright in the sky. He knew that he'd have to be careful every step of his way, but he couldn't deny the thrill he now felt—as intense and exciting as the night when he had gone to Cadayle's rescue.

Bransen knew that he shouldn't be enjoying the danger so profoundly. The Book of Jhest didn't allow for such thrills. But he didn't deny it; and the young man, whose life had been so empty for all these years, didn't push the excitement away.

Courting disaster and basking in the glow of danger, the Highwayman set out, circling the town to the north, the one region of Pryd Holding he did not know.

He kept imagining that he would find his true sire on the road—hadn't Bran Dynard left Chapel Pryd on a northerly route?—but of course, he did not. He kept thinking of Cadayle as well, and he knew that his roundabout course would take him to her eventually. It always did.

He crossed fields of grain, and followed the aroma of a baked treat very near to the windows of one cottage. He glanced all around and approached. The yard was unkempt, the fields overgrown, and the garden ill tended. But the smell kept Bransen moving for the window, where he even dared to peek in.

A peasant woman perhaps ten years older than he went about her chores, a pair of young children yapping at her feet. She wasn't particularly beautiful, but neither was she ugly, with the blond hair and blue eyes so common among the folk of the region and a body still relatively shapely despite the obviously difficult conditions around her. Bransen studied her for a few moments, but then his nose drew his eyes to the middle of the room. On a small table sat a pie, steaming in the morning air. Blueberry, by the smell of it.

The Highwayman considered how he might get to that treat and take a slice, but it was just a mental exercise, for he had no desire to take anything from the peasants of Pryd, who had next to nothing.

He was still musing about the pie, glancing left and right and trying to figure out how he might get in the front door without being noticed, when he realized his error. For the woman turned around and gave a shriek.

The Highwayman looked at her and held up his hands, bidding her to silence and trying very hard not to seem threatening to her in any way.

"Oh, but ye're to scare a sort to death!" the woman proclaimed. "I thinked yerself to be a goblin or a powrie!"

Bransen stared at her, hardly believing the obvious relief in her tone as she apparently recognized him.

"And what's bringing yerself to me house, Mister Highwayman?" she asked, seeming completely unafraid.

Bransen's mind whirled around corners he didn't know existed. Had his reputation spread so quickly among the peasants that he was considered by them to be a friend? For surely, this woman, helpless if he chose to attack, was showing no more fear of him than she might show to her own farm dog.

"Ah, it was me pie, wasn't it?" she asked with an exaggerated wink. "Come on in, then. I'll cut ye a good piece to fill yer belly."

Bransen looked all around to make sure that no one else was in the area, then with a shrug pulled himself through the window and took an offered seat at the table.

"I came to steal a scent of your pie, not to take food from your family," he said.

"Bah, ye've earned that and more."

"What do you know of me?"

"I know that ye kicked them beasties bothering poor Cadayle. I know that them tax collectors—Bestesbulzibar take them all!—keep looking over their shoulders for fear that ye'll strip them naked and run them into town! Hah, what more am I needing to know than that?"

As she finished, she pulled out a knife, cut fully a quarter of the pie, and heaped it onto a wooden plate. "Eat up, Highwayman. And if ye're still hungry, I'll chop ye another slice!"

Bransen couldn't deny the growling in his stomach and so he did begin to munch on the wonderful berry pie.

The woman sat across from him and shooed her children off into a corner. She stared at him all along, only turning her head to yell at the children whenever they became unruly. After a minute or so, she began telling him all about her miserable life, of how she rarely had enough to eat, of how her husband was off in the south and probably dead, of how her neighbors wanted to help her—and some were helping to tend the fields—but they were almost all in similar straits. She had few kind words for Laird Prydae, Bransen noted, and few for the Church of Abelle, though if she harbored any ill feelings at all toward the Samhaists, she kept them to herself.

She rambled on and on as he ate the pie, and she gradually shifted the conversation to the subject of her missing husband, repeatedly saying that he'd "been gone so long. So terribly long," and how lonely she was. Naive Bransen didn't even catch on to her leading statements until he finished the pie and she moved to cut him another piece, insisting he stay.

He politely declined and started to rise.

"Ye don't have to be going," she said, and she put her hand on top of his.

For a moment, the dashing Highwayman found that he couldn't draw his breath.

"I knew ye wouldn't hurt me the moment I saw ye at me window," the woman went on, her voice husky. "But there be a part of me that was hoping ye might be wanting more sweets than pie."

Bransen lifted her hand to his lips and kissed it gently. "My sweet lady," he said, "would that I could. But time is short and I've much to do." He kissed her hand again, then on impulse, moved in close and kissed her on the cheek—or started to, but she grabbed his face and brought her lips to his, and with an urgency he had never known before.

Finally Bransen extracted himself from her clutches.

"Let me see that face!" the woman purred, reaching for his mask.

But he was too quick, and ready for her now. With a jump and a spin, he was back at the window. "Truly a lovely pie," he said with a salute, and then he leaped outside and ran off.

He looked back a short while later to see the woman, face flushed, staring at him from the window.

Many emotions coursed through Bransen at that moment, not the least of which was a warm feeling that went from head to toe. It wasn't just the passionate kiss that had excited him but the mere fact that this woman, this ordinary Pryd peasant, knew of his deeds and obviously approved!

Full of spirit and full of confidence, the Highwayman dashed across the outskirts of Pryd Town, moving from shadow to shadow as always, but not too concerned that he might be seen—which he often was, peasants pointing and calling his name, and a couple even cheering from afar.

He came in sight of Cadayle's house at long last, approaching the lane from the north. He saw her before he got close, for she was out in the fields, down the long sloping hill behind the cottage, with the family's donkey.

Bransen looked all around, at last spotting some wildflowers, and he pulled them from the ground and hurried down the hill to join his love.

Cadayle nearly jumped out of her worn leather shoes when she finally saw him, standing there calmly and leaning on the donkey.

"Greetings this fine noon, fair lady," he said, grinning mischievously, one hand on the donkey as the beast contentedly munched the grass, the other behind his back.

"What are you doing about in the light of day?"

"Do you think that I vanish with the sunrise? A creature solely of the night, am I?"

"You've made few friends among the soldiers of Laird Prydae."

Bransen shrugged. "They are not the friends I want," he said, and he pulled his hand from around his back, presenting Cadayle with the flowers.

Her eyes widened in surprise, but she did smile and gradually reached for them.

Bransen teased and pulled them back away. "For a kiss?"

Cadayle's smile disappeared and she stepped back. "A kiss?" she echoed. "For my own flowers?"

"Your own?"

"You just picked them on the hill."

"How could you know that?"

"Because they're still dripping of dirt, and I saw them on my way down here. I kept Doully here from eating them, for I could see them from my window. Pretty they were in sunset, but now I'll not have that pleasure again, will I?"

Bransen could not have been more crestfallen, and it showed on his face; but Cadayle just laughed and jumped forward, taking the bouquet. "You are an easy one to tease," she remarked, and she brought the sweet-smelling flowers to her nose and inhaled deeply.

"But, fair lady," Bransen said, regaining his composure, "I named a payment." He started forward, but Cadayle held him at bay with her outstretched hand.

"A kiss is not a payment," she said. "It's given by choice. My own choice."

Bransen stepped back and studied her. "Then it is true," he said, feigning sudden and complete despair. "There is another man who calls Cadayle his lover!"

"What?"

"Ah, I have heard the rumors, my lady. All about town speak of them."

Cadayle waved him away dismissively.

"They speak of Cadayle and a queer little man who works with the monks," Bransen pressed, thinking himself quite clever.

But Cadayle's face went very tight.

"Yes, a creature they call the Stork," Bransen went on, not reading the signs. "Cadayle loves the Stork!"

He finished with a wide smile, one that Cadayle's hand promptly wiped away with a stinging slap.

For a moment, Bransen's heart fell and broke. Had the mere notion of Cadayle with his other self so disgusted her?

But the truth spilled forth in a burst of venom from her that shocked the Highwayman. "Do not ever speak of poor Bransen in such a manner ever again!" she demanded. "Do not mock him!"

"I—I did not," Bransen tried to reply.

"I thought you a better man than that!" Cadayle fumed. "Bransen Garibond's infirmity is no matter of jest, nor is it his fault in any way. You mock me by calling me his lover—but I would be, do not doubt, if he were a healthy man!"

Those simple words nearly knocked Bransen from his feet and had his heart thumping in his thin chest.

"I thought you different from the others," Cadayle continued, despite the Highwayman's holding his hand up to try to calm her. "When you fought Tarkus Breen and his bullies, when you slew him, I thought it in defense of Bransen as much as in the defense of Cadayle."

"It was," he managed to interject.

"But you mock him."

"I do not."

"Then what?"

"I feared that I was walking over a line in trying to court you," Bransen improvised. "I thought it prudent to discern your true feelings for the one called Stork."

"I hate that name. He is Bransen."

The Highwayman conceded the point with a low bow and asked in all sincerity, "Then you do not love him?"

"Perhaps I do."

"But you will not marry him?"

"Marry him?" Cadayle echoed with obvious incredulity. "He can hardly care for himself. How is he to care for a family? Bransen will stay with the brothers of Abelle. It is the only place for him, I fear."

"And what for Cadayle, then?"

"That is for Cadayle to decide."

He dipped another conciliatory bow. In the middle of it, it occurred to Bransen to pull off his mask and reveal himself to her. How he wanted to!

But he could not. He could not so endanger Cadayle as to reveal himself, and he realized that he had not the courage to do so. She had not declared her love for him, after all, but had merely not denied the possibility.

Bransen wished that he were a braver man.

"You are not the only one who cares for Bransen," he said.

Cadayle didn't seem convinced, but neither did she remain overtly angry. "Do you wish me to leave?"

Cadayle paused and stared at him for a long while, then said simply and soberly, "No."

"But no kiss for the flowers?" Bransen dared to tease.

"Next time, perhaps," she said, and she managed a smile. When his grin widened, though, she added, "Perhaps not."

"My lady, do not play with my heart."

Cadayle laughed.

"You dare to mock me?"

She laughed again, and he joined in.

A moment later, Bransen remembered the monks had planned to begin returning soon after lunch. "I must be on my way," he said. "But I will visit again, on my word."

"Day or night, it would seem."

"A man's heart forces him to take risks."

It was tough for Bransen to turn away from that smiling face, but he knew that time was running short. He ran with a spring in his step, flush with hope and joy, all the way back to the river, where he changed back into his woolen tunic and shuffled his awkward way back to Chapel Pryd.

Brother Reandu was already back at the chapel, waiting for him, seeming very afraid and more than a little angry. "What are you doing out beyond the chapel wall?" he scolded, and he grabbed Bransen by the arm and rushed him inside. "And what have you got in that sack?"

A wave of panic swept over Bransen. The game was over, he realized.

But a call from across the chapel's courtyard caught Reandu's attention.

"Come along and be quick!" Master Bathelais ordered Reandu. "Laird Prydae has ordered a sweep of the town to collect funds for Prince Yeslnik!"

"You go and finish your chores," Reandu said to Bransen, and the monk hurried away, apparently forgetting about the small sack.

Bransen breathed a deep, deep sigh of relief.

He made his way back to his room and fell upon his cot. The laird had ordered yet another round of taxes to be collected?

Bransen lay down and closed his eyes, seeking sleep.

He thought that the Highwayman would be busy that night.

Sweet dreams of fields and flowers and Cadayle swept through him. His body felt again the warmth of the peasant woman's kiss, but his mind substituted his love for the farm woman. Somewhere deep inside, the sleeping Bransen knew that her kisses would be sweeter.

The exertion of the day, the tumult of emotions, and the energy used in maintaining the harmony of his life energy, were more than Bransen had bargained for, and he was awakened not later that night, but the next morning, by the calls of a brother for him to get up and get to his chores.

So he did, and during the course of that day, he learned that Laird Prydae's collectors had been especially energetic the previous night.

Perhaps the Highwayman had missed an opportunity.

But the visiting Prince Yeslnik still had to get the treasure out of Pryd Holding.

When Yeslnik's carriage left Castle Pryd to great fanfare two days later, all the monks were in attendance.

And with the chapel emptied yet again, the Highwayman, too, was out and about.

CHAPTER 31

The Sparkle in His Eyes

Bannagran tried hard not to laugh, but his chuckles kept slipping past his tightly closed lips.

"Do not underestimate the seriousness of this," Laird Prydae warned. "Men like Prince Yeslnik do not take well to embarrassment." Despite his obvious sincerity, Prydae couldn't help but chuckle also. Prince Yeslnik's coach had rolled back to Castle Pryd. The angry young man had leaped from it, running screaming to Laird Prydae that he must capture and kill this "Highwayman beast!" Yeslnik had quickly recounted the encounter with the Highwayman, how this mysterious figure dressed in black had leaped atop his royal coach and had robbed him at sword point of all the monies Prydae had just collected.

Princess Olym had added that this robber had initially dispatched the powries who had initially stopped the coach.

"Do not forget that the prince's wife was quite smitten with the beast," Bannagran replied. "Or that Harkin, the driver, was quite grateful. Had the Highwayman not arrived, the three of them would have been slaughtered by the dwarves and Harkin's wounded friend would surely have died—I noticed that Prince Yeslnik made no mention of the powries at all."

"The man is angry."

"Wounded pride will do that to you."

"He will take that anger back to Laird Delaval. That and an additional tax exacted from Pryd."

"My liege, we cannot go back to the people for more money and goods," Bannagran warned. "They will not stand for it. Every tax collector would need a band of warriors to accompany him on his rounds, and there would be bloodshed, I warn you. Much bloodshed."

Laird Prydae considered those words carefully, knowing their truth but knowing, too, that he could not send Yeslnik back to Laird Delaval empty-handed. How he wished that the young prince had just kept going, all the way to the great river. That would have bought him some time, at least, before he needed to go and collect more revenues for his protecting Laird Delaval. Now he understood the truth, and that realization only made him even more angry at this Highwayman. He would have to take the money for Delaval out of his own riches.

"Post a reward," he told Bannagran.

"The people love the Highwayman."

"The people love money more. Post a reward, a substantial one. Promise that anyone who provides information leading to the capture of the outlaw will dine at the castle for the rest of his life. Offer a thousand gold coins. Offer complete access for the informant and his family to the brothers of Abelle and their healing gemstones."

Bannagran raised an eyebrow at that.

"Master Bathelais will not refuse me in this."

"I will spread the word through every tavern and every road," Bannagran promised.

Prydae walked over and dropped a hand on the sitting Bannagran's shoulder. "You have been my friend and companion for as long as I can remember," he said. "I need you now. I charge you with capturing and killing this outlaw. He is undermining my rule, Bannagran, and this latest theft jeopardizes the very life of Pryd Holding."

Bannagran's eyebrow arched again, showing that he thought his friend might be exaggerating a bit on that last point. There was no doubt, however, that the mere presence of this Highwayman was raising the ire of the common folk against Prydae.

"The people will not be pleased when he is dragged in and executed," Bannagran noted.

"Bernivvigar will kill him for us, I am certain. And the people will forget, soon enough. But we must get him, and soon. He has embarrassed us—could it be that he will attempt to attack me? To murder me in my sleep?"

Bannagran furrowed his brow. After all, the Highwayman had only killed one man in all of his exploits, and that with the man's own knife.

"Destroy him, my friend," Prydae ordered. "Use every soldier and every resource at our disposal. Find him and kill him, and very soon."

Bannagran nodded.

Y ou should not be here," Cadayle said. "You should not be anywhere near the town this night. Laird Prydae's men are everywhere, searching for you."

"How do you know that I was the one who saved Prince Yeslnik this day?" Bransen asked.

"Saved? Robbed, you mean."

"Robbed? Nay, I call it a reward, my lady. First I killed all the powries that would have killed the good young prince, then I took a reward."

"That is not what they are saying."

"Do you believe that any nobleman would be brave enough to admit that he was rescued? And by an outlaw highwayman?" Bransen said with a laugh. "No, Prince Yeslnik's pride will not allow him to include that little detail in his recounting of the encounter."

Cadayle managed a smile—and her smile truly lit up Bransen's heart!—but she glanced all around nervously, as if expecting Laird Prydae's soldiers to leap upon her.

"Perhaps I should have let the powries finish him and his wife before taking my reward," Bransen went on. "But then, of course, the innocent drivers would have been slaughtered as well, and that I could not allow."

"But you would have allowed the prince to be killed?"

The Highwayman shrugged.

"And his wife?" Cadayle pressed, clearly distressed.

"Well, perhaps not, though I am not very fond of the lairds of Honce and their ignoble henchmen."

"They are our protectors."

"They protect themselves," the Highwayman argued. "I have seen Laird Prydae's castle, and I assure you, the man wants for nothing."

"He is appointed by God, so say the priests. His line is blessed, as are the lines of all the lairds."

The Highwayman laughed at her, but inside, Bransen thought her words no laughing matter. He had come to understand the "sanctity" of the lairds, anointed by both monk of Abelle and Samhaist alike, each trying to gain favor with the powerful noblemen. The Book of Jhest had told Bransen a different story. The Jhesta Tu mystics outright rejected any special relationship between the secular leaders, of tribes and kingdoms and holdings, and God. But the peasants of Honce didn't see that; not even Cadayle, whom Bransen considered very intelligent and aware—mightily so, compared to the other peasants.

"Then I suppose that God will not be pleased with me for taking . . . this," Bransen answered, pulling forth the jeweled necklace he had pilfered from Olym.

Cadayle sucked in her breath, and the glittering of her eyes rivaled that of the stones in the starlight.

"Lady Cadayle," Bransen began. "Beautiful Cadayle. If you are to try to convince me that Princess Olym Delaval's neck is more fit for this than your own, I pray you save your breath and your effort. If God has blessed any woman with the beauty to properly complement this necklace, then surely that woman is you."

She raised her gaze to match his stare, and still she said nothing.

Bransen moved forward slowly, unthreateningly. She was afraid, he could tell; she was even shivering a little, and not from the chill night air. Bransen reached up and draped the necklace about her thin neck, reaching behind with both hands, and even moving closer to look over her shoulder as he worked the clasp.

He could feel her breath on his neck, so warm, and after he had secured the clasp, he stayed in place for a while, basking in the feel and smell of Cadayle.

Finally, he leaned back so that he was right before her, his hands still upon her shoulders.

"I cannot keep this," she said, and he put a finger to her lips to silence her.

"Of course you cannot," Bransen agreed. "But wear it this night, and secretly for as long as you desire. No doubt Laird Prydae and Prince Yeslnik will offer a fine reward for the piece. When they do, say that you found it at the side of the road, and collect your due. For your mother, if not for yourself."

"I cannot."

"Of course you can," said Bransen. "I will scatter a few coins near to the oak at the forward end of this very lane. Say you found the necklace there. The fools will believe that I dropped some of the booty."

"But—"

"What else am I to do with it?" Bransen interrupted. "I have no need of coin, am well fed and well housed."

"Then why do you steal?"

"Because I know that I am among the few who can so make such a claim of health and comfort. Because I know that Laird Prydae and all the other noblemen live in luxury while the rest toil for their benefit, even die for their benefit." He wanted to add, "And because it's fun," but he thought it better to keep that a secret.

"And I do appreciate beautiful things," Bransen added, and he stared intently at Cadayle, grabbing her eyes with his own, and he would not let go. "And truly that necklace is a pale bauble beside the beauty I now see. Upon you, it shines so much the brighter."

She blushed and couldn't hide her smile, and she started to look away. But Bransen wouldn't let her. He brought his hand up beside her cheek and slowly turned her to face him directly. He couldn't resist her, then, her smell, her warm breath, her beauty in the starlight, and so he leaned forward and dared to press his lips against hers.

To his amazement, she did not pull away from him, and her arms came up around his back, pulling him closer.

For Bransen, there had never been a moment as sweet.

Cadayle pulled back after a long and lingering moment. "I should not have done that," she said, and she broke free of his embrace.

"Oh, but I want to do it again!" Bransen blurted, and Cadayle put a hand over her mouth and giggled.

"But I do," Bransen said, and it was his turn to be embarrassed.

"Have you never kissed a woman before?"

Bransen thought on that for a moment, in light of his encounter with the farm lady. "One kissed me, once."

Cadayle giggled again. "Only one? A rogue like you?"

"And how many men has Cadayle kissed?" Bransen shot right back at her.

She grew very serious suddenly. "None before like that," she said.

Bransen felt his legs go weak. "One more kiss before I go?" he asked.

"Just one, and just a kiss, and then you must be on your way, Highwayman."

Bransen came forward in a rush, but Cadayle held him back long enough to calm him. Then she kissed him, long and soft and sweet.

The taste of her followed him all the way back to Chapel Pryd, all the way back to his dark and dirty hole.

Callen brought her hand to her mouth to hide her gasp, and she felt for a moment as if she would simply fall over. Never in her life had she ever seen any piece of jewelry as fabulous as the necklace Cadayle was wearing.

"You saw him again," Callen breathed.

"I found it by the side of the road," Cadayle said. "Along with these." She held out her hand, showing the few coins the Highwayman had given her to seed the story.

Callen's eyes went narrow. "You didn't find anything."

Cadayle squirmed, the observant mother noted. "Under the tree, Mother. There might be more. You and I can go look in the morning's light."

"Cadayle . . ." Callen said in even and controlled tones, her best Mother's voice. "You've not ever lied to me before."

Cadayle seemed to visibly break, then, her shoulders slumping.

"The Highwayman came to you again this night."

"Yes."

Callen took Cadayle's chin in her hand and lifted her face so that their stares locked. "And what did you give him for the necklace?"

Cadayle's eyes went wide in shock, which brought a wave of relief to the older woman.

"I did kiss him," Cadayle admitted a moment later, and Callen scowled. "But not for the necklace. I kissed him because I wanted to."

"Would you have kissed him if he hadn't given you the jewels?"

"Of course!" Cadayle blurted, and then she seemed embarrassed and low-ered her gaze once more. "I mean, it wasn't the necklace that made me choose to kiss him."

Callen pulled her close for a hug, then pushed her back to arms' length. "But you cannot keep it. You know that."

"He told me to turn it over to the laird and prince for the reward they will likely offer. Still, I feel as if I'm stealing. Perhaps I should just give it back for no reward."

"You're to do no such thing!" Callen snapped, and Cadayle shot to atten-tion. "No, you do as the Highwayman bade you. Laird Prydae and Prince Yesl-nik aren't to miss any reward, and God and the Ancient Ones know that we could put the coin to better use, for our sake and for that of all our hungry neighbors."

Cadayle brought her hand up to the precious necklace and her look went wistful, revealing to the observant Callen that her daughter wasn't truly en-amored of the idea of parting with the gift.

"You know that you cannot keep it," Callen said softly. "Wouldn't Berniv-vigar be happy to find you wearing such a thing?"

"I know," Cadayle replied halfheartedly.

The younger woman went to the other side of the small house then and began undressing, then slipped into her bed under the blankets.

Callen noted that she was still wearing the necklace. Callen just smiled about it, however, and was both glad that her daughter had apparently found love and terribly afraid of this man who had become the object of Cadayle's affections.

CHAPTER 32

Trinkets and Revelations

Any feelings of levity Bransen held about his exploits and the frustration he was causing to Laird Prydae were lost the next day when, out in the courtyard of Chapel Pryd, he saw the results of that frustration. Soldiers were everywhere, it seemed, moving about the streets and banging on the doors. The Stork overheard one conversation along the roadside not far away.

"What do you know of him?" the soldier roared, and he grabbed a young woman by the front of her simple tunic and lifted her up to tiptoes. "You'd be smart to tell me all!"

"I know nothing, me lord," the woman cried.

"You haven't met this Highwayman?"

"No, me lord. Please let me go. Ye're hurting me poor neck."

The soldier roughly shoved her back, and she stumbled and nearly fell. She ran off, crying, while the warrior moved along to the nearest door and began banging on it.

Anger welled inside Bransen, and it was all he could do to suppress his urge to don his black outfit and have a word with that man and all the others.

The Stork bit his lip and forced himself to calm down. The laird was angry and his soldiers were bullying some folks, but it was nothing serious, he told himself. A smile wound its way onto the Stork's crooked face, and suddenly he found that he was thrilled that he was so troubling the powers of Pryd Holding, and even those beyond. He used the recollection of Prince Yeslnik's face to block out the image of the frightened young woman. Yes, that was a pleasing memory.

Bransen vowed to himself that he would step up his pace, that he would infuriate Laird Prydae beyond reason. How far could he push it? he wondered. How long would he have to go to force the laird to make concessions to him? He fantasized about that, about being called to a meeting wherein Prydae offered his surrender. Wouldn't he be a hero to the common folk then! And wouldn't Cadayle love him all the more?

That last thought brought a frown to him. Was it him she loved? Bransen?

Or was it someone else entirely, the mysterious rogue named the Highwayman?

It was all too confusing, and so Bransen let go of the troubling questions and fears and focused instead on the kiss. He could still feel Cadayle's warmth; it had taken him through a night of wonderful dreams. There was nothing about her that wasn't perfect in his eyes. Her face, her soft skin, her softer lips. The feel of her against him, the sound of her voice, her gentle touch.

All of it stayed with him as he finished his chores that day—a day in which he kept glancing to the west, willing the sun to hurry and sink behind the horizon. For in the night, he would see her again.

She couldn't deny her excitement as she noted his approach. She had known that the mysterious Highwayman would come out to her this night. She had seen his face after their kiss and had heard the sincerity in his voice. Even with all that, however, Cadayle couldn't help but doubt, and fear, that he would not return. That fear, above everything else, revealed to her the truth behind her jumbled thoughts. For she was indeed afraid that he would not come to her this night, and if that fear was realized, it would be a painful thing.

But the Highwayman did not disappoint. He approached the field behind Cadayle's house with a visible spring in his step, and Cadayle knew that he had seen her long before she was aware of him.

He danced up before her, dipped a quick and polite bow, and produced a small sack from behind his back, handing it to her.

"You and your mother will eat well this week," he said with that mischievous grin of his, one made more mysterious by the fact that he wore a mask above that toothy grin, and one that Cadayle was beginning to see in her mind long after the man had gone.

Cadayle fished about in the sack, discovering an assortment of meat and fruit and bread. She hid her excitement and her smile, and she wasn't really surprised. Almost every night, the Highwayman came to her bearing gifts, from the mundane, like the food, to the fabulous necklace she still wore upon her delicate neck.

When she looked up, she noted that he was staring at that necklace. "They've posted no reward," she said, bringing a hand up to it.

"They will soon enough," he assured her. "Their searches around Pryd Town have brought them nothing but the enmity of the peasants. Their frustrations will lead them to try to turn commoner against commoner because there are simply too many of you for the noblemen and their few warriors to inspect or to control, if it ever came to that."

That last line hit her hard. "Do not speak of such things," she said.

"It is a reality the lairds understand well."

"Please do not speak of it," Cadayle said again.

"If the common folk rose up—"

"Then many of them would be slaughtered," Cadayle interrupted. "Whether the lairds fall or not would be of little consequence to a man killed in the street. And I would rather live under the press of Laird Prydae than bury my ma in trying to defeat him. What we've got is not perfect, but it's what we've got, and nothing more."

The Highwayman paused, then started to say, "But," then just paused again and seemed to shrug it all away.

"They will post a reward soon enough," he did say.

Cadayle wanted to reply that she hoped it would be a long time before Laird Prydae did so, but she held her thoughts to herself. She liked wearing the necklace—more than she understood at that moment. It made her feel pretty. It made her feel, for just a few moments of conscious delusion, rich and powerful.

And it made her feel, most of all, as if this mysterious stranger, this hero who had saved her and her mother, this good man who was trying to help the lot of the always-over-looked rabble of Pryd, cared for her. Cadayle wasn't even sure how she felt about the Highwayman. Did she love him? She hadn't even seen him without his mask!

Cadayle looked at him then, carefully, and what she did know was that she was glad, truly glad, that he apparently cared for her.

"Are all the people feeling your generosity?" she asked. "Or just a few, like me and my mother?"

"All the people? I would be busy indeed in even trying to visit the homes of half! I share what I can and do not distinguish among the people—well, except for you, of course. For you, I always save the best that I find."

Cadayle was certain that she was blushing fiercely, and she lowered her gaze.

"The laird must be seeking you."

"With all of his men," the Highwayman answered.

Cadayle looked up at him with concern. "If he catches you, he will kill you horribly."

The Highwayman shrugged. "I have killed no man who did not deserve it, nor have I taken anything that did not rightfully belong to the people."

Cadayle's hand went back to the necklace.

"Well, the lairds should not so hoard the wealth, then," said the Highwayman. "They live in splendor, while all else suffer in squalor."

"They are the chosen of God."

The Highwayman snorted and Cadayle took a reflexive step back, not quite understanding what it was about her last statement that had irked him. Was it the concept relating to the lairds, or the concept of God? At that moment, Cadayle began to understand just how shallow her growing feelings for this man truly might be.

"Are you of the Church of Blessed Abelle?" she asked.

He seemed surprised. "Well, no . . ." The answer was less than definitive in tone.

"A Samhaist?"

"Never that!"

Cadayle looked at him curiously, hiding her great relief. She certainly had no love for Bernivvigar and his horrible followers. Her mother had never told her anything good at all about the Samhaists, and though neither had she overtly attacked Bernivvigar in her remarks to Cadayle, her voice when speaking of the man or his religion had always been tight, as if holding back visceral hatred. Cadayle had gotten that impression, at least.

"Do not think me a godless man," the Highwayman stated, drawing her from her contemplations. "I see good in much of what the brothers of Abelle attempt to accomplish, and many of their actions are wrought of generosity. But there is more to the world than they know, I am certain, and so I do not limit myself to the beliefs they present."

"You know better than the Church?"

The Highwayman shrugged in that confident way of his.

Cadayle let it go at that.

They talked some more, about nothing in particular, and nothing of any real importance, and Cadayle soon began to understand that the Highwayman was just stalling, stretching out the conversation in the hope of . . .

He was nervous.

So was she.

Her mother began to call for her, and she glanced back at her house, then turned to her masked suitor. "I must be going," she said suddenly, and she came forward and offered him another kiss, thinking to make it just a quick peck.

But he caught her and he held her, held them pressed together, and for a long and wonderful moment, Cadayle didn't try to wriggle away.

She skipped all the way home, like a little girl dancing in the sunshine after a spring thundershower.

Thoughts of Cadayle followed Bransen as he made his way across Pryd Town. Once again this night, many of Laird Prydae's soldiers were about, as well as tax collectors moving from house to house and pestering the peasants. Bransen was in no mood for violence that night, no mood for catching one of those money-grubbers in a dark corner and striping him of his ill-gotten coin and foodstuffs.

He did veer from his course at one point, however, when he noted firelight far to the east. He headed toward the campfire out of the main town, moving through a copse of trees and then across a small field to a second copse.

Several men sat around the fire, over which a pig was roasting. They were vagabonds, Bransen knew, dispossessed by the many battles and the weight of their disappointment. All had wild beards and all were incredibly dirty. These were the outcasts of Pryd Holding, the forgotten men wandering the shadows at the edges of the civilized town. Bransen had seen many such men, perhaps some of these very ones, at Chapel Pryd, coming in to beg for food or magical gemstone relief from their maladies.

Bransen crouched just outside the radius of the firelight and listened, his smile widening as he came to understand that they were talking about him and the inconvenience he was causing Laird Prydae.

"Bah, good enough for Laird Prydae, I say," one roughly grumbled, and he tore a piece of meat from the bone and popped it into his mouth.

"Tired I am of fighting," said another. "Watched three of me friends fall to the swords of Ethelbert. Three's enough."

"Three's too many," another agreed.

"Well, I'm not seeing how this Highwayman's to help us from having that number go up," the first came back. "Nor am I seeing how he's to stop meself from going back to the south at Laird Prydae's bidding."

"But ye're not for crying over Prydae's money losses, now are ye?" said the second, and they all laughed.

"Laird Prydae can afford the losses," Bransen heard himself saying; and without even thinking of it, the Highwayman rose and stepped into the firelight. How the men scrambled! One even drew out a small knife and waved it ominously in Bransen's direction.

"Hold, I pray you," the Highwayman said. "I come not as any foe but simply as another traveler this night."

"Ye're him!" one of the men cried.

Bransen shrugged.

"Ye're the one stealing everything," the first said.

"Not everything and not for myself, of course," Bransen replied. "Laird Prydae has more than enough food and coin, I know, and so I am merely helping him to distribute his goods to those in need."

The men all looked at each other, and the one with the knife lowered it and put it away.

"Sit down, then," said the first of the group. "Take some food with us and tell us yer tale."

Bransen did take a seat on one of the fallen logs that formed the seats in their camp, and he did take a chunk of the offered meat. He didn't tell them any tales, however, and he just answered their barrage of questions with grunts and shrugs. To him, it was enough to simply enjoy the company, and he couldn't deny that he didn't mind at all the expressions of admiration, even awe, that were aimed his way. Again, the Book of Jhest's warnings about the failings of pride came to him, but he easily pushed them away.

For it all seemed like an innocent encounter of little importance, and so what matter if he indulged himself a bit by basking in their admiration? But then one of the men asked, in all seriousness, "Are ye looking for hire ons, then, Mister Highwayman? Are ye needing some strong men to help ye with yer work?"

The others all grunted and nodded and began whispering excitedly among themselves, but Bransen was too taken with the question to even begin to listen to those side conversations. This was a possibility he hadn't foreseen, and one that he found hard to dismiss. Could he form a band and lead it? Could he take these ragtag men, and so many others just like them who loitered about Pryd Town, and turn them into a formidable force?

He didn't know, and before he could explore it more seriously with some questions of his hosts, he noted something else, something that one of the men was holding: a skinning knife with a dull white bone handle.

"May I see your knife?" Bransen asked, holding out a hand.

"What?" the man replied, and he followed Bransen's gaze to the implement, then brought it up. "What, this?" He handed it over. "An old one and not much to see, but holding a fine edge, don't ye doubt!"

Bransen took the blade, thinking how much it resembled the one Garibond had always used back at the lake. That thought amused him, until he rolled the knife over and noted a stain on its handle, just below the blade, and a nick in the blade itself. Bransen froze, his eyes going wide. There could not be a second knife like this one, with such a similar stain and nick.

Bransen stared at it, remembering the many times he had seen this very blade, this exact knife, in Garibond's hand. He could picture his father putting it to use to cut the tasty flesh from a bass or trout; he could see it as clearly as if he were watching it then and there.

"Where did you get this?" the Highwayman asked, his tone changing dramatically.

He could tell that the vagabond caught the seriousness of that voice when the man stuttered, "W-what? That old thing? Had it all me life. Me da, he give it to me, he did."

Bransen turned a scowl upon the man. "I know this knife," he said. "And it was not your father's."

"Oh, ye're m-meaning the knife," the man stammered in a ridiculous correction. "No, no, the knife's not from me da. Found it, I did, years ago."

"Where?"

"Well, I'm not for remembering."

Bransen's sword seemed to leap into his hand, and he leveled it at the trembling man. One of the others screamed, a second shouted for him to be at ease.

"Come from the lake," the frightened vagabond stammered.

"From a house near the lake, you mean. The house of Garibond Womak."

The man shook his head and stuttered a few incomprehensible sounds.

"Aye, it was old Garibond's house," said another of the group. "I knew that one, Garibond Womak, and as good a man as ever I knew, he was."

Bransen lowered the sword. "Was?"

"Aye, Garibond once lived in the very house where come that knife."

"Where is he now?"

"Garibond Womak?" The man shrugged. "He's dead, from all I heard, and so he must be. Many went to the house and took what was there."

Bransen's eyes flashed with sudden anger.

"Aye, that's the way of it," another of the group insisted. "So many have so little. When one's dying, we're not to let his belongings go to waste."

"Garibond is not dead!" Bransen insisted.

"Then he's been gone a lot of years, and so it's the same," the man with the knife argued back.

Bransen shook his head. None of it made any sense to him. Garibond couldn't be dead. What had Brother Reandu said? That he had moved south . . . But Bransen remembered, too, that Brother Reandu would not meet his eyes. And Bransen thought of his last visit to the houses on the lake, of the strangers he had seen there, fishing and going about their business as if that was their home.

A fit of trembling began at the base of Bransen's spine and worked its way steadily up. Garibond dead? The thought hammered at him, for never had he even considered such a thing. Garibond was the foundation of all his life; and for ten years, Bransen had held fast the fantasy of going back to him, of showing him that his son was all right, after all.

"What more do you know?" he demanded of the group.

"I know that ye're holding me knife."

"Garibond's knife," Bransen corrected with a growl that told them the issue was not up for debate. But he noted the expressions coming at him from all the men, and most of those looks registered disappointment. They had invited him in to dine with them, though they rarely had enough to eat, he knew. They had offered to join with him.

They thought him a hero of the common folk.

Bransen tossed the knife down before the man. "Garibond is not dead," he said. "And when I find him, I ask that you return his knife."

"Bah, it's me own now," the man said defiantly, and he scooped up the blade. "Had it for ten years!"

The words nearly floored Bransen, and he staggered back as if struck, then turned on his heel and rushed out of the trees and across the field, running fast for Chapel Pryd, running away from the horrible thoughts that were dancing in his mind.

But they followed him, every step.

CHAPTER 33

A Woman and Her Jewels

Bannagran walked through the streets of Pryd Town muttering to himself, remembering his last conversation with Laird Prydae. He had not often seen his friend so animated and agitated. The continuing war threat to Pryd Holding had the laird on the edge, and this Highwayman character was threatening to push him right over. Every day at breakfast, Prydae spoke of nothing else, feverishly working with Bannagran and Rennarq to try to find some clues as to how they might apprehend the rogue. Every day, they related the same stories over and over again. Prydae had even bade Rennarq to ask Bernivvigar for help, something the secular ruler had always been loath to do.

Bannagran tried a rational approach now, focusing on the patterns of the attacks, from the first sighting of the Highwayman to the last. His thoughts and instincts kept going back to the first incident, the only one in which anyone had been seriously hurt, other than one of Yeslnik's drivers in the powrie attack. As chance would have it, with those very thoughts in mind, he spotted Rulhio Noylan—who had been among the five that the Highwayman had defeated—walking along the road by the market square.

The large warrior moved to intercept, and Rulhio saw him coming and abruptly turned.

"I would speak with you, young Noylan," Bannagran said, moving fast to catch up.

Rulhio's expression showed great fear when he glanced back at Bannagran, but no more so than Bannagran was used to seeing on the faces of young men, for usually when he spoke to them, it meant a trip to the south and the battle lines! Still, the young man did skid to an abrupt stop and stood waiting for the imposing warrior.

"You were there that night when Tarkus Breen was murdered?" Bannagran asked.

Rulhio swallowed hard and managed a slight nod.

"I wish to hear the tale."

"I told it in full," Rulhio replied shakily. "We all did."

Bannagran sensed suddenly that the man was a bit too defensive, and his instincts told him that there might be more to this than had previously been explained. Knowing aggression to be the arbiter of truth, the imposing warrior grabbed poor Rulhio by the front of his tunic. "And you will tell me again," he too-calmly explained, and he half carried, half dragged the terrified man off the main road, down a side alley where fewer witnesses could be found.

So the cringing Rulhio recounted the tale of that fateful night, a story that seemed strained now to Bannagran and not completely in line with what he had heard those weeks before. Bannagran purposely doubted every word, and searched for weaknesses in the logical chain of events.

"You and your friends were drunk?"

"Aye, he could not have defeated us if we were not," the terrified young man replied.

"And this happened out on the west road, out by Gorham's Hill?"

"Aye, as we told you. Way out there."

"Where did you come by the drink?"

"Inkerby's," Rulhio replied, naming a well-known tavern in Pryd Town, under the shadow of the castle and often frequented by soldiers.

Bannagran tried to hide his smile as he caught on. Why would five drunken men—troublemakers all, he knew—wander from Inkerby's, which was frequented by many of the local whores, all the way out to the western edge of Pryd Town. To his knowledge, none of the five in question lived out that way.

"Gorham's Hill is a long walk from town," he remarked, and he saw the sudden flash of panic in Rulhio's eyes.

"Well, we were drinking and needed to walk it off a bit. Me ma's not in favor of me—"

"You are often drunk," Bannagran interrupted. "And your mother knows as much."

"Just walking, is all."

"To Gorham's Hill? From Inkerby's?"

"Aye."

Bannagran went with his instincts. He came forward suddenly and brutally, grabbing poor, frightened Rulhio and lifting him off the ground. Two strides put them across the alley, where Bannagran slammed Rulhio up against the wall and held him in place, his feet a foot and more off the ground.

"W-what are . . . ?" Rulhio stuttered. "Why are—?"

"You tell me why you were out by Gorham's Hill."

"I just—" Rulhio started to reply. Bannagran brought him out and slammed him against the wall again, and Rulhio cried out.

"Hey there!" someone shouted in protest from the entrance of the alleyway, but when the newcomer saw who was down there—the legendary Bannagran—he ran off.

"My polite questioning fast approaches its end," Bannagran warned, and he pulled poor Rulhio out from the wall again, as if to slam him.

"Was the wench Cadayle!" Rulhio cried, and Bannagran froze, holding him aloft with ease.

"Cadayle?"

"She lives out there. Nothing but trouble for all of us. Teasing all the town men with her charms and protecting that ugly Stork beast who hides in the chapel."

Bannagran put him down, and Rulhio slumped back against the wall, which seemed the only thing holding him up at the moment.

"What are you blabbering about, man?" Bannagran demanded.

"We just wanted to teach her some respect."

"Who? Cadayle?"

"Aye, the wench."

"I know not of her."

"She's living out by Gorham's Hill with her ma," Rulhio explained. "Was Tarkus Breen's idea to pay them a visit. She fought him, here in town, defending that ugly little Stork."

"And so you went out there to teach her a lesson."

"Someone had to!"

Bannagran didn't argue the point with the fool. "And did you? Teach her, I mean?"

"We was going to."

"Did you find her?"

"Aye, we knew where she lived, her and her ma. We had her ready to learn, but then the—the Highwayman, he showed up, and . . ."

Bannagran pulled the man out from the wall. "He showed up and defended the women?"

"Weren't any of his business."

"And he beat you up and your brother?"

"Aye, and he murdered Tarkus!"

Bannagran nodded and roughly pushed Rulhio toward the alley's exit. "Show me this house by Gorham's Hill," he ordered. "I would like to see this woman, Cadayle."

Rulhio started to protest, but Bannagran shoved him again, hard enough to send him sprawling, and he got the message that this was not the time to argue.

Later that day, after sighting the house and Cadayle, Bannagran went back to Castle Pryd and alerted his spies. He thought to go to Laird Prydae with his hunch but changed his mind. Perhaps Rulhio's admission was important. Perhaps not.

Guldibonne Cob rested back against the trunk of a tree, relaxed and quite pleased with himself. For months the slender soldier had worked hard to get in Bannagran's favor, and now his efforts at last seemed to be paying dividends. All those who had fought in the ranks beside Guldibonne were back in the south, warring with the savages from Ethelbert.

But not Guldibonne. Bannagran hadn't sent him back, for he had given Bannagran reason to keep him around. Any errand, asked or unasked, the man had jumped to complete. He had scouted out the most tempting ladies in all the taverns of Pryd Holding, and even beyond Pryd Holding, and had brought them to his commander. It was all in the details, Guldibonne knew, and his attention to those little things had landed him this wonderful duty, watching the house of a pair of pretty women, mother and daughter, while his former comrades were off again at war.

He had gotten to know the lay of the land about Gorham's Hill very well during that first day and had found what he considered to be the perfect observation post, tucked in the boughs of a thick evergreen, with a view of the house, the lane before it, and the rocky field running wide behind. So comfortable was he that he even dared to take a bit of a nap that afternoon while the women were out tending their garden.

Guldibonne awoke soon after sunset, when the lights of candles and fires were just beginning to glow through the small windows and cracks in the wooden doors of the nearby cottages. The spy waited a bit, then carefully looked all about before heading to the window in Cadayle's house. He crept up right below the sill and slowly lifted his head to peek in.

The younger woman was there before him, partially dressed and unknowingly showing him much of her curving charms. But Guldibonne, as much of a lech as he was known to be, found his eyes drawn away from Cadayle's breasts, and up to her neck, where she was placing one of the most magnificent jeweled necklaces he had ever seen.

No peasant could possess even a single one of those glittering stones!

Trembling, Guldibonne finally managed to tear himself away from the amazing sight, and he lowered himself to the ground and slunk away. He hit the road and began walking, even started quietly whistling, in an attempt to appear casual and draw no attention. But this was too much to suppress— wouldn't Bannagran reward him magnificently for this information!

The man began to run full out, all the way to Castle Pryd.

CHAPTER 34

Behind Two Doors

So consumed was Bransen by the discovery of Garibond's knife that he did not go to visit Cadayle the next night. Of course he wanted to see her—he always wanted to be by Cadayle's side—but he knew deep in his heart that something simply wasn't right. Garibond would never have willingly parted with that blade, Bransen knew, for the knife was more than a utensil to him. It was a piece of Garibond's identity, a tool he had clearly valued because of how well it served him throughout his daily routine. He used it for cutting line and skinning fish, for taking small branches for firewood, and for eating his meals. He always carried it. Always.

Yet the man at the campfire claimed that he had possessed it for ten years. Doubts clouded Bransen's thoughts. Was it really Garibond's knife? Or was it, perhaps, that his own memory was not quite as reliable as he believed? He had seen Garibond's knife every day, practically, in the decade he had lived with him. But it was, after all, just a knife, of a simple and common design. And that was, after all, a decade ago, when Bransen was a child.

But why, then, Bransen wondered as he watched from the shadows of some trees, were these strangers living in the two houses of Garibond Womak? He could see them in the firelight behind the small windows of the lower cottage, milling about and making themselves perfectly at home. But how could they be at home in there? And where was Garibond?

He would find out, he decided. He would walk up and demand an explanation. But in what guise? As the Stork? The Highwayman?

He sat and he waited, so many questions spinning about in his thoughts. He watched as the scattered houses all around the area went dark, one by one, and as the upper house on the island similarly dimmed. All the forms moving in the lower house were adults, he could see, the two couples—two generations of a family, he believed. Gradually, the candles burned down and the windows darkened and the fire died out.

But even after the house was dark and quiet, Bransen sat there. He clenched his fists repeatedly at his side; he squinted against the stinging possibilities. He kept hoping that Garibond would walk up to the house, but he knew deep in the truthful recesses of his heart that it would not be.

The night deepened around him. No use in going to Cadayle now, he knew, for she was likely fast asleep. Almost all the town was fast asleep.

He watched the moon—the goddess Sheila to the Samhaists—pass her apex above him and wind down to the western horizon. And still he sat there, paralyzed by a fear more profound than any he had ever known, more so even than on that night he had first watched Tarkus Breen and his cohorts at Cadayle's.

"I must," he whispered to the night wind, and he pulled himself to his feet. "I must," he repeated, more loudly and assuredly, when he realized that his feet were not moving.

He thought of Garibond, recalling images of him as clearly as if he were seeing them all over again: at the lake; showing off a large catch; flashing one of his rare smiles; tousling Bransen's hair; splitting firewood; or just sitting calmly at the window, watching the world flow past.

Bolstered by the memories, the young man began to move, forcing one foot in front of the other. He owed this to Garibond, he reminded himself. He had to find out what was going on and where his father had gone. Outwardly, he just kept repeating, "I must."

Then he was at the door, and never had he seen a more solid barrier. He lifted his fist to knock, but lowered it, and then repeated the movement several times.

And then he began banging on the door, softly at first, but growing in intensity with each frustrated rap. "Answer me!" he called, and his fist slammed hard against the wood.

After several minutes, he had made up his mind to kick the door down, but just then he saw a light come up inside, and a form appeared at the window.

"Open the door," he demanded. "I must speak with you."

"'Ere, who are you, then?" asked an older man.

Bransen slammed the door hard. "Open the door or I shall knock it down."

"'Ere now, you be gone, knave!" the man at the window cried.

In response, Bransen leaped over, flashed out his sword, and put its tip near the man's face. "Knave it is," he said. "And growing angrier by the moment. Open the door, I ask and demand."

"You be gone!" the man shouted, and behind him, Bransen heard a woman cry, "The Highwayman!"

"We've got no coin for you to take," the man said, backing safely out of the sword's reach and sounding less sure of himself.

"I want not your coin," Bransen replied, and he lowered his sword. "Answers I need, and nothing more." He forced all sounds of fury and impatience out of his voice and calmly added, "My apologies, good sir. But please, it is important."

"If talk is all you need, then do it out there," said the obviously terrified man.

"How did you come by these houses?" Bransen asked.

"What do you mean?"

"We been here near to ten years now," the woman added. Bransen heard other voices from inside, off to the side and out of sight.

"How did you come by these houses?"

"Why is that your concern? You're not to take them from us!" the man answered.

"I've no need of any such thing. But I once knew a man who lived here on this lake. He was a friend, and I wish to know why I find you here now, where he should be."

There was some murmuring from within, a whispered conversation that Bransen could not follow.

"His name was Garibond," Bransen said, daring to utter it, though he was concerned about making any connection between Garibond and the Highwayman. But his mounting desperation would not allow for caution at that time. "Garibond Womak. A good and fine man."

More whispering ensued, and then, to Bransen's surprise, the door opened a crack. He moved over to see the two couples standing there in the light of a pair of candles, with the older pair just inside the door and the younger in the shadows behind them. None of the four seemed pleased at that moment.

"Ye knowed Garibond, did ye?" asked the younger woman, a short, plump, and dirty thing with a pug nose and dark rings under her sullen eyes.

"Aye, a good and fine man," said the man standing beside her, his arm draped across her shoulders. "From what I knew of him, I mean, and that weren't much."

"He had that damaged boy," said the older woman. "The one the monks took in when . . ." Her voice trailed off and she looked away.

"This was his house," Bransen blurted, growing nervous.

"For all his days," replied the older man who had addressed Bransen through the window.

Bransen started to nod, and then the words hit him hard as he came to understand their clear implication.

"'Twas Taerel, me da there, that buried him them ten years ago," said the younger woman, and she indicated the previous speaker.

"You must be mistaken," Bransen managed to say, trying hard to keep his jaw from quivering. "Ten years, you say?"

"Aye, was ten years," said Taerel.

"Garibond was dead when the monks came and took this . . . this damaged boy?" Bransen asked, trying desperately to destroy the logic of their claim.

"Was a few weeks later that the monks returned for Garibond," said Taerel, "with the soldiers."

The hairs on the back of Bransen's neck began to stand up.

"Aye," the younger man added. "I was just a boy then, but I'm never to forget that day. They went all through this house, tearing it up, and then they took him." He stepped forward and pointed down the lakeshore to Bransen's right. "Right over there's where they did it."

"Did what?" Bransen's words were hardly more than a whisper.

"They burned him," said the man, who was just a few years older than Bransen.

"Staked him up, branded him a heretic, and burned him alive," Taerel added.

"Bah!" snorted the younger woman. "And them's the ones who're saying that theirs is the gentle way and the gentle god, and not like old Bernivvigar. Bah!"

"The m-monks?" Bransen stuttered. "The monks from the chapel murdered Garibond?"

"Aye, Master Bathelais and the others. With the help of Laird Prydae's soldiers, of course. And it weren't murder if Garibond was guilty of heresy as they claimed, I'd say," said Taerel.

"Murder's murder," muttered the younger woman.

Bransen felt his knees go weak and he knew that he had to get out of there. His stomach began to churn. He half turned.

"Highwayman, you've got quite the tale growing about you," said Taerel. "All the town's talking of you, and glad they are that someone's telling Laird Prydae that he cannot keep taking all of our food and . . ."

The man's voice drifted off behind Bransen as he staggered away, back toward the trees. He couldn't believe what the four had just told him—Master Bathelais and the others would never do such a thing! But Bransen's inner denials rang hollow. He pictured again the knife held by the stranger at the campfire. He wondered suddenly why Garibond had never once come to Chapel Pryd to visit him. Never before had he even considered that fact, but why *had* his beloved father stayed away for all these years?

A sense of profound aimlessness washed over Bransen, a complete unhinging of all his focus and purpose that manifested itself in his lifeline of *chi*. He staggered and stumbled and fell more than once as he made for the copse, finally leaning heavily on one tree.

And still there was nothing but the confusion, the scattering of his life energy, the sporadic bursts and twitches—a profound aimlessness. Not even hopelessness, for hopelessness inferred some design and forward thinking, and in Bransen there was none of that. For all his life, he had lived with daily tragedy, with bullying and his helplessness, with the frustration of having a keen mind trapped in a damaged body. For all his life, the dominant feature had ever been pain.

But not like this. Garibond was dead. Branson knew it, he believed it, he held no doubt of it. Garibond, the uncomplaining man who had given so much to him, was simply no more. And all the fantasies that Bransen had entertained of returning to his beloved father whole and strong were no more. All the hopes that Bransen had about living again with Garibond—but in a completely different relationship, one in which he could care for his father as his father had always cared for him—were no more. But Bransen couldn't even focus on any of those things specifically. They were all there, spinning and intertwining in the scattered jumble of his mind, finally settling to a sense of emptiness, a hole he knew he could never fill.

He slipped down to the ground, all strength gone, tears filling his eyes.

The knock startled the two women, but before either could begin to react, a second, more impressive banging burst the door askew. Behind the kick came Bannagran, commander of the laird's garrison, the most notable and feared warrior in all central Honce.

Cadayle fell back, as did her mother, and the two started for each other suddenly, needing the comfort of each other's arms.

But Bannagran cut in between them and shoved them apart. And before the women could react or protest, a second unexpected figure strode into their house, one that froze them in place.

"A fine day to you, ladies," said Laird Prydae. Hulking soldiers moved behind him, blocking the morning sunlight as it tried to stream in through the now-open door. "I forgive your lack of preparedness for my visit."

"My liege," said Cadayle's mother, and she fell to one knee and lowered her gaze. Cadayle took the cue and did likewise—or started to, until Bannagran grabbed her by the hair and pulled her back upright. She reached back and pulled at the big man's wrist, but his mighty grip did not weaken at all.

"You were awake late into the night, I expect," Laird Prydae went on. "Meeting the Highwayman, no doubt."

"No, my liege," Cadayle started to say, but she just shrieked instead as Bannagran reached over with his free hand, grabbed the front of her nightdress, and tore it from her, leaving her naked in the room—naked except for a jeweled necklace.

Cadayle looked down at the floor and quickly lifted her hand to cover the stolen necklace.

"You leave her!" her mother cried from across the way, and Cadayle glanced over just in time to see Callen's approach stopped suddenly by a backhanded blow from Bannagran, which sent Callen flying to the floor. Cadayle instinctively started to react, but the big man pulled all the harder on her hair.

"Enough of this foolishness," Bannagran said. "You are fairly caught, young lass. Make your death an easier thing with a bit of cooperation."

Callen shrieked at the blunt remark and charged again, only to be thrown aside once more by the giant Bannagran.

"My liege, pray you get those soldiers in here to control this wench," Bannagran said with a chuckle, but he bit the words off suddenly, noting Prydae's transfixed expression. "My liege?"

Prydae stood there staring at the naked Cadayle, at the softness of her curves, at their odd familiarity. The laird was no stranger to the sight of a naked woman, and so he was not leering like some giddy adolescent. But he was transfixed, by a memory the sight of Cadayle had inspired. The curve of her belly, the way her wheat-colored hair cascaded in layers across her lowered face. He thought of a bonfire, of an adder, of an adulteress and a knave. His gaze went from Cadayle to her mother, who, like Bannagran and Cadayle, was now staring at him curiously.

"Callen Duwornay," Laird Prydae remarked, the name springing from memories he didn't even know he possessed.

The woman blanched, something that neither Prydae nor Bannagran missed, and fell back a bit.

"N-no, my liege," she stammered.

"Callen Duwornay," Prydae said again, more confidently. "Not the poison of a snake nor the powrie dwarves could kill you."

"No, my liege, I am—"

"You are Callen Duwornay, and that is your daughter," Prydae interrupted. He looked back to Cadayle, at her curves, as images of that long-ago night began to stir within him. He remembered Callen in the firelight—remembered her looking exactly as this young woman now appeared to him. He remembered her curves, and the regrets he had that he would never bed her; and as that last thought played in his mind, he felt a stirring in his loins.

"That one," he said breathlessly, pointing to Cadayle: "She comes to Castle Pryd."

"What of the old wench?" asked one of the soldiers moving into the room past the laird.

Prydae fixed his gaze upon Callen, who seemed too afraid to say anything at that terrible moment.

"What do you know of the Highwayman?" Prydae asked sharply.

"She knows nothing!" Cadayle blurted, and Prydae turned a fierce scowl upon her.

"But you do," he said.

"My liege, I will tell you everything I know," Cadayle pleaded. "But please, do not hurt my ma. She's done nothing. She knows nothing. She's innocent. Please, my liege."

Prydae motioned with his head, and Bannagran dragged Cadayle from the room as the other two soldiers descended upon Callen. Only when Cadayle was long out of sight did Prydae turn on the woman.

"How you survived is of no concern to me," he said. "I admire it, I would say."

"Please, gentle Laird Prydae, do not harm my girl," Callen said, her voice a whimper, her body seemingly broken by the weight of it all.

"Harm her? Nothing could be further from my intentions, Callen Duwornay."

Callen began to cry.

"My liege?" asked one of the soldiers flanking her.

"Give her to Bernivvigar," Prydae said, turning and exiting, hardly seeming to care about Callen. "Perhaps he will be merciful, perhaps not. It matters not at all to me."

The woman, too broken by the suddenness of it all, by the shock of being discovered and the horror of having her daughter so unceremoniously dragged away, offered no resistance, offered nothing at all, as the two men hoisted her up. She didn't, couldn't, walk as they started out, but that hardly seemed to matter.

They just dragged her.

CHAPTER 35

The Downward Spiral

He stayed near the edges of town as the sun climbed in the eastern sky. He knew that he should return to the chapel, knew that he was taking a giant risk in remaining out and about. The monks would go to his room when they noticed that he was not doing his daily chores.

But none of that mattered to Bransen now; nothing beyond the reality of Garibond's death mattered. He couldn't believe the tale those living in what had once been his home had told him. He couldn't imagine that Master Bathelais, scowling as he often was, could be so despicably cruel as to have murdered a man as fine as Garibond. And what of Brother Reandu? Perhaps Reandu wasn't as powerful in the order back then as he was now, but certainly he would have protested the execution. It made no sense to Bransen as he wandered through the shadows under the many trees that marked the outskirts of Pryd Town, and yet, he found that he could not deny that which was obvious.

The man at the campfire had Garibond's knife. The people in his house were sincere, and why would they lie, given that such a lie might well mark their doom at the hands of this masked stranger who had come banging on their door? Bransen knew that they couldn't be telling the truth, that Garibond couldn't be dead, and certainly not by the hands of the brothers who had been his protectors all these years. And yet he knew that they certainly were speaking honestly. He had seen it in their faces.

At one cluster of trees, the weary young man plopped down in the shade and leaned back against a white birch. He tried to sort through every memory he had of every encounter even remotely relating to Garibond these past ten years. He remembered Brother Reandu's face on the one occasion when he had mentioned his father, the initial shock Reandu had shown, the obvious discomfort behind his stuttered responses.

But what did it all mean? If Garibond was dead, murdered by the brothers of Blessed Abelle, what did it all mean to Bransen and for Bransen?

A myriad of emotions rolled through him, everything ranging from anger to despair to the feeling that he had to run and hide somewhere, somewhere dark and deep, where no one would ever find him. All the confidence of the

Highwayman flew from him, and he felt again the helpless little boy he had been. But what did it matter, after all? He thought again of his absence at the chapel, and of the implications should he be discovered, and he shrugged them away. How could he go back there, knowing the truth? He would have to face Master Bathelais and Brother Reandu. He would have to demand the truth from them, though he already knew it, in his heart at least. And then what? What could he say to them? What explanation could they possibly offer that would make any difference to the realities of their actions? For Bransen knew Garibond's heart as well as he knew his own, and if that man was a heretic in the eyes of the brothers of Abelle, then the brothers of Abelle were simply entirely wrong.

Bransen found a stream of sunlight flowing in through an opening in the trees, and he lay down, staring up at the fiery orb. He wanted the rays to permeate his corporeal form, to cleanse him of the impurities and anxieties, to empty him of his rage and his pain. He closed his eyes, and exhaustion overcame him.

He knew at once, when he awoke, that the day was nearing its end, and that any hope he might hold, of sneaking into the chapel unnoticed was long lost. Instinctively, he began concocting possible explanations and excuses to explain the absence of the Stork.

But then he stopped himself, coming to understand clearly that he truly had no intention of ever returning to the chapel as the Stork, of serving the wretched brothers of Abelle ever again. He would go back, perhaps, but as the Highwayman, formidable and angry and demanding the entire truth of Garibond's fate.

He wasn't ready to travel that mental course, and he winced against the tear in his heart. He wasn't ready. Not yet.

But what was he to do? Bransen glanced to the west and the lowering sun, its rim just beginning to brush the horizon. The world seemed so huge to him and so imposing. And he felt so small and so empty, without anywhere to go, without anyone on whom he could lean his weary frame.

No, that wasn't true, he realized, and before he even sorted out the emotion, his feet were already moving, propelling him to the south and west, toward the house of the one person in all the world Bransen felt he could still trust.

But when he got there, Cadayle was not at home. Nor was her mother, and the broken door spoke volumes to Bransen as he hesitantly stepped across the threshold and into the dark house.

He knew she wasn't there. Her smell wasn't there, the freshness she brought wherever she walked wasn't there, leaving the place dark and cold and empty. His eyes adjusted to the dim light and he slowly and deliberately scanned the room, afraid as his gaze roamed over every inch of space that he would find the body of his beloved.

Nothing was amiss, save the broken door. He saw no signs of struggle, no blood.

But they were gone.

Bransen's breath began to come in heaves, as he steadied himself and strengthened his resolve. He had come here thinking to lean on Cadayle; now he began to understand that it was she who likely needed him.

He would not, could not, fail her.

He turned and realized his error immediately as he found a pair of iron swords pointing at his throat.

"Easy now, Highwayman," one of the soldiers said.

The Highwayman noticed a third and then a fourth soldier moving around the sides of the small house.

"We knew you'd return, and now you're fairly caught," said the other, and he prodded his sword forward menacingly. "Laird Prydae will be speaking with you."

"Indeed," the Highwayman replied, the irony lost on the pair. He brought his hands up, palms out, in apparent surrender.

And then his foot flashed up, before him; and though the soldiers were but inches from him, so nimble was the Highwayman, so in control of his every movement, that his foot struck unerringly into the face of one, then the second, so quickly that neither registered the movement but just felt the sudden jolt.

Both staggered a step, though the blows were not heavy. It was no more than a momentary distraction, but that was all the Highwayman needed. Before his flashing foot even came back to the ground, his other leg propelled him backward, putting some distance between them, and in the same fluid movement, he drew his fabulous sword.

The soldiers hardly realized what had happened, but found themselves facing a swordsman with a blade twice as long as their short iron weapons.

One moved fast, coming forward before the Highwayman could bring that amazing sword to proper angle—so he hoped.

With a sudden surge, the Highwayman slashed down diagonally, driving the soldier's sword low and wide. A reversal brought his elbow smashing into the man's face. The Highwayman changed his angle so that the pommel of his sword connected squarely with the attacker's nose, shattering it. The man was out on his feet, but as the Highwayman squared up again, he launched a left hook that sent the unconscious soldier flying away.

Even as the man fell, the Highwayman came forward. The second soldier, obviously unsure, waved his sword around defensively.

He was too slow, and the Highwayman's blade slipped past, screeching as its tip connected with the man's bronze breastplate. A subtle twist and turn snapped the blade up, forcing the soldier to lean backward fast to avoid getting his face creased.

The enraged Highwayman pressed the attack, turning his sword and using it to keep the soldier's weapon at bay while he plowed forward, pushing the man right over. The soldier hit the ground and rolled immediately, trying to get up, but the Highwayman crossed to the side and kicked him in the face, once and then again. As the man flattened on the ground, the Highwayman stamped hard on the back of his neck, stilling him.

Then the Highwayman turned right, sword leading the way. He meant only to deflect the stabbing spear coming at him from the charging soldier, but his sword sheared the spear in half and scraped the man's breastplate, opening his throat as he came forward, unable to stop in time.

The soldier staggered past, clutching at the gushing blood, and fell to his knees and then to his face in the dirt.

The Highwayman had no time to concern himself with the man. Not then, for he completed his circuit and fell into a crouch facing the fourth and last attacker.

The soldier skidded to a stop, clearly terrified. He threw his sword to the ground and lifted his hands in surrender.

The Highwayman came forward suddenly, sword setting itself right on the top edge of the man's breastplate, poised to drive through his throat.

"Where is she?" the Highwayman demanded.

The man shook his head, looking stupid and out of his mind with fear.

"Cadayle—the young woman who lives here," the Highwayman demanded. "She was taken! You tell me where, or my sword will free your ugly head from your shoulders!"

"I do not know!" the man cried.

"You lie!" the sword jabbed in, forcing a squeal from the man.

"No! No!" the man begged, and he began to cry. "Please do not kill me. A wife I have, and children. Please, I beg of you!"

The words, so full of sincerity and terror, hit the Highwayman and reminded him that these men, these soldiers, even the tax collectors, were more than a part of the oppression that weighed upon the people of Pryd. They were individuals, real people with real lives and families and concerns.

But those concerns found no real hold on the Highwayman in that moment of outrage, overwhelmed by his fears for Cadayle and her mother and by his frustration at the loss of his beloved Garibond. He came forward suddenly and forcefully, bowling the soldier over onto his back and setting his sword once more at the man's throat.

"Your family will bring your body to the brothers of Abelle to be put cold in the ground or to the Samhaists for burning," he warned. "I'll not ask again."

"They took her and her mother," the soldier gasped. "I know not where they took the girl, but the mother was given to Bernivvigar. She will be tried and killed this night by the adder or the flames."

The Highwayman moved his sword tip back and stepped away from the man, his thoughts spinning. He glanced to the west, where the sun was almost gone, then back to the east and south, toward where he knew Bernivvigar held his audiences, his trials, and his murders.

He looked back down at the soldier, still crying, still lying there with his hands up defensively.

"Collect your companions and herd them into the house," he instructed, and when the man didn't immediately move, the Highwayman kicked him hard in the leg. "Now!"

The man scrambled to his feet and did as he was bade, while Bransen moved fast to the soldier whose throat he had cut. He turned the man over, fearing the worst, and was relieved to see that he was not dead, and that the wound, though still bleeding, wasn't gushing forth blood any longer. Still; it was a vicious gash, one that would need tending.

Bransen brought one hand to the wound, the other to the soul stone set under his mask on his forehead. He recalled the lessons of the Book of Jhest, the Healing Hands, and fell even deeper into the swirl of the gray gemstone. He felt warmth in his hands and was amazed to see the wound sealing. He stopped short, though, for he found that the effort was taking from his own control, from the solid line of his own *chi*. A wave of dizziness came over him, followed by a profound weariness.

But he shook it away, reminding himself of Cadayle. With a growl, he rose from the soldier and called to the man's companion to hurry up.

A short while later, the Highwayman ran off, leaving the four soldiers bound and gagged inside the house's dark walls.

CHAPTER 36

Buzzing in His Head

The spinning thoughts followed Bransen away from Cadayle's house, but as he met every different emotion with the reality that Cadayle and her mother were in trouble, anything other than simple rage was pushed away. Step by step, one thought by one, Bransen's mind became focused, crystalline clear, sharpening and narrowing his vision so much that it seemed to him as if he were looking down a long and straight tunnel. The tumult within his mind became something more like an internal buzzing, as if the top end of his life's line of energy were spitting jolts into his head.

Moving with a singular focus and complete determination, the Highwayman increased his pace, running purposefully but without any clear idea where he was going. And then he arrived, his head thrumming, the edges of his vision limned in red. Hardly formulating any plans, hardly considering any move he might make, the Highwayman looked out through a tangle of twigs and logs at the front of a tall, flat stone.

The buzzing did not relent.

Sometime later, he felt the heat growing around him, but it was as if the flames were not in proximity to him, but were distant. Without any conscious decision, the Highwayman's mind went to the drawer in the desk in the room above his hole. His fingers began to wriggle as if he were rolling a small stone in his palm, but he wasn't even aware of the movement. He felt the power of the gemstone as if he were holding a serpentine in his hand, though of course he was not. But somewhere within the buzz of his mind, the lessons of the Book of Jhest resonated, showing him the way to the same energy the magical stone provided.

And he needed it, though he wasn't even aware of the flames leaping all around him, devouring the twigs and logs. He sat there and stared out at the Stone of Judgment, peering around the yellow sheets of fire that flared barely inches from his face.

He knew the time drew near. He could hear the voices of people gathering around the bonfire, could see flashes of movement through the red shield at the edges of his vision. But they didn't matter. All that mattered was the stone before him and the man he knew would soon appear atop it.

The sight of the great bonfire roaring to life elicited horrible memories in poor Callen, a clear reminder of that night so long ago, a night that she had hoped she would never, ever have to recall. The crowd was comprised of different people but it all seemed the same to Callen, the jibes, the spit, the almost gleeful shouts.

As if in a dream, she allowed the guards to shove her out to a spot halfway between the fire and the large, flat stone. Bernivvigar's stone.

The hoots behind her told her that the snake handler had arrived with the sack and the snake, and Callen felt her knees go weak. Darkness filled her thoughts, memories of the confining sack, and the slithering serpent crawling over her, sharp fangs hooking into her tender flesh and pumping in their deadly, burning poison.

With a growl of defiance, Callen dismissed those recollections and divorced herself from her terror. This was not about her; she was not important. And so she would die this night, and for a crime that she had committed two decades before, a crime of passion and not cruelty, a misjudgment of her heart and nothing of malice.

But so be it, because this wasn't about her.

This was about her poor daughter. Nothing else mattered to Callen. Not her pain, not the viper that would await her in the sack, not her own death.

Were her previous crimes now being visited upon Cadayle? Callen knew that her daughter had played a dangerous game and had, in fact, brought this tragedy upon them both. But Callen couldn't so easily dismiss her own guilt. Had she passed more than her appearance to her daughter? Was there something in them that allowed for such mistakes of the heart? The irony of it all wasn't lost on Callen, because, indeed, hadn't Cadayle's foolishness with this outlaw Highwayman been much the same thing as Callen's behavior when she had cuckolded her husband?

Strangely, a wistful smile made its way onto her face as she considered that long-ago encounter. She had been given in marriage to a man she did not love and had been offered no say in the matter. That was often the way of things in Pryd, in all Honce, where practicality almost always overruled love. Her affair had not worked out well for her, or for her lover, but did she really feel that it had been an error? That affair had produced Cadayle, the beauty of her life. How could she consider that a mistake?

The wistful smile disappeared in the blink of an eye. Cadayle, the beauty of her life, was in trouble, likely to be executed, and there was nothing, nothing, that Callen could do about it. Cadayle had allowed her heart to lead her into a place of beauty, perhaps, into the warmth of love and the tingling expectation of merely seeing the Highwayman. But it had also led her into danger, a deep and deadly hole from which there seemed no escape.

Callen didn't know who to blame; Callen didn't care about blame. All that mattered was that she was never going to see her Cadayle again and that her daughter, her beautiful child, was in danger.

And there was nothing she could do.

Her contemplations fell away as a tall and straight figure walked out to the edge of the flat rock, towering over the gathering, seeming identical to the man he had been twenty years before and certainly with as much, and more, power than he had then commanded. At his appearance, the crowd fell into a fearful silence.

Bernivvigar spent a moment surveying them, his cold gaze freezing with fear any it fell upon. He nodded to the side, and she heard the scramble as men behind her began to ready the sack and the viper.

"Callen Duwornay," the old wretch began, not a quiver in his powerful voice, "we gather to execute the sentence imposed two decades ago. You did not admit your guilt then. You were given your chance to speak, though you said nothing. Now, we will not ask you again. You are doomed by your harlotry, and may the Ancient Ones forgive us all for delaying their proper justice and the gift of your corpse."

He snapped a wave in her direction, and the men flanking her yanked her back so forcefully that they pulled her from her feet.

But they stopped abruptly, and Callen followed their looks to Bernivvigar; and then, with them and with all the others, she followed Bernivvigar's gaze to the bonfire, rustling and shaking and taking on a life of its own.

Callen's eyes widened in shock as she saw the dark form step forth. Surely the old Samhaist had summoned a demon! One of the dreaded Ancient Ones had come to Honce to take her body away!

He saw the tall form of the old Samhaist but only in a strange silhouette, for sheets of fire rose up before his eyes. Even with his understanding and mimicry of the powers of the magical serpentine stone, Bransen realized that he could not remain within the inferno. If his concentration faltered for just an instant, the fires would set his hair and clothing ablaze and consume him.

But he did not falter. He thought of nothing but Cadayle, conjuring an image of her at the mercy of Laird Prydae. The buzzing in his head didn't lessen—quite the opposite—and even with the fiery yellow glow before his eyes, there remained that red haze at the sides of his vision, focusing him, directing the course of his rage.

That focus now was the solitary figure before him. Bransen stood up and the pile trembled, fiery branches falling down before him.

He thought of Garibond and the hideous wound inflicted on him by Bernivvigar, and the buzzing in his head intensified even more, like an angry bee trapped within him, prodding him with its sound and its stinger. Bransen's breath came in sudden gasps; he felt as if he would scream. His lungs burned as if they were on fire, as indeed he knew that they soon would be!

But he found his focus again, and he forced himself forward through the fire, ignoring the burning branches, ignoring the painful licks of flame. None of it mattered. None of his discomfort, his pain, his potential death mattered. All that mattered was that figure, now the focus of his ire, the symbol of all the injustices and all the hatred, of all the bullying and all the torture.

There he stood before Bransen, high on his rock.

Bransen crashed through the side of the bonfire. He heard the screams all around him; out of the corner of his left eye he saw Callen gasp and fall back, along with the guards supporting her.

But he strode forward, clearing the edge of the bonfire, stepping into the open in all his Highwayman glory right before Bernivvigar the Samhaist, right before the gasps and wide eyes of all the gathering.

He heard them crying out and whispering, "Highwayman."

They didn't matter. Nothing mattered, except that one figure.

"You dare interrupt this sacred ceremony?" old Bernivvigar roared down from on high. "You dare?"

Bransen drew the sword from his rope belt, but even without the weapon, the murderous intent was very clear in his eyes.

He strode toward the rock, and Bernivvigar surprised him, for the old man did not back away, did not show fear.

"To challenge me is to challenge the Ancient Ones!" he proclaimed, and he lifted his skinny arms up before him and uttered a quick incantation, the likes of which Bransen had never before heard. Bernivvigar's voice sounded like guttural grunting, but in a rhythm, as if someone were rolling stones down a jagged rocky slope in perfect timing.

Bransen didn't care. He drove forward, thinking to run up to the base of the stone and leap atop it, cutting the old wretch down in a single movement.

But he wasn't running fast, was suddenly barely moving, as if he were wading through deep mud. He glanced down at his feet, to see the grass itself reaching over his soft black shoes, grasping at him, knotting above the top of his feet. With a determined tug, Bransen tore one foot free, then the other. He swung his sword down in frustration, slicing a line in the grass, but any freedom he found was temporary as Bernivvigar's weeds and grass slapped and grabbed at him.

And the man was still chanting, and was no longer before him, Bransen realized. He followed the voice to the side and saw that Bernivvigar was standing on the grass not too far away, chanting and leering at him crazily, hungrily.

"Too long has the wrath of the Ancient Ones been bound inside the earth!" Bernivvigar cried; all about him, the people fell back in fear, for his voice was no longer that of a man, no longer that of a mortal creature. Somehow, Bernivvigar had gone beyond the bounds of his corporeal body, beyond the reach of the lesser beings about him.

Bransen, too, nearly swooned under the power of that voice.

"Feel the fires of the Ancient Ones!" Bernivvigar proclaimed, and he thrust both his hands out before him, his old, gnarled, and twisted fingers sparking and trailing wisps of smoke.

Bransen braced himself, falling once more into his concentration to deny the expected fires. But Bernivvigar was not aiming his strange magic Bransen's way, at least not directly. The ground beneath the Highwayman's feet began to slide and churn, and Bransen looked down in terror, noting that what had seemed ordinary grass was now smoldering with swirling red lava!

He didn't know what to do; he didn't know how to react. He scanned his memory of the Book of Jhest, looking for some clue, some hint as to what this old wretch was doing to him.

And then he heard a cry, sharp and shrill and full of a primal, tearing energy. His gaze slipped to Callen, who was on the ground on her back, the deadly viper coiled and ready to strike, just inches from her face.

Bransen wanted to call out to her, to tell her not to move. He wanted to leap before her, to take the strike if necessary, for he believed that with his training, he could withstand a snake's poison.

But the buzzing screamed in his head, a nest of bees, it now seemed. He knew that his shoes were smoking, knew that his feet were blistering, but he felt no pain: not even the bite of Bernivvigar's molten fires could penetrate the wall of his rage.

Without thinking, Bransen jerked his arm up and then snapped it forward, throwing his sword as if it were a spear.

He heard Bernivvigar's gasp, and the incantation stopped, before he registered that his sword had struck right through the Samhaist's chest.

Bernivvigar staggered backward, but did not fall to the ground. It hardly mattered to Bransen, for he charged at the man, in a great leap that brought him clear of the lava. His arms worked like the hooves of a charging horse, pumping and pounding, smashing Bernivvigar in the ribs, but strangely Bernivvigar was not grunting under the blows, and his skin seemed not to give at all beneath the weight of Bransen's punches, nor did his old bones crack in protest.

Bransen looked up to see Bernivvigar staring down at him and smiling, as if Bransen were but a child, an inconvenience. Bernivvigar lifted a hand and balled it tightly, and lightning-like energy crackled from his fist.

Bransen slugged him hard in the jaw, snapping the old man's head to the side. But Bernivvigar kept smiling and punched back. Though Bransen blocked the blow, he felt the jolt of energy surge through his body, stiffening him. Only his studies saved him, for he instinctively arched his body in just the right manner to serve as a conduit for the jolt, so that it ran down to the ground and left him relatively unscathed.

He punched again, and Bernivvigar swung.

Bransen ducked, leaning low, and with perfect balance, managed to kick his foot against the hilt of the sword protruding from Bernivvigar's chest.

A wince broke through Bernivvigar's mask of calm and confidence; and Bransen snapped off three quick kicks, all smacking the hilt and changing the angle of the blade.

Now the Highwayman found his rhythm, coming forward suddenly and popping off a series of short punches at the Samhaist. None connected heavily, and none would have done much damage anyway. But that wasn't the point.

Bransen was setting his feet; balance was the measure, he knew.

Bernivvigar swung again, and Bransen, knowing better than to block the enchanted fist, ducked. But even though the fist did not connect, it sent a jolt of lightning into him.

But that didn't knock the focused Bransen off balance, that didn't diffuse the buzzing.

He stepped sideways at Bernivvigar, grabbing the sword hilt, and accepted another powerful jolt and then another as he stepped away, turning his back as he tore his sword free.

Bernivvigar cackled mockingly behind him, but Bransen didn't hear it, didn't hear anything but the anger in his head.

Bransen started left, reversed the sword flow suddenly, and spun back right so quickly that Bernivvigar was still looking the other way when Bransen came whirling around, the sword high and horizontal, level with the old Samhaist's neck.

High into the air flew Bernivvigar's head, still wearing a smile of calm confidence.

Bransen was already moving the other way when the body crumpled behind him, when the head bounced down to the ground with a wet thump.

He dropped his sword and slowed his movement as he approached Callen and the snake, motioning at her to keep still. The snake hadn't struck yet, and it seemed as confused and overwhelmed as everyone else in the area—now far fewer people than when Bransen had emerged from the bonfire!

The buzzing continued, but within it, Bransen found a place of calm as he slipped between Callen and the viper, moving low and staring the frightened snake in the eye.

He moved his right hand across before him, and the snake's head swayed in concert.

His left hand snapped out, quicker than an adder's strike, seizing the creature right behind its triangular head.

Bransen allowed the snake to wrap itself around his left arm as he stood up, offering his right hand to the woman and pulling her to her feet.

He blew in the snake's face several times, and it seemed to calm. He gently set it down, where it rushed into the forest.

"You and you!" the Highwayman called to the two soldiers who had dragged Callen onto the field.

The men looked at each other and both edged away, as if thinking to run. But Bransen lifted his sword as if to throw it, and both froze in their tracks.

"On your head—if any harm comes to this woman, I will see you dead. All of you!" he shouted in rage, spinning to encompass the crowd. "Any who harm this woman will feel the wrath of the Highwayman! That wrath is boundless, I assure you!" He turned back to the two frightened soldiers, locking their gazes with his own. "I know your faces now. I know."

He turned to Callen. "Where is Cadayle?"

"Laird Prydae took her," she replied, her voice and body trembling. "He took her!"

"To the castle!" someone in the crowd called out.

"I seen him drag her in," said another.

Bransen looked all around, amazed once more at the reaction to the Highwayman. He pulled Callen close and hugged her tightly. "On my life, she will not be harmed," he whispered, then he turned and ran off, heading straight for Castle Pryd.

But then he veered as he saw the other structure beside the great castle.

The place he had called home for a decade.

The place, he now knew, that had never been his home.

CHAPTER 37

Their Pet Idiot

He sprinted through the streets of Pryd Town, chased only by the calls of those who spotted the man in the distinctive black outfit. He charged into the courtyard of Chapel Pryd, hardly slowing and brushing aside the one young, startled monk who made a move as if to try to stop him.

The main doors were open, but the Highwayman, knowing this building intimately, moved to the right-hand wall and to the small door set at its far end. This one, too, was unlocked, and Bransen charged through. He crossed the room above his own dungeon, to the door to the main corridor, and paused there, hearing voices in the hallway beyond and calls echoing.

With a growl, a memory of Callen at Bernivvigar's stone, and a mental image of the pains that Cadayle might then be suffering, Bransen kicked the door open and leaped out into the hall.

A pair of brothers confronted him at once, one holding high his shaking fist—clenching gemstones, Bransen understood—and the other waving an iron short sword, so ill cared for and infrequently used that it showed rust all along its black blade.

"You would be wise to escort me to Master Bathelais," he warned, his voice even, calm, and controlled. "And if you try to use that gemstone, I assure you that your head will bounce to the floor beside it."

The man thrust his fist forward a bit, in an attempt to be menacing, Bransen presumed.

Bransen's left hand snapped forward, clutching the man's wrist and yanking him forward. His right hand cupped over the gem-holding fist, turning it down and bending the wrist. The man shrieked in pain, all strength fleeing from his hand, and Bransen shoved him back—and now it was Bransen's fist that held the gemstone.

Even as he pushed the monk away, the other, inspired by the sudden action, perhaps, leaped forward and plunged his sword at the intruder's chest. A slight turn by Bransen had the blade going harmlessly by, and Bransen locked the man's sword arm tight against his side and sent his free hand, his fist balled, crunching into the monk's nose. He pumped his arm three times, connecting solidly with every punch, then brought his knee up hard into the poor man's groin. As the man lurched over, Bransen let go of his trapped sword arm and hit him with a right cross that spun him to the side and slammed him hard against the corridor wall, where he folded down in a heap.

The other young monk stood there transfixed and obviously terrified. That fear only heightened when the Highwayman snapped his magnificent sword out, putting its gleaming tip close to the trembling monk's bare throat.

"To Bathelais, at once, or I leave you dead on the floor," the Highwayman promised, and to his surprise, Bransen realized that he meant every word.

The terrified young monk scurried away, Bransen close behind. Bransen paused just long enough to turn and throw the gemstone at the head of the groaning, prostrate monk.

"What is the meaning of this?" Master Bathelais shouted, leaping from his chair when the door of his audience room burst open and a younger brother came stumbling in, to fall hard on the floor. Bathelais's eyes narrowed, but he did not back down as a second figure entered, one dressed in black clothes that proclaimed his identity.

Bathelais was not alone; Reandu, sitting across the hearth from him, also rose, sucking in his breath with the movement. Closer to the hearth, Father Jerak sat slumped in a chair, appearing oblivious to it all. One other brother was there, an attendant to the infirm Jerak. He had been standing just inside the door and to the side, though now he faded farther from the door, inching out toward his master and Brother Reandu.

"You dare to enter this holy place?" Bathelais said, and he squared his jaw and straightened his shoulders.

"It is no place that I have not been many times before," the Highwayman responded.

Bathelais stared at him hard, searching for a clue, but he needn't have bothered, for in that moment, Bransen reached up with his free hand and pulled the mask, and the gemstone, from his head.

"Do you not recognize your pet idiot, Master Bathelais?" Bransen asked.

Bathelais's composure couldn't hold any longer, and he widened his eyes, staggered back half a step, and nearly toppled over his chair. Across from him, Brother Reandu gasped and fell back into his chair, and the other monk cried out, "Stork!"

"It is imposs—it is impossible," Bathelais stammered, and the irony of listening to him stuttering was not lost on Bransen. "How? How can this be?"

Bransen came forward suddenly, sword tip lunging close to Bathelais's throat. "I have not time for explanations."

"We took you in!" Bathelais roared back. "We showed you mercy when—"

"Shut up," Bransen said, and he prodded the deadly sword ahead. "Mercy?" He spat the word, and then spat upon the floor at Bathelais's feet.

"You dare—" Bathelais started to protest, but he learned then that a sword tip against his throat was a sure way to silence him.

"Mercy?" Bransen echoed again. "You allow me to clean your chamber pots, and I am to fall to my knees in gratitude?" As Bathelais started to respond, Bransen poked his throat again with the sword, and then snapped the blade across, in line with Reandu, when he began to answer.

"None of it matters," Bransen explained. "I need you now, and you will help me."

"You are a fool," Bathelais managed, before Bransen prodded him again.

"An idiot, perhaps, if I was to believe the opinion of Master Bathelais," Bransen replied. "But it matters not. None of it. You are going to help me now, to repay me for the murder of Garibond Womak."

Bathelais's eyes widened so much that Bransen wondered if they would just roll out of their sockets.

"Yes, I know all about it," he said. "I know what you did soon after taking me in as your slave."

"He was in possession—" Brother Reandu started.

"Shut up," came the interruption. "I know everything there is to say on that matter, and the only reason that your heads are not rolling on the floor now is because I need you. Fail me in any way, and you die and all of your brethren in this chapel die also. Every one."

He studied Father Jerak as he finished—the man who had been in charge of the chapel on the day when Garibond had been murdered. Bransen thought to go over and cut the man's throat to show these others how serious he was, and he did take a step in that direction. But just one step, then the Highwayman stopped and pushed the thought out of his mind. To what gain?

Having passed that test, Bransen turned back to Bathelais and noted that the man shifted his glance, just briefly, to glance over Bransen's shoulder.

Alerted, the Highwayman dipped suddenly and lashed out with his foot, catching the creeping monk in the stomach and doubling him over. As soon as his foot came back to the floor, Bransen spun, his other foot connecting squarely with the side of the lurching monk's face, sending him flying away, crashing over a table and into a wall, where he lay very still.

Both Reandu and Bathelais started for Bransen at that moment, but they hadn't a chance and were backed again by the gleaming tip of the leveled sword.

"I am long past mercy, Master Bathelais," Bransen warned. "Hesitate again, and a monk will die." He pointed his sword at Father Jerak. "Hesitate again, and *he* will die."

"What do you want?" Master Bathelais asked.

"You and you," Bransen added, waving the sword at Reandu, "and the Stork are going to pay a visit to Laird Prydae."

As he spoke, Bransen pulled the black armband from his sword arm, revealing his birthmark, and began unfastening the black silk shirt.

CHAPTER 38

The Waterfall at River's End

You should not be here, not at this time," the sentry at the gatehouse of Castle Pryd said to the three unexpected visitors late that night. The man looked at the two monks—for all purposes, the two leaders of the Church in Pryd Holding—and then scrunched up his face in obvious disgust as he turned to regard the third visitor, the Stork, swaying and drooling and leaning on a long, narrow canelike implement that was wrapped in cloth.

"We have information regarding the man who has put this castle and town in a state of frenzy," Brother Reandu replied, and Bransen did not miss the not-so-subtle look that Bathelais shot him.

The sentry perked up at that, and stepped aside, calling to his companions to hold his post so that he could escort the trio into the keep.

The sentry and the monks huddled as they crossed the open courtyard, for a shower came up then, suddenly, with a crackle of lightning splitting the dark sky and big heavy drops splashing down.

Bransen shambled along behind them, trying his best to mimic the walk that had been his natural step all his life. He held his soul stone firmly in hand, his other hand tight on his "cane," which was, of course, his sword. He lolled his head and thrust each hip out before waving the respective leg forward. He babbled and moaned and let the drool flow from his mouth. In that moment, despite all the vital events that were churning about him, it occurred to Bransen how unpleasant a creature he was, how awkward this damaged physical coil appeared. Surely the outside world cringed at the sight of him, and while he did not relinquish his disdain for that shallow and unsympathetic attitude, he understood it more fully now. That thought only made him appreciate more acutely the one person who had fought against that flow, only made him realize the depth of kindness Cadayle had shown to him all these years.

He didn't let the steeling of his determination to rescue her interfere with his awkward gait. His focus held firm, and he kept to the course.

They entered the well-guarded keep at the rear of the castle, and those guards who met them moved back at the unexpected sight of the Stork. Bransen looked up at them and smiled stupidly, his head rolling, and that only intensified their disgust and drove them further aside.

"The laird is . . . engaged," the sentry reported back to the monks a moment later.

Bransen gave a grunt and secretly nudged Master Bathelais.

"This is more important," the monk replied, offering a quick glance back at Stork. "Take us to Laird Prydae at once."

"It would not be wise to interrupt—" the sentry started to protest, but Reandu cut him short.

"Do you begin to understand the importance of this?" the younger monk snapped. "The Highwayman is within our reach, right now, and any hesitation will cost us this one chance we have to put things aright."

"We understand fully," the man retorted. "The death of Bernivvigar is no small thing!"

"The death of Bernivvigar?" both Bathelais and Reandu asked together.

"His head lopped from his shoulders this very night by the Highwayman," the sentry explained. "He appeared out of the Samhaist fire, as if summoned from hell itself, so said the onlookers—half the town saw it! He walked through Bernivvigar's magic, and not even the Ancient Ones themselves could stop him!"

"Bernivvigar dead this very night," Master Bathelais murmured, and both monks widened their eyes at that remarkable news; both turned again subtly to regard Bransen.

Bransen managed to slip them a look reminding them that they, too, could easily find such a fate this night.

"That only strengthens our need and desire to speak with Prydae!" Bathelais said suddenly, with great animation. "Admit us at once, you fool, before all the holding is destroyed by the hands of this outlaw!"

The sentry babbled some protest, but he eventually led the monks past the surprised and curious looks of the other soldiers. A grand stairway swept up from the ground floor to a balcony that lined the left-hand wall. From the other end of that balcony, the stairs climbed to the higher levels of the tower.

The foursome climbed the first flight to the balcony and started along, with the sentry pausing at the door in the middle of the wall and knocking hard as the monks and Stork moved past.

Bransen turned as he heard the familiar voice booming behind him, to see a man well known to him come out of the room. Bannagran gave him only a cursory and disgusted glance, then turned to the soldier; but Bransen could not tear his eyes from the imposing warrior.

The monks moved away from him, but he didn't notice.

Brother Reandu called for him to keep up, but he didn't notice.

Finally, he broke the spell and turned, just as Master Bathelais swung around, fist up high. "Bannagran, to arms!" he cried. "The Stork is your Highwayman! Seize him!"

Bransen's eyes went wide in the face of the deceit, and he lifted his cane and waved it in tight circles to free its of its cloth casing. Or at least, he started to, for then a streaking bolt of lightning erupted from Master Bathelais's hand and slammed him hard in the chest, throwing him backward.

Bransen heard the cries of Bannagran and the sentry, heard the protests of Brother Reandu, and heard most of all, the continuing fury of Master Bathelais. He collected his wits and his focus immediately—he knew that he had to—and fell inside himself, visualizing the line of his *chi*. That spark of energy, that focus of life, was exactly the attack point of the lightning, as Bransen could see by the dispersing flares. He tightened his focus and forced his *chi* back into alignment. He used his Jhesta Tu understanding and his soul stone, countering the effects of the jolt.

And he did it all in the blink of an eye.

On instinct, Bransen dropped low, and the sentry who was charging him from behind flipped right over his bent back and tumbled down, but not before intercepting Master Bathelais's second lightning blast.

Bransen went around and thought to stand to meet the charge of Bannagran, but then stayed low instead, kicking one foot right into the leading foot of the warrior.

Bannagran tripped off to the side of the moving Bransen and stumbled forward, but recovered quickly, purposely running into the wall to secure his balance. He spun around, ready to meet Bransen's charge.

But Bransen wasn't charging. He hadn't come here to do battle with Bannagran or with the monks. He hadn't come here to exact revenge or to punish anyone.

He remembered all that keenly with battle so clear before him, and instead of charging forward to stab Bannagran or to thrust his sword into the treacherous Master Bathelais, the Highwayman leaped onto the railing of the balcony and then sprang from it just ahead of another of Bathelais's searing lightning bolts.

Bransen's muscles propelled him up and out, as he lifted his *chi* to lighten the resistance against that great leap, making it seem as much a flight as a jump. He soared across, catching the railing of the next ascending staircase and pulling himself over it in one fluid movement. He glanced back to see the commotion he had left behind: the man shivering on the floor from the sting of Bathelais's second lightning bolt; Bathelais shouting and pointing his way; Bannagran, with other soldiers now in his wake, running along the balcony to the base of the staircase.

Bransen ran to the top of the stairs and then a few steps along the next balcony before again leaping to the top of the railing and springing across, leaving his pursuit behind.

Below him, as Brother Reandu tended the wounded sentry, Master Bathelais watched that second flight with as much amusement as awe. He lifted his fist, holding the graphite gemstone, and followed the Highwayman's course.

"And now you die," the monk growled, thrusting his arm forward—or starting to, until something slammed against him hard, driving his arm across his chest.

With a great heave, Bathelais shoved back and extracted himself from the grasp of Brother Reandu. "What are you doing?" he demanded.

"Master, do not!" Reandu said. "He is just a boy."

"You idiot!" Bathelais growled, and he lifted his arm again.

And again, Reandu crashed against him, defeating his aim.

"Brother!" Bathelais roared, and he swung back and shoved Reandu away. But Reandu came right back at him, wrestling him away from the ledge and toward the wall.

Bathelais turned as he fell back, yanking Reandu around him and slamming his attacker into that wall first, then crashed hard against him. Bathelais jumped back, pulling Reandu from the wall, then slammed Reandu into the wall once more.

"I warn you," Bathelais cried.

"This is not the way!" Reandu argued, his words popping out in an explosion of breath as Bathelais rammed him hard into the wall. Dazed, he hardly noticed as Bathelais let him go and whirled, rushing back to the railing.

All the world was spinning for Brother Reandu, all his buried notions about right and wrong. Images of Stork flashed through his mind, of the boy's pleading with him to teach him to read, of the filth and disrespect the boy had long suffered at the hands of the "generous" brothers of Abelle.

He saw Bathelais lifting his arm to loose another lightning bolt, lifting the edges of his mouth in a smile that struck Reandu as very wicked.

He pushed himself out from the wall, shouting at Bathelais to stop. And indeed, the master did hesitate and half turned to regard Reandu's charge. Master Bathelais tried to get out of the way or to brace himself, but wasn't successful.

Reandu plowed into him, both of them going hard against the balcony rail, which buckled under their weight.

Bathelais tumbled over the edge and Reandu stood, waving his arms in an effort to keep from falling. He did manage to do that, then looked down in horror at his superior lying on his back on the lower floor, groaning and barely moving.

O ut of the corner of his eye, as he leaped to the next balcony, Bransen saw the fall of Bathelais. It hardly registered because it hardly mattered to him. He saw a figure on the last balcony above, rushing through a doorway and heard from within a woman's cry.

The Highwayman leaped out and high, lifting his *chi,* lifting himself toward the heavens. He caught his balance on the railing of the top balcony just as the dark figure disappeared into the room and the door started to close. Two strides and a dive had him there in time, shouldering the door open before the locking bar could be secured, and Bransen tumbled into the room. He came up fast, kicking the door shut, the locking bar falling in place.

Bransen jumped up, his back to the door, his sword at the ready.

There stood Laird Prydae before him, stripped to the waist and easing behind the side of a great canopy bed. Bransen could have had him dead in one leap, he knew, but he had to hold, for on the other side of that bed stood Cadayle, wearing only a sheer nightdress, her hair disheveled, her face streaked with tears, and her head back awkwardly, twisting to avoid the knife that was firmly held at her throat.

Behind her, eyes gleaming with open hatred and a wildness that Bransen had never before witnessed, stood Rennarq.

"Could it be?" Rennarq rasped.

"Let her go," Bransen demanded.

"The Highwayman is this creature?" Laird Prydae asked, his voice full of mocking disbelief. "All my holding has held its breath in fear of this damaged, half-goblin . . . thing?"

Bransen kept his eyes locked on Cadayle, ignoring the insults, trying to find some way out. He thought of throwing his sword, but Rennarq had Cadayle locked tight as a shield, with only part of his face showing around her tresses.

"A dangerous little boy, now aren't you?" said Prydae, and he reached subtly toward his mattress, under which he always kept a dagger.

Bransen noted the move and pointed his sword at Prydae threateningly, but held his advance.

"He loves this one, my liege," Rennarq noted, and Bransen glanced the old man's way to see a wicked smile splayed across his wrinkled face. "Yet another victim claimed by the weakness of the heart."

Bransen steeled his expression at that.

"Is that not so?" Rennarq teased him. "Will you charge at me, brave Highwayman, and cut me to death? Will you slay the Laird of Pryd Holding? No doubt that is your desire, but is it above the price that such an action must cost?" As he finished, he slapped his free hand across Cadayle's forehead and pulled her head back, revealing more of her vulnerable neck and the dagger firmly pressed against her tender skin.

Bransen found it hard to draw breath.

He jumped, they all did, when something or someone slammed hard against the door behind him. The locking bar held, and the door did not burst open.

"My liege!" they heard Bannagran cry outside, and he began to bang hard on the heavy wooden door.

"I'll have your sword, Highwayman," Laird Prydae said, and he extended his hand.

Bransen didn't move, didn't breathe. He stared at his helpless love, who shook her head, or started to, before Rennarq tugged her head back viciously and pressed in the dagger.

"Be reasonable, boy," Laird Prydae went on. "Surrender your sword to me and I will let the woman live. Else she dies, and you will live with that image for the rest of your days, short though they will surely be."

Bransen looked at him, at his extended hand, though he was too far away for Bransen to hand him the blade.

"Come along now," Prydae prodded, motioning with his fingers. "Put it on the floor and slide it across to me."

"Let her go or you die!" Bransen growled.

"Do you think we are afraid of death, foolish boy?" Rennarq answered, stealing Bransen's bluster before the young man could even begin to gauge Laird Prydae's reaction to the threat. For when Bransen glanced back at Rennarq, he saw a wildness there that laughed at his threat and a determination that Cadayle's throat would soon be open wide. There was no hope for negotiation to be found in those dark and angry eyes, Bransen knew, whatever Prydae might say.

The pounding intensified against the door behind him. The buzzing in Bransen's head began anew.

"Your sword!" Prydae demanded sharply.

Bransen had no answers. Cadayle was doomed if he lunged for either the laird or Rennarq. He couldn't get to the old man quickly enough, and he knew without doubt that Rennarq would put his knife to deadly use without hesitation.

"Boy, on my word, the woman will live," Prydae shouted at him, above the crack of wood that now sounded behind Bransen, as if someone had taken an axe to the door. "Surrender your sword now, before my patience comes to its end!"

Bransen's breath came in gasps. He searched his thoughts and his recollections of the gemstones, but found no answers.

Because there were no answers.

He forced himself to stand straight, then bent and placed the sword on the ground and kicked it across to Laird Prydae.

Cadayle whimpered at the sight, and that, too, was cut short by another tug and press by Rennarq.

Bransen stared at the pair, hardly paying attention to Prydae who scooped up the fabulous sword and readied it.

"Now move away from the door," Prydae demanded, and another sharp rap and the crack of wood accentuated his words.

But Bransen hardly heard them, keeping his focus on his helpless love and on the wretch who held her and who seemed so full of glee at the thought of tearing out her beautiful throat. A spasm nearly knocked Bransen from his feet then, as his emotions threatened to break the concentration that allowed him to hold himself in check. He tightened his grip on the soul stone and forced himself, for Cadayle's sake, to regain his complete control.

His line of *chi* burned brightly within him, excited by anger and terror, vibrating and humming. He could see it clearly as he closed his eyes and looked inside.

"Move aside," he heard Prydae demand, "away from the door."

He kept his eyes closed, kept his focus on that line of burning energy. He brought his hands down together in front of him, cupped his free hand, and clenched the soul stone all the tighter. His *chi* was a tangible thing to him at that moment, a real line and not an imagined one, like a wire that held him together, like a strong cord that kept him upright.

Like a spear.

With a deep exhalation, Bransen fell even further into himself.

"I'll not tell you again, boy!" Prydae screamed, but Bransen didn't hear him.

Behind him the door broke apart under another heavy blow, but Bransen didn't hear it.

Another deep exhalation, and the young man pictured a part of his life's energy blowing out from him, into his cupped hand. He collected it there, and felt its weight, felt its tingle.

"Move, boy!" Prydae screamed, distantly, it seemed to Bransen.

Cadayle's gasp sounded more keenly and more closely, but that, too, he pushed aside, as he breathed deeply yet again.

"Kill her!" he heard Prydae command.

Bransen's eyes opened, and he thrust his hands out toward Cadayle and Rennarq; and with that movement he threw his collected *chi*, a javelin of his life energy, a bolt of his inner strength.

Rennarq gave a gurgled cry as that tangible energy crashed into him, and his legs buckled, pulling Cadayle down behind him, hard to the floor.

Prydae leaped ahead with a shout, sword jabbing for Bransen's chest.

Bransen's left hand slapped the tip aside at the last moment and he turned to counter, but this was no novice he faced but a trained and seasoned warrior.

Prydae retracted the blade and thrust again, and though Bransen again managed to slap the side of the blade, the laird deftly twisted it, cutting a gash in Bransen's forearm.

Bransen heard a gurgled whimper and realized that Cadayle was hurt.

Prydae struck again, and this time he got the blade through enough to poke a hole in Bransen's side, forcing him to leap back—and he felt a jolt behind him that nearly had him flying forward to impale himself on Prydae's blade as the door got smashed again, this time with the axe driving down to crack the locking bar.

Prydae thrust the blade and Bransen fell back against the door and snapped his foot up to deflect the blade. Ahead he charged, thinking he might have an opening, but even as his foot first connected, Prydae was already moving out of reach, falling back and low in a defensive crouch.

"Well fought, boy, but you have no chance!" Prydae cried. To drive his point home, he tried to drive the sword home and might well have succeeded, had not the door burst open behind Bransen, startling them both.

Prydae fell back; behind Bransen, Bannagran roared.

Bransen turned, purely on instinct, leaning back, arms out wide, as he came around. He only half registered the flying, spinning axe, soaring in now for his chest as he came around. And still he leaned, bending his knees, head going back so far that he looked through eyes turned upside down and saw Prydae coming in at him.

A darkness flickered before his eyes, but Bransen did not consciously register it as the spinning axe.

He went down so low that his shoulder blades brushed the floor, and then every muscle in his body reacted to his demand, swinging him back upright, his legs straining to pull.

He immediately went to a defensive stance and started to turn sideways, expecting an assault from Bannagran in the front and Prydae behind. But Bannagran, his eyes and mouth opened wide in a silent scream, did not approach; and before Bransen even glanced back at Prydae, he understood why.

For there staggered the Laird of Pryd Holding, mortally wounded, Bannagran's axe buried deep in his chest.

Bransen dove to the side of the room, to Cadayle, whose throat was pouring blood. Beside her, Rennarq gurgled and twitched, and Bransen absently pushed him aside. For he posed no threat, the young Jhesta Tu knew. Bransen's spear of energy had ruptured Rennarq's *chi*, had shattered the line and sent it into uncontrollable spasms. The irony of it, that Rennarq was doomed to become the very storklike creature he so detested, made no impact on Bransen at that moment—not with Cadayle lying so still before him.

He could feel her life energy, her warmth, flowing out of her as he fell over her in a hug. He tried to compose himself, tried to bring the soul stone to bear and find some way to heal her.

But it was too personal, too horrible, and Bransen couldn't find his focus! And he knew that the soldiers were coming in and that Bannagran would fly into murderous rage. He pressed the soul stone to her wound and sent his thoughts, his heart and soul, into it.

But it was too little, he feared, and his trembling hands could not focus the power.

Then he felt a hand on his shoulder, and he nearly swooned, nearly broke apart on the floor.

"Bransen," Brother Reandu said quietly in his ear, and he placed his hand over Bransen's hand that held the soul stone. "Together, my friend," Reandu assured him. "Calm. Calm is the key."

Reandu kept talking to him, whispering to him, reassuring him. Bransen felt Reandu's energy flowing into his hand and into the soul stone, and used that flow as his own guide.

Bransen felt his hand grow warm.

The blood slowed to a trickle, then stemmed altogether.

Cadayle seemed so pale and so still. . . .

"Please," Bransen whispered, but Cadayle did not stir.

Reandu patted Bransen on the back as the young man fell over his beloved sobbing, and the weary monk rose to his feet and turned. Prydae was dead, he knew, and had known as soon as he had pushed his way into the room. Over by the body, Bannagran rose, his face twisted in a knot of rage and confusion. He started toward Reandu and Bransen, but the monk stopped him with an upraised hand.

"There has been far too much tragedy this day," Reandu said.

"One more will die," Bannagran promised.

"Because he was protecting the woman he loves?"

The simple question stole some of the bluster from Bannagran, and stopped his approach.

"Would Bannagran, loyal Bannagran, have done any less?" Reandu pressed.

"Laird Prydae is dead," the large man proclaimed. "Bernivvigar is dead. Rennarq lies torn on the floor, and your own Master Bathelais lies broken below. All because of this man, this Highwayman!"

"We gain nothing by continuing this," Reandu said.

Bannagran glowered at him, then glanced down at the sword on the floor. "Perhaps my satisfaction at killing him will be enough," he growled, and he started to bend for the sword.

He jerked back, as a rolling body rushed past, and when it went by, the sword was gone; and Bannagran glanced behind to see the Highwayman standing there, sword leveled and ready to plunge it through Bannagran's chest.

"You speak of satisfaction?" Bransen asked him. "Like my own satisfaction in killing those who maimed and murdered my father Garibond? Like my own satisfaction in watching Bannagran's own axe tear open the chest of Laird Prydae? Like my own satisfaction now, when I see mighty Bannagran fall dead on the floor? For, yes, I know that you were among those who murdered Garibond. Pray to whatever god you serve, Bannagran, and be quick!"

He ended with a movement that seemed the start of a thrust, but the shout of Reandu stopped him.

"No!" the monk cried. "No, Bransen, do not do this!"

Reandu came forward in a rush, pushing past to stand between Bannagran and Bransen. "I beg of you, my friend. This is not the way. You gain nothing by killing him, by killing anyone."

"And was Brother Reandu among those who murdered Garibond?" Bransen snapped back.

Reandu paled, all the answer Bransen needed, and for a moment, everyone, including Bransen himself, expected him to drive his sword through the monk's chest.

"Bransen?" Cadayle called.

The Highwayman looked past the helpless Reandu, past Bannagran, to see Cadayle propped on her elbows, her pretty eyes open and staring at him.

And judging him, in this critical moment. And the weight of that judgment forced him to judge himself.

He looked back at the terrified Reandu and the subdued Bannagran.

He lowered his blade.

Early the next morning, Bannagran studied the frail-looking young man standing before him, his mind flying between confusion, pity, and hatred. This man's actions had led to the death of his dearest friend, and for that, the mighty warrior demanded revenge.

To the side of the room stood Cadayle and her mother, Callen, holding each other, both crying, for they knew what would transpire here. Bransen had surrendered, on agreement that they would be spared, but that noble action did not lessen the blow they knew was about to fall.

"Do not do this, I beg you," said Brother Reandu, standing at Bransen's side. "There is no gain to be found here in continuing the senseless tragedy."

"We have already had this discussion," Bannagran said, cutting him short, and the warrior's eyes bored into Bransen, who did not look away, did not look down, and did not blink.

It all seemed so simple to Bannagran; he was willing to let the young woman and her mother go free—the Samhaists were in complete confusion and leaderless now, after all, and so there was no one to demand the death of the mother. As for the Highwayman, he was fairly caught and guilty of great crimes against Pryd Holding, indeed crimes that would undermine Pryd Holding!

Yes, the Highwayman had willingly surrendered to Bannagran, with the agreement that Cadayle would be spared. And so it all seemed a simple matter of beheading the fool or throwing him to the flames.

But that simplicity was undermined by the spectacle that Bannagran knew was unfolding right before Castle Pryd's closed gates. Hundreds, thousands, had turned out that morning to show their grief at the loss of Laird Prydae and to shout their support for the Highwayman.

Dangerous support, Bannagran knew, and he remembered his own warnings to his friend, Laird Prydae, when Prydae had expressed his determination to kill the Highwayman. Beyond that, Bannagran understood keenly that with the power vacuum, religious and secular, in Pryd Holding, the state of the holding would be his to wear as mantle or weight when Laird Delaval came to claim the land as his own. Bannagran's standing would greatly depend upon his actions this very morning.

He looked hard at the Highwayman and wanted to hate the man. He thought of his dead friend, killed inadvertently by his own hand, and he wanted to blame this man and to hate him all the more.

And yet Brother Reandu's words—of sympathy and understanding, of seeing poor Bransen's perspective in all this tragedy—had not fallen on deaf ears. Would Bannagran be honoring or doing a disservice to the memory of Prydae by executing this young man?

Or did it even matter?

He looked at Bransen for a long, long time, then barely believed his own words as he said, "Get out of Pryd."

Epilogue

Brother Reandu stood at the gate of Chapel Pryd long after the carriage had rolled out of sight, contemplating the momentous changes that he would have to steward. Master Bathelais had succumbed to his injuries, leaving Reandu as the highest-ranking monk in Pryd, behind the shell that was Father Jerak. Already, brothers were on the way from Chapel Abelle to discuss the disposition of their Church in Pryd Holding, which, it was commonly believed, would soon cease to be Pryd Holding.

For even as Reandu was preparing himself for the inquisitors of Chapel Abelle, Bannagran and the others at the castle made their preparation for the arrival of Laird Delaval himself, along with Prince Yeslnik, who, it was widely assumed, would be granted the holding as his own, under the auspices of Greater Delaval.

Reandu couldn't help but smile a little as he considered how greatly the old wretch Rennarq would despise this takeover by Laird Delaval. But Rennarq, after all, was now a babbling idiot, a storklike creature who could not control his movements. He could hardly eat, by all reports, gagging on every bite, and was likely to choke to death soon. Reandu had tried to help with his gemstones, but whatever the surprising Bransen had done to Rennarq was far beyond Reandu's meager powers to correct.

Good enough and proper justice for the brutal Samhaist, Reandu supposed, though he was not completely without sympathy.

He could not follow any course of sympathy at that time, though, for Reandu had much to accomplish in the short time before his superiors arrived. They would demand of him a complete report, and he knew that the report would not be viewed favorably if the chapel was not in perfect order. Every brother was hard at work, Reandu knew, and that thought reminded him that he, too, had much to do.

He turned toward the chapel, away from the road, but not without one last wistful glance at the long and empty lane. He missed Bransen already and lamented that he had not tried to learn more from the surprising young man. He hoped that the brothers from Chapel Abelle wouldn't take too close an inventory of Chapel Pryd, because he knew that he couldn't begin to explain his decision to allow Bransen to keep the soul stone he had stolen.

But Reandu, despite his fears, was still smiling as he considered his decision. Had he ever met a person in all his life as deserving of a gift from God?

"Farewell, Bransen Garibond," he said softly to the empty lane.

The simple wagon bounced along the flagstone road, the bumps rolling and soft as the wagon moved along at a leisurely pace. Holding the reins, Bransen didn't prod the horses, for he was in no hurry this day, no more than were Callen and Cadayle, flanking him. Tied to the back of the wagon, old Doully the donkey meandered along in step.

"I never knew the world was so wide," Callen remarked every so often, and her eyes were filled with a sparkle of adventure that backed up her claim.

"Wide and scary," said Cadayle, and she hooked her arm under Bransen's and moved a bit closer.

"Scary?" Callen replied doubtfully. "With the Highwayman here to protect us?"

Bransen smiled widely. He didn't look much like the Highwayman at that moment, in his simple woolen tunic and sandals and with not a weapon to be seen. But the black suit was there, tucked neatly under the wagon's bench, and beside it rested his mother's sword. His sword.

"And where shall we go in this wide, wide world?" Callen absently asked. "To where the wind begins and the gods do battle?"

"To whatever lands we find that are free of battle," Cadayle answered. "And few are those, these times in Honce."

"Then to Behr," Bransen answered, and both women looked at him in surprise.

"To the wide blowing sands of the southern lands, to the temple of the Jhesta Tu in the Mountains of Fire."

"You speak of places I do not know," Callen said. Bransen smiled, for in truth, he was merely spouting names that Garibond had told him in his youth and distant references in the book he had committed to memory so long ago.

"Are there any places we do know, beyond the boundaries of Pryd Holding?" Cadayle asked. Though her tone was light, there was substance to that question that was not lost on any of the three.

"To where the wind begins, then," said Bransen, and he gave the reins a little snap. "And where the gods do battle. That is something I wish to see."

And so they rode from the only place any of them had ever known as home, into new lands and new adventures.

The Ancient

A Few Years Ago ...

He walked across the windblown ice of the glacier known as Cold'rin, its frozen surface not causing him the slightest discomfort, not even in his feet, though he wore open-toed sandals.

He was Badden, Ancient Badden, leader of the Samhaists, who knew the magic of the world more intimately than any others in the world. Badden was the greatest of them; no creature alive was more connected to those magics than this man. So while he stood upon hundreds of feet of solid ice, he felt, too, the earth below that freeze, where the hot springs ran. Those very springs had led him to this place, and as he neared the edge of the glacier, the wide expanse of Alpinador opening before him, the old Samhaist trembled with excitement.

He knew.

He knew before he glanced down from the edge of the glacier that he had found it: Mithranidoon, the steamy lake of legend, the place where the god Samhain forsook his mortal coil and melted down into the earth, the source of all magic, the guardian of eternity. Samhain's servant was Death, men like Badden believed, who would bring the souls to the harsh judgment of the god who suffered no fool.

It was a clear morning. When Badden looked down his breath fell away from him, and many heartbeats passed before he could catch it once more. Below him was a fog-shrouded, huge, warm lake, perhaps twenty miles long and half that wide.

Mithranidoon.

The old man smiled at the rarely seen sight. He had found the holiest of Samhaist places and the source of his greatest magic just as his war with the Abellicans in Vanguard to the south had begun to ignite.

"Dame Gwydre," he mouthed, referring to the leader of the men of Vanguard. "You chose poorly in taking an Abellican as your lover." He ended with a chuckle, and no aged wheeze could be detected in the voice of the strong man, however many decades had passed since his birth. Most who knew him—or knew of him, for few actually knew Badden in any real way—believed that eight full decades and part of the ninth were behind him.

Ancient Badden slowly turned about to survey the area. He could feel Mithranidoon's strength keenly now that he had confirmed the location. Mithranidoon had beaten the glacier, and her power permeated the standing ice. He could feel it in his feet.

This place would serve, he thought, continuing his scan. Up here on the glacier he had easy access to the low mountain passes that would get him to the roads leading south into Vanguard. The vantage also afforded him solid defense against any advancing armies, though he recognized that no hostile army would ever get anywhere near to him. Not here, not with Mithranidoon feeding him her power.

"Mithranidoon," the old man said with great reverence, as if merely glimpsing the place from afar was enough to validate his entire existence, his sixty years as a Samhaist priest. But it wasn't enough, he realized suddenly, and he looked up to the heavens.

"You, there!" he said loudly, lifting his hand toward a distant, circling crow.

The bird heard him and could not ignore the call. Immediately it turned and swooped, speeding down, upturning its wings at the last moment to light gently on Ancient Badden's outstretched hand.

"I would see below the mists," the old Samhaist whispered to the bird. Badden stroked his hand over the crow's face and closed his own eyes. "To the scar Samhain rent in the earth."

Suddenly Badden launched the crow with the flick of his hand, his eyes tightly shut for he did not need them anymore. Ancient Badden saw through the eyes of the crow. The bird followed his instructions perfectly, sweeping down from the glacier, soaring vertically the hundreds of feet before it straightened out and rushed across the lake, barely a tall man's height above the water.

Ancient Badden took it all in: the caves of the trolls, lining the bank; the multitude of islands, dozens and dozens, some no more than a few rocks jutting above the steamy waters, others large and forested. One of those, particularly large and tree-covered, was dotted with huts of the general design common to the barbarians of the region, though not nearly as fortified against the elements as those found on the Alpinadoran tundra. Sure enough he spotted the tribesmen, large and strong, decorated with necklaces of claws and teeth, though, as they resided on a warm lake, they wore far less clothing than the average Alpinadoran barbarian.

Badden fell within himself and experienced the warm air coming off the spring-fed lake, warming the wings of his host.

So the barbarians had dared to inhabit this holy place. He nodded, wondering if he could somehow enlist them in his battles against Gwydre. Some tribes had joined him, if only for brief excursions against the Southerners, but none of those occasions had gone as Badden would have hoped. These Northerners, the Alpinadorans, were a stubborn lot, predictable only in their ferocity and wedded to traditions too fully for Badden to hold much sway over them.

The old Ancient chuckled and reminded himself why it was important for him to keep his eyes turned southward, toward the northern Honce province of Vanguard and to Honce proper herself. These were his people, his flock, the civilized men and women who had followed the Samhaist ways for centuries. They had followed unquestioningly until the upstart Abelle had brought them false promises in the days when Badden was but a child.

The Samhaist let those unpleasant thoughts go and basked again in the beauty of Mithranidoon, but he winced soon after as the crow continued its glide over an almost barren lump of rock. Almost barren, but not uninhabited, he saw as the bird sped past. It pained the old man greatly to see powries, red-capped dwarves, settled upon the lake.

But even that could not prepare him for the next sight, and when the bird passed another of the islands, Badden noted a familiar-looking design well under construction. Even here, they had come! Even in this most holy of Samhaist locations, the Abellican heretics had ventured and now seemed as if they meant to stay.

So shocked was Badden that he lost connection to the bird, and he staggered so badly that he nearly toppled from the edge of the glacier.

"This cannot stand," he muttered over and over again.

His mind was already whirling, calculating, searching for how he might cleanse Mithranidoon of this awful infection. All thoughts of enlisting the barbarians on the lake dissipated from him. They were all unclean. They all had to die.

"This will not stand," Ancient Badden declared, and in all his many years as leader of the Samhaists he had never once made such a declaration without seeing it to fruition.

PART ONE

In the Shadow of the Stork

I knew my course. How could I not? I had escaped my infirmities partly through use of the Abellican gemstone known as the hematite or soul stone, but even with that item of focus most of my liberation had come as a result of the training I had received by reading the book penned by my father. The Book of Jhest, the body of knowledge of the Jhesta Tu mystics, an order to which my mother belonged in the southern land known as Behr. If there was more freedom to be found from my affliction, I would find it there.

The road was obvious. All my hopes to free myself from the gemstone and the shadow of the Stork resided in one place to be sure.

That place lay to the south and east, through the port city of Ethelbert dos Entel, around the arm of the mountains and into the desert land of Behr. There I would find the Walk of Clouds and the Jhesta Tu mystics; there I would strengthen my understanding of the ways of Jhest to the point, it was my hope, where I would be free of the Stork.

It wasn't just my hope, but my only hope.

And therein lay my fear, deep and rooted and pervasive to the point of paralyzing.

We left Pryd Town, banished and glad to be. With war raging between the lairds there would be no easy passage, of course, but the ease with which I turned away from the road to Entel to the more hospitable lands surprised me, even as I justified it to Cadayle and her mother. Pretty words, grounded in logic and honest fears, made the change in course an easy sell to my companions, but no amount of apparent justification could hide the truth from me.

I changed course, delayed my journey to Ethelbert dos Entel and beyond, because I was afraid.

This is no new epiphany. I knew when I changed paths the true reason for my hesitance; it was not based in the many fierce soldiers Laird Ethelbert has spread across the land. Even as I offered that very reason—"too dangerous"—to Cadayle and Callen, I recognized the lie.

And now I accept it, for what is left to me if I travel all the way through the deserts of Behr to the land of the mystics only to find there that there is no deeper *understanding to be gained? What is left to me if I learn that I have progressed as far as I can ever hope to climb, that the shadow of the drooling, gibbering Stork will never be more than a stride behind me?*

My condition dominates every aspect of my life. Even with the soul stone strapped to my forehead, focusing my line of chi, I wage constant battles of concentration to keep the Stork at bay. I practice for hours every day, forcing deep-seated memories into my muscles so that when they are needed they will hopefully heed my call. And yet I know that one slip, one break of concentration, and all of my work will be for naught. I will bumble, and I will fail. And not just in battle. My concerns run far deeper than simple vanity or even the price of my own life. I cannot make love to my wife without fear that she may birth a child of similar disability to my own.

My one great hope is to be free of the Stork, to live a normal existence, to have children and raise them strong and healthy.

And that one great hope lies in the Walk of Clouds and nowhere else.

Is it enough to have the hope, even if it is never realized? Would that be a better existence than discovering ultimate futility, that there is no hope?

Perhaps that is the secret—the hope—for me and for all men. I hear the dreams of so many of the folk, their claims that one day they will go and live quietly in a peaceful place, by a stream or a lake or at the edge of the mighty Mirianic. So many claim those dreams throughout their lives, yet never actually find the time to execute their plans.

Are they afraid, I wonder, as I am afraid? Is it better to have the hope of paradise than to pursue it truthfully and find that it is not what you expected?

I laugh at the folly and preposterousness of it all. Despite all of my worries, I am happier than I have ever been. I walk beside Cadayle and her mother Callen and am warm and in love and loved.

My road at present is west and north. Not to Ethelbert dos Entel. Not to Behr. Not to the Walk of Clouds.

—Bransen Garibond

CHAPTER 1

The Would-Be King

Small and thin, Bransen nevertheless walked with the stride of a confident man. He wore the simple clothing of a farmer, breeches and shirt and a wide-brimmed hat under which sprouted tufts of black hair. He carried a thick walking stick, too thick, it seemed, for the fit of his fine hands. But it, like the hat—like the man himself—concealed a great secret, for within its burnished wood was a hollow, and within that hollow a sword, a fabulous sword, the greatest sword in all the land north of the Belt-and-Buckle Mountains. Fashioned of wrapped silverel steel, decorated with etchings of vines and flowers and with a handle of silver and ivory that resembled a hooded serpent, the sword would grow sharper with use as the thicker outer layers of wrapping were nicked or worn away.

It was a Jhesta Tu blade, named for the reclusive mystics of the southern nation of Behr. No detail of the sword had been overlooked, not even the prongs of the crosspiece, each resembling smaller snakes poised as if to strike. For to the Jhesta Tu, the making of the sword was a holy thing, a signal of deeper meditation and perfect concentration. This sword had been fashioned by Bransen's mother, Sen Wi, and whenever he held it he could feel in its details and workmanship the spirit of that remarkable woman, long dead.

A simple wagon pulled by two horses and a donkey tethered behind rolled beside him on the cobblestone road, driven by a woman who commanded Bransen's attention so completely that he was caught off his guard when another woman walked up beside him and tucked his silk bandanna up higher under his hat.

Instinctively, Bransen's hand snapped up to catch the wrist of the older woman, Callen Duwornay, his mother-in-law. He turned to her with a smile.

"I like the way you look at her," Callen said to him quietly, motioning with her chin toward her daughter. Oblivious of Bransen's stare, Cadayle sang while she steered the wagon.

"She is the most beautiful woman I have ever seen," Bransen replied quietly enough so that Cadayle couldn't hear. "Every time I look at her she seems more beautiful still."

Callen flashed him a wide smile. "A man looked at me like that once," she said. "Or so I thought."

Though she smiled her voice was filled with wistfulness and a hint of regret. Bransen understood the latter all too well, for he knew Callen's sad tale because it was intricately and intimately entwined with his own.

Callen had been in love once, but not with her husband. She met her soulmate after she had already been given in marriage, without choice and without say, as had been the custom twenty years before in Honce. The revelations of her adulterous affair had brought her a death sentence. As per the brutal Samhaist tradition, young Callen had been "sacked"—placed in a canvas bag with a poisonous snake. After being bitten repeatedly, her veins coursing with deadly poison, she had been staked out at the edge of Pryd Holding and left to die.

Bransen's mother had come upon Callen on the path and intervened, had used her Jhesta Tu magic to draw the poison from Callen and into her own body. But unknown to Sen Wi she was with child, with Bransen, and the poison damaged him severely.

Thus he kept close his second secret, concealed under a bandanna that he wore under his hat. The bandanna held in place a soul stone, a hematite, a magical gemstone enchanted with the Abellican powers of healing. While wearing that stone Bransen could walk normally with confidence. Without it he reverted to the clumsy and awkward creature often derided as "the Stork."

"Your lover betrayed you," Bransen said, but Callen was shaking her head before he ever finished.

"He had no choice. He would have been killed beside me if he had either denied or confirmed the affair."

"That would have been a noble deed."

"A stupid one."

"Speaking the truth is not stupid," Bransen argued.

Callen grinned at him knowingly. "Then throw away your hat and draw your sword out from that log you call a walking stick."

Bransen chuckled, accepting her point. "What was his name?"

Callen shook her head. "I loved him" was all she would say. "And he gave to me my Cadayle." She looked past Bransen then to her daughter. In that moment Bransen saw more clearly than ever the resemblance between Callen and her daughter. They had the same soft, wheat-colored hair, though Callen's was showing gray now, and eyes of similar brown hue, though rare were the times Bransen had seen Callen's eyes sparkle as they did at that moment, as Cadayle's always did.

Bransen followed her gaze to his beloved wife. "Then I forgive him his cowardice, whatever his name," he said. "For he gave me Cadayle, too, I suppose."

"As your mother gave you to her. As your mother gave life itself to Cadayle by saving mine when I carried Cadayle in my womb."

"When my mother carried me," Bransen said, looking back at his mother-in-law.

Callen sucked in her breath at his words. "I am sorry," she said.

Bransen waved her off. "Tell me true: Would you have stopped Sen Wi if you had known that drawing the poison would so damage me?"

Callen struggled for an answer as she glanced at Cadayle, which made Bransen smile all the wider.

"Nor would I," he said. "I would rather be the Stork with Cadayle beside me than a whole man without her."

"You are a whole man," Callen insisted. She reached up and tucked the hem of his bandanna.

"With the gemstone."

"Or without it," Callen said. "Bransen Garibond is a better man than any I've e'er known."

Bransen laughed again. "And perhaps one day I might walk without the soul stone. Such are the promises of the secrets of the Jhesta Tu."

"What are you discussing with your titters and giggles?" Cadayle asked from the wagon. "Are you stealing my husband then?"

"Oh, but if I could!" Callen replied.

Bransen put his arm about Callen and pulled her close as they walked side by side. It was not hard for him to understand the source of Cadayle's beauty, physical and emotional, and he knew himself to be a lucky man to have such a mother-in-law. To even think that someone would have so viciously tried to kill Callen—Bernivvigar the Samhaist had attempted to do so twice!—confounded him and filled him with outrage. Bernivvigar had also mutilated Garibond, Bransen's adopted father.

And now Bernivvigar was dead, cut down by the very sword in the log, by the very man holding the thick walking stick. Bransen was glad of it.

The conversation was ended by the sound of hooves coming down the road from behind, moving at a fast clip. That could mean only one thing on these roads in this day.

"Stork," Callen whispered to Bransen.

He was far ahead of her warning already. He closed his eyes and severed his connection—one that had become almost automatic at this point—with his soul stone. Immediately, the young man's fluid motions ceased, and he began to walk again in a gangly and awkward manner, literally throwing one hip out before him to swing his leg ahead. Now the walking stick became more than ornamental as Bransen tightened his grip on it and used it as a true crutch.

He heard the horses closing in fast from behind, but he didn't dare turn to observe for fear that the effort would make him fall flat on his face. Callen and Cadayle did look about, though, and Callen whispered, "Laird Delaval's men."

"Make way!" came a gruff command from behind a moment later. The riders pulled their horses to an abrupt stop. "Move this wagon off the road and identify yourselves!"

"He is speaking to you," Callen whispered.

Bransen struggled to turn about, finally managing it, though he nearly tumbled at several points. When he did come around he noted the astonished looks on the faces of the two soldiers, a pair of large, older men.

"What are you about?" asked one of them, a portly giant who sported a thick gray beard.

"I . . . I . . . I . . ." Bransen stammered, and he honestly couldn't get out any words beyond that, for he had grown unused to speaking without the aid of the gemstone. "I . . ."

Both men crinkled their faces with disgust.

"My son," Callen explained, and she moved to support Bransen.

"You admit that," asked the other soldier, younger and clean-shaven, except for a tremendous mustache that seemed to reach from ear to ear. Both men laughed at Bransen's expense.

"Bah, but go on now and leave him be," said Callen. "Wounded in the war he was. Took a spear in the back saving another man. He's deserving your respect, not your taunts."

The gray beard looked at them both suspiciously. "Where was he wounded?"

"In the back," said Callen, and the man put on a sour expression indeed.

"Good lady, I've not the time for your ignorance nor for your feigned ignorance."

"South o' Pryd Town!" Callen blurted, though she had no idea if there had been any real fighting south of Pryd Town.

That answer seemed to satisfy the pair, however, to Callen's relief—until the younger man fixed his gaze upon Cadayle, his gray eyes immediately lighting up with obvious interest.

"He's not really my son," Callen blurted, drawing his attention. "He's my daughter's husband, so I'm thinking of him as such."

"Daughter's husband?" the younger man echoed, staring at Cadayle. "He's married to you?"

"Aye," said the woman. "My beloved. We're for Delaval to see if any of the monks there might be helping him."

The soldiers shared a look. The younger one slid down from his saddle and moved beside Bransen and Callen.

"What's your name?" he asked, but when Callen started to answer for Bransen, the man held up his hand to hush her.

"Bra . . . Br . . . Brrrran," Bransen sputtered, spraying the man with every forced syllable.

"Bran?"

"Sen," Callen added, and the man hushed her with a scowl and a sharp retort.

"Bran?" he asked again.

"S . . . Sssss . . . Brranssen," said the Stork.

"Bransen?" the soldier asked, walking a circuit about him.

"Y . . . Y . . . Yes."

"Stupid name," said the soldier, brushing into Bransen, which sent the Stork into an exaggerated stumble, one hand flailing, the other desperately trying to get the walking stick under him for support.

The honesty of that awkward gait and those fumbling movements had the soldiers glancing at each other again with a mixture of disgust and sympathy. The younger one grabbed Bransen roughly and helped steady him.

"I'm sorry for your loss," he said to Cadayle.

"He's not dead," the woman replied, obviously trying hard to fight back her anger at the soldier for bumping Bransen.

"Sorry for that, too," said the man with a snicker. "Monks ain't to help this one. Better for him and for yourself if he'd've just died out on the field." He gave a derisive snort and walked away from Bransen, toward the wagon, visually inspecting it as he neared. "You're loyal for bringing him to the monks, I expect. But if he ain't for pleasing you, then you just let me know," he added with a wink and a lewd smile.

Cadayle swallowed hard. Callen moved immediately to Bransen and put her hand on his forearm, fearing that he would leap ahead and cut the fool down for the insult.

Abruptly other sounds could be heard from behind, plodding hooves and the creak of a coach.

"Or maybe she's liking those jerking movements in their lovemaking, eh?" the young soldier asked his older companion, who frowned at him in response.

"Just get the wagon off the road," the gray beard said.

"But the ground is uneven and full of roots," Cadayle complained as the younger man moved around to the side of the horses. "And our wheels are worn and will not—"

"Just shut your pretty mouth and be glad that we've not the time for other things," the younger soldier said to her. "Or the time to take the horses and wagon in the name of Laird Delaval." He gave a disapproving look at the wagon and team and old Doully the donkey tethered behind, adding, "Not that any of 'em're worth stealing."

"Don't, I beg!" said Cadayle, but the man grabbed the nearest horse's bridle and roughly tugged the creature to the side, guiding the wagon down a small embankment, where it rolled fast for a few seconds, coming to rest up tight against a tree.

Up on the road across the way, the gray beard walked his horse at Callen and Bransen, forcing them to move off the other side of the road, pulling his companion's horse beside him as he stepped farther along.

"Bow your heads for Prince Yeslnik, Laird of Pryd!" he instructed, staring at Callen all the while, making sure to keep his horse between the two wanderers and the approaching coach. As it rolled by, all gilded in shiny gold and pulled by a fine and strong team, Bransen noted the drivers, a pair of men he had seen before. He saw, too, the Lady Olym, Prince Yeslnik's annoying and spoiled wife, as she stared out the window.

He smiled as he glanced up at her from his half-bowed head. She regarded him with a start, which seemed a bit of recognition. Bransen winked at her for that, and she fell back, putting her gloved hand to her mouth.

That made Bransen smile all the more, but he kept his face aimed at the ground to make sure the gray-bearded soldier didn't catch on.

"He is a prince, you say?" Callen asked the man. "Or a laird, for you're calling him both."

"Prince Yeslnik of Delaval," the gray beard confirmed, moving his horse onto the cobblestones. Across the way, his younger companion rushed up the embankment to join him and quickly mounted.

"Named Laird of Pryd, soon to be Laird of Delaval," the younger man insisted.

"Aye, and the king of all Honce, don't you doubt," said his companion. "Ethelbert's soon to break, and when we're done with that one, we'll put the other lairds in place in short order."

"Aye," agreed the younger. "Now that we've got the river running free o' wild northmen and goblins, and Palmaristown's joined in Laird Delaval's cause, the ships're moving and it's not to be long. Ethelbert's city of Entel will find herself blockaded by the spring, and without his supplies and warriors flowing in from the southland he won't last long."

The gray beard shot his young and boisterous companion a scolding expression, clearly willing him to silence by showing him that he was wagging his tongue too much.

Bransen caught the nuance and understood that they were speaking of something terribly important.

To him, though, it all seemed meaningless banter, for he cared not at all which side won this fight, or what Honce came to look like thereafter. He had no love for any laird and could only hope that they would all kill each other in the last throes of the seemingly endless war. One thing did strike him, though: the notion that Prince Yeslnik had already been named as the replacement laird for Prydae, a man dead because of Bransen. It amused Bransen to think that Yeslnik was in line to become Laird of Delaval, and even king of Honce. The man was a fool and a coward, Bransen knew all too well. He had come upon the very coach that had just rolled past a long time before, when vicious bloody-cap powries had forced it from the road. Yeslnik, his wife, and their two drivers (one of whom had been seriously wounded) were surely doomed, but Bransen, the Highwayman, had come to save the day.

Of course, he had taken some reward for his efforts—much more than the stingy and ungrateful Prince Yeslnik had offered—and so the tale of his hero-ics had been buried by the prince's wounded pride.

Bransen closed his eyes and reconnected with the soul stone set under his black silk bandanna, leaving the Stork far behind.

"Laird Yeslnik?" he whispered under his breath as the two soldiers moved off. Cadayle called to the departing men, begging them to help her get her wagon back on the road, but of course they just ignored her.

"King Yeslnik?" Bransen asked quietly, shaking his head as if the possibil-ity was truly incomprehensible. And indeed, to him, it surely was.

Still, given his experience with the nobility of Honce, he was hardly sur-prised.

"We should have gone straight out for Behr, as we'd planned," Cadayle said to Bransen as he coaxed and tugged the horses to get the wagon back on the road.

"No choice to us," he answered, and not for the first time.

Cadayle sighed and didn't argue. Both of them had wanted to get out of Honce to board a ship in the port of Ethelbert dos Entel and sail around the Belt-and-Buckle Mountains into Behr. Bransen's greatest desire—at least, that which he expressed to his two companions—was to find the Mountains of Fire and the Walk of Clouds, the home of the Jhesta Tu mystics. Their centuries of wisdom had created the tome that Bransen's father had penned. Bransen's mother, Sen Wi, had been of their order. In their midst, Bransen believed, he would find the answers to his dilemma. There, he would attune himself more fully to his *ki-chi-kree,* his line of life energy, and would thus free himself of having to wear the soul stone strapped to his forehead. That soul stone allowed

Bransen to keep his line of life energy straight and strong; without it, his energy sputtered and flitted in every different direction, leaving him the crippled Stork.

The Jhesta Tu had his answers, he believed, and he prayed. But he could not go there at that time, as he had hoped, not through Ethelbert dos Entel, at least, for the place was locked down, and any man who entered the holding of Laird Ethelbert without proper authorization would find himself pressed into service or hanged by the neck.

And so the trio had come southwest instead of southeast and now neared Delaval, the principal city of the land, the seat of power for Laird Delaval, the man who would be king of Honce. Rumors along the road said that passage could be gained to Behr from that city, though it would be a roundabout journey indeed, sailing up the great river, the Masur Delaval (recently named for the ruling family), then through the southern expanse of the Gulf of Honce, and down along the broken region of small holdings known as the Mantis Arm.

It would be an expensive journey, no doubt, and perhaps one full of danger, but the roads simply were not an option at this time of intense warfare.

Or perhaps they were, but Bransen wasn't quite ready to make that all-important journey.

They were moving again soon after. Around a bend in the road less than a mile to the west the trio came in sight of the renowned city nestled at the base of southern hills, surrounding three fast-flowing tributaries that swept down through the streets and joined in a deep pool before the city's northern wharves. This was the head of the Masur Delaval, a river whose currents swirled and backed with the varying tides of the northern gulf.

The city itself was everything Bransen, Cadayle, and Callen had imagined, with rows and rows of stone and wooden buildings, many two or even three stories high. A stone wall surrounded much of the town, including all of the central region. Within it sat the most impressive structure that any of the three had ever seen, a castle so imposing and expansive that it dominated the landscape wholly, a series of three connected keeps whose walls towered so high and strong that Laird Delaval's designs on ruling the entirety of Honce as the one king suddenly seemed all too tenable.

By late afternoon, the trio had come to the outskirts, crossing through lanes bordered by trade shops of every type and with a large produce market set in a wide square just outside the city wall. A few peasants moved about the market, old women mostly, trying to get in a last purchase before the vendors closed their kiosks.

"Rotten goods," Callen whispered to the others, for Cadayle had come down from the wagon now to walk beside them, the three of them leading the team slowly. "Kitchen throwaways from the castle, no doubt."

"No different than in Pryd Town," Cadayle said. "The lairds and their closest take all the best, and we get what's left."

"Except the best that we never let go their way in the first place," Callen remarked with a wry grin.

"Or the best that a certain black-clothed highwayman took from them," added Bransen, and all three shared a laugh.

Cadayle was the first to stop, though, as she caught the undercurrent of the statement. She stared at her husband suspiciously until at last he looked her way with a puzzled expression.

"You can't be thinking . . ." she said.

"I often am."

"Of letting him out here," Cadayle finished. "The Highwayman, I mean. You keep yourself in the guise of the Stork while we're in Delaval."

"No guise, I fear," said Bransen as he reached up and popped the soul stone out from under his bandanna, quickly pocketing it. Instantly he felt the first twinges of separation, the first sparks of discord from his line of *ki-chi-kree.* "It is who . . . oo I ammm."

Cadayle winced at the stutter, despite her insistence.

"You hate seeing me like that," Bransen remarked, his voice relatively strong and steady. Cadayle looked at him in surprise. In response, he merely glanced down at his hand, still in his pocket, still holding the soul stone. He was getting much better at maintaining that connection even when the stone was not strapped to the focal point of his *chi,* up on his forehead.

Cadayle frowned, though, and Bransen immediately began his awkward gait.

"Don't you be thinking of stealing anything in this town," Cadayle whispered. "Laird Delaval frightens me."

Bransen didn't reply, but of course he was thinking precisely that.

They were turned away at the gate, for no wagons and horses were allowed inside other than those owned by the fortunate nobility who lived within the walls and the higher-priced merchants and tradesmen who had to pay dearly for a license to bring a horse or donkey or wagon inside. The guards did point them at a nearby stable outside the wall, however, and assured them that the proprietor was a man of high regard.

His reputation didn't matter much to them anyway. They had little of value in the wagon other than Bransen's silk clothing and the pack they simply would carry away with them. Doully was old and more a friend than a worker, and they had planned to sell the horse team upon their arrival anyway, for the poor beasts had seen too much of ill-groomed roads and broken trails.

"They'll both need shoeing, to be sure," Yenium the stablemaster informed them. He was a tall and very thin man with a dark complexion and darker beard that grew in every day. "Ye been walking a long way."

"Too long," said Callen.

The man stared at Bransen.

"Bringing him to the monks," Cadayle explained. "He was hurt in the war."

Yenium laughed aloud. "But they'll do ye no good," he said, waving his hands in apology even as he spoke the words. "Not unless ye got good gold to pay, and lots of it."

Callen and Cadayle exchanged sour looks, though neither was surprised, of course. It seemed as if some things were constant throughout the land of Honce.

"Our funds run short," Callen said. "We were hoping that you would have need of the horses and the wagon."

"Buy 'em?"

"They've walked too much of the roads," Callen explained.

"True enough," Yenium said. "And the donkey?"

"We'll be keeping that one," said Callen. "We've a long way to go yet."

Knowing their negotiations to be in good hands, Bransen let Cadayle lead him off to the side. Sure enough, Callen joined them shortly after, jiggling a small bag of silver coins and even a single piece of gold. "And he's to board Doully for us free for as long as we're in Delaval," Callen said with a satisfied grin. "A fair price."

"More than," Cadayle agreed and slung the pack over her shoulder. She was about to suggest that they go and see the city proper before the daylight waned but was interrupted by the blare of horns from inside the city wall. Cheers followed, and many of the peasants outside the wall began streaming for the gates, moving eagerly and chattering with obvious excitement.

Callen and Cadayle flanked Bransen and moved him along swiftly to beat the rush. Fortunately, they weren't far from the gate, and with a rather lewd wink at Cadayle, the young guard let them through. Not that the view was any better beyond the wall as thousands had gathered around the grand square, all jumping and shouting, lifting their arms high and waving red towels.

"What is it, then?" Cadayle asked a nearby reveler.

The woman looked at her as if she must be crazy.

"We've just come in," Cadayle explained. "We know nothing of the source of the celebration."

"The laird's come down," the woman explained.

"The king, ye mean!" another corrected.

"Laird Delaval—King Delaval soon enough, by the graces of Abelle and the Ancient Ones," the first said.

Bransen shook his head shakily, continually amazed at the manner in which the peasants always seemed to hedge their bets regarding the afterlife, citing both of the dominant religions.

"He's come down with his lady and all the others," said the woman. "Tonight the brave Prince Yeslnik's to be formally named as Laird of Pryd Holding. That and a host of other honors on the man. Oh, but he's handsome, and so brave! He's killed a hundred of Ethelbert's men, don't ye know?"

Cadayle smiled and nodded, hiding her knowing smirk well as she turned to regard Bransen, who of course knew better than to believe any such supposed heroics attributed to the foppish Prince Yeslnik. But Cadayle's smile disappeared in a blink, for Callen stood there alone with no sign of Bransen. Immediately Cadayle brought a hand up to her pack, realizing as she grasped it that it had been relieved of some of its contents. It was not hard for her to guess which things might have been taken.

She gave an awkward bow and moved away from the peasant woman, catching her mother by the elbow and leading her to a quieter spot.

"What is he thinking?" she asked.

"That with all of them down here . . ." Callen motioned with her chin toward the castle.

Cadayle heaved a great and helpless sigh.

Her husband was a stubborn one, she knew.

And that stubbornness was likely to get him killed.

B ransen didn't change into his black silk suit until he reached the shadows at the base of the stone wall to the castle's highest and most fortified keep. The exotic cloth had held up well through the years, and was still shiny, as if through some magic the dirt could not gain a hold on it. The right sleeve of the shirt had been torn away by Bransen, to make both his mask (for he unrolled the gem-holding headband down to the tip of his nose, with eyeholes cut in appropriately) and a strip of cloth that he tied about his upper right arm to hide an easily identifiable birthmark.

As he had expected, almost all of the soldiers had gone down to watch the pomp and ceremony of the anointing of Laird Yeslnik. The main gates were guarded, he noted as he crossed about the side streets and back alleys, as were all the entry points to the castle proper.

But Bransen was Jhesta Tu, or a close approximation at least, and he didn't need a doorway. So he moved to the back wall, out of view, and donned his black suit.

He glanced around, hearing the distant sounds of the growing celebration. He saw no guards in the area and held confidence that any who were supposed to be here, behind the structure and thus blocked from the merrymaking, were likely away from their posts, watching the happenings in the lower bailey.

He couldn't be sure, though, and that truth gave him pause.

"But you are the Highwayman," he reminded himself, his grin widening beneath the black mask.

Bransen fell within himself. He thought of the gemstones, of the malachite, and used the feelings its touch had inspired to reach that corresponding energy within his *ki-chi-kree*. If he had had the magical gemstone in his possession he could have floated off the ground, he knew, but even without it, even just remembering its powers, Bransen lightened his body greatly. He reached up with one hand and pulled himself up the wall.

Like a spider he scrambled, his hands and feet finding grooves in the stone. So weightless had he become that it mattered not how deep the ledge or how firm his grip. In less than a minute the Highwayman had scaled the seventy-five feet of the highest tower, all the way to the one narrow window on this back side of the structure. He peeked inside, then settled himself securely on the ledge. With a look all around at the wide and glorious rolling countryside south of Delaval, he slipped into the dimly lit room.

This was the tower of royalty, he knew at once from the many valuables— paintings, tapestries, vases, and a plethora of other trinkets and utensils and artworks.

The Highwayman rubbed his hands together and went to work.

It is long overdue, and less than you have earned," Lady Olym called back behind her as she entered her private bedchamber. "Your uncle should have named you Laird of Delaval and been done with it. His only son is not worthy, of course."

A murmur of protest came back to her from Yeslnik's room, too garbled for her to decipher—not that she cared to, anyway.

"Laird of Pryd Town," Olym said. If she was thrilled her voice did not reflect it. "Now I suppose we will have to live in that dreary place."

She pulled off her bulky bejeweled dress and an assortment of accessories. Stripped to her sheer nightdress, she sat down at her vanity, admiring her powdered face in the pretty mirror set atop the small marble table. One by one she pulled off her oversized rings, each set with a fabulous precious stone.

They paled in comparison to the necklace she wore, though, which was set with diamonds, rubies, and emeralds, one after another, three rows thick and from shoulder to shoulder. Olym gently stroked the precious stones, staring at them in the mirror as if in a trance. So fully did they hold her attention that she didn't even notice the black-clothed figure that had moved up to stand directly behind her.

Olym jumped indeed when a hand settled on her own and a soft voice whispered, "Allow me to help you with that, dear lady."

She started to scream, but the hand clapped tightly over her mouth.

"Do not cry out, I beg of you," the Highwayman said. "I will not harm you, dear lady. On my word." He brought his head down to rest his chin on her shoulder so that they could look each other in the eye through the mirror. For a moment Olym seemed to swoon, her chest heaving.

"On my word," the Highwayman said again, and he gave her a plaintive and questioning look and eased his hand away from her mouth just a bit.

Olym nodded her head, and the Highwayman pulled his hand away.

"You have come to ravish me!" Olym wailed.

The bemused Highwayman stared at her, for her tone sounded more hopeful than terrified.

Olym turned on him sharply. "Take me, then," she offered. "But be quick and be gone and know that I shan't enjoy it!"

Without the soul stone Bransen always stuttered badly, but never had he found words harder to find than at that moment, though the soul stone was, of course, strapped securely to his forehead.

Olym turned further about and threw back her head, the back of one hand across her forehead as if in despair. The movement thrust forth her breasts, of course, and the sheer nightdress did little to hide her obvious excitement.

"Take me, then! Ravish me! Have at me with your animal savagery."

"And force you to make little barnyard noises?" the Highwayman asked, trying hard not to laugh.

"Oh, yes, if you must! If that is what I need do to escape murder at the end of your blade!"

The Highwayman didn't quite know how to say, "But all I want are the jewels," so he stuttered again—until footsteps sounded in the hall, coming their way. "I beg your silence," he whispered, putting a finger over his pursed lips, fading into the shadows so seamlessly behind a tapestry that Olym had to blink and stare stupidly, wondering if he had ever really been there.

"Ah, wife," Yeslnik said, entering the room. "I am randy from the excitement of the day." He paused and looked at her admiringly, at her nearly naked form and obvious state. "Apparently I am not alone in my humor!"

Now it was Olym's turn to stutter. She glanced repeatedly at the shadows where the Highwayman had disappeared.

Yeslnik sidled up to her and pulled her tight against him, his eyes narrowing. "I am the Laird of Pryd Holding," he said, and then again and again. With each proclamation he squeezed Olym tighter to him.

"My laird," Olym said, looking past him as he turned, again to the spot where the Highwayman had gone.

Had gone and returned, she noted, for he stood there, leaning against her vanity, one arm bare and one blanketed in black silk crossed over his chest, a look of utter amusement on his face, his so-handsome face.

Olym took a deep breath and gave a mewling sound.

"Oh, my princess," Yeslnik gasped. "I am the Laird of Pryd Holding!" He shuddered as he squeezed her against him more tightly still.

"So you have mentioned a dozen times," a masculine voice said behind him. Yeslnik froze in place. "If you say it a dozen more, perhaps you will convince yourself you are worthy of the title."

Yeslnik spun about. "You!" he cried.

"I could be no one else," the Highwayman said with a shrug.

"How?"

"Your interrogation techniques leave much to be desired, I fear," the Highwayman said. "More so when one considers that if anyone here is a prisoner, it is not I."

"Not you?" Yeslnik stammered, trying hard to catch up.

"Yes you, not I," said the Highwayman.

"Not I?"

"Yes, you!"

"You?"

"Now you have it!" the Highwayman said, and pointed at Yeslnik and emphatically added, "You."

"Do not harm him!" Olym cried, and she threw herself in front of Yeslnik, her arms wide to hold him back—and also to give the Highwayman a complete viewing. "Take me as you will. Ravish me!"

"Olym!" Yeslnik cried.

"I will do anything for you, my laird," Olym wailed.

"Back to the barnyard, always there," the Highwayman remarked. Yeslnik stared at him incredulously.

"I will suffer his passion for you, my love," Olym said to her husband. "I will save you with my womanly charms."

"With your jewels, you mean," the Highwayman corrected. Faster than either of them could react, he came forward and snatched the necklace from Olym's neck, then, for good measure, scooped the rings from the vanity.

"Not again!" Yeslnik cried. In a moment of uncustomary courage (or more likely it was just his anger overruling his good sense), he threw Olym aside and raised his fists threateningly. He snapped his hand to the near side of the vanity, where Olym kept a sharp knife she used to scrape the dark hairs from her chin. Yeslnik stepped forward, waving the knife out before him.

The Highwayman dropped his hands to his side, sighed, and shook his head.

"You'll not make a fool of me again," Yeslnik declared.

"I fear you reached that marker long before I arrived," the Highwayman replied.

The Laird of Pryd Holding finally sorted that insult out and stabbed at the man in rage. The Highwayman turned, and the blade slipped past harmlessly.

Yeslnik retracted and stabbed again, and the Highwayman dodged the other way.

Yeslnik slashed across at the man's head, but of course the agile Highwayman easily ducked the awkward strike, then came up again and with even less effort sidestepped the next futile stab.

"Truly, Prince Yeslnik, you are making this more difficult," the Highwayman said. He ducked another slash, sidestepped another stab, then caught the move he had been waiting for, an uppercut thrusting the knife for the bottom of his chin.

It never got close. The Highwayman's left hand caught the prince's forearm, and his right hand clamped over Yeslnik's at just the right angle for the thief to buckle the prince's wrist, bending the hand forward suddenly. The Highwayman pressed, overextending the bend, driving Yeslnik's knuckles down toward his wrist. Under that strain and pain, Yeslnik could not hold his grip on the knife. Even as he realized he had let it go, the Highwayman's left hand shot out and slapped him across the face, backhanded him the other way, and slapped him a third time for good measure.

"Do you insist on making this harder?" the Highwayman asked, presenting the knife out, handle first, toward the prince.

Infuriated beyond reason, Yeslnik grabbed the blade and slashed wildly, again hit nothing but air. In sheer frustration he threw the knife. His eyes went wide indeed when he noted that the thief had caught it so easily.

Yeslnik turned and cried out, bolting for the door. "Take my wife!" he shrieked.

The Highwayman sprang into a sidelong cartwheel, catching his hand on the edge of the vanity, planting his other hand flat on its top, and springing away to intercept Yeslnik at the door.

"Your knife," he said, tossing the blade into the air.

Yeslnik's eyes followed its ascent as the prince skidded to a stop. To his credit Yeslnik caught the blade, but when he looked back down he found the tip of a fabulous and too-familiar sword an inch from his face. He gave a curious sound, strangely similar to his wife's earlier mewling, and let the knife drop to the floor.

The Highwayman shook his head. "Now what am I to do with you?"

"Oh," Lady Olym wailed, throwing her arm against her forehead and falling back, conveniently onto the room's rather large bed.

Both the Highwayman and Yeslnik sighed.

A noise from somewhere down the hall reminded them that the ceremony had ended and many of the castle's inhabitants were returning from the lower bailey.

"Under the bed," the Highwayman ordered Yeslnik abruptly, prodding the prince with his sword, guiding him around. Finally he stepped up and pushed Yeslnik forward.

"While you ravish my wife above me?"

"Oh," wailed Olym, and her knees drifted apart.

The Highwayman shoved Yeslnik harder for that, putting him down to his knees at the side of the bed. "You with him," he ordered Olym, and all humor had left his tone. "Under the bed!"

"But . . ." Olym protested, as sadly as any bride left at the altar.

"Under the bed. Now! The both of you." He prodded Yeslnik as he spoke, driving the man under with the tip of his sword. Grabbing Olym with his free hand, he yanked her off the bed. She fell heavily at his feet, but nothing other than her pride was hurt, he saw, as she looked up and reached for him desperately.

Yeslnik grabbed her and dragged her under the bed with him.

"In the middle," the Highwayman ordered. He dropped down and prodded at them with his sword, forcing them back from the edge. He looked all around, thinking to block the four openings of the bed. But alas, there was not enough furniture in the room to seal them in.

Sounds from outside the room heightened the Highwayman's urgency. Improvising, he leaped in a roll across the end of the bed, coming to his feet facing the foot. He looked from its thin legs to his sword and back. His eyes scanned the headboard. He could clear it and easily, he realized, as the movements sorted out before him. He had to be precise; he had to be quick.

But he was Jhesta Tu.

The Highwayman presented his sword before him and took a deep and steadying breath. Underneath the bed Yeslnik and Olym chattered but he left their voices far behind, concentrating on the task before him. Both hands grasped the hilt of the sword as he lifted it slowly before his right shoulder, keeping the blade perpendicular to the floor.

He stepped out with his left foot suddenly, slashing the blade down low, then reversed the swing so quickly that it passed over the severed bed leg before the bed had even dropped. Now he stepped right, finishing the move as his backhand took out the other leg.

The foot of the bed dropped as the Highwayman leaped back to the right in a twisting somersault. He came to his feet beside the bed, his back to it. Halfway up its length he continued his spin, his blade neatly severing the third leg.

Yeslnik and Olym cried out in protest, but their initial escape route, anticipated by the Highwayman, had been lost with the collapse of the bed's right side.

The Highwayman let go of the sword with his right hand as he came around. As soon as he faced the bed squarely again his legs twitched, lifting him in a dive ahead and to the side. He turned his free right hand under and caught the top of the headboard, allowing him to turn about as he lifted a straight-legged somersault that ended with a sudden tuck that spun him over and a more sudden extension that landed him upright facing the bed. But only for a moment, for he dropped and slashed to the right, and the fourth and final leg fell away, dropping the full weight of the bed onto Yeslnik and Olym, mercifully muffling their annoying cries.

The Highwayman stepped back and regarded his handiwork with a nod that reflected both surprise and satisfaction. He looked down at the small sack tied to his belt, bulging with coin and jewels, and nodded again.

"Do remember that I did not kill you, and it would have been an easy thing," he said to Yeslnik, bending low and peering under at the grunting and outraged man. "And do remember that I did not ravish your wife."

Yeslnik cursed and spat at him, but the Highwayman had perplexed himself with his own words. He leaned back to consider them and didn't even notice the feeble insult, verbal or watery.

"You remember that I did not ravish her," the Highwayman clarified, looking back at Yeslnik. "I do hope that dear Lady Olym will forget that fact, for I am certain that my lack of action angers her more than anything else I might have done, murdering you included."

"How dare you?" Yeslnik demanded.

"It is really quite easy," the Highwayman assured him, and with a tap of two fingers to his forehead, he rushed away to the window.

But darkness hadn't fallen yet, and the upper bailey teemed with guards.

Nearly an hour passed before Prince Yeslnik finally managed to squirm out from under the heavy bed. His howls took some time to get the attention of some servants, who at last rushed in and helped him pull the bed up enough to allow Olym to unceremoniously slither out.

"You!" Olym screamed at her husband. She made no effort to cover herself, though more and more people were charging into the room to see what was the matter. "You fancy yourself the laird of a holding, and you cannot deal with a single thief? You are a hero among men, and yet a single, small man chases you under your wife's bed like a frightened rabbit?" She moved to slap him, but Yeslnik caught her arm then her other one and held her fast.

"Would you be less angry if he had ravished you?" Yeslnik asked, more an accusation than a question. Lady Olym wailed—the first sincere wail she had offered that day—and collapsed onto what was left of her bed.

It seemed as if Yeslnik only then realized that the room was full of people, many of whom were staring at his revealed wife. "Out! Out!" he demanded, chasing them from the room. He gave a last, disgusted look at Olym and followed, ordering the guards to find the Highwayman and not return without the bastard's severed head.

Olym brought her hands to her face and sobbed for a long, long while as the room darkened. She was near sleep when soft lips brushed her forehead.

"Marvelous lady," said the Highwayman, who had never left the room. Olym's eyes popped wide open, and she thrust herself up to her elbows to face him directly.

"I cannot ravish a married woman, by the code of honor that guides me," the thief graciously explained. "But I assure you that the code is sorely tried when I glimpse a creature of such beauty." He reached up and gently stroked her face. Olym closed her eyes and swooned, falling back to the bed, her fingers kneading at the plush blankets.

"Think of me," the Highwayman bade her, "as I travel the wilds of the northland."

And then he was gone, sprinting to the window and going through so easily and swiftly that he was out before Olym had even glanced his way.

Not to fear," Bransen assured Callen and Cadayle the next day when they walked down the road out of Delaval, leading Doully the donkey. "For I told Lady Olym that I would be in the North."

"But our road is to the north," Callen replied. "And there you will truly be."

"Exactly," said Bransen and he flashed that grin, smug and disarming at the same time.

Sure enough, Laird Delaval's guards, at the request of Prince Yeslnik, streamed out of the city that same morning, heading south in search of the Highwayman as the Lady Olym had directed.

CHAPTER 2

Feeding the God Well

Samhaist Dantanna crouched low as he moved through the area of knee-deep white caribou moss. The plant could be mashed into a potent salve and made a fine tea, but Dantanna was looking for something even more valuable: dauba bulbs. They only grew among the moss, and never in great number. Even one bulb would make for a fine day's hunting, though, for the Samhaist could then prepare the most wonderful dauba stew, a brew that would take all the pains from his joints for a week and more.

Dantanna didn't like this land, Alpinador, far preferring the milder climate of Vanguard, south of the mountains.

It was not his place to question, though—at least not openly.

He had to keep telling himself that, for there was so much afoot in the world that Dantanna, still young and not completely jaded, did indeed wish to question. He bent low and brushed aside the moss as he quickened his pace. He knew there would be some dauba around this particularly thick strand of caribou moss—there had to be.

"That's a bootlace, not a vine, boy," came a gruff voice, and only then did Dantanna realize that he was not alone in the white field, though how in the world someone else had come in without gaining his attention he couldn't begin to fathom.

Until he looked up to see the weathered face, the thick mustache, and the pointed, feathered cap. Then he knew. The man standing tall and straight before him might have been forty or seventy—he had those ageless features that exude both strength and the wisdom of experience. So much experience.

"Master Sequin," he stammered, sidling back a few feet. The old scout didn't answer other than to stare unblinkingly and witheringly at the Samhaist. "I did not know that you were in the area," Dantanna said.

"Like to state the obvious, do you?"

Dantanna nodded stupidly. "I am Samhaist Dantanna—once we met, in Vanguard and near to where the Abelli . . ."

"Chapel Pellinor," the weathered Jameston Sequin said. Dantanna nodded, trying not to look too pleased that this great man had remembered him.

"I never forget a face," Jameston went on. "Or the name of a man I consider worth remembering."

Dantanna beamed all the more.

"What did you say your name was again?"

The Samhaist slouched. "Dantanna."

"You travel with old Badden?"

"Ancient Badden," Dantanna corrected, and (surprisingly to him) forcefully.

"You're a long way from home, boy."

Dantanna didn't begin to know how to take that. "There is the war . . ."

"The one your Ancient Badden started."

"Not so!" Dantanna protested with a severity that surprised him given his ambivalence, often disgust, at the fighting over Vanguard. "Dame Gwydre began it all. She chose and chose ill."

"Because she fell in love with a man?"

"Because she fell in love with an Abellican monk!"

Jameston Sequin chuckled and shook his head. "An offense worth all of this?" he asked.

Dantanna half shook his head and half nodded, giving no verbal response, because he knew that if he did he would never get any true resonance or confidence in his voice.

"Well, you fight your battles as you choose them," Jameston said. "I'll let the folk of Vanguard choose which religion, Samhaist or Abellican, suits their needs."

"And which for Jameston?" Dantanna asked, thinking himself sly for the instant it took Jameston to mock him utterly with a laugh.

The old scout brought his arm out in front of him, holding a sack, and still applying that withering gaze over Dantanna, he upended it before the man. More than a dozen pointy troll ears tumbled out onto the ground at Dantanna's feet.

"It's theirs to choose," Jameston said.

"As it is yours," Dantanna replied, still staring down at the multitude of ears—ears of creatures Ancient Badden had enlisted in the fight.

"If my choice is between a man and a troll, it's not a hard one, boy," Jameston said. "I said I didn't much care, and I don't, but you tell your Ancient Badden that I'm not for letting glacial trolls murder families in the name of Samhain or in the name of anyone else."

"Our struggle is . . ."

". . . none of my business," Jameston finished for him, "and none of my care. But when I see a troll, I kill a troll, and I don't ask who it's working for." He snorted derisively and started away.

"Master Sequin," Dantanna called after him. "If we meet again, will you remember my name?"

Jameston didn't stop or look back. "I forgot it already."

From a high perch on the very edge of the great glacier Cold'rin, Ancient Badden stared out across the miles of the southland. In his mind's eye, he looked past the frozen tundra of Alpinador to the thick forests of Vanguard. He envisioned the battles raging there, Honce man against goblin, Honce man against glacial troll, Honce man against the sturdy Alpinadoran barbarians.

His army, battling the men of Honce, punishing them for their growing acceptance of the heretics of Blessed Abelle.

A smile creased Ancient Badden's face, strangely white teeth (for one of his age) standing brightly in the midst of his wild black mustache and beard, a gigantic affair that poked out in a semicircle of sharp points beneath the old Samhaist's weathered face, its ends sharpened by dung and plaited with ribbons black and red. He would teach them.

Word had come that Chapel Pellinor had fallen—sacked as much by angry Honce men as by Ancient Badden's hordes. The few surviving monks were even then being dragged north, to this place, to be sacrificed to Ancient D'no, the worm god of the frozen lands.

Ancient Badden lowered his gaze to the clouds of steam at the base of the glacier's cliff face, where the ice met the hot waters of the lake called Mithranidoon. The mists seemed to him to thicken. An indication, perhaps, that D'no was pleased by the news? Or his imagination, his thrill, at the prospect of feeding the god so well?

Ancient Badden envisioned the hot waters beneath that cloud, the Holy Lake of Mithranidoon, the Rift of Samhain, the gift of the Ancient Ones to their children as a reward for their wondrous efforts here.

A particularly sharp retort turned the old Samhaist around, to view the crevice some fifty feet north of where he stood. A pair of giants, fifteen feet tall and with shoulders as wide as the wingspan of a great eagle, rolled heavy mallets up into the air, slamming them down concurrently upon the flattened head of a battered log, a sharpened wedge that drove deeper into the glacier with every smash. Once they had driven that one down to the level of the glacier, Ancient Badden would bless the spike and prepare its end with spells and fire, that another could be placed upon it and driven down, pushing the bottom one even deeper.

Over to the right of the giants, where the crevice was much wider and much deeper, several glacial trolls hung by their ankles, suspended beneath crossbeams by thin ropes. Their arms were weighted, forcing them into a diver's stretch, and their wrists had been expertly cut, their thin blood dripping down into the chasm and turning into a fine, coating mist in the windy gorge. Troll blood did not freeze, and the coating of it in the crevice would prevent the melted waters from mitigating the damage to the edge of the glacier. One troll, at least one, was dead and dried out now, Ancient Badden noted, but no worries, for the wretched little beasts were as thick as hares in summer Vanguard.

He scanned farther to the right, to the elaborate ice bridge he had magically constructed: it spanned the widest expanse of the chasm, with enough room on either side so that it would continue to allow crossing even when the rift had become as wide as intended. Ancient Badden couldn't help but smile as his gaze moved farther to the right, to the mountain wall bordering the glacier on the east, for against that dark stone loomed Ancient Badden's greatest work yet: his home, Devongel, a castle of crystalline ice, of elegant, winding spires and thick walls, of defensive and confusing mazes both practical and beautiful.

His smile disappeared when he looked back to the left, over by the working giants, and noted a smaller form, dressed in the telltale light green robes of a Samhaist, though surely nothing as elaborate as Ancient Badden's gown, decorated as it was with claws and teeth from various carnivores, and with leafy designs woven with threads green and yellow so that it looked as if the Samhaist could walk into a strand of brush and simply disappear. About his waist, Ancient Badden wore a thick red sash, tied on his right hip, with its frayed ends nearly reaching the ground. Only one Samhaist, the Ancient himself, could wear this holiest of belts, and Ancient Badden put his hand on that knot now, as the everannoying Priest Dantanna approached, to remind himself of that honor.

Wearing a sour expression, Dantanna circled wide of the giants and hopped the crevice, which, ten feet out from the spike, was no more than a crack, and neared Ancient Badden with a determined stride.

He bowed repeatedly as he covered the last dozen strides to his master, though not as quickly or as deeply as Ancient Badden would have liked.

"You have heard of Chapel Pellinor," Ancient Badden began.

"Burned and with its stones scattered," Dantanna replied, cutting off his words as if it pained him to speak them.

"Another victory over the Abellican heretics. Does that not please you?"

"Many men and women who were not Abellicans were killed in the fighting."

Ancient Badden shrugged as if it did not matter, which, of course, in the greater scheme of Samhain's universe, it surely did not.

"Killed by goblins and trolls and the barbarian mercenaries," Dantanna added.

Another shrug. "That is the way of things."

"Because we choose it to be! Once we battled beside the Honce men of Vanguard against the very army we now turn loose upon them."

"Once and not long ago, they knew their place," said Ancient Badden. Dantanna winced and quieted, the implications hanging heavily in the air. War was general south of the Gulf of Corona, laird against laird, with Ethelbert of Entel battling for dominance against the great Delaval. In that struggle, the true emerging winner seemed to be neither of the lairds, but rather, the Abellican Church, for the monks with their magical gemstones, powerful in both healing and destruction, had gained favor with every laird. Though possessed of magic of their own, the Samhaists could not match that Abellican availability of useful tricks.

"They look to the south," Dantanna dared to say after a few moments of uncomfortable silence. "The men of Vanguard see the turning tide amongst their Honce brethren."

"A tide turning away from us and from the Ancient Ones," said Ancient Badden. "It is a temporary thing, you understand."

Dantanna didn't reply, except that his face showed little in the way of concession.

"The Abellican monks dazzle with their baubles," Ancient Badden explained. "And provide comfort and even battle advantage. But they have little understanding of the proper preparations for the greater course. Death is inevitable—to lairds and to peasants. What answers might the foolish boys who follow the distorted memory of that idiot Abelle offer to mortally wounded warriors?"

"Fewer are mortally wounded because of their work."

"Temporary relief! Everyone dies."

Dantanna shook his head. "Then perhaps we have a role to play in complement with the monks," he said, or started to, for his voice trailed off and his eyes widened with fear as Ancient Badden put on the most fearsome scowl he had ever seen, a mask of danger and death, and the great Samhaist seemed to grow, to rise up above Dantanna, mocking him in his impotence.

But the growth proved short-lived, and Ancient Badden settled back easily, wearing a grin—though one that seemed no less dangerous. "You would like that, would you not?" he asked.

Dantanna tilted his head a bit, as if he did not understand.

"If we were to find a place beside the Abellicans," Ancient Badden clarified.

Dantanna began to shake his head, and his eyes darted about as if he was looking for a way to flee.

"How long did you think you could hide your allegiance to Dame Gwydre?" Ancient Badden bluntly asked.

"I know not of what you speak."

"Do not play me for a fool," Ancient Badden warned. "You counseled Gwydre extensively before her association with the Abellicans."

"Ancient, the Abellicans have been in Vanguard Town for years—before I ever came to know Lady Gwydre. Indeed, they were beside Laird Gendron before his death, when Gwydre was but a girl."

"With all their magical baubles, they still did not prevent his untimely death, did they?" Ancient Badden gave a little laugh. Dantanna winced, for it was widely rumored that the Samhaists had played a role in the "accident" that had taken the beloved Laird Gendron from the folk of Vanguard.

"And so Gwydre rose to power in Vanguard Town, a young, impressionable girl."

"Never that," Dantanna interrupted, and Ancient Badden's scowl put him back on his heels.

"And when your master died, Gwydre's ear was passed to you," Ancient Badden went on. "Your duty was clearly relayed: to keep Gwydre from the Abellican encroachment. Your own assessment if you will, Dantanna. Did you succeed or fail?"

Dantanna began shaking his head. "It was more complicated. . . ."

"Are you couching an admission of failure?"

"No, Ancient. Dame Gwydre has sought a balance from the beginning. She counts me among her trusted advisors as she counts—"

"The monks of Chapel Pellinor?"

"Yes, but . . ."

"One of them in particular," Ancient Badden said.

Dantanna swallowed hard, unable to deny the truth of it. Dame Gwydre had fallen in love with an Abellican monk, and the Church of Abelle had done nothing to dissuade the union—obviously for cynical, political reasons. Chapel Pellinor stood on the outskirts of Vanguard Town, by far the most important town north of the Gulf of Corona; Dame Gwydre commanded the army of the entire Honce province north of the Gulf of Corona, the region known as Vanguard. As her relationship with her lover monk had grown, so had grown the power of the Abellicans in Vanguard Town and across the land. Dantanna had not been able to resist that movement, and had come to believe that playing an amenable role was the only way he and the Samhaists could retain any semblance of influence over the feisty and headstrong dame of Vanguard.

He had improvised. He had taken his own initiative. He had gambled and had thought that he was carving out a suitable role for his Church—until the hordes had descended upon Vanguard from the north at the direction of Ancient Badden.

"You wear your answer on your face, foolish Dantanna. It is true, then."

"Dame Gwydre beds a monk, yes," Dantanna admitted.

"And you allowed it to happen."

Dantanna balked at the words, spoken as they had been as an accusation. "Allowed?"

"Yes, allowed. You saw the relationship budding years ago, and you did not stop it."

"Love takes its own course, Ancient. I tried to dissuade Gwydre. Indeed, I did. But her heart was set and immovable, and—"

"And you did not kill this monk."

That took Dantanna's breath away.

"Is the importance of this lost upon you?" Ancient Badden asked.

"No, Ancient. No."

"Then why did you not recognize your duty and fulfill it long ago? It has been many months since the commencement of the unholy tryst and yet this Abellican still draws breath."

"You ask me to murder a man?"

"Were you not so trained in the magic of poison? Do you think that training no more than an exercise in the hypothetical?"

Dantanna shook his head helplessly, his jaw hanging slack.

"Have you not the power to kill a single young monk?"

"I am no murderer," the younger Samhaist whispered.

"Murderer, bah!" Ancient Badden huffed, and he waved his hand and walked to the lip of the glacier, looking down the thousand feet and more to the mist rising off the lake. "An ugly word for a noble task. How many lives would Dantanna have saved if he had mustered his courage and done as his duty demanded? This entire war could have been avoided, or surely minimized, if Dame Gwydre had not been smitten by a heretic Abellican, you fool!"

"The war was one of choice," Dantanna dared to say.

Ancient Badden turned on him angrily. "Choice?" he roared. "You would cede the souls of thousands of Vanguardsmen to the heretic Abellicans?"

"We have our place . . ."

"Shut up," Ancient Badden said simply, and he turned back to look out over the southland. "You have failed, in the one task which meant anything, the one action that might have avoided years of strife and carnage. The misery, the death, the rivers of blood are all upon you because you had not the courage to strike a single blow."

"You cannot believe that," Dantanna gasped.

"I suppose, though, that I should thank you," Ancient Badden went on, as if he had not heard the comment. "The Ancient Ones saw fit to fill my divining pool with images of the battle of Chapel Pellinor. And the screams and cries. It was glorious, indeed."

"How can you say that?" Dantanna asked under his breath, despite himself and his fears.

"To hear men weeping like children!" Ancient Badden snickered. "To hear the cries of women who knew they were doomed for their heresy, who knew their children would be torn apart in retribution! Oh, the beauty of justice!

"And do you know the greatest victory of all?" Ancient Badden asked, spinning about and staring wild-eyed and wide-eyed at the stupefied younger Samhaist, who merely shook his head as if he was numb to it all.

"The captives!" Ancient Badden explained. "Lines of them, hundreds of them, perhaps, tethered together and marching for this very place."

Dantanna turned about to regard the giants, lazily pounding home the wedge spikes. He viewed the hanging glacial trolls, their thin blood dripping down into the melt, hindering the refreezing of the glacier. Another platform had been constructed near to them, this one with a crank and a long, long rope, one that would deposit the anticipated sacrifices deep within the chasm, where the white worm waited. When Dantanna turned back to Ancient Badden, the man's smug smile proved very revealing.

"They will feed D'no, and his frenzy and heat will facilitate the Severing," Ancient Badden confirmed, using the sanctifying term he had coined for his work on the edge of the glacier. "As D'no burrows and further melts the ice, we will feed him more. We will make him stronger and swifter, that he will reach to the stones about the ice to join our efforts with the earth magic of the Ancient Ones." He paused and regarded the younger Samhaist with a nod, one that seemed almost of approval. "I will allow you to offer many of them," he said, and turned back to stare out—mostly to hide his grin at Dantanna's horrified expression.

"Offer them?" Dantanna stammered. "You would murder them as food to further your ambitions here?"

"Murder," Ancient Badden said with a dismissive laugh. "A word you use so easily. Their lives are forfeit, by their own actions. They sided with heretics and so we—you—will exact proper punishment. Perhaps if I teach you to better wield that knife you were awarded, you will be less likely to fail us in the future when you are called upon by all that is holy to put it to proper use."

As he spoke, Ancient Badden summoned his magic to enhance his senses, and he clearly heard Dantanna's approach. Thus, he was not surprised when the man, standing right behind him, gave a shout and shoved him hard. Nor did Ancient Badden resist that push, lifting his arms gloriously wide as he went off the edge of the glacier, plummeting toward the mist below.

Dantanna gave a gasp and even offered a contrite wail as the supreme master, the Ancient of the Samhaist religion, tumbled toward certain doom.

Ancient Badden heard it and smiled all the wider, knowing that he had pushed the young fool to abject desperation. He closed his eyes and felt the wind thrumming about his falling form, his robes flapping noisily. He used that sensation of freedom from mortal boundaries to fall deeper into his magic.

Back up on the ledge Dantanna sobbed, his head in his hands, and so he did not immediately see the transformation as Ancient Badden assumed the most ancient form of all. His arms became leathery wings, his eyes turned yellow with a single line of black in the middle, and his face elongated into a snout, filled with fangs, and spearlike horns sprouted atop his head.

His shriek, the keen of a dragon, startled the sobbing Samhaist and those giants and other workers behind him—even one of the hanging glacial trolls, near death, looked up in horror. Dantanna sucked in his breath when he scanned far below to see a dragon swooping out from the mist, rising suddenly on the updrafts from the hot waters of the mystical Mithranidoon.

Dantanna scrambled to his feet and turned about, stumbling as he tried to flee. He got up but slipped again when he heard the sharp screech of the dragon. Seconds seemed to pass as minutes, every step became a chore—and most steps left him prostrate on the ice, trying to rise yet again.

Dantanna felt a thunderous slam against his back. He didn't fly forward, though he surely would have, had not a large talon-tipped foot closed about him to hold him fast. Flailing and screaming, he went up into the air a dozen feet and more.

Then he was falling, landing hard against the ice.

Again he was scooped in dragon claws. Again Ancient Badden lifted him into the air. And again Ancient Badden dropped him, though higher up this time.

Dantanna screamed in pain when he hit, his leg snapping under his weight, ligaments tearing, bones breaking. He tried to curl to grasp the wound tightly.

But the dragon grabbed him again, carrying him even higher.

Down he fell, landing with a crunching impact, his breath blown away. He tried to crawl but his bones were shattered and he was too far from consciousness to begin to coordinate his movements, foolishly flailing about. Somewhere in the back of his rapidly fleeing thoughts, Dantanna expected to be hoisted again. But it didn't happen, and he settled down into the deep, cold, gloomy recesses of darkness.

Sharp, agonizing stabs of pain in his shattered limbs awakened him some time later. He was hanging by his ankles from the very rope he had noted on the new platform suspended over the chasm. His hands were securely and tightly bound behind him.

"You failed," he heard, distantly it seemed, though when Dantanna managed to turn his head, he saw that Ancient Badden was standing on the edge of the platform only a couple of feet to the side and above. At the man's feet lay a sack, its contents of troll ears spilled. "A pity. I had thought to educate you. I had thought to build your resolve and your understanding."

As he spoke, the Ancient lifted his arm and signaled behind him.

Dantanna's eyes went wide, and he thrashed about painfully, pitifully. Ancient Badden watched passively as Dantanna was slowly lowered into the gorge, the younger man sputtering desperate pleas. The agony in his shattered legs did not even register any longer through the thickening wall of sheer terror. He screamed his repentance to Ancient Badden, but the old and wicked Samhaist had taken up an ancient song of praise to the great D'no, the white worm god.

Dantanna tried to settle his thoughts. He bent a bit at the waist to get a glance at the rope bound to his ankle, noting that it was the same one that bound his hands. He growled and tried to curl up to get near to that rope. He wanted to free himself, to fall the remaining distance and kill himself outright! Better that!

But Dantanna's executioner was no novice, and the young priest could get nowhere near the binding cord, nor could he hope to free his hands. In the dimming light he could see the myriad tunnels along the sides of the chasm. The ice was wet down here, as the pieces melted by D'no, blended as they were with the mist of glacial trolls' blood, could not fully refreeze. The web of tunnels. The burrowing of D'no.

From somewhere deep within the ice of the gorge's northern side came a guttural rumble, the growl of a monstrous beast.

Dantanna touched down on the wet ice, a trickle of water running past him. Now he scrambled more furiously, tugging his hands from side to side. Somehow he managed to pull one free, and the other slipped out of the noose. He rolled over and sat up, grimacing against the waves of pain emanating from his legs.

"Crawl, crawl," he gasped, working desperately at the ties about his ankle. His hands were numb and cold, though, and he couldn't get a proper grip on the rope. He cursed and fought harder. He heard a rumbling growl. Right behind him.

Dantanna's heart pounded in his chest. The growl became a hiss. He could feel the intense heat of D'no. He turned to face his doom just as the giant worm lashed at him.

———

From the platform above the crevice, Ancient Badden could see nothing of the feast. But he heard the screams. Indeed, he heard the horrified, delicious screams.

The rope tugged and jerked a couple of times.

The screaming stopped.

Ancient Badden motioned behind him, and the trolls operating the crank began turning it furiously, working with the frenzy of creatures who knew that they might be the next down the rope if they disappointed their mighty master.

Ancient Badden chuckled when the rope came up, to see the bottom half of Dantanna's leg still attached, the skin of the upper calf blackened by the heat of D'no.

Ancient Badden casually freed the limb from the rope and tossed it back into the gorge. Then, with a look of disgust at Dantanna's betrayal, he used his foot to sweep the troll ears into the chasm, as well.

"Eat well, Ancient One," he said.

CHAPTER 3

Rocks, Always Rocks

R ocks, rocks, it's always rocks!" the young and strong man complained, his muscular bare arms glistening with sweat. He was tall, more than halfway between six and seven feet, and though he had lost considerable weight on this multiyear journey, he did not appear skinny and he was certainly not frail, his lean muscles standing taut and strong. A mop of blond hair covered his head, bespeaking his Vanguard heritage, and he wore a scraggly beard, for even though his superiors disapproved of it, they would not enforce their rules against facial hair when they possessed no implement to easily be rid of it. He stood on a slope of brown dirt and gray stones—fewer near him now, since he had already tossed scores over the ridge so that they would roll and bounce down near to the wall the man and his companions were repairing. He hoisted another one, brought it near his shoulder, and heaved it out. It didn't quite make the lip and began to roll back his way. He intercepted it with a few fast strides, planting his foot against it and holding it in place before it could gain any real momentum.

"Catch your breath, Brother Cormack," said an older monk, middle-aged and with more skin than hair atop his head. "The air is particularly warm this day."

Cormack did take a deep breath, then gathered up his heavy woolen robes and pulled them over his head, leaving him naked other than a bulky white cloth loincloth.

"Brother Cormack!" the other monk, Giavno by name, scolded.

"Always rocks," Cormack argued, his bright green eyes flaring with intensity. He made no move to retrieve his heavy robe. "Ever since we came to this cursed island we have done nothing more than pile rocks."

"Cursed?" Giavno said, shaking his head and wearing an expression of utter disappointment. "We were sent north to frozen Alpinador to begin a chapel, Brother. For the glory of Blessed Abelle. You would call that cursed?" He swept his arm to his left, beyond the ridge and to the small stone church the brothers had constructed. They had placed it on the highest point on the island; it dominated the view though the square structure was no more than thirty feet on any side.

Cormack put his hands on his hips, laughed, and shook his head help-lessly. They had departed Chapel Pellinor in Vanguard more than three years before, all full of excitement and a sense of great purpose. They were to travel to the fierce mountainous northland of Alpinador, home of the pagan barbar-ians, and spread the word of Blessed Abelle. They would save souls with their gemstone magic and the truth and beauty of their message.

But they had found only battle and outrage and their every word had sounded as insult to the proud and strong northmen. Running for their lives more than proselytizing, the band had become lost in short order and had stumbled and bumbled their way along for weeks with the freezing winter closing in all around them. Surely the nearly two score monks and their like number of servants would have found a cold and empty death, but they had happened upon this place, a huge lake of warm waters and perpetual steam, a place of islands small and large. Father De Guilbe, who led their expedition, proclaimed it a miracle and decided that here, on these waters, they would fulfill their mission and build their chapel.

Here, Cormack mused, on a lump of rock in the middle of the water.

"Rocks," Cormack grumbled, and he bent low and picked up the heavy stone again, this time heaving it far over the ridgeline.

"The lake teems with fish and food. Have you ever tasted water so fine?" said Giavno, his voice wistful. "The heat of the water saved us from the Alpi-nadoran winter. You should be more grateful, Brother."

"We were sent here for a reason beyond our simple survival."

Giavno launched into another long sermon about the duties of a monk of Abelle, the sacrifices expected and the reward awaiting them all when they had slipped the bonds of their mortal coils. He recited from the great books at length. But Cormack heard none of it, for he had his own litany against the despair, an unsought but surely found reprieve, one that he hoped would bring him the greater answers of this muddling road called life. . . .

She glided from the boat as the boat glided ashore and with equal grace, her movements as fluid as the gently lapping waves. The moon, Sheila, was al-most full this night and hung in the sky behind and above Milkeila, softening her image further. She wore few clothes, as was normal for everyone on the hot lake of Mithranidoon, other than the monks and their heavy woolen robes.

Cormack felt his heavy robe about him now, and he became almost self-conscious of it, for it felt inappropriate in the soft, warm, misty breeze.

Milkeila's hand went to her hip as she moved toward him, and she untied her short skirt and let it fall aside. Still walking, she pulled her top over her head. She was not embarrassed, not uncomfortable, just beautiful and nude, other than the necklaces of trinkets—shells and claws and teeth—strung about her neck and a bracelet and anklet of the same design. A large feather was braided into her hair.

It was the first time Cormack had seen her naked, but it felt no more intimate to him than the last time they had been together, at the great meeting between the shamans of Milkeila's tribe, Yan Ossum, and a few select brothers of Chapel Isle. That's when he had known and when she had known. That's when Cormack had found a witness to his life, a justification of his heart and mind, a spirit kindred, a heart equally wide. All of the bantering, all of the posturing, between the shamans and the monks had played out like a sorry game to him, a juggling of positions with each side trying to gain the better ground.

None of it had impressed him and none of it had impressed Milkeila, and both had recognized the truth of it, the truth of it all, in each other's eyes.

So now she walked toward him with confidence, and all that she had revealed since stepping from her boat paled against that which she had already shown him. He looked at her eyes, at the sense of purpose on her face, at the trust that had already grown between them.

He fumbled with his robe. He wished he could have been as graceful as Milkeila, but sensations overwhelmed him now, and a sense of urgency came over him. They fell together on the sandbar and said not a word as they made love under the stars and moon.

Each had seen the potential of something greater in joining their religions, a wider and more perfect truth, and so it was physically between them, where their union seemed a more perfect form than either alone.

D o you not agree, Brother Cormack?" Brother Giavno said, and loudly, and Cormack realized that it wasn't the first time Giavno had asked him that. He stared at the older man stupidly.

"The glories of Blessed Abelle when the tribes of this lake are brought into our love," Giavno prompted.

"Their traditions are centuries old," said Cormack.

"Patience," Giavno argued, a predictable answer and oft given, but something about the last inflection as Giavno spoke the word gave Cormack pause. He looked over at his Abellican brother, then followed the older monk's wide-eyed stare to the water behind them.

Cormack saw the powries—bandy-legged, bandy-armed, barrel-chested

dwarves—floating in on their flat raft just an instant before they began springing into the water near the shore, bursting into a wild charge, brandishing
their weapons.

Cormack whirled about, took a few running strides and leaped high into
the air, crashing into a pair of dwarves before they cleared the surf. One went
down, the other staggered back, and Cormack set himself quickly and launched
a circle-kick that caught the standing dwarf on the side of its chin before it
could fully recover from the unexpected assault. Its dull red beret, the item
that defined the powries, who were also known as "bloody caps," went flying
away and that dwarf, too, tumbled under the water.

"Out, or they'll be sure to drown you!" Giavno cried, and he accentuated
his point by thrusting forth his hand and loosing the power of the stone he
clutched: graphite, the stone of lightning. A bright blue bolt sizzled past Cormack to strike the raft, sending powries tumbling, but as the bolt dispersed
into the water, Cormack felt a nasty sting about his legs.

Behind Giavno and beyond the ridge, another pair of monks cried out the
warning.

Cormack sloshed toward the rocky shore with all the strength he could
muster. He pivoted as he went and managed to somewhat deflect the barrage
of clubs that came spinning his way. More than one hit home, though, and by
the time he got out of the water, he sported a large welt on one arm and a
bruise on the side of his face that threatened to swell his right eye closed.

"To me!" Giavno called, to Cormack and the other pair, and just ahead of
the dwarves the young monk ran. When he reached his companion, he skidded low, grabbed up a stone, and turned as he rose, launching it at the nearest
pursuer. It hit the dwarf squarely in the chest, briefly interrupting its howl. But
only briefly, for the tough creature slogged through the strike and closed fast,
smacking wildly with its club.

Cormack didn't retreat; in fact, he surprised the dwarf by coming forward, within the weight of the club, rolling as he went to further absorb the
blow. It still blew his breath out, but Cormack fought through that and caught
the club as he turned, then turned further, taking the club with him and yanking it from the surprised dwarf's hands. He snapped off a quick smack against
the dwarf's head, then pivoted the club fast and sent it out spearlike at the next
powrie in line.

That one waved its arm to deflect the missile, but misjudged and whipped
his hand past too quickly. The red-bearded dwarf did block the throw, however—
with his face, or more specifically his nose—and his head snapped back.

"Yach, ye mutt," the powrie growled, reaching up to grab its busted pro-
boscis, and taking away a palmful of blood. The dwarf sneered and growled
louder and started for Cormack with more purpose.

But he stopped suddenly, looking confused, and staggered down to one knee.

Cormack had the time neither to acknowledge his luck nor to pat himself on the back for a perfect throw, for powries were made of tough stuff and such a strike wouldn't normally bring one down, temporarily though it might prove. As soon as he had let fly the missile, he retracted his throwing arm and drove it down to the side, slugging the initial target in the head.

The dwarf wrapped his strong arms about Cormack's waist and drove him to the side, intent upon bearing him to the ground. The monk worked his legs frantically, trying to stay upright, and repeatedly hit the creature with his pumping right hand. Blood flew, but from his knuckles and not the dwarf, for surely Cormack felt as if he was punching stone instead of flesh!

The monk didn't relent, though, nor did the powrie, taking him far from Brother Giavno and the other two monks and the group of a half-dozen powries bearing down on them. Another lightning bolt shook the ground, and the lead powrie began to dance wildly, arms and lips flapping, his thick red hair and beard straightening to full length and shivering in the air. He danced and hopped, managing another step forward, but then fell over.

The other five rumbled past, ignoring the rock missiles, and the club-fight began in earnest.

Cormack continued to work his legs frantically, continued to punch at the dwarf, but on one slug, the stubborn little creature turned about, purposely putting his face in line with the man's flying fist. Cormack scored a solid, stunning hit, but square dwarf teeth clamped upon the side of his hand and bit down hard.

Cormack thrashed and tore free his hand, breaking out of the dwarf's vise grip in the process. Even as he jumped backward, with the powrie coming in immediate pursuit, the monk launched a heavy left hook that snapped the dwarf's head to the side.

A right cross staggered the powrie even more, and gave Cormack the opportunity to square up against the dwarf.

"Yach, but I'm to scrape the skin from yer pretty face!" the stubborn powrie promised, and came on.

A trio of stinging left jabs put the dwarf back on his heels.

Cormack retreated a bit more; his reach was his advantage, he knew, and when he looked at his opponent, who seemed like a walking block of rock, he figured it might be his only advantage.

Giavno swung hard with his makeshift wooden mace. He scored a solid hit, but the powrie pressed him relentlessly. How the monk wished that he still had the mace he had carried when he had left Chapel Pellinor, a spiked weapon of wonderful balance and weight. But alas, that mace and all of their other metallic items were lost to them, corroded by the constant steam that floated about the islands of this hot lake.

Giavno hit the powrie again, cracking the block head of the weapon against the back of the turning dwarf's shoulder. The monk rolled his shoulders, thrusting forth his free hand in time to deflect the dwarf's smashing response. And as that powrie staff slipped by, the monk wrapped his arm over the dwarf's hands and bore in hard against his enemy.

Big mistake, Giavno realized as soon as he slammed against the dwarf, who didn't budge an inch. For now his advantage, the length of his arms, was lost, and the powrie fast squirmed and twisted free its hands, clamping them about Giavno's waist and tugging him along as it fell into a roll.

Another powrie closed on the wrestling pair, whacking away at Giavno with a weighted stick, raising welts under the monk's heavy brown robes.

Giavno grimaced through the pain and managed to turn about to see the two companions nearest him, both fighting valiantly and fiercely against a trio of dwarves, trading punch for swat. At one point in the roll, the dwarf loosened its grip, and Giavno quickly set his feet and thrust forward, scrambling toward his friends. As he had hoped, one of the powries broke away to intercept, launching a flying tackle at the monk and bearing him back to the two pursuing dwarves.

Still clutching his graphite stone, Giavno fell into its depths. He got smacked with a staff and punched on the side of his head. The dwarf who had tackled him twisted him about as if to break him apart. But Giavno held his concentration and sent his energy into the stone and through the stone, and jolting sparks of electricity fired out in all directions around him.

The powries fell back, were thrown back, and Giavno sprinted for his companions. He glanced over at Cormack with sincere, almost fatherly, concern, but reminded himself that Cormack had secured his position on this mission to Alpinador precisely because he had shown himself to be the finest young fighter at Chapel Pellinor.

Cormack would get back to the three brothers, Giavno told himself, and prayed.

A h, ye're that one," the dwarf said, nodding and smiling, and spitting a line of blood at Cormack's feet. "Yer blood'll make me beret shine all the brighter, then."

He howled and brought his staff up above his head, leaping forward.

But Cormack had anticipated the move and was moving as well, diving down to the side and lashing out with his top leg. He didn't hit the dwarf, but slid the kicking foot past him, then bent his knee and brought the leg back in at the back of the dwarf's knees. The powrie halted his swing and overbalanced backward for a second, as Cormack's calf drove in hard against the back of his knees.

That was naught but a ruse, though, as the unfortunate dwarf soon learned. For Cormack rolled out farther to the side, then reversed his flow, throwing his hips over and locking his scissors' grip on the dwarf. The powrie tried to fight the inevitable pull, but had no leverage against the prostrate and rolling man, and Cormack's trailing leg drove the dwarf forward and to the ground. The staff went flying and the powrie hit hard, just getting his hand under him in time to stop his face from smashing against the stones.

Cormack continued the roll to his back, extracting his legs on the last turn. He arched, put his feet under him, and snapped his muscles, lifting him to a standing position over the prone dwarf. He moved fast into position, where he could stomp the powrie's face into the stone, and even lifted his foot over the back of the still-stunned dwarf's head.

He hesitated.

He heard the splashing and turned in time to see the charge of the first dwarf he had decked, out in the water. It came out with fury—no, not fury, Cormack realized, but with terror.

For behind it emerged another creature, its smooth, bluish, almost translucent skin gleaming in the dull and hazy light, its black eyes peering at its prey intently under a protruding brow. A glacial troll, Cormack realized at once, and so too had the powrie, judging from the look of terror on his face!

No taller than the dwarves and far lighter, the glacial trolls were nevertheless the bane of all the island societies. Their thin limbs were deceptively strong, and their teeth pointed like little knives. And where came one troll, inevitably, came many, and Cormack saw that clearly now, the long waggling ears of the ugly goblinoid creatures poking from the surf all about the rocky beach.

The dwarf at Cormack's feet grabbed him by the ankle and tugged hard, and he didn't resist, but let himself fall backward into a roll, one that took him right over and back to his feet.

"Trolls! Trolls!" he cried, and he started toward the beach, yelling at the dwarf, "Faster!"

The dwarf threw his head back as he broke free of the surf and seemed to come on more quickly. Momentarily, though, for when the powrie jerked again, Cormack saw the truth of it.

The dwarf staggered forward, slowing, then slumped down to his knees and gave a great exhale.

"Yach!" cried the powrie on the ground before Cormack, and that one leaped to his feet. "Bikelbrin, me friend!"

That call had all the powries pausing and turning, as the truth of their predicament fell fully on man and dwarf alike. Ten of them stood against more than a dozen of the trolls, who were armed with spears tipped with sharpened, barbed shells and not the relatively benign sticks that the island inhabitants generally used to batter each other about the skulls.

The trolls closed on the kneeling Bikelbrin but so did Cormack, leaping down across the stones in full charge. He heard Brother Giavno shout, "To the abbey!" and understood that his three brethren would take that route, but he could not ignore the wounded powrie.

The glacial trolls neared, reaching for their embedded spears. Cormack put on a burst of speed, closing ground, and leaped, turning himself sidelong in midair as he cleared the dwarf. He was over the spears before the trolls could fully retract them. One let go of the shaft and threw its hands up to block, while the other stubbornly, and with a sickening wet sound, drew free its spear. That one took the brunt of the flying body-block as Cormack bowled both of the trolls over.

He landed atop them hard, smacking his hand painfully against a stone, and his forehead painfully against the back of that hand. A wave of dizziness washed over him, but he knew better than to succumb to it in the midst of vicious trolls! He rolled sidelong, right off the two, who scrambled and bit at him, one catching a tooth on his bare forearm.

Cormack tugged that arm free immediately and managed to slam it down hard on the troll's face for good measure as he regained his balance.

No faster than the other troll, however, which lowered its spear for Cormack's belly and thrust it forward.

The trained monk dodged aside and slapped the spear out wider with the flat of his hand. He started for the opening to strike at the creature, but instinct stopped him and turned him about.

Just in time to deflect the thrown spear of another troll.

Cormack jumped back, three on him now and a fourth coming in. To his left came a sharp retort, and one of the trolls he had bowled over stumbled forward and to the ground. Behind it came the furious powrie, running headlong and empty-handed, for he had thrown his staff, spearlike, into the back of the fallen troll's head. He called for Bikelbrin, but ran right past his wounded friend, leaping onto the second of the trolls Cormack had tackled, bearing it down under his thrashing and kicking form.

Cormack stomped hard on the back of the neck of the first fallen troll, ending its squirming. No mercy for glacial trolls, for everyone on that beach, human and powrie alike, knew that the trolls would show none. Up on the ridge, all of the powries had disengaged from Cormack's Abellican brethren and were charging down, and to the monk's relief, he saw Brother Giavno extending his clenched fist.

"To the abbey!" Giavno yelled again, and Cormack understood that it was for his benefit alone, a warning to him that his three friends would desert him here. A lightning bolt followed that warning, off to the side where it sent a trio of trolls hopping wildly and weirdly, the residual jolts waggling their spindly limbs in a frenetic dance.

A troll leaped at Cormack, and another went for the powrie and its wrestling companion. The young monk dodged a spear thrust, then a second. He turned sidelong, bent back and down as the third thrust angled high, past his head. Cormack's left hand, his inside hand, grabbed the shaft and he wrapped his right arm over it, just below the seashell tip, as he brought it down. He turned to face the troll and thrust his right forearm, now under the shaft, upward at the same time he drove his left hand down. The sudden movement and Cormack's redistribution of his weight snapped the spear at midshaft, and as soon as he heard the break, Cormack tugged the remaining troll weapon aside and crashed against the troll, grabbing a firm hold on the broken piece of the spear as he went. He felt that sharp piece drive into the troll's torso, and he wrapped his left hand about the creature, boring in harder.

The troll went into a frenzy and tried to bite at him, but Cormack stayed too low for that. The frantic creature wasn't done, though, and it used yet another of its many weapons, its long and pointed chin, and repeatedly drove the bony feature hard against the side of Cormack's head.

Both fell to the ground, Cormack on top, and he shoved up immediately to his knees, his movement pulling free the spear shaft. He flipped it in his hands as he went, and came right back at the troll, this time with the seashell head leading.

The troll scrambled and thrashed, slapped and squirmed, but to no avail, and Cormack fell atop it again, pushing the spear right through its chest. He tugged left and right, ensuring that the wound would be mortal, and finally he fell aside—to see the other troll, the one hit in the back of the head by the thrown powrie staff, standing over him, a rock in hand.

An explosion of bright white light filled Cormack's head as that troll struck. He covered and rolled and somehow even managed to get back to his feet without being hit again too badly.

But the troll was there, punching and biting at him, and all the world was spinning.

Cormack found his sensibilities just enough to punch out, a stunning right cross that through good fortune alone connected solidly on the troll's jaw, snapping its head aside and sending it back and to the ground.

Cormack tried to straighten, staggering left and right. He saw the powries and the trolls, one big pile of confusion and fury.

Then he saw the ground, rushing up to swallow him. He thought of Milkeila, his secret lover, and was sad to know that he would not rendezvous with her that night at their special place on the sandbar to the north, as they had planned. He thought it silly that he thought of that at all, for he didn't know why that image of the beautiful barbarian had flooded his thoughts at this critical time.

He knew then the reason. The thoughts, the image, were a blessing, a moment of peace in a roiling storm. He tried to say her name, Milkeila, but he could not.

The sounds receded, the light disappeared in a blink, taking her beautiful form with it, and Cormack drowned in a cold and empty darkness.

CHAPTER 4

The Crutch

Bransen rolled off Cadayle and onto his back. He threw his arm up over his face and even miscalculated that action, thumping himself hard on the forehead. Tears of frustration welled in his eyes, and with much trembling and shaking, he managed to guide his arm down to cover them. Cadayle came up to her side on one elbow to look over him.

Down below, Bransen's foot twitched and shot out to the side, smacking against the front support of their tent, nearly caving in the entrance. In ultimate frustration, the man managed to clasp the soul stone which lay at his side.

Cadayle gently stroked her husband's bare chest and whispered soft assurances to him.

Bransen didn't move his arm, didn't look at her.

"I love you," Cadayle said to him.

Despite his stubborn pride, Bransen reached over and clasped the soul stone that he had placed at his side. "You would have to, to suffer my . . . my clumsiness."

Cadayle laughed, but bit the chuckle off short, realizing that it wasn't being taken in the manner in which she was offering it. "We knew that it would take time," she said.

"It will take forever!" Bransen retorted. "And I do not improve! I dared believe that by now I would be free of the soul stone. I dared hope . . ."

"It takes time," Cadayle interrupted. "I remember the Stork, who could hardly walk. You can walk now without the stone tied to your head. You have improved."

"Old news," Bransen replied, and he finally did lower his arm so that he could look at his wonderful and understanding wife. "My improvements were dramatic and I dared to hold hope. But they have stopped now. Without the stone I am a clumsy oaf!"

"No!"

"Without the stone I cannot even make love to my wife! I am no man!"

Cadayle pulled away from him and sat up, shaking her head. As Bransen rambled on she began to laugh.

"What?" he asked at length, growing very irritated.

"I am unused to the Highwayman so full of self-pity," she said.

Bransen stammered and could not even give voice to his anger.

"You have brought down a laird and robbed the prince of Delaval—twice!" Cadayle said. "You are a hero of the folk—"

"Who cannot make love to my wife!"

Cadayle kissed him. "You make love to me all the time."

"With a gemstone bound to my forehead. Without it I am too clumsy."

"Then be glad that you have it!"

Bransen looked at her blankly. "I want—"

"And you will find it," she cut him off. "In time. But if you do not, then so be it. Be glad that we have the soul stone. Indeed, I am." She frowned. "But even if we didn't have it, even if you could not make love to me with any grace, do you believe that it would affect the way I feel about you? Do you think it would diminish my love and adoration for you?"

Bransen stared at her.

"If I could not make love to you," she challenged him, "would you throw me from your life to find a 'whole' woman?"

Bransen's stammer was powered by more than his physical infirmities.

"Of course you would not," Cadayle pronounced firmly. "If I believed you could, I would never have agreed to marry you."

Cadayle's expression softened. "I love you, Bransen," she said, her small hand stroking his chest. "The physical act of making love is sweet to me with or without the gemstone upon your head. There is no more to be said, and no more of your self-pity, if you please. I cannot suffer it from my beloved, who could kill a dragon protecting me. You have stepped yourself so far above the common man that self-pity from you is worse than irony. It is foolhardy and laughably ridiculous. You are the Highwayman. You are the best man I have ever known. A better does not exist. You are my husband, and every day I awaken and thank God and the Ancient Ones that Bransen Garibond found his way into my life."

Bransen tried to answer, tried to respond that it was he who should fall to his knees in thanks, but Cadayle silenced him by putting her finger over his lips, then bringing her own lips in to brush his softly. She moved atop him, then, straddling him and kissing him all over his face, whispering assurances all the while.

Bransen knew that he was the fortunate one here, but he let it go and lost himself in the softness and beauty of his beloved Cadayle.

366   R. A. SALVATORE

She's not to like this," the scraggly-faced old man said through his two remaining teeth.

Dawson McKeege shot the hunched old grump an incredulous look.
"They're all dead," he said, sweeping his arms out to the smoking ruins that
had been a thriving town only a few days before, and raising his voice so that
the others of the troupe could hear him well—before the arrival of Dame
Gwydre, who was said to be only a few hundred yards away. "How could anyone like this, old fool? Men and women and children of Vanguard, our brethren, our fellows, slaughtered before us by the monstrous plague."

"Goblins and them wretched blue trolls!" someone shouted from the side.

"Aye, and with Alpinadoran backing, not to doubt!" a third chimed in.

Dawson could only nod. The war had grown all about the northern fron-
tier of Vanguard, and now, if this was any indication, it had snuck in around
the edges. For this burned and broken town, Tethmawle by name, sat closer to
the Gulf of Corona than to the battlefields in the north.

The sound of approaching horses ended all the chatter, and the fifteen men
of the expedition turned as one to regard the procession galloping down the
road. The elite guards of Castle Pellinor led the way and took up the rear, sand-
wiching a trio of monks dressed in their brown robes, a pair of advisors lightly
armored and armed, and two women who both seemed at ease on their respective mounts, riding hard and not in the sidesaddle manner, which had become
fashionable among the courtesans of the holdings south of the Gulf of Corona. One of those women, the taller of the two, with hair going silver, but her
shoulders still tall and straight, held the attention of the onlookers most of all.

"She should not be out of the castle," Dawson muttered under his breath,
and he rubbed his weary eyes and tried to be at ease. He could not, though,
and he found himself glancing around nervously, as if expecting a host of goblins and trolls and other monstrosities to swarm down from the tree line and
score the ultimate kill in this wretched war.

The procession rambled up to the edge of the town, the soldiers fanning
out into defensive positions while the seven dignitaries trotted up to Dawson
and the others.

"Milady Gwydre," Dawson said with a bow to his ruler, his friend.

Gwydre rolled her leg easily over her mount and dropped to the ground,
handing the reins to one of the nearby men without a thought. She spent a
moment surveying the area, the smoking ruins, the charred bodies and the
bloated and stinking corpses of small gray-green goblins and blue-green trolls
littered all about the area.

"They fought well," the old coot near Dawson dared to remark.

Gwydre shot him a glare. "They are all dead?"

"We've found none alive," Dawson confirmed.

"Then it was no small force that came against them," said Gwydre. "How? How was such a sizable group able to sneak so far south?"

"Samhaist magic," one of the monks whispered from behind, and all three of the brown-robed brothers launched into quiet prayers to their Blessed Abelle.

Gwydre seemed more annoyed than impressed, and Dawson agreed with her completely.

"It is a wild land, milady," Dawson said. "We are not populous. Our roads are hardly guarded, and even if they were, a short trek through a forest would bypass any sentries."

"And their determination is aggravating," replied Gwydre. She walked past Dawson and motioned for him to follow, then held up her own advisors, even the Lady Darlia, her dearest friend, so that she and Dawson could move off alone.

As always, Dawson was impressed by how in control and command Dame Gwydre remained. She carried an aura of competence around her, one that had initially surprised many of Castle Pellinor's court. For Gwydre had been just a young girl that quarter of a century before when her father, Laird Gendron, already a widower, had been killed unexpectedly in a fall from his horse while hunting. Gendron, revered by the folk of this northern wilderness known as Vanguard, had held the scattered and disparate communities together with a "warm fist," as the saying had gone—a saying applied to Gendron, to his father before him, and to his great uncle who had been Laird of Pellinor before that.

"I cannot tolerate this," Gwydre said, her lips tight, her voice strained. "Chapel Pellinor's fall has created unrest, and the folk will be all the more unnerved when news of Tethmawle's fate spreads through forest trails."

"You fear they will question the fortitude of their dame?" Dawson asked, and Gwydre sucked in her breath and snapped an angry glare at him. But it did not hold, of course, for Dawson McKeege was perhaps the only person in all of Vanguard who could have spoken to Gwydre with that necessary candor.

"Do you remember when Laird Gendron died?" Gwydre asked somberly.

"I was with you when we received the news."

Gwydre nodded.

"Aye," said Dawson, taking the cue. "And so began the whispers, the laments of 'why hadn't the laird sired a son?'"

"The lower their voices, the louder they sounded," Gwydre assured him. "Those voices were part of the reason I so abruptly agreed to marry Peiter."

The admission didn't startle Dawson. "He was my friend as he was your husband. I suspect that he, too, heard those whispers, and couldn't suffer to see his beloved Gwydre so pained."

"I was a young woman, barely more than a girl," Gwydre admitted. "And never in my life had I done anything that would have, or should have, inspired their confidence. Even those years later when Peiter died, their doubts about me rightfully lingered."

"That was fifteen years ago, milady," Dawson reminded her. "And before your thirtieth birthday. Do you fear that they still doubt you?"

"We are in a desperate war."

"It is Vanguard! We are always at one war or another. The woods are full of goblins, the coast crawling with powries, the northland thick with trolls, and never in my life have I met a more disagreeable bunch than those Alpina-doran barbarians."

"This is different, Dawson," Gwydre said. Her tone quieted the man more than her words. For there lay a truth there that neither could deny. Dame Gwydre had taken a lover, an Abellican brother, and in the two years of her tryst, that particular Church's stature had grown considerably throughout her holding and by extension, throughout Vanguard—much to the dismay and open anger of the dangerous and powerful Samhaists.

"You fell in love," Dawson said to her.

"Foolishly. I placed my heart above my responsibilities, and all the land suffers for it."

"Those same Churches were going to fight, with or without your actions," Dawson argued. "As they fight a proxy war through the lairds in the South, where, it is said, three hundred men die every day."

Dame Gwydre nodded and couldn't deny the truth of Dawson's claims, for indeed, this same battle for religious supremacy over the folk of Honce was playing out throughout the Holdings of Honce Proper. There, the fight between Abellican and Samhaist was shielded from view behind the façade of the warring lairds Delaval and Ethelbert, but it was no less real and no less fierce.

In the South, the Abellicans were clearly winning, for their gemstone magic, both healing and destructive powers, was coveted by the many lairds feuding for dominance. In the quieter North, where few Abellicans and fewer gemstones haunted the wild land, the Samhaists had found refuge, so they had believed. Tied to the seasons and the world and the animals great and small through wise and ancient traditions, Samhaist wisdom served Vanguardsmen well indeed.

But then Dame Gwydre had fallen in love with an Abellican brother.

"There will be more Tethmawles," Dame Gwydre said solemnly. "One community after another will be sacked."

"I beg you not to tell that to your subjects, milady."

Gwydre shook her head to deny the dryness of Dawson's remark, and that action conferred to Dawson that she wasn't being melodramatic. She knew that she was losing to the hordes from the North, the legions of Ancient Badden.

"My council with Chief Danamarga did not go well," Gwydre admitted, referring to the powerful leader of one particularly friendly Alpinadoran tribe, with whom the men of Vanguard often traded, and who many times had graced Gwydre's table at Castle Pellinor. "He will likely keep his clan out of the fighting."

"That is good news," Dawson said. "His warriors are fierce."

"But he will not intervene on our behalf with the other tribes."

"The Samhaist influence is great among the Alpinadorans. But great enough to keep them allied with ugly goblins and the light-skinned trolls?"

Dame Gwydre shrugged and scanned the burned-out village. "We are losing, and Danamarga is a pragmatic man. If Vanguard is to be sectioned by the victors, then he would not serve his clan well to be left out of that gain."

"Vanguard is land. Without us it is empty land," Dawson argued. "What good will it alone bring to the Alpinadorans? What point is this war?"

Gwydre nodded her complete understanding. The Samhaists, so they believed, were egging on the monsters and the barbarians, but the underlying logic told Gwydre and her advisors that Ancient Badden didn't really want to wipe the Vanguardsmen from the region and chase refugees back across the Gulf of Corona.

"Ancient Badden and his disciples do not wish to minister to goblins and trolls," Dawson said. "Nor to the barbarians of Alpinador who loyally follow their own gods."

"Gods not far removed from the Samhaist deities," Gwydre reminded.

"True enough, but would you expect Danamarga and the other chiefs to relinquish their control to Badden's miserable priests? Of course they will not."

"Then this whole war is to teach me a lesson," said Gwydre.

Dawson shrugged, for he could not disagree. "It is to drive the Abellicans back across the waters and secure Vanguard for the Samhaists," he added. "We, all of us—indeed, even Dame Gwydre—are caught in the middle of a war of religions. And it won't end with Vanguard if Badden drives the Abellicans south. He knows that Laird Ethelbert and Laird Delaval have thrown in fully with the Abellicans, and it's not to his liking. He will chase the monks from Vanguard, then use us to cross the gulf and assail Chapel Abelle itself. Begging your pardon, dear woman, but that's no fight I'm wanting."

His dramatic tone brought a much-needed smile to Dame Gwydre's angular features, an impish grin that reminded Dawson of the beauty of the woman. Even now in middle age she retained much of that beauty, but the last year had weighed heavily on her, and too rare flashed that smile, reassuring and warm, superior but not condescending, and surely disarming.

So disarming.

It said much about Ancient Badden's hold on the land, and even more about the current state of the war, that Dame Gwydre's smile had not brought Chief Danamarga to their side.

"We must force upon Ancient Badden that wider fight you believe he desires, and before the battleground is his for the choosing," Gwydre said, and her eyes turned from Dawson to the south.

"An immigrant army," Dawson muttered.

"It is a fine season for the folk of Honce to turn their eyes to the open and beautiful North, I think," Gwydre confirmed. "Palmaristown, from all reports, has become the haven of rats and foul odors, and there are rumors that the refugees of the war collect en masse at Chapel Abelle, where there is little excess shelter and supplies. And yet, we have villages already built and ready to house those who would seek a better life, and a land as bountiful as any in Corona."

"Villages empty because all the men are fighting the war, or are already planted in the ground," Dawson reminded her, but he stole none of her momentum.

"It is the way of things," she said. "A man who comes here to fight for Gwydre is fighting, too, for his future. If he remains in the South, he will be swept into Delaval's army, or Ethelbert's, into a war whose outcome will have no bearing on the prosperity or security of his family. What will change for the folk of Palmaristown, or any other town, if Ethelbert wins? If Delaval wins? They are two lairds of the same cloth—their fight is one for personal gain and not over any manner of governance. But up here, the battle has more meaning. Up here, my warriors strike hard at the flesh of goblins and glacial trolls."

"And men," Dawson pointed out.

"Barbarians," Gwydre corrected. "Not the brethren of the men of Honce as we see in the South. Not a brother, perhaps, who through mere circumstance moved to a town now serving the other side."

Finally it seemed as if Dawson had run out of answers, and so Gwydre looked at him directly, flashed him that commanding grin, and said, "The gulf is calm, and the ships are waiting."

"Chapel Abelle?"

"That would be a fine place to start," said Gwydre. "The brothers there know of our desperation, and they do not wish to have a powerful Badden ruling Vanguard unopposed. Let them direct you to towns not yet emptied by Delaval's press crews."

"If Laird Delaval learns of my actions in stealing his potential soldiers . . ." Dawson warned.

"Do not let him know."

Dawson smiled hopelessly. When Dame Gwydre made up her mind it was not to be easily changed.

"They will come," Gwydre assured him. "You will convince them."

Dawson McKeege knew the meaning of Gwydre's "convince," and while it left a sour taste in his mouth, in looking around at the ruins of Tethmawle, it was not hard for him to weigh one evil against the other. Without hardy reinforcements, this wretched sight before him would soon become all too common.

H e fell down for the fourth time.

Cadayle ran toward him, but Bransen stubbornly waved her off. Trembling every inch of the way he managed to get over onto his belly and up to his knees. He did well to hide his grimace as he noted the sympathetic and concerned look that passed between Cadayle and Callen.

They were on the road north of Delaval, heading north-northwest along the bank of the majestic waterway that had recently been named the Masur Delaval. Though this northeastern bank was considered the "civilized" side of the river, the road, or trail actually, hardly showed any such signs. They were only three days out from Delaval Town, in a region untouched by the war, yet it was hard to call their path a road. Uneven, muddy, and littered with the large roots of the great willows that lined the river, the trail could trip up any but the most careful traveler. Every step proved a test of courage for Bransen, who stubbornly carried his soul stone in his pouch and not even in his hand, let alone strapped to his forehead.

Resting on his hands and knees to reorient and catch his breath, Bransen fought the urge to slip his hand into his pouch and produce the gemstone. He noticed a pool of red liquid and only then realized that he had slammed his nose on that last fall, splitting his lip as well. He spat a few times, red spray flying from his mouth.

He felt Cadayle's hand on his back and reminded himself that she loved him, that she was concerned for him, and rightly so.

"Don't you think that's enough for the day?" she asked quietly.

"W . . . W . . ." Bransen stopped and spat again, then reached for his pouch. He would have fallen over with the movement except that Cadayle caught him and held him steady. She grabbed his flailing hand and gently guided it to the pouch and the gemstone, then helped him bring the stone to his forehead.

"We've barely covered two miles," he protested in a voice clear and strong. Indeed, the sudden change shocked even Bransen.

"We should try to cross another five before dusk," said Cadayle. "We'll not go another single mile at our pace, and if you truly injure yourself . . ."

Bransen turned his head to eye her hard.

"I understand," she whispered to him, "and I know your reasoning. I wouldn't dare pretend that I have the right to disagree. But I beg of you to measure your pace, my love. You are tormenting your body more than it can take. You'll need more than the soul stone if you break your knee, and where will that leave me and my ma?"

"My patience is long gone with this creature known as the Stork," said Bransen.

"But mine is not."

Still holding the gemstone tight against his forehead, Bransen leaped up to his feet, catching himself surely and with incredible agility. He was the Highwayman now, the rogue who could scale a castle wall of tightly fit weatherworn stones. He was the Highwayman, who could challenge a laird's champion in battle and win.

Bransen pulled the gemstone away. Immediately, he swayed. He caught himself, though, and kept Cadayle at bay with an upraised hand. Then he stubbornly put his gemstone back in his pouch and let it go.

He took a step, awkward and unsteady. He nearly fell over, but he did not, and he even managed to glance back at Cadayle to see her and her concerned mother exchanging frowns.

Hand shaking, arm flailing, Bransen managed to get his fingers back around the precious gemstone. He brought it forth and collected, too, the black silk bandanna he used to secure it to his forehead.

"I did not wish to end with a stumble," he explained, securing it in place. He managed a strained smile, one that undeniably showed Cadayle and Callen that he was surrendering for the day for their benefit and not his own.

"I will be as patient as I can," he promised his wife. Despite his frustration his words were sincere.

"I love you," Cadayle said.

"With or without the gemstone," Callen added.

Bransen licked a bit of blood from his lip.

How could he be so fortunate and miserable all at the same time?

And how, he wondered as he brought his hand up to check on the security of the gemstone, could he both appreciate and resent its healing magic? The soul stone freed him from his infirmities, made him whole—heroic, even. And yet at the same time it trapped him and held him dependent to its powers.

He wanted to be free of it, but he could not tolerate the reality of that freedom.

"You are better than you were before you found the soul stone," Cadayle said. She waved her hand at the rough and root-strewn trail. "This ground trips you up, perhaps, but in your youth the flat grass of the monastery courtyard often left you on your face."

"*Ki-chi-kree,*" Bransen said.

"The promise of the Jhesta Tu," Cadayle agreed. "You will overcome this infirmity.

"You already have," she added. Bransen eyed her curiously. "You defeated it with your spirit long before you found any real control of your limbs. To others you were the Stork, some in jest and some in earnest sympathy. But you have always been Bransen. And you will always be Bransen, with or without the soul stone, whether or not you need the soul stone to walk a broken trail."

Bransen Garibond closed his eyes and took a deep breath, blowing out all of his frustration in one great exhale. "I never knew my real father," he said, and Cadayle and Callen nodded, for they knew well the tale. "He studied the Jhesta Tu. He has been to the Walk of Clouds. He copied their book—the same book that Garibond taught to me when I was young. He will have answers."

"Or he will show you where to look for them."

Bransen nodded, his smile genuine, and genuinely hopeful. "Garibond told me that he went to Chapel Abelle in the North. If I can find him . . ."

"Bran Dynard was a good man," Callen said, stepping up beside her daughter. "I owe him my life as surely as I owe it to Sen Wi. He knew why I was put out on the road to die, and why I carried the bites of the serpent. He knew that his superiors in his Church had witnessed my execution and had, with their silence, condoned it. And still he fought for me against the vicious powries, and he hid me away at great personal peril. You are much like him, Bransen. You carry his integrity and his sense of justice. Physical strength is nothing when weighed against that."

"I will find my physical strength," Bransen replied. "It is there—the soul stone shows it to me. I will overcome this infirmity."

Callen nodded. "I would never doubt you, and double blessed am I to have been saved by your father and again by you, the Highwayman."

Cadayle walked over and took Bransen's arm. "Five miles?" she asked.

"That would make seven for the day," said Bransen. "And we will do seven tomorrow."

Cadayle tilted her head back to get a better look into her stubborn husband's eyes.

"Two without the gemstone?" she asked.

"Two and a half," he replied flatly.

Callen's laugh turned them both to regard her, standing with Doully's reins in hand. "And they say that my walking companion brings a reputation for stubbornness," Callen remarked, shaking the donkey's lead.

All three were laughing, then, and even old Doully gave a snort and a whinny.

CHAPTER 5

Foul Chaps We'd Be

It called to him from the far corner of the darkness, a continual growl, a rolling "r." Finally it broke and rewound in its timbre like a wave flowing over itself just offshore.

It grew again in resonance and filled Cormack with its mournful vibration, beckoned him forward in the darkness. He followed, a purely instinctive and unthinking move. He knew not if the sound would take him from the abyss, nor, locked as he was in a state of near emptiness, if he even wanted to come forth from the darkness.

At that moment Cormack didn't want anything. He just was. A moment of pure existence or of nothingness, he couldn't tell. But the rolling "r" pulled him forward as if walking him to the edge of a cliff. He stepped off and fell through the blackness. His eye cracked open, and crystalline brilliance stung him. Sensations returned, and with them consciousness.

The light was the sun, sparkling off the water. The taste in his mouth was sand, for he was facedown on the beach. The sound was a song, a powrie chant.

With great effort Cormack rolled his head to the side. The bloody-capped dwarves were huddled in a circle, their arms locked over the shoulders of the next dwarf in the ring. They turned their living wheel in perfect cadence, a few steps left, a few back to the right, all the while singing:

Put me deep in the groun' so cold
I'll be dead, 'fore I e'er get old
Done me fights and shined me cap
Now's me time for th'endless nap
Spill no tear and put me deep
Dun want no noise for me endless sleep
Done me part and stood me groun'
But th'other one won and knocked me down

Put me deep in the groun' so cold
I'll be dead 'fore I e'er get old
Spill no tear and put me deep
Dun want no noise for me endless sleep

Cormack tried to lift his head to get a better perspective, and only then did the monk realize that he had been tightly bound, his hands painfully drawn up against his back, the rough weeds tight into his wrists. More than those shackles, though, loomed the noose of pain shooting through his head. As soon as Cormack got his chin off the sand, he dropped it back, grimacing all the way, as hot fires erupted in the back of his skull.

He closed his eyes tight and tasted the sand and tried hard to growl through the burning agony. He wanted to reach up and grab at the spot, but he couldn't wriggle free his hands.

Gradually it passed, and the powrie song continued, and their huddle circled left and right, just off the beach. This time Cormack slowly rolled his entire body instead of trying to lift his head alone, and he managed to gain a better perspective on the powrie dance. He realized only then that the dwarves were circling a particular spot, a particular thing. As he considered the words of their ditty he solved the riddle.

Cormack held his tongue, not wanting to risk interrupting the solemn ceremony. It went on for a long while until finally the ring of dwarves opened, revealing a cairn of piled stones. Still singing, the cadence marking their every movement, the dwarves turned as one so that they were no longer shoulder-to-shoulder, but formed instead a single file as they marched around and then away from the grave of their fallen comrade.

"So, are ye awake then?" the leading dwarf asked when they reached the beach and began to disperse. "Was thinking ye meant to sleep the whole o' the day."

"Better for him if he did, what?" the second dwarf added in a sinister voice indeed. "Better for him if he'd listened to his fellows and done run to their home o' rocks."

"More fun for us that he didn't," another put in, stepping out of the line and pulling his red beret from his hairy head. In the same movement the dwarf drew out a curved, serrated knife, its gleaming blade already marred by blood, and Cormack knew that he was doomed. Powries—bloody caps, as they were known—wore their most prized possession on their heads, and those red berets, through some magic that no race other than the dwarves understood, shined more brightly with the blood of fallen enemies. The intensity of a beret's hue constituted the powrie badge of honor, of rank and respect.

The dwarf with the knife approached. Cormack tried to hold steady his breathing, tried not to be afraid, as he glanced all around for his Abellican brethren.

But they were not to be seen. They were in the rock chapel, as the dwarf had proclaimed, and Cormack couldn't even free his arms to defend himself.

The tall and willowy woman burst from the forest, the wide leaves of the many ferns and low plants slapping against her bare legs as she rushed along the sketchy path. She had hurried from her village, intending to perform the midday service, the Fishermen Blessing, as her station demanded of her. As soon as Milkeila cleared the last brush and viewed the rocky expanse to the beach she knew that her service would be delayed, however, for none of the fishermen were in the water. They stood upon the high rocks, staring out over the calm lake to the southeast. Moving out onto the beach and toward those rocks Milkeila understood the distraction, for the sounds of battle, the sharp crack of sticks, the occasional cry of rage or pain, drifted across the flat water to her ears.

"Chapel Isle," one of her kinsmen said to her. She knew that already from the direction of the sounds, referring to the small and rocky island upon which the Abellican foreigners had built their simple monastery.

"The monks are longing for their homeland again," another fisherman said with a derisive snort, and others snickered at the thought.

Milkeila brushed from her face her thick hair, a rich brown hue that highlighted red before the sunrise and sunset, to peer intently into the fog, though she knew that she would see nothing definitive at this distance across the misty lake. Only on breezy days, when the perpetual fog was blown clear at various intervals, could the people of Yossunfier, this island, catch the slightest glimpse of the monks' home, and even then, it was nothing more than an indistinct blur in the distance.

There was simply too much mist this day, as almost every day.

"Better the powries than the monks," another of Milkeila's kinsmen remarked. The others grumbled their agreement.

Milkeila remained silent and did well to hide her discontent, for she hardly agreed. Nor had it always been this way between her people of Yan Ossum, Clan Snowfall, and curious southern Vanguardsmen who called themselves Brothers of Abelle. When the monks had first appeared at the lake they had befriended the barbarians, particularly the shaman class, to which Milkeila belonged (though back then, she had been merely a young and eager student). Many of her kin had quickly become disenchanted with the Abellicans because of their insistence that their way was the only way, that their religion was the true religion, and their demand of adherence to that strict order and rituals.

Milkeila's hand moved up to brush the necklace concealed under her more traditional one of claws and teeth and bright feathers. Under her smock the young woman kept a ring of gems, stones of varying color and type and magical property, given to her by one of the younger monks. She glanced around guiltily, knowing that her people would judge her harshly if they ever discovered her secret—and the other secret: that she was privately meeting with that young monk, being tutored in the general ways of Abellican gemstone magic. And much more than that.

The sounds of battle increased across the water.

"Looks like they have a good row going," one of the barbarians said. "We should prepare the boats and paddle in behind the fight. The pickings will be easy. Perhaps we could even go right to their stone church and throw the foolish Abellicans from the lake once and for all."

Others mumbled their agreement, but all present knew the impracticality of the suggestion. No raids could be executed without the proper blessings of the shamans and the careful planning of the elders, and none of that could happen in short enough order for this impromptu mission to occur. Still, the eager nods reminded Milkeila that she and her few rebellious cohorts were playing with danger here in their secret relationship with the Southerners, particularly Milkeila; she was shaman and had dared to take Cormack as her lover.

"Maybe the powries will do our work for us," the same man said after a few heartbeats, when enough time had passed for all of them to recognize the impracticality of his previous suggestion.

To hear her people cheering for powries over fellow humans left Milkeila cold. The Abellican monks had crossed a dangerous threshold early on, one they had stepped over by choice and not heritage. In insisting that the barbarians elevate the teachings of Abelle over their long-standing, traditional beliefs, the monks had, in effect, openly declared themselves heretics and had been branded as such by the elders and the shamans.

Milkeila recalled the day when she had warned the Abellicans about their unacceptable path and winced in her mind's eye to remember Brother Giavno's angry retort. "What do we care if our ways offend you?" he had roared. "Your place is in hellfire while heaven awaits the followers of Blessed Abelle!"

Milkeila hadn't known what "hellfire" might mean, but when Giavno had assured her that she and her people were doomed to sit in eternity beside the likes of the dactyl demons, she had fathomed the point of his rant quite clearly.

Fortunately not all the Abellicans were of similar temperament as that unpleasant one. Some of the younger brothers, one in particular, were quite open to the possibilities that there were other explanations and traditions worth exploring in sorting through the mysteries of life. Of like mind to Milkeila and her small group of friends, who often wondered about the world beyond the borders of the mist-covered lake, a world upon which they were forbidden to venture.

"Be safe, Cormack," the shaman whispered under her breath, her hand brushing her shirt above the necklace of magical stones, and in an even lower voice, she added, "My love."

The serrated blade was barely an inch from Cormack's throat when another dwarf grabbed the arm holding it.

"Nah," that second powrie said, tugging the first dwarf back from the bound human.

"I won't cut him wrong that his blood's spillin' too fast!" the first assured the others. "Let him die slow, and we'll all get our caps in the puddle, what?"

"Nah, ye're not for cuttin' him at all," said the other, and he moved in between the knife-holder and poor Cormack. He glanced back at Cormack as he did. Cormack realized from the dwarf's recently busted nose, blood caked on his thick mustache, that this had been one of his opponents before the glacial trolls had arrived on the scene.

"What're ye jabberin', then?" the knife-holder argued. "I come here to wet me cap, and wetting me cap's what I'm to do!"

"Ye got a dozen dead trolls for cutting."

"Bah, but troll blood's not much for brightening me cap, and ye're knowing it, ye danged fool, Mcwigik!"

"Best ye're to get, unless some o' them other monks come out o' their rock house, and that ain't for happening!"

One of the other powries added a complaint of his own, and another chimed in, but a second dwarf stepped forward in support of Mcwigik. Cormack recognized this one as the wounded Bikelbrin, whom Cormack had circle-kicked under the surf and had later leaped over when he had gone to intercept the ice trolls.

"Let him go, Pragganag," Bikelbrin said to the knife-holder. "If me thoughts're sorting out right, then this one saved me hairy bum."

"Trolls had ye dead," Mcwigik agreed. "We'd've put ye under a stone pile like we done to Regwegno there."

"Aye," agreed another, and to Cormack's horror, that one held up a heart—Regwegno's heart, apparently.

"But if there'd been no trolls it was us and them monks," Pragganag argued, though even he seemed to be losing steam here and let his knife's tip slip down toward the ground, enough so that Cormack was beginning to think he might indeed survive this ordeal. "Got me a crop o' burned beard," he added, tugging at the left half of his fiery red beard—or at least, the right side remained fiery red, for the clump in his hand had been blackened by one of Giavno's bolts of lightning. "And now ye're telling me that I lost half me beard for nothing? And when there's bright human blood right there, laid out and tied and ready for the taking?"

"Foul chaps we'd be to kill one what saved our hairy bums," Mcwigik growled back at him.

"Flattened yer own fat nose!" Pragganag shouted.

"Aye," said Mcwigik, and he glanced back and nodded—appreciatively!—at Cormack. "Got a wicked punch to him."

"And a wicked kick," added Bikelbrin.

"Then a good kill he'll be!" Pragganag reasoned. "And a brighter cap I'll wear!"

"But ye weren't the one to drop him, was ye?" Mcwigik asked. "Trolls bringed him down, and only because he leaped into the lot o' them to save Bikelbrin. The least ye can do is knock him down yerself afore ye're for taking his bright blood, don't ye think?"

Pragganag stood straighter, the knife slipping down to his side as he eyed Mcwigik and Bikelbrin suspiciously. "What're ye saying?"

Mcwigik grinned, his teeth shining white between the bushy black hair of his beard. He drew out his own knife and stepped fast behind Cormack. With a sudden swipe he took the bindings from the fallen man's wrists. He reached down and grabbed the man by the arm and roughly hoisted him to his feet.

A wave of dizziness buckled poor Cormack's legs as a ball of fire seemed to erupt within his battered skull. He couldn't focus his eyes and would have fallen back to the sand had not Bikelbrin rushed over to help Mcwigik keep him upright.

"Well, alrighty then," Pragganag laughed. He lifted his knife and advanced, grinning from ear to ear.

Mcwigik didn't even have to intercept, though, as a pair of dwarves behind Pragganag grabbed him by the shoulders.

"Not now, ye dolt," one said. "Fool monk can't even stand."

"Where's yer honor?" the other agreed.

"It's staining me beret!" Pragganag argued, pulling away, but he did indeed lower his knife.

"Now for yerself," Mcwigik said, turning Cormack to face him, hoisting the man again as he slumped back toward the sand. "New moon tonight—ol' Sheila's not to be found. Are ye hearin' me, boy?" He gave Cormack a little shake, which elicited a pronounced groan.

"Next time Sheila's not to be found ye get yerself back to the beach, and we'll come ashore so that ye can fight Pragganag here straight up," Mcwigik explained.

"Yach, but the human dog's not to come out to fight!" Pragganag argued.

Mcwigik tossed his fellow dwarf a dismissive glance and muttered, "It's the best ye're getting," before turning his attention back to Cormack. "Ye come alone and come ready to fight. And if Pragganag's beating ye, then know yer blood's forfeit."

"And what if this one wins?" Bikelbrin asked, giving Cormack another shake, which brought forth another groan. Across the way Pragganag snorted as if that notion was absurd.

"We'll get him something for his trouble, then," said Mcwigik.

"Yach, but ye're giving him his life now!" one of the dwarves behind Pragganag reminded. "Ain't that to be enough?"

"Aye, that's enough," said another.

"Nah," Mcwigik bellowed back, waving his free hand at them. "Making it more interestin'. If this skinny human's to win, then we'll give him Pragganag's cap," he added suddenly, on impulse.

"Aye!" Bikelbrin said, seeing all the faces except for Pragganag's, of course, brightening around him.

"To the dactyl's bum ye are!" Pragganag frothed.

But Mcwigik was quick to reply, "Are ye saying that ye can't take a skinny human one-to-one?"

"Yach!" Pragganag protested and threw up his arms, whirling away.

"Ye heared it all, boy?" Mcwigik asked Cormack, turning the monk's face to look at him directly. "Next time Sheila's not to be seen. Gives ye a month to get yer head put back together. Ye come out and ye come out alone."

Surely the world was spinning, and Cormack hardly registered any of it. But he managed a nod.

Mcwigik and Bikelbrin laid him back down on the sand, and Cormack's thoughts fell far, far away.

Onlookers ignorant of the shamanistic ways would have thought it a dance, though a pretty one to be sure. Milkeila's bare feet scraped across the sand, drawing lines in a prescribed pattern about her as she turned and swayed and sang softly. She crossed her right foot over her left, stepped down with her heel, then gracefully rolled her ankle to lift the heel from the sand and point her toe in. She went up onto the ball of her other foot and slowly twirled all the way around.

This was the circle of power.

Milkeila's hands moved in unison a foot apart out to her left. She chanted more loudly and dug her toe into the sand, connecting her to the power of the earth below her. Then she turned her palms up and lifted her hands to the sky, drawing that power up behind her movement. Her hands came gracefully down before her in a slow arc, and she repeated the process to her right side.

The energy lifted more easily this time, she felt in her soul, so when her hands were high in the sky, she turned about the other way, altered her chant to the god of the wind, and slowly turned her palms over as she found a stance of symmetry. She felt the wind gathered in her palms, so she slowly lowered them down by her sides, her thumbs tapping her hips and then moving lower to brush her bare legs below the hem of her short skirt. They pressed down past the outside of her knees and the sides of her shins as she dropped into a crouch, so low that her hands soon rested flat on the ground.

The shaman pressed the power of the wind into the soil, fanning the flames of the lava she had coaxed from far, far below. The ground around her, within her drawn circle, began to steam and to bubble. Despite what she had told herself before beginning the ceremony Milkeila couldn't resist sending her thoughts into the ruby that hung on the gemstone necklace. She felt the power there, teeming with strength, and sent it, too, into the ground.

One vent popped clear, shooting hot mist several feet into the air to the approving nods of the gathered clansmen and women. Several grabbed their pails of fish, knowing that the cooking circle was near completion.

Milkeila felt the warmth beneath her bare feet and knew that she had done well. But when her mentor, Toniquay, called to her as *"permid a'shaman yut,"* she felt more guilt than pride. For that was her title, the Prime Shaman of Youth, the most promising priest of her generation. She had earned that honor honestly, she knew, and was well on her way to the accolade before the Southern monks had ever come to Mithranidoon. But the fact that she had dared use an Abellican gemstone in this sacred ritual, or that she wore the necklace at all, or that she had given her heart to a man not of Yan Ossum, made Toniquay's prideful remark sting.

Lost in the swirl of thoughts, Milkeila realized that she should step out of the cooking circle when her feet grew very, very hot. She came out facing the water and walked through the gathering down to the surf.

"Always this beach," Toniquay said behind her. "This is Milkeila's special beach."

She didn't turn to face him, for she knew that she was blushing fiercely. This particular beach faced Chapel Isle and also faced the secret sandbar where she met with her lover.

"The magic is strong here, do you think?" Toniquay asked.

"Yes, shaman," she answered.

"It is the magic of the old gods that draws you to this spot ever again, is it not?"

She felt her cheeks grow even hotter at that double-edged question.

"I see it, too, *permid a'shaman yut,*" Toniquay said, his voice dipped in the syrup of sarcasm as he was so wont to do.

What did he see? Milkeila wondered. How much of the truth lay open to the wise and severe old man?

Despite herself, she lifted her gaze toward Chapel Isle, but only for the briefest moment before turning to face Toniquay. His knowing smile reminded her of her own whenever she chanced to catch some of the younger boys staring at her legs or breasts.

"A place of magic," old Toniquay remarked, and walked away.

Milkeila felt her cheeks flush hot again. She glanced over to see the fishermen and their wives preparing the meal, cooking the catch in the circle she had magically prepared by calling to the old gods of Yan Ossum.

And by extracting the power of the Abellican ruby.

CHAPTER 6

Keys to Debtor's Prison

The settlement on the mouth of the river where it spilled into the Gulf of Corona was called Palmaristown. It seemed to Bransen, Cadayle, and Callen that this was really two distinct cities and not one. Indeed, a solid wooden fence ran the length of the town, separating the ramshackle hovels in the region of the docks and the great river from the larger and more comfortable homes of the town's eastern section. That secure fence surrounded the inner town completely, with an open gate accepting the southern road from Delaval and a second one in the northeast, running inland just south of the gulf.

Guards walked their stations along a parapet built within that fence, with most concentrated in the west, looking out over the town's poor section and the bustling docks.

And they were indeed bustling, Bransen and his companions noted as they neared the southern gate. Ferries moved continually across the wide river, and so many sailing ships, including many of Laird Delaval's warships, were in port that several had to be moored out from the fully occupied wharves. Teams of dirty men moved to and fro, heavy ropes out behind them as they hauled skids laden with supplies, or thick trunks of trees brought in from across the river to the west, the region appropriately known as the Timberlane.

Drivers cracked whips on the heels of those poor laborers. The trio of visitors at the gate watched in astonished horror as one man fell to the docks beneath the weight of a heavy punch. He hit the ground, and the dockmaster began kicking him and stomping on him, despite his pleas, and none of the other laborers dared do anything more than look on.

"You haven't the stomach for it, then?" one of the guards at the gate asked the trio, obviously noting their horrified expressions. He looked at Bransen mostly, who moved without the soul stone this day in full Stork disguise. The guard crinkled his face at the sight and turned his stare to Cadayle. A rather lewd smile spread across his face.

"My husband," Cadayle said, stepping near to Bransen and taking his arm with her own. "Wounded in the war in the land south of Delaval."

"Fighting for?" the guard prompted. Across from him a pair of other sentries took note of the conversation and watched with sudden interest. They looked at Doully the donkey, too, particularly at the bulging saddlebags slung over her back.

"Laird Delaval, of course," Cadayle replied. "We are of Pryd Town, and Laird Prydae threw in with Delaval against Ethelbert, as has his successor, Laird Delaval's own nephew."

"Welcome, then," said the first. "You have nothing the Abellican monks cannot fix?"

"I . . . I . . . I," Bransen stammered and stuttered and drooled, and the sentry winced in obvious disgust.

"None have helped," Cadayle interjected. "Though many have tried. Perhaps here we will find our answers."

"Father Malskinner is mighty with the stones," one of the guards to the side remarked.

"Come through, then, and find your way," the first said, and waved the trio and their donkey through. "And don't you worry," he said to Bransen as the man staggered by him. "Those fools down there under the whip were brought from Ethelbert's lines."

"They are prisoners?" Callen asked with surprise.

"Until they die from their efforts, aye," the guard explained. He didn't seem bothered in the least by that eventuality. He glanced down at the docks and the bedraggled slaves. "I lost my brother in a ship fight in the gulf. I'd go down there and put the sword to the lot of them if it was my choice to make. But I'll take my satisfaction in knowing that these fools are helping Laird Delaval put an end to Ethelbert's claims. Every log they bring in from across the river, every crate of food or weapons sailing up from Delaval Town, works against the Beast of Entel. When Ethelbert falls, and fall he will, I'll take my satisfaction in knowing that Palmaristown played her part in his demise!"

"I only wish that my husband had not been so badly wounded that he might still aid in the effort," Cadayle said.

"Could be that his wife would offer comfort to guards loyal to Delaval," one of the pair across the way remarked, and his companion chuckled.

Cadayle took care to keep her response muted, neither too insulting in rebuff nor too accepting of the slight that it could coax the man on in his carnal quest. She clutched Bransen's arm tighter and led him through the gate, Callen and Doully coming up behind them.

Of all the towns they had traveled through none possessed the energy of Palmaristown. The city was not on the front lines of the fighting like so many of the settlements from Pryd to Delaval, and few wounded came through. Yet, Palmaristown remained in the very center of it all, for through here came many of Laird Delaval's soldiers, boarding ships to be carried across the Gulf of Corona to the distant eastern reaches known as the Mantis Arm. Here in Palmaristown the war was very real but very distant, an exciting event to be discussed in every tavern and on every street corner but without the torn bodies and missing limbs that cast the pall of harsh reality.

That sanitized reality reflected in the eagerness and excitement of the townsfolk. As word spread down the lanes before the trio many salutes and bows came at Bransen from afar.

They secured a tavern room quite easily, offered at half the normal price to the wounded soldier, and set out to find a stable and buyer for Doully, for the old donkey had seen too much of the road. Whispers preceded them, however, and before they even had the time to walk from the inn to the hitching post to retrieve Doully, they were met by a smiling young Abellican monk.

"Greetings, my friends," he said lightheartedly—so much so that Callen and Cadayle exchanged suspicious looks, for they were hardly used to helpful and cheery Abellicans.

"I am told that this poor man here has suffered terribly in service to Laird Delaval, may Blessed Abelle guide him to kingship," the monk went on.

"He was wounded south of Delaval against the men of Ethelbert, yes," Callen said, the hesitation in her voice reflecting her growing trepidation that Cadayle's lie was soon to be uncovered.

"I am Brother Fatuus of the Chapel of Precious Memories," the monk explained with a respectful bow. "Father Malskinner bade me to come forth and find this hero who walks among us, and to offer—" He paused and reached into a belt pouch, producing a quartet of gray soul stones.

"You would bestow healing to my poor son-in-law?" Callen asked, nodding appreciatively and coming forth to take Bransen's arm. "His wounds are grievous."

"As I see," said Fatuus. He turned a bit to the side and leaned forward in an attempt to view Bransen's back. "From the manner of his walk, I mean, as I have not witnessed any wound as of yet."

"The wound itself is long healed," Cadayle answered. "But the damage remains."

"A spear?"

"No."

"Sword?"

"No," Cadayle answered, and the monk crinkled his face with clear suspicion.

"Dagger?" he asked.

"A club," Cadayle decided. "He was smashed across the back, he told me, and he's had little control of his legs and feet since. And even his voice is lost to us, stuttering as he does."

The monk nodded and put on a pensive pose, as if he had any understanding at all.

Cadayle looked to her mother, who bit back a snicker.

"May I?" Brother Fatuus asked, extending his hand and the soul stones.

"Please, Brother," said Cadayle. She kissed Bransen's cheek and stepped away.

Fatuus began chanting to Blessed Abelle for guidance and strength. He closed his hand over the gemstones and gripped them so tightly that his knuckles whitened. He put his other hand up to Bransen's forehead and began to channel the soothing power of the gemstones into the wounded young man.

Bransen closed his eyes and steadied immediately, basking in the warmth of the wonderful enchantment. This monk was strong, he recognized immediately—more so than any of the brothers at Chapel Pryd. The healing energy flowed pure and direct, and Bransen felt as if he had his own stone strapped across his forehead. Using his Jhesta Tu training, Bransen opened up to the sensation and even dared hope, albeit fleetingly, that Brother Fatuus might offer some permanent benefit.

Bransen knew in his heart, though, that it would not be so.

A few heartbeats later, Fatuus relented and removed his warm and trembling palm.

Bransen opened his eyes, looked the man in the eye and said, "Than . . . Th . . . Th . . . Tha . . . k you." And he smiled and nodded, standing straighter, for indeed he felt much better (although he knew already it would be a very temporary sensation).

Cadayle came back to his side and said, "It is a fine thing you did this day," breaking Fatuus from his apparent trance.

He blinked repeatedly as he looked at the woman and her husband. "The wound is . . . is profound," he said.

"As many of your brethren have told us," said Cadayle. She looked at Bransen, and her smile came wide and sincere. "You performed very well, Brother. I have not seen him so straight since before the wound."

Already, though, Bransen began to bend, a bit of drool dripping from his mouth.

"It will not hold," Fatuus observed, and Cadayle offered a shrug and a forgiving smile in response.

"You must bring him to the Chapel of Precious Memories," Fatuus insisted. "I will beg Father Malskinner to allow others to participate. Our combined powers will lengthen the healing, I am certain."

"Of course," said Cadayle.

"Before Parvespers tomorrow," Fatuus bade them, referring to the ceremony of twilight. "We will be out all the day offering our services to the brave men on the docks."

"The slaves of war?" Cadayle asked. "Indeed, we saw them at their labors, being beaten like dogs."

"The filth of Ethelbert?" Fatuus replied, his eyes wide with horror. "Nay, not them, surely! Nay, nay, good lady, I speak of the privateers." As he finished he pointed to a pair of ships moored out in the open river to the north of the wharves, and sailing under no flag at all, none that Cadayle could see, at least.

"Privateers?"

"Free men," Fatuus explained. "Beholden to neither Ethelbert nor good Laird Delaval. They have sailed in at the behest of Laird Panlamaris the Bold, leader of Palmaristown, who seeks to enlist them in the united effort against foul Ethelbert and his swarthy minions."

"To bribe them, you mean," Cadayle reasoned.

"They will be compensated in coin, yes," said Fatuus. "And through the work of the Brothers of the Chapel of Precious Memories. God-given magic to heal their blistered feet and the many wounds brought back from weeks of toil at sea. It is the least we can offer to goodly Laird Delaval in his struggles against the Southern filth that is Laird Ethelbert."

Cadayle turned her look to Bransen, who, even through his Stork visage, wore a mischievous smirk. They were both well aware, after all, that the southeastern Abellican chapels served Ethelbert as these in the west and north served Delaval—and all in harmony and pragmatism.

Callen had barely closed the door to the room the three rented at a Palmaristown inn when Bransen grabbed up his gemstone and strapped it to his forehead under his black silken mask.

"Privateers," he said, not a hint of the Stork in his strong and steady voice. "Mercenaries."

"What are you thinking?" asked Callen.

"My guess is that my husband has decided that our load of booty is too dangerous to keep saddlebagged over poor old Doully," Cadayle replied, and Bransen nodded.

"I had thought to spread the wealth to the commonfolk about the region but feared that some of the jewels would be recognized," Bransen explained. "I've no desire to bring that pain to anyone—the same pain that both of you felt at the hands of Laird Prydae when I passed the stolen necklace to Cadayle."

"You need not remind me of that," Callen assured him. "Did I not bid you to throw the stolen coins and jewels into the river and be done with them?"

"And now I intend to do something along those very lines."

"By taking the treasures to the privateers and bidding them to double-cross Laird Delaval," Callen reasoned. "So you'd throw in with Ethelbert?"

"I care not if they all kill each other," said Bransen. "But there is a delicious irony in using that fool Yeslnik's treasures to buy off Laird Delaval's intended allies."

"As delicious as the Stork becoming a hero of the land against the interests of the lairds?" Cadayle asked. Bransen stopped putting on his black shirt and stared hard at her.

Cadayle merely shrugged, though, and offered him a warm smile. Her statement had been blunt, of course, but she, and perhaps she alone, had earned the right to talk to him in such a manner and many times over. Bransen could never be wounded by Cadayle's honest reference to the Stork, since Cadayle alone had stood by him before the creation of the Highwayman, when he had found the gemstone magic to allow him to free himself of the crippling bonds of his physical infirmities.

Bransen finished dressing in the black outfit his mother had brought from Behr, finishing by tying the torn strip of fabric over the distinctive birthmark on his one bare arm.

Bransen took up the fabulous sword, holding it reverently before his eyes as he studied the intricate vine and flower designs etched into its gleaming blade. The weapon had no equal north of the Belt-and-Buckle Mountains, and few swords even of the Jhesta Tu mystics in Behr could match its quality. Staring at the marvelous blade, Bransen was reminded that he would one day go there, to the Walk of Clouds, to learn from the masters.

He slid the sword into its sheath and slung it across his back, then took up the saddlebags full of Yeslnik's treasure and tossed them over his shoulder. He moved to the room's small window and peeked around the heavy curtain, considering the setting sun.

"The privateer captains might be ashore," Cadayle said.

"I will find them," Bransen promised, and Cadayle and Callen nodded, neither about to doubt this man who had delivered them from a life of misery beneath the boot of Laird Prydae.

He went out in the dark of night, hand-walking down the side of the two-story inn so fluidly that anyone looking on would have thought he was using a ladder.

The Highwayman didn't need a ladder.

He didn't bother with the bustle he heard emanating from the many taverns along the wall separating the two city levels, reasoning that if the privateer captains were in one of those establishments, they would return to their ships in any case.

He found the docks nearly deserted, with only a couple of slaves swabbing the planks halfheartedly, and with no dockmasters to put whips to their backs. Bransen paid them little heed as he moved through the shadows along the wharves to the smaller docks and the tiny boats. He secured one without incident and floated out from the wharf, gently paddling as the current caught him and dragged him along. That current took him toward the moored privateers, for the tide was receding in the gulf, which meant that he merely needed his oars to steer the craft, and not noisily row it.

He kept glancing back over his shoulders, locating the dark silhouette of a mast protruding into the night sky, and appropriately angled his oars, drifting slowly, slowly, and in no hurry whatsoever. He brought the rowboat up against a mooring line and tied it off there, then gathered up his bags and, with a quick check to ensure that his precious sword remained secure in its sheath, the Highwayman began his climb.

A few moments later he came over the rail, silent as death, dark as night, and carefully paced about the deck, seeking sentries and the general lay of the ship. He'd never before been on a ship and had never even seen one up close. It took a lot of his concentration to resist losing himself in the experience, for truly this craft was a work of art, so sleek and beautiful and ultimately functional. He studied the many ropes, climbing and disappearing into the mass of rigging. Many generations of sailors had perfected this design one rope at a time, he understood immediately, recognizing in general fashion the evolution that had led from simple, single-mast boats to this intricate and wondrous three-sail design.

He found a raised cabin aft and quickly discerned, from the shouting within, that the man inside carried great authority, and was likely the captain of the vessel himself.

Or herself, Bransen realized as he sidled up to a small window beside the forward-facing door and peeked in.

She stormed about a decorated desk, a rolled parchment in hand, a red bandanna tight about her head, with dark brown tresses flowing out behind and halfway down her back. She wore a puffy white blouse gathered about her slim waist and unbuttoned far enough down to be quite revealing with her every sudden turn. Black breeches and high boots completed her outfit, along with a dirk on her right hip, a curved sword on her left. She was not an unattractive woman, surely, and carried about her an aura of competence and danger.

He had come in late in her tirade, and she seemed too upset to speak in complete sentences, apparently, but it wasn't hard for the Highwayman to fathom the gist of her rant: the nature of the deal offered by Laird Panlamaris, representative of Laird Delaval.

"Five months o' sailing!" she cried. "Five! And feedin' a full crew and a hundred hungry soldiers to boot. And that through a gulf full o' powries! E'er ye seen a powrie, boy? Nasty little redcap hungry to open yer belly and tug out yer guts! Might that he'll eat 'em right there while ye're watch . . ."

She stopped and stared, mouth agape.

"Do go on," the Highwayman bade. "I admit that my own experiences with the wretched powries are rather limited, but from what I've seen, I'll not contra . . ."

The woman drew out her sword and leaped for him, thrusting for his throat.

But his own sword appeared in his hand, as fast as a blink, and he easily and gently guided her stabbing blade aside so that it poked into the jamb of the open door. She kept coming, and reached for her dirk, but there, too, he beat her to the quick, and the sailor grasped at an empty sheath!

The Highwayman held her stolen dagger up before her astonished eyes. He edged the privateer back at the point of her own dirk.

"Good lady, you have no fight with me," he said, and he flipped the dagger, catching it by its tip and presenting it back to the sailor.

She stared at him for many heartbeats before grabbing the presented hilt and yanking the dirk back from the intruder. She presented both her blades in a defensive stance as she continued to size up the stranger, clearly unsettled.

The Highwayman calmly replaced his sword in its sheath across his back, and the privateer seemed all the more frazzled.

"Who ye be?" she demanded.

"An independent rogue," he replied. "Much akin to yourself, I would expect."

"Ye're to lead with insults?"

"Hardly, milady. I hold my head with pride and would expect no less from you and the worthy sailors of these fine ships—ships flying under the flag of neither Ethelbert nor Delaval."

"We're in Palmaristown, which has thrown in with Laird Delaval."

"No doubt because Laird Delaval has shown the deeper pockets."

The woman tilted her head back and narrowed her eyes.

"Or because you believe that he will win out in the end and see a brighter future for those who do not oppose him," the Highwayman bluntly added. "In either event, I salute you. I hold nothing but respect for any who can thrive in these dark times. I hope you will come to see me equally worthy of your respect." As he finished, he pulled the saddlebags off his shoulder and tossed them at the privateer's feet.

The woman glanced down at them, but immediately lifted her gaze back to the surprising man in the black mask.

He shrugged.

The woman hooked her saber under the flap of the nearest bag and with a deft flick of her wrist, severed the tie and pulled open the flap in a single, fluid movement. A few coins rolled out, and several jewels showed, and despite her best efforts, the woman's eyes flashed with obvious interest.

"If you came to bargain, what a fool ye be to lay out the ante openly, and with yerself surrounded by potential enemies," she said.

Again he shrugged, so confidently, and the smile showing under his black mask clearly said that he believed he could rather easily retrieve his treasure.

"What army serves ye?" the woman demanded.

"I am independent, and I offer no threat to accompany my gift to you, good lady. I came here to present you with these coins and jewels, stolen from the castle of the Laird of Delaval himself."

The woman glanced at her crewman, who, throughout this entire ordeal, hadn't even moved. Nor did he notice his captain's look, fixated as he was on the marvelous and surprising intruder.

"You would be wise to keep them hidden while you remain on the river, or even in the gulf," the Highwayman said. "Delaval has sent word far and wide to find these, no doubt."

"Ye mean to push the burden o' them onto me?"

"If you do not want them, lady . . ."

"I said no such thing."

The Highwayman smiled wider.

"And what're ye asking in return for this . . . gift?"

"Nothing," he replied. "They are indeed a burden to me, as I remain in Delaval's lands."

"You would have us sail you to the reaches of Laird Ethelbert?"

The Highwayman paused, and almost agreed to that, thinking that he could then get around the spurs of the Belt-and-Buckle and into the famed city of Jacintha, in Behr, which would allow him an open road to the Walk of Clouds. Black wings of doubt fluttered up all about him, though, forcing him to admit to himself, yet again, that he was not ready for that ultimate journey.

"At another time, perhaps," he said. "I have business remaining here, though I do hope to reach Entel and beyond, all the way to Behr, in the near future. Should we meet again when my business is complete, I would beg of you to consider providing such passage."

"And for now?" the woman asked, looking down at the open satchel.

"I would beg you to hoist your sails and be gone from this place."

The woman looked at him suspiciously. "Ye be an agent of Ethelbert indeed, then."

"Independent," the Highwayman reiterated. "Truly so. I care for neither of the feuding lairds, nor for any of their lackey lessers. If all the nobles of all of Honce are murdered in their sleep tomorrow, I will raise a glass in celebration. But of now, it is Laird Delaval who has most aggravated me, and it does me pleasure indeed to stick pins into his sides, first by robbing his treasury, and then . . ."

"By buying off three ships he has employed for his efforts," the privateer reasoned.

The Highwayman shrugged. "The treasure is an offer of truce from another independent. Perhaps a prepayment for services needed some time hence. But I hold you to nothing at all. I come in salute—better that one such as you possess the coins and jewels than have me bury them in a hole. How should I ever live with myself if these treasures find their way into the hands of an innocent and oblivious peasant, who is then hanged by Delaval's people for possessing them? Here, I know, they are in competent hands of men and women wise enough to keep them safe and secret. So yes, I beg you to relieve me of my burden."

The privateer looked down at the bags again, licking her lips as she imagined the treasures within. If the hints showing on the open edge were any indication, she knew that this might well be the most profitable day of her life. With a sigh, she slid her weapons away and lifted her eyes to regard the Highwayman.

But he was already gone from her cabin.

It is an amazing transformation," Callen said early the next morning. Bransen had just awakened and was still rubbing the sleep from his eyes when Callen walked through the door of their rented room. Beside him on the small bed Cadayle hardly stirred other than to bury her face in her pillow against the intrusion of daylight.

"I did not know that you had been here before," Bransen replied, his voice steady, for he had slept with the soul stone firmly strapped in place on his forehead.

"Of course I have not," said Callen. "I'm only echoing the words of the townsfolk. Palmaristown has seen a great shift in the last few months. No Samhaists remain in the city, and there are few in the surrounding countryside by all accounts. And even the people here fast abandon the ways of the Ancient Ones."

"The Abellicans have the gemstones and the favor of the lairds across all of Honce," Bransen said.

"But the change is coming more quickly here than elsewhere—even than in Delaval itself from what I could see. I had no such expectation, since Palmaristown is on the border of the wilderness. Across the river is land untouched by the Abellicans by all accounts."

"And land unwanted by the Samhaists, likely," Bransen reasoned.

"Or perhaps the Samhaists are out there, just across the river, watching and biding their time."

Bransen shrugged, as he hardly cared. As he studied Callen more carefully, though, he recognized that she was more than a little unsettled by the sweeping changes, which surprised him given her unpleasant history with the brutal Samhaists.

"Perhaps the world will become a better place as the Samhaists recede into the shadows," he offered. "Not that I expect much better from the Abellicans."

"If they're not killing people it will be an improvement," Callen said, and Bransen smiled at her, glad that his words had apparently eased her troubled soul. He sympathized, and understood her inner turmoil, for indeed the changes sweeping the land were vast and profound, and Bransen recognized that few of the people had come to terms with them as of yet. Looking at it all from a removed point of view, it was more amusing than unsettling. He figured he really couldn't lose, for anything would be better than the present state!

"Did your tryst go well?" Callen asked.

"I believe it did."

"Those ships are from Bergenbel, the one holding south of the gulf that hasn't thrown in for either Ethelbert or Delaval. Both sides value that port, I am told, and so they pay dearly for the services of the privateers who have taken up the mercenary cause."

"Each believes that to be the path toward securing the holding, likely."

Callen nodded her agreement with the assessment.

"Then my visit with the flagship captain last night might prove more irritating to Delaval than I intended," Bransen said, his smile wide.

That smile grew all the wider later in the day when the trio started out of town. On a hill on the northeastern section they watched the Bergenbel privateers raise their sails and glide away from Palmaristown, heading north toward the open waters of the Gulf of Corona. At a nearby smithy, where they sold old Doully (for they could not bear to force the aching donkey to continue the journey), they found confirmation that the departure of the ships was the talk of the town, with many whispering that it would prove a harbinger for disaster.

"Ethelbert's bought them," explained the blacksmith, a hulking giant of a man with a red face and hair black and matted. "Word's out that they might have been spies from the dog, come here to survey Palmaristown's defenses."

"You are expecting an attack?" Cadayle asked.

"Preparing for it," the smith replied. "Who's to know what the dog Ethelbert will do? King Delaval's got him squeezed to the Mirianic."

They let it go at that, with Cadayle handing Bransen, in Stork guise, over to Callen and saying her farewells to Doully. They were some distance from the smithy, on an open stretch of ground reserved for visiting caravans, before any of them dared broach the subject.

"Just as you had hoped," Cadayle said.

Bransen grabbed the soul stone in his pouch and clutched it tightly. "If there were only a way for me to let Delaval know that it was the idiot Yeslnik's coin that bought off his privateers, my satisfaction would be complete."

"It's early in the day," said Callen. "You will think of something."

That brought a shared laugh from the three, but Bransen cut his short, and stuttered it and twisted it around, when he noted the approach of a city guardsman. With help from his two companions, the Stork staggered out through Palmaristown's northeastern gate, and down the open road toward Chapel Abelle, the seat of Abellican power.

A strange and unexpected feeling washed over Bransen at that moment. Suddenly it seemed real to him, this search for Brother Bran Dynard, his father—no, not his father, he decided, for that honor remained with Garibond. To this point, Bransen had considered this journey north a diversion as much as anything else, a delay against facing the hard truth of his road south. He had latched on to the idea of finding his father as much so that he wouldn't yet have to face the Jhesta Tu mystics and their answers (or more pointedly, their possible lack of answers) as out of any real desire to find and know the man who had sired him.

Now, though, with the road straight and clear before him and the last real city left behind, the idea of finding Brother Dynard suddenly seemed very real—and Bransen wasn't even sure what that meant. Would the man acknowledge him? Would the man crush him tight in a hug and be overcome with joy that his son had found him?

Did Bransen even want that? What might such a joyful reunion mean to the memory of his beloved Garibond?

So many questions swirled in Bransen's thoughts the moment that road came clear to him, the moment the idea of finding Brother Dynard became real to him. Questions of how he might react to the man, of how the man might react to him, and most of all, as time and wobbly steps passed, of why.

Why hadn't Brother Dynard returned for him?

Callen had many times called Bran Dynard a good man; Bransen could only hope that the answer to his most pressing question would bear that out.

Brother Honig Brisebolis rambled through the streets of the lower city, huffing and puffing and warning everyone to get out of his way. Wide-eyed and obviously in great distress as he was, few would pause to argue those commands from the three-hundred-pound rotund monk. Nor did the guards at the city's higher, closed gate hesitate at the monk's approach, rushing to swing wide one of those double doors to let the important Brother Honig ramble through without slowing.

Honig did pause just past the gates, however, as he stood on the crossroad. To the right, the south, lay the road that would bring him to Laird Panlamaris's palace, while the left road led straight to the square before the Chapel of Precious Memories. Honig's news would prove important, critical even, to both Laird Panlamaris and Father Malskinner.

"Laird Panlamaris might swiftly dispatch warships to intercept," he said aloud, trying to sort through his jumbled thoughts.

He turned left anyway, realizing that his first duties were to the Church and not the laird. He gathered up a head of steam, gasping for breath but not daring to slow.

"What is it, Brother Honig?" Father Malskinner bade him a few moments later when he burst into the man's spacious private chambers.

Honig tried to answer, but couldn't find his voice for his gasping, and wound up leaning on the father's desk for support.

"Did you meet with Captain Shivanne?"

Brother Honig nodded emphatically, but still couldn't quite reach his voice.

"Brother Honig?"

"They raise sail!" he blurted at last.

A perplexed Father Malskinner stared at him for a moment before rising from his desk and moving to a window that overlooked the river. As soon as he glanced out, he saw the truth of it, as all three privateers had their sails up and engaged. The father turned fast on Honig. "What is the meaning?"

"Shivanne makes for the gulf and beyond," he said.

"But Laird Delaval's soldiers and supplies have not even yet arrived."

Honig shook his head. "She will not wait. She laughed at my protests!"

"Laughed?"

"She was paid, Father. Well paid. 'A better offer,' she said."

"Ethelbert? Here?"

Again Honig wagged his head in the negative. "Captain Shivanne teased and would not say, other than to assure me that it was not Ethelbert, nor any agent of the foul Laird of Entel. A privateer, she called him, this man who brought her a treasure beyond Laird Delaval's offerings."

Malskinner stared at him pensively. "A third party in the mix of this war?" It sounded even more improbable—to both of them—as he spoke the words aloud.

"A thorn, more likely," Brother Honig said. "She said he wore a mask and suit of black, exotic material."

Malskinner's eyes went wide.

"She said that he moved as a shadow, and worked his blade with the skill of a master. A most magnificent blade, she assured me. A blade unlike any she had ever seen, and one, she promised, that would lay low a laird or would-be king."

"The man from Pryd Holding," Malskinner said with a nod of recognition. He moved swiftly for the shelving behind his desk, where he kept all the correspondences of the last months. In a matter of moments, he held the ones that had filtered up from Pryd Town, and the related messages sent out by Prince Yeslnik of Delaval, warning of a most notorious and dangerous figure known as the Highwayman.

Malskinner drew a deep breath as he read the last of those notes, the one informing him that Laird Prydae had been killed by this desperate fellow, who had then set out on the open road, destination unknown.

Flipping through some of the back parchments, the father of the Chapel of Precious Memories found the letter of detail sent by Brother Reandu on behalf of Father Jerak of Chapel Pryd.

"Bransen Garibond," he said to Honig as he digested the letter. He looked at the portly brother. "Of Pryd Town. It is rumored that he was connected to Brother Dynard and an exotic woman of Behr."

"Dynard?" Brother Honig echoed, shrugging and shaking his head.

"An insignificant brother," Malskinner explained. "He traveled to Behr and was there corrupted by the seductive ways of the beastly barbarians. Father Jerak properly dispatched him to Chapel Abelle, to see if his soul could be salvaged."

"Yes, yes," Honig said. "Killed on the road, if I recall."

"That was the rumor. I know not if Chapel Abelle ever confirmed it or not."

"We must tell Laird Panlamaris of this."

"At once," Father Malskinner agreed. "Have him send word far and wide to beware of this creature." He glanced back at the note. "And tell them to look for a damaged and small man."

"Damaged?"

Malskinner shrugged as he read through the description of Bransen, of his storklike gait and his drooling and stuttering. "An alter ego, a disguise of weakness, it would seem," he said.

"Your pardon, Father," came a voice from the doorway. Father Malskinner looked over to see Brother Fatuus poking his head in. "I could not help but overhear."

"Come in, Brother Fatuus," Father Malskinner said. "We are discussing a potential problem that has come to Palmaristown. You have noticed the privateers lifting their sails to the wind?"

"That is why I have come, Father. What did I hear regarding a disguise?"

Father Malskinner bade him approach, and handed over the letter of detail from Brother Reandu.

"Go to Laird Panlamaris," Malskinner ordered Honig. "Tell him everything and warn him to alert his guards to this storklike person."

"I have seen him," Fatuus said suddenly, and both of his brethren spun about to regard him as he stood there, mouth agape, holding Reandu's letter. "This man, Bransen. I saw him only yesterday. I tended him with a soul stone, though to little effect, and bade him come to us this very night before Parvespers."

"The creature described in that letter?"

"Perfectly described. He was named as a hero of the war, and so I went to him generously, as per your commandments on this regard."

Father Malskinner leaned back, then sat on the edge of his desk and nodded slowly. "It is true, then. The Highwayman has come to Palmaristown."

"The Highwayman?"

"A rogue of unusual talent and troublesome ways, it would seem," Malskinner explained. "It was he who paid the privateers to sail from us, by their own admission."

"Why would they divulge such information?" asked Brother Fatuus.

"Captain Shivanne freely told me," Honig interjected. "I went out to her this morning, as arranged, to tend to her crew. They were already readying for sail, and when I inquired, she told me. Indeed, I would say that she was rather proud of her gain—proud enough to rattle a bag of coins and jewels before me, and to tell me of her unexpected benefactor."

"Let us hope that this Bransen, this Highwayman, feels secure enough in his disguise to take you up on your offer of appearing before us," Malskinner said to Fatuus. "If so, we will take him quickly and with as little excitement as possible."

"Brother Reandu, speaking for Father Jerak of Chapel Pryd, takes pains to find kind words for this rogue," Fatuus said as he perused the remainder of the long letter.

"Laird Delaval would not likely see things in that manner," said Malskinner, and he waved Honig away. "Nor will Laird Panlamaris, who will face the wrath of Laird Delaval for allowing the ships of Bergenbel to sail unladen with Delaval's men and supplies. Find this man if he remains within Palmaristown, and if he does not, find out where he went. Perhaps if we offer him to Laird Panlamaris, that he might offer him to Laird Delaval, our failures will be forgiven."

Bransen didn't show up at the Chapel of Precious Memories before Parvespers that night, of course, and indeed, word came back to Father Malskinner even before the twilight ceremony that the man and his two female companions had exited the city through the northern gate, on the road to the central highlands.

Where lay Chapel Abelle.

The next morning, Brother Fatuus rode out that same gate, spurring his horse to the east with all speed to deliver Father Malskinner's warning to the brothers of Chapel Abelle.

So hasty was Fatuus's ride that he didn't stop to inquire about the curious Highwayman at the scattered farmhouses he passed, and so it was on his second morning out that as he rode hard down the lane past a small barn, three sets of eyes stared out at him.

"The one who tried to heal you with the gemstones," Cadayle said.

"He rides as if powries are chasing him," Callen added.

"Powries? Or the Highwayman?" asked Bransen.

CHAPTER 7

Tedium Undone

"Every day's one and the same," Mcwigik lamented, dipping his paddle silently into the water beside the small craft. "Weren't for the changes in the damned moon we'd not know that time's passing."

"Yach but she's passin'," said Bikelbrin, sitting opposite him. "Feeling it in me bones, I be."

"And meself in me broken nose," Mcwigik agreed and brought his hand up to touch his flat, wide nose, a bit flatter and wider still from the smash he'd been dealt twenty-eight days earlier. He had put a piece of white, gummy sap from the small, wide-leafed trees common to the islands across the bridge of his nose to secure it while it healed. He hadn't worn that gum bandage for a few days, but had put it back on just before the scheduled return to Chapel Isle. Pragganag and the others understood the reminder to be for Pragganag's benefit.

"Are ye to babble all then way, then?" said an irritated Pragganag, who was sitting in the back, testing the balance of his wooden-handled metal-bladed hatchet—one of the very few implements of metal still left intact after a century on the steamy lake. "Ye're to let the whole o' Mithranidoon know we're about, and won't it be the kitten's mewl to be chased by a fleet o' barbarian longboats?"

"All with sense've gone to bed," Bikelbrin replied.

"Which is saying what for ourselves?" asked Mcwigik, and Bikelbrin and three of the others in the small and stout craft laughed, the fourth being Pragganag, who narrowed his eyes so much so that his bushy eyebrows pretty much stole them from view as he glowered at Mcwigik.

Mcwigik took no note of him, and reached up to grab his bandaged snout.

"Yach, but that monk smashed ye good, what?" said Bikelbrin, and he and the others turned to Pragganag.

"Aye, and me nose's still for hurting when I'm laughing," Mcwigik said.

"Good thing yerself's the one what's telling the jokes then," Pragganag deadpanned, and the laughter began anew, Mcwigik joining in most heartily. As fierce a race as walked the world, powries typically relished these moments of ribbing, even if the best jabs came at their own personal expense.

The boat quieted then as the powries went back to paddling.

"We should build ourselves a barrelboat," Mcwigik said after a short pause, referring to the open-sea powrie craft, which resembled huge casks and kept most of their bulk beneath the surface. The interior of a barrelboat consisted of a series of benches set before pedals, and the tireless dwarves propelled their craft by pumping legs, with the pedals geared to turn an aft screw. Many a ship's captain had blanched white upon spotting a barrelboat, or even flotsam resembling such a craft, whose primary attack mode was, with typical powrie finesse, the ram. "Put her out on the lake, and wouldn't that make all the men shiver?"

"Ye can't be thinking it," Bikelbrin replied. "Ye might be making the trolls happy, but ye'd be startin' a war for winning, and not just for playing, don't ye doubt."

"Aye," one of the others chimed in, "ye send a barbarian boat to the bottom and give her crew to the trolls, and all the islands'd join against us and come a-calling. Our rock of Red Cap ain't that big."

Mcwigik offered an exaggerated nod to show that he wasn't being serious. He knew as well as any the agreed-upon protocols of the islands, and primary among those was the edict that no combatant, not powrie nor Alpinadoran nor Abellican alike, would be dropped under deep water. For Mithranidoon's opaque gray waters hid terrible things indeed behind her constant wall of tiny bubbles. Great fish and serpents had been spotted often, and the glacial trolls seemed to know immediately whenever someone went under.

No one survived Mithranidoon's deep waters for long, and the civilized "warfare" between the islands demanded certain rules of engagement.

"It'd be good to feel the screw beneath me feet again, is all," Mcwigik replied with a tone of concession.

"Aye," Bikelbrin and one other agreed, for only they and Mcwigik among the six on the boat had ever experienced such a thing, or had ever seen the world beyond the banks of this lake. The bloody caps had been on Mithranidoon for more than a century now, and though their numbers had dwindled a bit, from eighty to seventy-six, they had been fortunate to recover the hearts of almost all of the more than forty who had been killed—fallen to trolls and storms and barbarians—in the early days, before the silently agreed-upon protocols. The heart was key to an untraditional and magical form of powrie reproduction. Using it, an appropriate mass of stone (and the plentiful lava rock of Mithranidoon was perfect for the task), and a month of ancient magic in the form of sacred songs, the powries could create life itself, giving "birth" to the fallen dwarf's successor. Not often practiced on the Weathered Isles, where female powries were plentiful, Sepulcher, as this magical rebirth was called, had kept the strength of the community of powries on the lake, though they had but three females remaining among the lot of them—for Sepulcher, for some reason that no dwarf had ever figured out, almost always led to a male child, whether the hosting heart had come from a male or female.

Returning from their last trip to Chapel Isle, they had prepared and buried Regwegno's heart and some rock and begun the process. This very afternoon, right before they had departed, they had felt the first rumblings from the Sepulcher (the term also was used to describe the physical grave-womb). Regwegno's son would climb free five months hence, and judging from those initial trembles all expected this one would prove a scrapper to make his sire proud.

"I'm hardly for remembering it," Mcwigik admitted, "for I been a hundred five of me hundred thirty right here on the lake."

The dwarf behind him, the only one other than Bikelbrin who had come to Mithranidoon beside Mcwigik, gazed wistfully out to the northwest, toward the towering glacier wall, and lamented, "I make me brother Heycalnuck paddle out to the ice, just so I can feel the feel o' cold water. Never thought I'd miss the dark chill of the Mirianic, did I."

"Aye," Bikelbrin agreed.

"And I'll be finding it again's me hope," said Mcwigik, and even the wistful dwarf behind him stared at him incredulously for that comment!

"Mcwigik the fool," Pragganag said from the back. "The land's to be freezing yer blood solid inside ye, ye dope. Ye thinking ye're a glacier troll, are ye? Well, ye're thinking's to get yerself dead."

"Yach and aye!" said the dwarf behind Mcwigik. "We're not even for knowing where lies the damned Mirianic. East, say some, but west for others. How many hundreds fell on the march inland, the one the priests called glorious? Weren't for Mithranidoon and we'd've all been killed to death."

"By the cold, if not the barbarians, if not the monsters," Bikelbrin agreed, but there was a noticeably different timbre in his voice compared to the consternation of his fellow traveler.

Bikelbrin and Mcwigik exchanged a silent thought, then, a slight nod and resigned grin, for they often mused about leaving Mithranidoon, and of late had openly wondered how much worse death, even death without Sepulcher, could be compared to the tedium of life on the foggy lake.

One of the dwarves behind them began to sing, "When the stars come out to shine."

"Twenty boys, side-to-side in a line," another intoned, picking up the solemn chant of an old powrie war song, one that ended, as had the battle it described, badly.

"Yach, but not that one!" another cried. "Tonight's the night for fun, ye fools. We're not for war, but for sport!"

"Sport that's to get Prag's face broken," said the first singer, and all the dwarves began to laugh—except for Pragganag, of course. He stared hard at the others and slid his hatchet's metal head along a sharpening stone, the screech of it lost in their continuing laughter.

The night was dark, so they could hardly see the darker silhouette of Chapel Isle through the mist. They were quite familiar with their approach, though, and few could navigate as well as powries, even when Mithranidoon's mist was high enough to almost constantly obscure the stars.

"Ha, but it's lookin' like the monk's ready for a fight," Bikelbrin said after a long period in which only the quiet dipping of paddles in the warm lake water accompanied the ride. The dwarf lifted his paddle and pointed it ahead, where through the drifting mist a single torch could be seen.

"He's there with fifty o' his friends in wait, not to doubt," Pragganag grumbled.

"Then it's open hunting and me beret's sure to shine all the brighter," said Mcwigik. "Steady and straight to the beach, in either case, and if there's a bunch to be found, ye be quick in passing that axe, Prag, so we can open them up wide and fast."

Cormack never heard the craft's approach, for the wind was up this night and off the water, and the sound of the lapping waves against the rocky beach filled his ears. He had been out of the chapel for several hours by then; his second torch burned low, and his attention had long since left the unseen water. He sat in the sand, his back against a stone, staring up at the stars, which peeked out every now and then through the gray swirl. He worked two gemstones, a soul stone and a lodestone, through his fingers, tapping them together at intervals. The lodestone's power lay in magnetism, and Cormack had often come out with it, using its magical properties to look through it at the beach and shallows surrounding Chapel Isle. He had found many coins, and old weapons and tools, for with the lodestone he could sense metal—he could even use the power of the stone to telekinese small metallic objects to his waiting hand.

He hadn't found anything this night, but he hadn't really looked, using the lodestone as a pretense for getting out of the chapel without drawing suspicion. Once out here, the sun setting, he lost any interest in even pretending to search, as one question dominated his every thought: Would the powries come?

Even the pressing thought of impending battle had been lost to him soon after that, as the stars began to shine and before the mists climbed high enough to obscure them so greatly. Cormack often lost himself among the celestial lights, letting his mind drift back to his days in Vanguard at Chapel Pellinor and across the gulf in Chapel Abelle, the mother abbey of his Church. Those had been good and heady days those years ago. Full of purpose and meaning, Cormack had charged into Chapel Abelle with his eyes wide and his heart open, soaking in every detail, every premise, every tenet and every hope of Blessed Abelle's homily.

Did those ravenous and hopeful fires remain? the monk asked himself. He often found himself melancholy these long and arduous days, his love for Chapel Isle and this lake called Mithranidoon long lost. He did not cheer when the next level of the rock abbey had been completed, for it was a place that no one other than the brothers and their servants ever attended. He did not feel joy at the sermons of Brother Giavno or Father De Guilbe, even when they read from his favorite of Blessed Abelle's teachings. The messengers, he knew, could not inspire him, for while Cormack hated neither man (in fact, he was quite fond of Giavno), he knew in his heart that they had misinterpreted their purpose here in Alpinador. They had been sent to proselytize, to teach and to convert. Out here, the early hopes for their mission had not come to fruition. The barbarians would not hear their words any longer, and the rift would not mend. To Cormack's thinking, and he knew their neighbors on the lake better than anyone else at Chapel Isle, their failure would never reverse.

The fighting would not stop.

The barbarian souls would not be saved.

"Ah, Milkeila, alas, for you were my last hope," Cormack whispered, and his voice thinned even more as he moved to toss a pebble out toward the water, for there, coming at him through the uneven mist, loomed the hairy and wrinkled faces of the bloody-cap dwarves.

Cormack scrambled to his feet, brushing the sand from his pants.

"So ye came out," Mcwigik greeted him. The dwarf stepped closer and glanced all about, and Cormack retreated a step. "Alone?"

Cormack nodded, his eyes scanning the small band, then locking on the one in the back of the bunch, his planned opponent, who stood grinning wickedly and slapping a wooden club across his open palm. For a moment, panic set in, and the monk felt his knees go weak, his brain screaming at him to turn and flee with all speed!

"Alone?" Mcwigik said again, and he slapped the monk on the hip.

Cormack instinctively hopped aside, and all the dwarves bristled, and the man thought he would be overrun immediately. But the attack never came.

"Well?" Mcwigik demanded.

"Yes, alone," Cormack stammered. "I gave you my word."

"Ye did no such thing, but ye didn't argue," said Mcwigik. "Not that ye could've argued and still kept yer blood in yer body."

That brought laughter from the gathering, and Cormack swallowed hard.

"But that ye thinked it yer word, or counted it as such, says good about ye—for a human, I mean," said Mcwigik.

"Says ye got honor, or says ye got no wits about ye," Bikelbrin added, drawing another laugh. "Most with humans, we're thinking the second."

The laughing heightened, but Mcwigik cut it short. "Get it done," he said, nodding toward Pragganag, who came forward, weapon waving at the ready.

"Ye know the rules?" Mcwigik asked Cormack.

"No."

"Then ye do," snickered Mcwigik, and the other dwarves laughed again, except for Pragganag, who wore as fierce a scowl as poor Cormack had ever seen. "Pragganag's looking to finish ye, so if ye lose, expect to lose a lot o' yer blood. For yerself, ye beat him down as much as ye're wanting. Not a one of us'll get in the way. Kill him or bash his head in, or whatever ye're thinking to do—once ye've won, Prag's cap is yer own to claim."

"I ain't for liking that!" Pragganag grumbled.

"Ye're meaning to kill him, but we're just for giving him yer cap," Mcwigik argued.

"Me cap's worth more than his life!"

"Well then he can just kill ye and take the damned thing!" Mcwigik shot back.

"Only way the dog's getting it!"

Mcwigik started to respond, but then just offered a smile to Cormack and stepped out of the way. Cormack was about to ask a question, seeking assurances that he wouldn't get gang-tackled if he did indeed gain the upper hand, but he didn't even get the first word out of his mouth before Pragganag roared and charged in, smashing left and right with his club.

Cormack swung to his right, then again farther to the right, and a third time, which put him facing away from the furious powrie. He dove into a headlong roll, coming to his feet and springing forward immediately into a second dive and roll, for he felt the press of the charging dwarf. His third leap put him over some piled stones and gave him time to turn about on the far side, so that when Pragganag came roaring around the tumble, Cormack was ready and waiting.

"Are ye fightin' or runnin'?" the dwarf just asked before Cormack rushed forward, inside the reach of his club, and smacked him with a left, right combination that abruptly stole his momentum. The monk leaped straight back, and threw his head back farther to avoid a short swipe of the club. He slapped the back of it as it flashed past, driving it out and down, and managed a quick left jab to the powrie's hairy face before leaping back out of reach of the heavy backhand.

"Three hits for him," Mcwigik laughed.

But Pragganag just snorted, and if he had even felt any of Cormack's punches, it didn't show. He roared ahead, swiping wildly and repeatedly, and Cormack could only dodge and dart back.

"How long can ye run?" Pragganag teased, and came forward in a sudden rush and launched a mighty overhead chop.

Far enough to avoid that strike, the dwarf realized, and his eyes went wide as his club descended past his field of vision, to see that Cormack had already reversed course and was coming straight for him. The man leaped and lay straight out, feet first, and caught Pragganag with a double kick about the face and shoulders that sent the dwarf flying back and to the ground.

Pragganag rolled to his belly and started up, but he had barely made it to his knees before Cormack fell over him, driving a knee hard into the side of his head. Pragganag turned to face that knee directly as Cormack pumped his leg, but it took three smashes before the dwarf managed to bite the man, and even then, Cormack was able to quickly retract his leg so that Pragganag had hardly broken the skin.

Cormack fell over the dwarf and rolled about, looping his hands up under the kneeling powrie's arms and up behind the dwarf's neck. Normally this move would ensure victory, for the victim could be rendered helpless from the waist up, but normally Cormack wouldn't put the double vise hold, as it was called, onto a powrie dwarf.

Pragganag balled his legs under him and with tremendous strength lifted himself to a standing position, driving the human up behind him. Cormack tried to jerk and twist to keep his opponent off-balance, but Pragganag went into a sudden frenzy, spinning about left, then back fast to the right, then back and back again, stomping his heavy boots all the while.

Cormack felt as if he were riding a bull. His feet were off the ground more than on, and so he could do little to interrupt Pragganag when the dwarf took up a sudden run. Cormack fell lower on the dwarf's back, letting his legs drag, trying to halt the growing momentum, but Pragganag roared ahead, then bent low at the waist, lifting Cormack back up. At the last instant, Cormack understood the intent, and saw the cluster of large rocks fast approaching, but Pragganag slapped his arms in a cross up high on his chest, reaching back behind his shoulders to grab Cormack's wrists and hold him fast. Then with sheer powrie power, Pragganag ducked again and launched himself into a somersault, bringing poor Cormack right over the top.

Cormack hit the side of the largest rock, and Pragganag sandwiched into

Cormack. They hung there for a moment, like a splattered tomato, before both rolled down to the sand.

"Get up," Cormack told himself, trying to untwist, trying to get air back into his lungs. He hardly knew where he was, with bloody-cap dwarves howling all about him, but he kept his wits just enough to realize that it wasn't a good place, and that if he didn't get up soon, he'd be murdered where he lay.

He just started to his knees when the club flashed in. Purely on instinct, purely through the long hours of training he had received in the arts martial, Cormack snapped his left forearm up vertically to intercept that blow. The crack sent a wave of nauseating agony ripping through him, but his trained muscles continued the practiced move. He dropped his arm straight down, catching the shaft of the club in his left hand as he twisted about sidelong to his attacker, his right hand knifing up to catch the club right at the powrie's hand. Tugging down with his left and shoving upward with his right, Cormack gained the angle and tore the club from the dwarf's grasp. He kept the club turning, bringing his right hand right over his left; then he let go with his left as the club came back to horizontal, now directly across his chest.

Cormack gave a grunt and drove his right hand back, stabbing the fat end of the club right into Pragganag's eye with a thunderous crack. The dwarf's head snapped back and he stumbled several steps.

Cormack pursued, spinning the club out far to his right and then driving it hard against the side of the stunned dwarf. Still backpedaling, Pragganag tried to twist and block the blows, but wound up falling right over—to the appreciative howls of Mcwigik and the others.

Cormack went in for the win, thinking to drive the dwarf prostrate and pin him helplessly until he surrendered. Pragganag rolled his shoulder in tight, then burst back out, launching a backhand, and one that Cormack would willingly accept. The man curled only a little, bringing his left arm up to again absorb most of the blow, thinking to come in right behind it with another smash of the club.

But he didn't absorb it.

An explosion of fire ripped through Cormack's arm. He staggered backward, dropping the club and grabbing at his torn skin. He hardly understood what had happened until the dwarf leaped to his feet and faced him directly, the bloody axe swinging easily at the end of his left arm.

"What?" Cormack said, still backing until he fell to his bum in the sand.

Pragganag laughed at him and approached, and Cormack dropped his hands and all pretense of defense—for how with his flesh might he stop the swing of a metal-bladed axe?

"I'm wetting me own cap first!" Pragganag insisted to his fellows, closing the last few steps. He brought his axe up high and stepped in behind the descending blow, driving it down with enough force to sever the man's arm if he had lifted it to block.

And indeed, Cormack did lift his right hand, for when he had dropped his arms down beside him, he had brushed against his small belt pouch. Now he held the lodestone, and he saw the metallic axe head through its magic as clearly as if he were looking at the noontime sun on a cloudless and mistless day. Desperation drove the monk more than any actual thought, and he sent his energy into the gemstone, bringing its magic to an immediate crescendo.

He thought to call the axe head down toward the stone, but instead, again purely on instinct, he let the stone go to its target again. When Cormack opened his hand, the charged lodestone bulleted out with tremendous speed, firing true to the call of the metal axe head.

The sharp report echoed off the stones of Chapel Isle and rolled out to all corners of Mithranidoon. Good fortune was with Cormack, for the gemstone hit the axe as it descended past Pragganag's head, and the force of the blow broke the head from the handle so cleanly that it flew back into the dwarf's ugly face.

The stone flew away—far, far away—and Pragganag staggered back, a crease of blood showing about his cheeks and nose. He tried to stand straighter, growled against the pain and the numbness that was spreading across his stout form.

He was kneeling and didn't know it.

He was lying in the sand and didn't know it.

Cormack grasped his torn arm again and stumbled over to straddle the dwarf. He reached down and pulled the dwarf's beret free, then grabbed a clump of Pragganag's hair and tugged his head up out of the dirt.

"I'm not for knowin' what just happened," Mcwigik said, and he and the others crowded in a bit and seemed none too happy with the sudden reversal of fortune.

"You said I knew the rules," Cormack reminded.

Mcwigik thought it over for a moment, then turned to his fellows and gave a hearty laugh, one that echoed through the dwarf ranks.

And still Pragganag showed no signs of resistance or consciousness, prompting Mcwigik to say in all seriousness, "Do ye mean to kill him to death, then?"

Cormack looked down at the mass of hair and blood, then simply let go, Pragganag's face thumping back into the sand. The man stepped away and a pair of powries went to their fallen comrade, unceremoniously hoisting him to his feet. They gave him a couple of rough shakes and one spat in his face.

"Yach, but what in the dark waters . . . ?" Pragganag sputtered, his words hardly decipherable through his fast-swelling lips.

"What, what?" said Mcwigik. "He popped ye good in the head, ye dope. Put ye down good."

"I'll be paying him back."

"Nah, ye'll be shutting yer mouth and"—Mcwigik paused and moved to the side, scooping Pragganag's beret from the sand—"making yerself another cap."

Pragganag yanked one arm free from the dwarf holding him, and when that fellow tried to grab him again, Pragganag slammed the back of his fist into the dwarf's eye. "No, ye don't!" Pragganag yelled at Mcwigik as the dwarf moved toward Cormack, cap in hand.

"Ye got yer bum beat, and yer cap's the price," said Mcwigik.

"It is all right." Cormack tried to intervene, for what was he to do with a powrie's bloody cap anyway? But Mcwigik wasn't listening.

"The dactyl demon it is!" Pragganag protested, and he tore himself free of the other dwarf holding him, then held that one back with a hateful scowl before advancing on Mcwigik.

"The human keeped his word in coming out, but yerself's not got that honor?" Mcwigik asked.

"Ye ain't to give him me cap!"

"It is all right," said Cormack, but no one was listening.

Mcwigik turned sidelong to the advancing Pragganag and lifted his right arm up high and back, holding the cap away. He brought his left arm in against his torso, defensively, it seemed.

"Ye give it!" Pragganag demanded, and when Mcwigik kept the cap away from his reach, he slugged the dwarf in the face.

His mistake.

For Mcwigik had retrieved something else when he had grabbed up the cap, and his left arm shot across, neck height to Pragganag.

Pragganag started to shout something, but all that came out was a bubbling bloody gurgle, for that sharpened axe head, quietly retrieved by Mcwigik as he walked over, had cut a neat line indeed across poor Prag's throat.

Mcwigik stepped back and calmly presented the beret to Cormack, while Pragganag slumped down to his knees, choking and grasping at his torn windpipe and artery, his blood spraying high.

Cormack went for his pouch and his remaining stone. "I can heal him," he declared, rushing past Mcwigik—or trying to, for the powerful powrie stopped him dead in his tracks with an outstretched arm.

"No, ye can't. Ye can take yer damned cap and dip it in his blood. Then ye can put it on yer head and get ye gone from here. We're done playing, boy, and the next blood what's spilling'll be yer own." He thrust the beret into Cormack's hand. "Dip it!" he ordered in a voice that brooked no argument.

As he stumbled off the beach a few thumping heartbeats later, wet cap in hand, Cormack heard Mcwigik instruct the others—to their relief, apparently, judging from their responses—to take Pragganag's heart.

By the time he reached the small stone archway that led to the main door of the chapel, Cormack heard the now-familiar powrie burial song carried up by the breeze, its strange and somehow gentle intonations and harmony (given the gravelly voices of the singers) mingling with the sound of the waves so that Cormack would not even have known it to be a song had he not heard it before.

CHAPTER 8

To Prove a Point

The five-man craft drifted through the mist with hardly a sound other than the occasional flutter of the single sail in the slight breeze or the splash of water. Androosis sat forward, his long legs hanging over either side of the prow, which angled up high enough so that Androosis's feet remained comfortably high above the water. At eighteen, he was more than ten years younger than the other Alpinadorans on the boat, three weathered helmsmen and the oldest of the group, the shaman Toniquay. No hair remained on Toniquay's head, and his light skin was stretched thin with age and dotted with many brown spots, presenting an imposing appearance indeed, as if he had already gone into the grave and returned. The few teeth remaining in his mouth stuck at awkward angles and shined yellow, and the thin mustache he wore seemed no more than a shadow, depending on the light.

Another man curled against the aft rail, working the rudder and the sails, and the other two sailors sat in the middle of the fifteen-foot craft, just ahead of Toniquay. Each held a paddle across his lap, ready to assist at the command of the navigator.

Long lines stretched out behind the boat, each set with a multitude of hooks. The catch had been thin thus far, with only two rather small silver trout thrashing about in the many buckets in the flat hold between Androosis and the paddlers.

"Too calm a day," said Canrak, the gnarled man working the rudder. Though he was not an old man—in fact, he was the youngest other than Androosis—his face was so wrinkled that it seemed as if someone had piled separate slabs of skin one atop the other in the shape of a head. Add to that a thick black beard that grew in places where it shouldn't and didn't grow in other places where it normally would, and Androosis thought the lean and gangly Canrak possibly the ugliest human being he had ever seen. Quite the opposite of Androosis, who, with his fair skin and yellow hair, had caught the eye of almost every young woman of Yossunfier. Tall and strong, with wide shoulders and a solid frame, Androosis also stood out as one of the more promising young warriors among the tribe, and that fact, he knew, had played no small part in Toniquay's decision to carry him along on these long fishing excursions.

"She is calm and flat this day, but never too much so," Toniquay replied. "Mithranidoon is a blessing, storm or still."

He was replying to Canrak, but Androosis knew that the nasty old shaman had aimed those words his way. Toniquay knew well of Androosis's friendship with Milkeila, and he had led the outrage against her those weeks before when she had dared suggest an expedition to the shores beyond Mithranidoon. Subsequent to Milkeila's bold suggestion, it was no secret that the tribal elders had purposely carved up the tasks to keep the suspected conspirators apart. In fact some of those elders, like Toniquay, had been boasting of their wisdom quite openly. When the five had boarded the boat this morning, Toniquay had whispered to Androosis that "this is where you will learn the truth. Not in the wandering hopes of a young woman frustrated because she has found no willing lover among her peers."

Androosis had let the ridiculous insult to Milkeila pass without response, something that still weighed on his proud shoulders. But he didn't want a fight with Toniquay—certainly not! Because on Yossunfier, there could be no such fight. The structure of Androosis's people, Yan Ossum, was akin to that of all the Alpinadoran tribes. Elders carried great weight and respect, with the older shamans being the top of the hierarchy, second only to the Pennervike, the Great Leader of Yan Ossum, himself.

"Do you believe that we are wasting our time out here, friend Androosis?" Toniquay asked, catching the young man off-guard. He turned to view the smug shaman, and found four sets of eyes staring hard at him.

"A time on Mithranidoon is never wasted, master," Androosis obediently replied, and turned away.

"Well spoken!" Toniquay congratulated, and then in more solemn and dire tones he added, "Do you truly believe that?"

She felt the roiling lava far below her bare feet, but she did not summon it to her this day. For Milkeila had no duties to attend at that time and was utilizing her magical bond with the earth for no better reason than to remind herself of her powers—magical energy considered quite proficient among her shaman peers and elders. The woman needed that reassurance at this time, for she had seen Androosis board the boat with Toniquay that morning. Milkeila was no fool; she understood the significance of Toniquay's unusual trip out to Mithranidoon.

A handful of Milkeila's friends had joined her in shared fantasies of leaving Mithranidoon, a wanderlust sparked by the arrival of the Abellican monks three years earlier. To that point, none of them had even known that a wider world existed beyond the shores of Mithranidoon, not one inhabited by other men, at least.

It had mostly been idle chatter, of course, teenage restlessness. To Milkeila, though, there had run a string of honesty in that chatter. She wanted to see the wider world! Her relationship with Cormack had only strengthened that desire, of course, since it could never be an open marriage here on Mithranidoon—the elders, particularly surly Toniquay, would never allow such a thing!

The six conspirators had let the matter drop for more than a year and had relegated the plan to a far-distant place when Milkeila had surprised them all by reviving it only a couple of months previous.

The young shaman had recognized her mistake almost immediately. She and her friends were all coming of age now, soon to be celebrated as full adult members of Yan Ossum, and youthful fancies had been lost to more serious responsibilities. Milkeila held no doubts that at least one of the six, Pennerdar, had run to the elders with the news, and while the elders had not confronted her directly, she had noticed the extra glances, none favorable, Toniquay often tossed her way. Oh, but he had given her a fine glower that very morning, right before he had summoned Androosis to join him in the fishing.

"Androosis," Milkeila mused aloud. The sound of her own voice broke her concentration and connection to the earth power far below. Of course it was Androosis singled out for Toniquay's special trip onto Mithranidoon, for he alone had shown some interest when Milkeila had suggested a journey to the world beyond the lake.

Milkeila took a deep breath and unconsciously glanced to the southeast, toward Chapel Isle, fully obscured by the mists. With renewed focus the shaman reached deep into the hot powers flowing below the lake. She lifted her hand to fondle the secret gemstone necklace, seeking the added power there. A sense of urgency gripped her; if she could unlock the secrets of the stones, if she could find a way to blend their powers with her own, then perhaps she would find some answers to the questions she knew Toniquay would eventually throw her way.

The power tickled her but would not come true. She could not join the magic as she had joined her soul to Cormack. She spent many minutes straining until she felt the shaman magic flowing through her powerfully, begging for release as if it would simply consume her flesh and blood. At that moment of magical climax, Milkeila reached into the gemstones. . . .

Nothing.

Earth magic burst from her form, a sudden and flashing gout of flame rushing out in a small circle around her. Several leaves curled and crisped, and wisps of smoke rose from the ground in the aftermath.

Milkeila stood there gasping, both physically and emotionally drained. She looked around at the circle of destruction and shook her head, recognizing that it was no more than she could summon at any time. She brought the gemstone necklace to her lips and kissed it, thinking of Cormack, of the promises they had shared. She knew in her heart that they were not so different, these religions of earth and gemstone. And she believed, as Cormack believed, that the greater answers lay in the joining, in the whole.

If ever they could get there.

Milkeila looked back out at the lake, in the direction where Toniquay and Androosis had gone, and her stomach churned with doubts and fear.

A ndroosis turned back to regard the man and started to respond but bit it back, seeing that there was no compromise here, that Toniquay was goading him into open admissions that could be used to further split apart the group of young conspirators. If Androosis answered correctly here, then no doubt Milkeila would feel the weight of that response. If he did not, Toniquay would use it as further proof that the young adults of Yan Ossum were running wild and contrary to the traditions that had kept the people thriving for generations untold.

So Androosis said nothing.

"Tend the lines," Toniquay ordered him, not blinking an eye.

"They've nothing on them," Canrak said from the back, but Toniquay still did not blink.

"Bring them in, then," the old shaman said. "Let us learn if we can waste our time more productively."

Androosis studied Toniquay for a long moment, and still the old and withered man did not blink. Did Toniquay ever blink? Would he die with his eyes wide, and remain like that through eternity under the cold ground?

Androosis moved deliberately, finally, past the sloshing trout and between the oarsmen. He purposely focused on the back of the boat as he passed Toniquay, for he could feel the shaman's eyes boring into him, every step.

Canrak quietly laughed at him, but he ignored the fool—everyone on Yossunfier thought that one a fool—and methodically began hauling in the long lines.

Before they were even aboard, Toniquay motioned for the two men before him to dip their paddles. "Bring us right, half a turn," the shaman ordered Canrak.

Canrak nodded and grabbed the rudder, but paused and looked at Toniquay curiously. "Half right?"

"Half right."

"Yossunfier's left and back."

"Do you think me too stupid to know that?"

"No, elder, but . . ." Canrak stopped and licked his lips. "Half right," he said, and turned the rudder appropriately, which presented an obstacle for Androosis as he hauled the long line to Canrak's right. The young man moved outside the angle of the turned rudder, looking intently at the obviously disturbed Canrak all the while.

"Half right and bring us straight, and open the sail wide to the breeze," Toniquay ordered. "And paddle, the both of you. Strong and straight."

"We are not that deep," Canrak dared say, but if Toniquay even heard him, he didn't show it.

Canrak turned directly to Androosis then and gave a concerned look, but the young man, not nearly as experienced with the ways of Mithranidoon, had no response. He kept hauling, and tossed one or two sour looks back at Toniquay, who had his back to him and paid him no heed at all. This wasn't about fishing, Androosis now fully understood. Toniquay hadn't come out here to secure the day's catch. This trip was about Androosis, wholly, and about the conspiracy of the young adults who so desperately wanted to get off this smothering lake.

Even so, the boat's turn had Androosis surprised, as it had obviously unnerved the other three. Beside Androosis, Canrak licked his lips repeatedly and kept his hand tight on the tiller, obviously anticipating, and hoping for, Toniquay's command to change course yet again.

But the shaman didn't make a move or utter a sound, and the small craft glided through the mist. Canrak's warning that they were "not that deep" echoed in Androosis's thoughts.

A dark form loomed in the water, ahead and to port, a rock, prodding up like a signpost warning intruders.

"Holy Toniquay," Canrak started to say, but was interrupted when the shaman said, "Androosis, to the front."

"The line . . ." Androosis started to reply.

"Leave it, and go forward to watch our depth."

Androosis scrambled past the old shaman and the two paddlers. He stumbled and knocked over one of the buckets, spilling water and a trout onto the flat hold. He started for the fish, but met the disapproving glare of Toniquay as he bent and thought better of it, practically falling all over himself to get back to the prow.

He leaned far over, putting his face near the water, trying to get an angle in the light that would give him the best view to gauge the depth. They weren't that shallow at all, he realized to his relief, though another rock showed off to port, protruding several feet into the air above the water level.

He turned back to report such to Toniquay, and met the shaman's bemused expression, the man pointing past Androosis, dead ahead.

When he looked forward again, Androosis understood—everything. Less than fifty running strides away loomed a dark and foreboding beach, sharply inclined and covered with black, sharp-edged lava rock. Just a short distance up and away from the steaming water, the rock mingled with fingers of ice and snow, creating a stark contrast of white and black, each segment of the mix appearing as hardened as the other. A few scraggly tree skeletons showed among the stones, but they hardly constituted a sign of life, seeming more like a warning, warding away any living thing.

The mist blew across Androosis's field of vision, alternately thick and thin, and in a moment of clarity, he picked out among that desolate landscape a series of caves.

He knew this place for what it was, then, and he spun on Toniquay as if to scream an accusation.

"This is the destination of your dreams," the shaman said. "This is the promise of foolish Milkeila. Look well upon the desolation."

"This is one spot," Androosis sputtered.

"Too close to the trolls," the man paddling to Toniquay's left quietly, almost inaudibly, remarked, and he lifted his paddle from the water and brought it across his lap. His companion did likewise, and both stared at the shaman eagerly, as if in anticipation of an order that would get them fast away from this dangerous place.

"There are many such spots," the shaman retorted, ignoring the paddlers' words, actions, and expressions. "And you would need to stumble upon just one to be slaughtered. Nay, you would not even have to find one to arrive swiftly at your grave, fool. We are not like our mainland kin. We have lost their ways of survival, as our blood has lost its thickness. As it has thinned from the warmth of Blessed Mithranidoon. I warn you now, with this fate clear before you, our patience . . ."

A splash in the water just to the north of their position interrupted Toniquay's rant.

"Glacial troll," Canrak warned, his knuckles white on the tiller, and the two paddlers stared hard at the shaman.

Another splash sounded. As he glanced fast over his shoulder, Androosis thought he caught some motion near the caves.

"Do you understand now, young one?" said Toniquay, trying hard to keep himself calm and collected, obviously. "You think this all a game, a play for excitement."

"Holy Toniquay, we must be gone," Canrak dared say, and the shaman spun about and glowered at him, even lifted a hand as if he meant to strike at the man.

But the paddlers weren't waiting for the order any longer, and by the time the shaman turned back forward, they had already splashed their paddles into the water, the man to the right pulling hard, the one to the left reversing his motion, so that even without Canrak's work on the tiller, they set the boat into a standing turn.

And Canrak did work the tiller to aid them, despite the look from Toniquay. Another splash sounded, then two more in rapid succession. It wasn't about decorum or who was officially in charge. It was about simple survival.

Even the stubborn shaman seemed to understand that, for when he turned back fully, he did not berate the three, but kept his focus squarely on Androosis. "Mark you well the lesson of this day," he warned, waggling a long and bony finger at the man.

The square sail fell limp for a long while as frantic Canrak finished the turn, then went to work on the ropes, but the paddlers fell into a swift and efficient rhythm, and the small boat began to move away from the shore into the safety of the mist. After a few moments they all began to breathe easier.

But then both paddlers jerked suddenly. One nearly went over the side before falling back into the boat, his hands empty, while the other put up a brief tug-of-war, hauling his paddle in with all his strength, so much so that he lifted the top half of the troll clutching the other end right out of the water. The Alpinadoran sailor screamed, but to his credit, he did not let go of the paddle—the precious and vital paddle!

Of course, that didn't help any of them a moment later when a second troll speared out of the water, rising high into the air like a fish leaping for an insect. With tremendous momentum, it climbed up higher than the sailor holding the paddle, and as it descended, it grabbed him by the collar. Before the others in the boat could react, the sailor, the two trolls, and the paddle went over the side.

Androosis started for the spot, but stopped and spun about as another troll lifted into the air before the boat, angled to land on the prow. Androosis timed his heavy punch perfectly, catching the aqua-colored creature square on the jaw as it landed, and before it could gain any traction. The troll's head snapped to the side as the young barbarian followed through with all his weight, driving the creature over the rail and back into the water. It thrashed about on the surface for a heartbeat, then dived down, and Androosis knew it would be back, leaping high once more.

He couldn't wait for that. Behind him, the boat erupted in fighting as one troll after another flew up into the air and crashed down inside the hold.

Canrak and the other sailor flanked Toniquay, who held his hands up before him, his eyes closed as he issued an ancient chant to the barbarian gods. A trio of trolls pressed them hard, clawed hands changing strikes against the small knife of the paddler, and the gaff hook Canrak had collected before coming forward.

Androosis rushed back to join his companions, scooping up a water-filled bucket as he passed. He threw that bucket into the face of the nearest troll, who stumbled backward, and then Androosis closed fast to hit the beast with a left hook, smashing his hand against its chest and driving it over the rail. The creature grabbed at him desperately as it fell back, and caught Androosis's strong arm with both its hands. It couldn't get enough of a grip to resist the throw, but it did manage to hook its clawlike fingernails under the skin of Androosis's outer forearm, and that skin peeled down as the troll fell away.

Androosis clutched at his bleeding forearm, but only momentarily as another troll leaped aboard. He met it with a heavy punch, but this one swung as well, and it carried a club. Fist and weapon came together hard, the barbarian's knuckles shattering under the weight of the blow. He howled and retracted the hand, but went forward instinctively, lowering his shoulder to bowl into the creature before it could strike again with the club.

He and the troll tumbled to the deck, Androosis rolling fully atop the diminutive creature, freeing up his left hand for punch after punch, trying to get his hand past the troll's flailing arms.

Toniquay tried hard to shut out the tumult around him and concentrate on his spellcasting. He called upon the ancient gods of his people, upon Drawmir of the North Wind, gathering the offered power in his hands as he put them up over his head and began moving them harmoniously in a circle. He opened his eyes when Canrak cried out in pain, and saw a spear stabbing through the navigator's shoulder—and saw, too, yet another troll leaping high out of the water to the side of the boat. Its trajectory would have brought it crashing against Toniquay, but he reacted by thrusting his hands out in the troll's direction, throwing forth the gathered wind.

The flying troll looked like it had been flung by a sling, suddenly reversing direction and spinning back out over the water. It landed awkwardly, with a great splash. Toniquay paid it no more heed, turning his attention to the more immediate fighting, and to the sail.

The sail.

The shaman worked his hands again, more quickly and less powerfully this time, and filled the sail with a conjured gust of wind, swiftly driving the boat out toward the deeper water.

He did it again, and a third time, but then he went flying forward as a troll sprang onto his back, clawing at his face and bearing him down to the deck.

Androosis finally got a punch cleanly through, smashing the troll's face, and the back of its head cracked hard against the wooden deck. Clearly dazed, the creature slowed momentarily, enough for Androosis to set his broken hand below him and lift himself up. He reached back behind him with his free left hand, then let himself fall as he thrust out below him, throwing all of his weight behind the punch.

The troll's long and crooked nose shattered under the weight of the blow, and the creature again cracked its skull against the boat's decking.

Androosis rolled off, seeing that the creature was finished, and, now nursing two injured hands, stubbornly regained his footing.

Canrak was down, the troll above him stabbing repeatedly with its crude spear. The poor tiller flailed and blocked, both his arms torn and shredded, blood covering him. More blood than Androosis had ever seen. More blood than Androosis would have ever believed possible from one skinny man.

He shook off the shock and charged back, kicking the troll off Toniquay as he passed. He stumbled as he went under the sail, but didn't let that slow him as he threw himself at the spear-wielder.

Forgetting his more serious wound, he slapped a backhand with his right, trying to grab the weapon's shaft, but a wave of agony assailed him and he couldn't hang on. That cost him dearly as he came against the creature in his successful tackle, for it managed to extract the spear and angle it so that it caught Androosis on the right hip and drove down.

Fires of pain exploded all along that hip and down his leg, but again he ignored them, forcing himself to understand the consequences of failure here. He bore the troll to the deck and went into a frenzy, battering it with his hands and arms, driving his knee against it hard. He took as many hits as he gave, and the troll even lurched upward, trying to bite him.

Androosis merely tucked his chin in low and drove his forehead right at that biting mouth. He cut himself open on the troll's sharp teeth, but he smashed the creature into oblivion in the process.

Toniquay's cry startled him and turned him shakily about, just in time to see the troll he had kicked leap up against the sail, thrashing at it with clawed hands. Toniquay came in fast behind.

Too fast, for as he collided against the troll, it thrust forward and the shaman could not halt his momentum. Both he and the troll went through the sail, tearing the fabric as they went. They hit the deck hard and rolled apart, and the troll sprang up and rushed to the side, right over the side, taking with it the bulk of the sail!

Androosis and Toniquay exchanged horrified looks, and both started for the side rail, until the cry of the remaining paddler turned them back toward the prow, where the poor man was being hauled by a pair of trolls.

Toniquay turned fast and began waving his arms to summon his magic. But then he lurched and doubled over and grasped at the spear that had hit him in the gut.

Androosis staggered past him, but knew he would not get to his companion in time, and he could only gasp and look on helplessly as the two trolls and the Alpinadoran rolled over the prow and disappeared under the water.

Behind Androosis came another splash, and he turned to see that the troll he had smashed had also gone over. He slumped down next to Toniquay, saw the spear embedded in the shaman's gut, and had no idea of how he might help the man.

A sudden jerk on the boat had him back to his knees, looking aft with concern at the long line he hadn't completely brought in. He crawled to it and peered out, to see the paddler bobbing along behind them, apparently caught in the hooks. Androosis grabbed the line and began hauling the man toward him, but he knew before he got the poor man against the taffrail of the boat that he was too late. He grabbed the man by the shirt and half hauled him over, but as the man's head lolled back, Androosis stared into wide-open, lifeless eyes.

Horrified and gagging on bile, Androosis dragged the man up higher on the rail. But he lost his grip and fell backward onto the deck and lay staring up at the sky. Beside him, Canrak whimpered pitifully, and amidships, near the mast and torn scraps of sail, Toniquay growled and grunted.

Androosis felt consciousness slipping away. He fought against it and lifted his head to regard the man half hanging over the back of the battered boat. He tried to reach out and grab the man, but he found that he could not, found that he was inexorably sinking backward to the deck.

He stared up at the sky, but he saw only blackness.

PART TWO

The Long Road Unbidden

*P*erhaps it is because in order to simply survive I had to remain so much more in tune with the workings of my body, or perhaps it was my Jhesta Tu training, but whatever the reason, I find that I am more apt than the average person to understand the subtle clues offered to me by my unconscious soul. So many things we reveal to ourselves without ever realizing them!

The lightness of my step when I departed Palmaristown, for example, whether in the guise of the Stork or in that of the Highwayman, buoyed me; I felt as if I could leap a hundred feet off the ground. With the road straight before me to Chapel Abelle, the hopes of seeing this man, my father, Bran Dynard, filtered throughout my being and lifted my spirit.

Consciously, I wasn't even thinking about such things. Consciously, I told myself, berated myself, that this entire journey was no more than procrastination. The real road was south and east, but I was—deliberately—a long way from there.

But despite my pangs of guilt, I felt that buoyancy clearly and acutely, a sense of excitement, and not just because I had successfully deflected and delayed facing my deepest fears. Nay, on this road to the mother church of the Abellican Order, I felt as if I was moving forward on my journey, as if I was taking a very important and exciting stride.

I wondered if I was betraying Garibond, my beloved father-in-practice, who had raised me and tolerated my infirmities without complaint, who had loved me without condition and without embarrassment. My road seemed to be leading me to the man who had sired me, and my road was walked with eagerness, so what did that reflect upon Garibond and his sacrifices?

And what did I really expect from this man, Bran Dynard?

And why hadn't he come back for me? More than two decades had transpired since his departure from Pryd Town, and he had not returned for Sen Wi or for his child.

As I ponder these many angles, my mind jumbles and shakes and darts in directions unasked for. And to all of them, I have no true answers, I recognize, for I will not know how I feel about Bran Dynard until I have met him. I will not know his answers to my concerns until he has explained them. I will not know the effect upon the legacy of Garibond until long has passed, I am sure.

Indeed, that is the most unanswerable question of all, because the truth is clear and yet clouded by guilt, that most opaque of veils. I loved and still love Garibond with all my heart and soul. I would throw myself upon a pyre of flames to save him, without hesitation! I would do anything, anything at all, to have him back.

Of my sire, I am less certain. Of Bran Dynard, I have only expectations with which to guide my preconceptions.

Well, only those and the Book of Jhest, the tome he penned—or copied, at least. For the contents were such that no one without understanding of the book could properly relay its subtle shades. Perhaps that book remains the paradox of my inner conflict, the source of both excitement and trepidation.

For I would desperately desire to meet the man who penned that book, that marvelous tome which freed me from my abject helplessness, even if he had no connection to me in blood or otherwise, other than the connection I feel in my heart to that which he wrote. On this level alone, I am truly comfortable with my journey.

How could it be otherwise? I desire to meet the man who penned the wondrous book as I desire to meet the mystics of Behr who live the lessons of that book in their daily existence. And this journey is even safer than that, for whatever the outcome of my meeting with Bran Dynard, the Walk of Clouds remains. Hope remains.

Is this then a comfortable step for me? For all of my other fears regarding this stranger, I hold few or no familial expectations, so I suspect that I cannot be disappointed in that manner, and whatever philosophy Bran Dynard may express now, or whatever he might offer or not offer to further my recovery, he has already given so much to me that I cannot hold any anger against him.

Or maybe I do. Perhaps my anger at his refusal or inability to return to Sen Wi and to me will prove a stronger angst than I anticipate, a thorn more deeply embedded in my heart than I now understand.

And so with a resigned sigh, I must admit it may be that the only real comfort of this journey is that it allows me to put off the even more terrifying march to the Walk of Clouds.

—BRANSEN GARIBOND

CHAPTER 9

Work Brings Freedom

Dawson McKeege stood at the prow of his two-masted coast-runner, *Lady Dreamer,* taking in the grand oceanic and coastline view that never grew old for him. For before the craft loomed a three-hundred-foot cliff facing, mighty stone all brown and gray, and atop it, as if growing right out of the rock, stood Chapel Abelle, the heart of the growing, influential Church.

This was the spot where Blessed Abelle had first demonstrated the power of the God-given gemstones. This was the spot where—on guidance from God, it was said—he had learned to make permanent the magical properties of those rocks he had found after being shipwrecked on a distant island in the deep southern Mirianic Ocean. Alone and as removed from civilization as any man had ever been, Abelle had had little expectation of surviving, and seemingly no chance of ever returning to Honce.

But the magical stones had showered down from the heavens, the gifts of God to him, and as he had sorted through their magical properties, this young philosopher had come to understand them fully.

With those stones, Abelle had walked hundreds of miles across the ocean, so it was said, and through the power and potential of the gemstone magic, he had changed the world.

Dawson wasn't yet formally confirmed as an Abellican. He had been raised in Vanguard among a thriving farming and hunting community dominated by the Samhaists, and the old ways died hard. Still, he couldn't deny the spirituality he felt whenever this sight, Chapel Abelle, so impressive and growing grander by the day, came into view.

Hidden among the cliffs was a dock facility, with tunnels that climbed through the stone all the way to the chapel above—tunnels reputedly cut by Abelle himself utilizing a variety of potent gemstones.

"Hail to the flag of Dame Gwydre!" came a shout from the docks as *Lady*

Dreamer edged in around the jagged rocks. A pair of monks stood in open view, waving at the approaching ship. Dawson recognized one as Brother Pinower and returned the wave with a familiarity and heartiness reminding him that the relationship between Gwydre and this Church had grown so very strong.

Of course, that very fact had led to the current war in Vanguard, and Dawson couldn't help but grimace as he considered his former spiritual leaders, the Samhaists, now striking so violently and with such vile foot soldiers as goblins and glacial trolls. Never had the man imagined that the supposedly wise priests who had guided his people, as brutal as their customs often were, could so betray their people as to enlist the aid of such wretched creatures.

"Weapons, metals, or foodstuffs?" Brother Pinower asked as McKeege's ship pulled up alongside the longest of the three wharves and tenders hopped to the dock to begin securing her. "You will be hard pressed to get any, of course, in this dastardly time."

"Lairds Ethelbert and Delaval continue their war, then?" Dawson asked, hopping down easily to the planks beside the Abellicans.

"'Escalate' would be a better word," Pinower replied. "Laird Delaval believed he'd gained an advantage, and so he strengthened his line across the breadth of it, thinking to push Ethelbert right into the sea."

"But it wasn't to be," said the second monk. "Ethelbert's got a few tricks left."

"Aye, and a few allies from Behr," Brother Pinower agreed.

"A laird of Honce is using the desert savages?" Dawson McKeege asked, shaking his head, feeling at that moment pretty much the same about Ethelbert as he felt about the Vanguard Samhaists.

"Desperate folk take desperate measures," Brother Pinower added, and all three nodded.

"I've a hold full of caribou moss," Dawson explained, referring to the white moss that climbed knee-deep in regions of Vanguard and was favored for packing open wounds, among its many other uses. In a time of war that particular purpose of the fungus would take precedence, obviously, but extract of dried caribou moss could also be brewed into a medicinal tea, and sheets of the moss often sold at exorbitant prices as roofing or siding material, both practical and decorative, for the fancy homes of wealthy merchants. Vanguard had many profitable trading goods to offer Honce proper, but in this time of war, none was more sought after than the caribou moss.

"The lairds will pay well for it," Brother Pinower admitted.

"They will pay Chapel Abelle well, then," Dawson explained. "For I've no time to cart my wares southeast or southwest, and my boat's back to Vanguard when she puts out from your dock, presently, unless I am forced to make a detour to Palmaristown."

"We have some goods, of course," said Brother Pinower. "And some coin."

"Some? The whispers say that your Church grows wealthy on the tributes of warring lords."

"Whispers," Brother Pinower replied with an exaggerated sigh. He ended with a smile as wide as the one Dawson offered in response.

"Come," Brother Pinower bade him, leading him off the wharf and to the gated entrance and the winding tunnels that would carry them up to the cliff top and the mother chapel of the Abellican Church.

As soon as he exited that dock tunnel into the courtyard of the abbey, McKeege understood those whispers of growing wealth to be understated. For Chapel Abelle was more than twice the size it had been on his last visit only a year before. Scores of laborers worked the grounds, extending and thickening the already impressive outer wall and constructing new stone structures—barracks and rectories and all manner of buildings. Chapel Abelle had become a town unto itself, McKeege realized, and when he thought about it, it made sense. Once Chapel Abelle had been a small church set on a hill above the medium-sized town of Weatherguard, but in this time of pressing danger, it had become a fortress, a welcomed one for the beleaguered folk of the region.

Dawson looked to the main church, which was now surrounded by scaffolding, monks swarming every region of it with tools and materials. No laymen worked this all-important building, he noted. Its construction remained for the brothers alone.

"Father Artolivan will be pleased to greet you this day," Brother Pinower assured him, hustling him toward the church entrance. "It would help if I could introduce you with your intent."

Dawson looked from the church to the eager brother, who was at least fifteen years his junior, with skin too soft and white and eyes tired already from endless hours spent huddled over parchments. Dawson figured that Pinower rarely ventured outside of Chapel Abelle, other than when he was stationed at the docks, or at work on the abbey, perhaps. The Vanguardsman wished that he had more time, then, so that he could sneak the young man away from his stuffy brethren and put on a good drunk and a better woman.

"Tell the good father that I come with value and leave with purpose, for Vanguard's in need of . . ." He paused there and let the thought hang in the air between them. Indeed, it seemed as if poor Brother Pinower would fall right over from leaning so obviously toward McKeege.

Dawson merely grinned, intensifying the tease.

Soon after, Dawson stood before Father Artolivan, an old friend of Dame Gwydre, who had secretly offered his blessing to her union with Brother Alandrais.

"I've come under full sail," the Vanguardsman said, "and will leave the same way."

"Always in a hurry," the old father of the Abellican Church replied, his voice a bit slurred as if he had partaken too liberally of the bottle.

It was just age, though, and indeed, Artolivan looked every day of his eighty years. Skin sagged about his face, and his eyes had sunk deeply, circled by darkness. He could still sit straight, but not without great effort, Dawson noted, and there remained little sparkle and sharpness in his gaze. The Abellicans wouldn't easily replace him, though. Artolivan, it was whispered, had once glimpsed Blessed Abelle (though he would have been but a young boy), and had been trained by men who had learned directly from the great man. He was the last of his generation in the Church, the last man alive known to hold direct ties to Blessed Abelle and the momentous events of that magical and inspiring time.

"That is the way of the world, I fear," the old priest went on. "None have time to give pause. Patient consideration is a thing of the lost past."

"War breeds urgency, Father," said Dawson.

"And what is your urgency?"

"I've a hold of caribou moss and no time to barter."

"So I've been told—of both situations. You seek coin, then, so name your initial offer."

"I seek coin only to use it for another good," Dawson explained, and that piqued Artolivan's curiosity, it seemed, as the old man cocked his head to the side. "I will use the coin—and have brought much of my own, as well—to bribe."

"You have come for able bodies?"

Dawson nodded.

"To harvest? To log? As wives or as laborers?"

"Yes," Dawson replied. "All of that. Vanguard is sorely pressed by the Samhaists. Dame Gwydre has victory at hand," he quickly added and lied when he saw old Artolivan's face crinkle with doubt.

"We are all sorely pressed, friend Dawson. War rages the breadth of Honce."

"Yet I see Chapel Abelle swarmed by laborers, many young men who have apparently escaped the fighting."

"Many who were captured and thus put out of the fight on honor," Father Artolivan explained.

"From both camps, no doubt," said Dawson, and Artolivan nodded and smiled. It made sense, of course, for neither Laird Ethelbert nor Laird Delaval had the time or resources to expend on prisoners of the conflict. Neither wanted to enrage the populace by summarily executing captives (many of whom were likely related to constituents and soldiers on both sides of the conflict). So the respective lairds would demand a vow of honorable capitulation, effectively ensuring that the captured soldiers would not return to their former ranks, and then send them here to the Abellicans, to gain the favor of the priests who held the sacred stones. Of course, both leaders, for fear of making honorable capitulation attractive, required the Abellicans to work their laborers brutally, and reward them not at all.

Perhaps there was a winner to be found in the war, after all, Dawson thought as he looked upon the grinning father.

Dawson's own smile didn't hold, though, as he considered the differences in the struggle that faced Dame Gwydre in the North, as he considered the scene of Tethmawle. Ethelbert and Delaval, both posturing to rule the holdings of Honce, offered quarter to the unfortunate soldiers of the other side.

That was not the case in Vanguard's war.

"I had not heard that the Samhaists were near defeat in Vanguard," the wily old Abellican father remarked. "Quite the opposite."

"They have called upon goblins and trolls to strengthen their lines," Dawson replied. "We are sorely pressed. Yet victory is at hand."

"That seems a rather strange interpretation. Three sentences, spoken one following the other as if the logic of them flowed as such."

"Their line cannot hold," Dawson explained. "If Dame Gwydre can counter their latest excursions with a forcible strike, the mishmash of warriors our enemies the Samhaists have assembled will turn upon each other. We have seen it in several regions already. Dame Gwydre is certain that a sudden and—"

Father Artolivan held up his hand to stop the man. "The details of war bore me," he said. "From this church, you will be paid in coin alone—at fair value, given the need for caribou moss at this time."

"Both armies will value it greatly," said Dawson.

Artolivan didn't even try to argue. "What you do with that coin is for you to decide," the priest went on. "The workers here are not free men, but they are many—indeed, perhaps too many. If some choose to sail with you back to Vanguard, you and I, nay, you and Brother Pinower, will reach a proper sale price."

Dawson grinned and nodded and dared to hope that he could fill his hold with able bodies in short order.

Aw, but he come through with a parade and all," exclaimed the excited middle-aged woman who looked much older than that. "Was as grand a spectacle as Oi've e'er seen, do you not think?"

Cadayle nodded politely and let her continue, and she did, for more than an hour, recounting the celebration on the day that Brother Bran Dynard passed through this unremarkable hamlet of Winterstorm.

Bransen and Callen leaned against the front wall of the single-room cottage. Despite his reservations, Bransen continued to listen, but Callen had long ago obviously dismissed the woman's rambling as a desperate attempt to garner some reward—even if it was just the satisfaction of having an audience for her chatter and gossip.

"Was the last we seen o' him, that brother, do you not think?" the old woman said, offering a dramatic upturn in her inflection that startled even the daydreaming Callen. "And so he went, and so goes the world."

"To Chapel Abelle?" Cadayle asked.

The woman shrugged, and when that resulted in a disappointed responding expression, the woman brightened suddenly and nodded too eagerly.

"You'll be staying to break the bread?" she asked. "I've a bit o' porridge, too, and stew from a lamb killed only a week ago and not yet holed by the worms."

Cadayle turned to her companions, who offered postures and expressions perfectly indifferent.

"Yes, a meal would do us well as we continue on our way," she said to the woman, who beamed a toothless smile back at her, then hustled out of the house to gather ingredients and utensils.

"She had no idea that such a man as Bran Dynard ever existed," Callen said when she had gone.

"Do not underestimate the memories of villagers," Bransen cautioned.

"The imagination, you mean," Callen replied. "Their life is tedium, year to year to year. We've brought them something they sorely need: excitement."

"A war rages within a few days' march," Bransen reminded.

"Diversion, then," said Callen.

Bransen looked to Cadayle for some support here, but all she could offer was a shrug. He accepted that as he had to accept the simple truth of it all. They had covered many miles from Palmaristown, walking a road strewn with hamlets very much the same as Winterstorm, a cluster of farmhouses and perhaps a tradesman's shop or two encircling a common hall. Now with more than half the distance between Palmaristown and Chapel Abelle behind them, Bransen had hoped that the answers to questions about lost Bran Dynard would become more relevant and with answers beginning to flow more openly, but alas, the song remained the same. While some, like this woman, would weave elaborate tales, the quantity of words did little to enhance the quality. Hope had turned to dust in the first few minutes of an hour-long, creative recollection that was at least ten parts poetic license to one part memory. In truth, for all of their inquiries, the trio had garnered nothing at all about Bran Dynard's journey to Chapel Abelle those twenty years ago.

But Bransen wouldn't let his hopes die, for when he considered the truth of his quest he recognized that he should have expected nothing more than that which he had found. Indeed, the hospitality the trio had been granted along this road had made the journey not so unpleasant. His answers, if they were to be found, would almost certainly come from Chapel Abelle itself.

"Chapel Abelle," he said to Callen. She smiled and put a gentle hand on his shoulder. "Soon."

Three," a disgruntled Dawson told Pinower. "They are slaves here, and yet they view what I have to offer as less than even that!"

"I might have expected a few more," the brother replied. "But truly, they have seen the battlefield—many have felt the bite of cold iron. We work them hard, but here they know they will outlive the war. You offer them more war."

"I offer them freedom!"

Brother Pinower chuckled at that. "Vanguard is at war. Everyone here knows that truth."

"The path I offer leads to freedom with land and standing."

"Or to the belly of a goblin. They have been known to eat their captives and enemy dead."

Dawson gave a sigh of surrender.

"Three?" Brother Pinower asked, his tone becoming suddenly hopeful. "Three more than when you arrived. And you can rest easy that Father Artolivan will not allow you to return with only that."

"He will send monks?"

"No, no, of course not, for we have none to spare," Brother Pinower answered. "Not in these times. But there are gemstones that might serve the brothers of Chapel Pellinor . . ."

"Chapel Pellinor has fallen," said Dawson.

"A temporary situation, we are confident. Already the newest rumors from the northland speak of cleanup and rebuilding, with renewed vigor and determination. And many of the brothers of Pellinor remain alive. We will bolster their ranks—your ranks—with gemstones and other supplies. I have already spoken to Father Artolivan about this, and he has given me all assurances."

Dawson nodded. "Dame Gwydre will appreciate such support. But I've a hold to fill with able men, and only three have thus far agreed—and agreed for more coin than I intended to offer. I need fifty, Brother, to make my journey here worth the time and expense of Dame Gwydre, even with your generous offer of gemstones and other supplies. We are in short supply of bodies only."

"Patience, then," said Brother Pinower. "The battles across Honce rage, and more workers come in every week. Perhaps I can speak to Brother Shinnigord, who directs the workers, to more freely use the whip, that your offer sounds a bit more enticing."

"That would be appreciated," Dawson said, and gave a bow.

Brother Pinower shrugged as if it was nothing. "We have too many workers at present," he said. "And more arriving, an endless stream. Perhaps Father Artolivan can be persuaded to address your concerns to lairds Ethelbert and Delaval, to enact an agreement that would allow us to sail any excess direct to Dame Gwydre."

"Now that, Brother, would serve Vanguard well, indeed," Dawson replied, and nearly choked, so fast did he try to get the words out of his mouth.

It was an offer he dearly wanted to pursue, but some commotion to the side turned the both of them toward the door to the chapel proper, where a young brother came forth along with a pair of the more senior monks of Chapel Abelle.

"Brother Fatuus of Palmaristown," Brother Pinower explained to Dawson. "He rode in hard this day with urgent news for Father Artolivan."

"News that would interest me and my cause?"

Brother Pinower shrugged and promised to return presently, and Dawson went back to the work groups to continue his offers. "Three," he muttered as he walked across the open courtyard, and he shuddered to think of the tongue-lashing Dame Gwydre would give him if he returned with such meager reinforcements as that!

CHAPTER 10

Gaoler's Price

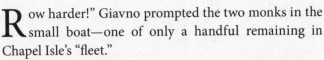

"Row harder!" Giavno prompted the two monks in the small boat—one of only a handful remaining in Chapel Isle's "fleet."

"Are we chasing ghosts?" one of the men dared ask.

"I saw it, I tell you!" Giavno insisted. "In the mist, drifting."

"Drifting? Or laying in wait?" asked the oarsman.

"Her mast was down," Giavno insisted. "Is down!" he cried, pointing ahead through the filmy gray steam. They all saw the boat, then, bobbing, mainsail torn down and with the craft apparently abandoned. "A prize for us to take back to Chapel Isle."

He looked back at the other two, grinning from ear to ear and certain that Father De Guilbe and the rest of his brethren would be quite pleased with today's catch, particularly since the monks had been forced to take men from their work on the chapel that they could construct more boats. When he turned forward again, though, his smile disappeared, for as they neared, the angle allowed him to see over the side of the craft, and it was anything but abandoned.

Giavno tried to tell the oarsmen to move more quickly, but all that came out of him was a gurgle. He did manage to wave his hand, at least, urging them on, and the paddling men brought the boat in swiftly.

Then they, too, gasped.

Three Alpinadoran tribesmen lay on the deck—the blood-soaked deck. Covered in blood, obviously much of it their own, the three did not react at all as the boats bumped, leading Giavno and his companions to believe that they were already dead.

"They must have ventured too near the glacial trolls," one of the oarsmen said. "We aren't far from the northwestern bank." He stood up as he spoke and stretched to grab the other boat with both hands, hooking his feet as he did to serve as a living grapnel. The other oarsman helped Giavno get across.

"Alive," the senior brother said as he bent low over the nearest Alpinadoran, a blond-haired and sturdy giant of a man. He fumbled with his pouch, producing a soul stone, and began praying over the man immediately.

A second monk came over as well, moving to the other injured Alpinadorans. "Alive, both of them," he announced in short order. "But not for long had we not found them, and might not be for long in any case!"

Giavno shortened his healing on the youngest man and moved to the others in turn, casting a minimal amount of healing energy into each to stabilize them and at least stop the more obvious bleeding. He didn't even have to tell his companions their role here as they tied off the drifting Alpinadoran craft to their own and went back to their paddles. They pulled with all speed, towing Giavno and the captured boat straight back to Chapel Isle.

The sound of voices gradually brought Androosis back to the world of the living.

"We are not animals," he heard Toniquay say from somewhere to the side—which side he couldn't be sure.

"Nor do we consider you such," came the reply in the accent of a Southerner whose first language was not Errchuk, the predominant tongue of Alpinador.

Androosis heard a rattle, maybe of bones, maybe of chains.

"There are practical considerations," said the Southerner.

Androosis opened his eyes. It took a long while for the grayness to slip aside and let light into his aching head. He saw a monk standing before him—of course, it had to be a monk. He was in a small room, a dungeon of sorts, smelling of torch smoke and lit only in the sporadic shadows of dancing flames. He was lying down on his side on a hard and damp bed of dirt, and a blanket covered him from waist to feet. He tried to turn onto his back to better view the monk and Toniquay, but the movement shot stabbing pains into him, and he grimaced and settled back onto his side.

"I am chained like a dog!" Toniquay said with a growl.

"It is our only means of securing you for our sake and your own," replied the monk, whom Androosis now recognized as Brother Giavno. Hope rose in the miserable barbarian when he noted another form behind Giavno and recognized it as Cormack.

Cormack would free him, he believed. Cormack was a secret friend.

"Rest and heal," Brother Giavno said. "Be at ease. We will negotiate with your clan to get you out of here as soon as possible."

"At once!" Toniquay retorted. "You have no right—"

"If I had not found you on the lake you would be dead," Giavno shot right back. "As would your companions. I could have left you there for the trolls, yes?"

Androosis couldn't see Toniquay from his angle, but he could well picture the man exhaling.

"I do not ask for your gratitude," Giavno went on. "But I will have your obedience. You—all three—remain in need of our healing stones."

"Do not use them on me!" Toniquay cried.

"If we had not then you would be dead."

"Better that!"

Giavno backed away a step and produced a rather wicked smile that seemed all the more nefarious because of the flickering orange light. "Very well," he agreed.

"Or on them," said Toniquay.

"Without the gemstones the man you call Canrak will die," said Giavno.

"If that is the will of our gods," Toniquay replied, seeming not at all concerned.

How Androosis wished that he could roll over and slap the prideful shaman!

Giavno gave a little chuckle.

"If you would unshackle my hand I could tend him," Toniquay said.

"But we will not."

Androosis gulped at the finality of that statement, made all the more clear as Giavno turned away and stooped to get under the low arch exiting the room, sweeping Cormack up in his wake.

"Hold firm, kin and clan," Toniquay said, reciting the mantra of Clan Snowfall. "We go with certainty."

Androosis heard a weak reply that seemed more of a whimper from farther across the way. His own grunt might have satisfied Toniquay's needs, but it was hardly one of assent.

There was nothing shy and retiring about Father De Guilbe. The road had been hard on him, harder still when he had to come to terms with the failure, or at least the sidetrack, of his important mission to proselytize the northland. But he had been chosen—indeed, had been promoted to father—as much because of his powerful temperament and physical attributes as any of his work on the tomes of Abelle or the philosophy of the church. Cambelian De Guilbe stood well over six feet tall, and even with the sparse diet of fish and plants the brothers realized on Mithranidoon he had retained much of his three-hundred-pound frame. It was said that he couldn't sing like an angel but surely could roar like a dragon. It was in precisely that voice that he ordered the bickering brothers Giavno and Cormack into his quarters, which encompassed the entirety of the highest finished floor of the chapel.

De Guilbe came out around his desk as the pair entered, motioning for them to shut the door. "Your doubts incite trepidation and fear in your brethren," he said, leaning forward as he spoke, a movement that wilted many a strong man.

"All respect, Father," said Giavno, "but there is no doubt. Brother Cormack is wrong and out of place."

Father De Guilbe's heavy eyes swayed to take in the younger brother.

"I object," Cormack said, trying hard to keep the tremor out of his voice.

"To?"

"His heart is too meek for the obvious and important task before us," Brother Giavno insisted, but Father De Guilbe held up his hand to silence the man and never took his scrutinizing gaze off Cormack.

"They are in the damp mud," Cormack said, and the way he blurted it showed that he was scrambling here to put his discordant emotions into substance and complaint.

"We live on a damp and dirty island, Brother," Father De Guilbe reminded.

"The dungeon is the least hospitable room."

"And the only secure one."

Cormack sighed and lowered his gaze.

"He would accept their repaired boat as a proper chamber for our guests," said Giavno. "Push them off the beach and send them on their way."

"Morality demands—" Cormack began.

"We healed them!" Giavno sternly cut in. Both he and Cormack looked to Father De Guilbe, noting that the man wasn't about to intervene this time, and indeed, was through that very silence inviting Giavno to continue with the scolding.

"The powers of God, through the gemstones, through the wisdom of Blessed Abelle, are the only reason the three barbarians continue to draw breath. We did that, working tirelessly from the moment I tied their broken boat to my own."

"A charitable act worthy of the Church of Blessed Abelle," Cormack interjected, and Brother Giavno glowered at him.

"He forgets why we were sent to Alpinador," Giavno said to Father De Guilbe. "He has lost purpose of our mission under the fondness he has developed for our barbarian neighbors." He paused and stared even harder at Cormack. "And our powrie neighbors," he added.

Cormack snapped a look at the man.

"Place it on your head, Brother," Giavno bade him. Cormack's expression shifted from anger to outright fear as he looked back to Father De Guilbe.

"Oh, do," said Giavno. "Everyone knows you have it with you, that you wear it whenever you believe no one is watching."

When Cormack studied Father De Guilbe he saw no concession there, just full agreement with Giavno's observations, and indeed, with his request. Hand trembling, the young brother reached behind and into the small pouch he kept on his back, secured to his robe's rope belt. He brought forth the powrie beret, the bloody cap.

Father De Guilbe motioned for him to continue, to put it on.

Cormack did, shifting it so that its band was tilted just a bit across his forehead, down to the right, where the top bulge of the beret flopped over.

Father De Guilbe chuckled, but it seemed more in pity than amusement.

"Why would you wear such a thing, fairly won or not?" Giavno asked.

"There is magic about it," said Cormack, and both of his listeners widened their eyes in surprise, and horror.

"When I wear it upon my head, I feel a greater sturdiness within my body," Cormack tried to explain. "This cap might show us why powries can accept such a beating and continue to fight."

"You wear it to understand our enemies," said Father De Guilbe.

Cormack started to agree and for a moment was truly relieved to be able to. But he stopped himself short, not willing to go so far in accepting that description of the powries—not after they had treated him so fairly and honorably.

"I wear it to expand my understanding of our neighbors," Cormack conceded, but he breathed easier when that seemed to satisfy Father De Guilbe.

"Keep wearing it, then," the father ordered. "In fact, you will face consequences if I see you without it."

Beside Cormack, Giavno snickered, and only then did Cormack realize that these two saw De Guilbe's order as a form of punishment in and of itself, a way to brand and isolate Cormack in the eyes of all the men on Chapel Isle.

"Let us return to the issue at hand," said De Guilbe. "These three barbarians owe their lives to us, would you not agree, Brother Cormack?"

Cormack searched about frantically for a way to dodge the obvious answer, but had to concede simply, "Yes."

"And they were healed through the powers shown to us by Blessed Abelle?"

"Yes, Father."

"Then their debt is beyond our magnanimity, of course."

Cormack replied with a puzzled expression.

"Their debt is not to Brother Giavno—or perhaps it is to a smaller extent," Father De Guilbe explained. "The gaoler's price—and we are not the gaoler, but merely the guards, is owed to Blessed Abelle and to God above him."

Cormack didn't like the way Father De Guilbe was framing the issue, but of course there was no way for him to disagree with the simple logic. "Yes, Father."

"Then the charity you desire is not ours to give," reasoned De Guilbe. "It is for God to determine, and fortunately, we are shown in the teachings of Blessed Abelle how such charity is to be bestowed. These three are prisoners of a higher power, who demands of them fealty. Absent that fealty, God would never have given us the blessed power to heal their mortal wounds—wounds, I remind you, which were wrought of no actions on our part."

"The price was not known to them," Cormack weakly argued.

"They were in no position to negotiate," Father De Guilbe replied. "And there was none to be had in any case. We were sent to Alpinador to show the light of God, and no man beyond Blessed Abelle himself has ever seen it more intimately than the three barbarians for whom you advocate. The truth has been shown to them, the light shines before their eyes."

"But—"

"If they refuse to see it, then they shall remain in the dark, Brother Cormack," Father De Guilbe said with complete finality. "Figuratively and literally."

Cormack could feel Giavno glowing smugly beside him.

"We will not mistreat them," De Guilbe said, turning to Giavno.

"Of course not, Father," the senior brother assured him.

"But our security demands their location, and there they will stay."

"For how long?" Cormack dared to ask.

"Until they dare to stare at the light, or until they are called to the afterlife, where they will see with it the folly of their stubbornness. We are agreed on that, I am sure."

Cormack lowered his gaze again. "Yes, Father De Guilbe," he said.

De Guilbe released them with a wave. Cormack instinctively reached up to the powrie beret.

"Wear it!" Father De Guilbe snapped at him ferociously, and Cormack nearly stumbled away in surprise.

"Wear it now and wear it always, Brother Cormack," De Guilbe demanded. "And never forget why."

Cormack again wore a puzzled expression.

"Why we came here," Father De Guilbe clarified sternly.

Cormack bowed and turned to leave, feeling moisture gathering in his bright green eyes. Brother Giavno's face was creased by a satisfied smile, but he did put a supportive hand gently and sincerely on Cormack's shoulder as they turned together for the door.

He ran his old fingers across the ice wall as he walked in the darkness. The moisture he felt there pleased him greatly, for it represented the fruition of his vision, the beauteous simplicity of his grand plan that would have seemed so complicated to any looking from afar.

The trolls' blood was performing as he had foreseen, coating the chasm carved by Ancient D'no (who was burrowing along the route proscribed by the giants and their mallets). The white worm's godly heat melted the ice; the trolls' blood prevented it from refreezing.

Soon Mithranidoon would be washed free of its infection.

Ancient Badden paused when he happened upon a torn head, its lower half bitten away and most of the skin pulled from the skull bone. Enough skin and hair remained for the old Samhaist to recognize it, though, and he bent and retrieved it, lifting it so that he could again look Dantanna in the eye.

"Ah, my old friend, do you understand now?" the Ancient asked with a chuckle. "Did the Abellican promises grant you immortality? Are the Ancient Ones impressed with your tolerance of the upstart heretics?"

Ancient Badden's features darkened into a fierce scowl. "Were you prepared for your death, fool Dantanna?" He let his fingers curl under the rim of the skull as he spoke, and squeezed tightly against the remaining brain and the ice-fly maggots.

"For centuries we have stood as the guardians of folly," he said, as if lecturing the man. "We have warned the folk and prepared the folk. We taught them to survive, to reap and sow, to treat their maladies, and mostly, you fool— and mostly!—we prepared them for the darkness of eternity. They must know the Ancient Ones to understand the paths they will walk when the specter of Death visits them. They must recognize their insignificance beside the gods that they will accept their dark fate as servants.

"But the followers of the fool Abelle come along and promise the mercy and benevolence of a forgiving god!" Ancient Badden roared, squeezing so hard that a bit of brain seeped out and slipped to the icy floor. "They tease with baubles and extrapolate from them what they consider infinite wisdom and wisdom of the infinite. But they did not know, did they, Dantanna? Empty promises and joy-filled fancies to tempt and cajole. Did the wretch Abelle greet you when Ancient D'no's teeth tore you from your mortal body?"

As if in answer he heard a rumble as he finished the question. Badden slowly lowered the skull and turned about to glance over his shoulder.

The white worm, a gigantic centipede-like monster, its back glowing fiercely with heat that could melt the flesh of a man to a puddle on simple contact, reared and clicked its formidable mandibles together. Small winglike appendages appeared just a few feet below its head, flapping and turning to hold it steady and upright.

Ancient Badden realized that this must have been the last sight Dantanna had known.

He laughed, then bowed. "God of the ice who denies the cold," he praised, and bowed again very low.

D'no gave a clicking sound, half hiss and half growl, and began to sway back and forth hypnotically.

Ancient Badden began to chant the oldest of Samhaist songs. No other man in the world would have survived that moment, but Badden knew the secrets, all the secrets, and his tone and cadence and inflection reflected centuries of knowledge and understanding of the wide world, of the great beast, the gods, and of this god, D'no, in particular.

The white worm gradually receded, backing for many feet before rolling over itself and scuttling away down a side tunnel.

Ancient Badden nodded at the confirmation of his powers and the truth of his beliefs. He held Dantanna's skull up before him one last time. "Blessed Abelle would have been devoured," he laughed, tossing Dantanna aside.

Cormack instinctively stiffened when he heard the soft paddling not far away. He stood on a sandbar some distance out to the northeast of Chapel Isle, a quiet and remote location that he had found soon after the brothers had arrived on Mithranidoon.

He listened carefully for further paddling, trying to determine the angle of approach. Was it his brothers, following him? If so, he mused, he hoped they would see the powrie beret first, think him a dwarf, and kill him from afar.

That would be easier than explaining to Father De Guilbe why he had come out here.

He heard the paddling again, faint but close, and he knew it could not be the brothers handling a boat that deftly and quietly. No, only the barbarians born and raised on Mithranidoon could so gently navigate the waves, so Cormack was not surprised when the longboat slid in against the sandbar a few heartbeats later and Milkeila climbed out.

She moved right to him, not saying a word, and wrapped him in a tight hug. "Too long," she whispered.

He detected sadness and anxiety in her voice and felt in her hug that she needed comfort. Cormack kissed her and crushed her tight.

"A powrie cap?" she asked, obviously taken aback. She moved back to arm's length and looked up at the man, for though Milkeila was a tall woman, Cormack stood a full head above her.

"A long and complicated tale."

"Then we haven't the time," said Milkeila, and she flashed a coy smile. "I was surprised by your signal but happy to see the light through the mist."

"There is magic in this cap, I will say," said Cormack. "When I don it, I feel . . . thickened. Strengthened. Not armored, perhaps, but as if I could withstand a heavier blow."

"Perhaps that is why the powries can withstand such a beating before relenting in battle."

"That and their temperament, which is akin to that of a cornered animal."

Milkeila smiled and nodded at that apt description. Having spent the entirety of her life on Mithranidoon, she had enjoyed many fights with the ferocious dwarfs.

"You lost three men," Cormack said, startling her and stealing her mirth.

Milkeila stepped back, sliding her arms so that she ended up holding Cormack by the forearms. "Five," she corrected. "How did you know?"

"We have three," said Cormack. Milkeila leaned forward eagerly, and Cormack added, "Androosis among them."

"You did battle?"

"We found them floating in a ruined boat. Trolls hit them and hard. Brother Giavno believes they were fishing in the northwestern waters too near the caves."

"Who are the others?"

Cormack shook his head. "They say little. One is a shaman, and by his dress high-ranking—"

"Toniquay," Milkeila interrupted.

"Stubborn," said Cormack.

"More than you would ever understand. They are alive, then, all three?"

"Healed in the dungeon of Chapel Isle."

A strange expression came over Milkeila's face, one that Cormack could not decipher other than to know it did not bode well.

"Dungeon?" she said, clarifying it all for him.

Cormack stepped back and shrugged helplessly. "Brother Giavno found them adrift. Had he not towed them to Chapel Isle they would have all died."

"Or my people would have found them," Milkeila interjected, her tone sharpening just a bit.

"They would have died even then," said Cormack, and how he wished he could have taken back those words the moment they passed his lips!

Milkeila furrowed her brow.

"They were very near to death," Cormack stammered, trying to climb out of the deepening ditch. "It took the efforts of several brothers working tirelessly with the gemstones . . . their wounds were grave."

"Too grave for the pretend gods of Yan Ossum barbarians, no doubt," the woman said dryly.

"I did not mean . . ."

"You did not have to," Milkeila said.

Cormack paused to draw a steadying breath. "The gemstones—the soul stones—are the most focused healing magic in the world. The lairds of Honce recognize this, truly. I do not diminish your gods." He grabbed her by the hands and pulled her close—or tried to, but she resisted. "You know I never would! But there are practical truths about the sacred stones and their related magic."

"My people are not without resources," Milkeila replied. "Our shamans are not useless fools sputtering meaningless chants to false gods."

"I did not mean . . ." he repeated helplessly.

"You did not have to," Milkeila said again, with a frown. "It is said among the islands that the monks see two ways to the world: their way and the wrong way."

"You do not believe that about me."

"Do not or did not?"

The two stared at each other for few uncomfortable heartbeats until Cormack added, "Is that statement not true of every clan on Mithranidoon's steaming waters? Could anything less be said of the powries? Of Yossunfier? Of Clan Pierjyk or Tunundar or any of the other tribes of your barbarian kin? The Alpinadoran clans cannot even agree amongst themselves—on anything, it seems!"

If Milkeila was impressed, she didn't show it.

"When will Androosis and the others be set free?" the woman asked.

Cormack swallowed hard—all the answer she needed.

"Then I am bound to tell my leaders that they are on Chapel Isle."

Cormack felt panic welling up inside. "You cannot," he begged. "I told you only because . . ."

"You cannot ask of me that I hold this secret. My kin are out upon the lake, every day, in search of the lost five. They travel to dangerous corners of Mithranidoon. Am I to hold quiet while some are lost to the trolls?"

"I would not have told you."

"Then you should not have told me! Not on that condition! You cannot ask that I pretend ignorance while my people sail into danger. And you cannot ask that I do nothing while my friend—your friend!—sits in your Abellican prison."

"You have to believe me," said Cormack. "I am trying to get them released. As soon as the healing is complete."

"Healing that sickens the heart of Toniquay, no doubt."

"He will allow no more now that his thoughts are back in the world of the living," Cormack admitted. "But he mends. They all do, and they are well fed. And I will press for their release, of course."

Milkeila's posture and the fact that she allowed Cormack to take her hands again revealed that she did not doubt him. But in the end she shook her head, unsatisfied with the promised resolution. "I cannot lie to my leaders. Not about this. I will not explain to them how I know, but they will be told that our lost brethren are on Chapel Isle. You cannot ask anything else of me."

"Their boat is beached on our shore," said Cormack, his tone noticeably short of enthusiasm. "Tell them you spied it from afar."

"My people will come for them," the woman promised ominously.

"I pray that a bargain will be struck," said Cormack. "Perhaps this is an opportunity for a better understanding between Chapel Isle and Yossunfier."

But Milkeila was shaking her head with every word. "There is no bargain to be found," she explained, her tone even and full of certainty. "My people will go to Chapel Isle in full force to demand the release. Anything less will incite war."

Cormack stuttered around a couple of insufficient responses before settling upon "What will Milkeila do?"

She stepped back and stood staring at him in the moonlight for a long while, obviously waging an inner struggle. "I am Yan Ossum," she said, and reached up to her neck to separate her second, secret necklace from her more traditional shamanistic attire. She pulled the gemstone necklace over her head and held it out to Cormack, who widened his eyes, too stunned to respond.

"I am Yan Ossum," Milkeila said again. "If there is to be war, I battle on the side of Yossunfier." She tossed the necklace to him, and he caught it. "It would be wrong of me to use your gemstones against you in that event. I would not so betray your trust."

"As you perceive I am betraying yours?"

Milkeila shook her head and managed a thin smile. "I am Yan Ossum, and you are Abellican. We both battle the limitations of our heritage—I am no more in Toniquay's favor than you are in the eyes of Father De Guilbe. But we cannot escape the truth of who we are, not in the event we both fear. My people will come for our lost brethren, and your brothers will not likely release them. And so we are left in the most awful place where our hopes collide with our realities."

Cormack stood there on the sand, staring at this extraordinary barbarian lass, a woman he had come to love, and he had no answers to her simple and straightforward logic. His shoulders slumped, his arms fell limp by his sides, and he smiled meekly, almost apologetically, back at her. He didn't know whether he should go to her and hug her again or kiss her to assure her that everything would be all right. It was a moot point anyway, for there was no strength in his legs at that moment, powrie beret notwithstanding, to propel him.

Her waning smile carried Milkeila back to her small boat, and she pushed it away from the sandbar and hopped aboard it with the grace only one of her heritage might know.

In moments, the mist enveloped her, and Cormack stood alone.

And never in his life had he been more aware of exactly that.

CHAPTER 11

Two Birds

"It is a lie," Brother Pinower remarked as Dawson, stepping lightly as if the weight of the world had been removed from his shoulders, started out of Father Artolivan's audience hall.

Dawson stopped with a small hop and turned to face the younger monk, but Artolivan spoke before he could reply.

"A tale of mutual benefit," the old priest said.

"A tale untrue," said Brother Pinower. "We know the fate of Brother Dynard."

"Do we?" asked Artolivan.

Pinower licked his lips and glanced over at Dawson. "We know at least that Dawson's concoction has no basis in any known facts, Father."

"Vanguard is a large and untamed place," said Artolivan.

"We make a leap of circumstance based on less than compelling reasoning, Father. To spin such a claim, without cause, seems the very definition of . . ."

"Prudence," Father Artolivan interrupted. "Play it out to logical conclusion in your thoughts, young Brother, absent this 'concoction,' as you deem it. The benefactors of your veracity would be?"

Pinower's gaze went from Artolivan to Dawson and back again, and again. After a few moments, he could only sigh, having no practical response.

With an appreciative nod to Father Artolivan, Dawson McKeege took his leave.

"Go with him," Father Artolivan instructed Pinower. "Supply to his tale the imprimatur of the Abellican Church."

Brother Pinower's expression showed his ultimate dismay, but he did not argue and did not respond, other than to bow politely and rush away in pursuit of the Vanguardsman.

Named because she sat below the peak of the northern cliffs and thus offered protection from the cold winds that howled down from the gulf, Weatherguard nevertheless still afforded her residents and visitors a magnificent view of Chapel Abelle, so strong and solemn and crisp against the steel-gray sky beyond the high rise.

Bransen, Callen, and Cadayle stood and enjoyed that view for a few moments when they first came in sight of the renowned abbey, with the two women flanking Bransen and holding him relatively straight, as he had been for most of their journey, particularly those parts when they neared more populated areas. Today he walked in genuine Stork form.

"Built by the hand of God, so they say," Callen whispered, awe evident in her voice. For how could it not have been? Many of Honce's traveling bards named this the most impressive structure in all the land, even above the magnificent palace of Laird Delaval.

Bransen slipped a hand into his belt pouch and clutched a soul stone. He had become quite adept at making this movement unobtrusive and even more so at accessing the power of the stone, almost instantly transforming himself. "We know the Abellicans far too well to make the mistake of listening to 'they,'" he reminded. "How might Chapel Abelle measure against the Walk of Clouds of the Jhesta Tu?"

"One day we will know, my love," Cadayle whispered to him. She nudged him gently to make sure he was aware of people walking by.

Anytime Cadayle rubbed his upper arm and said "my love," it meant that he should revert to his disguise. Bransen took the cue and let go of the gemstone. Any hint that he was faking his malady would surely land him on the front lines of the vicious war as both sides scrambled for more and more fodder to feed their kingly designs.

Cadayle and Callen helped Bransen to Weatherguard's long inn, a ramshackle old structure so warped and aged that the floor showed stains of the water that easily crept through whenever it rained or snowed. Still, the common room's hearth was enormous and well stocked. The fire, seeming like three separate conflagrations, worked its way through the jumble of logs piled high behind an iron grate, their flickering ends sometimes joining, sometimes flaring in opposite directions so that they resembled a trio of dancers acting out the tragedy of a failing love triangle.

The patrons in the room showed no such intrigue. Old men and women young and old littered the many small round tables set about the generous floor. Glances both scornful and bitter came at Bransen immediately as he entered. Only as he staggered storklike, drool wetting the corners of his mouth, did many of the patrons nod their understanding and let go of that resentment. Few men of Bransen's age remained in Weatherguard, and everyone in the room had suffered the loss of a husband or son or brother in the seemingly endless war between Ethelbert and Delaval.

"Wounded in the South," Cadayle explained to a gaggle of old women who stared incredulously as Bransen staggered into a seat.

"Ah," they all said together.

"A pity he weren't killed outright, then, ye poor girl," one dared offer.

Cadayle merely nodded, accepting their misplaced pity. She'd heard that one often enough.

Cadayle noticed then that one middle-aged man in the tavern seemed quite out of place. Sitting in a back corner, his weathered boots up on the table, he was surely of age and fitness to be at the front. He cradled a mug of mead in one hand, absently running the index finger of his other hand about its thick rim. And all the while he stared at her and at Bransen with more than a passing interest. Too much so!

Cadayle told herself that she was being ridiculous, that the man, like everyone else, was simply intrigued by the abnormality of the Stork. She settled into her chair beside Bransen, facing Callen.

Callen's glance over her shoulder was Cadyle's first warning. Before she even turned, a strong hand patted her shoulder.

"Well seen and well to drink," the man greeted, sliding up beside Cadayle near to the fourth chair at the table. He looked to her and then to it as if asking permission to sit down.

Cadayle glanced at her mother, who gave a quick nod.

"Do join us," the younger woman said.

The man settled in heavily, staring at Bransen all the while. "You look as if you've a long road behind you." He motioned to the bartender to bring a round of drinks.

"My husband cannot indulge," Cadayle said quietly.

"Make him unsteady on his feet, will it?" the man asked, and Cadayle glowered at him.

"Apologies, good lady," he said unconvincingly. He half stood and bowed toward Bransen. "Wounded in the war?" he asked, again too intently.

"In the South," said Cadayle.

"A pity, that. The towns are full of torn men. Arms and legs missing. Brains all scattered so that they can hardly speak. An ugly business is this war."

"One you seem to be avoiding," Callen said across the table, and Cadayle was glad indeed for the diversion.

The man gave what seemed to be a helpless chuckle. "I've come from Vanguard to the north across the gulf." He stood and tipped his heavy cap. "Dawson McKeege at your service, good ladies and yourself, good sir. Here on a brief—too brief!—respite. War's no less up there, I tell you."

"So you fled?" Cadayle asked.

The man laughed harder. "Nay, that wouldn't do. I've sailed under Dame Gwydre's banner to Chapel Abelle for supplies, you see? The gemstones of the Abellicans have proven well worth the journey. We're taming a land as vast and great as Honce herself."

"The brothers help you, then."

"Oh, indeed!" Dawson replied. "We've several working our chapels. Good men, one and all, though I've no doubt that more than a few found themselves in the northland for reasons of discipline and not choice."

Cadayle gave a pleasant and polite smile.

"Whenever the Church has one out of line, the road turns north, is my guess of it," the clever Dawson went on. "And don't be misunderstanding me! Pray no! We're all too glad to have them."

"Surely," said Cadayle, sharing a glance with Callen.

"And why might you be at Chapel Abelle?" Dawson asked. "Seeking help for your man, there, from their gemstone magic?"

Cadayle nodded.

Dawson returned it. "If they've the time, perhaps you'll find what you seek, though your man will likely find himself on a wagon heading back for the fighting if they manage the task."

Cadayle clutched Bransen's hand tightly. "He does not fear any battle," she said.

"Surely," Dawson replied. "Have you come far, then?"

"All the way from Pryd Hol . . ." Callen started.

"South of Pryd Holding," Cadayle quickly corrected. "Closer to Entel, even."

Dawson's eyes widened. "A long and trying journey, to be sure, with one so impaired." He paused as the barmaid came over and delivered a pair of pale ales.

"Don't ye let Dawson here bother ye," she said, exactly as Dawson had paid her to remark. "He's the lout of the North, so goes his reputation." She gave him a playful slap on the shoulder as she finished to diminish any real warning in her words, again, exactly as he had paid her to do. There was nothing like a charming rake to calm a stranger's fears, Dawson knew.

"But he's just harmless," the barmaid said in Cadayle's ear. "Always looking for a warm bed for his spike, don't ye know? And he's looking to yer friend there—yer ma, she is, I'm guessing, or yer older sister—and don't she look so pretty? My, but ye'll be a long time with yer charms following that one!"

Cadayle snickered despite herself. She lifted the ale to her lips and took a long and welcomed draw.

"Don't you be showing my dice, Tauny Dentsen!" Dawson complained as the barmaid whirled away, giggling. He looked back at Cadayle to find a warm smile waiting for him.

"How long are you to stay, then?" Dawson asked.

Cadayle and Callen exchanged uncertain looks.

"If you're to wait on the brothers, then some time, of course," Dawson reasoned. "Chapel Abelle is full of activity, readying for the new class of brothers who will enter her gates in but a few days. I doubt you will get Father Artolivan or Brother Pinower to even hear your request before the week is through."

"You know them?" Callen asked before Cadayle could.

"All of them, of course," said Dawson. "I told you that my Dame Gwydre is on fine terms with the brothers of Blessed Abelle. They've eyes on Vanguard, to be sure, as would any far-seeing man."

"And they have brothers up there," Cadayle added. "As you said."

"Aye, many have come for more than twenty years now."

Cadayle glanced at Bransen, a perfectly natural movement, and one that would not have been telling to Dawson had he not already known the true reason the trio had ventured to Chapel Abelle.

"So you're to seek the work of the brothers with their gemstones," Dawson said. "A reasonable request, and one that would likely be met with some sympathy were it not for these times."

Cadayle furrowed her brow. "What do you mean?"

"The brothers are exhausted," Dawson explained. "Overworked, particularly with the gemstones, as they tend constantly to the wounded of both the warring lairds. As long as you have a writ, you have a chance, I expect." He addressed Bransen directly. "You fought under Delaval's flag, yes? And his commander offered you a Writ of Plea for the Brothers of Chapel Abelle? The higher his rank, the better your chances, of course. A Writ of Plea from Laird Delaval himself would likely get you into their healing chambers."

"A Writ of Plea?" Cadayle asked, shaking her head.

"To be sure! A letter from a laird, or his commanders, begging special attention to a valiant warrior's wounds. Without it, you'll not get near to the leaders at Chapel Abelle, and they are the most powerful ones with the gemstones. They are not so—" Dawson stopped in a hush and sat staring sympathetically at Cadayle, then at Bransen. "So you do not possess a writ?"

A horrified expression came over the woman, and she looked to an equally surprised and upset Callen.

"All hope is not lost," Dawson was quick to add. "Have you a friend or relative among the brothers, anything to elevate your needs above the maladies of so many other poor souls? Was your man there particularly valorous?"

Cadayle stared at him incredulously.

"I recant!" said Dawson. "Dear lady, forgive my foolishness. Of course he was, but what I mean is . . . well, is there a witness to his bravery? A letter of honor if not a Writ of Plea?"

Cadayle's expression answered that clearly in the negative.

"Then a relative among the brothers?" asked Dawson. "Think hard, I pray you. A friend? An acquaintance, even? Anyone who can speak for your poor man there to elevate him from the throngs of wounded."

"We have come in hopes of healing, to be sure," Callen said, drawing the attention of both Cadayle and the man, and both looked equally surprised. "But also in search of one who might well speak for us."

"A brother?"

Callen nodded. "From Chapel Pryd, far to the south. He traveled to Chapel Abelle many years ago, so it is rumored, and we came here specifically in the hopes that he would help my daughter's poor husband."

"Your daughter?" said Dawson, and he seemed as if his breath had flown. "Surely I thought her your sister!"

Callen blushed and smiled, despite the obvious ploy.

"Well, if this brother is here, then you shan't have wasted your time, I expect," said Dawson. "I know all the brothers presently at chapel. What is his name?"

After another quick glance at her mother Cadayle said, "Brother Dynard. Brother Bran Dynard."

Dawson furrowed his brow and fell back in his chair, a look of knowing his expression.

"You know him?"

"No," the Vanguardsman replied. "But I know of him."

"He is at Chapel Abelle?" asked Callen.

Dawson managed a glance at Bransen as he looked to the older woman, and he recognized the sure signs of interest there, how the swaying man was actually managing to lean forward a bit.

"No," Dawson answered, and out of the corner of his eye he saw the clear signs of disappointment on the debilitated man's face. "Not here. Not for a decade and more at least."

Cadayle rubbed her face.

"He is in Vanguard, of course," Dawson said. Both women sucked in their breath, and Bransen turned sharply toward him—so much so that he nearly tumbled out of his seat.

"Aye, across the Gulf of Corona to the north," said Dawson. "Serving Dame Gwydre's flock."

"Then he is alive," Cadayle breathed, words she hadn't meant to utter aloud.

"Last I heard, indeed," said Dawson. "Would you go there, then? To Vanguard to find him?"

Neither woman had an answer to that, as was obvious from their respective, and equally overwhelmed, expressions.

"You cannot walk to Vanguard, of course," Dawson offered. "A month and more by land and through wild lands. The only way to Vanguard is by boat across the dark waters."

"And they sail from where? Palmaristown?" asked Cadayle.

"And the price of passage?" Callen added.

Dawson offered a warm smile. "Sometimes they do, yes, and I know not that there is ever a set price. No passenger boats make the crossing, you see. Trade ships, one and all, like my own *Lady Dreamer*."

"What price then?" asked Cadayle.

"For the three of you? Why, if I've room I'll gladly have you aboard. The price will be fine company and stories of the South. I can see by the looks of you that you've many interesting tales to tell."

"If you have room," Callen said.

"And I will, though the brothers have bade me to carry many of the war-weary prisoners," said Dawson. "Oh, they are not dangerous," he added, seeing a bit of alarm on Cadayle's sweet face. "Just poor souls fighting for one laird or another who got hurt or caught and by agreement of honor and convenience were put out of the war for its duration. The brothers take them in, both sides treated equally, but the ferocity of the battle has given them more than they can handle. Still, I expect I'll have room for three extras on *Lady Dreamer*."

Cadayle looked to Bransen and Callen for an answer, and Callen had one. "You are too kind," she said. "And we will surely consider your most generous offer. When do you plan to sail?"

"Tomorrow," said Dawson. "And I will hold three open seats. You will find Vanguard most accommodating. We've wood aplenty, and thus, Dame Gwydre has built entire towns in anticipation of emigration from the war-ravaged mainland. Most welcomed, I assure you, particularly with two so beautiful ladies among your trio."

He stood up then and motioned to the barmaid again, flashing a piece of silver and setting it on the table for her.

"I must see to my other arrangements," he said to the three. "A strong wind to fill your canvas, and moving seas to you."

He bowed and took his leave. Cadayle and Callen sat there, stunned, for many moments, each trying to digest all that had just happened.

"Can it be?" Bransen mouthed quietly to both of them, closing his hand on his soul stone once more. "Alive?" Even with the magical aid, the young man seemed to have a hard time sitting still and sitting straight.

Y̶ou confirmed my tale to them, of course?" Dawson McKeege asked Brother Pinower the next day, soon after he had noted Cadayle, Callen, and the man known as the Highwayman moving through the courtyard of Chapel Abelle and into the tunnels leading down to the dock where *Lady Dreamer* waited.

"As Father Artolivan demanded of me, yes," the monk confirmed.

Dawson grinned as he turned to regard him. "You disapprove?"

"I pride myself on telling the truth."

Dawson looked back out over the wall to the dark waters of the gulf. "In this instance the tale was better for all. Would this Highwayman be better off if he did not sail with me? Or would Father Artolivan be compelled to arrest him, surely to be hanged by the neck? You may have saved a life, good Brother. Isn't that worth a lie?"

"If the man is a criminal then it is not my province to deny justice."

"Criminal. Justice," Dawson echoed. "Strange words in this time, when men slaughter their own kin to further the aspirations of greedy lairds. Would you not agree?"

Brother Pinower sighed and looked out to sea.

"This is an easier course for Father Artolivan and for all of you. Perhaps you saved more lives than the Highwayman's, if it had come to blows. His reputation is impressive. If he is half the warrior Father Artolivan believes, he will serve Dame Gwydre well."

Now Pinower did look directly at the sea-worn man. "He goes to Vanguard under false pretenses. His anger will rise when he learns of the deception. You do not know that he will serve Dame Gwydre at all."

"Oh, he will," said a smiling Dawson. "For he goes not alone, and they, all three, will find themselves alone and vulnerable in a land they do not understand. Consider it his sentence for the crimes of which he has been accused. We will be your gaolers—it seems the way of things."

"If you say," said Pinower, staring out at the dark waters.

Dawson similarly turned. "Oh, he will," the man mumbled.

CHAPTER 12

Cold Seat of Power

Tinnikkikkik recognized the sense of dread emanating from his hundred glacial troll forces, and indeed felt it himself, for this place was surely unnerving. It was more than the cold air. This temperature hardly bothered the trolls, who swam in the icy waters of melting glaciers and ran about naked on Alpinadoran ice and snow even in the nights of deep winter. The warm waters of the lake below this glacier made them more uncomfortable than the cold, even this high up on the river of ice.

It wasn't the almost preternatural cold, it was the aura of the place. Tinnikkikkik had been in many houses sculpted of ice in his five decades but certainly never before in anything remotely like this one. Great crystalline corridors wound about each other in confusing twists and turns, some climbing higher, some lower, and ice or not, this was easily the largest man-made structure Tinnikkikkik or any of his tribe had ever seen, let alone entered. And it looked all the larger for its sweeping stairs, winding up to side towers that seemed grand indeed though they might only contain a couple of rather smallish rooms.

In addition to the size and grandeur of the palace, the simple truth of its construction only added to its imposing aura. For no picks and flat-blades had built Devongel, as it was called, and no strong arms, human, giant, or otherwise, had lifted the blocks into place to form the thick walls. Devongel had been pulled from the glacier upon which it stood through magic.

And no torches lit it, though it was not dark inside. It wasn't bright, but neither was it as dark as it should have been, even on a clear and sunny day, which this was not. A deep blue light glowed from the structure's ice, only enhancing the cold and empty feel of the palace.

Ancient magic had built this place and lit this place, earth magic, the power of the Samhaists. A different manifestation of the same magic that had compelled Tinnikkikkik to lead his people here, he knew deep in his heart, and though he might recoil at being so magically manipulated, even that realization had not stopped him from coming. He tried to tell himself that he followed the call despite his reservations because he was the bravest of his people—and indeed he had shown that to be the truth through many, many battles. His rank as boss confirmed that, for it was not an inherited title among his tribe, or any of the troll tribes.

Mumbling and shifting all around Tinnikkikkik, particularly the shuffling feet, warned him that the nervousness was threatening to overwhelm his forces. He stood straight—at over five feet, he was taller than most glacial trolls—and let his scrutinizing, roving gaze sweep in the entirety of the band, holding them with its intensity, though they surely wanted to flee.

The troll boss lifted his hand, palm up, before his chest and face, signaling his charges to stand straighter.

"Where do we go, boss?" the troll next to him dared ask, its tinny voice echoing off the cold and sheer walls and other flat facings. Perhaps it was design, perhaps magic, but the echoes seemed to grow in both volume and intensity above the original for a short while before diminishing to a long hissing whisper of sound.

Tinnikkikkik and all the others hopped every which way, trying to get a handle on the cacophony, and finally, in frustration, the troll boss just turned and slapped the speaker hard.

Strangely, that sharp slap did not echo.

But a single set of footfalls did, suddenly though not seeming so, as if they had been around the band all along but the trolls were only now noticing them. They drummed out a steady and slow cadence, and they seemed to be coming nearer, though from which direction was any troll's guess. The band huddled together more closely, every bloodshot eye turning intermittently to Tinnikkikkik, their leader, their boss.

He knew that, and so he stood as tall as he could manage, and did not flinch when Ancient Badden at last came into view, walking along a descending and curved ramp. He wore his trademark light green robes, his great beard spiked with dung, and though his footfalls sounded sharply, he wasn't shod in hard-soled boots, but in his usual open-toed sandals.

He moved slowly but somehow seemed to cover an enormous amount of ground, cleverly stopping just before Tinnikkikkik and the others, which left him higher on the rise. Since Ancient Badden was well over a foot taller than the largest of the trolls, he now towered over them even more, looking like an adult in the process of supervising a band of unruly children.

He spoke to the boss, using the troll language and inflection perfectly (for of course, it was magic that gave him the language more so than practice). "You long in come to me. I call to you long ago. Too long."

Tinnikkikkik shook his head obstinately. "Long walk."

"Long time."

"Only twenty suns."

"Twenty suns," Ancient Badden echoed with a sigh and a shake of his head. "In twenty suns I march my army all the way to the big water."

"Not with fight."

"With fight. Twenty suns? I call you. You should be here in five!" Ancient Badden found the troll language, with its minimal use of tense, thoroughly exasperating. It made sense to him, though, for the trolls never seemed to quite grasp the concept of passing time and rarely seemed to think farther ahead than their next step.

"No, long walk," the stubborn boss replied.

It seemed to Ancient Badden that the ugly little creature was gaining confidence with every word. That wouldn't do.

"Too long," the Samhaist said slowly and deliberately.

"No, long walk," the troll replied.

Ancient Badden stood very straight, even seemed to lean back just a bit. His eyes rolled up so that only the white was showing, and he whispered something Tinnikkikkik couldn't make out.

"What?" the troll boss started to ask, but as the ice floor beneath him melted suddenly to water, it came out as "Wha-aaaaaaaaaa!"

Trolls jumped back at the splash, and Tinnikkikkik went right under—which wouldn't have been a serious problem for a glacial troll except that the floor almost immediately refroze as soon as he was fully immersed.

The doomed troll did manage to thrust one hand up, the tip of his longest finger just prodding through the solid floor. And there he hung, stuck in the ice, encapsulated by the magic of Ancient Badden.

The other trolls shrank back, talking excitedly as one, and all terrified more than angry.

"Too long," Ancient Badden said to them, and when he got no response, he said it again, louder.

A hundred troll heads, all pointy ears and thin lips and sharp yellow teeth, began wagging their agreement.

Ancient Badden herded them before him. He would have to appoint a new boss, he knew, and send this force off at once, for there was a town he wanted overrun before the turn to winter, a last excursion by trolls exclusively to let Dame Gwydre and her Abellican playthings understand that there would be no rest through the cold months.

There would be no rest for the folk of Vanguard until they expelled the Abellicans and gave themselves back to the Samhaists.

It was as simple as that, as simple as a troll frozen in ice.

My coat's not even for fitting me anymore," Bikelbrin grumbled. He shook his shoulders, emphasizing the looseness of his heavy furred overcoat. "Gone all skinny living on that damned lake, I did."

"Too much fish and berries," agreed another of the party of four, a young and muscular dwarf named Ruggirs. "I hate fish and berries."

"All we e'er known," agreed Pergwick, who had been birthed from the heart of the brother of the powrie who had served as the donor for Ruggirs's own Sepulcher—which made Pergwick and Ruggirs true brothers in powrie tradition.

"Ye'll be feasting on good and bloody meat soon enough," Mcwigik assured them. "Enough o' the lake for me. Too much o' the damned lake for me!"

"Aye, but the season's later than ye thinked," Bikelbrin noted. "Long past midsummer and moving to cold fall." He finished with a shiver to accentuate his point, and to remind them all once again that they were ill equipped to handle the cold of the turning season. Mcwigik and Bikelbrin had the coats they had worn in that long-ago expedition that had brought them to Mithranidoon and had rustled up a pair for their two companions. But though the dwarfs had taken great pains to preserve those original garments, the material had frayed and the fur flattened. They were still in sight of Mithranidoon, moving generally south and east, and already the wind nipped at them through the holes in their coats.

They had wrapped their feet in layers of rags but that hardly helped. Toes were tingling, and night had not even fully fallen.

"We'll be needing a fire," Mcwigik remarked, but he ended with a sigh as he considered his words and looked all around, for the landscape, though in full summer bloom, showed little that could be used for such an endeavor. There were a few bushes to be found, though no trees readily available, so the dwarfs broke their march early and began gathering brush. When night came in full, moonless and dark, Mcwigik finally managed to get a fire going. Knowing it wouldn't last long, they piled rocks about the brush. The flames winked out soon after, consuming the meager fuel; warmed stones would have to do. They huddled about the stones and each other, and it wasn't so bad.

But the howling started soon after.

"Wolves," Mcwigik explained to the two younger powries, who had no experience with such creatures.

"They saw our fire," Bikelbrin reasoned. Pergwick and Ruggirs glanced at each other with obvious concern, something the other two didn't miss.

On Mcwigik's orders, they made a cairn of the heated stones and each sat against it facing in a different direction.

"Ye hold yer place," Mcwigik said repeatedly as the howling circled them and the two younger powries appeared as if they would break and run. Every now and then a darker shadow slipped past one or another's field of view, or starlight shining eyes stared at them from not so far away.

"Ye think we've the weapons to beat them?" Bikelbrin asked his friend candidly.

"I got me Prag's axe, and that'll put a dent in a wolf's skull," Mcwigik answered.

Pergwick jumped up suddenly and backed a step, which sent him tumbling over the cairn atop Ruggirs, who similarly scrambled to his feet. Mcwigik was about to scold them, but as he turned he saw the cause of the younger powrie's concern. Not five feet from the cairn, teeth bared, eyes shining, stood a large canine creature.

Mcwigik came past the tumbled two fast and yelled at the wolf, pumping his arm threateningly.

The wolf snapped and barked sharply, and Mcwigik found himself falling back over the other two, who both screamed as the wolf advanced.

But then it yelped as a rock pegged it on the flank, and it ran off.

"I ain't for fighting that!" Pergwick cried.

"So we seen," said Bikelbrin, the rock-thrower.

"Mcwigik fell, too!" Pergwick protested.

"Yach, he just caught me by surprise, he did," Mcwigik said, brushing himself off as if that motion might polish up a bit of his lost dignity. "Ain't fought one in a hundred years and more!"

"A record ye're not to keep for long," Bikelbrin remarked, stepping up beside him, another rock in hand. "The beastie ain't gone far."

More howling ensued, as if on cue.

The four spent many hours on the edge of their wits, jumping at every sound, but no wolves came that close again, though the howls and growls showed that the hungry canines were never far.

And if that wasn't bad enough for the tired and cold group, the rocks cooled long before the night had even reached its midway point, and the wind from the west didn't catch any of Mithranidoon's heated mist.

Gradually, they all drifted off to sleep, but so late into the night that the blazing dawnslight awakened them less than an hour after Pergwick, the last to find slumber, had closed his eyes. Even Bikelbrin, who had been the first to manage sleep, hadn't realized three hours of it.

They all looked to Mcwigik, the chief conspirator in this breakout from Mithranidoon. He certainly didn't appear as boisterous and determined as he had the previous morning when he had led them to the boat and off their island home.

"What're ye thinking?" asked Bikelbrin.

"And how many days're ye saying it's to take us to find the Mirianic?" Pergwick dared interject, drawing a glare from Bikelbrin, though—surprisingly—Mcwigik didn't react at all to the question.

"A month to two, he said," Ruggirs answered. "And each night's to get colder and longer, aye?"

"Not so," Bikelbrin replied. "It ain't like that."

"But generally so," said Pergwick, and Bikelbrin had to concede that point.

"More than a month or two," Ruggirs said.

"But what are ye knowing about it?" Bikelbrin demanded. "Ye never been!"

"But I'm knowing that me toes are hurting, and so're yers," the younger dwarf argued. "And hurtin' toes're meaning slower steps, and slower steps're meaning more steps and more days, and I'm not for thinking . . ."

"We're going back," said Mcwigik, and all three looked at him in surprise.

"We ain't to make it," the chief conspirator said, looking directly at Bikelbrin and shaking his head, his face a mask of disappointment. "We ain't the tools, the weapons, or the clothes. If them wolves don't eat us alive, they'll tear the skin from our frozen bones to be sure."

"The lake's not so bad," said Ruggirs, but no one paid him any heed.

"I'm wanting the smell o' the Mirianic in me nose as much as any powrie alive, don't ye doubt," Mcwigik went on. "But I'm thinking we're dead long before we near the place."

"If we even know where it is," Pergwick dared interject, and so downtrodden was Mcwigik, and so surprised by the sudden turn was Bikelbrin, that neither argued a point that would have brought them both to fury only a day before.

So they gathered their supplies and turned back to the north, and found their boat shortly after sunset. They returned to the powrie island without any ruckus, without any questions, but a few of the dwarfs who had known their plans did offer a superior I-telled-ye-so smirk.

The bitter defeat stayed with Mcwigik for many weeks.

CHAPTER 13

Consequences

Brother Giavno grimaced against the line of fiery pain coming from a deep gash across the meat of his upper arm. He had only avoided the brunt of the hurled spear at the last instant, so close a call that it had poignantly reminded Giavno of his mortality, had pulled him from the battle for a few troublesome seconds as he pondered eternity. With great effort and determination, though, the monk had stubbornly held on to the large rock he had carried this far up the chapel's stairs. He stumbled through the upper room's open door and across the small bridge that led to the parapet of the outer wall. Before him monks cried out frantic instructions and scrambled to and fro, trying to avoid the near-constant rain of rocks and spears and other missiles that flew up from below.

Over to the side of the bridge, a pair of brothers worked desperately to dislodge a ladder, the top rung and the tips of its posts visible above the wall. Giavno shuffled as fast as his burden would allow, and didn't even pause to confirm when he arrived, just threw his back against the wall immediately below the ladder posts, then heaved the rock up to his shoulder, and over farther, until it dropped from the wall and tumbled down, guided in its fall by the ladder.

He heard a shout of warning from below, followed by a scream of surprise fast turning to a howl of pain, followed by a crash. Then he dared stand, and turned to look out and regard his work.

A wave of nausea rolled over him, but, as with the pain in his arm, he gritted his teeth and pushed through it. One man lay on the ground, squirming in pain, his legs obviously shattered and his back probably so. He couldn't have been far from the top when Giavno's rock went over, and the more than twenty-foot fall had not been kind.

Kinder than the rock, however, which the lead climber had apparently eluded, but the spotter, or second climber, had not, taking it squarely on the head.

She, too, lay on the ground, but she wasn't squirming, her head split open and her brains splattered about the base of the ladder.

Giavno swallowed hard. This was his first confirmed kill and a woman at that (though Giavno understood that these barbarian women could fight as well as any man he had ever known in the southland). Given the ferocity and determination of the barbarian attack, this first kill would not be Giavno's last.

"Pull it up! Pull it up!" Giavno ordered the other two monks, for the falling rock and falling barbarians had scattered the attackers momentarily. He began to haul, and the others, emboldened by his courage, dared stand up and grab at the sides, hoisting the ladder straight from the ground.

Down below, barbarians rushed back in. One tall man leaped high and managed to grab on to the bottom rungs, and his weight halted the monks' progress.

A fourth brother came to the spot, though, grapnel in hand, and with Giavno's help, they secured it to the third-highest rung. The attached rope strung down to the small courtyard, feeding into a sturdy cranking mechanism the brothers had constructed to haul large rocks up from the lower portions of the island. The team down below went to work immediately, bending their backs against the poles and methodically walking around the base, cranking in the rope.

The ladder creaked and groaned in protest, but even the weight of a second barbarian who had leaped up to join his companion couldn't suppress the pull. With the wall acting as a fulcrum, the ladder's top dipped and the bottom, two men and all, raised up and out from the wall base. Their feet soon fully ten feet from the ground, the two barbarians stubbornly held on, with more barbarians rushing over and leaping up to secure them by the legs and feet. The sheer human ballast countered the crank and the ladder held steady, three rungs over the wall top, the rest suspended outside the chapel.

Only momentarily, however, for the ladder snapped apart under the awkward strain, dropping the barbarians in a heap.

"Now!" cried a monk far to Giavno's right, and he turned to regard the men there on the wall. Using the distraction of the commotion outside, they sprang up as one and hurled a volley of stones down at the piled barbarians, scoring many solid hits. The Alpinadoran attackers at the base of the wall withered under the barrage, their formations breaking apart and many of them retreating. They had just started to reorganize when a bolt of lightning blasted out of a lower window—Father De Guilbe's work, no doubt.

That proved enough to shatter the attackers' sensibilities, and they ran off as one, though even under that terrible assault, they did not leave a single barbarian behind, not even the woman Giavno had killed and another felled by De Guilbe's lightning bolt.

Brother Giavno spun about and slumped down, putting his back against the cool stone of the parapet. They had won the day, he knew, but he understood, too, that this would be only the first of many such days. The brothers did not have near the firepower to break out of their chapel against so large a force, and the barbarians didn't seem to be going anywhere anytime soon. Indeed, the size of their force had confirmed the monks' worst fears: that the many barbarian tribes of Mithranidoon had come together in common cause—something that had been unthinkable only a few hours before.

The brothers and their servants were badly outnumbered here, and every rock and every spear they had thrown at the attackers was one less they'd have at their disposal in the next round.

"Father De Guilbe has asked for you," a monk who appeared at the opening back in the main keep informed Giavno.

The weary brother nodded and hauled himself up from the stone. He glanced back at the distant barbarians to see them setting up large tents down by the beach before the dozens of boats that had brought them here.

From the top of the wall above the main gate to the small chapel compound, Cormack stared out at the bloodstains. Not so far away, he could see the hair and pieces of scalp of one unfortunate Alpinadoran who had caught a rock on the head. A woman, he had been told by one of the other brothers.

He couldn't see in much detail from this distance, but the small tuft of hair blowing in the gentle wind could well have been Milkeila's.

The monk resisted the urge to throw up. She could be lost to him forever. She could lie dead at the beach, her head split apart. Because she had been out there, he was certain, standing strong among her kin, standing determined that the imprisonment of the three men would not hold.

Father De Guilbe was wrong, Cormack knew in his heart and soul. To proselytize in the name of Blessed Abelle was a good thing, but not like this, not under penalty of a dungeon cell. Even if the men in captivity agreed to recant their own faith and follow the ways of Abelle, even if they came to do so with all their hearts and souls, it would be a hollow gain for the Church, and certainly not worth this fighting.

Cormack put his arm up on the stone railing and rested his chin in the crook of his elbow, staring helplessly at the distant tuft of hair, hoping and praying that it was not Milkeila's.

But even if his prayers were answered, it would do little to mitigate the realization that at least one woman, young and strong and full of pride and certainty to match Giavno's own, had died this day who should not have.

Not over this.

"Brother Cormack!" He knew Giavno's voice all too well these days. He slowly turned to face the man, trying to keep his agitation off his face.

"The fight has ended," Giavno said from the keep's main door, some twenty feet back of the main gate on the surrounding wall. "Be quick to your work. We need water to wash our wounds."

Cormack motioned toward Giavno's torn upper arm. "Have you been tended?"

"I go to Father De Guilbe," the man replied, though his voice softened in response to Cormack's honest and obvious concern. "He will use a soul stone."

"Quickly," Cormack bade him. Giavno nodded and disappeared inside the keep.

He is a good man, Cormack reminded himself. Despite his current anger at Giavno over the barbarian prisoners, despite his rage that it had come to this—a prolonged and lethal battle and siege—Cormack understood that Giavno's heart was good.

But the man's thoughts were misplaced. And if "good" men could precipitate this kind of foolish and worthless slaughter, then . . . The thought made Cormack grimace.

He pulled himself up and noted the commotion inside the courtyard that surrounded the main keep, where brothers ran to and fro to shore up the wall in places where it had been damaged, or where the work on it had never been good enough to begin with. Truly even he had to appreciate the efforts of the Abellican contingent, no matter his feelings regarding their current choices and mission, for the work on this chapel fortress was remarkable to behold. They had built a circular tower keep, easily the tallest structure on the lake at more than thirty feet, and when the battling had begun those two years ago, the brothers had constructed, and so quickly, the surrounding wall, a dozen feet high in places like Cormack's present position, the front gate, but more than twenty feet high in other areas. A series of bridges had been fashioned to traverse to those higher areas from inside the upper stories of the keep, allowing the brothers to bring in reserves quickly and efficiently wherever they might be needed.

This had been the first true battle where the enemy had come against them in such numbers and with such ferocity, and it seemed to Cormack that the fortress had held up amazingly well.

He scrambled down to the ground and went around to the left side of the tower, to a small and square supplementary building. From there, he opened a bulkhead and headed down a natural tunnel that had been widened by the monks, with stairs carved into the slippery and downward-sloping stone. He passed a side tunnel leading to the prisoners' dungeon, and grimaced as he heard the shaman of the trio chanting loudly, in open defiance.

They knew of the fighting, Cormack realized. They knew that their people had come for them.

Cormack pulled a torch from its wall sconce and hustled along, past another corridor and down another descent, at last coming to a heavy door barred on his side with three separate iron poles. He opened two smaller hatchways on the door—one for him to peer through and a second that allowed him to thrust his torch into the cave beyond before going in. The flickering of that torchlight amplified many times over once it had passed through the portal, for this cave sat at the base of the island, just above the water level, and the floor of its lower reaches was the lake itself.

The quick check before opening the door was more a ritual than actual security, for the brothers had done well to secure that cave as well, building a gridwork gate that allowed the fish to enter but kept out anything larger, like the fast-swimming glacial trolls.

The warmth of the misty air washed over Cormack when he opened the door, and the smell in this cave was particularly thick with fish, for the monks had been down here angling extensively in preparation for what they knew to be a siege, and they had cleaned their catch at the water's edge and thrown the scraps back in to attract more fish and the common crabs.

Cormack welcomed that warmth, and the smell, hoping that he would lose himself in the heavy sensations and forget the horrific battle he had just witnessed. If he had been able to do that, he would have lingered for some time down in this sanctuary.

But he filled several waterskins and headed right back out, and in his mind he still heard the screams, and the smell of fish had not replaced the smell of death.

They will come again," Father De Guilbe said to Brother Giavno. "And again after that. Stubborn lot."

"Foolish lot," said Giavno. "Our walls are too strong!"

"I appreciate your confidence, Brother," said De Guilbe, "but we both understand that our enemies will adapt their tactics accordingly. In this first exchange we had several wounded, yourself among them."

"It is just a scratch," Giavno protested. He turned his arm, presenting it to De Guilbe. Soul stone in hand, the father pressed his fingers against the wound and began praying to Blessed Abelle.

The warmth permeated Giavno's body, as comforting as the arms of a lover. In that magical embrace he wondered how these idiot barbarians could not understand the beauty that was Abelle. Why would they, why would anyone, not embrace the power and goodness that could afford such wondrous magic as this? Why would anyone not appreciate such healing and utility, and with the promise of everlasting life beyond this mortal coil?

He closed his eyes and let the warmth flow through his body. He could understand the hesitance of the Samhaists, perhaps, for an embrace of Abelle would rob them of their tyrannical power hold. But not these barbarians of Alpinador—well, other than their shamans. For the average Alpinadoran, Blessed Abelle offered everything. And yet, they had rejected the monks at every turn. The men in the dungeon would rather be killed than accept Abelle! And it wasn't just because one of them was a shaman of some high standing, Giavno knew. The other two were just as stubborn and unyielding.

But why?

"What is troubling you, Brother?" Father De Guilbe said, drawing Giavno from his contemplation.

Giavno opened his eyes and only then realized that the healing session was long over, that he was holding his arm up high before him for no reason at all. He cleared his throat and straightened before the father. "I told you that it was but a minor wound," he said.

"What is it?" De Guilbe pressed. "Does such battle leave an evil taste in your mouth?"

"No, I mean, well, yes, Father," Giavno stuttered. "It seems nonsensical to me that the barbarians would throw themselves against our fortifications over such a matter. Their companions are alive only through our work with the gemstones—they cannot deny that truth. And all that we have asked in return is the acceptance of the source of that healing magic by those three."

Father De Guilbe spent a long moment staring at his second. "You have heard of the Battle of Cordon Roe?"

Giavno nodded numbly at the preposterous question. How could anyone, let alone any Abellican, not know that cursed name? Cordon Roe was a street in Delaval City where the word of Blessed Abelle first came to the great city at the mouth of the river. The first monks of Blessed Abelle in that most populous center had set up their chapel (though it was really no more than a two-story house) on Cordon Roe and preached the words of faith.

"What do you know of Cordon Roe, Brother?"

"I know that the brothers who traveled there were well received by the people of Delaval City," Giavno answered. "Their services quickly came to encompass the entirety of the street, and on some days the surrounding avenues were clogged with onlookers."

"It was a promising start in the early days of our Church, yes?"

"Of course."

"Too promising," said Father De Guilbe. "Blessed Abelle had sent the priests to that largest city in Honce not long after the word of Chapel Abelle had arrived there. They were granted entrance by the Laird Delaval, our current Laird Delaval's grandfather, if memory serves me correctly, and indeed he proved to be their first patient, the first recipient of gemstone magic in the city, as he was afflicted with some minor but aggravating malady. So Laird Delaval granted them access and allowed them their prayers and their practices. And the people responded, as we know most will to Blessed Abelle once they have felt the power of the gemstones."

"And that angered the Samhaists," Giavno said.

Father De Guilbe nodded solemnly. "And threatened Laird Delaval himself," he explained. "And so was the garrison of Delaval City turned upon our brethren, and Cordon Roe became a fortress within that fortress city."

"Every brother knows of this."

"But do you know that the father of Cordon Roe brokered a deal with Laird Delaval to allow the brothers safe egress from the city?"

"I had not heard of that," Giavno admitted.

"It is not common knowledge. The story goes that the Samhaists inspired the mob of the city to descend upon Cordon Roe, and the brothers of Abelle, refusing to use the gemstone magic to kill their attackers, were overrun and murdered."

"Yes, all ten!"

"No, Brother. It did not happen like that. The brothers brokered a deal with Laird Delaval, but as they were preparing to leave he came to them with altered terms. They could leave or they could stay, but they must renounce Blessed Abelle and embrace the Samhaist creed. Under those conditions, no further penalty would be exacted upon them."

Brother Giavno's eyes widened with horror as he considered the awful price. He licked his suddenly dry lips and said, "And they refused, and so Laird Delaval's forces overran them?"

"They refused, and unwilling to kill in the name of Abelle they killed themselves, all ten, and a hundred of their peasant followers committed suicide as well, robbing Laird Delaval and the Samhaists—most importantly, the Samhaists!—from claiming victory at Cordon Roe. Pity their fate not at all, Brother, for their action, their ultimate dedication to their faith, broke Laird Delaval's heart. Within five years another contingent from Blessed Abelle arrived in Delaval City, this one invited by the laird himself, and with promises that they could practice their faith unhindered by him or by the Samhaists."

Brother Giavno swallowed hard, trying to digest it all.

"They killed themselves rather than renounce Blessed Abelle," Father De Guilbe explained. "And we name them as heroes. Now we face barbarians who do the same, and you would name them as foolish?"

"Your pardon—" Giavno started, but De Guilbe continued over him.

"The three downstairs are not so unlike our long-lost brethren, though of course they are misguided in their faith. Do not begrudge them their stubbornness, Brother, for if the roles were reversed I would expect of myself, and of you, no less dedication. Death is not our master. That is the promise of Abelle. Our . . . guests hold faith in a similar promise, no doubt, as do those who line up against us and throw themselves at our wall. There are many reasons to die, some good and some not so reasonable. This is a good one, I think, and so do the barbarians, and so we know they will come on again and again after that. I respect them for their dedication. I will respect them even as I kill them."

"Of course, Father," said a humbled Giavno, and he lowered his gaze to the floor.

"This is not Cordon Roe," De Guilbe went on, his voice growing stronger and more deliberate. "And we of the Abellican Order have grown stronger and more secure in our faith. We will hold these walls, whatever the cost to our enemies. With the Covenant of God's Year Thirty, there are no restrictions regarding our own defense placed upon us as were upon our lost brethren of Cordon Roe."

"What do you mean?"

"You witnessed my lightning blast?"

"Yes."

"When the barbarians come at us again, we will return their stones and arrows with a barrage of magic that will shake the waters of Mithranidoon!" Father De Guilbe asserted. "If we kill a dozen, a score, a hundred, so be it. Chapel Isle will not fall to the unbelievers. We are here and we are staying, and the men in our dungeon will remain there, will rot there, as the bodies of their kin will rot on the rocks before our walls. No quarter, Brother. Mercy is for the deserving, and unlike our lost brethren of Cordon Roe, we are not docile. We are warriors of Abelle, and woe to our enemies."

Outside of Father De Guilbe's door, Brother Cormack leaned back against the stone wall and put his head in his hands. The rousing speech had Giavno and the attendants in the room cheering, and that applause, that vicious affirmation of the elevation of the Brothers of Abelle above all others, tore a hole in Cormack's heart.

He thought of Milkeila, and pictured her lying dead on the stones.

He left the bucket of water right there outside the door and rushed back to his own tiny room, where he prayed for guidance, all the while almost hoping that a spear would find his heart in the opening moments of the next attack.

CHAPTER 14

No Choice to Be Found

After an uneventful and swift sail through the gulf, the growing late-summer westerlies filling her sails, *Lady Dreamer* slid into dock at Pireth Vanguard, the oldest Honce settlement in the land of the same name. Callen, Cadayle, and Bransen stood at the bow, watching the boat glide into place beside the long wharf.

"We'll find him," Bransen whispered quietly, his hand about the soul stone in his small belt pouch, his other hand clutching Cadayle's. In response Cadayle gave a comforting squeeze.

"And you'll get your answers, and some peace," said Callen. "None are more deserving of that."

"We will get off first, ahead of the commotion," Cadayle decided.

"Begging your pardon, good lady . . . ladies and sir, but Captain McKeege would see you in his cabin," came a voice behind them, turning them, all three (for Bransen, in his surprise, swung about, and not awkwardly), to face a young sailor they recognized as *Lady Dreamer*'s cabin boy, nicknamed Dungwalker by the uncouth crew.

"Shouldn't he be out here directing the docking?" Callen asked.

Dungwalker shrugged. "Any on the boat can do it. Captain's in his cabin, and he sent me to find you and tell you."

"Lead on, then," said Cadayle, and to her two companions she offered a dismissive shrug. "Meet with him here or out in the town. It's all the same."

They followed the cabin boy to the captain's quarters, located under the flying bridge at the rear of the top deck. Dawson was alone inside waiting for them with an opened bottle of rum and four metal cups set out on his desk.

"Fair seas," he said in greeting when they came in, the cabin boy taking his leave and closing the door behind them. "As fine a sail as we could have hoped for at any time of the year."

He motioned for them to sit at the three chairs he had placed in front of his desk. As the two women helped Bransen, Cadayle noted a curious-looking smirk on Dawson's face. She wasn't sure what it might portend, but somehow it seemed out of place to her.

"I hoped you would join me for a drink," Dawson explained when they had settled in. He poured some rum in his own cup, which already contained some, Cadayle noticed, and then in Callen's and Cadayle's. He paused, holding the bottle over the cup set before Bransen.

"Better that you don't," Callen remarked. Dawson nodded and pulled the bottle back, then dropped into his chair.

"To good friends," he said, lifting his cup.

"To finding Brother Dynard," Cadayle added before she tapped it.

"Dynard, yes," Dawson agreed after he had sipped. "I'm not sure which chapel, but they'll know at Pellinor."

"A long journey?" asked Callen. "If it is, we should secure a wagon for Bransen."

"A journey of two weeks, and one I'll make with the others. We'll take you three as far as Tanadoon, a small town just a few miles inland. They've many new houses waiting for folks, any folks, to take them. We will be putting the few families of our new soldiers there, too. So you'll have neighbors among some of the folk you've met on our journey, and all of you with your own houses and large plots of land." He gave a little laugh and explained, "Aye, we've got more wood for more houses than we've people to put in them! Here's to hoping you come to love this land as I do. It's a hard life, but one worth living, to be sure, and Vanguard would welcome the addition of such fine folk as yourselves." He lifted his cup again in toast, but he was alone this time.

"I do not know that my husband could manage it," Cadayle said.

"Of course," Dawson replied, and again Cadayle caught a flash of that strange, too-knowing smile. "I should be quick then in my search that we can get you three, and maybe Brother Dynard, back across the gulf before the winter snows."

"That would be good, yes," said Cadayle, drawing a poke from Callen.

"Don't be so ungrateful, daughter," Callen scolded.

"Everyone grows impatient when his grasp nears the goal," Dawson said with a grin. "No steps as desperate as the last three to the gate, eh?"

The procession of more than a hundred people, including most of Dawson's crew and a garrison from Pireth Vanguard, set out later that same day down the road, no more than a flattened trail, to the new town of Tanadoon.

New indeed! The smell of freshly cut wood greeted the caravan as they entered the southeastern gate of the wood-walled village. Neat and tidy houses all in a row greeted them inside, all looking very much the same. A few were occupied by families who had resettled from within Vanguard, but most sat empty and waiting.

"As you were promised," Dawson called out when all of the folk were inside. "Even you men who have no kinfolk with you can claim a home as your own—two men to each, if you've not family, please. Though you'll not be staying beyond this one night. But know in your hearts that you've a place to return to when your debt to Dame Gwydre is paid."

There was no cheer at that, which surprised Cadayle as she surveyed the dour bunch. Most of them were prisoners of Laird Delaval, a few from Laird Ethelbert, and none seemed overly pleased to be here.

The trio found a small home soon enough, settling in under the shadow of the northeastern corner. It was sparsely furnished, but had enough straw for them to make comfortable enough beds, and Dawson's men brought a fair number of supplies—foodstuffs and barrels of water and even a rough map of the area that included directions to a nearby stream.

"It is not so bad," Callen announced later that evening, the three sitting about a single candle, sharing a loaf of sweet cake. "All of it, I mean. The house and the food and the welcome of our hosts. A good and generous man is Dawson McKeege."

"Too much so I fear," said Cadayle, but Callen scoffed at her and waved the suspicions away.

The next morning, the men who had come to serve Dame Gwydre marched out of town for distant battles, a few leaving wives and children behind, totaling a score of folk or so to add to the like number already settled in Tanadoon and the handful of sentries patrolling the town's wall. The village had been built to hold near to three hundred people easily, but there couldn't have been a quarter of that number left after Dawson marched.

"I'll return presently with word of Bran Dynard for you," Dawson promised Bransen from atop his small chestnut stallion. He tipped his cap to Cadayle, then more assuredly and boldly to Callen (which made Cadayle blink more than once as she regarded her mother!), then cantered out to the head of the military line, and out through the same gate they had entered the afternoon before.

"I hate the waiting," Bransen whispered.

"He'll be back as soon as he can," Callen assured him with surprising confidence, drawing another blink from Cadayle.

"Mother?" she asked.

"He's a good man," Callen answered. With that she spun away and practically skipped into their chosen house.

"She's taken a liking to Vanguard," Bransen said dryly.

"It is a difficult place for the Stork," Cadayle replied, stealing his mirth.

Bransen turned on her. "Every place is difficult for the Stork," he said, trying hard to keep his voice low so that he would not jeopardize his disguise. Clearly agitated, that was no easy chore!

"I know," said Cadayle. "The sooner we are out of the reach of Ethelbert or Delaval or any of them, the better."

"We should have found a way to Behr instead of coming north," Bransen lamented, and turned away, feigning a stumble as a couple of other "towns-folk" walked by.

"We seek answers, so we go where the questions lead us," Cadayle replied. "Now it is Vanguard, but perhaps we are not so far from Behr as you believe. Dawson has been there several times, to a city he called Jacintha. The sail takes the whole of a season, but it is one he's made before and promises to make again."

Bransen quieted at that and seemed to Cadayle to relax quite a bit. She helped him back into the house, where they would spend the next few days anxiously awaiting Dawson's return with the word, as promised.

He came in with little fanfare but great commotion at the end of the next week, surrounded by a score and more of soldiers, including several of the men who had sailed north with Bransen, Cadayle, and Callen. Most of his entourage, though, was of longtime Vanguardsmen, all toughened by years of battle. The way they rode, the way they dismounted, the way their weapons came easily to their hands, spoke volumes of that.

"A fine morning made finer by the sight of you," Dawson said when the trio came out to greet him. He stayed up on his horse, as did the armed and armored warriors flanking him, several to either side.

Bransen stuttered to say something, but lurched suddenly and appeared as if he would have fallen had not Callen and Cadayle grabbed him at the last minute (in a perfectly choreographed maneuver).

"You need not do that," Dawson said.

"Well we're not to let him fall on his face now, are we?" asked Callen.

"I meant that he did not need to do that," Dawson explained, and all three looked at him curiously. "You, Bransen Garibond. There is no need to wear your mask of the cripple here."

Bransen stuttered and drooled, and he wasn't faking, for he had let go of the gemstone.

"Do not mock my husband!" Cadayle retorted.

"Your husband, the Highwayman?" asked Dawson.

"I know not what you mean," Cadayle said, and she straightened Bransen, steadying him on his feet, before taking a resolute step toward Dawson. "Have you come here to mock us? You promised us news of Brother Bran Dynard. . . ."

"He is dead."

That stole Cadayle's momentum, and Bransen let out a little squeal, as if he had been punched in the gut.

"I am sorry—truly," said Dawson, and he seemed sincere despite the confusing atmosphere here. "Bran Dynard died on the road more than twenty years ago on his way to Chapel Abelle. He never made it. The brothers think it was a powrie attack, which seems likely as the Holdings were at relative peace in those times, but powries remained thick about the land."

"Dead?" Bransen mumbled. He thought of the Book of Jhest, his salvation, and it seemed so incongruous to him that the man who had penned that magnificent work could have been killed so senselessly on the road so long ago. *The man who had penned it,* he mused, and he realized that he was referring to his father. He didn't know how to feel, or what to feel; nothing made sense to him at that stunning moment of revelation. He wanted to deny Dawson's claims, but wasn't even sure if his desire to do so was because the man had penned the book and might have some answers for him, or because the man was his father.

His father! Dead! Bransen was not as surprised as he would have guessed. So long, no word. A man he had never known. Would never know.

"How did you discover this?" Cadayle demanded. Suddenly she seemed to be stuttering almost as much as her husband, and that fact alone drew Bransen from his emotional jumble.

"The brothers told me back at Chapel Abelle."

"You lied to us!" said Cadayle. Next to her Callen let out a little shriek, covering her mouth in horror.

"I did and I admit it, but I did it for your own good," Dawson calmly replied. "And stop your lurching and drooling, man! Did you really believe that you could travel the length and breadth of the land in such an obvious guise? Word was run to every chapel in Honce to beware the man they called the Stork, for he slew Laird Prydae and left Pryd Holding in turmoil."

"That is a lie!" said Cadayle.

"Please, good lady, I am not your judge," said Dawson, and now he did dismount, though several of the fearsome guards around him bristled at the movement. "Nor did the brothers of Chapel Abelle wish to pass judgment. But they would have had no choice—indeed, they thought they had no choice. But I offered them one of mutual benefit."

"Liar!"

"And your husband's alive because of it!"

"Enough!" Bransen said, startling them all with the sudden power in his voice.

For a few moments all held quiet, then Dawson bowed low and said, "Welcome, Highwayman. Your reputation precedes you."

Bransen stared at him hard.

"If I had said nothing, if I had left you there, the brothers of Chapel Abelle would have taken you in chains and handed you to the nearest laird faithful to

Laird Delaval. They wished no such thing, but they were bound, surely so. You can understand that."

Bransen didn't reply, didn't move at all.

"You were passed on the road by Brother Fatuus from the Chapel of Precious Memories of Palmaristown," Dawson explained. "He arrived bearing news of the Stork, the Highwayman. They watched your approach before you ever neared Weatherguard. I offered them a deal, for your sake, for my dame's benefit, and to relieve the brothers of their regrettable duty."

"To take me here to fight in your dame's war," Bransen reasoned.

Dawson shrugged sheepishly. "We are in desperate need of strong warriors, and as I said, your reputation preceded you. The acting steward of Pryd Holding warned all of your prowess with the blade. You are a deadly sort, I am told."

"I want no part of your war," said Bransen, and Cadayle grabbed his arm tightly.

"There is no choice to be found, I fear," said Dawson. "You have nowhere to go, nor do your beautiful companions."

"You threaten them?" Bransen growled. The soldiers stepped their mounts in closer.

"Our fight is a good one," said Dawson. "Not like the meaningless slaughter in the South. We battle goblins and glacial trolls, evil little brutes, all. And heathen barbarian murderers, who steal in at night and slaughter our children in their sleep. We battle Samhaists, and I have heard you have no love for them, either."

"You seem to hear a lot."

"True enough," Dawson said, and he bowed, turning the sarcasm into a compliment. "I regret my lie, and I humbly apologize. Without it you would be long dead by now, your beautiful wife widowed, but still the need to so lie left a sour taste in my mouth. But that lie is irrelevant now, for the deed is done."

"Just let us leave," said Bransen.

"To go where?"

"Anywhere that is not here."

"Will you swim across the gulf, then? Or run west all the way around it, through wild lands where monsters and hungry hunting cats and bears are thicker than the trees? Be reasonable. There is no choice to be found."

"We will find a boat sailing south to Honce. Or to Behr, even."

"None will leave before the winter's end."

"Then we will wai . . ."

"Enough!" said Dawson, his visage suddenly hardening. He quickly mounted his steed. "Enough, Highwayman. You are fairly caught, and already convicted in the South, where the sentence would be death. I offer you this alternative. You will march with Dame Gwydre's forces—many of the same men who shared your boat ride to Pireth Vanguard—in a goodly campaign. We are desperate here. I am not asking you for this service."

"Meaning?"

"Meaning that if you refuse your life is forfeit."

Bransen narrowed his eyes and squared his shoulders.

"And so are the lives of your companions."

If Dawson had spun his horse about and prompted it to kick Bransen in the face, the impact would have been no less staggering.

"How dare you!" Bransen demanded, but Dawson tugged his horse around and began walking it away, and the mounted guards pressed in on Bransen and the two women in his wake.

"Say your good-byes to them, Highwayman," Dawson insisted. "We leave now. Serve us well through the winter campaign. If we fight back the Samhaist horde, you will be returned, and all crimes forgiven. I offer you passage anywhere in the world *Lady Dreamer* can take you." He stopped his horse and turned about, locking stares with the fuming Bransen. "That is the best offer you will ever get, Highwayman. I can legally have my soldiers kill you, and them, right now, by order of Dame Gwydre herself. Now gather your things and say your farewells. We've a long ride this night, and a longer one tomorrow."

Not since he had learned of Garibond's execution had Bransen felt such a profound emptiness within him. Lost opportunity, was the only thought he could hear. He didn't know what to feel and then didn't know what to make of that! That confusion brought guilt, and that guilt brought more confusion, and truly, Bransen seemed to be spiraling downward.

Dawson McKeege had duped them so easily! The cage the clever man had built around them, both with soldiers and by simple location, seemed as unbreakable as any Bransen had ever known. He sat in the small house the trio had taken as their own, his back to the door, his soul stone strapped under his black silk bandanna about his forehead.

"We could find our way out through the back window and over the wall," Cadayle said to him as she tied the silk strap about his upper right arm—which was really just an ornament now that his identity was fully revealed. "We'd be gone into the thick forest before Dawson and his men ever knew we'd left."

Bransen shook his head slowly and deliberately. "Gone to where? That forest is without end. Even if you and I could make our way, your mother is not a young woman."

"Then you go out," Cadayle said. "Be gone, Bransen, I beg. You are not for war; your heart is not the heart of a soldier. When you are fighting men—Alpinadorans—who have not wronged you, will you revel in the kill?"

"No choice to be found," Bransen said, echoing Dawson's words.

"Run!" Cadayle begged him.

"And that will leave you and Callen to the mercy of Dame Gwydre. You heard Dawson's warning."

"Dawson will not harm us."

"He will, milady," came Dawson's voice from the doorway. "Regrettably, but certainly."

Bransen narrowed his eyes as he stared at the man. He instinctively grasped the hilt of his fabulous sword at his side. But he could not deny the truth of Dawson's logic, that the monks would have killed him to avoid the wrath of Laird Delaval.

"You do not appreciate our desperation," Dawson went on, walking into the room. "We are pushed to the gulf. Entire villages have been slaughtered by the Samhaist aggressors and their monstrous minions. Entire villages! Women and children and even the animals. I have no love of deceiving you: I feel not clever or happy with the act. But doubt not my words of warning, for your own sake."

He looked at Bransen. "Now," he said. "We go," he announced simply, walking through the door.

Stunned with the sudden turn of events, Cadayle wrapped Bransen in a desperate hug. Callen came over and joined in, the shoulders of both women bobbing with sorrow.

Bransen pushed them back just enough so that he could stand. He kissed Cadayle on the cheek and wiped away her tears, though more were sure to replace them in short order.

"I will return to you," he promised. "Never doubt." With that, Bransen set her back firmly and followed Dawson through the door.

CHAPTER 15

Echoes of Cordon Roe

"Concentration!" Brother Giavno warned above the tumult of the battle raging again about the chapel's strong walls, which mostly involved crude spears (sharpened sticks) volleying against stones thrown from on high, coupled with a continual exchange of taunts and the incessant thumping of barbarians pounding on the fitted stones with heavy wooden mallets in an amazing attempt to weaken the integrity of the fortification. "It is most important, to your very survival."

The two younger monks looked at each other with obvious concern—and why should they not? For they were about to go into the middle of the barbarian attackers!

"Brother Faldo, you must maintain the power of the serpentine," Giavno repeated yet again. "At all costs! Accept a spear to your chest, but do not allow the magic of that gem to dissipate!"

Faldo rested the huge and surprisingly lightweight shield on one shoulder and nodded sheepishly. Behind him, the other young volunteer, Brother Moorkris, moved closer and took his companion's hand and together they shuffled for the secret door set in the wall, just to the side of the main fighting. Moorkris held out his open palm toward Giavno, as he had been instructed, and Giavno nodded for Faldo to enact the serpentine shield.

A moment later, a blue-white glow encompassed both young monks, and Giavno gave promising Brother Moorkris a ruby, the stone of fire.

"Charge into them," he whispered, and he nodded to the pair working the door.

It opened fast and Giavno shoved the two terrified young brothers out, then fell back through the door quickly and spun about, throwing his back against the stone. He knew they wouldn't long hold their nerve.

And he was right, for the pair had barely moved from the outside of the door before the barbarians took note of them. Faldo did well to keep low behind his shield and to keep his thoughts on the serpentine, maintaining the magical protection. A spear hit the shield, then a second, but this was of barbarian make, woven of thin wood into layers behind a leather front, and those weapons did not get through the clever tangle.

But the Alpinadorans didn't hesitate in the least and charged right in, and Faldo got rammed hard as a shoulder slammed against his shield, sending him lurching back and nearly upending him.

To his credit, he maintained the serpentine barrier, but the jolt broke his grip with his companion just as Moorkris sent his energy through the ruby and conjured a tremendous fireball.

With the connection to Faldo broken, Moorkris had no protection from his own blast, and like the poor barbarians caught in the area of conflagration, he was engulfed in his own flames.

It was all screaming and burning and shouting then, and Brother Faldo, confused and dazed and having no idea of where to turn next, stumbled back through the smoke toward the door. He felt someone punch him in the back, but he managed to stagger through, and Giavno and the others quickly shut and secured the portal behind him.

"I held the barrier," the devastated young brother started to explain, blubbering through his mounting guilt as he came to understand that his failure to hold on had immolated his friend Moorkris. He couldn't finish the thought, though, as he just fell over, for that punch in the back was not a punch at all, but a spear that had driven deep into his kidney.

"Get him to Father De Guilbe," Giavno yelled at the other two, and he rushed for a ladder that would take him up to the parapets. When he got there, he found that his comrades were no longer raining stones on the attackers, and when he peered over the wall, he understood.

For the Alpinadorans were running off, and just below Giavno no less than seven bodies—whether men or women, he could hardly tell—either lay very still or writhed on the ground in mortal agony, their clothing melted to their blistered and bubbling skin. He recognized the monk he had sent out there by the shape of the still-burning robes, and his instinct to run out and retrieve Brother Moorkris lasted only the heartbeat it took him to realize that the young and promising young Abellican was already dead.

With a heavy heart and a heavy sigh, Brother Giavno started for Father De Guilbe's quarters, praying that Brother Faldo, at least, would survive.

He paused at a group of several brothers, all staring hard at the gruesome scene below. "Go out through the secret door and see if any of our enemies can be saved. Be quick about it, and return at first sign that their companions are coming after you."

He thought that an insignificant command, easily followed and without consequence—other than perhaps the notion one or two of their charred enemies might be pulled from the grip of death. But he could not have been more wrong, for as soon as the brothers moved out to the writhing wounded, the barbarian forces from across the way howled and charged with fury beyond anything Giavno could have anticipated. The monks made it safely back inside, with one grievously wounded Alpinadoran warrior in tow, but they had to secure the door fast, and calls for renewed support along the parapets rang out almost immediately thereafter.

For the Alpinadorans came on with abandon, throwing themselves against the stone, smashing at it and seeming not to care about the rain of stones that came down upon them.

"Bolster that portal!" Giavno cried, and nearly as many brothers had to work at piling stones behind the battered secret door as were up on the walls trying to repel the attackers.

Of the three fights so far, that battle was the most lopsided, with another handful of barbarians dead, and several more badly wounded, and not a monk seriously injured.

But for Giavno, that last battle was the most unnerving of all, the one that told him in his heart of hearts that these enemies who had come against Chapel Isle were willing to die to a man and woman to retrieve their brethren.

He had never seen such ferocious dedication.

Nor had Cormack, who had watched it all—the fireball, the retrieval, the second wave of wild assault—with horror. "We cannot win," Cormack muttered many times during and after that second battle, for only then did he understand, truly understand, what "winning" might mean.

He saw Brother Giavno hustling toward De Guilbe's door shortly thereafter, and thought to follow and plead with them to abandon this madness.

But his feet would not move to the commands of his brain. He had no heart for another round of verbal battle with those two.

The three monks stood in a line, side by side, in De Guilbe's office, facing the father and Brother Giavno, who stood before the first, demanding his report.

"They are not eating," the young monk sheepishly replied to Giavno's question.

At the other end of that short line, Brother Cormack winced at every word. He knew it to be true. Androosis and the others would not eat—not a morsel. The captured shaman had decreed that they would die before acceding to the wishes of their wretched captors.

"Then make them eat," Giavno said to the man, who retreated a step from the sheer intensity of the senior brother's angry tone.

"We have," he stammered in reply. "We held them and forced food and water into their mouths. Most they spit back."

"But they got some," Giavno reasoned. "That is good. Their bodies will likely outlast their determination."

"Likely," Cormack mouthed under his breath.

"When we returned to them the next day, they were covered in vomit," the young monk explained.

Giavno glanced back at Father De Guilbe and gave a disgusted sigh. "Bind them more tightly," he ordered as he turned back to face the young monk. "That they cannot get their fingers down their throats."

"Yes, Brother," the young monk answered, lowering his gaze.

"The fourth has been placed with them?" Father De Guilbe asked, referring to the barbarian who had been caught in Brother Moorkris's fireball. The man would carry horrible scars for the rest of his life, but through the miracle of the gemstone magic, his life had been saved.

"Not yet, Father," the monk replied. "Brother Mn'Ache fears that his wounds will fester if he is laid in the dirt."

"Then put a blanket under him," Giavno intervened, and from Father De Guilbe's nod, Cormack could see that the man was of like mind.

"He recovers well, and should be ready for the dungeon in . . ." the young monk tried to explain, but Giavno cut him short.

"He recovers in the dungeon or he recovers not at all. I will not have a dangerous enemy in our midst when again his people attack. Would you have him climb out of his cot and murder Brother Mn'Ache while he was distracted at tending one of us?"

"He is bound."

"Now, Brother," Giavno ordered. "To the dungeon with him. Be gone!"

The young monk hesitated for just a moment, then whirled about and sprinted away.

"It is an unpleasant business," Father De Guilbe admitted. "Hold faith, all of you. Keep in mind that our Brother Mn'Ache was able to save two lives during the night, that of the burned barbarian and that of Brother Faldo."

"Brother Faldo is not yet awake," Giavno replied. "Nor is Brother Mn'Ache certain that he will recover."

"He will," said De Guilbe with a confident smile, and he motioned for Giavno to move along.

The next monk in the line, the one standing right beside Cormack, offered details on the work at shoring up the walls and cutting stones and the like to hurl down at the barbarians. With confidence he assured, "They will not breach our defenses."

The assertion was ridiculous, of course, and spoken more as a cheer than a proper evaluation, but it seemed to satisfy the inquisitor brothers, for Giavno patted the monk on the shoulder and moved to stand before Brother Cormack.

"The water supply is inexhaustible," Cormack reported with a shrug before Gaivno could even inquire, as if to ask of Giavno why they bothered to bring him to these meetings. His only oversight was that of supplying water and fish, after all.

"And the fish?"

"The lake is full of them. They come to our hidden pond to feed, and are not so hard to catch."

"Triple the catch," Father De Guilbe unexpectedly interjected.

"Father?" Cormack asked.

"Triple—at least," the man answered. "Our barbarian enemies will not relent, but they will pay too heavy a price to continue throwing themselves at our wall, I am sure. They will look for other ways to strike at us, and if they come to understand that we have this inexhaustible resource at our disposal, they might try to interrupt it. That, we cannot have."

"Yes, Father," Cormack said.

"On your travels to the pond, do you look in on our guests?" De Guilbe asked.

Cormack shrugged noncommittally.

"You are not prohibited from doing so," Father De Guilbe prompted.

"Sometimes," Cormack admitted.

"And it is as was described here?"

"They will not eat," Cormack admitted, and the floodgates opened then. "They grow weak. There is no bend in them, Father. They will not recant their beliefs and embrace ours—not at the price of their very lives—"

"Cordon Roe," Father De Guilbe interrupted, aiming the remark at Brother Giavno, who nodded, and Cormack grimaced at the reference.

If De Guilbe could see that apt analogy, then why would he insist on keeping the Alpinadorans as prisoners? For the end result would be their deaths or continued misery—how could it be otherwise?

Cormack wanted to shout those questions at these two monks, but the door swung open and the same monk who had just left to fetch the burned Alpinadoran and bring him to the dungeon burst in.

"A messenger!" he cried, clearly out of breath. "At the front gate. A messenger from our enemies approaches."

"Bring him in?" Brother Giavno asked of De Guilbe, who thought about it for a few heartbeats, then shook his head.

"No, he will learn too much of our inner defenses," the leader decided. "Let us go to him and greet him at the wall instead."

He started out immediately, Giavno beside him, and Cormack and the others, having not been ordered to stay behind, swept into their wake.

As soon as he climbed the ladder to the parapet above the chapel's gate, Cormack realized he was looking at one, if not the, leader of the barbarians of Yossunfier. The man was a shaman, obviously, for he wore the same ornamental necklaces as Milkeila, only grander by far, with his loose clothing decorated with shells and other trinkets, so that they rattled with his every step. He was old, well into his sixth decade of life, at least, and Milkeila had told Cormack enough about Alpinadoran society for him to understand that age was no small matter in the hierarchy of the tribes.

"I am Teydru," he said, his voice clear and strong, and Cormack sucked in his breath, for he had indeed heard that name before, and knew then that he was standing before the absolute spiritual leader of Milkeila's people.

"You come uninvited to this place, Teydru," Father De Guilbe replied rather curtly. It seemed even more snappish and stilted due to the man's lack of command of the common Alpinadoran language.

"You have three of my people," Teydru went on, unrattled.

"Four," De Guilbe corrected, and that seemed to shake the man just a bit. "And all of them alive only through the holy gifts of Blessed Abelle. Only through our work and healing powers."

"Better they had died, then," said Teydru, and out of the corner of his eye, Cormack caught De Guilbe's silent sneer.

"Leave this island," De Guilbe said.

"Return to us our brethren and we will be gone."

"Your brethren are alive only through our efforts. They have felt the warmth and love of Abelle."

"They embrace your faith?" Teydru asked, and his tone told the monks that he didn't believe it for a moment.

"They begin to see the truth of Blessed Abelle," De Guilbe countered cryptically.

To Cormack, there was great irony in that statement, for Father De Guilbe had proclaimed it without the slightest recognition that he, himself, would never begin to see the truth of anything other than Blessed Abelle. He was a man of complete intolerance demanding tolerance of others.

"Bring them forth to speak!" Teydru demanded, and De Guilbe crossed his arms over his chest, staring down at the man from on high.

"You are in no position to bargain," the monk reminded the shaman. "You have attacked us three times, and three times you have been repelled. That will not change. Your people die at our walls, but we remain. You cannot win, Teydru."

Unshaken, the shaman replied, "We will not leave. We will not stop attacking you. We will have our brethren."

"Or what? Or you will all lie dead at the base of our walls?"

The chide didn't have quite the effect De Guilbe was trying for, obviously, for Teydru squared his shoulders and proudly lifted his chin.

"If that is what our spirits demand," he answered, not a quiver in his voice. "We will not leave. We will not stop attacking you. We will have our brethren."

Cormack licked his lips and managed to pry his gaze from the imposing barbarian to glance at Father De Guilbe.

"We will kill you all," the monk promised.

"Then we will die with joy," said Teydru, and he turned and slowly walked away.

Father De Guilbe and Brother Giavno lingered for only a very short while before heading back to the father's office.

"They cannot defeat us, so they try to bargain," one young monk said hopefully to a group gathered not far from Cormack. "They will give up and leave soon enough."

"They will not," Cormack corrected him, and many sets of eyes turned his way. "They will fight us to the last."

"They are not that foolish," the man argued.

"But they are that faithful," said Cormack, and he headed for the tunnels and the pond, and this time he paid more attention to the details of the four prisoners and the dungeon holding them as he passed.

Four tense days passed before the next attack, just when some of the brothers were beginning to whisper that the barbarians would besiege the chapel rather than assault it again.

No such luck, and the reason for the delay became apparent very quickly: that the barbarians had been training, and thinking, and better preparing. Nowhere was that more evident than when a pair of brothers went out into the throng, much as Faldo and Moorkris had done. The horde retreated from them at full speed, while others, farther away, launched a barrage of spears and rocks at the brothers that had them scrambling back toward the wall.

Pursuit came swift, and to the credit of the monks, they had maintained their concentration on the serpentine shield throughout, and so they were ready to counter with a dazzling fireball.

But those nearest Alpinadorans, obviously expecting the blast, quickly veered aside, and more impressively, they had come in wrapped in water-soaked blankets! A couple were wounded—only minimally—but suddenly the two poor brothers found themselves under brutal assault.

From the wall, Giavno, Cormack, and the others cried out for them to get back to safety, and run they did. They couldn't outrun the spear volley, though.

Lightning bolts lashed out from the wall, along with a barrage of stones. Several barbarians fell, grievously wounded.

But so too did the brothers fall, side by side.

They would have survived their wounds, likely, had not the monks on the wall continued their barrage at the approaching horde. For the attackers wanted prisoners, that they could exact an exchange. They couldn't get near the fallen brothers, though, in the face of that barrage, so they settled for the next best option.

The Alpinadorans rained another volley of spears at the defenseless duo.

On the far side of the chapel, the western wall, a second wave crept up and then broke into a howling charge, knowing that most of the monks were across to the other side, trying to help their fallen.

"Go! Go! Go!" Giavno yelled at Cormack and some others, and the group leaped down from the wall and rushed across, to see brothers on the opposite parapets already engaging the ferocious enemy. A series of lightning bolts shook the ground beneath their feet as they ran to bolster the defense, and Cormack understood that the immediate threat had been eradicated, though the fighting hardly quieted.

The others ran ahead of Cormack as he slowed to a stop. He glanced back at Brother Giavno and the continuing battle at the eastern wall, wincing almost constantly from the terrible screams.

He went to the side structure of the keep, and to the bulkhead, where he picked up a torch and slipped down into the tunnels.

The sound of the fighting receded behind him, but it would take more than a closed bulkhead door to cleanse poor Cormack's sensibilities. That reality only made him move with more purpose, however, down the side tunnel to the dungeon where the four barbarians sat miserably, side by side. Cormack considered the task ahead of them and wondered if they could possibly succeed. Beyond weary, half-starved by choice, and one still recovering from immolation, Cormack had to wonder if they would even be able to stand up once he freed them of their bonds.

"Your people come on again," he said. "Men and women are dying up there."

Androosis lifted his head toward the monk, and Cormack simply couldn't read the expression on his face. Did he feel betrayed? Was he angry with Cormack? Confused?

"You would have us renounce our faith," the shaman said in a voice parched and dry and so very weak. "We would die first."

"I know."

The simple answer elicited a curious look from both the shaman and Androosis, and that gave Cormack some hope. He set the torch in a sconce and moved around the wooden wall. "We will venture deeper," he said as he loosened Androosis's bonds.

"Because you fear my people will overrun your pathetic castle," said Toniquay the shaman. "You move us away in desperation!"

Cormack hustled fast around the barrier to stand before the still-bound shaman. "Your people will not get through the wall. Not now and not ever. They will be killed to a man and woman at the base of the stones, unless we end this."

"You doubt the power . . ."

"Shut up," said Cormack. "More than twenty of your kin are dead already. More are dying right now. They will not relent and they cannot prevail. Their loyalty to you is commendable—and foolish."

"What would you have us do?" Androosis interjected, and Cormack was glad of that, for Toniquay was about to issue another stubborn retort, and time was too short for such bickering. He moved around the wall again and freed all three, with Toniquay last.

As they were freeing themselves of the rope, and climbing out of the mud and the piss and the feces, Cormack went back to the sconce and retrieved the torch.

"Follow closely, and as fast as you can manage," he instructed.

"And if we do not?"

Cormack swung about with a heavy sigh, drawing out a knife as he turned. "This ends today, now," he said. "I will show you the way out of here, or . . ." He brandished the knife. "It ends today."

"And why are we to believe you?"

"What choice have we?" Androosis asked, and motioned for Cormack to go.

To Cormack's relief, they all followed, with Androosis helping the burned man, even lifting him in his arms and carrying him along. That gave Cormack pause—would they even be able to execute the planned escape?

They went through the door at the tunnel's end, into the chamber where the lake comprised most of the floor.

"You are all strong swimmers, I would expect and hope," Cormack said, placing his torch down and starting to strip off his heavy cloak. He paused, though, and considered the action. "I cannot," he said.

Androosis shot him a concerned look. "We are not going back," he said.

Cormack shook his head, showing the four that such was not what he was talking about at all. "I cannot go into the water and open the grate, as I had intended," he explained. "If I return to my people with wet hair, they will know of my involvement."

"Grate?" Androosis asked.

"A simple netting, with minor reinforcement," Cormack explained, pointing to the northwestern corner of the underground pool. "Beyond it is a short tunnel—an easy swim to freedom."

Androosis stared long and hard at Cormack. He placed his companion down gently and waded into the dark pool, walking in until the warm water was up to his waist before ducking under. While Canrak, the fourth of the barbarian party, lent an arm of support to the burned man, Toniquay stared unrelentingly at Cormack.

"You are so afraid of my people," he said with a twisted grin.

Cormack brushed him off with a smirk and shake of his head, never taking his eyes off the spot where Androosis had disappeared.

"If it is not true, then why?" the shaman demanded.

"Because my God would expect no less," said Cormack.

Androosis came up with a splash, sucking in a deep breath of air. "The way is clear," he announced. "It is a short swim, with open water beyond."

"What about him?" Cormack asked with sincere concern, and he indicated the barely conscious newest prisoner.

"I will get him through," Androosis promised. He walked over to Cormack then and dropped his hands on the monk's shoulders. "You are a good man," he said simply, and that was all Cormack had to hear to know that he had indeed done the right thing. The cost to him might prove great, but whatever Father De Guilbe might do could not begin to approach the cost to Cormack's sensibilities had he continued to do nothing.

Cormack came out of the side chamber a short while later, to find the battle still on in full, still loud and chaotic, still, he hoped, providing him the cover he needed.

He went to battle and prayed with all his heart that it would be the last.

CHAPTER 16

Mitigating

They called him a multitude of names, and seemed to create a new one whenever he put his sword to work. The Dancing Sword, the Bird of Prey—any and all adjectives and superlatives to toss upon this warrior who stood so clearly above all others. Whenever a new title was bestowed, all knew to whom it referred, for there was only one it fit. All the conversations came back to the name by which they all knew him, the name used in his introduction to the soldiers. The Highwayman, he was called, and more than one sturdy soul shuddered to think of meeting this man on a darkened highway in southern Honce!

True to form, he danced this day, running about the battlefield, leaping and spinning, lashing out with his feet as he soared through the mobs and always striking mortal blows as he landed. Like a small tornado he rushed through the battling throng, and as the enemies—this day they were exclusively the blue-skinned and ugly little trolls—were easily distinguished from his comrades, there wasn't the slightest hesitation in his movements and strikes.

He ran past one man and troll in a death clench and struck fast and hard and true, and the troll howled and thrashed and toppled to the ground.

Its killer was already gone, to another man, fallen, with two trolls standing over him and stabbing down at his supine form as he scrambled desperately and futilely to block.

The Highwayman leaped between the two surprised trolls, his feet kicking out to either side. He connected squarely on both, snapping their heads back. One went flying to the ground, while the other somehow managed to stay on its feet.

The standing one died first.

The Highwayman charged at another, and as soon as it recognized him, his black mask and outfit, it shrieked and threw up its hands in a pitiful defense.

Feeling another troll rushing at his back, he leaped high and spun, coming around to circle-kick the defending troll with a sweeping strike that spun it out to the right. In midair, he flipped his blade from his right hand to his left, and allowed the momentum of his turn to guide the strike as that fabulous and decorated sword of wrapped metal plunged into the troll's chest. The Highwayman retracted immediately and flipped the blade back to his right in a reverse grip, and stabbed out with a backhand as he came fully around, timing it just right to slash across the chest of one pursuing troll, and send the second pursuer stumbling backward.

He flipped his sword to right his grip as he rushed past the bleeding troll, launching a heavy left-hand blow to lay the dying creature low as he pursued its backpedaling companion. That one, shield and small sword in hand, brought both up to block, but the man drove on, smashing away with abandon, his sword too fine for the meager defenses. A piece of shield went flying away, a piece of troll arm following. The blade of the troll's sword fell free to the ground, the head of the troll fast following.

The warrior known as the Highwayman skidded to a stop to catch his breath and survey the field. Only one concentration of trolls remained intact, a group of about twenty formed into a tight wedge on the far side of the fighting.

Behind the black mask, the man narrowed his eyes.

Twenty trolls.

He yelled and charged.

And he kept yelling, demanding their attention. A spear flew at him and he snapped his sword across, knocking it harmlessly aside. He caught a second hurled spear with his free hand and threw it down. He turned sideways, still moving forward, and leaned back, letting a third slip past, then angled and dove into a roll, under a fourth, and came up in a leap, above the fifth missile.

The volley grew more concentrated and coordinated, a barrage of rocks flying out at him.

He yelled in rage, in glee, in sheer ferocity, his sword and free hand working wildly as he turned and ducked and leaned, and he came right through the volley, showing not a scratch.

The troll wedge formation, appearing so formidable just a few heartbeats before, broke apart, the creatures running away from this madman they also knew by many names, all inspiring terror.

The closest one, then second, then third, fell in rapid succession to his flashing, marvelous blade, and he continued the chase for a long while, though he only scored one more kill, to drive the group far from the field.

He was angry at being out here, angry at being tricked, angry at being away from his beloved, but Bransen couldn't deny the elation of this furious fight against an irredeemable enemy.

All of that anger flowed into his arms, bringing them strength and speed.

And no amount of troll blood would satiate him.

Y ou did well in tricking that one," Brother Jond Dumolnay said to Dawson McKeege as they watched Bransen dance away in pursuit of the fleeing monsters. The monk continued his work on one of the wounded Vanguardsmen as he spoke, pulling open the man's tunic to reveal a gaping hole in his chest, blood gushing forth. Jond took a deep breath at the imposing, horrible sight and went to work with his soul stone, summoning its healing powers to try to stem the flow.

"It was for his own good, as much as our own," McKeege replied, more than a little defensively. "Your church would have turned the man over to Laird Delaval, and he'd have been sacked with a snake, to be sure."

Brother Jond continued his prayers, paused and looked at the continuing flow, then went back to his prayers—but only momentarily, for he saw the bleeding stem and nodded in relief that the man was now somewhat stable. Jond sighed and rocked back on his knees, dropping his bloody hands on his thighs.

"They would have sacked him?" he answered McKeege, and both of them knew the conversation to be a necessary and very welcome diversion. "Not if they understood his skill with the blade! They would have sent him posthaste to the south to do battle with Laird Ethelbert, I'd wager."

"The whispers have it that this Highwayman rained particular embarrassment upon Prince Yeslnik, one of Laird Delaval's favored nephews. No, if Delaval had gotten his hands on that one, Bransen would not have had the chance to prove his worth—and I doubt he'd have battled for Delaval. He had a bit of a run-in with the Laird of Pryd—word's that he killed the man."

"Laird Pryd himself?"

"His son, Prydae. You're knowing them?"

"I know—or knew—the father," Brother Jond explained.

"And?"

"Probably deserved it," Brother Jond admitted with a helpless chuckle. "If the son was much like the father, I mean."

Dawson McKeege gave a laugh at that, hardly one to disagree. By his estimation, most of the lairds of Honce, titles handed down through generations, weren't of much worth, which of course only made him appreciate his beloved Dame Gwydre, that notable exception, even more.

"Here comes your new champion," Jond said, indicating the returning Bransen. "It will take the Masur Delaval itself to wash the blood from his blade, I fear."

"Bloodier with every battle," Dawson agreed.

"A dozen huzzahs for Dawson's wit," said Brother Jond.

Bransen approached, looking at Jond. When he took note of Dawson, though, he veered suddenly, his face growing very tight.

"It is appropriate for a returning fighter to report his findings to his commander," Dawson reminded.

Bransen stopped and stood very still for a few heartbeats, composing himself.

"In fact, you should consider it required," Dawson pressed.

Bransen slowly turned to regard him. "The beasts are in full disarray and retreat," he said. "They'll not return anytime soon."

"Good enough, then," Brother Jond interjected lightly, his favorable relationship with both men serving to diffuse the obvious tension. "Myself and my Abellican brethren near the limit of our magical energies. Another assault would see less magical tending of the wounded, I fear."

"Curious," said a voice from the side, and all three turned and nearly gasped to find Dame Gwydre sitting astride her roan mare. "From all that I have heard of Brother Jond, I would be certain that he would find more energy within himself, somehow, some way, if a man lay wounded before him."

"Milady," said Dawson, stumbling to his feet. "When did you arrive on the field?"

"Be at ease, my friend," she replied, waving him back.

"You are much too kind, Dame Gwydre," Brother Jond said, lowering his gaze.

"I only hear the whispers, good brother," she replied. "I do not create them. Your reputation overrides your humility, and all of Vanguard is blessed and pleased that you are among us."

Despite himself and his sincere humility, Brother Jond couldn't suppress a wisp of a smile at that.

"And you," Gwydre said, addressing Bransen. "The Dancing Sword, is it?"

"That is not my name."

"It is Bransen Garibond," Dawson said, shooting a scolding glance at the impudent young warrior. "Or perhaps he prefers the Highwayman, the name attached to him for his misdeeds in the South, the name for which he would have been sacked or hanged by the neck."

Bransen smiled at the man, more than willing to take that bait. "The Highwayman will do, indeed."

"Your exploits are not unnoticed . . . Bransen," said Gwydre. "When this is ended, should you choose to leave Vanguard, I promise that my note of appreciation and pardon will accompany you, though whether the Southern lairds would honor such, I cannot say."

"Should I choose?" Bransen quipped. "What prisoner would willingly remain in his dungeon?"

"A bit of respect!" Dawson warned, but Gwydre motioned for him to be quiet.

"Vanguard is no dungeon, Bransen Garibond," Dame Gwydre said. "She is home. Home to many, many good people. You are free to view it in any manner you choose, of course—never would I deign to take that choice from any man."

"Yet I must fight for her, whatever my feelings."

"Fight for yourself, then," Dame Gwydre retorted. "For your freedom, such as it may be, and for the benefit of your young and beautiful wife, who does not deserve to see her husband put in a sack with venomous snakes. I care not why you fight, but I insist that you do. And while you may not see the good your fine blade is doing, we surely do. And while you may not care for those families given a chance to live in peace and security because of your actions against the Samhaist-inspired hordes, we surely do."

With that, she turned her roan mare and walked it away.

Dawson wore a pitying smirk as he shook his head, regarding Bransen. "One day you'll lose that stubborn pride," he predicted. "And you'll see the truth of Dame Gwydre, the truth of all of this, and you'll be shamed to have spoken to her such."

Then Dawson, too, walked away.

Bransen stared at him as he left, unblinking, his eyes boring holes into the man's back.

"You fought brilliantly today," Brother Jond said to him. "I had thought the line lost and expected that we would be the ones driven from the field."

Bransen looked at Jond, a man he had found it difficult to hate, despite his anger and his general feelings for Abellicans.

"That may mean little to you," Jond went on. "What field is worth the effort, of course, and you care not if Gwydre wins or Gwydre falls." He looked at the man lying before him. "But had we been driven from the field, this man would not have survived his wounds, and a woman not so unlike your wife would grieve forever."

"Dame Gwydre does not care why I fight," Bransen answered him, holding stubbornly to his anger. "Why would you?"

"Dame Gwydre has bigger things to care about than a single man's heart and soul, perhaps."

"And Brother Jond does not?"

The monk shrugged. "My victories are smaller, no doubt, but no less consequential, and no less satisfying."

Bransen started to snipe back, but held his tongue and just waved his free hand in defeat, then walked off to be alone.

Brother Jond watched him go with a knowing smile. Bransen's anger was real, but so was his compassion.

And in the end, Jond held faith that the compassion would prevail, because he had seen more than Bransen the warrior, this Sworddancer or Highwayman, as he was alternately known. After the previous battles, Bransen had helped Brother Jond and the others in tending the wounded, and his prowess in such matters was no less than his fighting ability.

Indeed, later that very night, Bransen and Jond worked side by side on the wounded.

"You hate them," Jond remarked.

"Them?"

"McKeege and Dame Gwydre, for a start," Jond explained. "My brethren in the South, as well. You are a young man too full of anger."

Bransen regarded him curiously, in no small part because this wizened monk wasn't much his elder, and to hear Jond calling him a "young man" seemed a bit strange.

"I am not as angry as you believe."

"It pleases me to hear that," Jond said, sincerely.

"But I have seen more dishonesty and evil than I ever expected," Bransen went on. He paused and bent low over a severely wounded woman, placing his hand on her belly and closing his eyes. He felt his hand grow warm, and the woman's soft moan told him that his effort was having some effect—though he couldn't begin to guess whether it would be sufficient balm to get her through the tearing and twisting a spear had caused in her bowels.

After a short while, Bransen opened his eyes and leaned back to see Brother Jond staring at him.

"What do you do?" Jond asked. "To heal them, I mean. You have no gemstones, and yet I cannot deny what my eyes show to me. Your work has a positive effect on their wounds, almost as much so as a skilled brother with a soul stone."

"My mother was Jhesta Tu," said Bransen, and Brother Jond crinkled his face. "Do you know what that means?"

The monk shook his head, and Bransen snickered and said, "I did not expect anything different."

"Jhesta Tu is a . . . religion?"

"A way of life," said Bransen. "A philosophy. A religion? Yes. And since it is one not of Honce, but of Behr, I would hope that the Abellican Order has no reason to hate it. But of course they do. Why control people's lives only a bit of the way, after all?"

"There is no end to your sarcasm."

"None that you'll ever see," Bransen promised, but he was smiling as he spoke, despite himself, and Brother Jond got a laugh out of that, too.

"I know that your journey here was the result of a lie," Jond said a long while later, as the two finally neared the end of the line of wounded. "But I cannot deny that I am glad you have come. As are they," he added, sweeping his arm and his gaze out over the injured.

Bransen wanted to offer a stinging retort, but in the face of the suffering laid out before him, he found that he could not.

"As am I," came a voice from behind, and the pair turned to see Dame Gwydre, stepping into one of Brother Jond's conversations for the second time that day.

Bransen stared at her and did not otherwise respond.

"Greetings again, Lady," Brother Jond said. "Your presence will surely uplift the spirits of these poor wounded warriors."

"Soon," she promised. "For the moment, though, I would speak with your companion."

She matched Bransen's stare, and motioned for him to join her outside the tent.

"Your anger is understandable," she said when he joined her outside. She led the way, walking across the encampment through a light rain that had come up.

"I will sleep easier knowing that you approve," he said, taking some solace in being able to so casually and impudently address this imposing and powerful figure. He felt as if he had scored a little victory in that retort, though he quickly scolded himself silently for such a petulant and childish need, particularly when Gwydre took it all in stride, as if it was deserved or at least understandable.

"The wind has a bit of winter's bite in it this evening," she said. "The season is not so far away, I fear. Our enemies will not relent—glacial trolls feel the cold not at all. But my own forces will be more miserable by far."

"A fact that little concerns you, I expect," Bransen said, and this time he did elicit a glower from the Dame of Vanguard. "Other than how it might affect your holding, I mean."

"Do you understand and accept why Dawson brought you here?" Gwydre asked quietly.

"I understand that I was deceived."

"For your own good."

"And for yours." Bransen stopped as he spoke the accusation, and turned to face the lady as she similarly swung about to regard him.

"Yes, I admit it," she said. "And though I knew not of Bransen Garibond, this Highwayman legend, when Dawson left Pireth Vanguard, and though I had no idea that he would so coerce you to come, I admit openly that I approve of his tactics and of the result."

"You would say that standing out here alone with me?"

Gwydre laughed at him. "Openly," she reiterated. "I know enough of Bransen to recognize that he is no murderer."

"Yet my anger is justified."

"Justified does not mean that it is not misplaced," said Gwydre. "I see that you have forged a friendship with Brother Jond and some others."

Bransen shrugged.

"If I granted you your freedom right now, with no recourse should you decide to leave, would you?" she asked. "Would you collect your wife and her mother and be gone from Vanguard?"

"Yes," Bransen said without hesitation and with as much conviction as he could flood into his voice.

"Would you really?" Dame Gwydre pressed. "You would leave Brother Jond and the others? You would allow the troll hordes of the Samhaists to overrun Vanguard and slaughter innocent men, women, and children?"

"This is not my fight!" Bransen retorted, somewhat less convincingly.

"It is now."

"By deception alone!"

Gwydre paused, and held up her hand to silence the agitated Bransen. "As you will," she conceded.

"You will let me leave?"

"No, I cannot, though surely I would like to—for you and for all of the soldiers," she said. "There is too much at stake, and so I insist that you remain."

"Dawson McKeege would be proud of you," Bransen replied, his sarcasm unrelenting.

"I do not wish to allow this war to go through the winter," Dame Gwydre said and turned and started off yet again, Bransen in tow. "The cold favors my enemies."

"Please, end it."

"I am considering creating a select team of warriors to strike deep into our enemy's ranks, perhaps to decapitate the beast. The hordes are held together by the sheer will and maliciousness of Ancient Badden, a most unpleasant Samhaist."

"A redundant description, from what I have seen."

"Indeed," Dame Gwydre agreed. "Do you agree with my reasoning?"

"You're asking me to join your attack force."

"I am tasking you with exactly that."

Bransen stopped, and Gwydre did as well, glancing back and allowing him all the time he needed to think it through.

"How far and how long?" he asked.

"Somewhere in the North," she replied. "Probably a journey of more than two weeks—and that if the enemy is oblivious to your passing."

"If I go, and if this beast, Ancient Badden, is killed, I would have my free-dom," Bransen said. "Even if this assault does not end your war, as you hope. I would have my freedom with your blessing and imprimatur to return unhin-dered to the lands of southern Honce? And you will provide a ship to sail my family home."

"You are in no position to bargain," she said.

"And yet, bargain I do. Even if killing Ancient Badden does nothing to end this war, I will have my freedom."

"You will not walk away," Dame Gwydre said.

"If you believe that, then you have nothing to lose."

"Agreed, then," she said. "Bring me the head of Badden and I will have Dawson McKeege take you back to Chapel Abelle, along with my insistence that you be forgiven your past indiscretions, though I cannot guarantee that the Southern lairds and Church will heed that imprimatur."

"Allow me to worry about that."

Dame Gwydre stared at him a moment longer as she gathered her cloak up tight against her neck, and with a slight nod, she walked away.

Bransen stood there for a long while watching her go, and thinking that at least he had a direction before him now, a place to go with the hope that it might indeed end in the near future.

It did not occur to him that Ancient Badden would prove to be the most formidable foe he had ever faced.

CHAPTER 17

The Cost of Conscience

They repelled the assault but not without cost, for this last attack by the determined Alpinadorans had left several brothers seriously wounded, one critically. The cost to the Alpinadorans had been even more grievous, with many carried from the field.

"Fools, all!" Father De Guilbe scolded, shaking his fist at the departing horde. None of the monks around him dared utter a word in response, for never had they seen their leader so obviously flummoxed. "Will we kill you all? Is this the choice you force upon us, fool Teydru? If you are concerned for your flock, why do you throw it to the hungry wolves?"

By that point, almost all of the Alpinadorans were back at their beachfront encampment, and though De Guilbe was yelling at the top of his lungs, it was fairly obvious that they could not hear him well enough to make out his words. Still, he ranted for several minutes, his diatribe turning mostly against Teydru, before he at last turned to face his own brethren.

"Idiots!" he said with a snarl, and many brothers nodded their heads in agreement, and one whispered, "They will not break through our walls," in support of the father's general thesis.

Father De Guilbe took a deep breath then and settled back against the stone parapet, letting the tension drain from his battle-weary body. "We will be working the soul stones long into the night," he said, mostly to Giavno. "Determine a rotation and be certain that our wounded brethren are tended dusk to dawn."

"Of course," Brother Giavno replied with a respectful bow.

"And if they come on again this day, conserve your magical powers," De Guilbe told them all. "Let us ensure that we have the energy to heal our wounded. Repel the fools with stones and hot water."

With that he took his leave, moving to the ladder that would take him to the courtyard. He had just started down when one of the brothers up high on the main keep yelled out, "They break camp!"

Father De Guilbe stood there for a moment looking up at the man, as did all the others, before they rushed wholesale to the wall to view the spectacle.

As the lookout had reported, they watched tents being struck, the distant barbarian encampment bustling with activity.

"Where are they moving their supplies?" Father De Guilbe yelled up to the lookout.

"To the boats!" he yelled back excitedly. "To the boats! They are taking to their boats!"

Father De Guilbe paused for a moment, then spun back to the wall to stare out at the distant camp. "Did we break their will at long last?" he quietly asked, and all of those around him murmured their hopeful agreement.

Soon after, all the brothers of Chapel Isle, save those already working the soul-stone magic on the wounded, gathered at the highest points on the southern battlements, staring out hopefully. Within an hour of the battle's end, the first sails rose up on the Alpinadoran boats and the first paddles hit the warm waters of Mithranidoon, and a great cheer erupted across the chapel.

"Perhaps they are not as foolish as we believed," Father De Guilbe said to Brother Giavno, both men smiling with the expectation that they had come through their dark trials.

That sense of victory was soon enough shattered, however, when a breathless young monk rushed into Father De Guilbe's audience chambers.

"They are gone!" he stammered.

"They?" Brother Giavno asked before De Guilbe could.

"The barbarians!" the young man explained.

"Yes, we watched them break camp," Giavno said.

"No, no," the man stuttered, trying to catch his breath long enough to explain. "The barbarians in our dungeon. They are gone!"

"Gone?" This time it was Father De Guilbe asking.

"Out of their chamber and down the tunnel. The door to the pond was open and the grate has been dislodged," the monk reported. "They are gone! Through the water and out, I am sure."

De Guilbe and Giavno exchanged concerned looks.

"Now we understand why our enemies broke camp and departed," Brother Giavno said.

Father De Guilbe was already moving, out to the hall and down the stairs. As they came out of the keep, rushing around to the entryway to the lower levels, Giavno spotted Brother Cormack and waved at him to join them.

"This is my fault," Cormack said unexpectedly when they entered the now-empty dungeon.

The others turned to regard him.

"I should have recognized their ruse," Cormack improvised. "Their unwillingness to eat."

"What do you know of this?" Brother Giavno demanded.

"It was an enchantment, do you not see?" Cormack asked. "They were not starving themselves in protest, to die before converting to our ways. At their shaman's instruction, they were starving themselves that he, or one of the others, could thin himself appropriately so that he could slip his bonds. Oh, but we should have guessed!"

"You babble!" Giavno said.

"Let him continue," bade Father De Guilbe.

Cormack held up his arms and shook his head. "Their magic is tied to the natural way," he tried to explain. "Perhaps—yes, I think it likely—their imposed starvation was merely so that they, their shaman, could enact some spell to further thin his wrists and hands."

"Those bindings were tight," another monk protested. "I tied them myself."

"That was many days ago," Cormack reminded. "The captives were far heavier then—all of them."

"You cannot know," Giavno said.

"Agreed," said Cormack. "But somehow they managed to slip their bonds. It all makes sense now, I fear—their starvation, their confidence, their impudence. When first we encountered these people, before the lines of intransigence and battle were etched, I learned much of their ways, and I know their magic is tied to the natural. Their shamans have spells to make their warriors appear taller, to strike fear into their enemies. It is said that their greatest spiritualists can shape change into animal form, much like the great Samhaists of legend."

"So you believe that their refusal to eat was a design to allow them escape?" Father De Guilbe asked.

To Cormack's ears, the large man didn't sound very convinced. Nor did Giavno, scowling at him from the side of the small dungeon, appear overly enthusiastic for Cormack's improvised lie. But now Cormack had to carry it through, of course. "It makes sense in the context of what I know about their type of magic," he said. "I should have guessed this ruse."

He shook his head and moved aside, hoping to take their scrutiny off him before more holes could be shot into his theory. To his great relief, Father De Guilbe merely said, "Perhaps your assessment is correct. Clever fools, though fools they remain." He turned his attention to the other two lesser brothers in the room. "Search the whole of the keep, of the tunnels and the compound," he ordered. "Likely they went out to the open lake—that would explain the departure of their stubborn kin. But if they remain, find them posthaste."

The pair started right out, sweeping Cormack up with them as they began their exhaustive search.

"And doubly secure that grate," Father De Guilbe called after them, and he paused to listen to the receding footsteps. "Brother Cormack thinks he has sorted out the mystery," he said to Giavno when they were securely alone.

"Perhaps he has," said Giavno as he moved around the wooden wall that had served to hold the bindings of the prisoners. "Though I wonder," he said when he got to the back, "if the shaman reduced his wrist and hand enough to slip his bonds, then why are all four of the binding ropes cut?"

Father De Guilbe gave a noncommittal shrug as if it did not matter—and at that, it really didn't seem to. The Alpinadorans were gone, escaped, and the men and women of Yossunfier had left Chapel Isle, bringing the whole ordeal to an end. That Cormack would be proven right or wrong seemed of little consequence. With a wave of his hand, a dejected Father De Guilbe left the dungeon.

Brother Giavno certainly understood that malaise. What had they been fighting for, after all? The souls of four men had been taken from them, somehow, some way, whether through Alpinadoran magic, or simple stubbornness, or . . .

A slight smile creased Giavno's face as he considered the torn bindings, as he considered the explanation offered by Brother Cormack.

The unsolicited explanation.

I should never have doubted you," Milkeila said breathlessly as she stood on the sandbar in Cormack's arms under a brilliant, starry sky.

"Speak not of it," Cormack bade her.

"But Androosis has already written songs to Corma—"

"I beg of you," said Cormack, hushing her with finger pressed to her lips. "That battle, that siege, all of it, is nothing I wish to relive or remember at all."

"It was painful to you to see the truth of your Church brothers," Milkeila reasoned. "And to betray them."

"And to see the truth of your people, no less stubborn."

Milkeila moved back to arms' length, scrutinizing Cormack sternly. "We did not hold prisoners," she reminded him. "We did not invade your lands insisting that you convert to our ways!"

Cormack hushed her again, and tried to kiss her, but she avoided him. "I know," he said. "And you know how I feel about it." She started to argue, but he wouldn't let her get a word in at that point. "And you know what I just did. Have you forgotten so quickly?"

"Of course I've not!"

"Then kiss me!" Cormack said playfully, trying desperately to turn this conversation to a lighter place.

Milkeila recognized that and smiled, and did indeed kiss Cormack, surrendering to him as they slid down together to the sand bar. As they fumbled with their clothing, Cormack paused and brought forth the gemstone necklace. Milkeila didn't argue with him as he placed it over her head.

Sitting idly and alone in a small boat out on the lake, Brother Giavno listened to their lovemaking as he had listened to their conversation, marveling at how well sound traveled across the dark waters on a night so clear.

He wasn't really surprised that Cormack had been the one to betray them, of course, but it stung him profoundly nonetheless. The young and handsome brother, so full of fire and potential, strong of arm and strong with the gemstones, simply did not understand the meaning of what it was to be an Abellican brother as they moved toward completion of the first century of their Church. Cormack's way was the art of exhaustive compromise, and that in a world full of enemies who would accept such Abellican concessions only as a pretense for their continued road to dominance.

For the Abellicans were at that time involved in a great struggle with the Samhaists, who would not forsake their old and brutal ways. Were it not for that ancient cult, Cormack's overly abundant tolerance of others—even of powries—might itself be tolerated within the Church.

But that was not the case. Not now. Not with all of Honce aflame as laird battled laird and both churches, Abellican and Samhaist, struggled mightily for supremacy. The other races, human and otherwise, had no choice but to pick sides. Neutrality was not an option.

Nor was tolerance for barbarians who would not see the truth and beauty of Blessed Abelle.

Brother Giavno had always liked Cormack, but hearing the man fornicating with a barbarian, a shaman no less, was more than his sensibilities could handle.

Cormack glided his craft easily onto the sand, lightly scrambling out and dragging the boat the rest of the way out of the water. Another boat rested nearby, flipped over, and the two handlers, whose job it was to make sure that all the craft were properly stored and secured whenever they were not in use, rested aside the paddles of the first returned craft and hustled over to help Cormack.

"Father De Guilbe wishes to speak with you," one of them told the return-ing sailor monk. "And what did you catch for us this day?"

Cormack held up a pair of trout strung on a line—fish that Milkeila had given to him, as was their custom whenever they met on the sandbar.

"You always do better when you're out alone," the other boathandler said. "They should put you out there every day!"

Cormack grinned and nodded, thinking that meeting Milkeila at their special place daily wouldn't be so bad a thing. None of the three on the beach understood the prophetic nature of the remarks, however.

With a noticeably lighter step, Cormack trotted back up from the beach to the chapel, and indeed all of Chapel Isle seemed as if a great weight had been lifted from it, as if perpetual stormclouds had at last parted. The three-week siege had taxed the brothers greatly, and though they were not all thrilled that their prisoners had escaped, and less thrilled that four of their ranks had been lost to battle and several others would be a long time in recovering, life got back to somewhat normal fairly quickly.

It occurred to Cormack that the work on the walls hadn't been this fre-netic since the early days of construction. Frenetic and with true zeal, he realized, for the brothers were going at their labors with a renewed sense of purpose, as if they were finally, finally, doing much more than the simple tasks necessary for day-to-day survival. They had built the chapel for defense and as a celebra-tion of Blessed Abelle. Now they had seen it through its former purpose first-hand. They had witnessed what had worked and what hadn't; already many plans had been drawn up for strengthening the walls and giving the brothers more and better options for repelling any future attackers. Mingled in with those practical plans were the requisite glorious design features, the marks of pride and gratitude to their patron.

"Purpose," Cormack whispered as he crossed into the courtyard. He won-dered then if that need to find meaning wasn't in some twisted way responsi-ble for the continuing warfare among the various peoples and powries of the Mithranidoon islands. Without the ever-present enemies, could the folk of the islands find meaning in their lives?

It was a truly chilling thought for the gentle-hearted man, but he didn't let it weight the spring in his step.

Brother Giavno's look at him as he entered Father De Guilbe's office did exactly that, however, a withering gaze that immediately sent Cormack's thoughts back to the beach, to the second, overturned boat, which had obvi-ously been recently returned.

"Fa . . . Father De Guilbe, I was told that you wished to speak to me," Cor-mack managed to stutter, though his eyes never left Giavno as he spoke.

"Where have you been?" the leader of Chapel Isle replied, and Cormack couldn't miss the undertone of his voice, so full of disappointment.

He turned to regard the man, and paused just a few moments to collect his thoughts and to try and sort all this out before answering, "Fishing. I go often, and with Brother Giavno's blessing. I landed two this day—one of good size—"

"You fish from your boat or from another island?"

"The boat, of course—"

"Then why were you on an island?" Father De Guilbe demanded. "It was an island, was it not? Where you met with the barbarian woman?"

Stunned, Cormack shook his head. "Father, I . . ." This time De Guilbe did not interrupt, but the stammering Cormack couldn't find a response anyway.

"You freed them," Father De Guilbe accused. "During the frenzy of battle you slipped into the tunnels and freed our four prisoners."

"No, Father."

De Guilbe's sigh profoundly wounded the young monk. "Do not compound your crime with lies, Brother." He paused and sighed again, shaking his head, before finishing, simply, "Cormack."

"Four souls for Blessed Abelle released to pursue heathen ways that will surely damn them for eternity," Brother Giavno put in harshly. "How will you reconcile your conscience with that, I wonder?"

"No," Cormack said, still shaking his head. "We thought they were not eating in protest, but it was an enchantment, perhaps. Or . . ."

"Brother Giavno followed you out onto the lake, Cormack," said Father De Guilbe, and again, his omission of Cormack's Abellican title struck hard at the young monk's sensibilities. "He heard you with the woman—all of it. And while your lust could be rather easily forgiven and atoned for—brothers often surrender to such urges—the action which precipitated your tryst is a different matter."

Cormack stared at him blankly, and indeed, that was exactly how he felt. He replayed his conversation with Milkeila in his head, and quickly recognized that an eavesdropping Giavno had heard more than enough to erase any doubt, or to defeat any protests coming forth from him. So he stood there and took Father De Guilbe's stream of anger, and he felt an empty vessel through it all, though he would not let that venom fill him.

"How could you betray us like that?" De Guilbe demanded. "Men died to protect that treasure: the souls of four Alpinadoran barbarians. Four of your brethren are dead, and a fifth might soon join them! What would you say to their families? Their parents? How would you explain to them that their sons died for nothing?"

"Too many were dying," Cormack said, his voice barely above a whisper, but the room went absolutely silent as he started to speak and all heard him well enough. "Too many were still to die."

"We would have held them!" Brother Giavno insisted.

"Then we would have murdered them all," Cormack retorted. "Surely there is nothing holy in that action. Surely Blessed Abelle—"

The name had barely escaped his lips when a bolt of lightning erupted from Father De Guilbe's hand and threw Cormack back hard to slam into the doorjamb. He crumpled to the floor, disoriented and writhing in pain.

"Strip him down and tie him in the open courtyard," Father De Guilbe instructed, and Giavno waved a couple of monks over to collect the fallen man.

As Cormack was dragged away, Brother Giavno faced Father De Guilbe directly. "Twenty hard lashes," De Guilbe started to say, but he stopped and corrected himself. "Fifty. And with barbs."

"That will almost surely kill him."

"Then he will be dead. He betrayed us beyond redemption. Administer the beating without remorse or amelioration. Beat him until you are weary, then hand the whip off to the strongest brother in the chapel. Fifty—no less, though I care not if you exceed the mandate. If he is dead at forty, administer the last ten to his corpse."

Brother Giavno felt the deep remorse in Father De Guilbe's voice, and he sympathized completely. This business was neither pleasant nor pleasurable, but it was certainly necessary. The fool Cormack had made his choice, and he had betrayed his brethren for the sake of barbarians—barbarians who were assailing Chapel Isle at the time of Cormack's treachery.

That could not stand.

Brother Giavno nodded solemnly to his superior and turned to leave. Before he got to the door, De Guilbe said to him, "Should he somehow survive the beating, or should he not, put him in a small boat and tow him out onto the lake. Leave him for the trolls or the fish or the carrion birds. Brother Cormack is already dead to us."

More than two hours later, the semiconscious Cormack was unceremoniously dropped into the smallest and worst boat in Chapel Isle's small fleet as it bobbed on the low surf at the island's edge.

"Is he already dead?" one of the monks asked to the group congregating around the craft.

"Who's to care?" another answered with a disgusted snort—which pretty well summed up the mood. Many of these men had been friends of Cormack's, some had even looked up to him. But his betrayal was a raw wound to them all, and too fresh a revelation for any to take a step back and see any perspective on this other than the harsh sentence imposed by Father De Guilbe.

For other friends of theirs, like Brother Moorkris, had died in protecting the prisoners and the chapel. Arguing about whether or not Father De Guilbe's decision to keep their prisoners and accept the siege and battle was not their prerogative, nor had any found the time to do so. Their jobs had focused simply on survival, on beating back the enemy whatever the reasons for the enemy being there.

On a logical level, some might come to understand and accept Cormack's treacherous actions. On a visceral level, the fallen brother had gotten exactly what he had deserved.

"If he's still alive, he's not long for it," another brother said.

Giavno stepped forward and tossed a red beret, Cormack's powrie cap, into the boat atop the prostrate, bleeding man. "It is a wound to every heart on Chapel Isle," he said. "Cast him out that the currents might take him to a cove where the beasts will feast, and when he is gone we will speak no more of fallen Brother Cormack."

Giavno turned and walked away and a group took hold of the small craft, guiding it toward the water. One man paused long enough to take the beret and set it upon Cormack's head, and when he looked at the curious stares coming at him for the action, he merely shrugged. "Seems fitting."

They all laughed—it was either that or cry—and brought the boat out onto the lake, giving it a strong shove to get it away from the island far enough so that one or another of the many crisscrossing currents caused by the underground hot streams that fed the lake would catch it.

"If it washes back in, I'll tie it to another and tow it far out," one brother volunteered, but that wasn't necessary. As a brilliant orange sunset graced the western sky, the stark, low silhouette of Cormack's funereal boat at last moved out of sight.

CHAPTER 18

Dame Gwydre's Trump

He walked with a sure and determined stride that mocked time itself, for he had seen seven decades of life and could pace men one-third his age. He stood tall and broad-shouldered, but his thick muscles had slackened, and his skin, so weathered in the northern sun, had sagged a bit. Still, no one doubted that the large fist of this man, Jameston Sequin, could flatten a nose and take both cheekbones with it!

His hair was long and gray, his beard not so long and still showing hints of the darker colors of his earlier years, and his great and thick mustache stood out most of all. He wore a tri-cornered cap, one he had fashioned, one that had been considered unique when he had fashioned it. Long and narrow, it trailed back from a round-pointed front to a flattened back that was just a bit wider than his head, and he kept a black feather along its right side, bent low to follow the line of the hat.

At one of Vanguard's archery contests half a century before, one won by young Jameston, of course, the man had received more than a bit of teasing regarding his rather unusual cap—until, of course, he had explained that the pointed front allowed him to properly line up his shots. Within a few months, and to this day, the Jameston, as the hat was called, was quite common among Vanguard's hunters, thereby adding to a legend that needed no enhancement.

It was said that he was of Alpinadoran descent, or mixed blood at least, but his long nose and protruding brow spoke of ancestors along the southeastern coast of Honce. His eyes were green, and his smile, though a bit snaggletoothed now, was infectious and strangely disarming, given the man's imposing stature and often withering glare.

He was smiling now, as much out of curiosity as anything else. "This far north?" he asked himself (a not unusual occurrence) as he moved far enough down the side of one mountain to better view the combatants in the dell below, which included men, apparently Vanguardsmen.

Now more interested in the fight, which he had presumed to be another skirmish between the various troll or goblin tribes, Jameston quick-stepped closer, but to a higher perch with a better view.

His first instinct at that point was to charge right in, for a quick glance made him realize that the small group seemed sorely outnumbered and sure to be overwhelmed. Before he had taken a step, though, he understood that such impressions didn't begin to tell this tale. The goblins, with a dozen lying dead already, were the ones in need of support.

Jameston drew Banewarren from his shoulder and set an arrow on its resting string as he watched the play. One man in particular, dressed in black from bandanna to boot, had the old scout nodding with approval. The man raced the length of the line, leaping and spinning, his thin sword cutting graceful and precise lines through the air and through the goblins alike. Wherever that man passed, goblins fell dead, and though an Abellican monk stood back from the action, ready to heal this man or any others who needed his magical services, Jameston doubted he'd expend much of his healing energy on this one.

A second, burlier figure crossed the black-clothed man's wake as he rushed out to the far left of the human defensive formation, and Jameston smiled even wider. For this one, Vaughna por Lolone, he surely knew. "Crazy V," he whispered, her nickname, and he laughed aloud as she lived up to it yet again, throwing herself with abandon into the midst of the goblins.

Jameston moved to find a better vantage point, testing the pull of Banewarren with every long stride.

Vaughna carried two iron hand axes as solidly as if they were extensions of her living arms. She punched out with her left, lifting the angle of the blow to clip a goblin forehead and jerk the creature's head back. Her second hand came in fast at the exposed neck, but she had flipped her axe into the air, hitting the goblin's exposed throat with her stiffened fingers instead.

As it staggered back gasping, Crazy V put her face right in front of the beast's, opened wide her eyes and mouth, and screamed wildly. As she did, she blindly caught her descending axe, dropped her shoulders back, and delivered a chop into the goblin's side, bending it over in pain.

Crazy V drove across with her left but brought it up short, evading the wounded creature's flimsy defense. For she stepped out with her left as she swung and pivoted on that foot, bringing a trailing right-hand backhand all the way about to chop the goblin almost exactly across from the first serious wound.

Then she spun away as if to leave but turned about suddenly and unloaded a barrage of chops, left and right, on the creature, melting it into a pile of torn muck.

Blood-spattered and unbothered, Crazy V twirled about and sought her next target, and even took a step that way before an unusual, red-feathered arrow whipped into the goblin and sent it flying into a tree, where the arrow drove through and pinned the dead thing upright.

Crazy V's face erupted in a gleeful look of recognition and she yelled again, just because. Only one man in this region was known for such fletching. She rushed off to find something to hit, because she knew that between this Highwayman and his sword and their newest arrival, there soon would be few remaining targets!

Bransen was careful that his dance did not venture too close to the ferocious Vaughna; he always took pains to avoid that one. It had nothing to do with his personal feelings, though the crass and crude woman often left him shaking his head. Rather, it was because her fighting style was so unpredictable, so out-of-control, it could interrupt the flow of his own, meticulous motions.

He stayed nearest to Brother Jond, both to ensure that the monk was free to continue his gemstone healing and the occasional magical offensive strike and because of the friendship they had forged in previous battles.

The remaining two members of the strike force, a middle-aged crusty old warrior named Crait and a redheaded young bull named Olconna, fell somewhere on the spectrum between Bransen and Vaughna. Neither could match his grace or her ferocity, but both performed an effective enough combination of the two.

Bransen, out of targets now that Vaughna had charged into the middle of the goblin line and had, predictably, broken it, sending goblins running every which way, paused and managed to glance over at Crait and Olconna, fighting side by side behind Brother Jond.

Crait dodged one blow coming in at his right, and moved so far to the left that it appeared as if he had opened himself up to a devastating spear thrust. But when the goblin took that opening, it found only Olconna's shield, and the creature's failure allowed Crait to fast-step forward behind his partner's block and plunge his bronze short sword into the goblin's chest.

Crait rolled to the left after the kill, sliding right in front of Olconna, his sword and shield slashing and bashing, but only as a ruse.

For he kept going and Olconna rushed into the void as he passed, and the goblin couldn't refocus its attention fast enough.

Bransen nodded his admiration. These two had been fighting together for a long time now, and had made quite a name for themselves farther to the east and north, where the battles along the coast had been more scattered but no less fierce.

This one was over, at least, or soon to be, and Bransen leaped past Brother Jond and charged off Olconna's right flank in fast pursuit of the now-fleeing monsters, hoping to get at least one more kill.

He managed two, and fast closed on a third when a red-fletched arrow beat him to the mark, throwing the goblin to the ground. Bransen looked around to spy the archer, but no one was in sight, and none of his friends, still back in the dell some twenty paces behind him, held any bows.

He finished the squirming goblin with a stroke to its neck, then rolled it enough so that he could push the beautifully crafted arrow right through. When he arrived back with his friends to present it, he found Brother Jond holding a similar one.

"Our day's gone brighter," Vaughna explained, in that voice of hers that always seemed to be on the edge of hysterical laugher.

"It is him?" Olconna asked, his voice thick with unabashed awe.

"Aye, that'd be the mark of Jameston," Crait answered.

"Jameston Sequin," Brother Jond explained to the obviously confused Bransen. "A hunter of great renown, who splits his time between Vanguard and Alpinador. It is said he knows the trails better than any man alive, and it will prove a fortunate turn for us if he is indeed about."

"There is the greatest understatement I've ever heard," Vaughna chimed in, and her tone made it clear that she was talking about more than a blessing for their mission. She nearly swooned (which seemed almost comical to Bransen, given her fire-spitting demeanor) as she pointed across a small lea, jumping up and down like a little girl getting her first view of a king. "It is him! It is him!"

"He's worth all that?" Olconna snickered.

The approaching man's legs seemed just a bit too long for his frame, giving him as determined and forceful a stride as one could imagine. His face, weathered and creased, showed nothing but strength and a commanding pragmatism. Bransen could see simply from the set of the man's jaw that this one, Jameston, wasn't loose with his words.

"You're a long way north of Dame Gwydre's lines, and you don't look like Samhaists to me," Jameston said when he neared the group. "Especially not you," he added, nodding his gray-bearded chin at Brother Jond.

"Hardly that," the monk agreed.

Jameston's gaze fell over Bransen, his face crinkling in a strange manner. For the first time since he had donned his mother's black silk suit, Bransen felt a bit self-conscious about his unusual dress.

"We did not come north just to find Jameston," Vaughna volunteered. "But we're glad to see you."

Jameston glanced at her for just a moment before offering a wink of familiarity, his face brightening. "Crazy V," he said. "Been a lot of years."

"Too many."

"And you, too, Crait," Jameston went on.

"I'm surprised you remember me," the old warrior replied.

"Not so hard a thing to do," Jameston answered. "How many might be living who have seen the fights you and I can claim as experience?"

Crait thought it over for a few heartbeats, then answered with a laugh, "Two?"

"Might be," said Jameston. "Might be." He stepped over to accept Crait's extended hand, the two clasping wrists with the respect old warriors often reserved for other old warriors.

Brother Jond cleared his throat, and after a curious glance at him, Crait began the introductions, though Vaughna interrupted him as soon as he had named Olconna and presented Bransen and Brother Jond.

"You wandered lost?" Jameston asked.

"Here on purpose," Vaughna corrected. "The fighting has been terrible in the South. Entire villages are gone."

Jameston nodded solemnly. "I've seen Badden's charges march out and figured as much."

"The Samhaists know no moral boundaries," Brother Jond put in, but Jameston's sudden grin silenced him, for it showed the grizzled old hunter to be far beyond the influences of proselytizing Abellicans and Samhaists alike in their unending struggle to collect every man's soul.

"You are a scouting band?" Jameston presumed.

"Half right," said Vaughna, and Brother Jond cleared his throat as if to remind her not to speak too openly. But this was Jameston Sequin, after all, and the woman just cast the monk a dismissive glance. "Dame Gwydre sees that we have to stop this war."

"And negotiating with the Samhaists won't get you far," Jameston reasoned, and let his knowing gaze encompass them all, and Bransen found it hard not to be naked under that man's imposing stare.

"You've come to kill Badden himself," the old hunter said, and the undercurrent of humor in his voice had the five exchanging worried glances.

That was all the confirmation Jameston needed.

"We will find him, and we will kill him, yes," Bransen announced unexpectedly, and stepped forward beside Vaughna. "He has earned the sentence."

"A hundred times over before you were ever born, boy," Jameston replied.

Bransen tried to recover fast from the response, which was both easy agreement and somewhat condescending—maybe. He just couldn't be certain, for this man, this apparently legendary hunter, had him in a continually unbalanced state.

"Never been enamored of that one," Jameston went on, beating Bransen to the dialogue. "Only thing I've found stupider than men who claim to speak for the gods are the people who listen to them. My apologies, Brother," he added to Jond.

Jond half shrugged, half nodded, seeming at least as off-balance as Bransen.

"Help us kill him," Vaughna blurted on impulse.

"Never been one to pick sides," Jameston replied.

"But you have been helping Dame Gwydre," Vaughna protested. "You have been sending reports south, so it's said."

"Counts of goblins and trolls and the like," Jameston agreed. "And the second count I made of them, after I left them, was always less than the initial."

"So you've already chosen your side, then," Vaughna laughed.

"Killing goblins and trolls isn't a side," Jameston deadpanned. "It's a religion. Might be the only religion worth fighting for."

"Well, since Ancient Badden has thrown in with the beasts, he has chosen sides contrary to your . . . religion," Brother Jond reasoned.

Jameston gave him a sidelong glance and a snicker. "Ten days of marching east of here would get you to a hot lake called Mithranidoon. Taking the trails west of that, into the mountains, will bring you Cold'rin, the glacier the hot waters hold back. Atop that is where you'll find Badden and his high priests. I'll take you to him—what you do once you get there's your own choice to decide."

He ended with a nod that brooked no debate, took his arrows from Bransen and Brother Jond, and threw one more wink Vaughna's way before hiking off to the east.

The party of five just shrugged and followed. What else was there for them to do?

A fter they made their camp that night, Vaughna and Jameston sat together, chatting and laughing like old friends.

"They were once lovers," Olconna remarked to Crait, the two of them on the far side of the encampment, cleaning and sharpening their weapons.

Crait laughed heartily. "More than once, if I'm knowin' Crazy V!"

Olconna shot him a curious glance, and his face crinkled. "You as well?"

Crait laughed again. "And I'm knowin' Crazy V!" he said.

Olconna looked back at the sturdy woman, shaking his head.

"That a problem for you?" Crait asked bluntly. "Make you think less of me, does it?"

"She's not so pretty," Olconna said.

"Bah!" Crait retorted without the slightest hesitation, and he, too, turned to regard the woman. "She's the most beautiful woman I ever seen."

Olconna put on a most incredulous expression.

"And if she's e'er to offer you a ride, you'd be a wise man to take it!" Crait added with a wink.

"Like everyone else?" the younger man asked sarcastically.

"Oh, but don't be going to that place," Crait replied. "You spend your days killing people and you're to judge one who takes a ride now and then?"

"But . . ."

"Ain't nothing to 'but' about," Crait cut him short. "Look at her, boy, and look at her well. Crazy V. She's living every moment with fire and filling her soul with memories and experiences most folk will never begin to imagine. She can outfight, outspit, outswear, and outfornicate almost any man alive and any woman I ever heard of. She'll go to her grave without regret. How many of us can say that?"

Olconna started to reply—several times—but he fumbled with the words, and all the while he stared at Vaughna.

Crait sat quietly, staring at the young warrior who had become his protégé of sorts and thinking that he had just given Olconna one of the most valuable lessons of all.

PART THREE

Part of Something Bigger

I resist.

I do not know where it comes from, what deep-seated instinct or sub-conscious component of my being precipitates the apathy, but for all the truth and truthful desperation of Dame Gwydre's plea I resist her call to arms. She is correct in everything she said. I do not doubt that, had I stayed in Honce proper, the Church or the lairds would have caught up with me and brought me to an untimely and painful end. I do not doubt Dawson's words that the brothers of Chapel Abelle knew the truth of the Highwayman and were prepared to capture or kill me. I have seen Abellican justice before.

I do not doubt that the Dame of Vanguard is desperate or that her people are suffering terribly under the weight of encroaching hordes, bounded (as they are Samhaist driven) by no moral constraints.

And still I resist.

I have seen the result of the troll raids, a town burned to the ground, every soul slaughtered. I am revolted and repulsed and angered to my heart and soul. I feel Dame Gwydre's outrage and her desperation and know that if she felt any-thing different she would be a lesser person. I see her trembling with outrage, not because of the tentative nature of her survival and title, but because she truly feels for those people who look to her for leadership—that alone, I know, elevates her high above the average laird of Honce proper.

And still I resist.

Who am I? I thought I knew, for all my life the answer was so self-evident that I never bothered to ask the question. At least not in this manner.

The Book of Jhest and the gemstones freed me from my infirmities and rede-fined me in a physical sense. That much is obvious. But now I come to know that the blessing of the inner healing is forcing upon me a second remaking, or at the very least, a very basic questioning of this man I am, this man I have become.

Who am I?

And what am I beyond the confines of my strengthened flesh?

Quite contrary to my expectations, this strengthening, this healing, has led me to a more uncomfortable place. It has forced upon me a sense of obligation and responsibility for others.

For others. . . .

For all of my youth and into early adulthood there were few others, and those—Garibond, some few brothers of Chapel Pryd, Cadayle on those occasions when I was graced with her presence—were important to me almost exclusively because of what they could do for me. They were in the life of Bransen Garibond because Bransen Garibond needed them.

It is difficult for me to admit that there was something comfortable and comforting in my infirmities. While the other young men were competing in this game we call life, whether simply running against each other, or seeing who could throw a rock the farthest, or in the more formal competitions to gain a position in the Church or in the court of the laird, I was excluded. It wasn't even an option.

There was pain in that exclusion to be sure, but I would be a liar if I didn't admit that there was also a measure of comfort. I did not have to compete in the endless battles to determine the hierarchy of the boys my age. I did not have to suffer the embarrassment of being honestly beaten, because no one could beat the Stork honestly!

My infirmity was no dodge, of course, but I cannot be certain that I would have eschewed a dodge had I needed one. I cannot make that claim because I never had to face that choice.

Then, suddenly, I was freed of that infirmity. Suddenly I became the Highwayman. Even in that identity I cannot claim purity of intent or righteousness of motive.

Who did the Highwayman truly serve in his battle with the powers that were in Pryd Holding? The people? Or did he serve the Highwayman?

The world of the Highwayman is not as simple as that of the Stork.

—BRANSEN GARIBOND

CHAPTER 19

Uncomfortable Riddles

A splash of water brought a cough. With that convulsion Cormack slid back from the deep darkness of unconsciousness. He felt wet along one side and sensed that his lower legs were floating.

The first image that registered to him was that of a glacial troll face, not far from his own, the creature hanging on the side of a (of his, apparently!) small boat and forcing its edge under the water to swamp it.

Cormack reacted purely on instinct. He rolled up to his elbow, facing the troll, reached across with his left hand, and grabbed the creature by its scraggly hair. He kept rolling, using his weight to push that ugly head back, then turned under, rolling his shoulder and hopping to his knees, thus driving the troll's head forward and down. It cracked its chin on the side rail but slid over so that Cormack's weight had it pinned on the rail by its neck.

Up leaped the man. The quick movement freed him enough to lift one leg and stomp down hard on the troll, eliciting a sickening crackle of bone. Cormack nearly overbalanced in the process and tumbled overboard.

Overboard? How had he gotten on a boat, out in the middle of the lake? Burning pain from his back reminded him of his last awful conscious moments, and the rest began to fall in place even as he tried to sort out his present dilemma.

They had cast him out, set him adrift, and now the trolls had found him.

The boat rocked, and Cormack had to work hard to hold his balance. The aft was almost underwater, lifting the prow into the air. Cormack started to turn back that way when he noted a troll scrambling over the prow and coming down at him.

He feigned obliviousness until the last second, then jammed his elbow back, cracking it into the creature's ugly face, crunching its long and skinny nose over to one cheek and tearing its upper lip on its own jagged teeth. The monk retracted and slammed his elbow back again, then a third time, for the troll's weight wouldn't allow it to simply fall away on the steep incline.

Cormack turned and knifed his free hand into the troll's throat, clamping tight. The troll scratched at his forearm, drawing lines of blood, but he held fast, choking the life from it. Or he would have had another of the creatures come over the aft, further tipping the boat.

Cormack turned fast but didn't let go, dragging the diminutive creature along to launch it at its companion. As the two trolls tumbled, Cormack leaped forward and stomped his foot hard on the newcomer's exposed head. He grabbed the second in both hands, by the throat again and the groin, and lifted it up over his head, then slammed it down on its companion.

He stomped and kicked desperately until one went completely still, but Cormack was out of time and he knew it, for yet another troll appeared at the low-riding aft. When the creature pushed up onto that rail the rear of the boat submerged, water flooding in.

Cormack turned and scrambled to the high-riding prow, trying to counteract the weight and lift the rear.

He was too late, so he went to the very tip of the prow, glanced around quickly, and dove away. He counted on surprise, for though he was a strong swimmer he certainly couldn't outdistance glacial trolls in the water!

But he had to try.

Milkeila sat on the sandbar that she often shared with her Abellican lover, remembering fondly their last moments together. She didn't know why Cormack hadn't come out to see her after that encounter. It really wasn't unexpected that time would pass between their trysts, for, given both of their responsibilities to their warring peoples, they more often than not sat alone on the sandbar.

But something nagged at the woman this day, some deep feeling that things were amiss, that something was wrong.

She rose and walked to the eastern end of the sandbar, the point nearest to Chapel Isle, and peered into the mist as if expecting some revelation or maybe to see Cormack gliding toward her in his small boat.

All she saw was mist. All she heard were tiny waves lapping the sand and stones of the bar.

Her gut told her that something was wrong. She had nothing else.

He swam for his life, legs and arms pumping furiously. Cormack had shed his heavy robe as soon as he hit the water and wore only the knee-length white pants and sleeveless shirt typical for his order. That and the stubborn powrie cap, which clung to his head as if by magic. Whether he dove under or kept his head up in the splashing water, that bloodred beret moved not at all from its secure perch.

Cormack knew that he had put about fifteen long strides between himself and the troll and its companions. He tried to do logical estimates of the remaining distance to the small island he had spotted. He could only pray that his dive had surprised the vile creatures, and that he would find the island quickly.

Good fortune showed him that the island wasn't as far as he had believed— not nearly—but on the flip side of that revelation was the knowledge that what he had taken to be an island was really no more than a couple of large rocks protruding above the water.

He could get to them—he did get to them—but what sanctuary might they provide? The highest point of the largest rock sat no more than four feet above the waterline, and the whole of that "island" proved no more than a dozen strides across its diameter.

Cormack crawled up onto it anyway, having little choice, for the trolls were not far behind. He had no desire to do battle with them in the water where they could dive and climb and maneuver with the grace of a fish compared to the lumbering human. He had barely set himself when a splash alerted him to the first of the pursuing beasts.

The monk moved to the highest point, crawling on all fours, and found a loose rock on his way. He pivoted and threw with all his strength, smacking a troll right in the face. The creature shrieked and began flailing wildly as its thin blood streamed over its nose and jaw.

Cormack seized the opportunity, skipping down and launching a barrage of punches and kicks on the troll. He had it turning, spinning, and hooked its arms behind its back and bore it down hard. With frightening viciousness, the man grabbed the troll's hair and began lifting its head, smashing it repeatedly on the rock.

He had to break away, though, as another exited the water. It slashed at him with clawlike fingers, but the monk was too quick, leaning out of range as he squared up.

Another troll broke the water, closing in savagely.

Cormack kept his focus on the first, trading harmless slaps and parries, but all the while he watched the second out of the corner of his eye. That troll leaped in with typical recklessness, but Cormack had set himself appropriately.

He dropped his weight fully on his right leg, then threw himself forward onto his left, closing the distance with the charging troll. Pivoting as he landed, he lifted his right foot into a well-aimed circle-kick that connected solidly with the troll's face, snapping its head back.

Cormack held the pose, leg up, and snapped off a couple of more kicks, though the troll was already beyond consciousness. As he did, he worked his arms frantically to fend off the first troll, which was trying to take advantage of his distraction.

Brother Cormack had been trained by the finest fighters in the Abellican Church, an order that had grown increasingly militant in recent years and had learned well to defend itself.

As the second troll slumped down to the stone, Cormack settled once more into a defensive posture against its furious companion. He didn't hold the defense for long, though. He outweighed the troll by fifty pounds at least, and as this flight and frenzy had settled more rationally into his consciousness, a stark reality became obvious to the man.

He had nothing left to lose.

So he waded right into the troll, oblivious of its swinging arms. In close, he unloaded a series of heavy punches, left and right, accepting a couple of hits in response. But while the troll was scratching and stinging him, he was inflicting real damage, and the clutch lasted only a matter of a few seconds before the troll crumpled before him, where he summarily smashed it into oblivion.

More trolls came from the water to battle him, but there was no coordination to any of it, just a line of victims. Cormack took them on, punching until his knuckles had become one mass of blood, until his feet bled from nicks caused by smashing troll teeth, until his arms felt as if they weighed a hundred pounds each, so great a weariness came over him.

But good luck and sheer rage drove his fury just long enough. When the last of the trolls, the seventh to crawl from the lake, fell limp before him, Cormack slumped to his knees on the stone.

Gasping for breath, Cormack tried to take a survey of his wounds, which included many deep cuts from claws and teeth. He knew that he had to get down to the water to cleanse them—troll bites were notorious for becoming pussy and sore—but he simply didn't have the strength at that moment. He was certain that if just one more troll crawled out of the lake he would surely be doomed.

The sun climbed higher in the eastern sky. The minutes became an hour, then two. The hot waters of Mithranidoon fought back the cold chill of Alpinador. At last Cormack managed to get down to the water and cleaned his wounds and drank deeply. He knelt there, letting his mind whirl through the events that had brought him to this desolate place. The memories of his last hours at Chapel Isle flooded back to him, and he looked again upon the deep disappointment etched into the face of Father De Guilbe, and even the regret evident in Giavno's voice.

Even as the man had scourged him senseless.

There was no going back. His banishment was not a trial or a penance; it represented finality and not forgiveness.

There was no going back.

Cormack was alone, in the middle of a lake full of monsters and trolls, surrounded by enemies. He looked at the steamy waters, and for a few moments he hoped that a group of trolls would rise up from the depths and overwhelm him. For in those dark hours Cormack's future loomed before him, empty, uninviting, terrifying.

He had all that he could drink, obviously, and he might even catch a fish, but to what end?

He peered out into the direction from which he had come, hoping against all logic that he'd see his boat out there, capsized but floating. He knew it would not be so; trolls were expert at destroying craft when they put their minds to it, and the best he could reasonably hope for would be a splinter or a plank washing up against his empty little piece of rock.

Cormack thought back to his fateful decision to free Androosis and the others, the choice that had landed him here, battered and sure to die. For a moment, he regretted his choice, but only for a moment.

"I did the right thing," he said aloud, needing to hear the words. "Father De Guilbe was wrong—they were all wrong." He paused and put his hands on his hips, looking around in an attempt to discern this portion of the lake. It was simply too steamy, though Cormack got the distinct feeling that he was farther to the north. So he turned south and a bit to the east (or so he believed) that he might be somewhat facing Chapel Isle.

"You were wrong!" he shouted out across the waves. "You *are* wrong! Faith is not coerced! It cannot be! It blossoms within—truth revealed in the heart and soul. You are wrong!" Cormack sat down upon the stones, though he felt energized by his outburst, by his proclamation, by the verbal reinforcement of his moral choice.

A slight splash to the side turned his attention that way, where he saw his Abellican robe bobbing in the water against the stones. He retrieved it and laid it out on the stones to dry, and in doing so took note of his powrie beret still set firmly on his head. He put his hand up to touch it. There was, indeed, some magic within that cap.

Cormack looked to the troll bite on one arm to find that it was well on the way to healing, showing no signs of infection. He considered the deep wounds on his back from the whipping. He should not have survived those without tending and yet he had come through them, floating alone in a boat.

The beret, Cormack knew in his heart. The powrie beret somehow acted in a manner to the soul stone and was possessed of magic.

The fallen monk chuckled helplessly. There lay a common thread here, he knew. From the powries to the Alpinadoran shamans to the Abellicans and even the Samhaists there lay a common magic, a bonding of purpose and power.

A singular God for all?

Were the names the various peoples tagged upon their gods really important distinctions? At that moment of epiphany on an empty island, staring certain mortality in the face, Cormack realized that they were not.

But what did it matter? He had nowhere to go, and his plight was only confirmed a short while later when a plank of wood from his boat washed up against the rocks. He retrieved it as the sun sank in the west behind him.

His stomach roared with hunger when he awoke the next morning. He gulped down lake water to try to quell the emptiness. Facedown near the water, hands cupping it and bringing it up to his dry lips, Cormack nearly fell over when he saw the troll right beside him. He fell back, scrambling to find some defensive posture, and cut his elbows and knees in his desperate thrashing before he finally realized that it was one of the dead ones from the day before, bobbing high in the water.

Cormack splashed in to his waist and came beside the troll. He dared to push down on it to try to force it under the waves and was amazed at its buoyancy.

He glanced back at his empty island, certain to be his grave site. He looked out to Mithranidoon and saw another dead and floating troll. Cormack blew a long sigh.

Was it possible?

CHAPTER 20

The Gathering

They came in through a variety of means, either running with steps magically lightened and lengthened, or in the form of a fast cat, or even, in the case of the older and more powerful, in the form of birds, flying across the mountain updrafts. They came from their respective parishes, their "Circles," to the call of their leader.

From Devongel Ancient Badden watched each approach, his magical attunement with the land informing him whenever a brother Samhaist crossed into his domain. Their number swelled to twenty, to thirty, and finally, to thirty-two, meaning that all but one of the Samhaists of Vanguard had survived the last months of war, and that one dead priest had died gloriously in the first battle of Chapel Pellinor.

Ancient Badden was pleased.

When they were all together he gave them a complete tour of the grand— now grander—ice palace he had constructed. He even took them to his room of power at the top of the highest tower, where a well reached deep through the castle floor, deep through the glacier, and deep into the energy of the hot springs far below.

"Bask in it," he bade them, and they did, many nearly swooning in the orgy of earth power of this near-perfect conduit to the Rift of Samhain, the holy lake of Mithranidoon.

Ancient Badden led the procession out of Devongel and onto Cold'rin Glacier. He showed them the work at the chasm, where the white worm god continued its destructive work, where the misting blood of trolls prevented the natural repairs. He even sacrificed a pair of prisoners so that his brethren could hear the feasting of the worm.

From their smiles Badden knew that he had been wise to summon them. Morale demanded it. What could be more pleasing to his fellow Samhaists than the strength of Devongel and the fearsome power of D'no?

"Gwydre reinforces from the south," one of the younger Samhaists, whose domain was near to the Gulf of Corona, reported when the group gathered north of the chasm. Badden bade them to share their knowledge. "Nothing substantial as yet, but . . ."

"It will remain nothing substantial," another insisted. "I have been south to Honce proper. The fighting between Laird Delaval and Laird Ethelbert does not abate. Indeed, it is more furious than ever. I had thought Delaval to be gaining the advantage, but Ethelbert has unleashed legions of Behr barbarians. They have cut a fine line across the northern foothills of the Belt-and-Buckle Mountains, moving so near to Delaval's throne that he was forced to bring back most of his frontline forces who were pressing the city of Ethelbert dos Entel."

"That does not bode well," yet another interjected. "Delaval will not be pushed from his city—he will win out in the end, but now that end seems more distant."

"Why do you think that ill?" Ancient Badden asked.

"It prolongs the war."

"And . . . ?" Badden pressed.

"The pain of war is not unnecessary," another Samhaist reminded. "Everyone dies. That some will have their lives shortened is not our concern."

"Easy, friend," Badden said, and he looked back to the other. "And . . . ?" he repeated.

"I only fear that the followers of Abelle grow stronger with every passing year of war," the younger man admitted. "Their gemstones are greatly coveted by the lairds—all the lairds—and every man they heal moves them deeper into the heart of the people."

A couple of the others gasped that the young one would speak so boldly to Ancient Badden, but to their surprise Badden seemed unconcerned and far from angry.

"You think in terms of years, young one," he said, and more gently than anyone expected. "Consider the decades before us. The centuries. Fear not the followers of Abelle.

"We will win in the end because we are right," he continued. "We will win because the order of society depends upon it. There can be no lasting victory for the followers of that fool Abelle, because any gains they make unwind the order. They are gentle—they do not inspire fear in the people. Absent that, anarchy ensues. History tells us as much again and again. As the people begin to lose their fear of the severity of honest justice, they will become lax in their morals. Every woman a whore, every man a fornicator and adulterer. Promises of eternal paradise will not stop a wife from cuckolding her husband! Declarations of a merciful god invite sin and, ultimately, anarchy.

"The monks of Abelle will have their day in Honce," Ancient Badden predicted solemnly, and almost all of the gathering gasped in unison at the admission they had all feared. "They will win, my brothers, but only until the structures of Honce society fall away. It will take a generation, perhaps a few, but the cuckolds and other victims will call out for us. Do not doubt it. Let the fighting rage south of the Gulf of Honce. What you perceive as victory for the monks is also the distraction that will prevent Gwydre from gaining help from the lairds. Let them have Honce proper while we secure ourselves forever in Vanguard. We will always be ready, be assured, to answer the pleas of the victims of the concept of a merciful god and the false promises of sweet eternity.

"Because, my brethren, in the end, it is order that holds civilization together," Badden concluded. "And because, my brethren, that order needs severity."

A cheer went up around the Ancient, one heartfelt and full of awe. Badden knew that he had yet again reaffirmed his position in his order. He was the Ancient, and none would challenge him.

"Go," he bade them all. "Return to your Circles and observe. The trolls and goblins who sweep the land do so because the people of Vanguard deny us. When, in any of your Circles, they stop denying us, when they deny Gwydre and her lover, we will redirect our attacks to another Circle."

All around him, Samhaists began to bow repeatedly.

"We cannot tell the common folk the truth of the monks and their false mercy because they are too stupid to properly recognize the greater truth," said Badden, "that severe justice to the criminal is mercy to the goodly man. We are the merciful ones. They, the followers of the fool Abelle, invite chaos and ruin."

He returned the bow to his minions, then walked through them back toward his house. Behind him, several raced off on magical legs, several cracked and re-formed their bones to become swift-running animals, and the greatest became as birds and flew away.

CHAPTER 21

A Heroic Mistake

"Badden surrounds himself with formidable allies," Jameston Sequin tried to explain to the group of five road-weary heroes. "You should have come north with an army to properly execute your plan."

"We could not have supplied such a force," said the pragmatic and experienced Crait. "And the attraction it would have wrought would have had us fighting trolls and goblins and barbarians every step of the way."

"By the time we reached our goal, if ever we did, we'd be lucky to have even this many remaining," Brother Jond added.

"Then it seems as if your goal was never really in reach," said Jameston. "You do not appreciate the power of your enemy. He is Badden, Ancient Badden, the Ancient of all the Samhaists. They regard him as a god, and not without cause. His powers are extreme."

"Ever see that monk use his gemstones?" Crait interrupted. "Or that one swing that sword of his?" he added, nodding his chin toward Bransen.

"I have and was impressed—at both!" Jameston admitted. "But have you ever witnessed a dragon of despair?"

"A dragon?" Bransen asked.

"Ancient Badden is near to a god among the Samhaists, and not without cause," Jameston said. "Have you ever battled a giant? Not a big man, but a true giant? You will if you deign to approach Badden. Creatures thrice the height of a tall man and several times his weight, with power to snap your spine with the ease that one of us might snap the shaft of an old arrow."

"We could not bring an army," Brother Jond said with finality. "Nor can Dame Gwydre's people continue under the duress of Badden's pressing hordes. We know the desperation of our plan—and to a man and woman we accepted it. Why can't you?"

Jameston started to respond, but thought better and bit it back, offering a conciliatory, helpless laugh. "We should stay to the populated lands as much as possible," he said instead. He crouched and drew his dagger, then etched a rough map on the ground. "We can get right into southern Alpinador along a fairly defined road, here, just east of the mountains. There are a couple of villages—reasonable Alpinadoran tribes—where we can resupply."

"How do we know that they won't send word of us to Badden?" asked Vaughna.

"If they even know of Badden," Jameston replied, "they owe him no allegiance. Do not make the mistake of believing that the Samhaist has captured the hearts of the Alpinadorans. They are a proud collection of tribes with their own histories, beliefs, and practices. I know of no Alpinadoran Samhaists, not one."

"Yet barbarians have been known among Badden's invading hordes," Brother Jond pointed out.

"Opportunism more than loyalty, I am certain," said Jameston.

"It is too great a risk," Brother Jond decided. "Let us keep to the shadows."

"The glacier where Ancient Badden has made his home is a long and difficult trek, through wild lands that are already beginning to feel the chill of winter."

Brother Jond nodded, and Jameston shrugged his agreement.

They set off soon after, heading generally north. They came under the shadows of a range of towering mountains on their west. Though Jameston heeded the demands of Brother Jond, over the next couple of days they often came in sight of a rudimentary road, and on several occasions, they saw the rising smoke from Alpinadoran campfires.

"Grace or muscle?" Vaughna remarked to Crait on one such occasion, when Jameston and Brother Jond had moved down to better view a village, leaving Bransen and Olconna in full view on the back edge of a bluff.

Crait snickered.

"Ah, but I like the way that Highwayman moves," Vaughna added. "It's all like a dance, like the wind under a moon."

"But the redheaded one . . ." Crait prompted, understanding where Crazy V would go.

"Arms to hold a lover aloft," she said. "A determined swing that's not to be blocked or parried. . . ."

Crait laughed aloud, and the two men at the bluff turned to regard him.

"Good thing for you I'm not the type to blush," Vaughna whispered.

"To make others blush, though."

"Aye, that's the fun of life," said Vaughna. "Grace or muscle?"

"The Highwayman's got himself a wife, a new one, and a beloved one," Crait reminded.

Vaughna sighed, clearly disappointed. "Muscle'll do," she said, and Crait laughed again.

Jameston and Jond returned, and the half-dozen moved along as always and set camp as always—except that night Olconna found an unexpected visitor.

His step was lighter the next day.

One afternoon as they passed through a stretch of pines and rocks, just below the snow line and in air cold enough so that they could see their breaths, Jameston whispered to the group that they were being watched.

"The P'noss Tribe," he explained. "Small in number but very fierce. They range from the road below to the passes above. This is their territory."

Bransen put a hand on his sword hilt, a movement Jameston did not miss. The scout shook his head. "We would be foolish to tarry, but they will let us pass through as long as we keep going. They trust in my respect of them."

The group continued along, single-file, and the five unfamiliar with the land kept glancing left and right, as if expecting to see painted barbarian warriors hiding behind every tree, spear in hand.

"Try not to look so terrified," Jameston chided them. "You will just make our hosts nervous."

The rest of the day passed without incident. Jameston kept them up high in the mountains that night, and the cold winds howled at them, and a few snowflakes even drifted about. But Jameston Sequin knew this place as well as the Alpinadorans who called it home. He had a blazing fire going and warmed rocks for the five to keep them comfortable as they slept.

B ransen watched the man carefully long into the night and marveled at the simple serenity on Jameston's face. He seemed fully at peace out here, like a man who had long left behind the trivial troubles of feuding lairds and Churches and petty human squabbles. As Jameston sat upon a boulder and stared up at the night sky, Bransen got a sense of a man truly at peace, of a man who had found his place in the universe and who seemed truly comfortable in that place. It occurred to Bransen that there was something Jhesta Tu about Jameston Sequin.

A thought crossed Bransen's mind. For a fleeting moment he considered the notion that Jameston Sequin might be his father. Was it possible that McKeege was wrong, that Bran Dynard had survived the road and had used his training from the Walk of Clouds to become this legend in the northland?

Bransen gave a little snort at his own absurdity, wondering how in the world that notion had infiltrated his mind. Wishful thinking. . . . He wanted Jameston Sequin to be his father. He wanted *someone* to be his father, particularly someone he could admire. Bransen had tried to dismiss the notion that Dawson McKeege's proclamation regarding Bran Dynard's fate had hurt him profoundly.

Jameston walked over and stirred the flames of the low-burning fire. The orange light danced across his weathered face, shadowing his deep wrinkles and reflecting off his thick mustache.

Bransen saw experience there, and competence and wisdom, and it only confirmed Bransen's earlier recognition of serenity. This wasn't Bran Dynard, though Bransen wished that it could be true.

He would settle for being spiritual companions, if indeed they were.

O ver the course of the next few days the road all but disappeared, and no more villages spotted the landscape. Jameston's temperament sobered considerably. Taking that lead, the other five began to feel the gravity of their situation.

They were getting close, they all believed, though none asked Jameston openly about it. They just did as the scout suggested, moving along in a straight line to the north, a few hundred feet up in the foothills of the seemingly endless mountain range. Jameston had to give them the directions far in advance for he was increasingly absent from their line, moving all about to scout the region and pick their course. On one such afternoon, with Bransen leading the five through more rows of tall and dark evergreens, the quiet emptiness was lost to a sudden sharp sound. Bransen pulled up and slid low behind some brush staring out.

"The crack of a whip," Brother Jond whispered, moving in beside him.

Bransen resisted the urge to say that he would expect an Abellican to recognize such a sound but decided against it. He had come to like Jond. In any case, what was to be gained by creating tension among the tight-knit group?

A motion to the side turned them both to the right where Vaughna crouched behind a stump. She looked at them and pointed down and farther to the right. Following her finger, the pair did note some movement among the lower trees, though they couldn't make out anything definite.

"Stay here," Bransen whispered to Jond. He waved to Vaughna, and then to Olconna and Crait, who were similarly crouching in some brush up above the woman, to do the same.

Bransen reached inside himself, to his Jhesta Tu training. He surveyed the landscape, falling away before him, and potential paths appeared to him as clearly as if he were drawing it all out on a map. He belly-crawled out from the brush, popped up into a crouch, and darted to a tree some ten feet from Brother Jond. He paused only briefly before rushing out again, to the left this time, then down again to a pile of stones before belly-crawling his way to a lower stand of trees.

Soon he was out of sight of the others, sliding from shadow to shadow, for it was darker down here with the sun beginning to dip behind the mountains.

A long while passed.

Movement alerted the four to Bransen's return—so they thought. For the form that emerged from some trees in a running crouch was that of Jameston, not Bransen. He moved to the pair highest up, and Jond and Vaughna joined him there.

Jameston's sharp eyes instantly assessed. "Where is Bransen?"

Brother Jond motioned to the valley in the east. "Scouting."

A concerned look crossed the scout's face.

"What is it, then?" Crait asked.

"Trolls, mostly," the scout answered. "Many of them, escorting a line of captured men and women to the north."

Four sets of concerned eyes turned east immediately.

"How many trolls?" Vaughna and Olconna said together, both voices full of eagerness.

Crait couldn't help but grin as he considered Olconna's tone. Play hard, fight hard, he thought, for that was always the way he had regarded Crazy V. She was rubbing off on his young companion already, apparently.

"Too many," Jameston argued. "A score at least, though the line is too long for me to get an accurate count. I dared not tarry, fearing that you five would run down heroically to intervene."

"Are you saying that we should not?" Vaughna protested. "If there are men and women down there . . ."

"The Highwayman returns," Olconna announced. They turned as one to see Bransen picking a careful path back up the mountainside. He rushed in and skidded down in the midst of the group.

"Trolls with prisoners," he breathlessly announced.

"So we've been told," Vaughna replied. "Too many trolls, so says Jameston." She eyed the scout out of the corner of her eye as she spoke, as if in challenge.

But Jameston wasn't taking that bait. "You wish to get to Ancient Badden, and we are only a couple of days from his glacial home. If you engage this group here and now you risk being killed or captured. You also risk having some escape to carry a warning to that most dangerous Samhaist. You have no chance of succeeding if Badden knows you are coming, of course, and little even if he does not. How many trolls are too many trolls, in that case?"

"One troll's too many," Crait grumbled, but the helpless shake of his head accompanying the statement showed that he had no practical answer to Jameston.

"For the greater good you would ask us to let the prisoners be tortured and murdered?" Brother Jond reasoned.

"I'm not envying your choices," said Jameston, and he turned to Bransen as he spoke, for the Highwayman was shaking his head. Jameston knew well where this was leading.

The snap of a whip crackled through the air.

"If we hit them hard and fast, we might have them all dead or fleeing in short order," Bransen offered.

"We've got the high ground to start our attack," Olconna added.

"But if any are getting away—" warned Crait.

"Then they'll think we came from the south to rescue the captives," finished Bransen. "And will they even report the disaster to the Ancient? Would they dare face him with such failure?"

"A score—at least," said Jameston.

"Then you need only kill three or four to do your share," Vaughna interjected. She hoisted her two axes onto her shoulders. "We can't let them walk right past us."

"There is the greater good to consider," Brother Jond protested.

"Spoken like an Abellican, to be sure," Vaughna replied with a snicker.

Brother Jond sighed and looked to Bransen.

"We cannot just let them pass," Bransen agreed. "I'd not sleep well on hard ground or soft bed alike for the rest of my days."

"True enough and more," said Vaughna. "We're arguing as if we've got a choice, and none of us here is thinking that."

Jameston's eyes narrowed. "Do not underestimate trolls," he warned.

"Killed a score of the ugly things already," Vaughna retorted. "More than that. Let's hit them and hit them hard."

All heads nodded. Jameston just gave a resigned sigh and started to lay out a plan, but Bransen beat him to it, sending the scout down north of the group to pick off any trolls who would flee that way.

With Olconna and Crait moving farthest to the south, Bransen, Vaughna, and Brother Jond traveled straight down the hill. Bransen took the lead, directing the movements of the other two so that they remained out of sight until they were right above the path, the line of monsters and miserable captives rapidly approaching.

"You're not too worn out to give a good fight, are you?" Crait whispered to Olconna as they settled into position.

Olconna looked at him curiously, even incredulously.

Crait's smile nearly took in his ears. "Told you it was a ride worth taking," he whispered.

Olconna's cheeks turned as red as his hair.

———

With grace and speed and perfectly silently, Jameston moved undetected into position behind a clutch of boulders a dozen feet up from the trail and just ahead of the lead troll drivers.

One in particular caught his eye, a nasty-looking beast with half of its face torn away. It swung a whip easily, with practiced efficiency, and the way the others—trolls, and not just the miserable prisoners—cowered against its every word told Jameston that this was likely the leader of the group.

He drew out his finest arrow and set it to his bowstring. With steady arm, he drew back and settled perfectly. He didn't want to shoot prematurely and ruin the surprise, but the moment the trolls became aware of the attack that ugly beast would die.

Jamestone nodded to himself. He still didn't agree with the decision to engage, but he couldn't deny that it would be great sport.

Thirty or more," Brother Jond whispered breathlessly as he slid in between Bransen and Vaughan just above the road.

Neither could disagree with his assessment. Trolls milled all about the line of a dozen or so prisoners. The estimate of a score seemed inadequate indeed.

"Call it off," Brother Jond whispered, grabbing Bransen by the arm.

For a moment Bransen seemed as if he would agree. But how? To their right Olconna and Crait were already settled, and too far away to be called back. And now the troll line had advanced and was right below them, barely a dozen strides away. There was no chance that they could sneak back up the hill unseen.

Bransen motioned farther back along the troll line to a cluster of the brutes about two-thirds of the way to the end. "Hit them harder," he whispered. Vaughna nodded, and even Brother Jond had to concede that they truly had no options here.

They had committed. They had made their choice up on the hill. The trolls and prisoners flowed before them. They took up their weapons and set their feet under them. The first strike would be crucial.

Olconna and Crait had already surmised the higher-than-expected count and the challenges it would bring. They crouched low behind some brush, glancing over to their left, the north, waiting for the trio to begin the assault.

When that delayed longer than expected, the pair wondered if perhaps the added numbers had turned them about, but it was a brief consideration and nothing more, for as the largest cluster of trolls, nearly a dozen, moved under the trio's position, Bransen and Vaughna leaped down on them, axes and that fabulous sword swinging hard.

"Cut the back!" Crait growled, echoing their earlier conversation, when they had decided their best action to be swinging around the rear of the troll line and driving the creatures forward in to a confused muddle. The toughened old warrior leaped up and started down, but paused as soon as he realized that Olconna wasn't moving with him. He looked at his partner, and saw that Olconna was looking past him, was looking to the south.

"By Abelle's skinny arse," Crait swore when he glanced that way, when he realized that this group of trolls and prisoners was merely the lead, and that many, many more trolls were approaching from the south.

"Be quick, for we've got no choice!" the old warrior yelled, and tugged at Olconna's arm, and the two charged down at the surprised creatures below.

The first few frenzied moments of that attack played out exactly as Bransen had hoped. He and Vaughna cut deep into the troll ranks, slashing and chopping the group apart. Any cohesion the trolls might have found in mounting a defense seemed scattered. Another troll fell before Bransen's slashing sword.

To the north a squeal of agony told the attackers that Jameston would not disappoint, and for a few moments all three believed that whether it was twenty or thirty or a hundred trolls the day would be fast won!

Brother Jond's cry brought them back to reality, though, followed as it was by shouts from Olconna and Crait.

Bransen managed a moment's reprieve to look that way, and his heart surely sank. Olconna was in full flight, running toward him with a look of utter desperation. Behind him, straddling a dead troll, Crait stood with his back to Bransen, his arms up to ward off a barrage of flying spears. And beyond those came the trolls, so many more trolls, running and hooting.

"Free the prisoners!" Bransen yelled. "Give them troll weapons—anything!" He leaped toward the nearest humans as he shouted, but they shied away from him. Broken by days, weeks even, of tortured capture, not one of them appeared to be in any condition to fight. Those nearest fell to the ground, cowering, whimpering as Bransen approached.

A pair of trolls came in hard at him, but Bransen, too full of rage at that moment, turned aside both their spears with a single downward slash of his blade. He stepped in behind it, stiffening the fingers of his left hand and thrusting them into the throat of the troll on his left while retracting his blade from the double parry and slashing it back across, sending the troll on his right spinning to the ground.

He turned toward the south. Crait was down and squirming. Though it seemed as if he would make it, Olconna lurched suddenly and grabbed at his calf, where a spear had hit home. He stumbled down to one knee. Another spear clipped him across the side of his neck, and a fountain of red exploded about him. He fell facedown to the ground, curled and covered, groaning with pain.

Bransen rushed back to Vaughna and Brother Jond, pressed on two sides by trolls. Hope surged in him again as he marveled at Vaughna's prowess, at the accuracy and power of her strokes. Behind her, Brother Jond lifted his fist and sent forth a bolt of bluish lightning, cutting the air above Crait and Olconna, meeting the troll charge head-on. As he let fly the bolt, so the mob of trolls let fly a volley of rocks, filling the air with missiles. Vaughna grunted and cursed as more than one smacked her hard.

Bransen had better luck—at first—twisting and dodging and snapping off a series of precise parries that deflected one rock, two, and then a third. With the third, though, the rock clipped aside but kept coming at him, right at his head. Bransen ducked it.

Almost.

It clipped him on the forehead and rebounded away. He staggered for just a moment before shaking it off. "Jameston, cover our backs!" he shouted, and started forward, going right by Vaughna. He ripped off a series of slashes and stabs that overwhelmed the nearest troll and kept on moving, determined to drive back the mob, to protect his two fallen companions.

Another lightning bolt reached past him, slamming the lead trolls, but another rock soared in for Bransen's head. He ducked fast to the side and came right back up.

His bandanna and gemstone fell free.

He took a couple more strides, more on inertia than conscious thought, and by the end of the second, he stepped awkwardly, badly twisting his ankle and knee. "What?" he tried to cry in surprise, but he only got out, "Whaaaa. . . ."

He knew. The Stork knew.

Bransen staggered and stumbled. The trolls closed in on him, and he tried to lift his sword to strike. He thought of the Book of Jhest, tried to recall his lessons, tried to fight through the sudden disconnect between his body and his mind. It was too sudden, too unexpected.

Bransen stumbled and fumbled. He dropped his sword and didn't even know it, swinging his arm across as if he still held the blade. A rock smacked him in the face. The nearest trolls, both carrying clubs, ran to flank him, either side, and whacked him hard, driving him to the ground. One flew away, though, a hand axe stuck deep into its forehead.

Vaughna and Brother Jond came forward in a rush, protecting Bransen. Hardly slowing as she neared, Vaughna bent and scooped up his sword and waded into the trolls, axe and sword. She scored a kill, and wounded two others.

"Net!" Brother Jond yelled, but before the word even truly registered to Vaughna she saw the trap, a huge net thrown by a trio of trolls. Instinctively she slashed at it. Bransen's fine sword sliced through one of its thick strands. But more nets were already airborne. The trolls pressed in from in front and from behind.

If it had been twenty, they might have won.

If it had been thirty, they might have won.

CHAPTER 22

Fed to the Fishes

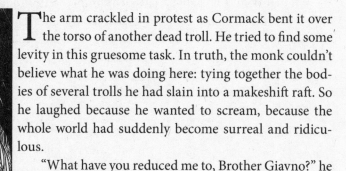

The arm crackled in protest as Cormack bent it over the torso of another dead troll. He tried to find some levity in this gruesome task. In truth, the monk couldn't believe what he was doing here: tying together the bodies of several trolls he had slain into a makeshift raft. So he laughed because he wanted to scream, because the whole world had suddenly become surreal and ridiculous.

"What have you reduced me to, Brother Giavno?" he asked aloud. He paused, surprised by the name he had put to his lament. Giavno hadn't passed judgment upon him, after all. That had fallen to Father De Guilbe, so why had he just used Giavno's name?

Because Brother Giavno represented to him all the promise and all the failure of the Abellican Church. So much potential and such shortsightedness all wrapped into one complex package. Just thinking of the man made Cormack's back ache, and yet, strangely, he found that he bore the man no ill will. He couldn't agree with the premise of his missionary brothers, and certainly not with their coercive and borderline evil methods, but he understood their perspective. He understood it all.

So he would stand against it. Out here, on a barren lump of rock in the middle of a steamy lake, tying trolls together into a macabre raft. Cormack laughed for real this time. It was that or cry, and he preferred to laugh.

Using strands of dead plants washed up against the rocks and contorting the stiffening troll bodies to complement each other, he soon enough had his bobbing craft constructed. He waded out with it to where the water was waist-deep, then pressed down on it to test its ballast. Dead trolls proved surprisingly buoyant—much more than a human, he thought, though of course he had no idea of how long his craft might last. Wouldn't it be fitting for him to float out into the middle of Mithranidoon only to discover that troll buoyancy lasted only a short while? He chuckled again.

To stay here was to die. That much he knew. Either trolls would come out of the water to attack him, or he'd waste away with little to nothing to eat, or he'd parch under the sun. Or a great storm would come up and wash him into the water—winter was closing in on Alpinador, after all, and even the warm waters of Mithranidoon were not immune to terrible storms.

So he had his raft. He had no other chances to take. Cormack gathered up the plank of his destroyed boat to use as a paddle and pushed off, drifting into the mist on a squishy pillow of flesh. He had no true idea of where he was on the lake, no idea of which way lay Chapel Isle, or Yossunfier, so he played his hunch and paddled out generally in the direction he considered south.

The plank wasn't much of an oar. Mithranidoon's strong crossing currents, brought on by the many hot springs that fed the lake and the constant battles between the colder surface water sinking into the heated depths, had Cormack swirling all over the place. The mist proved especially heavy this day, and the man couldn't see more than a few feet in any direction. Eventually, he just surrendered to the whims of the lake and reclined on the troll raft.

Sometime later, a slight twitch beneath him surprised him. He moved up to his elbows. The raft twitched again, then again more insistently. Cormack moved to the edge and peered into the dark waters, expecting to see a troll tugging at the raft. He fell back, swallowed hard, and knew he was horribly doomed, for a great fish had glided by just beneath him, a fish longer than he was tall.

Breathing hard, the man knelt on the center of the macabre raft and took up his paddle. He had to get out of here, had to get anywhere that was not open water. The raft jerked one way then shuddered as something large bumped it from below. Suddenly it began moving sidelong against all of Cormack's efforts, caught not by a current but by the gigantic fish!

He scrambled to the edge; his face blanched as he saw the beast just below him, its large mouth clamped about a dangling troll leg. Cormack took up the plank in both hands and stabbed hard at the fish. The whole raft bobbed under the water suddenly then popped back up, its integrity beginning to fail. Cormack saw the fish swim off with the troll leg in its mouth.

He rubbed his face. The raft continued to spasm as more and more of the huge fish nibbled, bit, and bumped it. He grabbed the plank and repeatedly smashed it down hard upon the water, trying to frighten the beasts away. For a few moments things did calm. Cormack held his breath, hoping he had escaped. But the raft was falling apart around him, and when he moved to hold it together he saw them, the great fish, circling and waiting.

"Oh, Giavno, what have you reduced me to?" the distraught monk asked into the stifling Mithranidoon fog.

Yach, pull 'er left, ye fool!" Kriminig chastised the four dwarves rowing the boat. Cranky old Kriminig, all gray beard and wrinkled face, stood at the prow, clutching his bloodstained beret, which was the shiniest among the powries of Mithranidoon. For none had seen more battles and none had scored more kills than Kriminig.

He closed his eyes as the boat began its turn and let his thoughts flow through his beret. All powrie caps shared the magic of bestowing toughness; wounds healed faster for the wearer, and the brighter a beret, the more cushion it would offer to its wearer. A few of those berets gained added benefits, as the layers of blood on the fabric and wisdom of experience for the wearer brought added insight.

For dwarves like Kriminig, the berets could serve almost as beacons, though weak lights in a thick fog, where he could sense the magic of another powrie cap. An injured dwarf would spark the magic, and that magic resonated.

Out on the lake fishing this day, Kriminig had felt such a pang, and though curious that it was coming from a direction opposite to their home island and far distant, and though he was confident that no dwarves other than the eight on his boat were off the island, he was certain of the feeling.

"A powrie's in trouble," he declared, leaving no room for debate.

"But our kin're all back at the home," another had argued.

"Then more've come to the lake," said a third, and so the debate went, round and round, and only one on the boat knew that he had an answer to the curious riddle. But Mcwigik, sitting in the back with the fishing net, thought it best to keep his suspicions to himself. A couple of the others, though, had heard rumors about Pragganag's cap, and cast curious glances Mcwigik's way.

"Just ye keep rowing," he said to them. "There might be something interesting to find."

"Too much left!" Kriminig grumbled. "Ease her back to starboard!"

Mcwigik rubbed his ruddy face, wondering if they'd come upon a fight between the monks and the barbarians.

He looked around frantically, lifting his head as much as possible, though he didn't dare stand or even kneel on the rocking troll raft. Even if he spotted another island, Cormack knew that he was doomed: there was no way he could outswim these giant fish even if he managed to surprise them and get a good lead as he had done with the powries.

One came up right before him and bit at a troll hand protruding in the air. Cormack saw those fish teeth all too clearly as they tore the fingers apart. If only he had an enchanted amber! He could use its magic and run across the water, barely disturbing the surface.

If only . . . !

This surely wasn't how the young monk had pictured he would die. He had always recognized that he might not live to a ripe old age. When he had signed on to the mission in Alpinador, Cormack had known well that several other brothers had been killed by the barbarians. He wasn't afraid to die, particularly if it happened in service to Blessed Abelle. Better to live life with a purpose, even with the risks, than to hide in a hole and hope for old age.

But he didn't want to die like this, anonymously, and for no better reason than to feed some fish.

One came up and bit him on the side of his calf, tearing his skin. He swung about fast and slammed his fist into the side of the fish. While that action did send the thing back under the water, the movement also further diminished the integrity of the raft. Another troll body broke free, leaving Cormack on only three remaining ragged things.

He felt his robes weighing him down as he often bobbed into the water, and he thought to take them off. To what point?

All the fear and the anger went away then, suddenly. Resigned to his fate, Cormack stopped himself from removing the soaked and heavy robes. He would let them drag him down to the depths. Better to surrender to it and get it over with.

He hoped he would lose consciousness quickly, that the pain wouldn't be so intense.

He took a deep breath, then blew it all out and set himself to plunge into the water, thinking he would just keep swimming down.

Just as he was about to go, though, he heard a splash that he recognized as an oar dipping into the lake.

"Here! Here!" he yelled, and he began smacking at the fish again with renewed urgency. "Here!"

A fish as long as Cormack was tall leaped up before him, coming for his face, but the agile monk reacted with fury and speed, smashing it in the side of the head with a right cross that turned it aside. He hit it again several times as it thumped onto his raft and rolled into the water.

But now he was in the water, the troll bodies all floating apart. His robes pulled him down as he worked his weary arms furiously to try to tread water. He tilted his head back as far as he could, gasping for breath. He got a mouthful of water instead and felt himself submerging.

A strong hand grabbed his shoulder, though, and hauled him back up. A giant fish brushed against his leg, and he slammed his head as he went up over the side of a boat. Then he was lying on the wood, eyes closed, only semiconscious, and curled defensively. He coughed and felt water pouring from his mouth.

"Well, what d'we got here?" he heard in that distinctive powrie dialect and the typical dwarf voice, which sounded somewhat like a receding wave rattling a beach of small stones.

"Name's Cormack," said another, a voice the monk recognized. "Won the cap fair and square."

"So take the cap and throw the fool back to the Mith trout," said the first, the last thing Cormack heard.

CHAPTER 23

Captives

"Don't let him fall," Brother Jond implored Vaughna as she struggled to keep Bransen marching in the line of prisoners. They knew well what would happen if that occurred, for one of the other prisoners had tumbled from exhaustion and the cold and the thin air earlier that day up high on a mountain pass. The trolls had descended on that poor soul immediately, whipping and kicking, and when the woman hadn't been able to get up (they prevented anyone from helping her), they had beaten her, laughing at and mocking her all the while, then left her for dead.

"What is wrong with him?" Vaughna asked, for she had never seen anything like Bransen's awkward, storklike gait.

"He got hit too hard in the head," Brother Jond replied. It was the eighth time he had answered that same question to Vaughna and to Olconna, whom he was now helping along the march. Olconna had taken a few fairly serious hits, and Jond initially feared that he would not survive. Most of those wounds had proven superficial, though, and Olconna's growing reputation for toughness had proven well earned. Now, though in pain and needing support, he moved along without a whimper of complaint.

Bransen listened to the conversations very distantly. He had thought to slur out some rudimentary explanation early on in the march, but had forgone the effort, realizing that there was nothing his companions could do. Brother Jond had retrieved the bandanna, but the soul stone was not to be found, and the trolls had stripped the monk of all of his possessions, particularly the magical gemstones.

Crait lay dead back at the scene of the battle. All of the four surviving heroes sent by Dame Gwydre had been hurt, Bransen the least of all, Olconna by far the worst. But without the gemstone, Bransen couldn't count himself as fortunate. He stayed within himself, focused on his Jhesta Tu training, and forced his *chi* somewhat in line. He didn't exhaust the process, though, understanding that there were limits to his concentration and that after a while his stork affliction would win out.

But he had to keep going, had to keep his focus intense enough so that he would keep putting one foot in front of the other. And he and his three remaining companions had to hope that the trolls would make a critical mistake, and in that event, Bransen was ready to fully immerse himself in Jhesta Tu and try to find at least a few moments of effective fighting.

Their hopes for such an error had waned throughout the remainder of that day and long into the night, for this group of jailers proved quite skilled, and the troll numbers overwhelming. At camp, the prisoners were separated into small groups, and every one lay facedown on the cold ground, a spear poised at the back of his or her neck.

Their only hope was Jameston. Only Jameston Sequin could get them out of this, though Bransen had to wonder what in the world a single man might do against the awful power of Badden and his minions. He tried not to think of that, tried not to succumb to the reality that he would never see his beloved Cadayle and Callen again.

The next day the line of prisoners was marched through a long, descending, barren pass overlooking a river of blue-white ice. As they neared the base of that path the ground became more slippery, and no matter how hard he focused or how hard Vaughna tried to help him Bransen fell repeatedly. The first time he thought his long trial would end with the trolls descending upon him to whip him to death. But many of the weary humans were slipping and falling. Unbeknownst to Bransen and the others they were too close to their destination for the trolls to allow any to die.

They moved out of the rocky mountain pass and onto the glacial sheet, and surprisingly, the footing was actually better there and far more consistent than on the ice-speckled mountain trail.

They had trudged on for nearly an hour when a gasp from in front brought all eyes up the slope to the southeast where a large castle appeared as if made completely of ice. Glistening minarets and towers reached up from foreboding bluish, nearly translucent walls. More dread-filled gasps issued throughout the group as they neared, both from the scope and aura of sheer power emanating from the castle and because this was the first time that any of them had actually looked upon a giant.

These were giants, as Jameston had warned, and not simply large humans. Thrice Bransen's height, the behemoth humanoid creatures mocked his warrior pride. No matter how fine he became with his weapon, no matter how strong he honed his muscles, no matter how fine and precise his reactions, how could he ever hope to do battle against such a behemoth?

Bransen shook his head and mumbled, "N . . . N . . . N . . . No," throwing the negative and distracting thoughts aside. For before him lay the ultimate challenge, the final pinnacle, perhaps. He had no doubt that this was the abode of Ancient Badden, the key to his freedom, or more likely by far, he now understood, the gateway to the afterlife.

Jameston Sequin had survived for so long in hostile lands because he knew when to run away. He had put six arrows into the air at the beginning of the battle and had scored three hits he knew to be mortal, sending a fourth troll spinning down to the ground in agony.

The frenzy had grown too confused after that, however, with human prisoners and trolls scrambling all over each other, and of course, his companions in the mix. Then had come the reinforcements, and all hope washed away.

Bitterness filling his heart, Jameston had found few options: charge in and die or be captured, or flee. He ran. He took little heart in noting that most of the group was still alive when the prisoner caravan passed beneath his perch a short while later, for he knew their destination.

He watched the second group of trolls moving across soon after and cursed under his breath repeatedly for his foolishness in not at least demanding a wider scouting of the area before the impulsive attack. He couldn't have stopped the stubborn would-be heroes, but perhaps he could have delayed them!

The scout shadowed that caravan the rest of the day and tried repeatedly to find some way into the troll encampment that night. But this was no novice group, and no openings presented themselves to the skilled hunter. He couldn't get near to his companions.

The next day proved even worse, for the two troll groups tightened up as they hit the more difficult and broken mountain trails that led high above Toonruc's Glacier. He watched helplessly as one woman stumbled and fell out of line to the ground. The trolls fell over her, beating and whipping, taunting and kicking, leaving her bloody form heaped on the ground.

As soon as they had moved out, Jameston rushed to her and was surprised indeed to find her still alive, though barely. He used his waterskin to clean the gashes, then pulled off his small pack and pulled out some bandages and herb salves and went to work on her many wounds.

She survived that ordeal with many groans and whimpers, but never opened her eyes. Jameston feared she never would open them again. He looked along the trail to where the trolls and their prisoners had disappeared and heaved a great sigh. Then he tenderly lifted the battered woman in his arms and moved off the way he had come.

It would be a long journey back to Vanguard, he knew, but that was this poor soul's only chance, and he had to inform Dame Gwydre that her team of assassins had failed. The prospect of a Vanguard ruled by Ancient Badden did not sit well with Jameston.

Bound, dirty, cold, and bone-weary, the prisoners were forced into a side-by-side line out in the middle of the glacier, just south of the enormous ice castle that graced the mountainside on the eastern edge of the ice river, and just before an enormous chasm in the glacial ice. Not far away, a pair of giants pounded wedges deep into the ice, but even their brute force could not intimidate the prisoners more than the old, but hardly feeble, man who stood before them.

Bransen knew it to be Ancient Badden, for he, who had slain the vile Samhaist Bernivvigar, surely recognized the Samhaist robes of station. The sheer power exuded by the old man, a commanding presence that seemed to mock any who stood near to him, reminded Bransen clearly of his long-ago encounter with the imposing Bernivvigar.

Only this one was stronger, he understood. Much stronger.

Ancient Badden let a long, long time slide past silently. The trolls stepped nervously from foot to foot, occasionally tittering, though not one dared speak. The prisoners tried hard not to meet Badden's withering gaze, but whenever one did he or she knew true hopelessness.

"Him first," the Samhaist instructed, pointing to Olconna, who was doing much better than his friends had anticipated. "Take the rest away. Keep them alive and keep them miserable that they will more welcome their deaths."

A trio of trolls grabbed Olconna and hustled him forward. When he tried to resist they tripped him facedown to the ice, his hands bound behind his back. He landed with a sharp crack. Olconna only groaned, but when he rolled to his side he left a stream of bright-red blood on the blue-white surface.

Bransen glanced at Ancient Badden to gauge his response; if the man had even noted Olconna's fall he didn't show it. Instead, his gaze had locked on a troll off to the side, the one that carried Bransen's sword strapped diagonally across its back. The Samhaist stared at it curiously for just a moment, then reached out his hand and grasped suddenly, as if he were grabbing the troll by the throat.

And indeed, magically, he had done just that from the way the creature suddenly stiffened and reached up with its own hands. Ancient Badden retracted his hand, and the troll stumbled toward him at such an angle that it obviously would have fallen over had not the Samhaist's magic been holding it on its feet.

As the troll came in Badden grabbed it by the throat with his real hand and with surprisingly little effort lifted the squirming creature into the air and turned it about. He regarded the decorated sword for only a moment before pulling it free, then dropped the troll back to the ground.

Ancient Badden's eyes sparkled as he studied the magnificent weapon. He said something to the troll that Bransen and the others couldn't hear. The troll responded more loudly, but in a language that none of them understood. Badden pushed the troll away and took up the sword in both hands, waving it before his eyes, his expression that of someone who had just realized a great treasure.

That expression changed abruptly. Ancient Badden sniffed at the air, eyes narrowing. Bransen managed to keep from throwing himself off balance as he glanced back to note Badden's souring expression, to see the Samhaist bring the sword blade up horizontally under his nose and sniff it, as a hunting dog might sniff.

Unaware of the changing mood, the trolls began herding the prisoners away from the gorge. Bransen and the rest started away, but Ancient Badden called a command for them to wait. As they all, troll and prisoner alike, turned to regard the man, he again took up his conversation with the troll who had delivered the sword. That creature whirled about and pointed in the direction of the prisoners, in the general area of Bransen.

Ancient Badden calmly walked over and spoke not to Bransen but to Vaughna at his side. "I am told you wielded this blade in the fight," he said.

Vaughna glanced nervously at Brother Jond and Bransen. "I did," she said, not knowing what else to say.

Badden motioned, and the trolls dragged her forward. "This blade," Ancient Badden announced, "has the scent of the blood of a Samhaist elder on it." His glower fell squarely over Vaughna. "This blade killed a friend of mine."

Vaughna seemed to shrink at the remark. She turned her head as if to look back at her friends for support. Bransen tried to call out that the sword was his, but the Stork was unable to make his cry any more than an undecipherable keen.

"I only acquired it recently," Vaughna stammered, seeming to shrink next to the Ancient one. "I never met a Samhaist elder."

"You have now," Ancient Badden replied. Without warning he stabbed the sword into Vaughna's belly. Her eyes registered shock briefly before she doubled over, howling and holding her spilling guts, and sank to one knee. Her companions recoiled in disbelief.

Ancient Badden motioned to the trolls, then to Olconna and to another group, followed by a nod of his chin toward Vaughna. His well-trained charges knew what to do. As one group moved to lift Olconna to his feet and shove him back to the others, a second group fell over Vaughna, dragging her forward trailing blood and bile.

She fought as well as she could which wasn't much, given her condition and the odds. The gutsy woman did manage to squirm about to regard Olconna as he was dragged the other way. "Every moment precious," she gasped to him, despite the pain, despite her imminent demise.

One troll ran to retrieve a rope, looped over a pulley at the end of a beam that was hanging out over the chasm. Bransen and the others watched in horror as the trolls tied the rope about Vaughna's ankle and dragged her to the edge of the chasm and left her there as Ancient Badden strolled over, sword still in hand.

The trolls around the prisoners began herding them again, but Badden stopped them. "Let them watch," he said with a wicked edge to his voice.

Hot with horror and revulsion, Bransen fell within himself. He fought to find his Jhesta Tu edge to cry out that it was his sword. The second the sound escaped his lips something smashed hard into the side of his head, dropping him to the ground. He looked up in surprise to see that it was Brother Jond's fist and not that of a troll.

"Do not insult her sacrifice," the monk whispered harshly.

It took the dazed Bransen a few moments to reorient himself. He looked back at Ancient Badden and the chasm where Vaughna hung upside down by one leg, trying to curl up, to grab her bleeding stomach. Bransen's heart sank, every fiber in his body tense with disbelief and shock. Brother Jond pulled the transfixed Bransen back to his feet.

Ancient Badden stood on the ledge before Vaughna, his arms upraised. He began a chant, calling forth the power of the "great worm of the ice."

"What is he doing?" the thoroughly shaken Olconna asked, or started to, for before he finished, a thundering, rumbling roar shook the ice beneath their feet.

Hanging over the chasm, Vaughna looked down, and her face drained of all color, despite being upside down. She began sputtering and tried to swing herself toward the edge while the trolls began to turn a crank, lowering her from sight. From somewhere below a great beast roared again with obvious excitement. Vaughna began to scream beneath the lip of the chasm, beyond sight. The trolls kept turning the crank, easing the woman a long, long way down. More screams, more roars, and then suddenly it went very quiet.

Suddenly the rope jerked so forcefully that the heavy beam bent and seemed as if it would break. It held, and the trolls began hauling up the rope—no need for the crank anymore.

"Justice is done," Ancient Badden pronounced, turning about to the gathering, a supreme and contented smile on his old face. He motioned to the trolls to begin herding the remaining prisoners away.

Suddenly another squeal from the chasm turned the stunned prisoners about yet again, this time to see the end of the rope. Vaughna's leg dangled from it, the flesh of her mid-thigh ripped and shredded where some nightmarish monster had swallowed the rest of her.

"By Abelle," Brother Jond muttered fervently, head bowed.

CHAPTER 24

The Anvil over Their Heads

They're wanting ye to use yer long legs and wade out for better fishing," Mcwigik explained to Cormack.

The man sat on a large rock on the northeastern side of the powries' nearly barren island, staring at the misty waters.

"We're not going to kill ye," Mcwigik assured him, handing him a weighted net. "Not unless ye do something asking us to kill ye."

"I do appreciate the rescue, and your generosity in allowing me to live."

Mcwigik shrugged. "I'm thinking that the bosses are wanting Prag's son to get old enough to see if the boy can win his dead father's cap back."

"The bosses? Aren't you one of the bosses?"

"Yeah, but I'm wanting to keep ye alive just because."

"Just because."

"Yeah."

Despite his troubling situation Cormack managed a little grin at that cryptic admission from the rough powrie. He had grown somewhat fond of the dwarf.

"Ye don't give us any reason to kill ye, and we won't kill ye," Mcwigik reiterated. "Now go get us some fish." The dwarf hocked and spat on the rocks and turned and started away.

"And what happens when you go to battle?" Cormack asked, stopping the dwarf in his tracks. Hands on hips, Mcwigik slowly turned about. "When the powries row out to do battle with the monks or the Alpinadorans, what am I to do?"

"Ye're a long way from getting us to let you go along," Mcwigik replied, completely missing the point.

Cormack gave a little laugh. "I could never go to such a fight, and you know it well."

"Yach, but ye fought them barbarians all the time."

"Not by my choice," said Cormack. "Never by my choice. Not against them and not against you powries."

Mcwigik hocked another large ball of spit, this time landing it near Cormack's feet. "I'm knowing ye better than to think ye're afraid of a fight," he said.

"There is no point to the fighting!"

"No? How about the trolls, then? Would ye—"

Cormack cut in. "I'll help you kill all the trolls you can find."

Mcwigik smiled approvingly. "Yeah, we seen what was left of yer boat. Durndest boat any of us e'er seen. Might be a big part of why th'others're letting ye stay."

"But I cannot stay," said Cormack.

"Up for a long swim, are ye?"

"I cannot remain here for long, anyway," the fallen monk went on, ignoring the sarcasm. "This is no place for me."

"Ye wanting us to put ye back with the monks?" asked Mcwigik. "Aye, might that we can, but that ye'll have to earn. So go get the fish, and keep getting the fish—"

"I can never go back there," Cormack interrupted. "They would not have me, and I would not have them. They set me adrift, thinking they had left me for dead, but somehow I didn't die."

"Not somehow, ye dolt," said Mcwigik. "Was the cap on yer head." Cormack reached up to adjust his beret in acknowledgment.

"So ye're not wanting to go back there, and ye're saying ye can't stay here . . ."

"Yossunfier," said Cormack.

"The barbarians?"

"Yes," the monk replied. "I would have you drop me there."

"They'll kill ye."

Cormack pursed his lips. "Nevertheless, that is where I would like to go."

"Well, ye ain't for going there with us," said the dwarf. "Not a place we go near. Those folk ain't like yer monk friends. They know the water and know when anything's near their island. They been there a hundred years, ye know. And more, lots more. They're not using stones to throw lightning like yer own. Nah, their magic's quieter but worse for us if we venture near."

"Then give me a boat so I can go there alone."

Mcwigik spat again, this time hitting Cormack in the foot. "Ye're daft. Boats're worth more than yerself."

"I will return it in short order."

"Then how're ye getting back to their island after ye drop it back here?"

"I'm not going back to that island or any island," Cormack said, half under his breath, and it surprised him to see Mcwigik stiffen at that remark, a look of intrigue suddenly upon his face.

"This has never been my place."

"What're ye saying, boy? Say it plain."

"I have a friend—several, perhaps—on Yossunfier who wishes to be gone from this lake. Lend me a boat so I can retrieve her."

"Her? Haha, but that's telling me a lot."

"We'll come right back with the boat. Then, with your agreement, you can take us to the shore and never think of us again."

Mcwigik started to respond in several different directions. Cormack gathered this by the way the dwarf's mouth worked in weird circles with no real sounds coming out.

"Yach, just catch the durned fish!" he finally blurted, waving a hand at Cormack dismissively as he stormed away.

Cormack had no idea what all that might be about, so he took up the net and waded into the warm lake waters.

You keep looking out to the south," Androosis remarked, walking up beside Milkeila. "You fear that something has happened to him."

It was a statement, not a question, and an observation that Milkeila could not dispute.

"We took care to make it appear as if our escape had been of our doing," Androosis tried to assure her. "I doubt that our friend's complicity is known to the monks."

"And yet he does not signal . . . in any way," said Milkeila.

Androosis put a hand on her shoulder to comfort her. Barely had his hand touched her when Toniquay yelled, "Your duties!" They broke away from each other and turned as one to regard the shaman, who was striding their way. "You spend far too much time seeking an Abellican," Toniquay scolded.

"An Abellican who saved us," said Androosis. He shrank back as soon as he uttered the words, surprised by his own outburst at this powerful figure.

"It is true then, what they say," Toniquay said to Milkeila. "You have fallen for this Abellican named Cormack." He snapped a glare at Androosis, too, daring the young man to say again that Cormack had saved their lives.

"He is a friend," Milkeila replied coolly. "A loyal one."

"Friend," Toniquay spat derisively. "A mere friend does not betray his own brethren. Nay, there is more at work here than friendship. His betrayal bespeaks fires in his loins."

Milkeila didn't respond at all, didn't blink or sneer or speak.

"Your duties await," Toniquay reminded her, adding as she walked by, "You would do well to prove yourself."

"I am shaman—"

"For now."

The warning did indeed shake the woman, visibly so, and she turned and hurried away.

Toniquay turned his withering gaze back to Androosis. "And you," the shaman said, "would do well to learn and accept your place. My patience nears its end for Androosis. I took you to dangerous waters. Men of honor paid with their lives!" Androosis's stunned expression spoke volumes, clearly arguing that the disaster on the boat was hardly his fault.

But Toniquay wasn't hearing any of it. "We went out of our way to try to save you, young and spirited one. But no more. Prove yourself or you will be banished—if you are fortunate and the elders are feeling generous."

"Yes, Toniquay," Androosis replied obediently, hanging his head in humility.

The shaman walked away, eyeing the young man's every step sternly.

A somber mood accompanied Brother Giavno and the rest as they went to work collecting the larger stones from the area of the island they had come to regard as their quarry. Giavno winced and couldn't help but recall the last time he had been down here, when powries had arrived and Cormack had battled them so magnificently, so bravely.

The loss of Cormack was no small thing to the brothers of Chapel Isle. The manner in which it had occurred had left them all, particularly Giavno, tasked with delivering the very likely fatal beating, feeling empty and desolate. No one had spoken the fallen brother's name since he had been pushed out adrift in the small boat. No one had to.

It was written on all of their faces, Giavno clearly saw. To a one they had been shaken. To a one Cormack's betrayal had asked primary and devastating questions about their purpose and place in this foreign land and among these foreign societies.

Why had Cormack done it? Why had the man betrayed them, betrayed the very tenets of their mission, according to Father De Guilbe's interpretation?

Giavno thought he had the answer to that, echoed in the sounds of Cormack's lovemaking to the barbarian woman. Love was the strongest of human emotions, Blessed Abelle had taught, and more people had been brought down by love than by hate. While there was no specific prohibition of marriage in the Order of Blessed Abelle, such relationships were scorned among the brotherhood. If you gave yourself to the Church, it was to be wholly so. Worse still, to foster a love affair with a heathen, with a barbarian shaman, was far beyond the bounds of acceptability.

Cormack had earned his beating, Giavno believed, and had told himself a million times since that awful day. He could still feel the tug of the whip as its barbed ends dug into and hooked on the flesh of Cormack's back.

He shuddered, and only then realized that one of the brothers had been asking him a question, and probably for some time.

"Yes, Brother?" he replied.

"The stone?" the younger man inquired.

"Stone?"

The monk offered a curious stare at Giavno for just a moment, then nodded as if he completely understood (which he likely did, for the cause of distraction was quite common at that time) and motioned toward one large rock that had been set off to the side.

"Is it too large, do you think?" the monk asked.

Giavno looked at him curiously. "No, of course not."

"I cannot carry it alone," the monk replied.

"Then get someone to help you."

"They are all busy, Brother Giavno. I thought that perhaps you could help, either with your arms or through use of the malachite stone in lessening the weight."

Giavno was about to reprimand the brother for being so foolish; Giavno was overseeing the work detail and not participating. But then he caught something in the young brother's eye, a look of both hopefulness and sympathy, and when he glanced out at the wider scene, he realized that more than one of the other workers had taken a subtle, covert interest in this distant conversation.

Brother Giavno smiled as it hit him fully: They were trying to distract him. As the work was keeping their minds off the tragedy of Brother Cormack, so they had thought to include Brother Giavno in that blessed busyness.

"Yes, Brother," Giavno addressed the young monk. "Come. Together we two will carry the stone to the chapel, and what a fine addition to the wall it will be."

Together, he thought, for all that the brothers of Blessed Abelle had was each other. So far from home, so far from kin, without that mutual bond they would all surely lose their minds.

That was what had made Cormack's betrayal so particularly difficult.

Ye might remember Bikelbrin, and these are me friends, Ruggirs and Pergwick," Mcwigik said, splashing at the water's edge behind Cormack.

Cormack nodded to each in turn, wondering uneasily what this unexpected meeting might be all about.

"We'll take ye to her," Mcwigik announced, and the fishing spear fell out of Cormack's hand. "Not sure how we'll do it, but we'll find a way. But we got a price."

Cormack held up his arms, fully displaying his now-ragged brown robe. "I have little, but what I have—"

"Ye know yer way about out there," Mcwigik interrupted. "That's the price."

Cormack looked at him curiously.

"The four of us're done with this rock, and have been for a long time," the dwarf explained. "We're wanting to be gone from the lake, but we're not for knowing the land about. Been a hundred years since I walked those paths, but for yourself, it's not so long. So we'll help ye get yer girl, and in exchange, ye'll take us along."

"My road will be south, no doubt, out of Alpinador and into the Honce land of Vanguard—maybe even across the gulf and into Honce proper, itself. I'm not sure how well-received a powrie might be . . ."

"Ye'll take care of it," Mcwigik said. "So start thinking on how we might get ye to yer girl, and then we're off this rock, all six—or five, if she's not to come."

"Or nine or ten, perhaps even twelve," said Cormack, "if her friends decide that they, too, wish to see the wider world."

"Bring a hundred," said Mcwigik. "A thousand! Long as me and me boys get to get out o' here and to places more interesting."

Cormack settled back on his heels. He could hardly believe the sudden turn of events. One moment, he was floating on a raft of tied troll carcasses, about to be eaten by fish, and now he was looking at escape, at what he and Milkeila had dreamed of for a long, long time.

He nodded—stupidly, he figured.

"We can find Yossunfier at night," Mcwigik said. "And we're thinking to go in one of the next few."

Cormack nodded again, no less stupidly. Mcwigik thumped his hands on his hips and walked off.

Cormack retrieved his fishing spear. Oddly, he couldn't hit another thing the rest of the afternoon.

For the Enjoyment of the Ancient

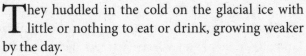

They huddled in the cold on the glacial ice with little or nothing to eat or drink, growing weaker by the day.

The fortunate ones continued to huddle in misery, for every couple of days one was grabbed from their midst and dragged to the crevice, to be wounded and lowered into the gorge as food for the beast that lay below.

Ancient Badden presided over those ceremonies of sacrifice, and he seemed to truly enjoy it. How much like Bernivvigar he appeared to Bransen. The same feral look consumed him in those moments of inflicting agony upon others.

The only other time they saw the old wretch was during the daily troll sacrifice. This was done differently, with several trolls hanged over the gorge with slit wrists so that their blood rained into the dark chasm.

"They hang them in different places every day," one of the human prisoners observed. "Like they're trying to make sure that the whole chasm gets coated in troll blood."

"Thin blood, that," another of the prisoners chimed in. "Mix it with water, and the water won't freeze."

None of them had the wherewithal to put it together from there, because, really, what did it matter to the doomed prisoners?

Bransen, however, noted every detail. His entire existence at that point centered around his mental acuity, as his physical limitations had only increased with the brutal conditions. He tried to put all his Jhesta Tu training and discipline to the side for the time being, as if he was storing it for one furious moment. That was his only hope. He had to find exactly the right time and hope that such an opportunity would present itself.

One gray morning Bransen knew that his last chance had come.

Only Brother Jond fought for him when the troll guards came to drag Bransen away. Even Olconna mitigated Jond's protests, quietly telling the monk that maybe it was for the better that Bransen's misery be ended. Whether they fought for him or not wouldn't have mattered in a practical sense, but Olconna's attitude stung Bransen profoundly. He had more important things to think about, however, as the trolls dragged him to the edge of the chasm. He lay helpless as Ancient Badden approached, carrying Bransen's sword.

This was his moment, Bransen realized. He had to somehow call upon the powers of his training, had to strike fast and sure, get that sword and finish Badden as he had done with Bernivvigar. But he had possessed a soul stone on that long-ago occasion; every step and movement wasn't a battle for him then as it was now. Still, he had to try!

"This one?" Ancient Badden asked. His incredulous tone allowed the prisoner to ease back from his shining moment of fury. "Hmm," Badden mumbled, glancing from Bransen to the gorge. "No," he decided.

Bransen breathed a sigh of relief, though he knew any reprieve could only be temporary. Every one of the prisoners was being kept alive for one purpose. "No, if we feed him to the worm, he will likely infect the beast with . . . with whatever malady it is that so wrenched his limbs. Bring him south."

Ancient Badden started off in that same direction, crossing an ice bridge to the southern rim of the chasm, then walking off the hundred strides or so to the glacier's cliff edge. The trolls dragged Bransen behind.

Bransen knew he had avoided being sacrificed but not escaped execution. His resistance was not a conscious decision; it came from pure instinct, simple and unafraid, as only a man who realizes death is both imminent and unavoidable might discover. All of his muscles twitched in magnificent harmony, moving together for the first time since he had lost the soul stone, lifting him suddenly to his feet, his wrists and ankles breaking free of the hold of the four escorting trolls as he twisted and then hopped upright.

He snapped a circle-kick against the side of a troll's knee and slugged the creature in the jaw as he came around, launching it away. He leaped straight up as the other three closed on him and kicked out to both sides with perfect balance and stunning power—literally stunning, as the kicks sent two trolls staggering and stumbling to the ground.

The remaining escort leaped onto Bransen's back and began clawing, but the man executed a high somersault and stretched out to full extension as he came over, ending his turn so that he landed flat on his back atop the troll. He wrenched the creature's arms from his chest and throat and twisted them at the wrist as he rolled off the creature. When he hopped back up to his feet, he gave sudden jerks that broke both of those wrists cleanly.

Bransen spun about as two of the first three came in at him. The leading enemy was right upon him as he turned, and got its hands about his throat, choking him. Bransen hooked his thumbs under those of the troll and tugged out and down, then folded his legs under him so that he fell to his knees, taking the troll down with him. He used the suddenness of that impact to viciously drive the troll's thumbs over and down, breaking both.

Bransen hopped right back up, but he felt the pangs of the Stork within, the moment of Jhesta Tu–inspired coordination fast fading. He barely slapped aside the clawing strikes of the last of that group, and worse, several more were fast heading his way. Worst of all for Bransen, Ancient Badden had taken note of the fight.

The ice under Bransen's feet suddenly turned to water, and he plunged down, and only avoided continuing deep into the glacier by throwing himself to the side. Instinctively, Bransen rolled himself out of the water—and a good thing that was, for it froze again almost immediately.

Across the way, Ancient Badden cackled with enjoyment. Trolls fell over Bransen, beating and clawing him. His glorious moment of concentration was lost, falling to the curse of the Stork once more. He still tried to flail, for what it was worth, but the four trolls now bearing him held him tightly and a pair of others walked alongside, punching him hard every time he moved.

They dropped the nearly unconscious man at Ancient Badden's feet near the edge of the glacier and moved fearfully away.

"Do you see it?" Ancient Badden asked him. Lying helpless, Bransen saw only the sky and the tall man towering over him. Badden reached down and took him by the front of his shirt and with surprising and terrifying strength hoisted him upright. Bransen looked out on a long, long drop, hundreds of feet and more, to a wide and long lake that was almost completely blanketed by fog.

"Mithranidoon," Ancient Badden explained. "It's called that even by the Alpinadoran barbarians. A Samhaist name in this northern land. Do you know why that is?"

Bransen didn't even try to respond, for he wasn't even sure what he was seeing or feeling or hearing. He had all he could handle to merely keep himself from falling into a deep and dark place. He could not allow that to happen. Not now.

"Because the magic of this place cannot be denied—not even by the barbarians," Ancient Badden proclaimed. "Even they understand that our name for it—Mithranidoon—is the most fitting. Even they accept that this is, as it long ago was, a Samhaist holy place. And yet it is not under my dominion. Not yet. Not until I wash away the vermin who have deceitfully come to call Mithranidoon their home, as if any but the Ancient of the Samhaists holds any claim on Mithranidoon!"

Bransen tried to commit Badden's words to memory, though he expected that they would mean nothing to him in short order, since he would be dead.

Still, that part in him that would never surrender kept working, kept plotting, kept trying.

"The great worm does its burrowing work," Ancient Badden said, and it was obvious to Bransen that he wasn't talking to him anymore, was just speaking out loud to hear the glory of his words. "The blood of trolls ensures that the god-beast's work is not reversed by the cold. And soon Mithranidoon will be cleansed."

Ancient Badden's voice had risen with each word, in glorious proclamation, and he ended with a self-deprecating chuckle, as if a bit embarrassed by his outburst. "I cannot allow you to participate," Badden said to Bransen. "I am sorry, but you will not share in the glory of my victory. My god-beast is too precious to me to allow it to eat you.

"Of course, none of this matters to you," Ancient Badden said, his voice lowering as he threw Bransen from the cliff.

In all me days, I ain't seen anything as stupid," Mcwigik grumbled, and pulled on the oar to complement Bikelbrin, who was sitting beside him. "Ye're taking us to get cold so we won't be getting cold?"

"It is called acclimating," Cormack explained.

"It's called stupid."

"You said you want to get off the island and the lake."

"Get off and stay off! But not to sleep against the ice."

"We might have to," said Cormack. "Winter hasn't come in yet, but it's drawing near, and even this time of year can bring freezing winds and deep snows to the higher passes."

"Then we won't go to the higher passes," Mcwigik argued.

Cormack exhaled and tried to relax. He knew that part of the dwarf's agitation was due to the dramatic adventure they might soon be undertaking. He and these four powries, along with Milkeila, he prayed, and perhaps some of her friends, were bound to leave Mithranidoon. This was not the best time to undertake such a journey, but the thought of spending another several months on the lake surrounded by nothing but powries was more than Cormack's sensibilities could handle. It hadn't taken him long to decipher that Mcwigik and his fellows felt the same way, either. They all wanted out—now.

"Shouldn't yer lady friend be with us?" Mcwigik asked.

"Shouldn't you take me to her so that I can find out?" came the sarcastic reply.

"In good time—when others' eyes ain't on ye so much."

"The more we get to the cold, the better. It will thicken your blood."

"Yeah, acclimating," said Bikelbrin. Behind him Pergwick chuckled.

"Stupid," muttered Mcwigik under his breath, but he let it go at that. For all his complaining, everyone there knew well that he wanted to get away from Mithranidoon as much or more than anyone else.

In fact, Mcwigik picked up his rowing pace as soon as the conversation ended, nudging Bikelbrin to match him.

Instinct replaced conscious thought as Bransen plummeted from the ledge. Arms flailing, body twisting, the man's sensibilities were too consumed by sudden terror to consider his Stork limitations. The Book of Jhest resonated in his thoughts, and he reflexively twisted to get his arms nearer the sheer ice wall.

Then those arms worked desperately, frantically, catching, grabbing, pulling, scraping—never enough to jolt him or send him tumbling, for that would have been a fatal mistake, but enough to continually jerk against the fall. It took him a couple of heartbeats to align his sight properly below and put his arms in synch, reacting to the edges and bumps as he registered them. But once he found that balance and timing he began to literally pick his path below him and devise the best strategies.

He manipulated by the angle of his grabs and slaps and the constant twists of his waist, and his handwork became more intrusive and stronger. He spotted one bigger ledge just below, and reacted fast enough to hook his fingers a dozen feet above it—not to break his fall as much as to give him the leverage to turn vertical. His feet hit the ledge hard; his legs bent to absorb the blow, and he did not resist as he fell right over backward, having somewhat slowed his descent.

Then his hands went back to work, and he kicked his feet against every possible jag as well, working furiously to counter the force of his fall. Some two dozen feet from the ground, though, the glacial wall sloped in and away, and the already plummeting Bransen could only free-fall that last expanse. He knew that he was going too fast to attempt to roll out of it as he hit, so he flattened himself out horizontally and spread his arms and his legs.

He slammed into the muddy ground, and the bright sky winked out.

Ha! Looks like yer eyes seen right," Mcwigik said when the group of four dwarves and Cormack came around an ice and boulder jag at the base of the glacier to see a man lying flat out on his back, driven more than halfway into the muddy ground.

"I'm guessing that hurt," Ruggirs said, and all four of the powries chuckled. Cormack, though, saw nothing funny in the tragic fall, and rushed to the man, though in looking up at the towering glacial cliff face, he knew that this one was certainly dead.

The man's strange black clothing made him even more curious, and when Cormack got beside him, the lightweight nature of the smooth fabric had him scratching his head, as it was totally unfamiliar to him.

Cormack nearly leaped out of his shoes when the man stirred.

"Yach, but he's a tough one," remarked Mcwigik, coming up behind Cormack.

After the shock wore off Cormack immediately went back to the man, bringing his ear close to the fallen one's mouth to see if he could detect any sounds of breath.

"He is alive," Cormack announced.

"Not for long," Mcwigik chortled. "Better for him that the fall had snuffed out his lights for good."

"Aye, that had to hurt," Ruggirs said again.

Cormack continued to inspect the man, to try to determine the extent of his injuries. In truth, he was thinking that the most merciful thing he could do would be to smother this one and end his pain, but the more he looked, the more his estimate of injuries lessened. He pulled off his powrie cap and set it over the man's head.

"It's to take more than that," Mcwigik grumbled, but Cormack ignored him and kept moving the fallen man, one leg or one arm, or rolling him up to a near-sitting position. Through it all, the injured man made not a sound.

"I don't think he fell all the way," Cormack announced.

"Yach, but he buried himself half into the mud!" Mcwigik argued.

"He could live," Cormack replied. "His wounds are not as bad as we expected."

"Ye're not for knowing any such thing."

"Nor are you for knowing that I'm wrong," Cormack shot back. "This man can live. If I had a gemstone . . . We have to get him to Yossunfier. Help me now, without delay." The powries all looked at Cormack incredulously, and none made a move.

"We cannot just let him die!" Cormack yelled at them, and all four burst into laughter.

Cormack took a deep breath to calm himself. Screaming at the powries now would likely just get him stranded here or worse and would do nothing to help this poor fellow. "Please," he said quietly. "There is a chance I can save him. We humans don't just bury hearts and pop out of the ground again."

"Ye'd be smart to watch yer words," Pergwick warned, but Cormack waved him away.

"I know, I know," he said. "But it is important to me to try to save him."

"Ye know him?" Mcwigik asked.

"No, of course not."

"Then what do ye care?"

"I just do," the increasingly impatient Cormack retorted. "Please, just get me to Yossunfier that I can at least try to save him."

"Yach, but ye're just wanting to take yer girl along with us—again," Mcwigik argued.

"She already is coming with us by our agreement."

"Then ye're wanting her with us sooner, and we already told ye . . ."

"She will be of great help to us," Cormack admitted. "All of her people will. Save this man and help ourselves, I say."

"We get near to Yossunfier, and we're to see the sky full o' barbarian barbs," Mcwigik grumbled. "Ye think it's an easy thing, but ye're a blind fool. Them barbarians see us coming, and we'll all be dead before we step on their beach. Now, are ye thinking that'd be a good thing for your flat friend there?"

Cormack took another deep and steadying breath, and looked all around, feeling as if the answer was right there before him, waiting to be unveiled.

He smiled. "There may be another way."

You wonder why I have allowed you to live this long," Ancient Badden said to Brother Jond after having the monk beaten and dragged to him in the ice castle.

Brother Jond looked up at him blankly, trying to appear as impassive as possible. He was terrified, of course, but he didn't want to give the wretched Samhaist the pleasure of seeing him squirm.

Ancient Badden stared at him for many heartbeats and nodded his chin as if prompting the man to respond, which Brother Jond would not do.

Badden's visage melted into a profound scowl. "You would think that an Abellican monk would be my first victim, of course, since your Church has been the scourge of the land these last seven decades." In fighting off the urge to respond, Brother Jond couldn't suppress a slight smile, and that only made Badden scowl all the more.

The Ancient broke into a sudden giggle, cackled through a quick chant, and waggled his necklace at the monk. The floor beneath Brother Jond's feet turned from ice to water suddenly, plunging him in.

But not deeply, for Ancient Badden cut the spell short and reversed it, freezing the floor around Brother Jond's legs, up to mid-thigh. The contraction of the ice squeezed him so hard that he could feel the blood rushing up from his legs. He felt suddenly sick to his stomach and light-headed at the same time. His eyes bulged as if the rush of blood would simply launch them from their sockets. He tried to remain silent, but a soft groan escaped his lips. The ice tightened some more.

Now Ancient Badden towered over him. "Ah, but I would so love to tear your limbs from your torso." He brought the side of Bransen's sword against Jond's cheek with a stinging slap, then turned the blade as he flashed it past, just enough to draw a deep cut across the monk's face. "Or to open your belly, side to side, and slowly draw out your entrails. Have you ever seen the face of a man so tortured? It is the most exquisite mask of agony."

"And you declare yourself a man of God!" Brother Jond blurted before he could reconsider his reaction.

"Ah, so he speaks," Ancient Badden laughed at him. "I had thought you a mute, which would be an improvement for any Abellican, of course. I am not a man of your childish and benign creation, fool. I am a man of the Ancient Ones, of the truths of life and death. You are too cowardly to face those truths, so you cannot begin to comprehend the way of the Samhaist! I almost pity you and all the others born after Abelle, who were raised in the echoes of his lies and false hopes."

Brother Jond narrowed his eyes, but his threat was so impotent as to be laughable, which of course, Ancient Badden did.

"I said 'almost,'" Ancient Badden reminded. He waggled his necklace, and the ice gripped on Jond's legs even more tightly.

"I keep you alive because you may be of use to me," the Samhaist offered. "As my armies press—"

"Your hordes of monsters, you mean."

Badden shrugged as if that hardly mattered. "They serve a greater purpose."

"They are—"

Brother Jond stopped suddenly as Ancient Badden kicked him squarely in the face. His head snapped back and forward, and a couple of teeth flew from his mouth along with a gush of blood and spittle.

"If you interrupt me again I will hurt you more profoundly than you have ever experienced, more so than anything you could ever have imagined," Ancient Badden warned.

Dazed, temples throbbing, legs aching, Brother Jond could not even bring a defiant stare to his face.

"As my armies press into Vanguard and drive Dame Gwydre to Pireth Vanguard, she will seek parlay," Ancient Badden explained. "As her principal consort is one of your feeble Abellican associates, your presence among my prisoners will grant me a greater ante." The Samhaist bent low and stared into Brother Jond's face, and when Jond tried to turn away, Badden punched him hard, grabbed him by the chin, and forced him to lock stares.

"Does that please you? To know that you will help facilitate the downfall of your religion in the region of Vanguard? Nor will it end there, I promise. When the war in the southland is ended, so too will be the tricks of your kin that so enrapture the dueling lairds. The reality of the conflict will weigh heavily upon the grieving people, and we will be there. For the Samhaists know Death, while the Abellicans deny it. The Samhaists understand the inevitability, while the Abellicans offer false promises. That will be your downfall."

Brother Jond's face became a mask of apathy.

"What is your name?" Ancient Badden asked. No answer.

"It is a simple question, one carrying great importance," said Badden. "For if you do not answer, I will bring in one of the prisoners and torture him to death before your eyes. It will be an hour of screams that will echo in your mind for the rest of your days, short though they will be."

Brother Jond glared at him as he started to motion to the troll attendants. "Brother Jond Dumolnay," he said.

"Dumolnay? A Vanguard name, or of the Mantis Arm, perhaps."

Brother Jond didn't answer.

"Mantis Arm," Ancient Badden decided. "If you had been raised in Vanguard you would better know the Samhaist way and would never have fallen for the lies of the fool Abelle."

"Blessed Abelle!" Brother Jond corrected, spitting blood with every syllable. "The Truth and the Hope of the world! Who mocks the Samhaist death cult and your use of terror to control the people you claim to serve!"

"Claim to serve?" Ancient Badden said, and laughed loudly.

"Then you do not even pretend!"

"We show them the truth, and they may do of that truth what they choose," the Samhaist growled back. "We bring order and justice to rabble who would eat each other if they were not instructed not to!"

Brother Jond couldn't suppress a grin, glad, despite the beating, that he had irked the Samhaist enough to garner such a rise of emotion. "Justice?" he said with a sarcastic laugh.

Ancient Badden went silent suddenly and stood up straight, staring down at the ice-trapped monk.

Brother Jond took a deep breath to steady his nerves, guessing that he had gone too far here. But it was too late for any retraction, he understood, too late to bring the Samhaist back to a level of calm. So he followed his heart and put his fears behind him.

"I will see your demise, Ancient Badden," he declared. "I will see the victory of Blessed Abelle in Vanguard and throughout Honce!"

"Indeed," the Ancient replied calmly—too calmly. His arm swept across, slashing Bransen's sword, drawing a line in Brother Jond's face and taking both his eyes and the bridge of his nose in the process.

The monk howled and screamed, thrashing in agony.

"I doubt you will 'see' anything," Ancient Badden said to him, and walked away.

CHAPTER 26

Well Found in a Dark Place

Milkeila wasn't consciously thinking of anything as she walked on the beach one dark and breezy night. Resignation filled her thoughts and filled her heart, so much so that she had abandoned her hopes of what might have been, in full knowledge that her reality simply could never approach those hopes and dreams.

She didn't know how many days had passed since she had last seen her beloved Cormack. Too many, though, for her to ever expect to see him again. Either he had been found out as a traitor and imprisoned or put to death, or he had buried himself in guilt over his stark actions and had abandoned his wayward course—a course that included Milkeila.

For several days, the woman had tried to concoct some mental scenario in which she could lead her people to go and rescue Cormack; she had allowed herself to fantasize about again besieging Chapel Isle and forcing the monks to relinquish their unfaithful brother.

That could never happen, of course, and she didn't even know if such was Cormack's condition. So, for the sake of her own survival, Milkeila had let it all go, had exhaled and exorcised Cormack from her heart and mind.

And always, Toniquay was there, looking over her shoulder, reading her emotions and reminding her, ever reminding her, of her responsibilities to the traditions. She was shaman, and among the Alpinadoran tribes that was no small thing.

She walked the beach this night, the wind blowing aside the mists enough to afford her a wonderful view of the starry canopy above, the water gently lapping the rocks and the black volcanic sand of Yossunfier's beach, and she was at peace. Until she saw a single light in the southeast.

Milkeila's heart skipped a beat. She thought it must be Chapel Isle—perhaps a lantern at the top of their ever-growing tower. But no, she realized, it could not be. The light was not far enough away.

A boat, perhaps, she silently cautioned, and she stood perfectly still and tried to not allow the movement of the small waves to distort her perception. After many heart-wrenching moments, she realized that the light was not moving. It was on the sandbar.

Milkeila had to consciously breathe and steady herself. She started for the boats immediately, but her swift stride slowed as it occurred to her that the light could be a trap. Perhaps Cormack had been discovered as a traitor and had been tortured into revealing all! Perhaps a group of monks had lit her and Cormack's private signal beacon to lure her to the sandbar and capture her.

Those thoughts continued to swirl in Milkeila's head even after she had appropriated one of the smallest Yossunfier boats and had started quietly paddling out from the shore.

Her heart raced as she came to confirm that the light was indeed coming from the sandbar, or near to it, but she was a bit concerned that Cormack would burn such a light for so long on so clear a night. Certainly it could be seen from Red Cap or Chapel Isle, and after so many minutes, perhaps even some of Milkeila's own people would decide to go and investigate. Of course, all of this was based on the presumption that it was indeed Cormack.

Milkeila gave one long and powerful pull with her paddle, then put it up and bent low in the small boat so that her silhouette wouldn't stand out against the horizon as she glided toward the sandbar. Peering through the thin mist, she saw a form, and the way the tall man paced left no doubt in her that it was indeed her beloved Cormack. She started to sit up, even to call out, but she bit back the call as she noted another form on the sandbar, short and thick. A powrie.

Milkeila sat up and speared her paddle into the water to create drag and slow the boat. She was still drifting, the current and her momentum bringing her very slowly toward the sandbar. She didn't know what to do! She wanted to see Cormack—more than anything in the world, Milkeila wanted to be certain that her lover was all right, wanted to feel his strong arms about her again.

But what was this? Why would Cormack bring a bloody-cap dwarf to their private place? A groan from the far side of the sandbar made her realize that there were others, as well, and soon she was close enough to see another powrie over there, kneeling over something—a man, perhaps?

Despite her caution, Milkeila couldn't turn away from this. Cormack's movements showed her that she had been seen, and the man rushed to the point on the sandbar nearest to her and softly called out her name, waving frantically for her to come ashore. And she did, and Cormack wrapped her in as tight a hug as she had ever known.

"Powries," she said, her voice as shaken as her sensibilities.

"Quickly, here," Cormack said, taking her by the wrist and dragging her along to the back side of the sandbar, where an injured man lay on the ground,

a second powrie beside him. As if that wasn't distressing enough, a third powrie sat in their boat, just a short distance away.

"Cormack, what are you doing?" Milkeila asked, and when the monk didn't
answer, she just stated, rather severely, "Cormack!"

He stopped and swung about to face her. "We found him. You have the
gemstones? He will die."

"Who?"

Cormack dragged her over. "This man."

"Who is he?"

Cormack shook his head. "We found him at the base of the glacier, half-
buried in the mud."

"We? You and the powries?"

"Yes."

"Cormack?"

The monk paused and took a deep breath. "I was expelled from Chapel
Isle, beaten and left for dead. This powrie—"

"Mcwigik's the name," the dwarf interjected.

"Mcwigik saved my life," Cormack explained. "They've taken me in."

"Every dwarf needs a dog," Mcwigik mumbled.

"We were going to come and get you," Cormack continued. "We're leaving
the lake."

"You and the powries?"

"A few, yes. But we found this man, and he will surely die . . ." As he finished, Cormack reached for Milkeila's tooth-and-claw necklace, and twisted it
out of the way to reveal the string of gemstones he had given to her. "Help me,
I beg," he said, and reached to remove the magical necklace.

Milkeila instinctively bent and helped him do so, following Cormack as
he rushed to the supine man, fumbling with the gems to find the powerful
soul stone. He went to work immediately, pressing the stone against one egre-
gious wound, where the man's leg was swollen and possibly broken. Milkeila
put her hand atop Cormack's and began a prayer of her own, using the soul
stone connection to the wounded man to impart her energy into the gem to
heighten Cormack's work. The man groaned and stirred a bit.

They went to the next wound and then the next after that, and with each
application of gemstone magic their bond tightened. They shared smiles after
every victory, though they had no idea of whether or not these little bits of
mending would win the largest battle of all and keep this stranger alive.

"He's wearing your cap," Milkeila remarked.

"Magic in a powrie beret," Mcwigik said from the side.

If either Milkeila or Cormack heard the dwarf, neither showed it, for they had locked stares and hearts and to them at that moment, the outside world didn't exist.

"He fell from the glacier?"

"And somehow he is not dead," Cormack answered. "The mud, I guess, for the ground at the glacier's base is soft."

"It is a long fall," the woman replied, obviously doubting.

"And yet he lives," said Cormack with a shrug, as if nothing else really mattered.

They had worked their way up over the most obvious wounds by that point, and Cormack put the soul stone on top of an area of swelling on the battered man's forehead. Again he sent the gemstone's magical energy flowing into the stranger, and again Milkeila put her hand atop his to help.

But then the supine man did likewise, his hand snapping up to grab Cormack by the wrist. His eyes popped open wide and Cormack instinctively tugged away.

"No!" the stranger started to say, but the monk and Milkeila had moved too forcefully for him to prevent them from pulling the stone from his forehead, and as soon as that happened, he lost all strength and the two healers fell back, staring at him.

"Gemmm . . . gem . . . ge . . . ge . . . ge," the wounded man pleaded, his jaw shaking and drool sliding from the side of his mouth.

"I think ye forgot to put his brains back in," Mcwigik quipped, seeming very amused by the man's sudden and pathetic attempts to sit up or even to communicate.

"Ge . . . Ge . . . Gemmmm," the man cried, reaching out at the recoiling duo.

"I'm thinking he lived by landing on his head," Mcwigik said, and his two powrie companions chuckled.

"He wants the soul stone," Cormack surmised.

"The poor man," said Milkeila.

The stranger kept stuttering and drooling and shaking so badly that he seemed as if he would just collapse.

"Give it to him," Milkeila said.

Cormack looked at her incredulously.

"He cannot run away with it," the woman reminded.

Cormack reached out and put his fist, clenched over the soul stone, in the stranger's shaking palm. As soon as the man tightened his grip about Cormack's fist, Cormack relaxed his grasp and let the gemstone fall to the wounded man.

Shaking fingers immediately stilled and closed over the gemstone, and with a great and collecting exhale, the wounded man lay easily on the sandbar. Many heartbeats passed.

"I think it killed him to death," Mcwigik said, but then the man reached his hand up and pressed the gemstone against his forehead.

"Or not," muttered the dwarf, and his voice reeked of disappointment.

Many more heartbeats slipped past and the stranger remained motionless on the ground, his hand pressed against his forehead. Then—with hardly an effort, it seemed!—he sat up, still holding the gemstone to his forehead, and said in an accent that was obviously from south of the Gulf of Corona, "Well found in a dark place and know that you have my eternal gratitude. I am Bransen."

They hadn't hit anything vital, he believed; the wound was not mortal. It hurt, though. How it hurt, and it was all poor Olconna could do to turn his focus to his surroundings and not the cut in his belly.

He had managed to secure a knife; he surely would have preferred a sword, but the knife he had hidden away in his boot would have to suffice.

He couldn't deny his fear as the giants lowered him head-down into the ice chasm, a thick rope tied tightly about his ankle. But Olconna had spent the better part of his adolescence and all of his adulthood in battle, and had faced tremendous odds again and again. Always he had found his answer, his way to victory or at least to escape, and he had no reason to believe that this time would be any different. Ancient Badden had erred, Olconna believed, because he had allowed the man to greatly recover from the wounds he had received in the fight when he had been captured.

He brandished the knife. He forced himself to extend downward and stretch the wound, as he couldn't hope to battle whatever beast might be down here while doubled over.

It was darker now, for he was well over a hundred feet down from the ledge, but not pitch black. Olconna forced himself into a slow turn, taking in the myriad edges and jags of the chasm walls, trying to pick out a shape among them that foretold something else.

"Faster," he muttered under his breath, wanting to be on the floor and free of the rope before this beast appeared. In the back of his head, Vaughna's last words, "every moment precious," played over and over like a constant echo of regret. For the man, cautious in everything but battle, hadn't lived that way—until he had encountered Crazy V. The notion weighed on him for a short moment, but Olconna turned that fear that he had lost his chance into determination that he wouldn't let it end now, that he would find a way to gain some years where Vaughna's words would guide him as sound advice.

But a moment later Olconna heard a low rumble, like a huge rock rolling down a hill. The beast smelled his blood, just as that old wretch Badden had predicted before he had stabbed Olconna in the belly.

Olconna slowly turned at the end of the rope, his gaze passing the long and open stretch of corridor. He noted a movement down there, a quick glimpse of something large, something awful. He tried to battle his momentum, to stop and face the beast, but he kept going around. He managed to twist about, eliciting terrific pain from his torn belly, to catch a few quick views of the approaching monster. It looked like a gigantic worm, or more accurately a caterpillar, for the many small legs scrabbling at its sides. Giant mandibles arched out in semicircles before its black, round maw—the type of toothy orifice often found on sea creatures, which seemed to pucker as much as open.

"Faster!" Olconna said again, cursing the giants who were lowering him, but as if on cue, the rope stopped.

He hung there, twenty feet from the ground, too high to try to free himself, for the fall would surely leave him helpless in the face of the monster. But too far, he believed, for the approaching beast to get at him. He managed to steady his turn properly so that he could face the crawling nightmare.

They'll let me bleed out up here, above it, he reasoned, and he decided then that if the worm came under him he would cut free his ankle and drop upon it, all caution be damned!

That thought rang as a beacon of hope in his mind, turned his fear into action, into violence, as he had trained to do for all of his life.

But the worm reared up like a cobra, and before Olconna even appreciated that fact it lashed out.

Olconna tried to respond with the dagger, but so shocked was he that he didn't even realize that his weapon arm was gone until he saw it disappearing into the awful beast's mouth!

Now he screamed. There was nothing else. Just the pain and the helplessness—that was the worst of it for a man like Olconna.

No, not the worst. The worst of it were Vaughna's echoing words, a creed for her, a lament for him: Every moment precious.

The worm took its time, lashing and tearing, and Olconna felt no less than six more stabbing and slashing bites before he finally slipped into that deepest darkness.

Cormack sat on the rail of the beached boat, his shoulders slumped as if all of the air had been sucked out of his lean body. Before him, Milkeila paced nervously back and forth, continually glancing at the surprising man in the black suit.

The man who had just informed them that their entire world was soon to be washed away.

"Are you to let him keep the soul stone?" Milkeila asked, pacing.

"It is your stone."

The shaman stopped and turned on her lover curiously.

"I would counsel that you let him keep it," Cormack decided. "It is the most important of gems, I agree, but if what Bransen says is true, then he is all but helpless without it."

"And with it, he walks with the grace of a warrior," Milkeila added as both watched the young man, who stood across the sandbar going through a series of movements and turns, the practice of a warrior, as brilliant and precise as anything either of them had ever seen. Cormack in particular appreciated Bransen's movements, for his training in the arts martial as a young brother of the Order of Abelle had been extensive and complete.

Or so he had thought, but in watching Bransen, Cormack recognized an even deeper level of concentration than he had ever achieved, and by far.

"I believe his every word," Milkeila admitted, and she seemed surprised by that statement. She turned to see Cormack nodding his agreement.

"It is too outrageous a story to not be true."

"We have to tell them—all of them," said Milkeila. "Your people and mine."

"And even Mcwigik's," Cormack added. "At the very least, Mithranidoon must be abandoned."

Milkeila lamented, "A wall of falling ice to wash us all away."

CHAPTER 27

Three Perspectives

"O n pain of death!" Brother Giavno said again, becoming dangerously animated. Out on rock-collection detail, Giavno and his two companions had been the first to note the approach of Cormack and the strange-looking man in the black suit of some exotic material—Giavno thought it was called "silk," but as he had seen the stuff only once in his life, and many years before, he couldn't be certain. The stranger wore a typical farmer's hat, but Giavno noted some black fabric under that as well.

"Greetings to you, too," Cormack replied.

"How can you be alive?" one of the other brothers asked, and Cormack tapped his beret.

"God's will and good luck, I would say," the fallen monk replied.

"You know nothing of God," Giavno growled.

"Says the man who whipped him nearly to death," Bransen, at Cormack's side, quipped. "A godly act, indeed—at least, according to the mores of many Abellicans I have known. It is strange to me how much like Samhaists they seem."

Giavno trembled and seemed about to explode. Behind him, over the rocky ridge, some other monks called out and soon a swarm of brothers was fast running toward the rocky beach.

"Why did you come here, Cormack?" Giavno asked, seeming as much concerned as outraged—a poignant reminder to Cormack that he and this man had once been friends. "You know the consequences."

"You thought me already dead."

"A death you earned with your treachery."

"Your definition, not mine. I followed that which was in my heart, and many of the brothers here, I would wager, were glad of it. I find it difficult to comprehend that I was alone in my distaste for our imprisoning of the Alpinadorans."

"What you find difficult to comprehend is that you make no rules here, or anywhere in the Church. If Father De Guilbe wished for your opinion on the matter, he would have asked. And he did not."

"Ever the dutiful one, aren't you?" Cormack replied, and Giavno narrowed his eyes.

"Alive?" came a shout from behind, and Father De Guilbe, surrounded by an armed entourage, appeared over the crest of the hill. "Are you mad to come back here?"

"How would I know differently?" Cormack asked. "I remember little beyond the sting of your mercy."

"Play not coy with me, traitor," said De Guilbe, and unlike Giavno, there wasn't a hint of compassion or mercy in his tone. He turned to the nearest guards and said, "Take him."

"I would not," said the man standing beside Cormack.

Father De Guilbe dropped a withering gaze over him—except he did not shrink back in the least. "And who are you?"

"My name is Bransen, though that is of no consequence to you," Bransen replied. "I am a man here not of my will, but of misfortune, and I come to you only to repay the debt that I owe to this man, and to the people of some of the other islands."

De Guilbe shook his head as if not comprehending any of it, and Bransen let it go, for it was of no consequence.

"I bring a grave warning that your world is about to be washed away," Bransen said. "It is my duty to tell you that, I suppose, but whether you choose to act upon it or not is of little consequence to me."

A couple of the monks bristled, obviously focusing on the last part of his quip and not the more important announcement. Of the group, now twenty brothers, only a few raised their eyebrows in alarm, and even that became a past thought almost immediately, as one of Father De Guilbe's entourage announced, pointing at Bransen, "He has a gemstone!"

Cormack glanced at Bransen in alarm, but the man from Pryd Town seemed bothered not at all.

"Is this true?" asked Father De Guilbe.

"If it is, it is none of your affair."

"You walk a dangerous—"

"I walk where I choose to walk and how I choose to walk," Bransen interrupted. "Feign no dominion over me, disingenuous old fool. My father was of your order, a brother of great accomplishment. No, not any accomplishment that you would understand or appreciate," he answered De Guilbe's curious look. "And more to your pity."

"From Entel?" Father De Guilbe asked. "Your swarthy appearance bespeaks a Southern heritage."

Bransen grinned knowingly at the obvious ploy.

"It matters not," De Guilbe said. "You are here with a criminal and carrying contraband."

"Contraband?" Bransen said with a mocking chuckle. "You presume to know how I came about this gemstone. You presume that I have a gemstone. You do not understand Jhesta Tu philosophy, yet pretend that you have any understanding of me, or of what I will do to your guards if you send them forth, or of how I will come back in the dark of night and easily defeat any defenses you construct, that you and I will speak more directly at your own bedside."

It took a while for all of that to digest, and Giavno at last broke the uncomfortable silence by berating Cormack, "What have you brought to us?"

"A man to deliver a message, and then we are gone from here."

"The glacier north of your lake is home to a Samhaist," Bransen announced. "The Ancient himself. Ancient Badden, who wars with Dame Gwydre of Vanguard."

"How do you know?"

"Because I was there, just yesterday," Bransen answered. "Badden claims dominion over this lake and works to ensure that all here, yourselves included—and especially, if he should ever learn that Abellicans reside on this most holy of Samhaist places—will be washed away on a great wave of his murderous wrath. If he executes his plan there is for you no escape. If he is not stopped this place you name as Chapel Isle will become a washed stone on an uninhabited hot lake."

"Preposterous!" said Giavno, while the monks around him whispered and shuffled nervously, and looked all around for someone to settle their fears from the sudden shock.

Bransen shrugged, as if unconcerned.

"We are to believe you?" Father De Guilbe asked skeptically. "You come to us beside a traitor. . . ."

"A man I hardly know, but one possessed of more sense than you it would seem. I have come to deliver a message as repayment to this man you name as traitor and yet who feels obligated to you still. Whether you act upon that message or not is not my concern. I hold no love for your Church. Indeed, from what I have seen you are more than deserving of my contempt. But I am Jhesta Tu, and so such feelings as contempt have no place in my world."

He turned to Cormack, but before he could address the man, Giavno assailed him, "Jhesta Tu? What is Jhesta Tu?"

Bransen eyed the fiery man out of the corner of his eye. "Something you could never begin to comprehend."

"Take them!" Giavno yelled, and immediately a pair of guards, brandishing short swords, leaped at Bransen and Cormack.

They never got close. Bransen, expecting it, even coaxing it, leaped at the first, kicking his right foot out to the man's right side, then sweeping it across. It posed no real threat to the monk, but had him distracted so that that the real attack, a snap-kick from Bransen's left foot, caught him right in the chest, blasting out his breath in a great gasp. Bransen landed lightly back on his right foot and propelled himself forward and left, beside the staggering monk's awkward thrust. He snatched the man by the wrist with his right hand, drove his left hand brutally against the monk's straightened elbow, then quickly covered the man's sword hand with his own, bending the monk's wrist over painfully and stealing his strength—and his grip on the sword.

The blade didn't fall an inch before Bransen snapped it out of the air, and he spun away, back-kicking the wounded monk in the side to ensure that there would be no pursuit, and also to shift his own momentum, driving him to intercept the second approaching guard.

The short swords collided repeatedly in a series of arm-numbing parries that ended with Bransen looping his blade over that of the confused monk. A twist and jerk sent the short sword to the ground, and left the tip of Bransen's sword at the stunned monk's throat. And it all happened in the space of a few heartbeats.

Bransen laughed and straightened, moving his blade back from the terrified man. He hooked the fallen sword with his own and deftly flipped it into his left hand, then turned to Giavno and flung both swords, spinning end over end, to stick into the ground right before the monk.

"You have been warned," Bransen announced. "Ancient Badden will destroy you."

He turned and walked away.

Cormack lingered a short while longer, looking mostly to Father De Guilbe. His expression was one of apology, perhaps, but mostly it was filled with pleading. But there was no more to say, so he followed Bransen back to the boat.

Both Cormack and Milkeila accompanied Bransen onto the forested island of Yossunfier. Many more people came out to greet them before they even got their boat ashore. The whole of Milkeila's tribe, it seemed, came down to the waterfront, shielding their eyes from the morning glare, whispering among themselves at this surprising group approaching their island home.

Many scowls focused on Cormack and his obvious Abellican attire, but

Androosis was there, along with Toniquay and Canrak, instructing his kin that this particular monk was no enemy of Yossunfier.

As the trio glided in near the beach, strong hands grabbed the craft and ushered it up onto the beach. Toniquay stepped front and center before Milkeila as she exited the boat, the higher-ranking shamans deferring to him because of his intimate knowledge of this situation and these participants.

He stared at Milkeila for just a few moments, then scrutinized Cormack, his expression giving the man no indication of how much his actions had ingratiated him to the barbarians. Then Toniquay's gaze fell over Bransen, but only for a moment.

"What do you presume?" Toniquay asked Milkeila. He waited just a short while of uncomfortable silence before adding, "Do you believe that your friend has earned the right to step onto our land simply because he, unlike so many of his kin, took a moral road? Do you think that all past wrongs will be simply forgotten?"

"It was at great personal cost!" Milkeila replied, instinctively defending her lover, who put a hand on her arm to calm her. "But that is not why we have come. Cormack signaled to me and I answered his call."

"Signaled?" Toniquay said suspiciously. "And how did he know a way in which he might signal you, Milkeila? And how did you know to answ . . ." He stopped and waved his hand and shook his head. His point had been made that the woman would surely have to answer for her apparent secret relationship with this Abellican, but Toniquay was more interested in hearing Milkeila's tale at that time.

"Why is he here?" the shaman asked.

"Cormack found this man, Bransen," Milkeila replied, and she put her hand on Bransen's shoulder. The man in the black suit nodded, though he obviously understood little of the conversation.

"Bransen fell from the glacier," said Milkeila.

Toniquay looked at her skeptically, and doubting murmurs grew all about them. "Then he would be dead," Toniquay said.

"But he is not," said Milkeila. "Whether through simple luck and soft mud, or his extraordinary powers—and he is truly blessed—I know not. But he is here, and he was up there, and he comes to us with a dire warning. The Ancient of the Samhaists has taken the glacier as his home, and plots now to destroy all of us who dwell upon Mithranidoon."

"Samhaists?" Toniquay echoed. He had heard the name before, in the private discussions among the shamans about people who lived beyond Mithranidoon's warm waters. The Samhaists, so it was rumored, had given this place its name, though that had been centuries before. In the lore of Yan Ossum, shamans had gone south to teach their magic to the men of Honce, long before the many battles and wars between the two peoples. In Alpinadoran mythology, Samhaist magic was a direct offshoot of the Alpinadoran Ancient Gods, though in Samhaist lore, the order, and who taught whom, was of course reversed.

"This stranger is from outside of Mithranidoon?" Toniquay asked. "Strange then that he arrives just a few years after the Abellicans. Before them, none had come to us from the outside since the powries, before my father's father was born." Even as he denied the possibility, though, Toniquay had to admit that the man's clothing was fairly convincing, and unlike anything he had ever seen.

"He is an Abellican spy," someone from the side yelled, a sentiment that was echoed through the crowd.

"He is not of my former comrades," Cormack answered. "He is no Abellican, and has only been to Chapel Isle on one occasion—yesterday—to deliver the same message there that we deliver here. This is no trick, Toniquay. On my word, for what that is worth to you. I found this man in the mud on the northern bank of Mithranidoon, injured. He came to us with a tale that you must hear, that my people must hear, that the powries must hear. For if he speaks truly, and I believe that he does, then all of us are in dire peril, and will soon be washed from our homes."

Toniquay stared hard at Cormack for just a few moments and then motioned to some of his nearby tribesmen. Soon the trio found themselves surrounded by armed Alpinadoran warriors.

Cormack immediately turned to Bransen and grabbed the man by the arm. "They are honorable, but careful," he said in the common language of Honce.

"I insist that you remain with us while we investigate your claims," Toniquay explained.

"Be fast, for all our sakes," Milkeila answered.

Toniquay nodded his agreement and motioned to the warriors, who escorted Bransen and Cormack to a nearby hut, while Milkeila stayed with Toniquay and the other shamans.

She knew what they would do, and was not surprised when several of the more powerful shamans called down high-flying birds. Weaving spells, they each bound their sight to that of an individual bird, then sent the winged creatures on their way, and for the next several minutes, the powerful elders saw through the eyes of their familiars. Unlike Ancient Badden's heightened powers, though, these shamans couldn't control their familiars, and so they were at the whims of the aerial creatures.

Still, it didn't take very long for more than one of the birds to climb above the glacial rim, and the ice castle gleamed in the midday light.

To her surprise, a most pleasant one, Milkeila was allowed to leave

Yossunfier with her two companions. She had not been forgiven, Toniquay assured her, and would ultimately have to answer the many questions her arrival with the men of Honce had raised, beyond the worries of some strange "Ancient" plotting atop the glacier.

Now, though, given the revelations, they all had more important issues before them, so Milkeila, Bransen, and Cormack paddled off for Red Cap Island, while Toniquay and the others plotted as to how they would best bring all the Alpinadoran tribes of the islands together again in an even more urgent cause.

Father De Guilbe rubbed his face and leaned back in his seat, breathing hard.

"It cannot be," Brother Giavno said, shaking his head in denial.

"Exactly as the stranger said," De Guilbe confirmed. He tossed a soul stone back onto his desk, the same stone that had just allowed him an out-of-body journey, where he had willed his spirit to fly up to the great glacier looming over Mithranidoon.

"They are boring a chasm that will collapse the front edge of the glacier into our lake," he explained.

"Ancient Badden?"

"It can only be. The castle of ice has the Samhaist tree design."

"Then Cormack was not lying, and the stranger is . . . ?"

"Of no concern to us at this time," Father De Guilbe answered. "We must be gone from this place posthaste. Our time here was not profitable—we claimed not a single soul—and so we will continue our mission elsewhere."

"We will allow Ancient Badden to destroy the lake and all who live upon it?"

"What choice have we, Brother?"

Brother Giavno trembled and lifted his hands several times, as if about to divulge some plan. But alas, he had no answers.

"Prepare the brothers, prepare the boats," Father De Guilbe instructed.

The differences between the reactions of the three peoples were not lost on the foursome of Bransen, Cormack, Milkeila, and Mcwigik. In fact, the reaction of the supposedly vile powries as compared to that of the humans proved startling to the two men and Milkeila—startling and embarrassing.

"Yach, but ye done good!" Kriminig the powrie leader congratulated Mcwigik after he had led Bransen and the others to his boss so that the stranger could tell his tale. "That beast up there's thinking to be dumping on us when we're not knowing, but now that we're knowing, we're the ones to be doing the dumping!"

"You know of Ancient Badden?" Cormack dared interject.

"Ye just told me of him," Kriminig replied, as if he didn't understand the point of the question, and while the dwarf leader began barking commands at his charges, readying them for a fight, the three humans found a moment of quiet discussion.

"He believed us without reservation," Cormack whispered, his tone clearly marking the distinction of that reaction to those of the monks and the Alpinadorans.

"Or maybe he is just happy for a fight," Milkeila said, and she swung about to the wider commotion going on around them, the many excited discussions springing up among the powries.

"Bah, but I'm sad to hear this killer's surrounded himself with trolls," one said. "Their blood's not much for shining me beret."

"Aye, but he's got a swarm o' them, they're saying," another piped in. "We'll get a glow out of it. The folks of the other islands won't be needing their share, don't ye know?"

"Yach, and there'll be bunches o' them folks about, too, won't there?" the first replied with a wink. "More than a few're going to be bleeding bright red."

"And who's to say they won't be turning on us when this killer's chopped down?" asked a third.

"A few hundred trolls and a few hundred men, and only two score of us," the first said with a sigh. "It'll take me all the day to collect the blood!"

"Ha ha!" the others laughed, and they swatted each other on sturdy shoulders and rolled along their way, as only powries could.

That last comment had brought a look of alarm to both Milkeila and Cormack, though—until Mcwigik and Bikelbrin shuffled over.

"Bah, but don't ye be thinking me kin're to start any trouble up there, other than the trouble that . . . what did ye call him? That Ancient?" said Mcwigik. "No trouble, I tell ye, other than finishing the trouble that one's already started."

"They are willing to fight beside the monks and the Alpinadorans, then?" asked Cormack.

"Ye heard Kriminig say just that," said Bikelbrin.

"Sure, and a fine row it'll be, we're all for hoping," Mcwigik added. "Though we're not even knowing if yer monks're coming along for the play. Did ye hear them say that?"

Cormack's lips grew very tight, all the confirmation anyone there needed to understand that he was filled with doubts about whether his brethren would march alongside the rest or not.

"Yach, but it's not to matter," Mcwigik said generously, and he slapped Cormack on the back. "That Ancient up there's made himself an angry swarm o' powries, and we're meaning to show him that doing so wasn't the smartest thing he's ever done!"

"Hope he's not too old and withered," said Bikelbrin. "Me beret's needing a bit of a gloss."

CHAPTER 28

The Meaning of Home

Brother Giavno stepped out of the small boat onto the shore of Lake Mithranidoon for the first time in more than a year. He glanced back in the direction of Chapel Isle, the place that had been his home for these last few years. Not much of a home, and not much of an island, Giavno knew, but still there was in his heart a great lament, a profound sense of loss. Nothing more than a cursory glance at his dour companions told him that he was not alone in these feelings.

He let his gaze drift north along this, the western coastline of Mithranidoon. Cormack was up there, he knew, along with his strange collection of friends and perhaps with more allies culled from the various islands. He meant to go against Ancient Badden, and that was a noble cause, whatever the reason.

A splash behind him turned Giavno back to the lake, where the last boat, bearing Father De Guilbe and a foursome of Chapel Isle's best warriors, neared the shore. As the five debarked, Giavno was left wondering how many years, decades, centuries even, might pass before the construction at Chapel Isle was once more inhabited by disciples of Blessed Abelle. Their monument would stand against the wave should it come, Giavno believed, and even if someone else, powrie or Alpinadoran, happened upon the island, they would more likely use the sturdy chapel fortress than tear it down. So maybe, someday long in the future, the Abellicans would return and continue the work done by Giavno and De Guilbe and the others.

"Form them up at once and let us be far away from this place," Father De Guilbe instructed Giavno as he walked past. "I would find Dame Gwydre before the onset of winter, and that will be no easy road."

"Of course, Father," Giavno replied, and a part of him agreed. Another part, though, had him looking to the north yet again, and wondering about Cormack and the others. He recognized the expediency of De Guilbe's decision to abandon their mission and return where they were likely needed, but that didn't stop him from feeling as if he and his brethren were, perhaps, abandoning their neighbors in this time of dire need. For despite all of their fighting, even the deadly siege put upon Chapel Isle by the Alpinadorans, Brother Giavno did think of them, and of the powries, as neighbors.

That was the surprising paradox that dominated his mind and his heart.

"Brother Giavno!" Father De Guilbe shouted, shaking the man from his contemplations. He nodded and rushed off to rouse the brothers.

He was glad that it was not his place to make these decisions.

They glided out of the mists of Mithranidoon like the ghosts of their warrior ancestors, painted with berry dyes of red and yellow and blue, carrying spears and clubs, and decorated with trinkets and necklaces of teeth and claws and paws and beaks and feathers—so many feathers. Their flotilla numbered boats in the hundreds, each boat carrying as few as one or as many as a half-dozen of the proud Alpinadorans. Most stood up as the boats reached the shore, as if in defiance to the task and enemy that awaited them.

Even Milkeila, intimately familiar with her people, even Bransen, who had seen the armies of southern Honce, even Mcwigik, who was never much impressed with anything human, gasped at the spectacle of the many diverse tribes of Mithranidoon coming together as one. And for Cormack, this marvelous sight served to reinforce his understanding that proselytizing these people, with their traditions, heritage, and pride, was no more than a fool's errand, and a condescending one at that.

For Milkeila, though, another emotion accompanied it all, based on her certainty that she was looking upon her people for the last time, likely forever. Even if she managed to survive the coming battle, she knew that it was over for her. Her small group of friends, co-conspirators dreaming of leaving Mithranidoon only two years before, had been split apart from her in more ways than physical. She stood with the man she had come to love, but inside, Milkeila had never felt more alone.

Still, the spectacle before her made her proud to be, or to have been, of Yan Ossum.

At the center of the Alpinadoran force came the shamans, Teydru and Toniquay prominent among their ranks. More than just spiritual leaders, Alpinadoran shamans were considered the wise men of their respective tribes, the advisors on all matters important.

"They will direct the attack," Milkeila explained to her companions, indicating the select group.

"They will likely wish to speak more with Bransen then," said Cormack, "as he has seen the passes and the glacial structures." He was about to add that he would help Milkeila in translating the exchange, but the woman just shook her head.

"They have seen them," she explained. "Both the way to Badden and his defenses. If we were to be a part of their execution, they would have summoned us as they debarked their boats."

"What's that to mean?" Mcwigik demanded. "Got all me boys together just to be a part of it."

Milkeila calmed him with an upraised hand, and cautiously made her way along the beach to speak with Toniquay.

"The powries wish to help," she said to her superior. "They have brought the whole of their force to join in our march."

"Our march?" Toniquay quipped, his expression sour. "You have plotted to leave us, and conspired of late to expedite your journey. Because you brought us this information, Shaman Teydru has seen fit to grant you your wish without prejudice or punishment. You have paid your worth to us and are free to go."

While those words might have once sounded as welcome to the young woman, in this time and place they hit her as mightily as a bolt of lightning. She had known it was coming, indeed, but still, to hear the declaration spoken so clearly and directly unnerved the poor young woman. The black wings of panic fluttered up all around her, threatening to drown her sensibilities in their confused jumble of flapping. She felt alone, suddenly. Homeless and without family, stranded on the beach of a hostile world, all security stolen.

She looked over to her tribesmen, trying to sort through the jumble to spot Androosis, or some other friend who had expressed similar desires of leaving Mithranidoon.

"Your young friends will not be joining you," said Toniquay, as if he had read her mind (and indeed, that was not beyond his power). "They have offered no compensation for the freedom they desire—not even Androosis, though there was debate about whether or not he, too, should be given free leave."

Milkeila stood there for a long while, trying to find her breath.

"I would have thought this news exciting and welcome to you," Toniquay teased, for of course he had anticipated exactly this.

Milkeila regained her composure, albeit with great difficulty. "Of course," she said, for what choice did she have? A decision so rendered by the shaman council was not an invitation to debate.

"The powries have come in whole to join in your battle with Ancient Badden," she restated. "They are fierce allies and ferocious enemies, as you are well aware. They would know their place in this, among a force so many times their size."

"How generous of them," Toniquay remarked, contempt thickening his voice. "Better than the cowardly monks, at least, who debark far to the south and run down the road of the same direction. They stand strong only behind thick walls of stone, it would seem."

"Their place?" Milkeila pressed, knowing well that Toniquay could launch into a diatribe of many minutes, and one that left him far from her original question, if he was not quickly reined.

"They have no place among us," Toniquay answered bluntly. "If they wish a place in the battle, then it is to the side, and out of our way."

Milkeila started to argue, but Toniquay was hearing none of it. "We do not train beside powries, nor are we to expect our warriors to trust any of them. The same is true of the monk and the stranger."

"And of Milkeila?"

"You trained beside us once."

"But the trust?"

Toniquay paused and let the question slide away before reiterating, "Their place is not among us. They, you, all of you, would do well to stay far to the side of our march."

Milkeila couldn't help it as her misty eyes were drawn out to the lake, toward Yossunfier, which had once been her home.

Once and always and nevermore.

They were not properly outfitted to survive the climate off Mithranidoon, even now before the onset of winter, so the Alpinadorans, led by their shamans, who had used the views of eagles and hawks and crows to spy out and map the passes, wasted no time in their march. Long and swift strides carried their formations up the mountain passes beside the glacier; shamans and other leaders shouted encouragement and bolstered the warriors with magic and herb-treated waters to hold their spirit and their strength. There would be no camp, no respite. Their swift pace would end when they met the enemy.

Behind them came the powries, and among them Bransen and his two now-homeless companions, still trying to figure out where they would fit into this upcoming battle.

Before they had even reached the glacier, sounds of fighting erupted far ahead, at the front of the Alpinadoran line. The ranks tightened, powries eagerly adjust their berets. But those ranks quickly loosened up again, and when the trailing group crossed the battlefield they discovered that the army had happened upon, and had summarily overrun, an encampment of no more than a dozen trolls.

"Here's for hoping that one or more got away to warn their friends and set them all about us," Mcwigik grumbled. "Sure to be the only way we're to find any fightin' this day!"

"Aye, the tall ones'll run all the way through Badden's door," Bikelbrin, at Mcwigik's side, lamented.

Bransen glanced at Milkeila and Cormack, the three of them understanding that they were the only ones among this group who hoped the prediction would prove true.

And Bransen, who had been at Badden's camp, who had seen the hundreds of trolls and the giants there, knew it to be an unrealistic hope, and one that would soon enough be destroyed.

They ran over another group of trolls soon after. A volley of Alpinadoran spears flew out to the east soon after that, taking down a pair of scouts.

The barbarian horde didn't even slow to retrieve the missiles.

Good fortune gave Bransen and his companions a fine vantage point as the real battle commenced. The path wound down and around a huge outcropping before spilling onto the glacier, and the powrie contingent, Bransen's trio among them, was up high and still back of the stone when the leading Alpindorans swept onto the ice like a breaking wave, washing over those nearest trolls before smashing into a more coordinated defensive formation. Spears crisscrossed in midair, with the trolls taking the brunt of it, as their spears were too small and light to get through the Alpinadoran wicker and leather shields.

The Alpinadoran warriors poured over the front troll ranks, their towering line of broad-shouldered men and women, most well over six feet in height, dwarfing the diminutive, light-featured trolls.

But the trolls did not break and flee, and those in the back scrambled all over each other trying to get to the front ranks and into the fight. Like a horde of rats, they leaped and bit and scratched and kicked, flailing so wildly that they were as likely to strike their own as they were to hit their enemies.

More barbarians swept onto the glacier, lengthening the line and filling in the holes as some of their kin fell away.

In the back, watching from on high, Milkeila chewed her bottom lip, her knuckles whitening about the handle of the stone axe she carried.

"They are winning," Cormack pointed out to her, and draped an arm across her sturdy shoulder.

"Yach, but we're not to even get to the ice afore the fight's done," Mcwigik complained.

"Aye, and all that fine spilled blood'll seep into the cracks by then," added Pergwick, he and the young Ruggirs hopping over to join Mcwigik and Bikelbrin and the humans. "Or mixed with the scraped and melted ice to be even thinner!"

"Come on, ye bleating sheep," another dwarf called, and as they turned to regard the shouter, he waved them his way. Apparently they weren't the only ones concerned that the fight would end before their arrival, for before that yelling dwarf, a line of powries was going over the ledge and out of sight, picking their way, the group learned when they got to the spot, down a steep but climbable descent that would get them out onto the glacier just to the south of the Alpinadoran position.

Glancing over the ledge and following the line of powries climbing down (with amazing deftness, he thought, given their short limbs), Bransen could pick out the point of demarcation. Few trolls stood in that area of the glacier, focused far more heavily to the north and the barbarians.

For a brief moment, Bransen's eyes flashed wickedly, wondering if the enemy had left open a flank they might exploit.

But as the leading powrie dropped down the last few feet to land upon the ice, Bransen's excitement turned to dread.

A rain of heavy, large stones complemented the dwarf's arrival. The northern, left flank, far from open, had been charged to the giants, half a dozen of the behemoths, standing tall now behind a wall of ice blocks that had obscured their position. With their light, bluish skin, white hair, and wrappings of white fur, they blended well with their shiny and eye-stinging environment, but that camouflage did nothing to diminish their overwhelming aura of strength now that they had been spotted.

Bransen started to call the dwarves back up, but stopped, stunned, as they seemed more excited and eager to get down than they had before the giants had risen up.

"Giants!" Bransen pleaded with those dwarves around him, a call seconded by Cormack.

"Bah, them ain't giants," Mcwigik said with a howl.

"Not like the giants we got on the Julianthes," Bikelbrin added, using the powrie name for the Weathered Isles, their Mirianic Ocean homeland.

"Not half," Mcwigik agreed, "but I'm betting their blood runs thick!"

That was all the others had to hear, and Pergwick and Ruggirs nearly tumbled from the ledge as they fought and scrambled over each other to get to the descent. After the dwarfish tumble rolled away, the three humans stepped up to the ledge.

"You do not seem convinced of your course," Cormack remarked to Bransen, and the Highwayman smiled at his own inability to keep his emotions from his face.

"I came here to buy freedom for myself and my family," he replied honestly. "Badden's head for a journey south."

"We'll make sure that you get the foul one's head, then," Milkeila assured him.

Bransen snickered. "All who came north with me are lost. Either dead or trapped in that castle. Dame Gwydre would not refuse me my reward even should I return now, before the task is complete."

"But Badden must be stopped," Cormack said.

Bransen look at him skeptically.

"Do you deny his evilness?" said Cormack.

"Not his, not that of your Church. Not of the lairds—not one of them," said Bransen.

Cormack stiffened at that poignant reminder of the lack of familiarity between them.

"Then you agree that he, Badden, is worth killing," said Milkeila, her voice taking on a distinctively sharper edge.

Bransen looked at her carefully, his expression measured, and caught somewhere between amusement and condescension. "That is not the question. The question is: Is Badden worth dying over?"

Below them, the powries encountered a group of trolls and the fight was on. "He is," said Cormack, and he started over the ledge, moving swiftly down the steep decline. Milkeila shot a disappointed look Bransen's way and followed.

Bransen passed them easily, using his Jhesta Tu training and his marvelous control of his body to run down the cliff.

CHAPTER 29

Despoilment, Inevitability, and Questionable Triumph

By the time Bransen got down to the ice shelf, most of the trolls were either down or scattering and more than half of the powrie contingent was already in a full sprint to the edge of the chasm just south of their position. Both their courage and commitment stunned Bransen, for not only were they charging headlong into the waiting giants, but they were putting themselves into a position where they would be afforded one less avenue of retreat, where, if the battle went badly, they would find no escape.

It wasn't stupidity, or ignorance of battle techniques, that launched them to the chasm, Bransen knew. They weren't going to retreat. They were either taking the fight right to Badden's castle across the way, or they were going to die trying.

His surprise and confusion over their level of commitment nearly cost Bransen his life, as a troll spear flew in for his side. At the last moment, and with the prompting of a cry from Milkeila, the Highwayman half turned and snapped a backhand against the spear, just below its stone head. The force of the blow flipped the light spear into a near-right-angled turn, and the nimble Bransen flipped his hand and snatched it from the air, his legs moving perfectly to catch up to his shifting shoulders.

He sent the missile back out at the nearest troll, though he didn't know if that was the missile-thrower or not. The creature flailed wildly and tried to fall away, and indeed did fall away, though not as it had intended, embedded as it was on the end of the spear.

Bransen thought to yank that spear back out of the squirming troll as he ran past. But he shook his head, confident that his hands and feet would prove to be all the weaponry he needed at that time. He skied into a pair of trolls, spinning a circle-kick as he came in. That one foot turned both their spears aside, and as he came around fully, Bransen quick-stepped forward, snapping off quick left and right jabs into the faces of the respective trolls. He pressed forward, staying inside the optimum reach of their weapons. He spun to face the one on his left and drove his elbow back behind him to further smash the face of the other.

A fast left-right-left combination knocked the troll facing him back and to the ground; then Bransen similarly dropped, turning sidelong and coiling his legs as he did. The troll behind him, now below his prostrated form, had just begun to recover from the elbow to the face when Bransen swept his lower, left leg across, hooking the troll behind the ankle and sliding its foot forward, while Bransen's right leg straight-kicked for that same knee.

Legs weren't supposed to bend like that, as the troll's howl of agony proved.

Bransen thrust his left arm down below him, driving his upper torso up from the ice. He tucked his legs again and spun with the momentum, right into a standing, turning position that allowed him to circle-kick the descending troll right in the face.

Its head snapped over backward with such force that its neck bones shattered.

A roar from behind turned Bransen around just in time to see a giant topple over, grasping both its knees. The powries wasted no time, swarming over the behemoth with glee, stabbing it and slashing it and wiping their berets across the wounds.

Bransen's jaw dropped open in disbelief as he lifted his gaze to view the fight beyond the fallen giant, to where a group of powries was rushing to and fro and back again, in and around the legs of a futilely swatting giant who never got close to hitting any of them.

Oh, but they were hitting the giant! Great, reverberating smacks, and always about the knee. They looked like wild lumberjacks chasing animated trees. The giant danced and tried to keep ahead of them, but they'd only reverse direction, dart between its legs, and whomp it yet again. They howled with excitement and sheer enjoyment, and that only infuriated the beast more, it seemed, and its swings became more frantic, and more futile. Other powries joined in the dance, chopping, always chopping, at the giant's legs. Down it went, to be swarmed and finished.

Bransen remembered his feelings upon first seeing the giants. How puny and helpless he had thought himself. But the powries had long ago found the answer to the imposing, seemingly impregnable behemoths. One after another, the giants fell. And the powries rolled along, berets glowing in the afternoon sun.

Cormack and Milkeila collected the stunned Bransen as they rushed to catch up. "We'll be at the ice castle within the hour!" Cormack predicted.

Accurately, Bransen knew.

Toniquay sang great songs of rousing tenor, heroic deeds, captured and amplified and now enhanced magically to provide more than a morale boost,
but an actual physical boost to the listener. And the warriors of Alpinador, the
brave men and women of the many tribes that inhabited Mithranidoon, lived
up to their heroic heritage. With coordination and fury, their line drove deep
into troll ranks; whenever one group broke through and spearheaded out in
front, those to either flank appropriately stretched behind them, so that instead of having any group get caught out alone and surrounded, the length of
the barbarian line surged forward in a series of small wedge formations. One-
against-one, there was no contest to be found. The larger, stronger, better-
armed Alpinadorans stabbed ahead with impunity, skewering troll after troll.

And yet, Toniquay and the other leaders observed, their progress proved
painfully slow. Waves of trolls came against them. Mobs of the monsters rushed
in, leading with a barrage of flying spears that set the barbarians back on their
heels and forced them to pause and cover with their wicker and leather shields.

Toniquay looked to the distant ice castle, their goal, and then to the west,
toward the dipping sun. They would not get to the castle in daylight, he surmised to his dismay, and the night would not be kind.

A cheer in the southern end of the Alpinadoran line turned Toniquay that
way, and when he noted the fierce fighting there, he did not at first understand.
As he focused, though, he heard the bolstering cry "Another giant is down!"

He swept his gaze out farther to the south, to the powries, the fallen monk,
the stranger, and Milkeila. The shaman's tight old face crinkled with confusion and consternation; were these to be the saviors of Mithranidoon?

All he had for weapons were his hands and feet, and Bransen really didn't
see how either would do any damage to the giant battling the powries
before him. But he had to try.

A dwarf rolled right around the behemoth's treelike leg, ending with a
solid, two-handed wallop of his heavy club against the front of the giant's knee.
As the behemoth lurched and howled, Bransen closed the last dozen running
strides and leaped high. Good luck was with him, for even as he lifted, the
dwarf, having gone around to the back of the giant's leg, drove in a dagger,
then smacked it hard with his club. The giant lurched backward this time,
distracted and overbalancing just as Bransen crashed in and began launching
a series of heavy punches. Over went the giant, crashing down to its back on
the ice, and Bransen hopped up to a crouch, sprang into a forward somersault,
and double-stomped his heels into the giant's eyes.

The giant howled and swatted him, launching him away, and only good
fortune and a beam of wood prevented Bransen from going over the lip of the

chasm. As soon as he had steadied himself, his legs dangling over the ledge, he looked back in fear, expecting the behemoth to rush over and finish him, but the damage had been done, and now powries swarmed over the supine giant, hacking with abandon.

Cormack slid down low and clamped his hands on Bransen's shoulders, desperately steadying him. Bransen started to assure the man that he was all right, but a shriek from the north, a supernatural, preternatural piercing screech, cut him short.

When he looked at the small dragon swooping across the lines of cowering barbarians, Bransen knew at once that it was Ancient Badden. Leathery wings propelled the beast with great speed, its long hind legs and talon-tipped feet snapping down to keep the warriors ducking and diving aside.

It screeched again, and there was magic behind that powerful wail, for many men fell to their knees, screaming in pain and grabbing at their ears. A dragon claw caught a woman by the shoulder and jerked her from the ground with such force that one of her boots was left behind! With that one foot holding her tight, the dragon's other foot raked at her, talons tearing clothing and skin with ease.

The creature banked and rolled back under, and with a sudden halt of its momentum, hurled the broken woman like a missile through the throng of barbarians. The dragon breathed forth a line of fire, immolating some and creating an obscuring fog.

Spears reached up at it but they seemed to bother the beast not at all, for they did not penetrate its armored body, or what seemed like a magical barrier encompassing that body. The defiant dragon issued that deafening, earsplitting screech again, sending more warriors to their knees in pain.

"We have to help them!" Cormack cried, tugging Bransen back from the ledge. He scrambled to his feet, as Bransen did behind him, and started for the Alpinadorans.

"That is Badden," Milkeila mouthed in horror-filled understanding.

Bransen grabbed Cormack by the shoulder, tugging him about. "The castle," he said.

"We have to help them!" Cormack implored.

"We help them by taking the castle," Bransen replied. "It is the source, the conduit, of Badden's power."

Cormack glanced back at the desperate fight to the north, but desperate acquiescence was in his eyes as he turned back to Bransen.

"Go on! Go on!" Bransen shouted to the powries, for he saw that the way was clear. "To the castle doors, for all our sakes!"

But few powries heeded that call, entranced by the allure of bright giant blood, and with still more behemoths to be tripped up and slaughtered. And the hesitancy of the behemoths—obviously they had fought the tough little powries before—only made the dwarves hungrier.

"Mcwigik!" Cormack called, and the dwarf skidded to a stop and turned to face the humans. "To the castle!" Cormack yelled, pointing emphatically that way.

Mcwigik put on a sour look, but he did stab out his arm to stop Pergwick from running by. Cormack nodded and started off, Milkeila and Bransen close behind. By the time they crossed the glacier to the ice ramp leading into the castle, Mcwigik and his three cohorts trailed in close pursuit.

A strange sense of urgency came over Bransen, then, and he overtook Cormack, moving from a trot to a sprint for the front of the large castle. He looked all about as he ran, though his path was straight. Were Brother Jond and Olconna still alive?

How much he suddenly cared about the pair and the other prisoners surprised Bransen, and he silently cursed himself for his hesitance back on the path. How could he have considered turning aside? He lowered his head and ran on faster, right to the base of the ice ramp that led up through the carved towerlike guardhouses that flanked the opening to the castle's bailey. But there, right at the base of the ramp, he skidded to a stop, and he quickly put his arm out to block Cormack from running by him.

"It is warded," he explained.

"How do you know?"

Bransen shook his head, but did not otherwise answer. He fell within himself, finding the line of his *chi* and willfully extending that life energy down to the ground beneath him. He felt the power there, clearly, and discordant with the teeming magic that had constructed and now maintained this castle.

"He says that it is trapped," Cormack said to Milkeila when she came up beside them, the four dwarves huffing and puffing close behind.

Milkeila nodded her agreement almost immediately. Her magic was quite similar to that of the Samhaists, both drawing their energies from the power of the world beneath their feet. She stepped up tentatively and began chanting and rattling her claw and tooth necklace.

She nodded again and looked back to Cormack. "Our adversary has collected the muted countering energies to his construction together in this one place," she explained. "It is a powerful ward."

"Can you defeat it?" Cormack asked.

"Or can ye bleed it?" asked Mcwigik, and Cormack looked at him curiously, and all the more curiously when he noted Milkeila nodding and smiling.

The shaman tentatively walked up the ramp, rattling her necklace before her as if it served as a guard to the release of Samhaist magic. As she neared the opening to the castle bailey, she began to softly chant while jiggling her necklace with one hand and running her other hand in the air right near the doorjamb without touching it. Immediately the gleaming ice began to sweat and drip, and little flames seemed to dance within the ice itself.

Bransen felt it all profoundly. He understood Milkeila's counter; she was calling to the ward in measured volume, bringing it forth in bits and pieces to release the pressure. He nodded as he came to understand the trapped flames in the doorjamb, designed to burst forth with tremendous energy if any crossed through without the appropriate magical commands.

As his understanding of both the ward and Milkeila's apparent answer to it crystallized, Bransen joined in the effort, channeling his *chi* to tease out pieces of the warding magic. Now the jamb was sweating all about so profusely that a steady drip fell from the overhead ice beam like a moderate rain.

"Yach, but ye're to drop the whole thing!" Mcwigik grumbled.

"Exactly what the trap was designed to do," Bransen explained. "But Milkeila and I have diffused it enough so that . . ." With a grin back at the dwarf, the Highwayman darted ahead past Milkeila through the opening. Flames burst forth all around him, a sudden and sharp release of energy, but nowhere near what it would have been initially.

"The explosion would have taken down the front wall," Milkeila explained, leading the others through the puddles and the portal to join Bransen. And not a moment too soon, for they found their friend already engaged with another contingent of the stubborn and pesky trolls.

The first spear thrown his way had become Bransen's weapon as he sprinted right into the midst of the creatures, who quickly formed a semicircle about him. Holding the light spear in his left hand only, Bransen thrust it out to the left, and as he did, he hooked its back end behind his hip. Using that leverage, he swept the spear across in front of him, catching it in a reverse grip with his right hand. He kept the spear head moving left to right, as if he meant to put the thing right around his back, but instead rolled it in his fingers, deftly flipping it to a forehand grip with his right before stabbing it out that way. The troll on that flank, taking the bait that the spear would fast disappear behind the man, had just lifted it club and begun its charge when the thrusting spear pierced its chest.

Bransen bent his arm at the elbow powerfully, sending his hand straight up, and he flipped the spear back across his shoulders. He caught it with an underhand grip with his left and subtly altered the angle of momentum, rolling it completely around to stab out in front of him, again left to right. He loosened his grip, letting the spear slide forth as if in a throw, but caught it firmly lower on the handle with his left and grasped it at midpoint with his right, then stabbed diagonally out to his right more powerfully, retracted, reangled and stabbed straight ahead, then again, turning his hips to put it out right of his position in three short and devastating thrusts.

Three trolls fell away. The others of the group fell back on their heels, confused and frightened, and just as Bransen's friends rushed past him, overwhelming the lot of the trolls. Only an unlucky turn, a broken spear hooking at a bad angle, caused a wound on any of the companions, catching Pergwick painfully in the hip.

The dwarf shrugged off any attention, though, and matched the pace of the others as they charged across the courtyard to the castle's inner door. Again Bransen took the lead, and again he thought to filter out his sensitivity to magic to seek out wards. But the door slid aside and out jumped a man dressed in Samhaist robes and holding a short bronze sword. For a brief instant, Bransen thought it to be Ancient Badden, and he instinctively pulled up.

That proved a fortunate delay, as the Samhaist sent a gout of flames out through his hand to engulf his sword blade and came forward with a series of mighty sweeps, extending those flames out before him.

Mcwigik ambled by Bransen and nearly right into them, before finally stopping with a shout of surprise. He shouted again when Bransen leaped atop him, then sprang from the dwarf's sturdy frame, soaring high and far, lifting his *chi* as he went to carry him far above the expected mortal boundaries. He threw his spear at the man as he went, but the Samhaist was appropriately warded against such missiles and it did not penetrate.

It was no more than a diversion, anyway, and Bransen soared up and over. The surprised Samhaist turned his blade upward to try to intercept, but Bransen was too high. He landed behind the Samhaist, turning as he descended, and as the man tried to turn, Bransen shot his arm through the gap in the man's bended elbow, then knifed his hand up behind the Samhaist's neck, catching a firm grip. He turned with the Samhaist, staying right behind him and up against him, and as soon as the man tried to reverse back the other way, throwing back his shoulder and arm instinctively to break his momentum, Bransen similarly knifed his other arm in the same manner as the first. Now with both of his hands clamped behind the Samhaist's neck, "chicken-winging" his opponent's arms out behind him in the process, Bransen easily turned the man and tripped him up.

They fell together, the Samhaist facedown and with no way to free up his arms to break his fall. Bransen added to the impact by shoving out with his hands just before the Samhaist's face hit the ice.

Bransen sprang up, running right over the man to grab the fallen sword. He was content to leave it at that, but of course, the powries were not. They came in stabbing and slicing, pounding the poor fool back to the ice in short order, so they could dip their berets in his spilling blood.

Through the open door went Bransen. Milkeila came in right behind. "We need to find Badden's place of power," she said. "There must be one greater than all the others."

Before Bransen could agree, Cormack rushed past and shouted, "Brother!" Both Bransen and Milkeila turned his way. The pair then followed Cormack's gaze to the side where a group of miserable prisoners huddled, most prominent among them a man wearing Abellican robes.

"Jond," Bransen breathed, and he thought again of his hesitation back on the ledge, and his serious considerations of just turning around and going south to find Cadayle and Callen.

The Highwayman's face flushed with shame, and even more when Brother Jond called out, "Bransen Garibond, have you come to save us, friend?"

Friend. The word bounced around Bransen's mind, an indictment made all the more damning because Brother Jond didn't even understand that it was one. Cormack was to him by then, working the ropes to free the man and the others around him.

"Not one will be able to aid us in this battle," Milkeila was saying when Bransen finally joined the couple at the prisoners' side.

"Well found, friend," Bransen said to Jond, and he couldn't suppress his horror at seeing the man's maimed face, scarred slits where his eyeballs once were.

The blind monk followed the voice perfectly and fell over Bransen, wrapping him in a hug, sobbing with joy and appreciation.

"No time," Milkeila said. "That beast is outside, killing my people! I am certain that his power is concentrated in here through some conduit to the magical emanations beneath this glacier."

"A dragon is he!" one of the other miserable prisoners proclaimed.

"Horror of horrors!" another chimed in.

"Whenever Ancient Badden appears to us, he comes down the ramp across the foyer," Brother Jond blurted, shaking his head and pushing Bransen back to arms' length, as if trying to sort it all out.

Bransen recognized the desperation on his face, the need to help here, to try to repay Badden for the injustice that had taken his sight.

"Please! Help me!" came a cry from behind, and all turned to see the Samhaist Bransen had clobbered, crawling on his elbows toward them, the four powries close behind. "Help me!" he said again, reaching plaintively toward the human intruders. As he spoke, Bikelbrin came up beside him, spat in both his hands, and took up a heavy club, lifting it for what was sure to be a killing blow.

"Hold!" Cormack yelled at the dwarf, and he rushed back. "He can tell us."

The warriors of the tribes increased the number and ferocity of their attacks on the dragon. As one, they dismissed their fear and threw their spears, or rushed to engage the beast whenever it swooped low enough for them to reach. They hardly cared for the trolls, then, for next to this monster, those creatures seemed no more than a nuisance.

But the dragon seemed unbothered by it all, seemed pleased by it all. Toniquay and the other shamans, chanting more fiercely to inspire and protect and strengthen their charges, throwing whatever offensive magics they could conjure at the beast, understood better than their noble and ferocious warriors.

And in that understanding, they trembled with fear.

For the dragon not only seemed impervious, but seemed to grow, in size and in strength. No spear penetrated its scaled armor, and no warrior stood against it for more than a few heartbeats. Tearing claws and snapping maw, thunderously beating wings and snapping, clubbing tail drew a line across the Alpinadoran ranks, laying men and women low with impunity.

"How do we even hurt it?" Toniquay heard himself asking. Hoping to answer just that, the shaman completed his spell, bringing forth a bird sculpture he had just magically fashioned from the ice. He held it up before his lips and blew life into the small, crystalline golem, then thrust out his arm, launching it away at the dragon.

The gleaming ice bird flashed overhead, gaining tremendous speed before crashing hard into the dragon.

If the great beast even noticed the animated missile, it did not show it, and the ice bird exploded into a million tiny and harmless droplets of water.

Toniquay winced, and then did so again as he saw another man lifted into the air in the dragon's rear talons. Those mighty feet squeezed powerfully and with such force that the poor warrior's eyeballs popped from their sockets, blood and tissue flushing out behind.

Toniquay could only suck in his breath in horror.

They hustled up the ice ramp, Brother Jond leaning heavily on Bransen and the four dwarves bringing up the back of the line, carrying the captured and battered Samhaist by the wrists and ankles.

The ascending corridor wrapped around to the right as it rose, crossing over one landing and then another, both circular and both centered by the same wide icy beam that seemed the main support for this part of the castle structure.

"I'm not thinking he's long for living," Mcwigik said, and the people in front paused and considered the poor fellow, and winced as one as the dwarves just let him drop facedown on the floor.

"Don't ye even be thinking of it," Mcwigik warned them, and Bransen laughed at the accuracy of the dwarf's guess, for he too could clearly see the silent debate between the two over whether or not they would use their healing magic to help the man.

"We cannot just let a fellow human die," Milkeila remarked, as much to her fellow humans as to the dwarves.

Ruggirs walked up beside Mcwigik, stared hard at the humans, then stomped on the back of the Samhaist's neck. Neck bones shattered with a sickening crunch and the Samhaist twitched violently once or twice before lying very still.

"Yer magic's for meself and me boys, and don't ye even think o' using it on one of them that we're fighting when there's fighting afore us," Ruggirs explained.

"Yach, but it's not looking like he was hurt that bad after all," Pergwick said from behind the angry Ruggirs, and Bransen understood the statement to be for the sake of the humans and nothing more, a way to accentuate Ruggirs's point.

"But ye was right, Mcwigik," Pergwick went on. "He weren't long for living."

Mcwigik waved his hand at the humans, bidding them to move along.

They wore expressions of shock (even outrage, in the case of Milkeila and Brother Jond), but they did indeed move along, for they hadn't the time to discuss the powries' tactics.

At the top of the ramp, they came into another circular room, and recognized that they were in the highest tower of the many-turreted castle. Here, too, the support beam ended, but at floor level and not at the ceiling, for it was no support beam in the conventional sense at all.

It was the base of a fountain, one that sprayed a fine and warm mist into this room. That mist contained power, Bransen recognized immediately, and so did Milkeila. That mist was the stuff of Samhaist and shaman earth magic, the exact conduit Milkeila had sought.

The water stream lifted about six feet into the air, before collapsing back in on itself and splashing down into a two-tiered bowl, and though that base was also made of ice, it seemed impervious to the warm flow.

"This is his source of power," Milkeila stated, moving closer and lifting her hand to feel the splash and spray. "This is where Ancient Badden connects to his earthly power."

"You can feel it?" Cormack asked, and Milkeila's expression showed clearly that she was surprised that he could not.

"I can, as well," Bransen said. "It is not so unlike the emanations of your gemstones. It teems with energy, with *ki-chi-kree*."

Cormack rubbed his face and looked over at Brother Jond, who sat silent and expressionless. What Bransen had just said, the comparison of Samhaist magic to Abellican, would be considered heretical to the leaders of the Abellican Church, but Jond seemed not to mind, nor to disagree.

And Cormack certainly didn't. Adding the fact that Bransen had also included his own mystical powers, this strange concept of *chi,* only reinforced to Cormack that he was right in this, that all the Churches and magical powers were in fact pieces of the same god and same godly magic.

As he considered that, he felt an acute sting, a memory of his whipping, across his torn back.

Bransen closed his eyes and stepped up to the fountain, then washed his bare arm through it.

"If that is Badden's source of power, can we, too use it?" Cormack asked. "Perhaps to counter the Ancient?"

"We cannot use it as he uses it," Milkeila replied. "The powers he garners from it are . . . beyond me."

"This magic is not focused and stable, as with the Abellican gemstones," said Bransen. "It is fluid and ever-changing, and we cannot access it as Badden does—certainly not in the time we have."

"What, then?" Cormack asked.

"Despoil it," both Jond and Milkeila suggested together.

"I will weave spells into it, to divert it from whatever course Badden has fashioned," the barbarian shaman explained, and she stepped right up and began softly chanting, singing, an ancient rhythm of an ancient blessing.

Similarly, Bransen held his arm in the flow and sent his *chi* into it, trying to stagger the infusions and twist them in a wild attempt to somehow alter the magic within the water.

And most straightforward of all came the powries, all four. "Ye heard her, boys," said Mcwigik. "Put a bit o' the dwarf into it!" They lined up around the bowl, unbuckled their heavy belts and dropped their britches, and began their own special and to-the-point method of despoiling the magical water.

"Hope he's not drinking it," Bikelbrin noted with a snicker.

"Yach, but I hope he is," Pergwick added. "We'll give him a taste o' the powries he's not to forget, what!"

H e soared over their line with impunity, roaring and breathing forth lines of fire, ignoring their feeble spears thrown by their weak, mortal muscles. He was Badden, Ancient of the Samhaists, the voice of the ancient gods, who blessed him with the power of immortals, in this case, the strength of a true dragon.

He pondered that if he killed enough of them up here, he might not even need to drop the front off of the glacier and flood the lake. It was a fleeting thought, though, for after the contamination these heathens had brought, the lake would be better off for the purification, in any event! Besides, he would *enjoy* it. As he enjoyed this slaughter of unbelievers. He raked the line; he roared with divine joy.

A spear dug deep into his side.

Ancient Badden's roar changed in timbre. More spears reached up and stung him profoundly. He answered with another gout of fiery breath, and indeed, those nearest barbarians shied away from the flames. But those flames were not nearly as intense as the previous.

Badden's serpentine neck swiveled to offer him a view of his distant castle. Something was wrong here, he knew. Something was interrupting the flow and strength of his magic. Another spear pierced him, shooting lines of hot pain. The dragon roared and beat his long and leathery wings, propelling him across the barbarian ranks and beyond.

The barbarians cheered behind him and threw more spears and clubs and rocks—anything to sting the defeated beast. Then they threw taunts, and more than one noted that the dragon seemed as if it had diminished in actual size.

Feeling the painful sting of a dozen wounds, and feeling even more acutely a sudden distance to the power that fed his draconian form, Badden knew those observations to be more than illusion.

There was little for Cormack to do as the other six, in their own special ways, despoiled Badden's fountain conduit. Too late, he thought to take the gemstone necklace from Milkeila, for now he did not dare interrupt her concentrated efforts.

Nor did he want the gemstones at that time, the former Abellican monk had to admit, to himself at least. The sense of betrayal was too raw and too sharp. His communion with the gemstones had always before elicited a feeling of kinship to Blessed Abelle, the man who had founded the Church less than a century before. But now, clearly, the representatives of that dead prophet considered Cormack's worldview as heretical.

If he used the gemstones in this tremendous battle, would he feel the consternation of the spirit of Abelle?

He considered that perhaps he was making too much of it all, was allowing his anger and disappointment to overrule his judgment. He looked over at Milkeila and could see the strain on her face from her continuing efforts. The magic she battled was tangible, and formidable.

With a sharp inhale, Cormack steadied himself and took a step toward her, determined to dismiss his excuses and offer whatever help he could. But he stopped before he had really even started, for through the translucent wall above and behind Milkeila came such a blossom of orange and yellow that Cormack instinctively pondered that he was seeing the birth of the colors themselves. He watched, mouth agape, unable to even call out a warning, as those colors, the fires of dragon breath, turned the icy wall to water and steam, and through the glowing cloud came the beast itself, framed in hot-glowing mist that made it seem as if it were entering through some extradimensional portal!

The powries cried out and scrambled to pull up their pants; Bransen re-acted with snakelike speed and precision, diving to the side, out of the way and collecting Milkeila as he went, still deep in her trance.

Cormack could only stand there and gape as the dragon's serpentine neck swept down and the beast rolled right over it, tucking its wings. As it came around, it was not the lower torso of a reptilian dragon that showed, but the legs of a man, feet adorned with painted toenails and vine-tied sandals. Badden continued his transformation as he completed the somersault and it was a man and not a dragon that landed on the floor before the fountain.

But not just any man; it was the Ancient of the Samhaists come calling.

He landed with such a thud that it seemed as if he must be many times his apparent weight, and the same magic that perpetuated that strange perception reached out from Badden and into his magical ice floor. Huge ripples rolled out from the man, waves of ice, as if the floor had been caught somewhere between the state of a solid and of a liquid. Those ripples rose like waves and crested sharply and with tremendous energy, throwing dwarves and humans alike into the air violently. They crashed into the walls and bounced off the fountain, handheld weapons flying wildly. Milkeila splashed down into the fountain, and with the rumbling all about her, it took her a long while to sort out which way was up and get her head above water.

She fared the best, however, for the only place in the room, other than at Badden's feet, that was not violently rolling and crashing was within that very pool. The shaman grimaced as Mcwigik and Bikelbrin flew past her, grabbing at each other for support until they were split apart from each other by the intervening fountain tower, both ricocheting, spinning out toward the walls. She cried out in pain as her beloved Cormack flew straight up into the air, more than a dozen feet—and only his considerable training allowed him to sort himself out enough in his descent to prevent landing on his head.

She winced at watching Bransen, not flying about, but maneuvering over the solid waves as a boat might defy heavy surf, and she gasped in shock to see one wave break right over poor Ruggirs, smashing down on the dwarf with tremendous force, blowing out his breath in a great and profound groan. The ice wave blended right over him, burying him in the floor.

Not far from her, Ancient Badden cackled with enjoyment, and stamped his foot again, giving rise to another series of waves, ones that crashed into the rebounding first set and sent the whole of the room into frenzy. Even the walls began to ripple and buckle! Now all of Milkeila's friends flopped and bounced about uncontrollably, except for buried Ruggirs and one other.

To the Jhesta Tu, Bransen's posture was known as *doan-chi-kree,* the "stance of the mountain," a place of complete balance and perfect calm, where the straight-standing mystic reached his line of life energy, his *chi,* below his *ki,* his groin, and down to *doan,* the floor beneath his feet. That line of life energy became the mystic's roots, his stability, and in such a state, a Jhesta Tu could not be moved by a charging giant.

The floor rolled to Badden's command beneath Bransen's feet, but Bransen moved with it, his legs bending and straightening accordingly and so perfectly that his upper body remained perfectly still. He locked stares with Badden. The Ancient stomped his foot again. But Bransen would not be thrown.

Milkeila drew courage from that image and shook herself from her stupor. She reached into her magic again and thrust it into Badden's fountain, demanding that the violence end.

She felt as if she was trying to hold back the great Mirianic Ocean itself! But she shook away her despair and pressed on, blocking out all the distractions, focusing solely on the task at hand.

The room began to quiet.

A ncient Badden broke off his stare and looked over his shoulder at the woman, feeling her intrusion into his magic as keenly as if she was reaching into his stomach and tugging at his entrails. The Samhaist roared, as much the voice of a dragon as that of a man, and stabbed his hands out to the fountain's centering geyser. The roiling waters froze solid suddenly, encasing Milkeila's hands and forearms in a crushing grip.

Badden whipped his arm in a sudden circle, and the icicle responded likewise, turning over itself as it rushed around, twisting Milkeila right over.

She felt her shoulders pop from their sockets, then wrenched her back as the ice stopped its swing abruptly, locking her top half fast in place while her lower body whipped around.

Waves of nausea and dizziness and floating black spots filled her gut and head and eyes, and when the ice returned again to its liquid fountain form, the helpless woman dropped into and under the water, with no sense of direction or awareness at all.

Badden chuckled as he felt his magic flow more fully once more, but he knew that the diversion of this foolish woman had cost him. For in the moment of calm, the humans and dwarves had closed.

The Ancient snapped the fabulous sword off his back, took the hilt in both hands and sent it out to arms' length. With a maniacal cackle, the man went up onto the ball of one foot, hooked that balance point into his magical energy and began to spin. Not to spin like a young girl at play, but to truly whirl about, gaining speed and momentum with every turn. His form blurred; he altered the angle of his blade so that there was no possible approach.

Pergwick howled in sudden pain and fell away, desperately clutching at his head to hold his scalp in place. He went down to the floor, looking frantically for his lost beret.

Mcwigik and Cormack, side by side, fell away without getting stung, but Cormack shouted anyway, in frustrated outrage and not in physical pain, for he found himself separated from his fallen Milkeila, and he couldn't see her above the rim of the fountain bowl. He tried to maneuver around the side, but got all tangled up with the ducking and retreating Mcwigik.

"What whirlpool's he swimming in?" the dwarf barked in absolute surprise.

Bransen, too, slipped out of reach, but in a more controlled manner, taking a full measure of his adversary, and Bikelbrin dove over the side of the fountain, splashing down into the water. He had just regained his footing when Badden suddenly extended his reach, using the narrow sword as a focus for the release of his magical energy.

The prone Pergwick skidded across the room. Cormack and Mcwigik went flying away in a confused tumble, and Bikelbrin flew back into the center pole of the fountain with such force that his sensibilities kept right on flying.

Dazed and hardly conscious as he hit the water once more, the dwarf flopped over the drowning Milkeila. On pure instinct, he hooked his arm under the woman's head and rolled himself onto his back, atop her back, using her bulk to keep his own head above the water. He kept his arm hooked to hold himself steady, and that alone saved the gasping Milkeila, for the weight of the dwarf rolled him back and his arm brought her head out of the water.

Ancient Badden had never felt a purer release of magical energy, as satisfying as any release any man might know. He stomped his foot to accentuate the magic, sending the room into a series of crashing ice waves once again.

Before he could congratulate himself, however, Ancient Badden looked into the face of one who had not been moved by his magical thrust, and who seemed not bothered in the least by the current rocking.

Bransen Garibond held his ground. "You have my sword," the Highwayman calmly explained, and Badden looked at him in abject disbelief.

"It is you!" the Samhaist replied. "I threw you from the glacier!"

"Highwaymen bounce," Bransen replied.

"You were a babbling fool—an idiot who could hardly stand!"

"Or I was a clever scout, taking a measure of Ancient Badden and his forces before bringing doom upon them."

Badden stood up straight and shook his head—or started to, for faster than a striking serpent the Highwayman struck. He sprang forward and snapped off a left and right jab for the old man's face, connecting solidly both times.

He leaped back immediately, throwing back his hips and keeping his belly just an inch ahead of the thrusting sword. As he bent double with the move, Bransen drove down his forearm to knock the blade downward.

But Badden had anticipated that, and he cunningly turned the sword so that Bransen's arm hit the razor edge.

Bransen did grimace, but simply rolled his hand down lower, changing the angle and driving the blade out wide. Then he rushed back in, slamming against Badden, one hand holding the man's sword arm, the other hand grasping the old man's face.

And Badden responded by snapping his free arm up behind Bransen. First he crushed the man into him, and with strength beyond anything Bransen could ever have believed possible!

Badden grabbed the back of Bransen's hair and bandanna and tugged back violently, and Bransen growled in pain and in the sudden horror that he might again lose that precious gemstone. He raked his hand straight down, fingernails drawing lines of blood on Badden's face, then reversed and hit the old man with a series of short and devastating uppercuts, crunching bone beneath his pounding fist.

Badden reflexively let go of Bransen's hair to bring his free hand in to stop the barrage, but the moment he did Bransen shot out to the side, going after Badden's sword arm, going after the sword, furiously.

But even though he got the leverage, the proper angle, he couldn't pry the weapon free, and he realized his error, realized how vulnerable he had left himself, right before Badden's fist smashed him in the back, driving his breath from his body. This was no mortal he faced, but some magical monstrosity! He needed the sword, but he couldn't hope to get it. Badden pounded him again, and Bransen's legs went weak.

"Fool!" the old Samhaist chided.

Bransen fell within himself as yet another explosive and thundering punch crashed against his back. He found his line of *chi,* found his center. . . . He thought of Cadayle. He centered all of his fleeting thoughts on her, using her image as a focal point for holding on to his fast-flying consciousness. Something flew past him, and he was jerked backward. Another form rushed by— Cormack. He heard the slap of punches; he managed to glance over his shoulder to see Mcwigik tight about Badden's leg, biting the man hard on the thigh, and to see Cormack facing Badden straight up, raining a rapid barrage of punches against the man's face. That one was no novice to fighting.

But neither was he—were they—a match for Ancient Badden.

Bransen guessed Badden's move—to pull free the sword and be done quickly with all three—so as soon as the Ancient started, Bransen reacted with sudden fury and all the power of his training behind him. He lunged for Badden's sword hand, grasping the wrist and cupping his other hand over the Ancient's clenched fist, snapping with all his strength, with all of his leverage, with every ounce of Jhesta Tu and gemstone magic he could possibly muster. One chance, he knew. One moment of focused power.

Ancient Badden's hand bent back over his wrist, his wrist-bone shattering. Bransen drove his own hand up over Badden's fist, catching the serpent hilt of his mother's sword and pulling it free.

He got slugged one more time but anticipated it and was diving into a forward roll even as Badden's fist hit him, thus absorbing much of the blow. He rolled head over, coming numbly back to his feet, and he spun about just in time to see Cormack launched in a sidelong somersault by a vicious backhand.

Staring at Bransen with hate-filled eyes, clutching his broken hand in close at his side, the Ancient clawed his free hand down on the stubborn, gnawing powrie, and with frightening strength plucked Mcwigik free.

He lifted the dwarf to throw him at Bransen, but the Highwayman was already there, coming under the would-be sentient missile. He stabbed, and quickly slashed upward, cutting under Badden's arm. The Ancient still managed to throw Mcwigik, but suddenly he had so little strength behind it that the dwarf bounced and turned and roared right back in. Or would have, if there had been a need.

Bransen worked like a dancer, spinning, swinging his arm, changing the angle of his deadly blade with such skill and precision that Ancient Badden never once blocked or turned effectively enough to prevent the Highwayman from hitting him exactly where Bransen had wanted to.

The sword slashed across Badden's belly, came around and poked him hard in the biceps, and as he lurched, his arm lowering, slashed him across the chin, drawing a sizable line across half his throat in the process. Over and over, Bransen rolled the blade, diagonal down, left and right, and lines of bright blood erupted all across the Samhaist's light green robes.

Now Badden wore a mask of fear, and he stumbled backward, trying pitifully to get his arms up. Bransen kept hitting him, slashing him, even lifting a foot to kick him. Back went the Ancient, who suddenly seemed little more than an old man, to fall into an awkward sitting position against the wall. And Bransen was there, suddenly, sword edge against Badden's already bleeding neck. Ancient Badden laughed at him, blood dripping out with every chortle.

"You seem happy for a man about to die," said Bransen. Behind him, Cormack cried out for Milkeila, and Bransen heard splashing.

"We all die, fool," Badden replied. "You will not likely see near the years I have known."

"Or the failure," said Bransen.

"Ah yes, the triumph of your Abellican Church," Badden retorted, and indeed, Bransen's face did crinkle at that.

"My Church?" he asked incredulously.

"You have thrown in with them!"

Bransen snickered at the absurdity of the remark.

"Do you think them any better?" Badden asked, his words becoming more labored. "Oh, they find their shining moment now, when their baubles so impress the young and strong lairds. But where will they be when those lairds are old and lie dying, and those baubles offer nothing?

"We Samhaists know the truth, the inevitability," he went on. "There is no escape from the darkness. Their promises are hollow!" He laughed, a bloody and bitter sound.

"A truth you are about to realize intimately," Bransen reminded him.

But Badden's laugh mocked him. "And as these Abellican fools rise ascendant, buoyed by their empty promises of forever, do you think they will be any better?"

But now Bransen was back on level emotional ground. "Do you think that I care?" he chided right back, and that brought a curious look from the old man.

"Then why are you here?"

Bransen laughed at him and stood straight. "Because they paid me," he said with a cold and casual tone, "and because I hate everything for which you stand."

His sword came across, and Badden's puzzled expression remained on his face as his head rolled across the floor.

Epilogue

The six survivors and Brother Jond collected the rest of the prisoners and led them out of Ancient Badden's ice castle.

Outside, the battle had ended; with the dragon chased off, the troll lines had broken, and now both barbarian and dwarf lined the chasm, throwing stones and blocks of ice and spears down at the monster that prowled its depths. From the roars that rose, it seemed as if many were hitting the mark. For the great white worm would not flee into one of its burrows to escape the barrage. It would not back down from the threat, though it had no way of scaling the chasm wall to get at its attackers.

Its mighty bulk and power could not protect it from its own lack of brains.

Mcwigik and Bikelbrin rushed off to join in the fun, and even Pergwick, holding his cap against his head, and his cap holding his scalp in place, followed.

"You are from Vanguard?" Brother Jond asked Cormack, who supported him as they moved across the ice.

"Years ago," Cormack explained. "And Chapel Abelle before that. I was a member of Father De Guilbe's expedition."

That sparked recognition in Jond, and a great smile creased his face. "I had thought the feel of your clothing to be that of an Abellican robe!"

"I am not Abellican anymore, Brother."

Jond stopped and faced Cormack, though of course he couldn't actually see the man.

"I was cast out," Cormack admitted. "I questioned the limitations."

"Limitations?"

"The Abellican Church's refusal to explore those traditions and magic outside the domain of the Church and the gemstones," Cormack honestly offered. "There is more beauty to be found in this world, a wider truth than that which we have come to represent." Brother Jond gave a curious "hmm," and Cormack had no idea if he was offending or intriguing the man. "The woman who accompanied us into the castle is a shaman of an Alpinadoran tribe," Cormack explained.

"I gathered as much."

"I love her."

"Hmm."

"And I see in her true and divine beauty—I see it in our other friend as well, this man named Bransen."

"Ah, the Highwayman, yes," said Jond. "He is a unique one."

"And possessed of godly powers."

Brother Jond shook his head, unwilling to make that jump.

"Powers akin to those of our gemstones," Cormack clarified, and Jond now nodded.

"I witnessed his healing hands," Jond said. "And his grace is rather amazing. But he is no man of God. Not yet, though I suspect that his nature compels him to look that way. For all his life, our friend Bransen cared only for Bransen, and absent in him is a sense of community and greater good. No, not absent," he quickly corrected. "Simply not yet developed. I hold out great hopes for that one, if he doesn't get himself killed too soon."

As Jond put forth those observations, Cormack looked out at Bransen, who was paralleling the powries toward the chasm. The monk's words, so very much like his own to Milkeila regarding the Highwayman, rang true indeed.

"We will get you back to Chapel Pellinor and Dame Gwydre," Cormack promised.

"Perhaps I might put in a good word for Brother Cormack."

Cormack winced at the title Jond had used, both because he doubted that any good word would do any good, and because he wasn't sure that he wanted it back.

"They ran, you know," he said. "Father De Guilbe and the others of Chapel Isle—our chapel here in Alpinador—did not join in the greater cause with the Alpinadorans and the powries. Instead, they fled south, bound for Vanguard."

Brother Jond started to reply—to offer some justification, Cormack knew. But instead he just sighed and shook his head, and Cormack realized that this wasn't the first time this man had been disappointed by the actions of fellow Abellicans.

Cormack didn't press him on it, though. He hooked his arm under Jond's shoulder to support the man, and led him away.

Ye been wanting this for a long time, mate," Mcwigik said.

Pergwick, a thick white bandage running about his head, chin to top, and under his replaced beret, lowered his eyes and kicked a stone. "Ruggirs was me brother," he said. "We slapped blood together that if either got killed to death, th'other would watch over the Sepulcher and care for the kid. It'll be me brother, too, ye know."

"Aye, there's that," Mcwigik agreed. "But I'm not for waiting the years ye're to need. The lake's made me batzy already, I tell ye!"

"Not asking ye to wait, and I'm thinking that yerself and Bik are to open things up for the rest," Pergwick replied, looking up and seeming much more at ease. "Kriminig and the others've said as much—that we'll all go south when word comes back from Mcwigik that there's a place for us. I'm guessing that more'n ourselves have had too much o' Mithranidoon."

Mcwigik nodded and clapped Pergwick on the shoulder. "Good enough, then, and I'll be smiling when I see ye again."

Pergwick grinned and began to nod, but Mcwigik cautioned him with an upraised hand.

"Don't ye go shaking yer head too rough!" the dwarf said.

"Aye, we're not wanting yer brains to go flying out. Ye're not for much to spare," added Bikelbrin, walking over and carrying a large sack full of supplies.

"What do ye know?" Mcwigik asked, and Bikelbrin motioned to the side, where Cormack, Bransen, Milkeila, and Brother Jond stood in a group, all carrying sacks.

"Where'd they get the goods?" asked Mcwigik.

"The barbarians," Bikelbrin replied. "They ain't too happy with the girl, but they know she just saved their homes."

"An easier road for us all, then," Mcwigik reasoned.

"More food to start, at least. As for the rest, we'll be seein'."

They both patted Pergwick on the shoulder, then moved to join the others. The group of six was off the glacier that same night, moving determinedly south. The weather stayed warm over the next couple of days, and they encountered no trolls, and so they made great progress, despite the soreness from their fight with Badden and the more serious wounds, which Milkeila's people had treated very well. Even Brother Jond, sightless though he was, walked with a spring in his step and took up hearty and spirited conversations with the two powries.

"You will return to your wife?" Milkeila asked Bransen a couple of days out.

"The moment I deliver this"—he jostled the small pack tied to the side of his pouch, one that contained the head of Ancient Badden—"and she grants me the passage, as promised."

"You will sail far away?"

"As far as I can."

"To where?"

That question seemed to startle Bransen.

"Are you running to something or away from something?" Milkeila asked, as Cormack walked over.

"The two are not mutually exclusive," Bransen replied.

"But the distinction is important."

Bransen shrugged as if he didn't agree.

"You are a man of marvelous skills—important skills in this trying time," Cormack added.

"All times are trying."

"Then all times call for heroes, else all will be lost," Milkeila said.

Bransen snorted. "The way of the world is the way of the world and beyond any one man."

"That seems a pointless outlook," said Cormack.

"It is one I have come by through bitter experience."

Milkeila quickly added, "You have been given a great gift and have never thought to turn it to the benefit of all?"

Bransen considered his time in Pryd Holding, when he first earned the title of the Highwayman, when he spent his days stealing from the laird and distributing the booty to the unfortunate peasants, crushed under the weight of his heel, and he could not help but laugh. That laugh quickly soured, though, for he could not help but admit that even then, the good of the people was more a vehicle for his own ego than truly for the good of his people.

"We just saved the people of Mithranidoon," Milkeila reminded.

"And with positive ramifications that will spread throughout the whole of Vanguard, no doubt," Cormack added. "You cannot deny that we did indeed just change the world for the better. The bloody head you hold in your belt pouch is no small matter—perhaps it is in the measure of the centuries, but it certainly is not a small matter to the people of this day and age and region."

Bransen snickered and waved them away. His road was to his beloved Cadayle and to Callen. His responsibilities were to them, and to himself. The idea that he owed anyone else anything seemed on its surface preposterous—how many people in the world had ever shown the young Stork compassion and service?

As the two walked off, Bransen looked around at his fellow heroes and poor Brother Jond, the only other survivor of the band that had come north on the command of Dame Gwydre. He thought of Crait and Olconna and couldn't help but grin as he considered Crazy V.

He tried to deny it but could not. He had found a strange comfort and warmth in being a part of that lost group. And as much as Bransen told himself that he was only along on the mission for the sake of Cadayle and his family . . . He had hesitated at the bluff overlooking the glacier, yes, but in the end, he had gone down to do battle with Badden.

And in the process, he had formed a new bond with this competent group. He couldn't deny the warmth.

He felt like he belonged.